D1042931

The Vampire Files

VOLUME ONE

P. N. ELROD

ACE
2003
50TH
ANNIVERSARY

ACE BOOKS, NEW YORK

An Ace Book / published by arrangement with
the author

PRINTING HISTORY
Ace trade paperback edition / October 2003

Library of Congress Cataloging-in-Publication Data

Elrod, P. N. (Patricia Nead)
The vampire files / P. N. Elrod.
p. cm.
Contents: v. 1. Bloodlist ; Lifeblood ; Bloodcircle
ISBN: 0-441-01090-3
1. Fleming, Jack (Fictitious character)—Fiction. 2. Private
investigators—Illinois—Chicago—Fiction. 3. Detective and mystery stories, American.
4. Fantasy fiction, American. 5. Occult fiction, American. 6. Chicago (Ill.)—Fiction.
7. Vampires—Fiction. I. Title.

PS3555.L68V36 2003
813'.54—dc22   2003045118

ACE®
Ace Books are published by The Berkley Publishing Group,
a division of Penguin Group (USA) Inc., 375 Hudson Street,
New York, New York 10014.
ACE and the "A" design are trademarks
belonging to Penguin Group (USA) Inc.

PRINTED IN THE UNITED STATES OF AMERICA

10 9 8 7 6

To the good friends who made this possible.
You know who you are!

CONTENTS

BLOODLIST

Throughout the whole vast, shadowy world of ghosts and demons there is no figure so terrible, no figure so dreadful and abhorred, yet dight with such fearful fascination, as the vampire, who is himself neither ghost nor demon, but yet who partakes the dark natures and possesses the mysterious and terrible qualities of both.

—*Montague Summers*
The Vampire: His Kith and Kin

1

Chicago, summer 1936

THE car was doing at least forty when the right front fender smashed against my left hip and sent me spinning off the road to flop bonelessly into a mass of thick, windblown grass.

It was a well-engineered accident, involving no small skill on the part of the driver. A body, depending on its size and weight in relation to the speed and position of the car usually does two things: it either goes under the car or bounces over it. Going under, it can get dragged, leaving a lot of bloody physical evidence all over the road and vehicle. If it gets flipped up and over, the driver risks a dented hood and roof or a broken windshield or all three. The professional hit-and-run artist knows how to avoid such risks and will try to clip the target with just the front bumper or fender; that way he has only some scratched paint to touch up or at most a broken headlight to replace.

I had been hit by such an expert. There was minimal pain, though, and that was swiftly receding. The idea my spine had been broken was the first real thought to surface in my cobweb-clogged brain since I woke up on the beach. I'd been groggy then, with only enough stuff working in my head to shakily stand and blink down at my soaked clothes. It never occurred to me to question why I was on a beach and in such a condition, and I was still in a thought-numbing state of shock when I climbed a short, sandy rise and found the road. There was no rational decision on what direction to go in, my legs took me left and walked. When I heard a car motor rumbling up behind me I stuck out a thumb and walked sideways.

The small dot down the road swelled into a dark green Ford with a big lumpy-looking man at the wheel. While still a little distance off, the car slowed abruptly, its headlights raking painfully into my eyes. I shaded them, blinking stupidly as the motor gunned, gears shifted, and the thing shot forward. The driver held a straight course, as though he'd changed his mind about picking up a hitchhiker, then he swerved at the last possible second. If my brain had been running on more than one cylinder, I might have been able to jump away in time.

The landscape stopped spinning and I lay belly-up, staring at an unnaturally brilliant Milky Way a few feet from my nose, wondering what the hell was going on. I tried moving a little, the initial pain of the impact was gone, but I was cautious of broken bones. Everything worked perfectly, though—I'd been incredibly lucky. Twisting onto my stomach, I stared down the road.

The Ford stopped, the motor cut, and the lump behind the wheel was just levering himself out the door.

The only cover for fifty yards was long grass. The beach was just across the road, but this particular stretch was clear of concealing rocks. Except for the car, the only option left was a stand of trees on my side, which was much too far away.

The man was coming up fast and had a gun in one hand.

Anything was better than waiting for it. My feet dug into the ground and I bolted for the trees like a frightened rabbit. He spotted me, changed course, and yelled for me to stop. After hitting me with the car, he couldn't have really expected me to do him any convenient favors.

In an open space a gunshot doesn't sound like a gunshot, not like the ones you hear at the movies. All I heard was a flat, unimpressive crack, then the impact sent me sprawling.

It'd been a lucky hit; we were at a slight angle to one another and the narrow part of my body was toward him. The bullet entered my lower right back, just above the pelvic bone, traced through my vitals and out the front, just above the belt buckle. I doubled up and instinctively tried to hold things in, but there was nothing. The sharp, hot pain was already vanishing and my hands came away clean from what should have been a bloody mess.

My would-be killer trotted up, turned me over, and stopped short as I stared accusingly at his stupefied face. He was puffing hard and looked ready to say something but gulped it back. He quickly leveled the gun with my eyes. The business end looked as big as an open manhole. His finger was ready on the trigger; orders were being sent from his brain to the tiny muscles, telling them to contract. Before they could respond I grabbed the gun and twisted it out of his hand. His finger was caught in the trigger guard, there was a soft pop, and he yelped with surprise and pain as one of the bones snapped.

He fell back, trying to get away, and I seized an ankle, jerked, and pulled him down. His left fist swung up and slammed into my face, but with little effect. I managed a weak, backhanded swat and left him half-stunned. In another second his arms were pinned to the ground and he was utterly unable to break free. It was easy to hold him still even though he was built and muscled like a wrestler and outweighed me by a good eighty pounds. He looked up at my face hovering inches from his own and whimpered.

The man's heart and lungs were thundering in my ears like a train. All my senses were sharp and new and wonderful. I could even smell the blood, an exciting scent when mixed with the sour tang of fear. On his thick, rough neck the skin seemed oddly transparent where the large vein pulsed. First it disturbed, then it tantalized. My mouth sagged open, dry and aching with sudden thirst. I felt drawn to it like a cat to milk.

He gagged and his bladder let go as my lips brushed his throat, then he passed out.

I jerked back, wondering what the hell I was trying to do. Pushing away until I no longer touched him, I lay facedown in the spiky grass, shaking like a fever victim until the thirst faded.

With a hand under each arm, I dragged him backward over the irregular clumps of grass and sand to his car. I felt strong enough to carry him, but didn't relish coming into contact with his wet pants. Fortunately the key was in the ignition, so I was spared a search of his lower pockets. I opened the passenger door and stuffed him inside.

My mind was more or less functioning again and full of questions. Who this stranger was and why he wanted to kill me seemed like good ones to start with, so I picked his coat pocket and went through his wallet.

The driver's license was issued to a Fred Sanderson of Cicero. The name might have been fake; it meant nothing to me, but the town struck a sour note in my general memory. A bare ten years had passed since the Capone gang invaded the place and took over. Big Al was in jail now, gone but not forgotten if Sanderson was any example.

Except for five dollars and the phone number of someone named Elsie, there was nothing informative in the wallet. I unbuckled Sanderson's belt and slipped it from his well-muscled waist. He was heavy, but in solid condition. As I'd thought, the leather strip had been specially constructed to overlap on the inside. Working it open, I took careful count and transferred the five hundred dollars hidden there into my own pants pocket without a single pang of conscience. After what he'd put me through he owed me, and I needed the operating funds.

I looked long and hard at his face. The heavy jaw and thick lips were frustratingly familiar, but nothing clicked in my memory.

It was very bright now, the sky all strange with the sun and stars shining improbably together. It was confusing until I realized it was the moon that was flooding the place with such brilliance. Like ice water, fear spread out in my guts and left me shaking at the edges. The night was too bright, it was wrong, totally *wrong*.

Distraction. I needed distraction. Where was I?

East of us were tall buildings in the distance. I was still more or less in Chicago. The last thing I recalled was some phone call launching me out of the hotel I'd just checked into. I'd left at midafternoon to do something and ended up that night soaking wet on a deserted patch of Lake Michigan shoreline with some crazy trying to kill me. Wonderful.

I felt my head for lumps, found a swelling behind one ear, and smiled with relief. A concussion of some kind; that would account for the initial disorientation, the memory loss, maybe even make my eyes overly sensitive. I'd only imagined the gunshot and had taken care of Sanderson on adrenaline alone.

Almost as an afterthought I checked my wallet and was surprised to find it in place and intact. I thought I'd been mugged. The papers were out of order and damp, but everything was there, including the money and change

left over from the precious twenty I'd used to pay for the hotel room. It was
when I returned the wallet to its inside pocket that I noticed my shirt front.
A big burn hole was in it just over my heart, surrounded by water-diluted
red stains. There was a smaller hole down, next to my belt buckle.

I tore the shirt open and found an ugly round scar just left of the breastbone. It was large, but looked freshly healed.

The lapping of water on the shore sounded loudly in my ears. Far out
on the silver lake, the streamlined shape of a rich man's yacht glided slowly
east and disappeared behind an intervening point of land. My left hand
twitched and clenched. I made it open again. The palm had more than a
dozen puckered red circles on it. More scars, and I couldn't think of how I'd
acquired them or what might have caused them. At least they didn't hurt.
My right hand was also damaged with a narrow pink welt like a neatly
healed cut just above the knuckles. It, too, was painless. Cautiously I spread
a hand over my heart. It should have been banging away like a trapped bird,
but there was nothing, nothing but the scar and still night-cool flesh.

I rebuttoned the shirt, not wanting to look or speculate anymore and
stared helplessly at the lake. It gave no answers or comfort so I opened the
driver's door and slid behind the wheel. I rubbed my face and was surprised
at the heaviness of the beard there. Reaching over, I swiveled the rearview
mirror around and stared with an icy shock of comprehension at the empty
glass.

No.

Please, God, *no*.

Death had come to me that night, unexpected and unfair. Death had
changed me, then left, taking with it the memory of that supreme moment
we all must face. Eyes shut, I hung on to the steering wheel and vainly tried
to adjust emotionally to what had once been a distant and purely intellectual concept. In a way I was more frightened by the idea that someone had
wanted to kill me than by the fact that they'd succeeded. It was too much
to take in, the best thing was to shut down the feelings for the moment. I'd
get used to things soon enough, not that there was much choice about it
now. In a larger sense it was what animals and mankind had faced since old
Adam found himself outside the garden: adapt or die.

Having died already, there was only one alternative left, even if it was
mentally distressing.

For something to do I tied Sanderson's arms behind his back with the
belt and used his flowered necktie on his ankles. Rooting around in the
glove compartment turned up several road maps, so I was able to make a
good guess about our present location and figure out how to get back to my
hotel.

It was a tight fit behind the wheel, we were about the same height, but
my legs were longer. I didn't bother adjusting the seat, that was always more
trouble than it was worth. The starter started, the engine kicked and caught,

THE VAMPIRE FILES: VOLUME ONE

and I eased it into first. Thirty minutes later I stopped in what looked like a safe, secluded place and cut the motor. We were about a mile from my hotel according to the maps; an easy walk through the sleeping neighborhoods. This was a dead-looking business district, with a few tired stores, some dusty warehouses and empty lots decorated with weeds and broken glass. From the look of things, the Depression hadn't been kind to the place.

Sanderson was awake, but playing possum, the altered rhythm of his heart and lungs betraying his condition. He was either very controlled or too scared to flinch when I plucked his yellow silk handkerchief from his front pocket. I used it to rub my prints from the steering wheel, dashboard and gearshift, and stuffed it back in his pocket. His gun was weighing heavily in his own pocket as I leaned across the seat and gave his cheek a solid pat.

"You can open your eyes now, I know you're awake." My tongue played over teeth which had receded to their normal length. At least I'd be able to talk without lisping. "I said you can open your eyes." I gave him a hard shake.

They popped wide.

"Name?"

"F-Fred Sanderson."

"Sure it is. What are you doing in town, Fred?"

"Visiting friends."

"They got a boat?"

He shut up until shaken again. "Yeah, so what?"

"Why'd you run me down?"

"Wha—"

"You heard me, why did you try to kill me?"

The heavy jaw snapped shut again, his eyes rolled toward the door, and he struggled against his bonds. I lost my patience then, and for the first time took a great deal of pleasure hitting a man. I pulled the punches, though. I wanted to persuade, not kill him, and it took surprisingly few blows to soften him up. Despite his tough looks, he had no tolerance for pain.

"Frank Paco—said—I—just a job—" he burbled through a bloody nose.

"He your boss?"

"Yeah." Sniff.

"He wanted me dead? Why?"

He coughed messily.

"*Why?*"

"You wouldn't talk."

I got the handkerchief again and wiped his nose. "Neither are you."

"He wanted the list, you wouldn't tell him where, so he—" He froze. "How did you—it was right in the heart—"

"I got a bulletproof vest. Come on, keep talking."

Sanderson looked anything but convinced. "You *know* all this." His voice was rising with panic. "Why do you ask, you *know* all—"

"What's the boat's name?"

"*Elvira.*"

"What's the list? What's on it?"

"I dunno—honest, I don't. *You* got it, you know what's—"

"How did I get it?"

"I dunno."

"*Answer.*"

"It was Benny Galligar. You got it from him. *You* got it! I dunno nothing, I swear! Just lemme go!" He was all but screaming, and the panic had him rolling around, trying to break free. I tapped him again, did it too hard, and that ended the questioning for the night. Shoving the exasperation to one side, I went over the car again for prints and found it was registered to International Freshwater Transport, Inc. It might not be of much use, but I filed the name away for future reference.

Outside the car, I wiped the handles clean with the bottom of my coat and repeated the action on the passenger side. Sanderson's head was lolled over, leaving his neck taut and vulnerable, with the bloodsmell rising from his body like perfume. I stepped back quickly before something regrettable happened, and hurried down the street.

Sooner or later, God help me, I would have to feed.

The hotel night clerk was half-asleep when I asked for my key.

"That's two-oh-two?" he mumbled, groping for it, but there was no key hanging next to the number. "Hey, you're not Mr. Ross."

"No, I'm Jack Fleming and I want my key."

"Fleming? Oh, yeah, we had to move your things out. Don't worry, I got them right back here."

One thing after another. "Why'd you move them out?"

"Well, you only paid for the one night and when you didn't come back, we couldn't leave the room go empty. There's a convention in town an' we gotta rent the room while there's business. You know how it is."

"Yeah, I know. Can I have my stuff?"

"Sure, no problem." He hauled out a battered suitcase and a smaller, but no less battered case that held the means of my livelihood, a typewriter. I found my clothes intact, if sloppily folded, and my portable seemed to be in working order. While I checked my things, the clerk had woken up and was checking me.

"Been having some trouble?" he asked cautiously. His eyes trailed with open curiosity from my unshaved face to my damp, grubby clothes.

"Something like that." I pulled out another coat from the suitcase, turned my back to the clerk, and changed the old for new.

"Jesus Christ, are you all right? There's a big hole and blood all over your back!"

It was annoying. In sparing the guy the sight of my punctured shirtfront,

I'd given him the full benefit of the back, where the bullet that killed me had exited. I buttoned up the fresh coat and tried to bluff it through.

"Hey, you shoulda seen the *other* guy."

"No kiddin', there's—"

"Yeah, well, don't worry about it," I snapped. "The less you know, the better for both of us, if you know what I mean."

"Yeah, sure." He backed off unhappily. Perhaps as a long-time resident of Chicago he knew exactly what I meant.

"Do I owe any on my bill?"

"Just for one more day, that's all."

"You could have left things alone for another day, couldn't you?"

"Huh?"

"Couldn't you have left my stuff up there for one more day?"

"Mr. Fleming, you were *gone*—"

The man's tone alerted me. "Gone for how long?"

He looked in his book. "It was right here, you checked in Monday, then left your key with the day clerk—"

"Did I get any phone calls?"

"I dunno, we don't keep records of that. The switchboard girl might know. Anyway, when you didn't come back by checkout time Wednesday, we packed your things up. It's Friday now and we couldn't keep the room not knowing if you were coming back or not, not for no three days we couldn't."

Friday morning.

I paid up and left the hotel on shaking legs.

I wandered around for a couple hours, unhappy and frustrated by the lapse of memory. Perhaps it was the shock of being killed. Some people could block out horrible experiences in that way, and being murdered had to rank pretty high up on the horrible-experience list.

List. Whatever the hell that was.

Benny Galligar. I might have known him from New York.

It was getting brighter, the added light hurt.

The moon was long gone, the stars were fading, and things were brilliant enough right now that if I were still out when the sun came up, my eyeballs would fry in their sockets. I spotted a hand-painted hotel sign at the end of the block and hurried for it.

At the cost of fifty cents, and that was a severe overcharge, I got a monk's cell with a single dirty window overlooking a narrow alley. I locked the door, the lock a piece of bent wire that slipped through a metal eyelet screwed into the frame. The door still sagged open, so I shoved a rickety chair under the knob, but it was even money it'd give away the first time someone breathed on it wrong.

Despite the limited view, the sunlight might still find a chink in the dirt and come in. I thought of sleeping under the bed, but one look at the floor changed my mind. I had joined the ranks of the Undead, but still retained firm ideas about basic sanitation A thin blanket hung over the window dimmed things, but not by much.

I dragged my clothes off, poured water into the washbowl, and splashed my face and neck. Shaving would have to wait till tomorrow, there was no time tonight. It was creepy, anyway, not being able to see my face peering out from the mirror. I examined myself without one. Purple and black bruises were all over my stomach and flanks, with many short rows of small crescent marks that had cut the skin. I could guess they had come from brass knuckles. My wrists were encircled with raw-looking weals, indications I'd been tied down. Large crescents overlay the smaller ones, probably the result of some well-placed kicks.

I'd seen bodies like this before, but only in the morgue when I'd been covering a gang killing. The sight was always sickening. Considering the amount of damage I'd taken, the shot in the heart might have been an act of mercy. The bullet mark was still there, but looked less ugly than before. I felt for the exit hole and found a large rough depression on my back. Both were painless. The small circles on my left palm were still a puzzle, but they were quickly healing as well, the angry red softening to pink.

The sheer violence that had been directed so personally at me was more than enough to leave me emotionally stunned. *Why* it had happened was a total blank and overwhelmingly disturbing on every level.

I rubbed down with a wet towel and pulled on clean underwear and threw out the old. Of the bullet Sanderson had fired, there was no sign, except for the holes it left in my clothes. For some reason I thought about what my mom once told me concerning underwear and accidents and smiled, then my limbs went all stiff and sluggish. The sun had just come up.

Pulling the pillow and spread from the bed, I walked into the closet and shut the door. I dropped the linen on the floor to foil any light leaks and to put something between me and the dirt, then I dove headfirst into the pillow and didn't come up.

Maybe I expected something like sleep or straight black oblivion, but it wasn't that good. Frozen in place for the day, the body was utterly still, but occasionally it sent a sensory message along to the brain.

Hard floor.

Footsteps somewhere in the building.

Something crawling on the right hand.

The brain noted it all, but wouldn't or couldn't respond. It was busy dreaming.

Water, floating, darkness, pressure, blinding light. Cheap birth symbolism, but the midwife had brass knuckles and a gun. She had Sanderson's grinning face and stood aside so the doctor could aim his own gun and blast me back into the dark forever.

Heat, bad air, clothes soaked with a thousand years of sweat. Voices, yelling, wanting something. Where is it? Where did you put it?

Fighting them, but no control.

Her hair was a dark nest on the pillow, soft and thick in my fingers. Sky blue eyes flushing deep red as I gave her blood and she gave me heaven on earth in return. Where are you? Where—

—did you put it? Just tell us, we'll let you go.

Liar, I forget. I don't know. I'm dying.

I'd always bring her flowers. She didn't eat candy. She never ate. Our private joke.

Leave me alone, I don't have it, but they kept at me, killing an inch at a time.

Books tumbled open, the words clear and sharp and utterly false. Thousands of books lined up in uneven rows like an army before the uniforms are issued. One thick black book, almost, but not quite true. Her thick dark hair—forget the books, just love her, that's all she really wants. Give her—

—the list, where did you put it?

Where did you go? Why did you leave me?

A boat, a big one, but the water still closes over us all, pulling us down into the cold—

—and stiff, I've got to move. If I can just move I'll stop dreaming. God, let me sleep or wake, but not this.

No control.

A man screaming.

Falling.

Dying.

No control.

Sunset.

Release.

2

I pushed the pillow away and forced air into the dormant lungs. The dream dance whirled away into nothing, leaving a cold, stiff, frightened man to deal with the memory. Why hadn't she told me about the dreams? She told me what to do when death-time came, but never mentioned this. Maybe it was just trauma, maybe it would fade eventually, for now there was nothing I could do but try to shrug it off and get dressed.

It was something of a trick to shave without looking, but if I got nicked I never felt it. It'd be interesting when it came time for a haircut, I'd yet to see a barbershop without a mirror.

My other suit was too heavy for the weather, but the heat didn't seem to be bothering me. In a way it was disturbing not to be sweating. I took down the blanket, tossed it on the bed and cracked the window for the sake of appearance. The spread and pillow joined the blanket, and I shut the door.

My shoes squeaked coming downstairs. The dip in the lake hadn't done them any good. I dropped the useless room key at the front desk and went outside.

The first trash can I found became home for my bullet-ridden blood-stained clothes. The labels and laundry marks got thrown into a storm drain farther down the street.

A mercenary street kid charged me a nickel for directions to a district full of pawnshops. Most of them were closed by now, the ones still open didn't have what I needed. I leaned against a doorway, tired and restless. My senses were painfully sharp, matching my teeth. I pushed the canines back in their sockets with shaking fingers. I'd have to feed soon or drop in my tracks.

The last open shop looked no more promising than the rest, but the first thing I saw inside was the big steamer trunk in the middle aisle. It was a good three by five feet and solid looking. Except for some travel stickers and dust, it was almost new. My satisfaction was apparent to the sharp-eyed owner and it took ten minutes to haggle the price down to a reasonable level. Once in agreement, money changed hands and I was hauling the trunk out the door.

No cabs were in sight so I was resigned to walking the six blocks back to the hotel. The trunk was awkward with its bulk, but oddly lightweight because of my new strength. I went as quickly as I dared, hoping other pedestrians would be alert enough to get out of the way in time.

"Hey, buddy, c'mere a minute."

Startled at being addressed, I paused, then cursed myself. Just like any hick fresh off the farm, I was about to be mugged. The man in the alley was in deep shadow except where his gun poked out, fat lot of good it did him with my night vision.

"Come on, put down the box and get over here. Now." He waved the gun.

I eased the trunk to the pavement. I was fast enough now to take the guy, but the gun might go off and bring the cops, and I had no desire to risk putting bullet holes in my last suit. Wishing hard I were any place else, I stepped forward.

The man shimmered, went gray, and vanished. So did the alley.

As though from a long distance, I heard his yelp of surprise and the slap of feet as he ran away. That was of minor concern, though; I was having trouble with my senses again. No weight, no form, and just this side of total panic; I could see nothing, but was aware of shapes and sizes close by. I felt the wind pushing me right through the wall of a building, my body oozing between the cracks in the bricks. I shoved away hard and launched myself through the wall of the opposite building, and stumbled to my feet in a ladies' clothing store.

It was great to have feet again and legs and all the other things that usually come with a solid body. I leaned on a table, delighted to have hands again. Reality was just wonderful. . . .

I looked around and wondered how I was supposed to get out.

All in all, dematerialization was tough on the nerves, but a hell of a great way to avoid a mugging.

My escape from the dress shop was a reluctant undertaking. Going through the doors the usual way required breaking a lock and perhaps setting off an alarm. At least the place was closed. My sudden appearance out of nowhere might spoil business for the owner though it would have made for an easier exit out a door. I wasn't sure I could repeat the trick. In retrospect it seemed more instinctive than conscious, like trying to swim when thrown into water for the first time. Don't panic and the body would do all the rest.

The third try was successful.

One second I was in the shop, the next, outside with the trunk and making sure my body was all there. Everything was intact, but I was very tired and my throat ached with thirst.

I turned the room light on out of habit, then squeezed the trunk through the door. Between it, the bed, and my belongings, it was beginning to look like a set from a Marx Brothers movie. I sank onto the creaking chair and miserably considered food. There was no way I could cheat around my condition. The mere thought of going out for even the rarest of steaks made me nauseous, but that in turn led to another thought.

Hurrying downstairs, I whistled up a cab. By the time one arrived I was twitching with restlessness. I forced myself to move sedately getting in and remembered to sit close to the door to be out of sight of the rearview mirror.

"Where to, mister?"

"The Stockyards," I lisped around my teeth.

We crossed water twice to get there, the opposing natural force pressing me hard into the seat as the cab lurched forward. The pressure was uncomfortable but bearable. The roaring emptiness inside was far worse.

"You all right, mister?" the driver asked as I paid him.

I nodded without speaking and kept my eyes down, not wanting to frighten him. I felt strange and no doubt looked strange. The last time I was this way a man had fainted, and a repetition of the experience would be inconvenient now.

The air was permeated with the smell of blood. There were other smells, but this was the one that cut through them all and gave me a direction to follow.

The place was full of people and noise, train whistles shrieked, cattle lowed and bellowed, men shouted and cursed—men were everywhere, including where I wanted to go.

I went in, anyway.

At this point I was challenged only once by a large specimen who, from the size of his shoulders, looked like he swung the sledgehammers that sent the animals on their final journey to the dinner tables. I couldn't understand what he was saying to me, except it was hostile in some way. He was nothing less than an annoying obstacle to walk past, but he stopped me with a slab of a hand.

This kind of behavior irritates me at the best of times, but I was now to the point of physical pain. I swatted his hand away and snarled some threat, a mild enough reaction considering how badly I felt. We locked eyes in anger for an instant and for the first time I became aware of another human mind.

I told him to leave, and from my brief contact with him knew he thought his sudden retreat was his own idea. I wanted to think about this, to examine and test it to make sure it was not just imagination, but something stronger and much more insistent was in charge. All it wanted was to end the desperate, empty agony that was turning me inside out. Clear thought blurred and faded, the body was taking over in order to survive. It needed privacy from the interference of others; sought and found it among the more distant cattle pens. It wanted a quiescent victim and chose the least alarmed animal from the dozen that milled around the enclosure.

Here, too, was a mind; an alien one to my own, with simple dull impulses I could override. It stood rooted as I approached because I wanted it to do so. I drew close and touched one of its big surface veins, nearly sobbing with relief. For what I had to do there was no conscious thought or the least anticipation of revulsion. This was now normal if I wanted to survive. I closed in, intuitively knowing what to do, cutting neatly through the thick flesh with my teeth to open the vein.

Warm and rich with life, it pulsed into my mouth.

No more than a minute passed and I had all I needed. I released the animal, physically, mentally, and gratefully. A little blood dribbled from the wound, but soon stopped and the cow mingled with others, apparently none the worse for wear. I leaned against a fence rail and wiped my lips clean with a handkerchief. The pain and tunnel vision were gone, it was like waking up from the day's bad dreams. I had only to shake off the memory and start functioning again. My first idea was to leave the Stockyards as discreetly as possible. My newly learned vanishing trick might come in handy, but I'd wait awhile on that one, wanting to get used to the idea.

Prosaically using my old dependable legs, I left the place and found a taxi, returned to the hotel, and had it wait. Upstairs, I threw my stuff in the trunk, carried it down, and checked out. The driver and I managed to secure the thing to the car. It stuck out the back, but was in no immediate danger of falling into the street.

I hunched down in the backseat and asked to be taken to the same train station that had welcomed me to the city two days ago. Correction, six days ago, but I'd think about the amnesia later, right now I felt like a finalist from a dance marathon. It was not enough to feed and shut out the sunlight, I had to have earth around my body and it would have to be soon. I had to go home.

Once at the station, I booked the trunk on the next train to Cincinnati. By the time a man came for it, I was already inside. To my delight I was able to vanish and reform without trouble and without disturbing the lock or thick leather straps. Gingerly perching on the typewriter case, I braced my arms against the sides and held the suitcase in place with my knees to keep things from rattling too much as I was bumped from one end of the station to the other. Packed in like a living pretzel, the trunk didn't seem nearly so large, but from the grunts and curses outside, the porter disagreed.

The trip, at least at night, was very boring. I initially suffered through a couple bouts of mild claustrophobia, but was far too weary to let the cramped quarters get to me. I kept movement to a minimum, not wanting to alarm the baggage man, but still shifted around, vainly seeking a more comfortable position. It was tempting to get out and take a walk, but I was abnormally tired and unsure of my ability to get back inside again. At least I didn't need air.

The train crawled toward Cincinnati, but the sun came up before we got there, and I was trapped in the dark with senseless memories for the day. It was just as bad as the last dream bout, but faded sooner, and when the train stopped I'd slipped into a semi-aware trance that brought no rest, but did abridge the passage of time. When night came again I was stationary and correctly guessed from the intrusive sounds that the trunk had been unloaded and was waiting to be claimed.

I felt marginally better just being in Cincinnati, and drifted easily from the trunk to reform in a crouch among the other baggage. When no one was looking I slipped out and blended in with the rest of the travelers, keeping my hat pulled low. This was my hometown and I had a lot of friends, the last thing I wanted was to renew old acquaintances. Once outside, I ducked into a cab and gave directions that took us north of town and down a narrow, unlit rural road. The driver got a little nervous after awhile and asked me if I was sure I knew where I was going. I was sure, as sure as an iron filing knows where the magnet is.

I had him stop and asked if he minded waiting.

"Waiting for what? There's nothing out here."

I took out a dollar bill and told him that was his tip, tore it in two, and gave him half. He still looked apprehensive.

"I'll have to keep the meter running."

That was fine. I left the road and walked up an overgrown private lane.

Grandfather's farm was deserted now and the place seemed smaller than I'd remembered. In truth, the land around had shrunk over the years, sold off a few acres at a time to make the taxes. My father refused to sell the house itself, though, or the immediate acreage, not that there were many buyers these days. Grandfather and Great-Grandfather Fleming and their families were buried here along with a lot of memories. Run down as the place was, I was glad it was still ours.

My parents lived in a smaller, more modern house in the city. Mom treasured her gas stove and indoor plumbing; no one lived out here anymore. I looked up at a corner window on the second floor that marked the room I'd been born in. This was my home as I'd never known it before, the house standing on the living earth I needed to survive.

Searching the barn turned up some old feed sacks in good enough condition to use once the dust and field mice had been shaken out. Taking four sacks, I doubled them one inside the other, making two sturdy bags. Another search turned up a ball of twine and a rusty shovel with a broken handle. It would do. What it lacked in leverage I could make up for in strength.

The cemetery grounds were still cared for, indicating Dad's occasional presence. I cleared a patch under the big oak tree of leaves and acorn husks and began shoveling dirt into the bags working over a large area so the missing soil would be less noticeable. When the bags were three-quarters full I twisted the ends and tied them up tight with the twine.

Despite the hard work I was no longer tired.

A big stone that hadn't been there on my last visit a few years back was marking Grandfather's grave. I went over to touch the cool gray granite. The previous wood marker had borne the same deeply chiseled letters that spelled out my own name.

In Memory of
JONATHAN RUSSELL FLEMING
1820–1908

I was glad no sentimental phrase was carved under the date; nothing would have been appropriate. A man like Grandfather or the family's feelings for him could not have been so neatly summed up.

When I was eight, my puppy died. Like me it had been the runt of a litter of seven, and for that reason it was my favorite. With the dreadful practicality to be found on working farms, the body was disposed of in the trash burner. Unable to accept the idea, I hid under the porch all day holding the limp little ball of fur and wishing it back to life again. When the family missed me, I ignored their calls. After all, they'd ignored me and it was only fair.

In the end Mom found me and dragged me out, promising certain doom on my backside as soon as I dropped my britches. Even at that early age I was mulishly stubborn, refusing to participate in my punishment and resisting all efforts to be separated from the puppy.

Grandfather interfered.

"Not this time," he told Mom. "I'll take care of him. I'm not as mad as you are." He took my hand and we walked down to the graveyard and sat under the oak tree.

"You shouldn't have hidden out, Jack," he said at length.

"No, sir. But they were going to burn Pete, and I don't want him to go to Hell." I held my breath; it was the first time I'd used a bad word.

Incredibly, Grandfather nodded. "I see what you mean. Would you feel better if we buried him proper?"

"Yes, sir, but I don't want him dead."

"Neither do I, but there are a lot of things we can't do anything about, and death is one of them."

"Why?"

The old man considered the question awhile, trying to gear the answer for an eight-year-old mind. "You like summer, don't you?"

"Yes, sir, no school."

"But if it lasted all the time you might get tired of it, don't you think?"

"I dunno."

"When school comes along in the fall and you get to see all your friends again, aren't you glad of the change?"

"I guess."

"And when winter comes you do different things because of the snow, and that's a nice change, too."

"Yes, sir."

"Well, now—this is the interesting part, Jack—dying is a change, too, just like the seasons. People live in the spring like you and your brothers and sisters, they grow up to a long summer and autumn, like your parents and me, and then sooner or later they die, and that's like winter. It's not a bad thing—it's only a change."

"But don't people go to Heaven?"

"Sure they do, but they have to change, they have to die to get there. Some folks are even glad of the change because it means they'll have no worries and something different to do. When your grandma was dying years ago she was hurting and tired; she was ready for a change. We were sad when she was gone, but we also knew she wasn't hurting anymore. We knew she's gone to Heaven and was happy."

Grandfather's voice had cracked. I was stunned to see tears rolling down his lined face. He pulled out a bandanna and wiped them away.

"Now, I don't know everything, but I'll just bet you Pete was hurting somehow and knew he needed to die, and when he did he didn't hurt no more. He didn't want to make you sad, but he just couldn't help it."

"So he changed?"

"Yes."

"So he's in Heaven?"

"I don't see why not, but it doesn't really matter what happens to his little body, it's all the same to him. The part of him that you loved isn't here no more—he changed. What really matters is that you know about this and that it's all right to feel sad. It's also good to be happy when you remember how he made you happy while he was around."

I thought about it hard while we buried the puppy near the oak tree, ringing the small grave with some stones. Halfway through the job I started crying, and Grampy loaned me his bandanna without a word and went on with the work. When he finished, he looked up at the northern horizon and took a deep, cleansing breath.

"I think winter is coming," he said, and winked at me. It was only September; I didn't understand. I did the next morning when we found he'd died in his sleep. I was the only one who didn't cry at the funeral.

I couldn't help but think of my own change. "What would you think of me now, Grampy?" I whispered at the stone. I could almost sense the big bones resting in their pine box, patiently waiting for the Second Coming.

I tossed the broken shovel back in the barn and stalked down the lane, the two thirty-pound bags swinging light in my hands.

The return trip to Chicago was boring, but easier to get through with the earth packed into the trunk with me. Rested and more confident about vanishing, I spent most of the night sitting on top of the baggage reading a dime magazine. I could almost ignore river crossings, and when daylight came I was able to truly sleep, or whatever it was. The dreaming had faded. The presence of the earth even dulled the next night's hunger down to a low-level ache.

It took a good half hour to claim my trunk. The Chicago station was very busy, just as it was when I first arrived. There was a week-old trail to pick up on, but I had a good idea about where to start.

The trunk was laboriously loaded into a cab, and the cab took me to a small hotel the driver knew about that was within walking distance of the Stockyards. It was a cut above the fleabag I'd last stayed in. For ten dollars a week I got heavier curtains, a fan that worked, a radio, and a private bath. Its proximity to the Yards must have had an effect on the price and the presence of luxury extras.

Not bothering to unpack or even drop off the key, I left the hotel to get some dinner. My visit this time was more discreet; I knew the lay of the land better and trusted my disappearing trick to keep me out of trouble. It was taking a little practice to get it just right, but I was catching on fast. Learning to wiggle my ears as a kid had taken a lot longer.

On the way back, I stopped at a newsstand, bought some local papers, a copy of the one I'd worked for in New York, and a street map. The vendor gave me directions to the nearest Western Union office. The place was open with two fresh-faced young clerks in command. I filled out a telegram to my parents saying I'd arrived in the Windy City and managed to land a terrific job at an ad agency and they'd advanced me some money for one of my ideas. Along with the message, I sent twenty-five dollars. They'd been having hard times since the Crash, and hardly a payday passed that I didn't mail them five bucks or so to help out, but this time the amount was conspicuously large. They might think I'd turned to bank robbery, which wasn't too far off the mark, but the truth was hardly something I could tell them about.

I went back to the hotel. While the tub was filling I read the headlines and funnies and jotted notes on the rates for the personal columns. Using the hotel stationery, I printed out my usual message, all seven words of it, then shut off the tub taps and went downstairs.

This place actually had a bellboy on duty. He was reading a comic book in an alcove with his wooden chair tilted back on two legs, making more dents in the floor. I asked him if he wanted to make four bits. He put away the book. It took a minute to straighten things out. His usual type of errand for a guest was to either locate a female companion or a bottle of booze or both, neither of which I had much use for at the moment. I gave him the four bits and enough money for him to place my message in all the papers I'd bought. It would run for two weeks. He promised to do it first thing tomorrow. I told him to bring me the receipts in the evening and he'd get another tip.

Upstairs, my room had steamed up slightly from the bath water, so I opened the window and turned on the fan the thoughtful management had bolted to a table. It stirred the air around and felt good against my skin as I stripped.

By now the bruising was nearly gone and the scar over my heart was fast disappearing. My body was making good use of the fresh blood I'd imbibed.

I studied the tub warily before stepping in, grimacing at the flash of apprehension it caused. It was only the free-running stuff I had to worry about, really. Nothing happened when I stepped in and soaped up, it just felt like something ought to. I sank back and thought about the beach . . . perhaps with the water around me I could go back . . . the stars had been so bright, the lake stretching on forever . . . silver and black. Before the peace of the beach there had been crushing darkness . . . hard pressure pushing from all sides, weight dragging me down . . . smothering pressure, growing worse—

I was on my back on the bathroom floor along with a lot of water. The pressure was gone, but my left hand twitched as though electricity were running through it. My body trembled uncontrollably. It lasted a moment more, scaring the hell out of me, then abruptly stopped.

If it brought this kind of reaction, I wasn't so sure now I wanted to remember my death. I dressed, nervously tried to push the incident from my mind, and vowed never to relax in a tub again.

It was past midnight when I stepped out into the humid air and turned right. The address I wanted had been in the phone book and the map said it was on the same side of the Chicago River as my hotel. After spending the last two nights cooped up in a trunk I wanted a long walk. At least it would save on cab fare.

Forty minutes later I reached the warehouse offices of International Freshwater Transport, Inc. There was no dark green Ford in the street. I didn't know whether to be disappointed or relieved.

The front door was a thick, no-nonsense steel thing. I tried to go through the metal, but found it to be more dense than building bricks or my trunk and couldn't pass until I slid under the thin gap between the door and threshold. I felt like sand dribbling through the skinny part of an hourglass.

This operation had no budget for extras. The reception office was a small area divided from the warehouse by wood planks nailed to two-by-four framing. There was a steel desk, some broken-in chairs, and a couple file cabinets, suspiciously unlocked. The papers inside were routine and therefore useless.

The desk held the promise of a single locked drawer that I opened with the help of a letter opener. Inside were two ledger books, the last year's and this year's, and a half-full fifth of whiskey. After looking at the books, it became obvious the drawer had been locked because of the whiskey. IFT, Inc. was just what its name suggested: shipments came in, stayed at the warehouse, and then continued to their destinations. Most of the traffic was between the U.S. and Canada, hence "international" in the title. Maybe it looked good on the letterheads. Maybe Sanderson's car was stolen, in which case I was wasting my time.

I flipped through more papers lying on the desktop. Nothing. The blotter on the desk was a giant calendar. It was the last week of the month and covered with old doodles and odd notes. The first Monday was circled in red with an underlined notation. The ink had gotten smeared by something wet, so the specifics were lost, but there was one clear name in the mess.

Mr. Paco. Something or other—Mr. Paco.

Sanderson's boss. At least there was a connection, so I went through all the papers again more carefully, but had to give up. Aside from the single name on the blotter he wasn't mentioned again, but I went through the tried-and-true motions. I noted down names and addresses, anything that might prove useful later on. Taking no chances, I wiped away my fingerprints on the unlikely idea they might call the cops when the broken drawer was discovered. Finished with the office, I checked out the warehouse.

It was big, of course, and despite my now-excellent night vision, gloomy, but that was only an emotional reaction. The actual level of light was more than sufficient. Predictably, it was filled with hundreds of wooden crates, each labeled and neatly stacked. Some were marked as farm equipment, others as spare parts, nothing there was of a perishable nature. I pried open a box and rooted around in the packing material, finding new metal junk that did indeed look like spare parts to something. The operation looked well organized and aboveboard, and nothing, absolutely nothing, was familiar to me.

It was a quarter to four when I got back to my room. I thought I should feel tired, but wasn't, that I should be hungry, but there were no pangs. All the things one usually felt after an extended errand weren't there, and I missed them. I missed being human; even the physical discomforts would have been welcome. I was depressed and couldn't even get drunk to forget it.

My trunk was unlocked.

I stopped being depressed and got scared instead.

The lid flipped up. I was hardly aware of doing it. My eyes vainly tried to focus on something that should have been there but wasn't.

My precious bags of earth were gone.

In their place was a folded piece of hotel paper. I grabbed it up. The paper was covered with cramped, precise handwriting.

Dear Sir:

You do not know me but, as you may gather, I know something of you. If you would learn more, meet me at the address below. I shall be there until dawn. You should have no difficulty locating the street, as it serves the Stockyards.

Hopefully,
A Friend

3

WITH great care I refolded the paper, thinking furiously. I knew no one in town, unless I counted Fred Sanderson, and the note sounded too high-tone for his ilk. The writer was certainly aware of my nature since he'd taken my earth. He also had to be crazy. Who else but a complete nut would want to make friends with a vampire?

My map verified the meeting place was indeed only a few blocks from the Stockyards, no more than a ten-minute walk.

I made it in four.

Clearly aware it could be some sort of trap, I wavered awhile, torn between curiosity and caution. Grabbing the trunk and running back to Cincinnati was an attractive option, but the identity of my correspondent would remain a mystery, and probably one I couldn't afford. Somewhere down the line I'd been very careless.

Curiosity and the need to recover my earth won out, but I still checked the area before going in. It was a business district, with small stores at street level and a scattering of offices on the upper floors. Many of them were empty, the rest were struggling hard to reach the prosperity which was supposed to be just around the corner. I circled the entire block of buildings slowly, making sure there were no surprises trying to hide in the shadows. Except for a few parked cars with cold motors, the place was deserted and asleep.

There was one lit window in the building I wanted, up on the second floor. Blinds were drawn over the glass. I could see nothing from the street.

Inside, I climbed the stairs as quietly as possible, but the caution was wasted. Between the old loose board and my shoes, the squeaks were deafening to my ears. At the landing were two doors facing each other with opaque glass panels set in them and numbers painted on the glass. The one with light shining on the other side was on the left. I went still and listened; in the room beyond a single set of lungs pumped shallowly.

Pressing hard against the wall to present a narrow target, I turned the knob slowly and pushed. The door swung open easily and without a creak. I could hear a heart now and it began beating rapidly. His lungs worked faster to keep pace. Given the circumstances, mine would be, too, if they still worked regularly.

The man's voice was belyingly calm. "I gather you found my note. Good evening to you, sir. Would you care to step into the light so we might better see each other?" He had a very distinct British accent.

I hadn't any better ideas and eased away from the wall. Inside was a small, plain room with a single wooden desk facing the door. The man standing behind it was in his mid-thirties, tall and on the thin side, with a bony face and beaky nose. His sharp gray eyes were fixed on me and gleaming with excitement.

On the floor next to the desk were my two bags of earth. He followed my look and took on an apologetic tone.

"I hope you are not offended by the theatrics, but it was the one thing I could think of that would guarantee your coming here."

I was angry and let it show. He stiffened and clutched at something on his desk. Whatever it was lay under an open newspaper. It was too big for a handgun and the wrong shape for a rifle. I made myself calm down; he'd gone to considerable trouble and risk to get me here, I'd at least hear him out. A few moments passed with the two of us waiting for the other to make a move. His breathing evened out and I relaxed my posture.

"You seem to know who I am," I ventured.

"I only know the name you gave on the hotel register. However, I do know *what* you are."

"And what do you plan to do about it?"

"That depends entirely upon yourself." He gestured with his free hand at a chair near the desk. "Perhaps you would like to make yourself more comfortable, Mr. . . . tell me, is it really Robinson?"

"Jack will do for now, and I like it out here well enough." I was acutely aware of the man's scrutiny, as if he were expecting something from me.

"Then it is true."

"About what?"

"That you cannot enter a dwelling without an invitation. I occasionally live here, you see."

I was liking the situation less and less. "Just tell me what you want."

"Yes, I see I'm being unfair, but I don't know you and have no reason to trust you."

"I could say the same thing." No invisible force like the want of an invitation was keeping me outside, only natural caution. I first wanted to know what he was hiding under the paper, and it did no harm to have him underestimating my abilities.

"Indeed, but then you are a much more dangerous person than I am if all the stories are true."

Great, the guy really was crazy. "How dangerous are you?"

"To you, at least during the day, I might prove to be very deadly."

He was perfectly right. He knew my hotel and might have means of finding out where I'd go should I decide to bolt for home, or I could walk in and grab my earth and discover the hard way what he had under the paper.

He watched me thinking it out. "I only said that to keep you here; I'm hoping you'll understand I need not be an enemy."

"What are you, anyway, some kind of—Van Helsing?" I nearly said Renfield and changed it only at the last second.

He was amused. "So you've read *Dracula*?"

"Yes, and seen the movie."

"What did you think of it?"

"They could have done worse."

"Was it very accurate?"

"In what way?"

"Concerning yourself, of course."

"I have yet to stalk around in a cape and tuxedo and drool over feminine throats."

"But you do have to drink blood?"

I found that very difficult to acknowledge.

"Why are you so uncomfortable with that concept?"

"Why are you so damned nosy? What do you want?"

"I apologize. I am being frightfully rude to treat you like a lab specimen. Please don't be offended that I got carried away."

The man seemed genuinely sincere. I shrugged. "I'm a journalist, I know how it is."

"Thank you. What paper do you work for?"

"I don't. I quit the one I worked for in New York and came here."

"And?"

"And nothing. I've been too busy to look for a job."

"How odd you should need one. I would have thought that over the years you would have accumulated sufficient funds to be very comfortable."

"You haven't quite got the right idea about me."

"What do you mean?"

"I mean I'm still new at this; I'm just four days old."

That made him pause. "You've been a vampire for only four days?"

"Nights, if you want to be accurate."

"How utterly fascinating."

"If you say so."

"Could you tell me how you came to be this way? Were you attacked by a vampire?"

The melodramatic question made me smile. I shook my head. "It's kind of a long story. . . ."

He took the hint. "May I have your word that you won't tear me to pieces if I ask you in?"

"It's not worth much since you don't know me."

He shrugged. "You took a chance coming here. I'll risk it."

A crazy man or a brave one. "You got it. Besides, this is my last good suit. I don't want to ruin it."

If the joke was funny, he didn't laugh. "Very well, Jack, enter freely and of your own will."

"Don't you think that sounds a little corny?"

"It does at that, but does it work?"

I walked in slowly, making a show of it. His heart was going like a hammer, but his face was calm; a frightened man, but good at hiding it. The idea that I was the inspiration for all this fear made me uncomfortable and nervous, so I'd have to put us both at ease. I stuck out my hand.

"Jack Fleming."

He carefully switched hands under the paper and gripped mine briefly. "Charles Escott."

"Glad to meet you."

"Please sit down." He again indicated the chair next to his desk. Good Lord, but we were so polite and formal.

I sat and tried to look harmless. After a moment, he sank into his own chair, his eyes never leaving me. Whatever he expected me to be like, he'd apparently overestimated my ferocity. I hadn't been ferocious in years. Escott's heart slowed down and I breathed a mental sigh of relief.

"It must be obvious that I am intensely curious about you," he said. "I would very much like to hear your story, if you don't mind telling it."

I chewed my lower lip and did my own sizing up of him, look for look and his surroundings. There were two doors: the one I used and another behind Escott. The walls were bare of any kind of decoration but white paint. The place gave no clue to his personality, the man himself was the only clue. Piercing, intelligent eyes, thin lips, nervous hands; he reminded me of one of my long-ago college professors. His clothes were neat and nondescript; not expensive, not cheap, ordinary and therefore unnoticeable. I'd already figured he'd been following me around. He must have been good at it since I'd been looking over my shoulder all evening.

"Do you plan to shoot me with whatever you have under the paper?"

"Sorry, I'm just naturally cautious." He drew the paper away to reveal a cocked and loaded crossbow.

This time the man knew his stuff. If anything could hurt me, it would be the wooden shaft lying ready in the contraption. I regarded it with some respect. "If it makes you more comfortable, you can keep it, just don't shoot me."

Escott's brows went up, surprised that I had given him such permission. It indicated that I could take the thing away from him if I chose. I was sure I could, but not anxious to force the issue. He took his hand from the trigger, but left the weapon within reach.

Having come to a sort of mutual truce, I felt more like talking.

"It started in New York a couple years ago," I said. "There was a big publicity build for the movie *Dracula*. It was quite a hit, women fainting in the aisles and that sort of thing. My editor sent me down to interview people who'd seen the show, and write up about how scared they were. It was all pretty predictable stuff, but then I met this girl who thought the whole thing was terribly funny. She was really beautiful. We got to talking about the supernatural. At first I thought she might be into spiritualism or astrology or some other silliness, but she wasn't. She was like a butterfly collector I once knew."

Escott made an expression indicating he needed that one explained.

"He had hundreds of butterflies, he knew all about them, and was willing to learn more, but he never actually wanted to *be* one. She was like that. She knew a lot, liked to talk, but didn't believe in it for a minute."

"I see. I gather you liked her."

"I fell in love the second I saw her." I left it at that, not knowing if Escott could possibly understand. I drew more air and went on. "We dated, just like a couple of kids, and one night she asked me over to her house. We ate dinner, at least I did. She never ate with me when we were out; I thought she was just kidding me along because of the movie. It was a private joke for us, you know? After dinner we listened to the radio, danced a little . . ." My voice was getting thick, I couldn't help it.

"Mr. Fleming, if this is too personal for you, you needn't go on."

I pulled myself together. "Thanks. You get the idea of what it all led up to, going into details—"

"I understand." He sounded as though he really did.

"After that, we were together all the time, at least at night. It was no joke, she really was a vampire, but it didn't seem to matter much. I was in total possession of my faculties, too. I did research on the subject, of course, and talked to her about it. None of the books I found on vampirism remotely mentioned anything about what we had or felt for each other. They were full of a lot of stories of helpless victims and bloodthirsty attackers; kind of sick stuff, really. If you want to get psychological you could call it symbolic rape. When you get into the Freudian end of things it really gets weird, but none of that had anything to do with the reality we shared."

"During this relationship did you—was there ever an exchange of blood?" He kept his voice carefully neutral.

"Yes," was my brief reply.

"The purpose of this exchange was to eventually make you like her?"

"If it worked."

"Worked?"

"She said it didn't always work or else the world would be hip-deep in vampires. Almost everyone is immune to it, you see. I think it's like a very rare disease that some people can't catch it even if they want to."

"You wanted to?"

"For us to always be together, yes, and she did what she could toward that end, but it was never certain. We'd have no way of knowing until the day I died, but at least until then we'd always be together."

"But something happened?"

The words were sticking in my throat. "We had a date. I went to her house to pick her up and she wasn't there. She didn't have a lot of possessions, but a few clothes and toiletries were gone and she left the rest of her stuff like she meant to come back. Later I got a card in the mail. She said she was having some trouble, that some people were after her because of what she was, and to look out for them. She'd come back when it was safe. That was five years ago." I left unsaid the weeks of worry, fear, and frustration and the months spent trying to find her. In five years the pain had not faded and the wound was still raw to touch.

He saw it on my face. "I'm very sorry."

"I think . . . maybe they found her." I got up suddenly and paced around the room, trying to work off the build of emotional energy. My back to him, I paused to look through the blinds at the empty street below. "You're the only one I've ever told the whole story to."

"I apologize for forcing the confidence. It shall not be repeated to anyone."

I believed him. "Thanks." After a while I got control again and sat down. "Life went on, I guess. I finally decided to leave New York. Last Monday I breezed into town, found a flop for the night, got a phone call and walked out. Sometime Thursday night or Friday morning last I woke up dead on a beach just west of the city."

He took a moment to digest it. "Who called you?"

"I don't know, it might be someone named Benny Galligar."

"How did you die?" He made it sound like an ordinary question.

"I was shot. Before that I was beaten up badly."

"Who did it? Why?"

"I don't know!"

"You don't—"

"Between Monday afternoon and Friday morning I can't remember a damned thing."

"How extraordinary."

"If you say so." Then I finished the rest of my story.

"How utterly extraordinary."

"You're repeating yourself."

"Yours is a fascinating case."

"You sound like a doctor. What are you, anyway? It's your turn to talk."

"Certainly I owe you that. I'm a private agent; people bring me their problems and I try to help them. The vernacular here would be private investigator, but I find that particular label and its attendant connotations can give people the wrong idea about my work."

"You mean you don't do divorces."

He stifled a smile and leaned forward clasping his hands together. "Mr. Fleming, if you have no objections, I'd like very much to help you discover what occurred to you in those missing days—to help you solve your own murder, if you will."

"Well, I don't know—"

"We could be of great help to one another."

"I'm listening."

"For instance, you're a newcomer to the city, but I know it very well. I know the people who run things and the people who control *them*. Capone may be gone now, but the gangs are still active and they are very powerful. Frank Paco heads one of them. If he had you killed he must have had a very good reason."

He straightened, reaching for the crossbow. I tensed and then relaxed. He'd been looking for a pipe that had gotten shuffled under the paper. "Do you mind?"

"No, go ahead."

"It sometimes helps me to think, mostly it keeps me awake." He tilted the chair back after the pipe was drawing, and stared at the ceiling. I stared at my shoes and thought about getting another pair the next night. These looked like something off a bum, but worse. The pipe smoke gradually added a pungent flavor to the air, but for some reason it made me uncomfortable and I considered pulling the blinds up to improve the air circulation.

He was staring at me with open curiosity, and I was beginning to think it was his favorite expression.

"Excuse me, but are you breathing at all?"

"Only when I talk. I'm afraid it comes with the condition."

"In the winter you shall have to remember to wear a scarf over your mouth or people might notice."

"I hadn't thought of that. Listen, do you mind answering some of my questions?"

"Not at all."

"How did you find me and know what I am?"

"I confess to a lifelong interest in the outré, but never expected to come face-to-face with a living, so to speak, example. I first saw you at the railway station and was instantly struck by the fact that we physically resemble each other, though of course, you're a bit younger."

"I don't think so. How old do I look?"

"No more than twenty-three or -four."

"But I'm thirty-six," I protested.

"Perhaps it's part of your changed condition. That *is* very interesting. But to continue, I enjoy watching people: I note their mannerisms, walks, faces, but I don't like to get caught doing it; that spoils the fun. People draw the wrong conclusions or become offended or both, so I practice covert observation."

"Come again?"

"I don't get caught watching. I follow them, face one direction and look in another—and I study their reflections in mirrors."

"I didn't notice any mirrors."

"True, but there were several panels of glass available that served just as well. Even the window on the door of the cab you took was useful. I saw your trunk and the porter, but could not see you. Something as unusual as that could not be ignored, so I followed you in another cab to your hotel. I listened as you registered and got your room number and the name you gave. When you came back down and went to the Stockyards I lost you there somehow, but by great luck you turned up again at a newsstand that was on your route home. Then you spent some time at a Western Union office, and when you left I tried to find out the nature of the telegrams you sent. To their credit, the employees were quite reticent, though one did mention you sent money to your mother. Then I had to leave, lest I lose you. I set up a vigil at your hotel, intending to call on you during the day to see if my suspicions were correct. You left again some time later, so I seized the opportunity to search your room.

"Once inside, I took the liberty of going through your luggage and found those two bags of earth. It gave me quite a turn because up to then I was still only half believing what my eyes had told me. Of course, you might have had some other reason for carrying them around, but it would hardly explain your lack of a reflection. I wanted to meet you and talk, but had to do so without placing myself in unnecessary danger. It would have to be under controllable conditions. My knowledge of vampires is, at present, limited to Stoker's book and that film. I had to hope they were correct.

Leaving you my note, I took your bags to guarantee your coming, and set my defenses."

"Just the crossbow?"

"And the hope that you could not cross the threshold without an invitation."

"That's it?"

He opened the desk drawer and drew out some garlic and a large crucifix. He was puzzled when I didn't flinch away, and his eyes went wide with alarm when I actually picked them up. I wrinkled my nose at the garlic, but then I never did like the stuff. I gave it back to Escott. "You can't win them all."

He fingered the cross with astonishment. "But I thought—"

"Yeah, I did, too, once. Look at it this way: I was basically a decent guy before someone killed me, and I don't feel any different now. Maybe if I were, say, the real Dracula with his life history, I'd twitch if I saw a cross, too. As for the garlic, in the part of Europe where it originated as a weapon against vampires it's a basic cure for just about everything. You got a cold, rheumatism, a headache? Try a little garlic. Troubled by vampires? Use garlic, it can't hurt. It can't help, either. What good is something that smells bad against someone who doesn't have to breathe?"

"That is a good point," he admitted. "Was I at least right about the threshold?"

" 'Fraid not. How do you think I was able to get into the hotel in the first place?"

"Oh."

"How did you get into my room?"

"With the aid of some highly illegal, but very useful lock picks, which also served well for your trunk. I must compliment you on that for a very good idea; a large trunk is certainly less noticeable than a coffin."

"It was the only thing I could think of. Besides, it beats taking a flop in a closet."

"I'm sure a coffin might bar you from the better hotels as well."

I gave him a look. He was joking.

"Why, though? Why get to know me? If you're crazy it doesn't show."

"Thank you, I think." He shook his head. "I'm not sure if I can explain why. Perhaps I suffer from terminal curiosity. If you'd been a different sort of person from what you are, I don't think I'd have taken the chance I did tonight."

"What do you mean?"

"Well, any man who sends money home to his mother can't be all bad."

"Good grief."

"How did you evade me at the Stockyards?"

"Like this." I vanished, floated through the door, reformed and came back inside. Escott hadn't moved a muscle, but his heart was thumping hard and his eyes had gone a bit glassy.

After a long time, he said, "That was very interesting, not to mention unnerving. Would you mind doing that again?"

I didn't mind a bit, it was good practice. He was still unnerved. When I thought I had enough control, I tried a partial disappearance while still sitting in the chair. It was all pure show-off.

"That is absolutely astounding," he said. He looked like a kid with a new toy. "I can see right through you. It's like a photographic double exposure. Can you talk while in this state?"

I moved my lips, there was still some air left to form words. After a second my reply became audible. Faint and hollow, I said, "Don't know, haven't tried."

"It seems the more solid you are the better the quality of sound." He stood and reached toward me. "May I?"

"Sure."

I was finding it interesting as well, though it was disturbing to see Escott's hand passing right through my midsection. I was certain I could feel it, like a tickling within.

"Rather cold," he commented. "And you have a tendency to drift."

"I have to concentrate when it's like this." I relaxed and materialized completely. "It's draining in a way."

"I should think so. Everything about you vanishes—your clothes and effects, that is—I wonder what your limits are." He held out his pipe. "Would you mind, just once more?"

I didn't. Escott took back the pipe and puffed on it. "Still lit . . . I find that interesting."

"Why?"

"It means things are unaffected when they go with you. That could prove to be very useful."

I pondered on what he wanted to use it for, disappeared again and came back. "There may be a weight or size limit. I tried to take the chair with me this time and couldn't."

"Perhaps you need more practice. We can research all this thoroughly, I'm sure. What you do is certainly not covered by the present laws of physics." Another idea struck them. "Are your teeth—may I examine them?"

I shrugged and opened my mouth.

"You're very fortunate; they're perfect."

"Erf-ik?"

"You've never had cavities."

"Uh-Ah-aah—"

"What?" He let go.

"But I've had cavities."

"Then you've no fillings."

"You sure? Check the back on this side."

He did and only found unblemished molars. "Your condition is not without its beneficial side effects."

I moaned, "This is getting strange."

"One more look?" He gently pushed back my upper lip and probed the gum area above the canines. "They would seem to be retractable . . . and very sharp." He tugged at one. "Extends at a slight outward angle . . . mm . . . about half an inch longer than the others." He released the tooth, and I felt it slowly slide back. "Extension probably the result of an involuntary reflex occurring when stimulated by hunger pangs. Is that correct?"

"Yeah, they come out when I need them."

"I might like to see that sometime." He fiddled with his pipe.

I found the man's clinical interest, at least on the subject of my dining habits, to be annoying.

Escott continued to poke and cluck to himself, oblivious to my growing irritation. It was like a medical exam, and I never liked medical exams. In the end, I had to take off my coat and shirt so he could see the bullet scars.

"There's hardly any mark in front at all now, but there *is* a large discoloration on your back . . . very slight, though, and it appears to have shrunk. From your description of the chest wound, I'd say you were shot at close range by a large-caliber bullet, perhaps a dum-dum."

"I took a forty-five auto off Sanderson."

"I'd wonder what you had that was making your coat pocket sag so. It would certainly meet the requirements."

"Here." I dug it out and gave it to him.

"And he shot you that second time without harming you?"

"It *hurt* and did not improve my suit. I didn't like it at all." I buttoned my shirt.

"I should think not." He looked out the window. "Well, well, it is getting rather late for you, and I'm a bit sleepy myself. Could we continue this discussion tomorrow at your convenience?"

"I'd like that, sure."

"In the meantime, I shall begin inquiries into your case."

"Well, go easy, you can see how rough these boys play. You better keep the gun."

"Very well, at least as evidence."

I picked up my bags of earth. "I'll be by a little after sundown."

"That would be perfect. Good night to you, Mr. Fleming."

"Good morning to you, Mr. Escott."

4

Not much of the night was left. If I rushed it I could pull out and find another place to stay before the sun caught me. Instead, I walked home, dumped the bags of earth back in the trunk, and got undressed. My instincts about people were fairly sharp by now, and I had a good feeling about the man. The question of whether or not to trust him had only been briefly considered. With something close to fear I realized I was alone, I needed a friend badly.

There was no hunger the next night, so I could skip visiting the Stockyards and go straight to Escott's office. the afterglow of the sunset made my eyes burn, though, and I made a mental note to acquire a pair of dark glasses at the first opportunity.

It was only eight. A fair amount of traffic still cluttered the street and my mind was on sunglasses, so I almost didn't notice the dark green Ford parked in front of Escott's stairway until too late. I approached the stair opening and at the last moment continued past without breaking stride. Two men were at the top just emerging from Escott's door.

I raced around the block to get a good look at them from behind. Peering around the last corner, I was in time to see them stowing a long, heavy bundle of carpeting into the trunk of the Ford. They were red and puffing; their burden seemed overly heavy for its size. The trunk lid slammed down and they dusted their hands off. The one on the left had a bandaged right forefinger. It was Fred Sanderson.

Their backs to me, they opened the doors and got in. Before those doors shut I was making a beeline for the trunk, crouching low. There was no time to try opening it. The engine was kicking over, giving me a face full of exhaust. Not having any better ideas, I vanished and seeped through the crack between the lid and the car's body before they pulled out. I cautiously resumed form again, making sure there was enough room to do so.

I was on my side, crammed uncomfortably against the rug which smelled of dust, grease, and other less pleasant things. It was difficult to hear well over the rumble of the car, but I was sure I detected muted breathing beneath the layers of nap. Reasonably certain it was Escott, I hoped we'd stop soon before he smothered. Under the present circumstances it was impossible to unwrap him.

After the first few minutes of the ride I lost all sense of direction and had to fight off motion sickness. We crossed water, and soon the sound of the wheels on the road steadied. There were no more stops and turns, and the speed was steady, so I gathered we were on a highway. This was worrying; if the ride were too long, I'd be stuck somewhere without my earth, but long before this could become a problem the car slowed and made a sharp right turn onto a very bumpy dirt road. We slid to a stop and the motor was cut.

I pressed an ear to the bundle and was reassured by the sound of working lungs, though I didn't think their owner was conscious yet. Outside, crickets and other small creatures made their little noises. Awkwardly close at hand, the two men lurched out of the car. Not wanting to be discovered in such a tactically poor position, I floated from the trunk and reformed where I hoped I wouldn't be seen.

Trees were all around, but too sparse to offer adequate cover. When I turned to face the car I thought the game was up, Sanderson was looking right at me, then his eyes skipped blindly past. He didn't have my night vision. His friend even gave him a flashlight to facilitate their work.

They opened the trunk and with a none-too-gentle wrench, hauled the bundle out, and dropped it on the ground. From their movements, I'd have to interfere soon, but dark or no dark, I didn't want to risk being recognized by Sanderson. I tied a handkerchief cowboy-fashion over my lower face, feeling foolish about the melodramatics, then turned up my coat collar and pulled down my hat.

The men were professionally matter-of-fact about their task. They yanked one end of the rug up and Escott's unconscious body rolled out onto the leaves and dirt.

"You want to do it here?" the other, younger man asked Sanderson.

"Nah, we might get blood all over us takin' him to the river."

"We could carry him in the rug."

"Georgie," came the patient reply, "we would then have to throw it in with him. The boss don't like wasting a good gimmick, he'll want to use the rug again someday, and then where would we be? Come and get the legs."

They grunted and lifted their burden. Before they'd gotten ten feet, I darted in and punched Sanderson for all I was worth. I felt and heard bones give under my fist. The big man's head snapped back, and he shot straight away from me and smashed against a tree.

His partner had little time to react, but he was fast. He dropped Escott's legs and clawing for his gun when I knocked the wind out of him with a gut punch. He doubled over with a *whoosh* and was made unconscious by a more restrained tap on the head.

I tore my mask away and knelt by Escott, checking him over. There was a swelling behind his left ear and a little blood from a cut lip, but he seemed otherwise uninjured. On a hunch, I searched Georgie and found a whiskey flask. I sniffed to make sure it was drinkable and dribbled a little into Escott's sagging mouth. I was surprised at my enormous relief when he coughed violently and opened his eyes. He was understandably dazed; it took a few more minutes and another swallow before he was up to asking questions.

"Dear me, how ever did we get out here?"

"By way of Fred Sanderson taxi service."

"They caught me like a bloody amateur," he complained, painfully probing his lump. "Did they get you, too?"

"Hardly. I hitched a ride when I saw them load you into the car. Neither of them looked like carpet layers." I indicated the discarded rug.

Escott was unsteady, but made a game effort to get to his feet. I helped him. "I am very much in your debt, Mr. Fleming. I hope that I may somehow—"

"Don't worry about it," I interrupted. "You could have aced me with a hammer and stake anytime today, but you didn't. We're even."

"But, my dear fellow, such an action never occurred to me." Escott was truly shocked.

"But *I* thought of it. The way I am now I gotta be careful who I trust, but I know you're gonna be square with me. Now before we get all maudlin, let's pack these two mugs in the car and get back home."

I left the flashlight with Escott and got busy manhandling Georgie into the backseat. Having had some practice at it, I removed his tie and secured his hands together behind him, then went back for Sanderson.

Neither of us had to venture very close to know something was seriously wrong. Sanderson's utterly loose posture was enough to alert Escott, who gingerly felt for a pulse. I already knew that to be a futile effort.

Escott turned the body face up into the light and his breath hissed sharply. I looked quickly away, sickened by what I'd done.

Twenty minutes later we were almost back in Chicago. Sanderson's body was in the trunk, wrapped in the rug. Occasionally Escott would check the backseat to make sure the now-blindfolded Georgie was quiet. I'd been silent, driving carefully to avoid the unwelcome attention of any cop with a quota to fill.

"You've got to understand," I finally said, "this is scaring the hell out of me."

"I do understand. A healthy dose of fear will certainly temper your actions from now on."

"That's not it. I'm afraid of what I've become. What I did back there— I knew what would happen if I hit him like that, and I did it anyway."

"Good."

I glanced at him, surprised. His face showed a dour expression that must have matched my own. "Good?"

"Mm. Do you honestly think I harbor any regret or pity for a man who would have been the agent of my death and was by your own guess responsible for yours? Your feeling of guilt is misplaced. Were our positions reversed I should give no more thought to the matter than a soldier does when he must shoot at the enemy."

Half a lifetime ago I had shot at the enemy. I hadn't liked it then, either.

"He would have met his death sooner or later, for such was his life, and then at the hands of someone with far less conscience. If it is any comfort to you, I'm sure he never knew what hit him."

"*What* is the magic word. What have I become? I'm no longer human."

"That is utter nonsense and for your own good I suggest you put it from your head as quickly as possible. Do you in all truth really believe the biological changes within you have stripped you of humanity? You still possess your mortal clay, you still have emotional needs. I think you are giving far too much credence to a fictional character created out of the imagination of an actor's manager."

I gave him a sharp look.

"No, I'm no mind reader, but I can follow your line of reasoning. The character Dracula was a monster. He was also a vampire. You are now a vampire, ergo, you are a monster."

"What makes you think I'm not? Maybe I should pull over and strangle the kid in the back."

"If you feel it's necessary, but you won't."

He was right, it'd been a stupid thing to say and said in anger.

"You're feeling guilty, hence this black reaction. Feel guilty if you must, but leave self-pity out of it, for it is the most destructive of all emotions."

"What makes you so smart?"

"I read a lot." He bowed his head in weariness, looking green at the edges.

"You still want to go on after this?" I said, meaning the investigation.

"Oh, yes, but not just this moment."

I heard something in the back and checked our prisoner from the mirror. "He's waking up," I whispered.

Escott nodded, tapping his lips with a finger. We kept silent for the rest of the trip while Georgie played possum in the backseat.

Following gestured directions, I negotiated the streets and pulled into a no-parking zone. We rubbed the interior down for fingerprints, got out, and Escott lifted the hood. He fiddled briefly with something as I kept a nervous lookout. We both jumped as the street was filled with the ear-splitting blare of the car's horn. Escott dropped the hood, swiped at it with his handkerchief, then grabbed my arm, and we hustled out of sight around a corner.

"What was that for?" I asked as we left the area.

"There's a police station not a hundred feet from the car. Once that horn gets their attention they can take Georgie in at least for disturbing the peace. After they find Sanderson they can become more creative in their charges."

"Why didn't you want to question Georgie about this?"

"He wouldn't have known anything useful. I'm already certain Paco ordered my untimely demise because I was clumsy somewhere in my investigations. I did quite a lot of poking around today and he must have got the wind up, and can only expect more of the same until one or the other of us has been eliminated."

"You're pretty cool about it."

"Only because my head hurts too much at the moment for me to be overly concerned about the future."

"You can't go back to your office, they might be watching."

"I have other places to . . . uh . . . lay low for the time being. However, I do have to return to my office to fetch some paperwork; it's too important to leave. I'd be most obliged if you accompanied me. I don't feel well at all."

"Be glad to, but what if some of Paco's men are there?"

"I'm inclined to think only Sanderson and Georgie were involved with this job, but we won't know until we get there, which we won't do unless we find a cab."

Taking the hint, I left Escott resting on a bench outside a barbershop and went looking, turned up a cab near a hotel, and returned to pick him up. He gave directions and paid the driver off some two blocks away from our goal. We walked the rest of the way, eyes peeled, and turned onto the street that ran behind his office. He approached the door of a modest tobacco shop, produced a key, and went in, motioning me to follow. It was full of crowded shelves and fragrant smells, the second floor was devoted to storage and full of dusty crates. Escott pulled one away from the back wall and made something go click. A three-foot-tall section fitted between the wall studs popped open like a door. Two inches beyond this opening was another apparent wall. He put his ear to it and listened.

I made a reassuring gesture, then realized he couldn't see it for we were in almost total darkness. "There's no one on the other side or I'd hear them," I murmured.

"Oh," he said. He pushed on the wall, opening another narrow door, and eased himself through. I followed. We were standing in a small washroom, but only for a moment. Escott went on to the room beyond.

I correctly guessed it to be Escott's living quarters behind the office. Except for a radio acting as a nightstand next to an army cot and the window blinds, the place was depressingly bare; even a hotel room had more personality. I found myself fidgeting as Escott moved smoothly around in the semidarkness. He pulled a suitcase from under the cot, opened a tiny closet, and was busily packing.

"You dropped a sock," I observed.

"On purpose. Should they send anyone here later I want them to draw the conclusion that I've departed in a great hurry, which is what I am no doubt doing. Besides, it was developing a hole."

He went to the office. His desk had been searched. He paused and grimaced at the mess, then stopped and grabbed up some scattered papers. "I'll have to sort this lot out later," he muttered. The crossbow was still on the desk; he picked it up and took it back to the bedroom. I wondered what his attackers had thought of it.

"This will hardly fit in my bag, I'll have to leave it in the tobacco shop for the time being. It is a bit too conspicuous to carry right now."

"How did you happen to have it in the first place?"

"It's a working prop left over from my acting days. I made it for a small part I had in the Scottish Play."

"The what?"

"*Macbeth,*" he said sotto voce. "As a weapon these days it is a little bulky, but it is powerful, lethal, and silent. I have smaller ones, but thought you might be more impressed with something large."

"You thought right."

"Then you're certain wood can harm you?"

"The lady I knew in New York mentioned it."

"Ah." Escott returned to the washroom and shoved the suitcase through the doors, along with the crossbow. He paused at the medicine cabinet, dropped some shaving items into his pockets, and then, to my puzzlement, tugged at the frame of the cabinet itself. It swung out, revealing a flat metal box standing on edge in the space behind. He opened it, making sure the papers inside were still intact before taking them away.

"Who did your carpentry?"

"Oh, I did it all myself," he said with some pride. "I love this sort of thing, don't you?"

As Escott locked the tobacco shop door, I asked, "Do you own this place?"

"Half of it. The other owner actually runs it. I help him financially through these hard times and he helps me by maintaining a good hiding place and, if necessary, escape route with twenty-four-hour access and egress."

"Are you rich?"

"Sometimes." He swayed a little. "Sorry, that bash on the head is making itself felt."

"Lemme take your bag."

"Only if you insist."

"Where to now?"

"I'm not sure. Not knowing just where I slipped up on my investigations, I can't be certain which of my other places would be safe."

"Then stay away from them and get a hotel."

"Mr. Fleming, I don't think you have grasped the tremendous influence the gangs have on this city. If I show my face at the wrong hostel I am very likely to get it blown off, putting to naught your efforts tonight on my behalf. Within hours, if not already, Paco and his men are going to know of my miraculous escape and be looking for me. It's very bad for their image when someone thwarts them, you see."

"Then you'll leave town?"

"I'm . . . not sure." Beads of sweat had popped out on his forehead and his face was gray. He was having some kind of delayed reaction. I caught his arm to support him.

"Hey, you're really sick. Come on, we'll sneak you up the backstairs of my hotel, you can flop there."

"But I really shouldn't—"

"You can't think in the shape you're in now. You'll be safe enough there under my name."

He protested mildly once more, but now and then everybody needs a keeper. I appointed myself his and dragged him off.

Once back at the hotel, Escott collapsed with a groan on the bed while I ordered up some ice and poured out a double from Georgie's permanently borrowed flask. With the whiskey on the inside and the ice on the bump outside, he went into an exhausted but healing sleep. I was stuck with the whole rest of the night and wondering what to do with it when someone knocked at the door. It was the bellhop returning with my change and receipts.

"You wasn't here when I came on, or I'da brought 'em sooner."

"That's all right, I was busy. You got them all?"

He held up a few pounds of newsprint. "Sure do."

I tipped him and told him I'd want copies of each paper every night and to put it on my bill. He grinned, knowing I'd have to tip him each time he brought them up. I winked back and took the papers inside.

I spent the rest of the evening reading. My notice appeared in the personal columns of them all and by some miracle the wording and spelling was correct.

DEAREST MAUREEN, ARE YOU SAFE YET? JACK

It was the same notice I'd been putting in the papers without a break for the last five years. If she were alive, if she only glanced once at it, she would let me know. After all this time I'd little hope left. Checking the papers for a reply each day and getting none had eroded most of it away. I fended off the inevitable depression of disappointment by sifting through the rest of the pages.

The war in Spain was heating up, FDR was confident the economic crisis was over, and there was an encouraging rumor on the fashion pages that hemlines were going up. The shoe ads reminded me it was high time I did something about my footwear, so I squeaked downstairs to look for my friend the bellhop. I gave him a picture of what I wanted with my size scribbled next to it, five bucks, and a silent blessing for not asking questions.

It was a longer night than usual, with nothing to do but listen to Escott sleep. The papers filled the time up, though, and I kept my eyes and brain focused on them or else I'd be seeing Sanderson's mangled face instead. Before turning in I wrote a note for Escott, telling him he was welcome to stay as long as he wanted and to put any meals on my tab. I opened the window wide, turned on the fan, and took to my trunk for the day.

He was gone when I woke up, but there was a note on the radio stating his intention to return after dark. I was uneasy but let it go and went through my nightly ablutions, dressed, and strolled downstairs to buy something to read. The bellhop had my shoes, and I let him keep the change for his tip. He was making a fortune off his oddball guest, but I didn't mind; he was honest, incurious, and the shoes more or less fit. We got on so well he loaned me his own copy of *Shadow Magazine*. When Escott let himself in later, he found me comfortably engrossed in something called "Terror Island."

"An intriguing title," he observed. "Here, I borrowed your key."

"Anytime, I've got other ways of getting in." I marked my place and put the magazine to one side. He cocked an amused eye at it. "I know the writer; I like to keep up with his work," I said, trying not to sound defensive.

"I have serious doubts that anyone can, he turns them out at an astonishing rate."

"Well, they usually have more than one guy working on the stuff."

"Not for this one so far. Certain elements of his style have been constant."

"You don't seem the type to go for stuff like this."

"You are the first person who ever thought so."

"I take it you're feeling better?"

"Apart from the slight headache and some bruising, I am quite myself again, thank you."

"What were you doing out in broad daylight?"

"I was safe enough after I retraced my steps by making a few calls on the phone downstairs—"

"Have a seat"—I dragged a pile of newsprint from the chair—"and tell me all."

"Thank you, I will. Yesterday I paid a visit to International Freshwater Transport and while enquiring about their rates, took a good look around, especially at the faces of their help. At least three of them had no obvious duties other than to watch me, and the names of the daily work schedule were suspiciously neutral."

"Neutral?"

"John Smith, John Jones, John—"

"I get it, go on."

"As I was leaving the warehouse, I spotted Sanderson. With your description of him in mind and the fact that his index finger was still well bandaged, he was impossible to miss. He looked twice at me as well, perhaps for a moment he thought I was you. I left and then spent time researching the business. Several hours and false trails later, I determined that Frank Paco does own the business, but is overly modest about it. IFT is not a growing concern, they seem to make only enough to keep their heads above water—excuse the pun—but not much more. They also do not appear too interested in improving things, either. They were not at all anxious to do business with me, and the rates they quoted were discouragingly high."

"So you think they have only a few select customers?"

"Yes, and to me that indicates smuggling."

"What kind?"

"Almost anything: stolen goods, drugs, people wanting in or out of the country . . . Such business can be most profitable if properly organized. Perhaps if we returned to their warehouse and opened a few crates we could discover the source of their profits."

"I'd be happy to try again."

"Anyway, after all these labors I was quite starved and stopped in at a little cafe I like, and there made my downfall. It was pure carelessness on my part; that and the fact that Mr. Sanderson was a man very skilled at following people. His young partner Georgie was with him and sat nearby nursing some coffee, while the more noticeable Sanderson remained discreetly in his car. Georgie heard me order my meal sans the American accent I'd used at IFT. He must have mentioned it to Sanderson, then they followed me to my office."

"How did you find this out?"

He coughed slightly. "One of the waitresses there is somewhat fond of me, I can't imagine why, and she happened to notice their car tagging behind me when I drove off, and didn't like the looks of it. From there I can deduce their later movements. Having found my office, Sanderson probably called his boss to inform him of my suspicious activities at the warehouse. Paco is not known for his tolerant attitude toward the curious, so he sent them after me. I think it was Georgie who did the actual violence to my person. His shoes were rubber soled."

"How could he sneak up behind you in that small area?"

"Sanderson was using his car for a distraction. He was racing the motor with the bonnet up as though there were some problem with it. When I went to the window to see what the noise was about, Georgie coshed me. They went through my desk, as you saw and fortunately for me, waited for darkness before taking me downstairs in the rug. You know the rest."

"Except what you did today."

"With that out of the way I went home for a change of clothes and to make more calls. Georgie is still in jail and his friend Paco has never heard of him. I've also found out Paco is no longer actively seeking me."

"Why not?"

"That is a good question. Perhaps he's under someone else's orders or something else has him busy."

"Who or what?"

He shrugged. "It or they have my gratitude in the meantime. I think I may have turned up an interesting possibility for you. If you've nothing better to do we can look into it more closely tonight."

"Are you kidding? I'll get my hat."

We went down and got into a black Nash that had been a luxury model a few years ago. The outside had some dimples in the metal running in an almost straight line from front to back, but the finish had been well polished and the interior was as clean and blank as his office.

"What are those marks? They look like bullet holes."

"They're bullet holes. I had them repaired, as they ruined the paint job."

"Bullet holes?"

"Bullet dents, actually."

"How'd they get there?"

"I understand someone took a few shots at the previous owner with a machine gun." He busied himself with starting the motor.

On the front seat between us was a hat, a brown derby with a red satin band. On one side of the band was a miniature stickpin in the shape of a diamond-trimmed horseshoe. He took his own hat off and put this one on. He was wearing dark gray so it figured he had some good reason to look so mismatched. He saw the question forming on my face and smiled.

"It's our passport," he explained, which explained nothing. He liked his mystery game, so I let him enjoy it. He was working on my case and whatever he wanted was fine with me.

We drove to an area he said was called the Bronze Belt, which was Chicago's version of Harlem. Once there, he cruised the streets slowly, scanning them for something or someone. I asked him which.

"Oh, definitely a person. One has only to make the right contact and one is in."

I nearly asked in what, but that would have been too obvious and I'd been thinking of something else, anyway. "Have you turned up anything on this Benny Galligar?"

"From my local sources I learned he is considered to be only 'small time,' though he specializes in safe-cracking and lately some bodyguard work. No one has seen him for a week or more but I have several inquiries going. He should turn up soon."

"Hope so, I'd like to know why he called me, if he did call me."

"He is originally from New York. The logical inference is that he knows you from there. If you can recall anyone with that name—"

"He'll be changing his name like other people change socks. I did know one or two Bennys, though. In New York you practically trip over them; maybe if and when I see him—"

"He was described as a small man, graying hair, lined and lived-in face, forty to forty-five, nervous manner, sometimes affects an Irish accent when he's in the mood—"

That rang a bell. "Wait, Benny O'Hara, sometimes he'd sell me a tip, you know, where to go to see something interesting."

"For a news story?"

"That's how it usually worked. I knew him as Benny O'Hara. How could he have known I was in town?"

"Perhaps he was staying at your hotel. I'll check on it. I've been there once, the night clerk remembers your last visit quite clearly, perhaps I can persuade him to go back a little further in his memory."

"Yeah, between him and the day clerk there must be something useful."

"Be assured, I shall try."

We paused for a red light and a skinny brown kid suddenly poked his face into my window.

"I thought this buggy looked familiar," he said, grinning at us. "You up here lookin' for a shine, Mr. Escott?"

"Hello, Cal. Actually I'm looking for a shoe. How are you?"

"Same old stuff, a day late an' a dollar short."

"I cannot overcome your time difficulties, but I can possibly aid your monetary problems." He passed a dollar over to Cal, who made it disappear.

"You're a real friend. Next time you need a shine, you look me up, it's on the house."

"Where will you be?"

"I could be anyplace, but if you go down three blocks and turn right one, the gents on the corner can tell you proper. You just say I sent you." He flashed his teeth, pushed away from the car, and went off with a quick, pavement-eating stride.

The light changed and Escott followed the directions, easing the big car into an empty space on the curb and letting it idle.

A group of dark men were standing just outside the cone of light from a streetlamp on the corner ahead. Escott told me to stay put and got out. The men had been talking and continued to do so, but their posture had subtly changed. It was apparent they were fully alert to our presence, but content to wait and let us make the first move. Two of them dropped their cigarettes and stood a little straighter, their arms hanging free so they could more easily get to the angular bulges their tight-fitting coats were unable to hide. Two more shifted their weight to the balls of their feet. They moved out and bracketed Escott when he got close enough.

His head moved slightly as he acknowledged them and there was some low conversation I couldn't quite hear because of the noise of the car. He said something to the armed men; the one on the left shot back a suspicious question. Escott touched his hat and looked reasonable. The man was dissatisfied with the situation, but Escott kept talking and once gestured back to the car, presumably about me. I had half a mind to get out and come over, but this was his show and he didn't look to be in any immediate danger, despite their belligerent attitudes. I sat and stewed and unsuccessfully tried to read lips.

The man on the left made a decision and sent one of the brackets into the building they were guarding. He came out after a minute with a report even more dissatisfying to the leader, but he nodded grudgingly to Escott. Escott came back and opened my door.

"We're in."

"What, the frying pan?"

"The Shoe Box."

"Is it a speak?"

"It used to be. Now it's a respectable nightclub."

"Just how sticky are things?" I gestured with my eyebrows at the men.

"Not very, nothing to worry about now. The gentleman we will see is a cautious fellow, but will welcome us as long as he has sufficient notice. He has a very strong dislike for surprises."

"Gang boss?"

"What a colorful way you have of phrasing things, no doubt due to your journalistic training."

"And the fact we're in Chicago, it seems to be a major industry here."

"For only a fractional percentage of the population, I assure you. Not everyone here is a boss, someone has to do the support work."

"Like him?" One of the brackets was walking toward us.

"Yes, well, let's go."

I shut off the engine, pulled the keys, and got out. He closed the door and walked away. "Aren't you going to lock it?"

"There's no need, no one would dare touch it now."

I made a casual glance around and noted a few dozen faces watching us from windows and doorways up and down the street; men, women, and even a few kids. They all had the same attentive look about them as the door guards. The Shoe Box was a well-surveyed fortress. I felt like a target in a shooting gallery, which led me to speculate if any of them were armed. Escott seemed comfortable, though, and he was nowhere near as bulletproof, so I told myself to relax. We followed the bracket into the building.

There was a small entry hall and then a long passage with a wood floor that acted like a drum to our footsteps. I heard loud and fast music vibrating through the right hand wall, mixed in with the thrum of conversation, clinking glassware, and laughter. We passed by a closed double door that led to the fun and went on to the back of the building, stopping outside another door. Our bracket said he could let Escott in, but he'd have to search me. If it would speed things along, I had no objections and held my arms out. He was efficient and had the quick, light touch of a pickpocket, which might have been his usual occupation when he wasn't pulling guard duty. He found my pencil, notebook, and wallet and nothing more lethal in my pockets than some change. He tapped my shoe heels, checked my hat, decided everything was harmless, and opened the door and stepped to one side.

It was a big room, furnished with sofas, overstuffed chairs, and low tables. One of the tables was really a fancy model of radio that cost more than I'd made in a year. It was playing softly, just loud enough to mask off the sounds coming from the nightclub. At the far end of the room was a small bar near a long dining table where a man was seated alone, eating what appeared to be his dessert. As we came in he tapped a napkin to his lips and turned to look at us.

His skin was sooty black, his hair cut close to the scalp with a short beard edging his jawline and elaborately trimming the mouth and chin. Dressed in light brown with a deep red silk shirt and tie, he looked almost foppish, but was easily getting away with it. He stood up, a big man and not one you could ignore.

Escott spoke first and in a voice rather louder than required to carry across the room. His tone was a mixture of anger and pity. "O thou Othello, that wert once so good/ Fall'n in the practice of a damned slave/ What shall be said to thee?"

Our host was still for a moment, staring at Escott, whom I was sure had need of a straitjacket and gag, then he responded in a rich voice: "Why anything/ An honourable murderer if you will/ For naught I did in hate, but all in honour." Then he barked out a short, delighted laugh and came over to wring Escott's outstretched hand. Both men were grinning.

"Charles, you s.o.b., what do you mean showing up like this with the derby? You could have mentioned your name to the boys! How the hell are you?"

"I am in good health and only wanted to see if it still worked. I would have called, but you'd moved and left no forwarding number or address I could acquire."

"Then it's your own fault. You should have come around more often. You gave my men a start with that hat routine."

"As I had intended—it keeps them on their toes."

"Well, it doesn't go with the suit, so dump it. Have you eaten yet? Dessert then; we've still got some pie and coffee."

"That would be fine, but please allow me to make some introductions. This is a friend of mine, Jack Fleming. Jack, you have the honor of meeting the best Othello I've ever had the pleasure of working with; Shoe Coldfield."

Coldfield stuck out his hand. "Any friend of Charles—and that's short for Shoe Box. I got no bones to pick on how I started out. Just watch my smoke, I'm going to be mayor of this town someday."

"Really now, you can do better than that," Escott said dryly.

"All right, governor then, but only if they raise the pay. How did you find the place?"

"We saw Cal, or rather he saw us."

"Smart kid, that."

"He's grown."

"He's eating regular."

We sat down at the table and coffee was brought in by a kid in a busboy jacket who was also doing duty in the nightclub. Through the walls I could still hear music, which made an uneasy counterpoint with the radio.

"What brings you here, Charles? Working on a revival?"

"I heartily wish. Should I return to the boards, you will certainly be the first to know. In truth, I need a favor."

"These days who doesn't? What's on your mind?"

"I'm working on a little problem for Mr. Fleming, and since yesterday, for myself, in which Frank Paco is involved."

Our host sobered up, taking a cautious tone. "Just how involved is he?"

"Yesterday two of his men tried to kill me, and were it not for Mr. Fleming's timely intervention, they would certainly have succeeded. He survived an attempt on his life only last week from the same source and has been laying low ever since."

"Can't say as I blame you. What do you need? Smuggling out of town?"

"Nothing quite so drastic. Let me apprise you of the whole situation." Escott told him the basic truth, but said that I sought him out and wisely omitted all the facts concerning my condition.

". . . so until Mr. Fleming knows what occurred during those missing four days he will always have this rather nasty problem."

"How do you think I can help? He needs a head-doctor."

"I was hoping you could help us get into Paco's house."

Coldfield shut right up, from sheer disbelief I suppose, since I was feeling the same way. "My mistake," he finally said. "*You* are the one who wants a head-doctor."

"Shoe, I am quite serious."

"If Paco is after you, you oughta be. Why get into his place?"

"For a good look around and to find out what he's up to."

"Hell, I can do that from here. What you want to know?"

"Some information on International Freshwater Transport might be useful."

"It's just his smuggling operation, everyone knows that."

"But what does he smuggle?"

"It used to be booze and he still brings in some of the fancy foreign stuff. If the price is right he'll take most anything, including people in or out of the country. Lately it's been machine parts and chemicals coming in."

"Is it possible to find out whom they go to and for what purpose?"

"I can try tomorrow, but can't guarantee anything. I generally keep my people away from his territory. I suppose you want specific names for the chemicals, p'fesser?"

"It could help identify what he's up to, but please do not expose your people to undue risk. Yesterday I only made casual inquiries and his reaction was most violent."

"Don't worry. You gonna put him out of business?"

"That would be nice."

"Yeah, we can dream, but he's got friends. Word has it he's been dealing with Slick Morelli out of New York."

"Is that name familiar to you?" Escott asked me.

"Sure, he's a big nightclub owner there, ran a lot of speaks, then fancied them up into top spots after Repeal. He sold a few and concentrated on one or two of the biggest. He always had the best acts and the prettiest girls. Of course, this is only what I've heard, I never had the chance to take a look." Or the money, I silently added.

"He hasn't changed much," said Coldfield. "He's done the same thing for one of the biggest clubs in town up on the northside; he's got a half-interest in it."

"The Nightcrawler?" asked Escott.

"Yeah, maybe he likes fishin' or something."

"Does he own a yacht?"

He nodded. "A nice one, too, if you can have any other kind. The *Elvira.*"

I stirred in my chair at the mention of a ship.

Escott noticed, but continued. "Who is the other owner of the club?"

"A fat guy named Lucky Lebredo. He oversees the gambling there."

Escott glanced at me. I thought about the name, then shook my head. He turned back to Coldfield. "Do you know of any connection between Paco and Morelli?"

He shrugged. "If there is, it's probably money. Paco likes to spread it around and always needs more, Morelli keeps his in a mattress and the Good Lord help you if you borrow from him. He takes his loan interest right out of your hide."

"Do you think Lebredo is involved with them?"

"I don't know. Maybe not, all he seems to do is gamble. He's got an adding machine for a brain, and a deck of cards is just another part of his body." He paused. Escott was looking at something we couldn't see, hovering just over the table centerpiece. We waited him out in silence until his eyes blinked a few times.

"You back?" Coldfield asked casually.

"Yes, just thinking, but I need more information."

"Then you're still serious 'bout going in?"

"Very serious."

"What did you have in mind?"

"Have you read the social columns?"

"Never miss 'em," he said with a trace of sarcasm.

"Then you may have noticed Frank Paco is hosting a reception at his estate this Friday. The place is going to be filled with politicians, hangers-on, and the man Paco plans to support in the next gubernatorial election."

"Yes . . ."

"The whole thing is certainly going to be catered."

Coldfield thought it out and smiled. "You mean you can cook, too?"

"No, but I can pass as a waiter."

"Not on this one you can't. You know damn well one of my joints is doing the food and service, and face it, Charles, you're just too white for this job."

"Then I can work as a white waiter."

"And stand out like a sore thumb. No sir, Paco likes his staff well done. Besides, what white man would be working for me? Whites work for white caterers, and once in a while they take on a colored kid 'cause he works cheap, but it just isn't done the other way around."

Escott's pride had been piqued. "Am I or am I not a character actor?"

"The best, but no blackface makeup is going to pass a close look, and your nose is all wrong, anyway. If you were me, would you want to take the chance?"

"I agree," I said. "Paco might know your face, Georgie could be out on bail by now, and if either of 'em spots you, you're scragged and so are the caterers."

Escott's eyes snapped at me a second, then he visibly calmed and shrugged it off. "Of course, you're both right. We'll have to think of something else. Perhaps I could get hold of an invitation or forge one."

"Not easy, they check 'em against their guest list. You'd have to be in someone else's party to sneak past, and then you still have your face to consider. Look, why does it have to be this Friday? Try some other night when Paco is gone and just break in. I can stick one of my boys on the catering staff to case the place for you."

"That is most kind."

"Great, anything to save your ass. Listen, how 'bout we all have dinner tomorrow night, right here."

"Dinner, yes, but it's on me—to make up for too long an absence. Hallman's, I think."

"You're joking, Charles. I couldn't get past the door."

"You most certainly will if it's my party. If you plan to run for governor you'll have to get used to breaking open some doors."

"When I do that, the cops get nervous."

"And well they should. Eight o'clock?"

"That's early for me, but I'll be there, and will try to have some dope on the warehouse from my boys."

"Please advise them to use all caution; that thump on the head I got was nearly fatal."

"Your skull is too thick. I heard something was fatal to Paco's chief gun, Sanderson. They found him in a trunk the other day. That anything to do with your problem? The papers are saying Georgie Reamer hit him with a sledgehammer." He was looking at me with interest.

I was careful not to look at Escott for a clue. How much Coldfield knew or guessed about last night would be my affair. I shrugged. "Hey, I used to be a reporter—don't believe everything you read."

We left without hindrance from Coldfield's men, one of them even nodded and smiled as we went out to the untouched Nash. I gave the keys back to Escott and we got in. The watching faces were still around, but were not as

interested in us as before. Word must have been passed that we were welcome in the neighborhood.

"He's some guy," I commented.

"Yes, I met him in Canada when we were both young and hungry. I
was already in an acting company when he walked into the theater with his
shoe-shine box and asked for work. We got to be friends and with a great
deal of argument, persuaded the manager to hire him on permanently. He
worked at moving scenery and in wardrobe at half-salary. Occasionally, I'd
do him up in white-face so he could carry a spear in the background when
we were short of players, but he was being wasted. If you could have seen
us in *Hamlet* as Rosencrantz and Guildenstern; he nearly sweated his
makeup off and gave the game away. At least it showed the other actors in
the company that he was more than capable, but our manager was a pigheaded old reprobate. He refused to even consider Shoe for the obvious
part of Othello."

"But he did play it?"

"Oh, yes, but it was a bit of a challenge for me to arrange it. The one
thing I did manage was getting him the part of understudy to the lead. The
manager allowed that much."

"Then the lead got sick?"

"Not precisely . . . I had to help him along. Between the chloral hydrate
the company Iago slipped him and the ipecacuanha I provided to treat his
symptoms, he was in no condition to play the Moor of Venice, and Shoe had
his chance. I must say he brought the house down with his performance."

"What about the lead?"

"He recovered in a week or so and no harm was done. By then he had received a telegram offering him a radio announcing job in New York and he left.
I'm afraid we didn't miss him much, a very unpleasant ham, he was."

"Was the telegram genuine?"

"Why, what a suspicious mind you have, Mr. Fleming."

5

I got my trip to the Stockyards out of the way and was ready and waiting
at a quarter to eight when Escott picked me up. He was in an ordinary suit,
which was a relief to me because Hallman's sounded like a white-tie-and-
tails joint and I was fresh out of tuxedos.

"I may have a problem at this place," I said.

"What would that be?"

"Let's just say that I have a very restricted diet."

He opened and shut his mouth. "Dear me, I'm afraid I never even thought of that."

"Neither did I. Doing business over food is a very normal thing. We take it for granted.

Escott considered it. "Yes, I can see—you must have a tremendous amount of free time to be unfettered with having to stop and eat every four or five hours."

"I'd gladly go back to it if I could."

"Would you rather skip this evening, then?"

"No, I'll just say it's stomach trouble and nurse a coffee. As long as we're on my case I want to be along every inch of the way, if it's all right with you."

"I've no objections. I've made more inquiries after Benny Galligar/O'Hara today, but with negative results."

"If he was in trouble with Paco, he's probably blown town by now."

"I agree. He's set a very sensible example for us."

"Yeah, too bad I ain't got any sense."

Hallman's was a white-tie place, after all. Escott must have noticed my lack when he went through my room last Monday, and I silently blessed him for his consideration in wearing a regular suit. Like many swank places in Chicago, Hallman's was cheek-and-jowl with less savory neighborhoods. The street it faced was a high-tax area with bright lights, expensive shops, and other classy restaurants, but cross the alley behind it and you were gambling with your skin. Sometimes it was a gang, sometimes a loan operator, but both types shared an avid interest in acquiring someone else's money. The cops had regular beats in the area, but could hardly prevent the odd out-of-towner from getting picked off by local hunters. When Escott got out of the car this time, he made a point of locking it.

A uniformed man at the canopied entrance guarded some potted palms and a red carpet that ran out to the curb. He held the door for us and bowed slightly.

"Good to see you again, Mr. Escott."

"Thank you, Mr. Burdge. Can you recommend anything tonight?"

"Any of the veal dishes, but stay away from the fish. Our regular fish chef is off tonight and his replacement did his training in the army."

"An inland army, no doubt."

"You got it."

We went in and checked our hats, telling the maître d' we were still expecting one more and would wait by the door. It wasn't a long wait; at eight a gleaming new black Nash drove up and stopped next to the red carpet.

"I see you have similar tastes in cars," I commented.

"Well, he did give me such a good deal on my present transport a few years ago that I couldn't turn him down. I must say he still knows how to make an entrance, a natural talent. The stage lost a very fine actor in him."

The chauffeur was out and opening the rear door of the Nash; Burdge, the doorman, stood a little straighter and held the door to the restaurant. It was some credit to his self-control that he wilted only a little when Coldfield emerged into the light. He was postcard perfect in a custom-tailored tuxedo with a satin-lined cape and a silver-headed stick. He carried the clothes comfortably, like Fred Astaire, albeit a much larger-sized Astaire with coal black skin and a beard. He sauntered up to the doorman, who was looking a bit confused as to how to handle the situation. Coldfield gave Burdge a look that banished any inclinations of refusing him entry, and then came in.

Escott tapped his hands together in soft applause. "Well played, sir. A pity it could not have been preserved on film."

Coldfield was pleased. "You said it, history is being made tonight." He nodded to me. "Ready to get tossed out with the best?"

"I'd like to see anyone try."

The maître d' was well trained; his eyebrows only bounced up an eighth of an inch and back down before he got hold of himself.

"Your usual table, Mr. Escott?" he asked. In a minute I understood why. Escott's usual table was in a discreet alcove off to one side of the main dining area. The man was only reminding Escott he wasn't trying to shuffle our dark companion out of sight. Whether he wanted to or not, I'd never know.

We sat and went through the business of ordering drinks and studying the menu. Playing my part, I read through it and shook my head.

"Anything wrong, Mr. Fleming?" Escott asked.

"I'm not up to eating anything yet. I got a bad burger for lunch and the thought of more food—" I made a queasy face and shrugged.

"What a pity, perhaps a little broth to recover? No?"

"No, thanks, I just gotta let things run their course so to speak. Don't mind me, you two go ahead and enjoy yourselves."'

They did. Escott had veal, Coldfield a steak, and I watched the other patrons between our bouts of conversation. The smell of food did make me feel a little sick, but it was the memory of eating that really nettled me. I'd finally made it into a fancy place with someone else paying the bill, and all I could enjoy was the decor.

We got our share of looks. One group quite obviously cut short their meal and left, their backs stiff with indignation. They wouldn't have minded or even noticed him if Coldfield had been part of the cleanup staff, but being a fellow customer was too much for their tender sensibilities. The maître d' would have caught their verbal wrath had he been by the door as they left, but being an alert man he'd removed himself from the area in time. This graceless show was not lost on the other diners, who had been wondering what to do themselves. Happily, they had the good taste to mind their own business, and the conversation buzz soon returned to normal levels.

"You may have pulled this off, after all, Charles," Coldfield murmured.

"So it would seem. I should like to live to see the day—"

"Yeah, I know, I know. Well, you at least got me in here—"

"No, you got yourself."

"I'm hell on doormen," he agreed. "But you're just lucky."

"How so?"

"He had a pretty good idea I wasn't Jewish."

Halfway through the meal a waiter came up with a telephone. "An important call for you, Mr. Escott."

Escott said hello into the mouthpiece and scowled a lot. I couldn't quite hear what was being said on the other end, even if I had any business in doing so.

He shook his head. "No, I couldn't possibly, this is a very bad time. . . . What? All right, then, but hurry." He hung up and the phone was taken away.

"What's the problem?" I asked.

"I shall have to absent myself for a few minutes. One of my sources of information wants to talk and will only do so face-to-face. He's coming by to pick me up."

"Can't he come in?"

"Not this one. He likes to keep on the move, so we have to go through this little comedy now and then. We drive around the block a few times, then he drops me off. Strange fellow, but often useful. If you gentlemen will excuse me, I should be back in time for dessert." He stood up with a quaint little bow that only the English can get away with, and left. Coldfield watched his departing back with an indulgent smile.

"How long have you known him?"

"Off 'n on, about fourteen years. Haven't seen much of him since he took up this private-agent stuff, but then I've been busy, too."

"Do you mind his kind of work?"

"Why should I? He doesn't seem to mind mine."

"What do you do?"

He gave me a look of mock surprise. "Why, I run a nightclub."

"At a considerable profit?"

"No point being in business if you don't make a profit."

"How long has he been a private agent?"

"Awhile."

"You play it close to the chest."

"That's how you survive in this town."

He never gave a direct answer to any questions that were too probing, and I asked quite a few before catching on. It must have been the reporter in me. After I figured things out, we stuck to neutral subjects and watched the place slowly empty. Then we watched the staff cleaning up. Our waiter hovered just within sight, broadcasting polite but clear signals that he thought it was time we left.

"Think he stiffed us for the check?" I said jokingly, looking at the clock on the wall. He'd been gone nearly forty minutes.

"No, they'll just put it on his account. He's been coming here for years."

I worried anyway. The phone call could have been a trick to get him outside. Coldfield read my face and told me to relax.

"Charles can take care of himself."

"I hope so."

We waited. A lone busboy in thick glasses shuffled around cleaning the tables. His walk and movements bothered me for some reason, and when I caught a glimpse of his blank face I knew why. His was the careful heavy-heeled, loose-limbed walk of the mentally retarded. He moved from table to table, cleaning up and wiping down, then looked at us and wondered why we hadn't left yet. He was about fifty, with overlong gray hair, a thrusting box-shaped forehead, and thick gray brows that grew across the bridge of his nose. His mouth was open slightly as he stared at us and then at the waiter, undecided on what to do.

"Maybe we should wait outside," Coldfield said.

The waiter came up and said something to the man, pointing to the kitchen. He nodded and went away.

"Yeah, we can do that."

We got up, much to the staff's relief, and went out into the warm, muggy air. The potted palms were inside by now and the doorman locked up behind us.

"Have you any idea who called him?"

He shook his head. "Come on, let's get my car."

Coldfield told his chauffeur to wait by the restaurant door in case Escott turned up, and got into the driver's seat and turned the key. He opened the other door for me and I barely shut it before we were moving. He swung sharply around the block, his lips tight. He was worried, too.

We made a futile figure-eight circuit of the two facing blocks, so he pulled up and parked next to the canopy and cut the engine. Tension was coming off of him like heat, but he kept it controlled. His door wasn't slammed shut in frustration as he got out, and I tried to follow his example.

We hung around awhile longer. There was an alley between the restaurant and another building and I heard noise coming from it, but it was only the staff leaving for the night. They filtered out the side door one by one and the manager locked up. I spotted the doorman and went after him. He'd seen Escott get into an old car with someone and they drove off, but I couldn't get him to be more specific. He hurried off to his ride home and I went back to Coldfield with the negative news.

His gaze traveled up and down the street, his hands clenched tight on the silver knob of his stick. "Damn him and his work," he growled.

I silently agreed. A car cruised past but didn't stop. Each new set of headlights put our necks to swiveling, but in vain.

Another sound came from the alley—footsteps—but it was only the middle-aged busboy. He carried a box, which I remembered seeing him fiddling with in the alley while the other workers left. He walked past us, staring at Coldfield either in recognition or because of his color, and went on to the parking lot, disappearing around the corner. Almost immediately after, we heard a brief cutoff noise coming from a surprised human throat. Coldfield, the chauffeur, and I exchanged looks and hurried to investigate.

The busboy had his back to the brick wall of the restaurant, protectively clutching his box. In a semicircle around him were three young men still in their teens. Clustered by Escott's Nash were four more of the same type: hard-faced and hard-muscled street kids with all the social conscience of wharf rats. It didn't take a genius to figure they'd been trying to steal the last car in the lot, and the poor busboy had interrupted them.

For a few seconds we were all frozen and staring in a sort of tableau, each side summing up the other, then the chauffeur smoothly pulled out a .38 and held it at ready. He started to say something, but a long, thin shape arced out and smashed down on his thick arm. He swallowed his scream as his knees buckled and fell on top of his dropped gun. One more kid lurched out from his hiding place behind us, swinging an iron pipe down on the man's bowed head.

The time it took to raise the pipe up and down *must* have been brief, but to me he looked like he was moving through cold molasses. Without really thinking, I stepped in, plucked the pipe away from the kid, and hit him in the stomach with my free hand. I remembered in time to pull my punch, though. I didn't want to rupture his internal organs.

The other boys took this as a signal to attack, three of them going straight for Coldfield, who defended himself with his stick, giving as good an example of dirty street fighting as I'd ever seen. He was big and holding out well enough, but we were still badly outnumbered. Two kids rushed in on me with knives, which I simply took away from them since they seemed so slow to me. I shoved them away and sent them staggering into a third kid, and the whole group went down. I used the breathing space to lift the chauffeur to one side, and grabbed his gun.

The three shots I fired at the sky did the trick. The punks disappeared like water into dry ground before the last echoes faded.

Coldfield was a little winded but none the worse for wear, except his tux would need some repair work. He came over and knelt by the chauffeur.

"Is it broken?"

The man felt the arm carefully and shook his head. "Nah, he caught me too high. Cracked maybe, be a hell of a bruise."

"We'll get the doc to look at it. I'll finish driving tonight. You okay?" he asked me.

I pretended to be breathless and nodded. "No problems."

"Goddamn punks. The streets just ain't safe anymore."

I was about to ask him if the streets in this town had ever been safe when I noticed the busboy cowering against the wall. "Hey! You all right?"

He hunched over his box, too shaken to move, the eyes behind his thick glasses were bugged halfway out of their sockets. I walked over slowly, try-

ing to say reassuring things so as not to frighten him more. He let himself
be led out into the glow from the street lights. His teeth were chattering. I
asked him where he lived.

He moved his head vaguely around. "Bad boys . . . hurt."

"Did they hurt you?"

"No." He stared at the chauffeur's arm. "Hurt?"

"Where do you live?"

"Number five." He held up five fingers and counted them off.

"That's very good. Where is number five?"

He counted again, this time going to ten in one rush and waited for my
approval.

Coldfield sighed. "I hate to say it, but maybe we should just look for a
cop who knows where he belongs."

"He might have an address on him. Have you got any papers?"

He looked blank.

"Wallet?" I tried. Another blank look. I pulled my own wallet out and
showed him. "You got one, too?"

He fumbled in his pockets after putting his box down and found one. I
opened mine and showed him the papers inside, but instead of following
suit, he just stared at it. Impatiently, Coldfield took it from him, and the
man instantly burst into tears of protest.

"Mine," he said feebly, and looked at me for help, his face streaming.
"Mine—"

Coldfield had backed away so he could get a better light on the wallet,
then he folded it, stalked over, and punched the busboy in the face, knocking him flat. His eyes were blazing. "You goddamn son of a bitch!"

The chauffeur and I gaped, then looked at the busboy who was just
coming to his feet, holding one side of his head. What we were seeing didn't
clearly register at first, but it looked like part of the man's forehead had
peeled bloodlessly away from the skull. He put his thumb under the loose
flap and tore it completely away and rubbed gingerly at what would soon
be a black eye.

"Do I get that catering job now?" Escott asked.

It took us all awhile to get on speaking terms again. I felt like punching him
myself, but Escott apologized profusely, especially to the chauffeur. His original plan had been to get into his car and drive up to us, but the punks had
interfered. Once the explanations were out Coldfield settled down.

"But I'm not sorry I hit you, 'cause I'd have done it anyway," he said,
still annoyed. I remembered he hated surprises.

"I don't blame you for it, old man." Escott opened his trunk and stowed
away the box which contained his clothes and makeup equipment. He
brought out a flask and passed it around, which did a lot to improve the
general atmosphere. "My question still stands: do I go in with the caterers?"

Coldfield sighed. "Yeah, why the hell not? If you get killed it'll even us up for tonight."

We went to the Shoe Box and Coldfield got busy arranging a doctor for his chauffeur. In the end one of his other men was summoned to drive him to the hospital, where the arm could be properly examined. He laid no blame on Escott for it, saying the car thieves would have been there anyway, and went off with his friend. As they walked down the hall I heard him giving a highly dramatic account of how he came by his injury and how the boss had stepped in and single-handedly saved the day. He'd probably get a lot of drinks out of that story, and Coldfield's reputation wouldn't suffer, either.

Drinks were waiting for us when our host had finished his business. He drained his own and sank into one of the overstuffed chairs. The radio was off and the club band apparently on break. The only noises now were the customers a few rooms away and someone banging around in a nearby kitchen.

"Hey, Fleming." He jerked me back from wherever I'd drifted. "Come on and have a drink. You deserve it after all that rumpus."

I joined them. Escott was perched on the edge of a couch, a sheet of paper in his hand and his forehead wrinkled.

"What's that?"

"A list of the stuff Paco has been shipping in and keeping, but don't ask me what they add up to; that's Charles's specialty." He went to the bar and made another drink. Returning, he nodded at my untouched glass. "Don't you like my booze?"

"It's fine, I'm just not much of a drinker."

"You're more a fighter. I was busy, but saw some, and I've never seen anyone move that fast in my life."

"It's amazing what you can do when you're scared."

He snorted and raised his glass. "Here's to being scared."

I was going to pretend to sip, but it was no good, he was watching me too closely. I braced myself and gulped. The stuff dropped down my throat and hit my guts like hot lead.

Coldfield read my face all too clearly. "I guess you really aren't much of a drinker."

"Bad stomach is all, always had it." I kept gulping at nothing, trying to keep the stuff down, feeling like a balloon about to burst. Escott provided some distraction as he shook his head over the paper.

"There is definitely something to this, but I need more information. Tomorrow I shall have to find out who actually ordered this and where it ends up after removal from the warehouse."

"All right, but just make sure you're at the caterers by six, or they leave without you. I'll let them know what you're trying to pull and tell them not to make a fuss. You goin' to do this act again?"

"Oh, yes."

"What about Fleming? You said you wanted him in, too."

"Not exactly. I shall ask Mr. Fleming to remain nearby with the car. If things get too warm for me, I'll slip out and he can drive us away." He looked at me. "Are you all right?" He'd been too absorbed to pay attention earlier, but now his eyes darted from the empty glass to my face and he understood what had happened.

I tried a weak smile, but kept my lips firmly together, telegraphing to him that I had an urgent problem.

Escott thanked Coldfield, said that we had to get moving, and hustled me out of the Shoe Box and into the car in record time. After a short block I asked him to pull over. I couldn't stand it any longer. He did, I opened the door and leaned out for the explosion. The booze shot into the gutter like a burst from a fire hose. I spat out the last drops, blinked at the dirty street below, and forgot to clutch the doorframe when the dizziness hit. Escott grabbed my arm to stop—

"Mr. Fleming?"

—me going over the rail into endless black water. A heavy hand on my neck forced my head down—

"Fleming?"

—retching, no air, blood pounding behind my eyes—

"Fleming!"

He yanked me upright and kept me from sliding under the dashboard. "What's wrong? Fleming?"

"A dream . . . on the boat."

"You remembered something—what?"

He had to wait a long minute for the shaking to pass, and my left hand was still trembling while I told him what I could. He looked at it, then up a me.

"Touched a nerve, has it?"

"It's almost over."

"Then you've had this kind of seizure before?"

"Seizure?"

"When I see someone going all boneless as you did, I call it a seizure, and you seem familiar with it."

"Yeah, I had one a few days ago when I tried to remember what happened before I woke up on the beach. It's like I'm not here anymore. I don't like that loss of control."

He made a sympathetic noise. "Was your last experience as dismaying as this one?"

"Unfortunately. Except last time I was trying on purpose to remember. This time getting rid of that stuff—"

"Spontaneously triggered the memory?"

"Yeah, what you said."

He *ah-hummed* like a doctor and motioned for me to shut the door, then worked the gears and pointed the car in the general direction of my hotel.

"What's on your mind?" I asked.

"Just an idea . . . I thought a reenactment of your final moments on the boat—"

"I get it, but it's kind of hard to reenact something if you don't know how it was enacted in the first place."

"We know you were beaten and shot."

"You want to beat me up and shoot me?" I said cautiously.

"It is only a suggestion, mind you."

"Let's keep it that way until I can think it over."

"As you wish. After all, I could lose my license by assaulting a client, even if it is in his best interest."

I watched the streets glide past, waiting for the tingling in my left hand to subside. "You still want me along tomorrow?"

He was surprised. "Why would you think otherwise?"

I made a fist and opened it, stretching the fingers. "Because of this. I might conk out on you."

"I'm willing to risk it."

"And because I've met some private inves—agents before, and usually the last thing they want is their clients breathing down their necks while they work."

"That is usually true, but then you don't breathe."

"Funny."

"Besides you are essential to our success. Surely you're aware of the extreme usefulness of your abilities?"

"For sneaking around unseen? Uh-huh, except I'm not too sure what I should be looking for."

"In this case, you might know it when you see it, like a half dozen crates marked as spare parts. You'll have much more freedom of movement than I. You need only to avoid getting caught."

"I figured that much, but how do I get there? I'm not up and around at six."

"You can use my car. I'll leave it at your hotel after I've finished my inquiries for the day. There will be a marked map on the seat showing you how to get to his place."

At a quarter to eight the next night I was out and following his neatly written and meticulous directions. In addition to the map was a sketch of the house and neighboring grounds, and an X marked a shrub-sheltered spot off the road where I could safely park. Paco took his privacy seriously. There were warnings about armed guards, high fences, and even watch dogs, all of which I intended to avoid.

The place was just far enough from town to give the illusion it was in the country. The land around was brilliantly lit by star and moonlight. There was no darkness for my eyes to rest in; even the deepest shadows under the trees had been reduced to soft gray patches devoid of mystery and fear. Darkness had been ended forever for me. Perhaps tonight I would see the man who was responsible.

Twenty careful minutes later I was crouched under the window Escott had designated, mentally keyed up but devoid of the usual physical signs of excitement. My lungs drew no quick gulps of air, my heart wasn't hammering in anticipation of action, I wasn't even sweating. My hands were paper dry. The only evidence of inner turbulence was the iron-hard stiffness that seized my spine. It did help me to keep very still while I waited; that alone was enough to make me invisible to the occasional patrolling guard. I was just another shadow in the bushes.

Escott softly called my name from the window. The coast was clear, inside and out. My body vanished, reappearing just behind him and still in a crouching position. I came out of it slowly, orienting. We were in a bathroom.

He'd been peering out the small window and then whirled with a stifled yelp. "My God, but that's unnerving," he whispered, and I tried very hard not to smile at his reaction. "Are you all right?"

"I'm fine." I stared in fascination at his makeup job—it was perfect. "How can you see through those glasses?"

He pulled out a sheet of paper with a rough sketch on it. "Here's the kitchen, where I'll be. . . . They've set me to washing dishes for now and I've got the window over the sink open if we need to talk. This is the dining room, the guests are still there, about thirty of them, give or take the odd gunman. The caterers are only allowed into these areas, the rest is your territory. Paco's office shouldn't be difficult to identify, but in particular you might seek out the basement. There is a locked door to it in the kitchen, but I'm willing to guess there's another entrance as well."

"You think the locked door is to protect more than just his liquor?"

"I certainly hope so. I want to know where he put all the money he borrowed from Slick Morelli."

"Anything in particular I should look for?"

"Whatever looks out of place in a normal house—or even this one for that matter. Perhaps even your list, if they're careless enough to leave it lying around. In the last week they could have acquired it from Benny Galligar."

"O'Hara."

"Whatever."

I nodded in agreement because he looked nervous. "Okay, don't worry about me. How long will you be here?"

"My group is supposed to leave around twelve. I'll have them drop me off near the car, and wait for you there. You should have as long as discretion allows."

It seemed like plenty of time and I said so. "You better get back to your dishes. If I turn up anything, I'll let you know."

"I've learned to be a patient man, Mr. Fleming. Good luck."

He slipped out the door and I was on my own, without even my reflection for company. I gave him time to get away, then floated out of the bathroom. Considering its proximity to the dining room and kitchen, it would have a regular parade of intruding patrons. Feeling my invisible way down the hall kept me safe, but I'd have to solidify soon to get some bearings. Two men walked past, their voices flat and muffled in my ears. I followed in their wake until they faded away. Pressing what would be my back against a wall, I tried a partial re-forming.

The confusing buzz of background noise became the familiar tones of clear conversation coming from a large room on my right, with double doors leading in to dinner. There was a T intersection down the hall on the left. I picked the left branch of the T and began opening doors.

There were plenty of closets, some small bedrooms apparently belonging to the permanent staff, and another bathroom. It was a water haul so I tried my luck with the other branch of the T and found more of the same, except for one encouragingly locked door. I ghosted through it and felt the floor drop away in a series of descending right angles. It was the other basement entrance. At the bottom landing was another locked door, which also proved useless for the owner.

Inside, I partially materialized and discovered the jackpot. It was a brightly lit laboratory crammed with the kind of stuff I'd last seen at college, when I'd slept through the required chemistry courses. It was nearly as big as my old classroom, but neater and newer looking. The one thing it didn't have in common with higher learning was the lantern-jawed mug sitting at his ease about five feet away from me. Only my lack of sudden movement and his complete absorption in a magazine kept him from spotting my intrusion. I vanished, got behind him, and reformed.

His face was unfamiliar, but his flashy clothes and callused knuckles were enough to identify his probable line of work. On a table next to him was a half glass of milk with crumbs floating on top and a plate of cookies that he occasionally dipped into. His magazine caught my eye—he was also interested in the Shadow's adventures and halfway through *Terror Island*. Someday I'd have to write Walter and tell him about his mobster fan.

Without disturbing him, I very quietly checked out the rest of the joint. At the far end a door with a glass panel set in it led to a dark service area for the furnace, and eventually went on to the kitchen stairs. There was also a locked wine cellar, a laundry, old furniture, and a lot of dust. Going back by way of the lab, I returned upstairs to the T, down its base, and explored another hall. This area was not very promising, with only some socializing rooms; nothing like an office until I got to the last door. It was locked, but no problem.

Paco liked to show off. The inside of his sanctum looked like a decorator's idea for a president's office. It was full of velvet and leather upholstery, black-stained wood, and gold-framed oil paintings of conservative landscapes. The only portrait was of a bullish-looking man with heavy features and pop-eyes. He looked enough like Sanderson to have been a close relative. It was hard to judge how tall he was, for the painting was done on a larger-than-life scale. No memories stirred for me and I wondered how good a likeness it really was.

My training as a detective was limited to what I'd learned watching movies, so I started looking for a safe behind the paintings, but with no luck. The desk drawers were locked, and since Escott didn't want any obvious signs of intrusion I left them alone and sorted through the papers left on top. Nothing important was on them, just some notes about the party and a few doodles.

I tried upstairs and found only more bedrooms and baths, gave up, and snuck back to the kitchen. I could make little sense of the noise and muddle of voices there, and drifted outside to look through the windows. The curtains were open and the sashes raised to let in some breeze. The kitchen was steamy and filled with people busy with mountains of food. Peering through one window, I was face-to-face with Escott, who was bent over a pile of dishes and up to his elbows in soap suds. I softly tapped for his attention and told him to go to the cellar door. He nodded dully, as if to himself, staying in character so well I had some doubts whether he'd really heard and understood. But a few minutes later, when I unlocked the door from the inside, he was turning the knob one second and standing next to me on the small landing the next.

I explained the problem with the laboratory: I could get in anywhere, but lacked his knowledge.

He pocketed the fake glasses and rubbed his eyes. "I can absent myself from the dishes long enough to have a good look. Lead the way."

We went straight to the glass-paneled door and from the safety of the dark on our side, looked in. His eyes lit up at the sight of all that equipment. He stared at everything for nearly a minute, then grabbed my arm and backed us away.

"What's it about?" I whispered.

He shook his head with a small, impatient movement. "I've got to get in there. Can you get rid of the guard?"

"How permanently?"

"Nothing fatal, if you don't mind—wait, he's moving."

We shrank deeper into the shadows, watching through the glass. The man left the magazine open on the table, massaged his back, stood, and stretched. He checked his watch, yawned, and unlocked the stairway door, then secured it again from the other side.

I darted forward, sieved through our door, and let Escott in. "You've only got a few minutes."

"How do you know?"

I pointed to the now-empty glass of milk. "He's headed for the can to get rid of that, so he won't take long."

"Excellent deduction," he approved, and went to work, prowling the length of the room, inspecting the variety of glass tubes and flasks, and poking nosily into cabinets. In one of them he found a handwritten notebook of some kind and in another was a small safe. He suppressed a bark of triumph, dropped on his haunches, and tried the handle. We were both surprised when it turned and the door swung open.

"What's inside?"

"Something odd," he said more to himself than me. He opened the book, scanning page after page, visibly puzzled.

"Anything wrong?"

Too occupied to pay attention, he re-examined some sealed glass containers that seemed to be filled with liquid chrome. He tapped one and the convex surface vibrated like a molten mirror. Leaving them, he searched for and located a supply of chemicals in a walk-in closet. He read the labels but opened a container anyway to make sure of the contents. A smell like rotten eggs drifted into the air, and he looked like a kid who'd just gotten everything he ever wanted for Christmas.

"Come on, what is it?"

"No real heat source except those Bunsen burners," he muttered thoughtfully, "but that could be talked around. Well, well! We can leave now."

"Glad to hear it."

He returned everything to its place except the book, and we got out about ten seconds before the guard returned. He got comfortable with his magazine again and began reading.

"Why isn't he at the party?" I whispered.

"Probably shy. Come on."

Back at the kitchen stairs, he sat on the second lowest step, pulled out a small flashlight and studied the book. Five minutes later he was shaking so hard with silent laughter he had to close it up to get his breath back.

He held it out to me. "If nothing else, this would be proof enough of Frank Paco's criminal tendencies, for is it not well-known that you can't cheat an honest man?"

"What is it?"

He rolled the Latin out slowly and with evident pleasure. "*Magnum opus.*"

"What great work?"

"Open the first page, read what is printed at the top."

" 'What is above is as that which is below, and what is below is as that which is above.' What's it about, burying people?"

"A kind of philosophy, a seeking for enlightenment which has since become corrupted and obscured by ignoble charlatans. You saw the mercury and sulfur. All that was lacking was a purifying furnace. This, my dear fellow, is alchemy."

"Alchemy," I repeated blankly. "Paco is trying to make gold?"

"Pah! The man hasn't the education."

"He's got a tame chemist, then."

"More likely a chemist *cum* physics." He shook his head. "Not a genuine one, but a fraud in every sense of the word."

"A con man?"

"Precisely."

"Somebody's convinced Paco he can turn lead into gold?"

"Not lead, but mercury. It's next up from gold on the periodic table. The notes in that book indicate they plan to use radium—"

"Radium?"

"—in some exotic process that will knock an atomic number or two from the mercury so they end up with either gold or platinum."

"That's impossible."

"In theory it seems quite possible, but that is just in theory."

"It *is* impossible?"

"Given the present state of science, yes, but the idea can be so beautifully profitable if presented in the right way to greedy and receptive ears. This is a confidence trickster of rare genius and no small audacity. It would be an honor to meet the fellow."

"But where can he get radium?"

"He doesn't have to get any—that's what I found in the safe."

"An unlocked safe? But radium is more expensive than gold."

"Astronomically more expensive and far more dangerous to have lying so casually around. Only four years ago there was a case of a Pittsburgh man who died horribly from ingesting a quack medicine containing radioactive salts. The radium they have tucked away in that unlocked safe is nothing more than a convincing substitute. No doubt it was purchased by the mark for a large sum of cash from the con artist's partner."

"So the phony radium and all this lab equipment are just so much window dressing?"

"A new twist to a very old game, don't you think?"

"Yeah, I also think that maybe Paco is wise to it and pulling the strings of the con man. He's got a lot of money swilling his booze upstairs and might take some of the greedier ones on a little tour down here."

"A good point," he admitted. "Again, I seem to have underestimated the opposition. All right, we discard the outside con man for the moment and put Paco in his place instead. He chooses a few gullible prospects from his guests, leads them to think he can make an unlimited quantity of gold by using radium as a modern-day Philosophers' Stone and offers them the opportunity to invest—"

"Or help buy the radium—"

"Then the experiments end in failure and Paco pockets the unspent cash."

"You think he borrowed the cash from Morelli to start with, just to build this lab?"

"It makes quite a convincing backdrop, does it not? I talked with Shoe again today and he was able to confirm that Paco had borrowed a quantity of cash from Morelli about a month ago, before you came to town."

"You don't think this is connected with me?"

"I really don't know. For the moment the most I'll say is that it seems unlikely."

"It's a beautiful situation, though."

"In what way?"

"Paco's left himself wide open—I mean if anything should happen to that lab . . ."

"Are you suggesting we do something precipitant?" He looked hopeful.

"Any objections?"

"After what Paco nearly had done to me, I don't give a bloody damn what happens to him so long as it's something terribly unpleasant."

"You got any ideas?"

"Yes, but I want Shoe's people well clear of this before we do anything. Is the car in place?"

"Just like you marked on the map."

"Good. I must ask you to go there and wait for me. The catering staff leaves at midnight."

"Sure, but what are you planning to do?"

We'd been too loud, or our voices had carried in some freak way, for the glass-windowed door to the lab opened and the basement lights flared on. Escott's back was to them, and his body shielded mine with shadow. He slipped his thick glasses back on and whispered a one-word order for me to hide. The last I saw of him was his startled expression as I vanished.

"Hey! Who are you?" Heavy aggressive footsteps approached and barked. "Hey! I'm talking to you! What are you doing here?"

"I wash up," Escott mumbled in the same voice he'd used to such good effect last night. I moved up behind the man; if there was going to be trouble, I wanted to be in a position to take care of it.

"Yeah? Well, what's to wash down here? You dunno, huh? Get back up to the kitchen. Gowan—move. It's more than your ass is worth if you come down here again."

They both trooped up the stairs. He pushed Escott out, locked the door, and clomped down again. He moved around the basement, checking to see if he missed anyone, but eventually returned to the lab with a weary sigh and shut off the lights. He sounded bored, which wasn't good. A bored man is on the lookout for distraction. Whatever Escott had in mind, we'd have to be careful.

I floated upstairs and outside, appearing at the window as before. Escott was busy scrubbing pans, trying to catch up on lost time.

"I'll be at the car," I whispered.

He nodded as though in time to some unheard inner music, and splashed another of pile of dishes into the soapy gray water.

The guards patrolling the estate were visible a mile off. I had no trouble avoiding them, but the dogs were another matter. They'd been on the other side of the grounds when I'd first arrived and were now making an importune circuit of my escape route. One of the men had a big mongrel on a short lead that caught my scent. Its ears went flat and he came charging, dragging his master. I like dogs, but this time my vanishing trick was never more welcome.

I was near a pine tree and used it to orient myself, hanging close to the trunk to keep from drifting in the slight wind. The man and dog approached and he let the animal sniff around. However, it did not like blundering into the space I was occupying, and at first contact the dog gave an unhappy yip and decided to seek something else to threaten that was a little more within his experience. He broke away and ran off, his master in hot and annoyed pursuit.

It was way past time to quietly beat it out of there. The commotion was drawing the kind of attention that was only welcome in a three-ring circus. I formed up solid again and, moving fast, got away from the clown-and-dog act and found the fence I'd climbed coming in. It was a long five minutes of tearing through brush, brambles, and long grass to reach the car and something of an anticlimax once there, since I had nothing to do until Escott came. For the next couple of hours I plucked greenery from my clothes, kicked at stones, and ducked every time a set of headlights appeared on the nearby road.

Shortly after twelve a large truck rumbled up from Paco's and stopped for a few seconds. A single tall figure hopped from the back, waved to someone inside, and was left in the exhaust as the truck drove off. There was a spring in Escott's step, as though he were on vacation and hadn't spent the evening washing dishes for a man who'd tried to have him killed.

"Sorry about that interruption," he said. "I'm certainly glad the fellow missed seeing you."

"You didn't get into trouble?"

"Not at all. I think the man was reluctant to inform anyone that a person of my apparent intellectual capacity managed to get down there in the first place, as it would make him look bad."

"Good, I didn't want to have to do anything he'd regret. You going to get rid of that face?"

"Yes, I'm beginning to sweat it off, anyway." He opened the Nash's trunk and turned on a small flashlight with a piece of red glass over the bulb instead of the usual clear covering. He noticed that I noticed. "You may have excellent night vision, but I must preserve my own as best I can."

He fixed the light so he could work, and hauled up a large metal box; the layered, unfolding kind used by fishermen to hold their lures and other equipment. Instead of spare hooks and lines, it contained a wide assortment of greasepaints, powders, brushes, sponges, and a dozen other things I couldn't identify in all the clutter. It was the only thing of his that was not starkly clean and neat.

Working quickly in what for him was very dim light, he removed the glasses, false forehead, some protruding teeth from his lower jaw, a ragged gray wig, and odd tufts of hair. He smeared cold cream on and wiped the rest of the makeup off on a thin towel that had seen better days, then closed the kit up. He shrugged out of the white dishwasher's coat and buttoned a dark shirt on in its place.

"Now we can get to work."

"My question still stands: what have you got planned?"

He reached into the trunk again and pulled out my answer.

"You're kidding. You *carry* that stuff around with you?"

"I try to be prepared and I am not kidding. You can put this where it will do the most good."

"Where? Up Frank Paco's—"

"Don't be crude. He has unwisely indebted himself to Slick Morelli to construct facilities to 'produce' his dream gold. You have suggested that if those facilities were destroyed—"

"Well, not in so many words . . ."

"This could be a setback he can't afford."

"Couldn't he just start over?"

"I think not, since his credibility in the criminal community would be destroyed as well once the story got out, and I can make sure it does. It's cost him a lot to set things up, and he might not be able to clear the debt with his creditor."

"He might get rubbed out."

"That is a possibility. If you have second thoughts let me know now, for this is a felony."

"My murder was a felony. Paco owes us both one, so let's go collect."

6

SILENTLY entering the house by way of the kitchen, I started to re-form, but became aware just in time to dodge two men making a late raid on the icebox.

"Did you see that?" a distorted voice asked.

"See what?"

"I thought something moved over there."

"Check it out, then."

I held still, even when something alien intruded into my amorphous body.

"Jesus, it's cold as hell in here. Shut that box up."

"You see anything?"

"Nah."

"Boss'll think you're drinking, you talk like that."

"I could use one."

I left them to their food and moved on to the basement. The lab was as I'd left it, complete with the "milk and cookies" guard. Try as I might, I couldn't work up any dislike for the guy, and it took a real effort to tap him a good one behind the ear so I could do my work undisturbed. To make up for the assault, I eased him gently to the floor and thoughtfully folded his magazine into his coat pocket. Then I went through the lab like a dose of salts, opening cabinets and leaving them open, dumping drawers and looking for papers that might be useful. Escott had been thorough, though, and anything really important would be upstairs with Paco.

Now I hauled out Escott's present, a single stick of dynamite with a five-minute fuse attached. It would do the job, but I wanted to be certain of the lab's utter destruction, and for that spent the next few minutes sloshing several gallons of alcohol all over the room. The walk-in storage closet was full of usable items, and anything marked flammable was added to the general mess. I made sure the air vents were wide open. There were no windows to the outside or I'd have opened them as well. After that I gave the gas taps for the Bunsen burners a good twist and listened to it hiss invisibly into the room.

Propping the dynamite on the one clean table in the middle, I lit the fuse with some nervousness. In the five minutes it would take to burn down I planned to be in the car with Escott and tearing down the road back to Chicago.

I hoisted the guard with the sweet tooth over my shoulders, my new strength making him seem remarkably light, then unlocked the lab door that led to the T-intersection and set it to lock again once it was closed. Trudging upstairs with my burden, I opened the second door into the hall and put the man down to one side. My back was to the hall while I was busy with the door. Too late, I heard the sharp clunk of a machine gun bolt being drawn back. My guess that the hallway would have less traffic than the kitchen was wrong.

"Freeze right there, buddy," a voice told me.

I had to obey and wondered how I could stall them. If I left now they might check the basement and, depending on their luck, foil the explosion or be blown up. There were two men behind me. One of them approached, and I raised my hands slowly.

"Stay outta my line of fire, Harry."

Harry grunted in acknowledgment. He searched me with quick, professional slaps. "He's clean," he announced, and stepped back.

"What's going on?" demanded another, more authoritative voice.

"We caught ourselves a burglar, Mr. Paco."

"Check out the lab, Harry."

I made a move to stop him, but was told again to stay put. Harry slipped downstairs. "The door's still locked, Mr. Paco," he called up.

"Then how'd he get Newton out, dummy? Get up here and check 'em. He's gotta have keys or something."

My muscles had gone all tight. Frank Paco's voice had touched a dormant memory in my brain. I needed time to think, to remember. . . .

"You! Turn around."

I turned slowly, enjoying first the puzzlement, recognition, and then shock on Paco's face.

"*Fleming,*" he breathed softly. Only I could hear him. I felt an awful smile crawling across my features.

The portrait in his office had been too flattering—the artist must have wanted his commission very badly. He'd caught the wide face and pop eyes, but had omitted the ingrained hardness and suspicious set to his mouth. Paco was shorter than Sanderson, but built much the same; stocky with muscle, rather than flab, and not afraid to use it, but now, because of my face, he fell back a step in fear.

"Mr. Paco?" the man with the machine gun said uncertainly.

The need to assert his authority overrode his confusion. Paco straightened and glared at me, rejecting his first instincts. And why not? As far as he knew, Jack Fleming died over a week ago.

"Who are you?"

"My name is Gerald Fleming. I believe you know my older brother, Jack."

Paco seized the explanation as I knew he would. Once more on firm ground, he was able to deal with the situation. "Yeah," he agreed reasonably. "I know your brother."

"You met him the other week, didn't you?"

"Yeah, we had some things to talk over. But you answer the questions here, punk. What are you doing in my house?"

"I thought we could talk."

"We'll talk and you better answer straight. What are you after?"

I said nothing and my bloodshot stare made him uncomfortable.

"This guy's some kind of freak. Take him out and get rid of him."

Harry and the machine gunner each grabbed an arm and marched me past Paco and down the stem of the T. "Get rid of me and you'll never find that list," I shot back. My escort hesitated.

"What makes you think I want it?"

"My brother told me you were after it. He gave it to me. I know you got him. I'll trade you the list for him."

Paco was chuckling. I'd given him a lot to laugh at.

"What if I got it already?"

"Then you wouldn't bother talking to me now." Maybe the bluff would stall things longer. I had no idea if there was enough truth in it to give him doubts, but I was almost certain I hadn't talked aboard the *Elvira*. He might still want his list. "I came here to look for my brother. You caught me square; but I'm willing to deal."

"I'll just bet you are." Paco came closer, his gaze absorbing my face. I hoped my reclaimed youth would pass the hard study. "I'll deal with you the same as I did with him." His hand came up and he tried to knock my jaw off its hinges. I faked the impact, snapping my head hard over and letting my knees buckle. The two men on either side kept me standing.

Not that I paid them much attention, my guts had gone cold. (They were going to kill me . . . they were going to beat me to death. . . .)

"You hear me, punk?" Paco's voice jolted me back to the hallway. "You start talking. You tell me how you got in here. You tell—"

"Frank?"

"What?" His head jerked around in irritation. Another man strolled up. He was in evening clothes, holding a glass, and his face had the broken-veined, dissipated look of a confirmed alcoholic.

"Ask him what he was doing in the lab. Is the lab safe?"

"He musta got in somehow to get Newton out, Doc," said Harry. "The door's locked now and I don't have no key to check."

"Oh, of course, hold my drink." The man fumbled in his pockets. "I have mine right here . . . um . . . somewhere."

"I told you, I was only looking for my brother," I insisted, needing to sidetrack them.

"Then why were you dragging Newton around?"

"I thought I could use him as a hostage."

Paco didn't believe that one at all, not that I blamed him. He threw a hard punch to my stomach. I doubled over, remembering to force air from my lungs. I sagged between my supports, gagging a little, and hoped my performance was convincing.

"How'd you get in here?" Paco repeated.

"Snuck past men—open window—"

"Frank, do you have your key, I must have left mine—"

"Not *now,* Doc!"

"You'll think not now if he's damaged anything down there."

Paco growled and slapped through his pockets. I straightened, worked saliva into my mouth, and spit right in Paco's face.

It was a more than sufficient distraction. Paco gaped at me, frozen in sheer disbelief. His big hand came up slowly to wipe it away. I found a perverse enjoyment in the situation and let it show.

"Leave it there," I suggested. "On you it looks good."

He went beet red, then hit me hard enough to knock me from the grip of my two supports. Stiff-legged, he bulled after me with his fists ready, and I made a big show of cowering and backing away. Paco struck again and again. I was only distantly aware of the blows, feeling impact rather than pain. He'd wear his hands out before he could do me any real harm now. I put on a good act, though, crying out, throwing my arms up, trying to protect my face and groin and each second moving farther and farther away from the basement door.

I heard it a split second before anyone else and, down already, I just covered my head and lay prone.

The blast roared up the stairs, knocking the bottom door to splinters and shattering every window in the house. The whole structure shook; plaster and framed pictures alike jumped from the walls to the bucking floor. The men in the hall were bounced away by the concussion, and the machine gun went off and tore holes in the ceiling.

Paco, Doc, and Harry were knocked flat, Paco actually somersaulting over me. People were yelling alarms in other parts of the house and beneath it all, like the purr of a tiger, I heard the fire. It was time to go.

I got my feet under me and stood in time to greet the reinforcements rushing in from the dining room. Spotted as the outsider, two of them grabbed me while a third aided Paco. He threw off the helping hands and came straight for me. He halted inches away, glaring.

"Take this bastard to my office. Somebody call the fire department."

They dragged me to the office on the other side of the house. Behind us Paco was talking to Doc.

"Get up, you goddamned lush. We got work to do."

I faked weakness, hoping they might get careless and take their eyes off me for a moment so I could disappear, but there was no such luck, not with the boss right behind them. They kept their guns locked on my head until Paco came in, dragging Doc with him.

Doc was the worse for wear and dropped onto a couch, holding his head. Paco went to the massive desk, unlocked it, and began cramming papers into a briefcase.

"What's Slick going to say about this?" Doc wondered out loud.

"I already know," said Paco. "And if you got any brains in that skull that ain't been pickled yet, you'll figure it out, too."

"What will we do?"

"A quick trip outta town with a few of my best boys until this blows over."

"An apt phrase."

"And this mug's coming, too. Slick and me screwed up with his brother, but I won't be taking any chances with this one. If I come up with his list and hand it over, Slick will cancel all my IOUs."

"Assuming you get this kid to talk."

"He'll talk. He don't have his brother's guts."

Oh, yeah?

"What about me?"

"Don't worry. I'll find a safe spot for you until we can set things up again." He snapped the case shut. "Come on."

They opened the door to a smoke-filled hallway. Paco's men were losing out to the fire. He slammed the door, coughing. "We'll take the back way," he said, and started for another door across the room.

Just as he touched the knob, the lights went out. Not knowing how long it would last, I took advantage of the situation. In seconds I knocked Doc and the other two men out cold. The sounds alerted Paco. He swung around, a gun in his hand.

"What's going on?" he demanded. "Doc? Sam? Answer me!"

I grabbed his wrist, pushing the gun away and squeezing. He grunted in pain, dropping the gun from suddenly nerveless fingers. He was trying not to scream. I eased off, but only a little.

"Fleming, it's you, ain't it? We can still talk. I can still give you your brother—" Now he did scream, my grip on his wrist tightened involuntarily and the bones snapped. He dropped the briefcase and sank to the floor when I released him.

"No deals, Paco," I whispered from the shadows.

"What d'ya want? Just tell me. . . ."

What I wanted he didn't want to know. The hate inside me was growing like a separate living thing, and I wanted to turn it loose on this man and let it tear him to bloody ribbons. I picked him up by the clothes and shoved him against the wall. He made a small movement with his left hand. I should have paid attention, but was too crazy to notice. He drew a slightly deeper breath and briefly held it, which was a warning, but then it was too late. The hard snout of a nickel-plated derringer was pressed up under my rib cage and he triggered both shots.

Two red-hot comets tore through me, leaving behind the harsh, ringing aftershock of pain. My body spasmed once for each bullet. I must have cried aloud in reflex, because it hurt like hell. Paco let his breath out in relief and waited for me to fall away.

Instead I slapped the gun from his fingers and laughed. It sounded ugly to me, and I could only imagine what it was doing to him. My lungs ran out of air and I was still laughing, shaking with it, drunk from the look of fear on his face. He fought to get away, but I hoisted him right off his feet and pinned him to the wall. There was just enough thin light coming from the windows for him to see my face. His pop eyes bulged even more, his head shook, and he looked ready to scream, but it was reduced to a whimper that seeped out of his mouth like dribble.

"What's on the list?" I said, giving him a shake to punctuate the question. His heels knocked loosely against the wall.

"N-n-numbers."

"What numbers?"

"C-code—don't know—"

"What do you want it for?"

He was struggling again. "You're dead, I shot you—"

"You're damn right I'm dead, you son of a bitch. You tell me why."

". . . dead, shot you—"

"What is the list for? Why do you want it?"

"Slick!" The name was screamed out. It could have been an answer or a call for help.

"What does Slick have to do with it?"

"He wants . . . Him—you get him. Lemme go, oh God, lemme go!"

"Who killed Fleming?"

"I dunno."

"Did you?"

"No!" The denial was too fast and forceful. "It was Slick! He said to do it. Him!"

"Why?"

"Shut him up. Please, lemme—"

"Where?"

"Yacht."

"The *Elvira*?"

"Yes."

"Who else was there?"

"Fred, he tried to tell me. Oh God, tried—"

"What? Tell you what?"

"You're dead. Go away, go away." Tears streamed down the man's cheek from his wide-open eyes.

The hot, living hate was banging around inside me, fighting to get free, clouding my brain like the smoke that was just starting to ooze into the room. He couldn't turn away from me, and then it was too late. He stiffened under my grip like a corpse. His mouth dropped wide and a gagging noise came out. The noise shaped itself, rose in volume, and lengthened into a full-fledged shriek that had no humanity in it. I let go and stepped away. Something else inside me released him as well, and the screaming died away. Paco dropped facedown on the floor and didn't move.

I stared, afraid and wondering what I'd done to him. I was cold all over and shaking, feeling drained and weak. Out in the hall someone ran up, shouting for Paco. The door opened, and smoke billowed into the room along with two blinded, coughing men.

Paco was still alive, but he didn't respond when I turned him over and there was a heart-sinking blankness in his eyes. As surely as I'd broken his wrist, I had shattered his mind. Considering what he had done to me and who knows how many other poor slobs who couldn't hit back, I felt no pity for him. I picked up his briefcase and retreated a few steps through the door we were to use before the lights went out. By then, the newcomers were tripping over unconscious bodies.

"What the hell? They're all out. . . . Mr. Paco? Mr. Paco?"

But Paco was still oblivious.

"We gotta get 'em outta here."

"The back way?"

"Too slow—open the window."

I quietly left while the men were busy lowering bodies into the flower beds outside. No one really noticed as I crossed the open grounds this time. All eyes were on the house. Some of them had been late-staying guests still in evening dress, others were servants, the rest looked like the thugs they were, and all huddled in little groups and stared at the smoke rising from the windows to the sky. Shouts from the other end of the house brought help to the men who were getting Paco out, saving me the trouble. I may have hated his guts, but I wouldn't have let him burn to death.

Turning away, I walked unchallenged out the front gates and down the road. In the distance I could hear the first fire trucks approaching.

Escott was standing on the fender of the Nash, craning to get a better view of things.

"You were successful?" he asked when he could see me.

"Yeah, it was a real riot."

"Anything wrong?" He dropped down.

"No." I got in the car and tried to pull myself together. I felt the same as when I'd hit Sanderson and turned his face inside out, only this time it had been Paco's mind. I wasn't sorry about it, but I was frightened that I had such an ability and of what it might do to someone who didn't deserve it.

Escott started the car and got us well on our way back to the city. He was looking at me, wanting to know what was the matter, but forcing himself to be patient. I shrugged and shook myself as though I'd solved a problem. It wasn't solved by a long shot, but I could at least push it aside for the moment.

He took my movements as an opening to conversation. "What is in your case?"

I'd forgotten it. "Some of Paco's papers. He seemed to think they were important enough to carry from a burning house, so I took them away instead."

"Dear me, yes, they should prove to be most interesting, indeed. But did he not see you?"

"Yeah, he saw me, but I passed myself off as my younger brother Gerald, who I invented just then, and he swallowed it."

"Then will he not be in pursuit of Gerald?"

"The explosion and fire were some big shock to him. I don't think he'll be looking for me at all. He was talking about finding a deep hole and pulling it in after him. If his boys are smart they'll be doing the same thing."

"If they're smart. What else happened?"

"I think I met the alchemist; they called him Doc. He was drunk, but still had more brains than the others, he nearly spoiled the boom. I last saw him being hauled out a window, guess he got too much smoke. He was worried about what Slick would say once the news was out, which was why Paco was leaving town. Morelli holds all his markers."

"He may have a difficult time collecting now."

"I . . . I started to remember things, Paco's voice—I nearly had another seizure, but snapped out of it. I found out for certain I was killed aboard the *Elvira* for some kind of coded list. Paco and Morelli were both after it, so it wasn't just the loan and money tying them together."

"At one point it was you and what you knew."

"When I didn't talk . . . I know they beat the hell out of me before Paco . . ."

(He raised the gun to my chest and fired. The flash filled my eyes, I fell . . .)

My head bumped hard against the dashboard. My shoes were stained with grass and damp. Escott said my name in a worried tone and brought the car to a stop. He pushed me upright against the seat, and I shook my head like a dazed prizefighter, my eyes blinking as I tried to regain the present.

"Fleming?"

"I'm all right." I was a little surprised; the guy was really concerned about me.

"You don't look it," he said.

My ears were ringing from the memory of the shot and I felt weak; my vision was fuzzy around the edges. The shock of memories coming back I couldn't help, but I could handle the cause of these new symptoms.

"I just—just drop me at the Stockyards. I'll walk home from there, if you don't mind."

He didn't.

Maybe I'd talk with him later, for right now things in my stirred-up brain could wait. We were both tired. For something to do I opened the briefcase and rummaged through the papers. There was a lot of junk I didn't feel like wading through just then. No doubt Escott would enjoy every bit of it later. Then I found an interesting item at the bottom of the case which I could immediately understand. If the printing on the homemade wrappers could be believed, I was holding five neat bundles of one hundred twenties—ten thousand dollars all in one lump sum sitting in the palm of my hand. After spending so many years living close to the edge, all that cash felt pretty damn good.

"Who says there's no justice?" I mumbled.

"What?"

"You want some?"

Escott spared a glance at the money and managed not to run us off the road. "Well, well."

"You think it's marked?"

"Knowing Paco, I think not, but it won't hurt to make a thorough check."

"You mean we keep it?"

"Why not? You once asked me if I were rich. I said sometimes. This is one of those times. A little extra cash is always handy."

"I thought you might be above this sort of thing."

He looked pained. "A Private Agent is entitled to whatever rewards his conscience will permit. If this is Paco's money, my conscience can become quite elastic. It is? Then I think we should consider this to be sufficient recompense for our work tonight. I shall put my share to good use, such as interior improvements to my home."

If he meant his two-room office, he could use a lot of help there. I looked down at the shredded cloth on my stomach. "I think I'll get some new clothes."

Escott looked at the holes. "I thought I smelled cordite. What happened?"

"I annoyed Paco."

He wisely decided to leave it at that.

After feeding and a good day's rest I felt a lot better, and the next night I made an effort to find a men's store that closed early, so I sifted through the ads in the papers, squinted at my map, and located a place nearby that might fill my needs. Then I went downstairs, got a handful of change at the desk, and folded myself into a phone booth. The operator put me through to Cincinnati.

"Hi, Mom. What's going on?"

After last night I needed a dose of reality, and happily used up my change talking to her and Dad about mundane things. We argued about money a little.

"Don't think we don't appreciate this, Jack," said Mom, "but you can't afford to be sending us twenty-five dollars all the time. You have to save a little for yourself."

I thought about the five thousand dollars Escott would be bringing by tonight. My current expenses were running about fifteen dollars a week, including rent and tips. My food, of course, was free. At that rate I could easily spare my folks twenty-five bucks a week for the next two years or more. Maybe by that time Roosevelt would have the economy back on keel.

"I'm saving a little. . . . How are my siblings?"

"What?"

"How's the family? Any new nephews or nieces?"

"Yes, Sarah Jane wrote just the other day. . . ." And she went down the line chattering about my three brothers and three sisters and the growing brood of grandchildren, then had to hand the phone over to Dad.

"Where are you staying so we can write you?"

"I'm just at a small hotel for now, and I may be moving on if I find a better place," I hedged. I didn't want them knowing I was staying under an assumed name. I asked him about the store and about his drinking buddies and what he thought about Hitler, safely distracting him away from questioning me. I'm a lousy liar at the best of times and my parents were always able to tell when I was trying to give them the business. The best thing was to keep my distance until I could figure out what was safe for me to tell them about my condition, or if I could tell them anything at all.

"What happened to all that reporting?" he demanded. "What's all this about an ad agency? I thought all those places were in New York."

"They have a few out here, and they pay good money to bright boys like me."

"Like—what—oh, your mom asks when you coming back for a visit?"

"When I get a vacation."

"When's that?"

"I don't know, I just started. Give me some time to get settled into things."

"You know you got work here if you need it."

"I know, and thanks."

"Well, this is costing you a fortune. Write next time."

"I will, don't worry."

He gave the phone over to Mom, who said pretty much the same stuff, then repeated it all over again to make sure I understood.

"And remember what I said about saving some for yourself."

"Yes, Mom."

"And be careful about what you eat. No drugstore hot dogs."

"No, Mom, I promise."

She said good-bye, gave the phone over to Dad again, and he told me to stay out of trouble, and we said good-bye.

I stayed in the booth for a while, my head down and a cold hard ache inside. I hadn't been really homesick since I first left for the Army as a kid. At least back then I knew I could return again, that home and things would be the same as ever, but that was a kid's thinking. Their lives had changed and I had changed and grown up. I didn't necessarily like the situation, but there wasn't a whole hell of a lot anybody could do about it.

I backed quickly out of the confining space of the booth and went outside, trying to put distance between myself and the loneliness. The depression followed, but its hold lessened with the distractions the long streets offered. Thirty minutes of roundabout walking put me in front of a men's shop that had advertised in the papers.

It was closed and no one would be in the back working late, which was exactly why I picked the place. I didn't need any hovering clerks asking awkward questions about my aversion to mirrors.

I slipped inside and got oriented. The front window shades were pulled, but the low level of illumination was more than adequate. Turning the lights on would have just annoyed a passing cop. After poking around, I located a pencil, receipt book, and a pair of gloves, not necessarily in that order, and proceeded to wait on myself.

Careful to print, I recorded the purchase of several shirts, ties, a couple of suits, some other odds and ends, and the real corker: a tuxedo, complete right down to the white fringed scarf to drape around my neck. I figured the scarf would make me look more like Fred Astaire than Bela Lugosi.

The clothes were high quality and with a price to match, but aside from rent and a few tips, I wasn't spending my money on very much else. I overpaid the purchases by three bucks since I was out of small bills, but thought it would be sufficient compensation to the shop owner for my inconvenient nocturnal intrusion. I could have just walked out with the stuff, but I'm basically an honest guy. Besides, if the incident were reported to the cops, they would probably do nothing. The stuff was paid for and then some. They'd have bigger fish to catch than some customer who took self-service very seriously.

After packaging everything up into a stack of long, flat boxes, I tried leaving by the back door in order to avoid witnesses to my impromptu Houdini act. There were alarms on all the doors, set to go off if they were opened, so I was forced to dematerialize to get out. Not all the boxes went through, the ones that didn't tumbled to the shop floor. I made several trips in and out after that, holding the larger ones close. Since I had to enter the back door of my hotel by the same method, I got a lot of practice in that night. The boxes all bore the name of the store I'd "burgled" and I didn't want to be seen entering the lobby at a late hour with an armful of incriminating evidence. Should the story of the honest thief make the morning papers, the last thing I needed was to have some night clerk putting things together. Maybe I was being overly cautious, but sometimes paranoia pays off.

Before midnight had rolled around, my new duds were hung up, their labels removed and flushed. Taking another short walk out the back way, I disposed of the boxes and wrappings in some isolated trash can.

Escott was sitting in my armchair smoking his pipe when I returned.

"You certainly waste no time." He nodded at my open closet and its new contents, and his eyes went to the top hat on the bureau. "Planning an evening out?"

"Maybe. From what I hear about the Nightcrawler Club, I figure a plain old suit and tie wouldn't get me past the hat check girls."

He murmured agreement. If he had questions about how and where I came by the stuff, he kept them to himself.

"Is this a social visit?"

"More or less. I was wondering if you had seen the papers."

I knew what he was talking about. "Yeah, but you know how these things can get distorted. Editors like to punch things up; it sells papers."

"True, but even taking that into consideration, there was quite a lot of copy devoted to Frank Paco's mental condition."

"He must have been running close to the edge. The fire may have pushed him right over—either that or he's faking to keep Morelli from collecting."

"Has your memory come back on anything since last night?"

"Haven't thought about it," I lied. "I've been busy."

"And I as well." He pulled five thousand dollars from his inside pocket and gave them to me.

"Clean?"

"Very clean."

"I'll try not to spend it all in one place. Don't I owe you something, though?"

"For what?"

"For this case, or are you working for free these days?"

He made a noise that was something like a laugh. "Mr. Fleming, I have already received a very exceptional fee for this case and it is safely lodged in my home, all five thousand of it. You have been more than generous, believe me. As it was, I had not planned to bill you anything at all, especially not after you prevented Sanderson from dumping my careless carcass into the river."

"All right, we'll call it even, then."

"You don't keep banker's hours. You have a safe place to keep your share?"

"Don't worry, it'll be locked away."

"Very well." He changed the subject again, but kept the conversational tone in his voice. "Did you know that several of Paco's key men have been arrested on suspicion of arson?"

"Fancy that," I chuckled.

"I've also been going through the papers you brought out."

"Is it good stuff?"

"It is excellent stuff. I made copies for future reference, and then anonymously turned them over to the right people. If Paco were in his right mind, he would certainly be in jail by now, rather than in hospital."

"Better that he's in the hospital; he can't make bail and leave the country."

"He does have a police guard on him."

"Couldn't happen to a more deserving guy."

"What did you do to him?" he asked in the same quiet tone.

I wasn't ready to talk about it. He could see that, but just sat there and waited.

"Was it something to do with your condition?" he said after a long time.

After all the activity last night I had needed to go straight to the Stock-yards, so he knew I hadn't touched Paco's throat. Such an assault might have driven the man around the bend, though at the time it hadn't even occurred to me to try. Escott was fishing around for something more subtle.

I avoided his eyes. "You've seen him?"

"I talked with a nurse who had."

"How is he?"

"The same as he was last night."

He wanted to know very badly.

"Was that a result of one of your powers?"

I caught myself avoiding his gaze again and stopped. "You make it sound like I'm Chandu the Magician."

"More like Lamont Cranston."

He was referring to the introduction of "The Shadow" radio show.

Every time it came on, the audience was reminded of his power to cloud men's minds. "Yeah, I guess it was something like that."

"What kind of control do you have?"

"I don't know, that was the problem."

"Are you going to learn how?"

"No!"

He gave me a few minutes to cool down. I paced the little room and looked out the window for a while. The street was still down there. I thought about Maureen and all the things she hadn't told me.

"Mr. Fleming . . ."

His formality was annoying. "Why don't you call me Jack?"

"I was going to wait until your case was cleared away. I prefer to keep things on a business level with my clients until they cease to be my clients."

I looked at him now. My mind was concentrated and I prayed controlled. His gray eyes had ceased their normal movements and were locked onto mine. It was so damned easy.

"Call me Jack."

His pipe dropped to the floor with a clack, and the tobacco inside scattered from the impact. The movement distracted me just enough. He blinked and his face resumed the expression he had a few seconds ago.

"Where's your pipe?" I asked.

He found it and apologized for the mess.

"But how did it get there?"

"I must have dr—" He let his breath out slowly. "You did it just now?"

"Yes, I told you to do something. The pipe falling was just a side issue. Now do you see why I want to leave this alone?"

"Induced hypnotism . . ."

"No—"

"Jack, this is not something you should avoid, this demands responsib—"

"Am I still your client?"

It was an oddball question and he wondered why I'd asked it. I told him.

"You see how it is? You weren't even aware of what I did. You think it's your own idea. If I told you to jump out the window singing 'Swanee' you'd do it."

"If it were hypnosis, I would not."

"Yeah, I know all that. You can't get a person to do anything against his will—but that's for the normal kind, and this isn't."

"How do you know that?"

"Because I saw what it did to Paco."

"Did you do it on purpose?"

"No—I don't know—it was an emotional thing as well. I don't know how it works, it just happened. It got away from me and I'm not going to try anything like that again. I have no right to."

"And how do you plan to control it if you choose to ignore it?"

"I don't know. . . . I'll work things out. I could avoid all this arguing by just telling you to forget all this."

"Then do so."

"No. I'm not going to go banging around in your brain with a monkey wrench and have you ending up like Paco."

Escott nodded thoughtfully and refilled and lit his pipe. "I almost wish other people were as morally minded as that, but then I should be out of a job."

It took me a minute to figure out what he meant by that beyond the obvious, but at times I could be pretty damn slow. His needling had been more of a test than curiosity. Apparently my reaction was satisfactory and I almost resented his game. Almost, because if our positions were reversed I might have done the same thing to him.

I tried to laugh, but it came out sour. "Yeah, I'm a goddamned Jack Armstrong."

He stood up. "If you've nothing else planned, would you care to go for a drive? I find it to be quite relaxing and I've found something you might like to see."

I didn't, so we did. He took the Nash as far north as the streets led without actually being in the lake, then took an east-west road. He went dead slow past a two-story brick building that took up the whole block. The place was dark except for a couple of upstairs windows.

"The Nightcrawler Club," he said, in case I'd missed the dark neon sign on the front. "I thought you'd like a look at it. They're closed on Sundays."

He drove down a block and pulled over. We got out and walked past the place, then around to the back. I noticed someone standing in the rear alley and told Escott to keep going. We turned away from the club, going north again until we were stopped by a railing that overlooked the lake. We stood only ten feet above the black water, but I hated any kind of height, and kept away from the rail. Escott leaned on it and stared at the garbage swelling against the concrete boundary of the land.

"Who was in the alley?" he asked.

"An off-duty waiter, maybe, but he was dressed fancy."

"We can try again later."

He pushed away from the rail and headed east along the water. There wasn't much to see: a few boats tied up, others were at anchor farther out; they all looked asleep at this late hour.

"Do you see anything there?" He pointed to something large on the lake. The last time I'd seen it was in profile. It's stern was toward us now, but I had no trouble reading the name.

"The *Elvira*."

"I couldn't be sure of her in the dark, but she is in the same spot she was in this afternoon. Morelli's on board now with his lady friend. He spends his free time there when he can."

"Must be nice."

"What does it bring to mind?"

I shook my head. "Sorry. Right now it's just another boat."

We walked on and made a big circle before coming back to the club. The alley was clear this time, but there wasn't anything worth seeing. It was wide enough for the delivery trucks, and had no more than its share of trash at the edges and the usual loading platform and steps that go with back doors. When I took an incidental breath, the place stank with a wet and used smell—nothing extraordinary—it could be found in any alley with bad drainage the world over.

I shook my head again to his unasked question. As a memory jog, the place was useless. We walked back to the car, or at least tried. The fancily dressed man must have taken a turn around the block himself. It was hard to tell who was more surprised. Automatically his hand went to his belt, where he kept his gun.

"What're you doing here? Get out!"

We were more than ready to oblige and moved away from him, but like a yapping dog, he trotted up behind to make sure we left. Things were peaceful enough until someone else stepped out the back door.

"What is it, Ed?"

"Couple of guys and they're leaving."

"Who are you with?" he said to us.

"Just ourselves, takin' a walk home," said Escott. He had an American accent now and sounded slightly drunk.

"And where's home?"

"Nonayur business. You want us out, we're out." Swaying, he grabbed my arm and started away.

"Ed."

Ed needed no further instructions. He came around in front of us and pulled the gun. I hoped it was too dark for him to see our faces clearly.

"What's the big idea?" protested Escott. "We're goin'."

"In a minute," said Ed. "Turn around and keep your hands out."

He marched us up to the loading dock, the second man joining us at street level. He also had a gun. With his other hand he was pulling out a lighter. While he fumbled to get it working, I felt Escott's muscles tighten. It wouldn't do us any good if those bozos got a clear look at us. While they were watching the sparking lighter, Escott released my arm and twisted backward, grabbing Ed's gun hand and forcing it down. I jumped the other guy and tried to do the same. He had the gun up and fired once, but I knocked it to the outside before it could do any damage. I didn't waste time pulling it away from him, but just hit the side of his head and stunned him. He went down hard and ceased to be a worry.

I checked Escott. Ed had lost his gun and they were both scrambling and rolling on the concrete to get it. I kicked it out of the way and when there was an opening in the punching and flailing, leaned in and knocked Ed cold. I dragged Escott to his feet, and we ran out of the alley for the car before the one wild shot could bring reinforcements. Escott had the keys out and ready. He opened the passenger door, dived in, and slid over. The Nash was started and in gear almost as fast.

He was breathless with a thin sweat on his face, but his eyes were gleaming happily. The man was crazy, he'd been enjoying himself back there.

"That was good exercise," he puffed. "At least we know they take their security as seriously as Paco."

"That could be a problem."

"But not for you, my dear chap. Thanks for the helping hand, that fellow was awfully fast."

"Anytime. Are you done for the night or do you want to take on any wandering longshoremen just to cap things off?"

"Another time. Believe me, I did not think they'd react so suspiciously. The one on the steps must have seen through my drunk act. A pity, it went over well enough on stage. I shall have to show you my press clippings sometime. Oh, dear."

He pulled the car over fast, the right front wheel bumping the curb as we jerked to a halt. He was still breathing hard and his damp skin was gray.

"Oh, damn. Oh, bloody damn." He pressed a hand against his left side. Blood was seeping freely between his fingers. "The bastard had a knife." He slipped sideways against me in a dead faint.

7

DR. Clarson was a small man with large brown hands that at first glance didn't look dexterous enough for the work they were doing. His tightly curling hair was cut close to the scalp. He was about fifty, but the gray at the sides made him seem older. His movements were economical, and if he had any opinions about patching up a white man in his tiny examining room at two o'clock on a Monday morning, he kept them professionally to himself.

Escott was out cold again on the exam table. The room was too small for anyone else but him and the doctor, so Shoe Coldfield and I had to be content to cool our heels in the waiting room outside. There were six old wooden chairs, each as scarred as the matching floor, a small table that must have served the receptionist as a desk, and some ancient file cabinets, also of wood. The place was very clean, though, and smelled sharply of antiseptic. Coldfield looked worried, but not overly anxious. However shabby the place was, he had trust in Clarson's medical skills.

I was restless and wanted to pace, but held it in check, trying to follow Coldfield's example of patience. He sat quite still on one of the chairs, his gaze straying to the doctor and Escott, alert in case he was needed. All I could do was fidget around on my perch on the table and try not to look at the smears of blood we left decorating the floor when we brought Escott in. Bloody damn had been right, my hands and clothes were covered with the stuff. From the literature I'd read in the past on the subject of blood and vampires, I should have been feeling something other than sick horror.

The blood on my hands got sticky, and I asked if there was a washroom nearby. Coldfield glanced up and led the way out to one down the hall. We cleaned up as best we could, but our clothes would be the laundry's problem.

Things hadn't changed at the office. We sat down again. I chewed on a nail, a habit I hadn't fallen into since I was a kid. It tasted lousy, so I forced my hand down with the other and kept still. I looked at Coldfield and wondered why he hadn't asked for explanations, as he was certainly entitled to do, but then I hadn't volunteered any. I looked at Clarson's back and wondered what was taking so long and if we should call an ambulance.

I had eased Escott down on the seat, pulled out a handkerchief, and pressed it against his side. It soaked through in what seemed like an instant, but I could see now that my reckoning of time had been distorted by fear. With his head level with his heart, he came to after a moment and said something unintelligible, then clearly said my name.

"I'm right here. I'll get you to a hospital if I can find one."

"No. Find Shoe . . . closer."

I had no better ideas and at least I knew where to go. Somehow I got over to the driver's side and drove like hell to the Shoe Box.

Half a dozen dark men jumped when we screeched up outside the place, and I could hardly blame them. A couple came up to the car, and I recognized one man from our previous visit. He stuck his head in the window, his eyes going wide and curious at Escott's huddled form.

"Is Shoe around? His friend Escott's been hurt."

He wasted no time on the tableau, but straightened and shouted to someone by the nightclub door, who disappeared inside.

"How bad is he?"

"Don't know—it's a knife wound; he didn't feel it at first."

"Yeah, that's how they are." He spoke from experience, but didn't elaborate.

Escott's eyes were open, but he didn't seem aware of very much. His lips were blue and a sheen of sweat covered his cold face. I knew shock when I saw it and wished to God Coldfield would hurry. After a couple of years of pressing the sodden handkerchief, I looked up and saw his face in the passenger window.

"Shit, what happened?"

"Knife fight. He wanted to come here."

"It's his lucky night," he said, and looked back at the club entrance and told someone to hurry. That someone was introduced as Dr. Clarson, who peered at Escott and got into the backseat, telling me where to drive. Cold-field got in the other side and we took off. Three blocks later I stopped in front of a dusty stairway leading into a dark building. The street-level sign declared the doctor's office was in room 201 and gave the hours.

Coldfield took over pressure duty while Clarson went up to unlock things and turn on the lights. Between the two of us, Coldfield and I got Es-cott up to the office, hopefully without inflicting more damage. Escott must have been in some pain by then; his gray eyes rolled up at the harsh white light and kept on going to the top of his head.

As the waiting telescoped, I became very conscious of Escott's soft breathing. Every few seconds I had to stifle the urge to get up and check things. Leg muscles would tighten, then forcibly relax as I willed myself to stay put so as not to break the doctor's concentration. Another twitch would bring up another excuse. For something to do I pretended to breathe. In that small and very quiet waiting room, Coldfield might possibly just no-tice its absence as Escott had.

Escott . . .

When there was a long, descending sigh in the next room, Coldfield went bolt upright in his chair and looked at me.

The doctor stood up straight and nodded over his work. His had been the sigh we had heard. We crowded into the doorway to see. Escott's clothes had been peeled away, leaving his trunk pale and vulnerable except for the bandages just under the line of his rib cage. Clarson washed up at a tiny sink in the corner and dried his hands carefully.

"How do I handle it, Shoe?" he asked without turning.

Coldfield looked at me. "You want to tell me now?"

I told him how it had happened and that it had something to do with Escott's investigation of my case. Clarson shook his head, giving his silent opinion of grown men trying to act like Saturday-afternoon serial heroes.

"He won't be kicking off just yet," he told us. "So I guess there's no harm in keeping this between us."

"What do we do now?" asked Coldfield .

"Leave him here tonight, let him rest. He lost a lot of blood and got some muscle cut up, but no internal stuff or he wouldn't be here." He didn't specify if he meant the office versus an emergency room or among the living.

"What about tomorrow?"

"We'll see in the morning. I don't want him moved for now. I'm keep-ing him quiet for a few hours, so you two can go on. I'll call you at the club if there's any trouble."

"Do you anticipate any?" I asked.

"Not really, infection at the most. I cleaned him up good, but knives can be dirty."

Coldfield and I thanked him and went downstairs to the car. There was some blood on the upholstery, but it was dry now. We were just getting inside when a long, bony body lurched at us from behind. It was Cal, the skinny kid who shined shoes, but now he was minus his box and easy smile.

Coldfield was surprised, which for him was the same as being annoyed. "What you doing out of bed, boy?"

"Jimmy told me about Mist' Escott."

"He's all right now—"

"Can I see him?"

"He's not even awake and the doctor says he needs rest. He's not hurt too bad, so come on and get in the car."

Cal looked wistfully up the stairs, then reluctantly got in between us. I drove back to the Shoe Box and Coldfield had me park around the back. Without being told, Cal got out and trotted ahead of us to the back door.

"He lives here?" I asked.

"Yeah, him and a few other boys his age. They earn their keep and it's respectable work."

"What about their families?"

"Some don't have any to speak of. Cal's dad was killed in an accident and his mama works in a bar so she can be close to the booze. When she climbs out of the bottle, Cal will move back with her, but until then he's got a home here."

"In a nightclub?"

The question should have annoyed him, but didn't. "My sister comes by to look after them. This place is a castle compared to where they've been. I make 'em work and when they aren't working, they go to school. I don't force anything they don't want; they can leave when they like, and some do, but the smart ones don't."

The headline, "Bronze Belt Boys' Town" jumped into my head. It would make a good story, but now was hardly the time for an interview.

"Want to come in for a drink?" he asked.

"Thanks, but next time. I need to get home and clean up."

"You got a way home?"

"I can walk."

"Not in this neighborhood, you can't. Come on, my turn to drive you." We went to his newer Nash and got in. He asked where I lived and I told him. "That's a pretty long walk."

"I like to walk."

"In some parts of this town, you're better off running."

"So I've noticed." I handed over the keys to Escott's car. "Here, I won't be by till late tomorrow, you take care of them."

"Sure. You still going to mess with Morelli?"

"I have to, now."

"Take some advice and don't." He didn't mention the consequences. He didn't have to since we were both thinking about Escott.

*   *   *

Back in my room I packed my dirty laundry up for the staff to work on. To save trouble explaining the bloodstains I just threw the shirt away. I spent the rest of the night flat on my back and staring at the ceiling from the bed. It was depressing having to sit through the long early-morning hours alone and not be able to watch the dawn and the change of mood a new day can bring. The only good thing was the oblivion it brought as soon as the lid of my trunk came down, and then an instant later it seemed, there was another fresh night ahead of me, as though the day had never happened.

I phoned the Shoe Box first thing and talked to Coldfield.

"You been out all day? I tried to call."

"Yeah. Call me for what? Is he all right?"

"He's weak, but insisted on going home. I thought you'd want to know, is all." He gave me a different address from the little office and I wrote it down. "You aren't going to tire him?"

"No, just apologize for putting him through all this."

"It's no one's fault but the s.o.b. with the knife."

I agreed and hung up.

The taxi dropped me at a row of two- and three-story buildings that looked old enough to have escaped the Fire, or had been built immediately afterward. Kids played in the quiet street, and parents sat on the steps and fanned themselves in the twilight. It was a respectable middle-class neighborhood. It hardly seemed suitable for Escott, but then again I couldn't think what else would have been right.

I rang the bell of a brown brick building of three floors and Cal opened the door.

"Hi, Mist' Fleming. Shoe said you was coming."

From somewhere close inside, Escott said, "*Were* coming, Cal."

Cal grinned and said it again correctly, standing back for me. It was a small entryway, with a rack on the wall to hang hats and coats. Directly ahead were stairs leading up into shadows. On their left was a hall going through to the back of the house. An open set of double doors were parallel to the stairs, and beyond them was a cramped sitting room, where Escott was lying on an old chintz-covered sofa. He was in a dark purple bathrobe; the color made him look more pale than he was. There were tired circles under his eyes, but he seemed glad to see me.

"Come and sit down. Will you have some tea?"

The question was for Cal's benefit; I politely declined. "You look better than last night. How do you feel?"

"I'll live through it. Shoe invited me to stay at his place, but I wanted to come home. We finally compromised, and he let me go, but only on condition that Cal stays over and keeps an eye on me."

"Good, I was afraid you'd be alone."

At second look, the place only seemed cramped. The high ceilings made the floor area appear smaller in proportion. The floor was highly polished, reflecting the lamplight and a few comfortable old pieces of furniture. Several pictures hung by long wires from the upper moldings. They were all large mediocre prints of naked women reclining on clouds with naked babies and doves, and were hardly consistent with Escott's character.

"Did this place come furnished?

He noticed where I was looking, his eyes crinkling. "Do you like them?"

"They're . . . interesting."

He didn't miss my expression. "You have excellent taste. They shall no doubt prove profitable to the junk dealer as soon as I can get around to it."

"They came with the house?"

"Yes, certainly. It has an interesting history. I have it on good account from my neighbors that the place was once a bordello."

"The previous tenants *are* gone?"

"Yes, the owner died some time ago, the place went for sale, and I was able to buy it quite cheaply, as no one wanted to live here. You know, I still occasionally have to turn away an old customer who hasn't heard the news yet. My life is not dull—sometimes odd, but never dull." He sipped his tea. "Shoe thinks I should talk you out of pursuing your own case and to turn it over the police."

"You know I can't go to them the way I am."

"I know, but Shoe doesn't. He obviously has decided that I have no further interest in it because of this little incident."

"I'm not too surprised; he mentioned it last night. I am sorry about this. If I'd been faster—"

He shook his head. "No one else could have been faster, I've seen it and you did save me, after all, and I am grateful. Forget about it, I'll be up and doing soon enough."

Cal came in with a glass of water and a small bottle of pills. "It's time."

Grimacing and accepting two, he washed them down quickly to get it over with, then Cal took the glass away to the kitchen. As soon as he was gone, Escott spit the pills fastidiously into a handkerchief and tucked it into the robe's pocket. He drank more tea to wash away their taste.

"What gives?" I asked.

"They're morphine. I've seen what it can do to people, and I'd really rather endure the pain. At least I know it will go away. Clarson is an excellent fellow and discreet, but he really should know better. I had an armful of the stuff this morning and could hardly do anything for myself."

I wondered what he could possibly feel up to doing in his condition. "Do you need anything now?"

"Only more patience."

"You aren't talking me out of this mess?"

"We're enough alike that I know better than to try."

"I'm going there soon."

"Tonight?"

"Tomorrow. I want to give them time to cool down from last night's fracas. They wanted to know who we were with. You think they thought we were Paco's men?"

"Possibly, or any of a dozen smaller gangs out for trouble. I'm inclined to think they were just naturally suspicious. What do you plan to do?"

"I was a journalist two weeks ago. . . . I'll just check things out like it was any other story and see what happens." Vague at best as an idea, but it had worked for me on other occasions and had turned into acceptable copy. I was hoping to turn this into my missing memory.

Escott was visibly tired, so I wished him well and left, walking around the city for a couple of hours. Coldfield was right about some places being dangerous, but I was a big boy now and could take care of myself. I was looking things over, getting acquainted with the streets and the personality of each block, slowly working toward the Stockyards and my inevitable stop there.

By now I had ceased to be too squeamish about the blood drinking. That oddball reaction had hit me on my second visit there. My first feeding had been done in a kind of panic; "you must do this or die." It had been quick, dreamlike, and with no time to think. My second visit had been more leisurely, and when it came down to brass tacks, I almost balked. The thought of opening an animal's vein with my teeth and sucking blood from the wound was nauseating, but out of necessity I had to push the thought from my mind and get on with the business. Intellectually, I still had trouble handling the process, but by now I was at least getting used to it. It helped to think of it in terms of a habit, like brushing one's teeth; boring, but it had to be done.

The blood completely satisfied my hunger and gave me strength, but its ingestion was a far cry from sitting comfortably around a table with friends and socializing into the small hours over real food and drink.

Leaving the yards, I wandered a long time until I found an all-night theatre and went in. Leslie Howard pined after Merle Oberon in *The Scarlet Pimpernel,* and I watched it three times in a row, until I was rooting for Raymond Massey to win. He never did, so I went home and read the papers until dawn.

The personals still carried my question to Maureen, but had no reply. I told myself again I was a fool to hope after all these years and should just give it up. As always, I gave a mental shrug. It wouldn't hurt for just one more week, it really wouldn't.

But it really did. The trick was to ignore the hurt and keep hoping.

The tuxedo fit well enough. I was one of those lucky ones who could buy things right off the rack, even pants. The new patent leather shoes were a bit snug, but they'd be well broken in tonight. A mirror would have been useful, for I was interested in how young I appeared. I'd fed heavily last night to obtain a good color as well, as I planned to pass myself off as Gerald Fleming again.

I transferred some cash into a new wallet and worked the stiffness from it. The rest of my money was locked in the trunk with my other personal papers. The wallet had a little pasteboard card with lines for printing one's name and address. I filled it in with the name of Gerald Fleming, a phony out-of-town address, and the name of Jack Fleming as someone to contact in case of an emergency. As a legal ID it was totally useless, but better than nothing at all. I draped the white silk scarf so it hung in front, and finished things off with the top hat.

I left by the back door, partially from paranoia, partially from the idea that if anyone in the lobby glommed me in this memorable getup they'd raise my rent. A few blocks away I caught a cab and had it take me to the lion's den.

Tonight the windows of the Nightcrawler were bright, and fancy people were streaming in and out even at this early hour. I paid the driver and trotted up the wide steps in order to slip inside with a knot of revelers, but found my way suddenly blocked by an agile mountain disguised as a man in a tuxedo. He had short blond hair, small eyes, and a chronically grim set to his mouth.

"Good evening," he said civilly. I mumbled a reply of some kind, noting he was giving me careful study. His eyes flicked to some grillwork set like an oversized vent in one branch of the U-shaped entrance. The darkness of the small room beyond wasn't quite adequate to hide the man with the gun who sat there. He nodded and the mountain stood aside and let me by. I pretended not to notice this exchange, as they decided I wasn't a dangerous character. It was favorable to be underestimated. I looked young and hopefully innocent—all that was needed was a touch of stupidity. Considering some of my antics from the past, that would probably be very easy.

The doorman did his duty, but I paused at the threshold with a brief attack of doubt and insecurity. Though it would have been too dangerous for him, I wished Escott was along. I missed his confidence. Despite the advantages I had now, I could still get scared. For just one second I nearly turned back, but a silly-looking woman with frizzed black hair and too much makeup caught a look at me and whooped hello. Her party had preceded me coming in and were already more than a little drunk.

"Whatcha waitin' for, a streetcar? Come on in, cutey," she shrilled.

I couldn't stand this kind of drunk, but went in before I started thinking again. She latched on to my arm.

"Isn't he cute? Hey, Ricky, isn't he cute, isn't he?"

Ricky said, "Yeah," and swayed a little. How had they qualified getting in if the watchdogs had been so careful with me?

"That's how I like 'em, tall 'n cute," she told Ricky reproachfully. I hadn't been cute since I traded my short pants in for an older brother's hand-me-downs, but let them drag me inside. Stepping away from the door, I heard the men behind us chuckling. Good. If they found my situation something to laugh at, they might also think me harmless.

As politely as possible under the circumstances, I detached myself from the lady's grip and checked my hat and scarf in with the first of the many stunning blonds that worked there. Platinum was the dominant color, apparently a requirement for employment. They wore short black dresses decorated with silver sequins in the pattern of a spider's web. Over their hearts were black, red and silver pins of stylized spiders, all of which were a nice gimmick to tie in with the name of the club.

With difficulty, I turned my attention from the girls to the rest of the place. It was very noisy. The barrage of conversation trying to be heard over the brassy orchestra was like a riot in a large dog kennel. With that image in mind it was easy to categorize the patrons. There were a few high-class ones with pedigrees, but the overwhelming breed represented were the mutts; well-dressed, but mutts all the same.

Another blond came up and led me to a table the size of a dinner plate and told me the waiter would be by shortly. The place was surprisingly busy for a weeknight, but well organized. In less than a minute a young man appeared and took my order for Irish coffee, which also appeared in less than a minute. I pretended to sip, though bringing it to my lips was an act of will, and I had to stifle a gag. For distraction I looked around and caught several unescorted young ladies giving me a hopeful eye. I wasn't that handsome—they were working girls. I had no inclinations for that at the moment, so my gaze slid past to the swaying couples on the floor below. The band wound up the music, the dancers dispersed, and the lights went down. A single spot picked out another platinum blond leaning against the grand piano. She was in something long, white, and silvery, a nice contrast to the brief black skirts of the other girls and a perfect complement to her long shimmering hair.

She sang something sad and shallow in a voice that was surprisingly good, filling the room and hushing even the worst drunks. As with any woman I noticed, I was comparing her to Maureen, looking for something wrong, but for once the lady was holding her own. She finished her song, and the lights faded and came up, but by then she was gone, leaving her audience wanting more. The band cut to another number and couples began to venture onto the floor again. I looked up and saw a pretty girl smiling at me, holding a tray full of tobacco products.

"Bobbi always knocks 'em dead," she observed with a nod toward the stage. I made a business of picking out some cigarettes and got her to talk a little. In two minutes I found out where she lived, when she got off work, the time of Bobbi's next number, the location of the gambling rooms, and the requirements to get inside, which were specifically a lot of cash and the willingness to lose it fast. Her interest cooled and she moved on, apparently having had experience with gamblers. I'd seen the type as well; men who would rather gamble than make love, more fool they.

And here I was trying to imitate them. I abandoned my table and drifted over to a guarded door marked PRIVATE. The large man there asked my name. I gave the one I was using that night and was slightly disappointed to get no reaction. He consulted a telephone, a buzzer sounded, and he opened the door wide.

It was another big room, but much quieter, lit by crystal chandeliers and dimmed by cigarette smoke. I'd been in places like this before, but never when they were in one piece. Usually I was hot in the wake of a police raid making a written account of the destruction and noting down who had been arrested for what. Prior to tonight I had never been able to afford this sort of decadence. It felt great.

At the money cage I bought two hundred dollars in chips, blanching inwardly at the small pile they made in my pocket. For something to do, I lit a cigarette and studied faces. Not one of them was familiar, which was all for the best, since I didn't want to be noticed right away. I wandered around, looking for Slick Morelli. He was either not there or my memory was not cooperating the way it had at Frank Paco's. Maybe I was expecting too much from my traumatized brain.

Giving it a rest, I found an isolated corner and got into a blackjack game, winning ten dollars and losing fifty before realizing I could cheat without getting caught.

The dealer's face had about as much expression as a dead fish, but he had no control over his heart rate. When the immediate noise level occasionally subsided, I could just hear it. Every time he dealt the house a good hand it beat just a little louder and faster, and after some concentrated practice at sorting out the internal signals my rate of winning rose marginally. I didn't win every time, that was impossible with the other players and the natural fall of the cards, but I had enough of an edge to win more than lose. In an hour I left the table a thousand dollars ahead, excited at the prospect of a new vocation in life.

Circling the room again, I looked at the new faces, checking out the suckers at the roulette tables and slot machines. One of the machine patrons was the singer, Bobbi. She looked just as good, if not better, close up as she did fifty feet away on stage. Now she was wearing a black sequin-trimmed wrap over her bare shoulders. It must have been to provide some modesty to her stage gown, but since the black material was practically transparent it had just the opposite effect.

She pushed a coin into the slot and hauled the lever down with just enough precise force, indicating long practice. She got a cherry and two lemons. Her face revealed no disappointment. Her moves were automatic: push in a coin, yank the lever, and wait, push in a coin . . . I was getting hypnotized. She won a small pot, added the money to the stack she kept ready, and started over again. I wondered if she'd rather gamble than make love.

She noticed me out of the corner of her eye. Just my luck, the first emotion I inspired in her was annoyance. "The floor show's in the next room, ace."

"Sorry, didn't know I was intruding."

"You shouldn't look over other people's shoulders."

I moved around to her front field of view and angled so I could look out across the room. Tapping out a cigarette, I offered her one.

"They kill the voice and stain the teeth," she told me, pulling the lever down with decidedly more force. I put my props away unlit and offered to buy her a drink.

"No, thanks, and before you ask me why I'm here, I'm supporting my crippled mother down on the farm."

At least she was talking to me. She didn't say anything I wanted to hear, but she was talking. I watched her play the machine. There was more strength than grace in her automated movements, but the view was very absorbing.

"You know Slick Morelli?" I asked.

She kept up the rhythm, but her eyelids flickered. "Doesn't everybody?"

"Where is he?"

"Somewhere around."

"Can you point him out?"

"You think I'm the party hostess or something? Go talk to one of the boys over there." She jerked her head in the direction of the door. The movement dislodged a wisp of hair. She paused long enough to brush it with her fingertips, using the gesture to glance at me before going back to the machine. I tried to keep my smile neutral and non-threatening.

"I hard that yacht of his is for sale," I tried. "The *Elvira*."

She laughed. Another coin, down came the lever. I didn't see the result. She put in another coin.

"Why not? He needs the money."

This time the lever stayed up. Her eyes slid over to mine. I expected blue, but they were hazel. She studied my face, trying to fit me into a category and finally deciding; it was anything but complimentary. "What do you want?" she said wearily.

"An introduction to Slick?"

She almost said why, but thought better of it. "Go talk to one of the boys."

"They're not as pretty. My name's Gerald Fleming . . . I think Slick will want to talk to me about my brother Jack."

The names meant nothing to her, which was a relief.

"Jack met him two weeks ago, they were aboard the *Elvira*."

Her heartbeat went up suddenly, but she kept her face straight.

"He's built just like me and much the same in the face, but he's in his mid-thirties."

Nothing new, she was still reacting to the mention of the yacht.

"Frank Paco and a guy named Sanderson were there, too. Fred's dead now and Paco is headed for a nuthouse. . . ."

She went white at those names, but still tried to cover it with a kind of defiance. "So what?" She wore a soft flower scent, but underneath the roses

I could smell fear. I asked her why she was afraid. She didn't deny it. "Death and taxes, what else?"

Slick Morelli or me?

She kept her eyes on the machine. "I think you'd better go now."

"I'd rather stay."

"Suit yourself, it's no skin off my nose."

"A guy could get discouraged."

"Good."

"I know Slick killed my brother."

She had a lot of control, but now the fear smell was drowning the perfume. She went on playing, pretending she hadn't heard.

"If you see him tonight, pass that on. I'll be around."

"You're not kidding, are you?"

"No."

"Why do you think he—"

"Because I was at Frank Paco's last dinner party, the one with the hot finish that made all the papers. I overheard things. Slick's name came up in the course of the conversation."

"Aren't you being kind of stupid to march in here like this?"

"Maybe, but Slick won't hurt me because I've got something he wants."

"What?"

"The same thing he wanted from my brother Jack, but didn't get."

"Okay, be cagey."

"The less you know the better it is. I don't think you want to be in the middle of things."

"So everyone tells me. Why should you care?"

"You remind me of someone."

"Thanks a heap."

"She was afraid sometimes, too."

She watched me, troubled and wary. I shut up and moved away, there was no more to say to her and I couldn't trust my voice. Maureen was still too strong within me and I was feeling guilty for being attracted to Bobbi. She was as beautiful as Maureen, but in a different way; she was also vulnerable and worked hard to hide it. She gave me a lot to think about and I drifted blindly for a while. I lit more cigarettes, but didn't inhale. My body allowed me air to speak with, but rejected all foreign substances but one, and I had tanked up on that last night. I puffed superficially and added to the haze.

In one of the alcoves a little way from the noise, a serious poker game was in progress. There were five players, but most of the chips were on one side of the table in front of a totally bald fat man with a tangled brown beard bunching along the edge of his jowls like a baby's bib. Just as I strolled up one of the players threw down his hand and folded for the night. He left with a sweat-slick face, his body giving off the kind of reek that only comes from a habitual gambler, the kind that loses. I was the only observer of the game, the fat man probably won far too often for it to be of any interest to onlookers.

The cards went down and he raked in another pot, neatly stacking his chips according to color with his short, flat fingers. There must have been nine thousand dollars in front of him.

"Care to join?" he said, not looking up.

"No, thanks, I'll watch." I didn't like poker, tending to agree with Ambrose Bierce, who defined it as a game played with cards for some purpose unknown. I'd been listening to heartbeats and knew my little trick would be totally useless at this table with these veterans of the bluff. To test it, I mentally played a hand against the fat man, looking over the shoulder of another player. I lost repeatedly, as he registered about as much emotional reaction as the felt-covered table. All hands were alike to him. Bored, I finally left, sliding quietly out of the alcove. The fat man's glassy soulless eyes followed me before they snapped back to his cards.

After patrolling the room once for Morelli, I went back to the blackjack table and settled in for some serious gambling of my own. As a game to play, it was much faster, and I enjoyed the mental workout it gave. Before I knew it, two hours were gone and I was the only player left. It increased my odds of winning, I had the dealer's reactions down well enough by now to practically read his mind.

I flipped up my last card—it was a straight blackjack, I got them occasionally. It was time to quit. Hardly believing it, I gathered up fifty-eight hundred dollars in chips. At this rate I could buy Dad a whole new chain of stores. My conscience wasn't chafing a whole lot. It was Slick Morelli's money and he owed me.

Shuffling the chips away, I looked up, my gaze locking on to Bobbi's face. She moved without hurry across the room, not smiling, not frowning, carefully blank. She sat on the stool next to me and gave the dealer a quiet signal. He closed the table and left.

"You gave up on me pretty fast. Why?" she asked.

"I thought that's what you wanted."

"I don't know what I want right now."

Dance music filtered in sporadically from the club room as the door opened and closed. I caught her scent again—roses and fear. It was strangely exciting. Her skin was very light and in the shadow beneath her jaw I could see the veins throbbing with life. I could smell that, too.

Keeping very still, I waited for her to look up at me. She was so very beautiful and the first woman I'd wanted in a long, long time. When she finally looked, I suggested we leave the room. She stood and let me follow her through an unmarked door at the back. We were in a dim hall, silent for her; for me it was filled with the uneven rhythm of her lungs and the booming of her heart. She let the wrap slide down from her shoulders as her arms went up around my neck. The length of her body pressed warmly against mine, just as I had wanted it. I caressed her hair, tilting her chin up and kissing her red lips.

But the passion was all one-sided. Her face was empty of all thought or feeling, her mind was in some neutral state, waiting for my next suggestion. I backed off in doubt, then, suddenly knowing it was wrong, I turned away.

As a living man I'd never forced myself on a woman, and I wasn't going to start now. My changed nature had provided me with an all-too-easy route to seduction. Maureen completely avoided the use of this ability. She had wanted a willing lover, not a slave.

Bobbi's arms hung loose at her sides, and gradually awareness returned to her eyes. If she had some clue of what I'd been doing, she made no sign. Perhaps she thought her own idea had brought us here. I put a hand on the doorknob, hers stopped me.

"I think I should go."

"No." Her voice was hardly above a whisper. "I had to tell Slick what you said."

"I know, it's all right. That's why he sent you after me."

"Was it that obvious?"

"Just unexpected."

"I can get you out from here. I'll tell them you got wise and ran."

"Too risky for you, though."

"I'll be all right." Her breathing was back to normal and she still held my hand. Her face was tilted up again and she was free from any form of suggestion now. I lowered my head and kissed her and felt elation when she responded. I wanted to stay there, but reluctantly had to draw away. There was a pleasant kind of pressure building in my upper jaw. It was different from hunger pangs, but just as intense, pushing out my canines. While things were still manageable, I pushed them back into place with my tongue. Now was not the time or place for that sort of thing.

"This isn't Slick's planning," she said.

"I know."

"Look, maybe I can meet you tomorrow—"

"Tomorrow night. I have to talk with Slick first."

"Why?"

If I tried to answer that one we'd be there all night, which under any other circumstances would have been most desirable. I shook my head and smiled a little. "I'll take you back before you're missed."

She crumpled. "I hate it when he makes me do this. He said it was a joke, but I know better. He wanted me to get you outside, for you to meet me out front so you're seen leaving the club."

"I'll oblige him, but we'll leave you out of it."

"But you're a fish on a hook now. Don't you see?"

"Like my brother?"

She was trying not to shiver. "I don't know about him, I really don't. Two weeks ago Slick spent several days on the yacht. He came back exhausted and in a bad temper, maybe your brother had something to do with it, but I just don't—"

She looked like she needed a pair of arms around her, and I did the best I could. "Don't worry about it, it's my choice. I'm leaving now, by the front door."

"He'll kill you," she said with certainty.

"No, he won't." It was too late for that, but a person doesn't have to have a bullet drilled through his heart to be emotionally dead. I smiled again, got hers in return, and felt alive for the first time in years.

I traded my chips for cash at a grilled window under the hard gaze of two gunmen and folded the money away. The cashier made a big point of inviting me back again tomorrow night. He must have figured my beginner's luck would have worn out by then.

The band was playing a last slow number and I emerged from behind the door marked PRIVATE. Bobbi had gone around by another door and was on the dance floor, floating in the arms of a man who was holding his face close to her gleaming hair. Some guys had all the luck. It might have been Morelli, but I was only guessing.

The tables had lost most of their patrons. One whole section had been roped off and the mop-and-bucket boys were busy cleaning it. I collected my top hat and scarf, giving the girl at the counter enough of a tip to wake her up, and left by the front entrance.

I wondered how much line they were going to give me before hauling me in.

The cool night breeze off the lake felt clean and moist. The place was probably an Arctic hell in winter, but now things were just right. There were still a few hours before dawn. If they planned to try anything, I hoped the night would be long enough to accommodate them. I turned left along the front of the club, walking slowly. Behind, two sets of shoes were keeping pace with mine. I stifled a smile.

Between streetlights I paused and glanced back. One of them was the walking mountain, the other was the guard from the casino door. I tried to not be overly optimistic that they were after me. They could be underpaid enough to just want my newly acquired money. I continued on and turned the corner. There were two more men standing in the way. One of them plucked a toothpick from his mouth and flicked it away. He must have seen that one at the movies.

The guys behind caught up with us and completed the quintet. To make it look right I tried to duck past them for the open street. They were fast and professional and didn't even muss my clothes, but then I was not using my full strength to fight them. With arms held pinned to my sides and the white scarf over my eyes, I was marched quickly back to the club.

From the length of the walk and the smell at the end of it, we were going in by the alley entrance. I made some stock verbal protests until one of them shoved my own handkerchief into my mouth. This was done only to shake me up. If I'd really started to yell for help, they'd have been a lot rougher. In silence I was dragged up some steps and over a linoleum floor. From the leftover smell of grease, I guessed it was a kitchen. We trod on wooden floor for twenty-eight paces, then I was stumbling up a flight of stairs. Knuckles rapped on wood and I was shoved forward.

The door shut. I stood on carpeting in a room with two sets of lungs; one right behind me, probably the Mountain and the other about eight feet in front. A light switch clicked, and I felt a gentle warmth on my face.

The scarf was yanked down. The warmth came from a flexible desk lamp whose bulb had been angled to shine right in my eyes. The rest of the room was dark, but it didn't matter; the man trying to hide behind the glare was quite visible to me.

He was medium sized and dark haired, with a pale olive complexion slightly marred by old acne scars on his cheeks. In his young thirties, he had a set of sweet dark eyes that should have been on a woman. He would have been handsome, but his nose was too pinched and he had what looked like a razor cut for a mouth. His stare was intense and I shifted uneasily.

He smiled approval at my reaction.

I checked the room over so as not to look at him. It was a plain working office, but with a nice rug, a couple of paintings of ships, and an expensive desk-and-chair set. On the desk was a phone and blotter, in the corner behind me stood a file cabinet. There was no other place to sit, though some dimples showed in the rug where chairs had been. He was smart enough to know how well such minor intimidations can undermine a person's confidence. He sat relaxed behind his desk, gave me a good once-over, then raised one finger as a signal to the man behind me. Hands probed, and my wallet, half a pack of cigarettes, and a book of matches were dropped on the desk. He opened the wallet, ignoring the money, and his eyes rested a moment on the little pasteboard card.

"I think you can consider this an emergency," he began. "Would you like us to put you in contact with your brother?"

Figuratively speaking, I could breathe a little easier. I'd worried he wouldn't have accepted me as Gerald. I didn't answer, but squinted at the light as though trying to see past it.

"I heard about you being at Paco's, he continued. "They said you wanted to trade the list for your brother. I know where he is and I'm willing to deal."

It was simply stated and the truth, but I didn't think he was dumb enough to think I was that gullible. He was only feeling me out.

"Are you willing to deal with me?"

"Only if you're Slick Morelli," I said.

He didn't answer except to move his hand slightly. The Mountain came up on one side and buried his knuckles in my stomach. That hurt a little— very little—and I faked the rest, going down on my knees as I had done at Paco's; no imagination, these guys.

"You can call me Mr. Morelli, Junior," he told me. "Now say thank you."

I was pulled to my feet and punched two more times before I got bored with the business and said what he wanted. There was a purpose to it all; get me to give in and obey him once and it would be that much easier for me to give in later about other things. He knew his business. I'd seen it done in other situations. The faces changed, but the technique remained constant. I let the Mountain hold me up and concentrated on breathing. Under the circumstances, they were both bound to notice if I stopped.

"Now, where is the list?"

Again, I said nothing; my memory had it in a place I could not reach. They'd killed me over it before, and they'd certainly try again—a difficult job in my present state, but not impossible. I had some control this time, though, and would stall to try and learn more, hoping my contact with them would trigger a memory.

Morelli opened a drawer in the desk, drew out a long black cigar, and fitted it into a silver holder. The skin on my head began crawling in different directions, my left hand twitched and I fell back a step into the Mountain. He held me firm as Morelli looked up and saw my fear. The reaction had come boiling up without warning, and it was all I could do to stifle the urge to tear away and bolt out the door. He finished lighting the cigar and blew smoke at the ceiling.

"Start talking, Fleming."

A film was over my eyes. I blinked uncontrollably. My hands jerked up to rub them clear.

("Start talking, Fleming.")

The Mountain's grip kept me on my feet or I'd be on my knees again.

(The cigar stink filled the little room. Its burning end pivoted from my eyes and pointed down to my left hand. The pain shot up the arm, into the brain, and came clawing out through my clenched teeth. I tried to tear away from it and the binding ropes. . . .)

The Mountain shook me out of it. My jellied legs found the floor and I stood under my own power, staring at Morelli with hot rage. I wanted badly to let it out, knowing what it would do to his mind; good revenge for my past pain, but it would accomplish nothing. My eyes tracked another cloud of smoke. His leisurely manner reminded me that he had all the time in the world, I only had until sunrise.

"What did you do to Jack Fleming?" I asked. "How did you get him?"

"I ask the questions, Junior." This was punctuated by another punch.

"Did you have Paco shoot him?"

I was on the floor now and felt the distant blow of a shoe in the back of one leg. I made an appropriate noise in response. The Mountain bent down to pick me up. For the first time he spoke, whispering in my ear.

"Tell him what he wants, kid. He won't let me let up."

So he was supposed to be my friend, he had some pity for me. Maybe if I cooperated he'd pull his punches. Bullshit.

"Where is the list?" Morelli pretended he hadn't heard his boy speak.

I was made to stand. Favoring my kicked leg, or appearing to, I shook my head. The Mountain hit again and that's when I overdid my act. It was by accident, or by sheer clumsiness, that my body pitched too far and too fast off balance and my head connected hard with the edge of the desk.

The thing was made out of very solid mahogany.

Lights flashed behind my eyes, there were waves of dizziness, and if I went under they'd think I was dead. They'd sink me in the lake again and this time I might not come up. My eyelids fluttered, I felt myself falling, but it was just the Mountain turning me over.

Breathe, keep breathing.

He was watching me closely. I looked back, concentrating on pumping my chest up and down and fighting the pain in my head.

Breathe, breathe until the worst of the shock passes.

"I thought he was gone for a second, but he seems okay, now," said the Mountain.

"Then wake him up." Morelli sounded infinitely put out. "And, Gordy, you be more careful with him this time."

He splashed a glass of water I didn't want in my face and I spit it from my nose and mouth like poison. The door opened and a chair was dragged in. They put it under me. Perhaps Gordy the Mountain was getting tired of holding me up.

"Tell him what he wants, kid," he urged.

My head was bowed, I gently checked the sore spot. There was no blood, but it *hurt*. It hurt far more than Paco's gunshots. I remembered the time and let the sleeve ride up my wrist for a glimpse at my watch. Not good, but better than I expected.

Morelli was still behind his desk, puffing on the cigar. The office was hot despite the air-cooling system, filled with smoke and the stink of sweat. Now I was glad they'd thrown the water; it would give the illusion that I, too, was sweating.

"I'll clue you, Fleming. You talk now, or you are dead meat. We will work you over and you will die. Talk and you will live."

For how long? I wondered.

"Where is the list?"

Same old song. I stalled and let Gordy earn his keep. He was not too creative, but he had a lot of endurance and muscle. He needed it since I kept falling from the chair as part of my act. It was a long and brutal quarter hour before I finally broke. I'd seen it done before in movies, in real life. I gave them the full treatment: sobbing, pleading, anything I could think of, and it was exactly what Morelli wanted to see. He was feeling good now; he'd ground a man down, opened his guts, and not left his chair.

I slid to the floor and made friends with the carpet, curling up to nurse bruises I didn't feel. It kept my face hidden and my voice muffled. Both were always dead giveaways whenever I tried lying. Between moans and groans I spun them a line of how Jack had passed the list on to his baby brother, but kept the details to the bare minimum; too many and they wouldn't believe it.

"Very good," said Morelli. "But where is it now?"

"I took a room at Jack's hotel and waited for him. I figured you'd already been there and wouldn't come back again, and there was a chance Jack would for his stuff."

"Smart, Junior. Keep talking."

"It's at the hotel, hidden in the basement. I'll have to show you where. You'll never find it otherwise."

They had a lot of trouble swallowing that one, and it took a large chunk of the time I had left to convince them they had to take me along.

My eyes were covered again, but this time they spared me the handkerchief. We went downstairs and waited in the kitchen. A car rolled up and stopped, its engine idling quietly. They opened the door, guided me down the concrete steps, and I was shoved into the backseat. I slumped low as if in bad shape—actually I was worried about the ever-present rearview mirror.

Gordy was on my right and another man was on my left. They each had a hand tightly gripping my wrists, taking no chances on my making a sudden move. Morelli sat in the front with the driver, occasionally giving a direction.

We crossed water once, twice, there were several turns, and we waited in silence for traffic signals. The car finally slowed and parked, the motor still running. The right-hand door opened and Gordy dragged me out. He pulled the scarf down and the first thing I saw was a gun ready in his hand. Next to him was the casino guard, who had a hand inside his coat like a latter-day Napoleon. His body blocked my view of Morelli in the passenger seat. Dead meat or not, he was careful not to let me see his face. It was fine with me, I was sick of it, anyway.

"Go and get it," he said.

The hotel was a block away on the same side of the street. Maybe the night clerk would remember me, but I wasn't planning to test him. I'd only gotten them back to this neighborhood because it made the story I told more plausible. I wanted them nowhere near my present hotel.

As before, they marched along, gripping my arms. I was in luck, for a change. They'd have to pass the entrance of an alley that ran between the hotel and the next building. There was a risk they might catch on to my unusual strength, perhaps they'd put it down to desperation. It wasn't getting any earlier; pretty soon I would be desperate.

We breasted the alley and I shook free, connecting a mild backhand hit in the gunman's stomach and pushing Gordy into some garbage cans. He recovered fast, and was up and after me before I'd gotten halfway down the alley. His friend was catching up as I came to the wood fence blocking the far end. I went over it with an agility that surprised me, landed like a cat, and pounded away, gaining a good lead.

The fence protected a street lined with residential flats, each with steps and railings and deep doorways. There were plenty of places to hide if necessary. I went to the right, wanting to gain more distance before vanishing. That was one trick they didn't need to witness. I was looking for a suitable place to duck when one of them did the unexpected. It must have been the gunman, Morelli had forgotten to tell him I was needed alive.

What felt like a sledgehammer blow caught me between the shoulder blades. The pain made me forget my aching head for the moment. I was in mid-stride when my body was lifted and thrown off balance by the impact. I tried to keep my legs under me, but the shock to the system was too much, and they buckled and failed. I rolled hard onto the sidewalk, carried on by impetus until I hitched up against the wheel of a parked car. The two men trotted up and turned me over.

I'm too much of a joker not to take advantage of such a situation. Besides, it was a way of getting them off my back. I gave it my best, pulling my hands up to cover what should have been the exit wound and hoping it was too dark for them to see the lack of blood. As they approached, I gasped, twitched convulsively, and slowly let my last breath shudder out in a horrible rattle. I stared at them with glassy eyes. They stared back, then Gordy bent down to feel for a pulse in my throat. He straightened and looked at his buddy, shaking his head.

"You're up shit creek," he pronounced.

I was right about it being the gunman and saw why I hadn't heard the shot; a bulky silencer was fixed to his weapon. It was enough to damp the sound down so the local residents continued to sleep.

A half minute later the car rolled up and Morelli erupted out before it stopped. He glanced once at his men, then glared down at me. I was sorry for not drawing my death scene out long enough to give him a cryptic message to worry about. He whirled on his men. Gordy pointed at the other guy, who had gone all white. Morelli went all purple, the neck tendons coming up as though to break through the skin. His body shook with rage and his breath came in short gulps. He'd gotten one last chance to find his precious list, and this guy had stupidly taken it from him. He snatched the gun away and, using it as a club, laid into him. When he finished, there was another body decorating the sidewalk. He gave the bloody gun to Gordy and stalked back to the car. Gordy picked up his buddy and followed a minute later.

"What about him?" he asked. They were out of my line of sight, but I could imagine his throwing-away gesture in my direction.

"Leave him. He's got no wallet, they'll think he was mugged. Leave him."

The car doors slammed and they drove away.

I lay on the sidewalk and counted my blessings. When I stood up and felt my aching head I was in the mood to consider everything else. I was out of the Nightcrawler more or less in one piece and Morelli thought I was dead. On the down side, my new suit was a disaster area, I was missing fifty-eight hundred bucks in gambling winnings and I still didn't know much more than when I'd begun. At least I had names and faces now.

The sky was getting lighter and I had to go home. I started around the corner to my old hotel, but thought better of it. There was a remote chance that Morelli might be there, or return the next day and find out about the guy in the ventilated tuxedo wandering in and asking for a cab. No, that was a very bad idea. I kept walking, moving quickly in hopes of finding some other open business, or better yet, an available cab. No such luck occurred and by now the light was hurting my eyes.

I was anxious enough to make an illegal entry into a closed drugstore on a corner and used their phone to call for transportation. There was still change in my pockets, so I left some on the counter for a pair of their darkest sunglasses and went outside to wait, scanning the street in worried hope. I was tied down to the place now, unable to move until the damn cab arrived.

The gentle gray light from the east was blinding, and I could hardly see the driver when he did arrive. Tumbling into the back, I promised him a two-dollar tip if he could get me to my hotel in as many minutes. With that for motivation, he poured on the coal.

When we reached the hotel, he had to follow me up to my room for the money, but I had to stumble down to the lobby again to pick up a key. My door was locked and my normal method of entry would have sent the man screaming into the streets. I was on a friendly basis with the night clerk, though, and that saved a little time. I persuaded him to give the driver the money and to put it on my bill. He did it with a smile, God bless him, gave me a key, and I fled upstairs.

The sun was up now. I was moving through syrup and going blind. I found the keyhole more by luck than anything else and shoved the door shut, sinking to the floor. My head felt ready to explode from the weak reflected sunlight filtering through the window. I crawled to my trunk, but it was locked. I tried to seep inside but couldn't; the light was searing my brain, I could hardly think. Where was the damn trunk key?

I groped in the closet, tearing the pockets of my old suit. Wrong guess. The bureau, I left them in a drawer. . . . Crawl over and visit them . . . Middle drawer, under the shirts . . . I groaned with relief as my stiffening fingers brushed them and clutched.

I fumbled forever with the trunk lock and was ready to just break it off when it finally flipped open. I pushed the lid up, forced my legs to straighten, teetered a second, and fell inside. The proximity of my home earth helped, and my arms had just enough flexibility left to pull the lid down again, shutting me safely away from the light.

Then consciousness was whipped away like dust into the wind.

Someone seemed to be knocking at my door, but too close and too loud. It was the trunk lid. Escott was the only one who knew I slept here, so I said come in and it opened a crack. I thought I saw a dim oval floating in a sea of purple sparklers.

"Are you all right, old man?" it asked. "I've been trying to call for an hour."

I shook my head, which made it ache more. I wanted him to go away and let me rest.

"Good Lord, you look like death warmed over. Let me help you out."

I started giggling like a fool and let him pull me up. It seemed that lately all I ever did was let other people haul me to my feet. I felt weak, though, and let him, until I remembered he was still recovering from that knife wound and the strain of lifting me wouldn't be doing the stitches any good. I put a hand on his shoulder for balance, got my legs out of the trunk, and stumbled for the bed, flopping on it. It felt great to stretch out. Something cool and wet was soothed over my forehead, a washcloth. Escott was a mind reader.

"That's an extraordinary goose egg you have there. How in the world did you get it, or are you up to questions yet?"

I tried to open my eyes again, rubbing them clear with the cloth. Purple sparklers still floated around, so I had to locate him from the direction of his voice.

"What's the matter?"

"I got caught by the sunrise, I can't see anything."

Considering the situation, I must have sounded idiotically calm. I felt his fingers propping my lids gently open and heard a match strike. I thought I could see it as it moved from side to side.

"You're tracking light and your pupils are reacting to it."

"Then maybe it's temporary."

"Are you in any pain?"

"Only from the goose egg."

"You have a nasty hole in your shirt," he observed calmly.

"It matches the one in the back."

"You must have had a very interesting evening."

This time I took the opening and told him briefly what happened last night, just leaving out the part about Bobbi and the blackjack game.

"Have things improved?" he asked, meaning my sight.

"A little, I think." But I was only being optimistic and kept involuntarily blinking to clear my eyes.

He waited a moment before cautiously suggesting the Stockyard as a remedy. I'd have to stop being so sensitive about my feeding habits.

"It might help," I agreed. It couldn't hurt.

He was apparently relieved at my reaction. "I'll be happy to guide you, but won't there be a bit of a problem with both of us trying to sneak in?"

"There's so much coming and going, we probably won't be noticed. Are you up to it?"

His voice, at least, sounded stronger. "I've had a good forty-eight-hour rest. The stitches are itching and that means they're healing. I've even sent Cal home."

"Okay, if you're sure. Can you help me change?"

He did and somehow got me down the backstairs to his car. I thankfully left the rest up to him. He parked us close in and then put something into my hand.

"What's this?"

"Your dark glasses. They were in the bottom of your trunk. Should we run into anyone they will lend credence to any story I give them about your blindness."

"As long as they don't become a permanent part of the act."

"See here, if any blood will do, wouldn't it be easier if I just found a friendly dog?"

I was appalled. "A dog? I *like* dogs, I couldn't—"

"It was just a suggestion," he said hastily.

I got out and waited for him. He took my arm and guided me slowly along the sidewalk, down curbs, up curbs, and from the noise and jostling of bodies, past the front gates of the Yards. The cattle stench was very strong now, I could hear them clearly and very close.

"Try to find a place that doesn't look busy," I advised.

He said nothing, plainly thinking me crazy since most of the place was busy all the time. There was a long, soggy walk for us before he finally found a spot that met the requirements.

"Fence," he said. "Shoulder height, wooden, there are several cows on the other side."

He didn't need to tell me, I could sense them. I felt for the fence, then glided right through it.

I guess I should have warned him.

He drew a shaky breath. "You could make a fortune haunting houses. That was quite an entrance."

I made no comment, my hands were already reaching out to a warm, shaggy body. I calmed the animal with soft words and felt my way toward its head. I knew just where to go in. If nothing else, my fingers could guide me to the right spot, but I paused and looked back to where he was standing.

"Escott?"

"Yes?" he whispered back.

"Would you mind not watching?"

"Er . . . um . . . not at all, old man." His feet scraped as he turned around. Maybe he didn't understand why I was so touchy about this, but at least he respected my feelings. I could trust him to stay turned.

The ache in my head subsided quickly. I stood slowly, feeling much stronger. The stuff spread a wonderful warmth all through my body like a slug of smooth liquor, but without the drunken side effects. I took off the cheaters and tried my eyes out. The purple sparklers were fading, and I could just make out Escott's outline above the fence and went over.

"I think I'm okay now."

"Your eyes—"

"They're better already."

"They're . . ."

"What?"

"Nothing, I'm glad . . . may we leave?"

Escott clearly did not care for cattle at all. We got back to the car without incident and scraped our shoes off. Things were improved enough that I was able to drive, but Escott was more tired than he wanted to admit and remained quiet. It was fine with me, since I wanted to think. My first waking hour had been too occupied with trying to recover and all my day time had been spent in total oblivion. I couldn't remember dreaming; perhaps I no longer did.

Physically I was all right; emotionally I was angry. It was still inside me, ready to be directed at Morelli or myself. I could have walked out of the club at any time last night, but stayed and went through the wringer again, hoping to find a memory. Except for the humiliation suffered at allowing another man to hit me when I could have hit back, I wasn't really hurt. Oddly enough, I felt no grudge against Gordy; the man's manner had been so completely neutral through the whole business that I thought of him only as a tool in Morelli's hand. I also remembered the bloody wreck of Sanderson's face. That had held me back, that and not wanting to tip my supernatural hand to them.

There was a kid I knew in the Army whose right hand had been shot clean off. I saw him years later wearing an artificial hand covered with a glove. He'd gotten into the habit of hiding it in his pocket and pretending it wasn't there, and each time you looked at his eyes they stared hard into yours demanding that you pretend as well. There was another kid in the same unit who'd lost a leg from the knee down. I met him again in New York while doing a story for the paper. He was the lead dancer and director of a polka troupe. He, too, was ignoring his injured limb, but in a different way.

My vampirism was just a peculiar condition, like a health problem. If I respected the rules it imposed I'd have less trouble, and that made it more acceptable to my confused brain. There were definite compensations for the rules, though. Otherwise I'd be at the bottom of Lake Michigan, forgotten and unavenged, along with who knows how many others. I'd changed in a greater sense than my grandfather could ever have imagined, but I'd been fighting it. That was why I'd been reluctant to have Escott watch as I fed. Had our positions been reversed I doubt if the thought would have even crossed his mind.

My anger had a direction now.

Morelli thought that kid brother Gerald was dead, and so did all his boys. It was a unique situation, certainly one of which I intended to take full advantage.

"I'm going after Morelli again," I said.

Escott nodded. "I can't think of a more choice subject for you to turn your talents upon. Have you worked out a plan yet?"

"Yes. In fact, you inspired it back at the Yards."

"Indeed?"

I explained my idea. With a chuckle he approved and added a few touches of his own. We changed direction to go to his house, picked up some stuff, then went back to my hotel. While I took a bath, he worked on my perforated tuxedo shirt.

"I certainly wish I could be around to see his face," he said, blowing lightly on the wet gore to dry it. Gingerly I put the shirt on, doubling my chin to get a good look at my front. A large part of it was covered with what looked like blood, but was actually some very realistic-looking stage stuff Escott had developed himself.

"The trouble with real blood," he said cleaning his paint brush, "is that it dries out, gets sticky, and goes brown, but this will stay nice and fresh looking. Unfortunately, it doesn't wash out, but in this case that hardly matters."

"Nope, the bloodier, the better," I agreed. It was good to be doing something positive, not to mention sneaky, like a kid out on a college prank.

I had good color again, but Escott opened his makeup case and toned it down, putting circles under my eyes and hollowing out the cheeks.

"At least your face has the right underlying bone structure for this sort of thing. I find nothing more tiresome than trying to thin down a full face."

"That's never been one of my problems." I'd always been on the lean side. "Did you learn all this in the theater?"

"Yes, in Canada. I was apprentice to the makeup artist of a Shakespearean company for three years. I was also props, scenery painter, set builder, and as you know, occasionally played a part. I'm especially fond of character parts. The Soothsayer in *Julius Caesar* was one of my best roles, though hardly an effective one, considering that Caesar chose to ignore me."

"Got any similar warnings for me?"

"My dear fellow, in all fairness, I should call Mr. Morelli and warn him. He is in for a rough night. There, you don't look quite so bad as Banquo's ghost, but you'll do. It's subtlety we are striving for, after all." He gave me the keys to his car.

"But I couldn't—"

"I insist. Tonight, at least, so that you need not be delayed waiting for a taxi. You can drop me back home again and go on to the club from there."

It made sense and I was very grateful for the loan. As he pointed out, I might have a problem getting a cab driver to take me as a customer the way I was got up now.

"Look, I know you must be tired—"

"Nonsense, it is *not* doing anything that tires me out."

"Well, I thought if you felt well enough tomorrow you might ask around for a car for me."

"That should be no trouble. I have a friend in the business. New or used?"

I gave him enough money for a good used one. I had no preference of model as long as it was dark in color and fairly anonymous. I drove him to his door and promised to tell him all the details tomorrow, then I turned the nose of the big Nash north and headed for the Nightcrawler.

Parking a block away and out of sight of the club, I carefully locked things up and went down the dark street, trying to look inconspicuous in the bloodied tux. It was damp and quiet; the hard heels on my dress shoes made a lot of noise against the sidewalk, at least to my ears. Having made a wide circle to avoid the front entrance, I eased into the alley, found it empty, and tiptoed up the concrete steps to listen at the kitchen door. A lot of activity was going on within, but I slipped inside anyway, feeling my invisible way along in the general direction of the twenty-eight-pace-long hall. They'd done me a favor with the blindfold last night, for it was very close to the method of travel I used now. I felt my way to the stairs and ascended, then partially materialized at the top to get my bearings.

The upstairs hall matched the one below, but was longer, running the length of the building. Just to the left and across the hall was a likely-looking door for Morelli's office. The rest of the hall had doors at regular intervals. Some were open with lights inside, and nearby a radio was playing, competing with the orchestra down below in the club.

Things seemed deserted for the moment, so I took the opportunity to check out the area. A partially solid form made it easier and quieter to move and my senses weren't so muffled, though it was almost like swimming in the air. I went to the office first; it was empty and I moved on to other rooms. There were several bedrooms, bathrooms, and a second set of stairs on the far east end. About a dozen of Morelli's boys seemed to be permanent residents, at two to a room. The place was like a hotel. The next door down from the office led to a much larger bedroom, probably Morelli's. I took a good look around, opening drawers and being generally nosy. He had a large tiled bath, a well-filled closet, and a door opening to a slightly smaller bedroom. From the decor and scent I knew it was Bobbi's.

She'd be downstairs, probably in the casino. If she'd been singing, I would have heard her. I wondered if she knew what had happened last night. Morelli might not have told her. It was something to hope for, anyway.

On the ground floor was another hall running roughly through the center of the building at right angles to the first, and it ended in a closed door. The hall served as a buffer zone between the casino and the nightclub. The door gave joint access to the hatcheck stand and the casino cashier. I got curious as to where they kept the money they raked in, and went back to Morelli's office.

After a short search, one of the boat paintings on the wall swung out on hinges, revealing a combination-lock safe. I was unfamiliar with such things, but had read a lot of lurid literature about them and seen a few in movies. I'd be able to hear the tumblers clicking into place and for the moment had nothing better to do. The office door was locked, so there'd be enough warning to vanish in case of an interruption.

Playing with the dial was harder than it looked, and about a minute after I started, heavy footfalls were coming in my direction. I pushed the painting back, stood behind the door, and disappeared.

They twisted a key and the doorknob at the same time and three bodies burst into the room, hitting the lights. There was silence for a while as they went over the place. I felt the tug of moving air when they whipped the door away from me.

"He must have got past us," said someone.

"He wouldn't have had time." It was Morelli's voice.

"Then maybe the trip is on the fritz."

They tested it out. I got the idea that the second the painting swung open it set off a signal elsewhere in the building. It was working fine, but Morelli left a man to keep an eye on things while they searched the rest of the place. The other two left. I waited a decent interval until he settled into a chair. From the noises he made he seemed disgusted with guard duty. I quietly materialized before him, and his expression when he looked up was worth a million. I had his complete attention, and that made the rest easy.

"Don't move," I told him.

He didn't.

"I'm not here, you can't see me, you won't remember me. Take a nap."

He folded his arms over the desk blotter, lowered his head and dozed off. I watched and listened, but he was genuinely asleep. I suddenly shivered all over and stifled a nervous laugh. Had it once been like this for Lamont Cranston? Only the Shadow knew. . . .

I went to the painting, swung it open, and waited.

My man woke up when the door crashed open. I could imagine everyone looking at the painting in vain, since it had been thoughtfully pushed back into place.

"Did you touch it?"

"I never went near it, Slick, honest! I been in this chair the whole time."

Morelli growled and they tested it again with no better results. There was a brief argument and in the end a second man was left to keep the first company. I waited long enough to give Morelli time to get downstairs, or wherever it was where he spent his evenings.

The two men were facing each other, one behind the desk, the other in the chair in front. They were quiet, but from the small sounds produced, a deck of cards was in use. The first man had already been primed, hypnotizing the second was just as easy. They both got sent off to Slumberland, and I repeated my act with the painting.

The next armed invasion was more fun. Morelli cross-examined his two stooges, unfairly accusing them of a lot of things, and then kicked them out, electing to remain there himself to do the job right.

It was exactly what I wanted.

I let him settle down. He made some calls on the house phone and then ordered up some coffee and a sandwich from the kitchen. He swept the cards into a pile and dealt out a hand of solitaire. I was behind him, partially materialized, and watched with interest. The hand didn't come out so he cheated until it did. I went away for a moment when his snack came and left him undisturbed as he ate. With what I had in mind, he'd need all his strength.

When he was quiet again, I moved in, covering him like a blanket. Previous experience informed me that in this form I was on the cold side. He began to shiver almost immediately. I clung around him as he got up and fiddled with something on the wall, probably the air vent. He paced up and down, then got on the phone and made an irritable inquiry on the state of the air-cooling system. We both waited until the return call came that stated everything was working fine. He slammed the phone down and poured another cup of coffee to warm up. I drifted away, coming to rest on the chair I'd occupied last night.

By very slow degrees I became visible, until I was sitting solidly in front of him, staring with blank, wide-open eyes. I thought my initial appearance should be underplayed.

His reaction was quite gratifying.

Perhaps he'd first noticed something just on the edge of his vision as he looked down at the cards, something that didn't belong. The eye automatically tracks movement, but I wasn't moving, only gradually becoming *there*.

His eyes snapped up and grew until they were as wide as my own. His heart boomed and his breath stuck in his throat, and he stayed that way for nearly a minute, apparently too terrified to look away or even move. I thought if I said boo (and I was very tempted) he'd go completely to pieces, so I kept still and slowly faded away.

Escott had said that my antics were unnerving. Now I was getting a firsthand look at their effect on the uninitiated.

Morelli was frozen in place for some time, his heart fighting against his rib cage. Cards and cold coffee forgotten, he got up and circled the chair. As soon as he touched it I blanketed him again to give a brief chill and then pulled away. He jerked back as though he'd been burned instead, and then he was backpedaling for the door.

I heard his steps retreating down the hall. While he was out I eased the door shut and locked it. Going to the desk, I gathered all the cards up into a neat pile, which I left in the exact center of the blotter, faceup. The top card was the ace of spades. I opened the hinged picture again, shutting it and vanishing just as the door was unlocked.

He wasn't the first inside; he left that to Gordy, whom I recognized by his sheer bulk. Morelli was upset, but too proud to show it in front of his men, or to explain why he'd called them back so urgently. They went over the room inch by inch, testing the safe out again with negative results. I spent the time wrapped around Morelli to stay out of everyone's way and to wear his nerves down some more. He was gritting his teeth to keep them from chattering.

Then he noticed the cards on the desk.

"Which one of you did that?" he demanded.

They were all innocent and said so. He shut up, probably brooding on the significance of the top card. In the end, he pitched all of them out, except Gordy. The chair went out as well and another was brought in. He left the door open and had Gordy stand in the hall to watch the stairs.

He fidgeted awhile, getting up and patrolling the room, then dropping behind the desk in disgust. He had no further use for the cards and just sat there, fully alert and listening. I decided to fulfill his expectations.

I appeared quite suddenly on the floor, recreating the position I'd been in when he saw me dead on the sidewalk last night.

It was a real sensation.

He shot to his feet, sending his chair over with a crash that brought Gordy in just too late to see me.

This time Morelli had him stay in the room.

He ordered up some more coffee and lit a cigar; just the thing for his nerves, as far as I was concerned. I waited patiently.

Gordy's suggestion for a game of pinochle was ignored. Neither man spoke much. Small wonder.

The coffee came and went. Morelli got up and said he'd be back in a minute. After all that liquid and the chills, I knew where he was headed.

He chose to go to the big tiled one in his own room. In his absence, I gently put Gordy to sleep and turned out the room lights. After making sure it was clear, I shut off the hall lights and then waited for Morelli to come out. When he did, he got very cold again. He hesitated in the fan of light from his bedroom, not wanting to venture into the dark hall.

"Gordy?" His voice was not normal, nor very loud. He had to repeat himself several times before Gordy responded. The office light came on.

"Yeah . . . Slick? Why are the lights off?"

"What the hell were you doing sitting in the dark?"

"I dunno, I looked up and they were out."

"Did you put 'em out?"

"No, boss!" He sounded hurt. "Maybe one of the boys is playing a joke."

"Then you go find 'em and tell 'em it ain't funny."

"Sure. Now?"

"Yes, now!"

Gordy trundled off, stopping at the other occupied rooms to talk with the boys. Morelli's teeth were chattering, so I gave him a break and preceded him into the office. He opened a desk drawer and brought something out that clunked heavily when he put it on the desk. It wasn't hard to guess what it was. Well, if it gave him a sense of security, fine. I'd just have to undermine it.

I partially materialized in front of him, my hands reaching out. He blanched, brought the gun up—it was a police .38—and let fly with all six chambers. In this halfway state I felt the bullets tickle through. They made sensation, but no pain. Nevertheless, I rocked back as though hit, and vanished. The room was full of smoke as his men charged in looking for something to shoot at, and they all asked questions, even the quiet Gordy. Morelli declined to answer and just said the gun went off by accident.

"Six times?"

For a gangster he was a lousy liar. "Shut the hell up and get out!"

They got out.

I hung around until four A.M. By then the club and casino were long closed, and the money counted and locked away behind the picture of the boat. Prior to opening the safe, Morelli had pressed a button under his desk, which I understood deactivated the circuit of the burglar alarm. At the time, everyone was out of the office while he twirled the combination lock open. No one was there to see me peering over his shoulder and getting all the numbers.

He was feeling better after shooting at me, and I'd been quiet for some time, which restored some of his confidence. All the same, he left two men in the office with the door open and strict instructions to keep their eyes in the same condition. Then he went to bed.

Twenty minutes passed, and things were quiet. I put the men to sleep, found the button, and turned off the alarm. It took another quarter hour of twisting the damned dial around before getting the combination right. I'd been off on the last number and had to experiment. It was frustrating work and bad on my nerves because I had to keep half an ear cocked on the hallway, ready to vanish if I heard someone coming. In retrospect, I'm sure the time spent was pretty good for a complete novice. It certainly was profitable.

I was an honest thief, taking only my fifty-eight hundred bucks in smaller, used bills, though there was considerably more inside. I shut things up again and put the alarm back on. They'd have a fine time trying to figure out how the money got lifted.

I wanted to make a final grand call on Slick before leaving and more than that, look in on Bobbi, but the clock said it was late and I had to allow for car trouble or unexpected delays of some sort on the journey home. Playing it safe, I left, but promised myself and Morelli another performance.

▲
9
▼

The next night Escott came by a little after sunset. He'd found a year-old dark blue Buick and said the dealer guaranteed it for at least a week. The interior was clean, the engine sounded good, and the outside only had a few dimples on the metal to show that it was no virgin.

"I had a devil of a time with the paperwork," he told me. "The dealer wanted you there to sign things before I could have the car."

"How did you get it, then?"

"I didn't. It was your cash up front that persuaded him. That, and the veiled threat of finding another dealer who was less particular. Just sign here."

I signed here. He gave me the keys and I gave him my thanks.

"It was nothing at all. Have you a driving license?"

"A New York one. I had to sell my old wreck to get me out here. Why?"

"I was curious if you planned to acquire one for Illinois."

"Good question. I would if I could."

"I could do something about that as well. We resemble each other a bit in build and features, I could work at forging your signature and just go in for you."

He seemed wistfully eager to break the law on my behalf and I said as much to him.

"Well, this is a unique opportunity for a new experience—is there something amusing in this? I am serious, the law does not look lightly upon forgery."

"I know, but you don't have to do this."

"I don't mind a bit. To me, this is rather like going to a speak during Prohibition—have fun, but don't get caught. Now, depending on the expiration date of your old one, sooner or later you will need a new driving license, or would you prefer to have the police ticketing you for want of one?"

"I doubt if I'd let things go that far, but I see your point."

"Good. Of course, you know your best cover is to remain anonymous. The less people notice you, the safer you are."

"You talk like I'm some kind of Bolshevik spy or something."

"They're called Communists now, or is it Socialists? But you have the right idea. Prior to your—shall we say—conversion those years ago, what was your attitude toward vampires?"

"I generally thought about Theda Bara if I thought about it at all, but other than that I didn't believe in them except as a myth."

"What better shield could one ask for?"

He had something there. We returned to my room, and while I told him about last night's show, he made my face up again.

"Suck your cheeks in. . . . All right . . . raise your brows. . . ."

"Wish I could see this stuff."

"Yes, I can do a very effective job, if I do say so. You're looking a bit more gruesome tonight, I'm allowing for decomposition."

"How thoughtful."

"I knew you'd appreciate it. I could bring a camera next time. It would be interesting to see if your image can be recorded on film."

"I have wondered about that."

"There." He made one last touch-up and I relaxed my stiff neck. "Now, as we say, 'break a leg.' "

"Hopefully Morelli's."

"Have you taken into consideration he's probably checked up on you by now? He might be wondering why the papers carried no account of a body being found on that street the morning you were 'killed.' "

"Well, this is Chicago and that kind of thing does happen."

"Not that often, but all too true at times. He's bound to have friends in the police and other departments who are in a position to find things out for him."

"I'll be careful, but as far as he's concerned, I'm a ghost and he's not about to tell anyone he's being haunted."

He chuckled. "Then have your fun—"

"But don't get caught."

I parked my car in a new location, locked it, and walked a quick two blocks to the club. The place was busier, if that was possible, and there were more men out front. They loitered around, the lines of their monkey suits spoiled by the bulge from various pieces of lethal hardware, and checked the face of each new arrival. Morelli must have really been impressed last night, but I couldn't figure how he thought posting extra guards could protect him from supernatural forces. I gave them all a miss and vanished while still across the street in the cover of a doorway. There was always some disorientation, but I was improving, especially when it came to moving in straight lines. The street was a wide-open space, that could easily be crossed, and when I came to the outside wall of the club, I went up like an elevator. Feeling around for an open window, I seeped in and materialized in Morelli's bathroom.

Its door was ajar. I edged an eye around the jamb and saw Morelli fixing his tie in front of a big mirror, getting ready for the evening ahead. It would be a memorable one for him.

I started things off by turning the taps on in the tub and flushing the toilet. He came quickly to investigate, probably without thinking, and stopped short when he saw the empty room. With slow cautious movements he shut off the water and looked around. It didn't take long, but by then I was in the bedroom, easing open all the drawers of his bureau.

From under the bed I followed his progress by watching his feet tour the room. He angrily slammed one of the drawers shut, charged the hall door, gave it a jerk, and glared outside. No one was there to receive it, so he closed the door and began checking the closet, Bobbi's room, her closet, and under the beds, drawing a blank each time. He then made a circuit of the walls, tapping on them with something hard. This was puzzling until I realized he was looking for secret panels. While he was busy inside the closet, I floated back to the bath and flushed the toilet again.

He was there in a shot, standing on the threshold, trying to keep one eye on the bath and the other on the bedroom. He rattled the flush lever uncertainly, took the top off and peered at the mysteries within. Out in the bedroom I flicked the lights off.

He noticed immediately. The switch was by the hall door. He'd have to cross a large dark space to get to it. If he waited long enough, his eyes would get used to the dark and he could cross with ease. He didn't. With more steadiness than I would have had, he left the comfort of the bright bathroom and crossed over. His heart was pounding, but he forced himself to walk at a normal pace. After all, there was nothing there in the dark that wasn't there in the light. Personally, I'd always found small comfort in that bit of logic. His sedate pace gave me plenty of time to materialize at his feet and trip him.

He went down hard, stifling a cry and throwing appearances to the wind. Scrambling to his feet, he was clawing frantically for the light switch while still a good ten feet away from it.

I wanted to use Escott's makeup job while it was still fresh, so when the lights came on I was practically nose to nose with Morelli.

At that point I think anyone coming into the room would have scared the hell out of him, but the fact that I was only inches away and not looking too healthy to boot could explain his reaction. He couldn't bolt out the door, I was in the way, but by now he was beyond coherent thought. He fell back from me with a scream and fainted away like some fragile heroine from a silent movie.

I couldn't pause to laugh, that kind of yell would bring his bully boys. I moved fast, pulling drawers onto the floor, ripping the bedclothes out of place, and then ducking into the closet. I used the last few seconds to relieve the hanging rod of a fine collection of suits and coats before disappearing.

Gordy yanked open the closet door; I knew it was him from his size and the quick way he moved. He surveyed the wreckage, made sure no one was hiding under the mess, then backed out. In the room there was quite a commotion as attempts were made to revive Morelli. His body was searched for an extraneous bullet or knife holes, and the other rooms were combed for intruders. None were found, and when Morelli did wake up he had no good explanation for his blackout or the tumbled condition of the room.

His patience ran out quickly, as well as his temper, and having been found in such an embarrassing state didn't improve things. He kicked all of them out except Gordy, who didn't talk much.

"Find out if anyone new came in tonight," Morelli told him. "Use this phone."

It took only a minute. "Six of them, boss," he reported. "They came in with a bunch of regulars and have been in the bar all evening."

Morelli growled and kicked one of the drawers. "Some jerk is playing jokes on us." I noticed the plural. He wanted to include everyone in his haunting to keep from being too isolated by the ghost. Otherwise it might mean the ghost had a legitimate grievance against him; which I did.

"I'll check up on all the boys." Gordy was keeping his tone carefully neutral. Perhaps the thought that Morelli was going nuts had crossed his mind.

"I want you to check up on Fleming."

"Sure, boss, which one?"

"Both, but especially the kid brother. Find out what you can, when he got into town, who claimed the body and where they are. Wake up people if you have to, I want to know tonight."

"Sure, boss."

They left the room together, stopping off at the kitchen to send someone upstairs to clean the mess I'd made. There was no point in troubling the hired help and I stuck with Morelli, literally. He was feeling cold again. Gordy went off to get his information, leaving Morelli to restlessly pace the club and casino while I hung around him like a pilot fish. He stood this for half an hour, then headed for the back exit. His car was ordered up and he left a message that he'd return at closing time. I enjoyed a short ride, albeit a blind one, and had no idea where he was going. He parked and got out, and I remained behind and materialized for a look around. We were at the waterfront, the car resting on a concrete pier that jutted out like a breakwater. It must have been a solid piece of construction going down to the bottom from the land, or I'd have felt the pressure I always experienced being over water.

Morelli was just disappearing over the edge of the pier, where steps went down to the water. I left the car and quietly followed. He was easing into a small boat. I pulled back before he could see me. Out on the lake, serenely anchored in deeper water was the *Elvira*. All by itself, my left hand twitched and clenched.

Morelli rowed clear of the pier. I was standing under a light so he couldn't help but spot me. He broke off rowing and gaped, the current slowly taking his boat off course. I kept still, a scarecrow figure in stained and tattered clothes, watching him. Gradually I faded to nothing. Limited though my acting experience was, I knew how to make a good exit.

I moved back beyond the light and reformed. Morelli was rowing quickly toward the *Elvira* where three crew members were standing by to help him aboard. Chances were they'd been watching him and hadn't noticed me, which was fine, I planned to be his exclusive ghost for the time being.

It took ten minutes to walk back to the Nightcrawler. I strolled slowly to give things time to settle, and went in by way of the bath again. The cleaning crew was efficient; the place was back to normal after my rampage. Next door, someone was talking in Morelli's office, Gordy from the sound of it. I lounged against the wall and eavesdropped; it was better than radio because I was the star.

Gordy was on the phone, vainly trying to get information on my nonexistent kid brother. He seemed an expert at delegating tasks, for he was calling people up, giving them the name of Gerald Fleming, and telling them to get a line on him. Almost as an afterthought, he threw in my real name. Some of the calls were to New York, and I wondered if I should start sweating. No mutually familiar names were mentioned and his tone indicated he was long used to dealing with the people on the other end. Somewhere out there was a very large network of eyes, ears, and busy little pencils. He hung up and we both waited.

In ten minutes the first incoming calls started. Locally, the police department never got a report of a body fitting Gerald Fleming's description, dead or otherwise. No area hospital had me with a gun wound lurking in any of their beds. When the hotels began reporting in I was glad for registering under another name. He received a single call from New York that stated I was an out-of-work journalist who'd left to look for greener pastures in Chicago. It was depressing to hear it put that way, but for once it was good to have a thoroughly undistinguished career.

The office door opened and someone else puffed into the room. The voice was naggingly familiar, but I just couldn't place it.

"Anything?"

"No, Mr. Lebredo." Gordy sounded respectful rather than neutral this time.

Mr. Lebredo lowered himself into a chair with a sigh. "What did Miss Smythe have to say about Morelli?"

"She said he couldn't sleep and that he kept the lights on all night."

"And you?"

"He's been acting pretty strange."

"So we've all noticed," he said dryly.

The phone rang. "Yeah? Go on . . . all right." Gordy hung up. "I'm beginning to think that the kid just dropped outta the sky. No one's heard of him."

"If his name really was Gerald Fleming."

"Slick said he was a younger version of the other guy. There's no doubt it was the brother and he was a green as a stick, he even had his name in his wallet. He was just a stupid kid."

"As you say." There was silence for a while. "Fifty-eight hundred was missing from the safe; fifty-eight hundred was what Morelli took from him. No one else has access to the safe that we know of, therefore Morelli might be trying to pull something. If it was for no other purpose than to buy a bauble to keep Miss Smythe happy, I shall let it go, but you keep your eyes on him as usual."

"Yes, sir."

"And don't forget the errand I want done. You've still got the address?"

"Yes, sir."

The man got up and left. I was curious about his looks and waited until he was down the hall, cracking the bedroom door a little. I was stumped for a moment because he was away from the original surroundings I'd first seen him in, but I did finally remember the fat poker player who'd invited me to join the game. He looked about my height, but had Gordy's weight, none of it muscular and most of it in his ass. Lucky Lebredo, half owner of the club, was apparently playing a game other than poker behind Morelli's back.

He waddled downstairs, and I quietly shut the door. Hours stretched before me, unbroken and uneventful. I could go back to the hotel and wait there until Morelli returned, but decided to hang around. I wanted to see Bobbi again and was hoping she might come upstairs sometime during the evening. It was a slim hope and a foolish one, but something to think about.

Hardly being in a fit state to greet her, I went to the bath, stripped off my coat and shirt, and scrubbed at the makeup. It was stubborn junk, but I left a lot on the towel as I rubbed my skin raw. Escott had used cold cream to clean his face, maybe Bobbi had some lying around. I decided to look and at the same time borrow one of Morelli's shirts.

I shut off the taps and went alert. Someone was moving around in the next room. I peered past the door; Morelli's mirror reflected most of the room, including Bobbi, who was just about to leave.

"Wait!" The word was out before I could think.

She whirled in surprise. "Who's there?" She backed against the door, ready to escape.

"It's me, Ja—Fleming. I'm in the bathroom," I added unnecessarily.

She visibly relaxed, then tensed again. "What are you doing here?" she hissed. "Slick'll kill you."

"You told me that once before, but he didn't." It was a relief to know Morelli hadn't told her of my apparent demise the other night.

"You've got to get out of here."

"It's all right, believe me."

"Why don't you come out?"

"I'm getting dressed and I'm bashful." It was true. I was very shy of that big mirror out there.

She made a noise, it might have been a laugh.

"Why don't you come over here?" I suggested.

"Where's Slick?"

"I left him aboard the *Elvira*. He said he'd be back around closing."

"I didn't know he was gone, I thought you were him in there. Why are you here? The way he looked the other night—"

"We came to an understanding."

"And what about your brother?"

"We're working things out." I wanted to change the subject. "Would you turn the light off?"

Her hand moved to the switch and paused. She looked like she wanted to question why, then thought better of it. We were both grown-ups. The light went out. I threw the towel in the hamper, picked up my shirt and coat, and shut off the light.

She was halfway across the room and had to stop, uncertain in the dark. Her arms were crossed, hands gripping the elbows hard as she looked in my general direction. If she was afraid, I could easily change her mind, but that would have been a cheat, and I hate cheats, so I held back and let her decide what to do. I already knew what I wanted to do. Dressed in something white with simple clinging lines and silver combs in her hair, she was unsettling and inspiring.

"You're very beautiful tonight." Not the most brilliant or original thing to say; she must have heard it often enough, but it was the stunning truth.

"Why are you here?"

A reasonable question. I didn't answer.

"Did Slick send you?"

"No. I thought you didn't like being too curious."

"I think I have a right to be this time."

"If you're worried about him, he won't be back for hours, so relax. I'd rather talk about other things." I cautiously moved closer, but didn't quite touch her.

"Like how you survived the other night? I saw how he was. How'd you get out of it? He'll kill us both if he finds us."

"I said we were working things out."

"Is a night with me part of the deal?" She had no illusions of her effect on men. She took it for granted in the same way other people breathe. Her question also left me fairly shocked.

"Good God, does he make you—"

Her jaw lifted and set, taking the wind out of me.

"I'm sorry—I—Slick knows nothing about me being here. I think maybe I should go now."

"You really would leave, wouldn't you?"

"Very reluctantly. I'm here because I wanted to see you again. I was going to wait in the downstairs hall after I—"

"And get spotted by half the staff? That makes a lot of sense."

"So who ever said I had brains?"

"But how did you get here? He *must* know."

I shook my head, forgetting she couldn't see me.

"You're doing this just to see me?"

"Do you want me to stay?"

She considered the question carefully. That was something else I liked about her, the way she listened and weighed facts, an ability no doubt sharpened by living close to people like Morelli. "Only if we lock the door."

"Consider it done," I said, and moved to do it.

"Fat lot of good it'll do. Slick isn't the only one with a key."

"I'll bet he's the only one who has any business using it, though, but he's not here, so let's forget him. What else would you like?"

"Does it matter to you what I like?"

For the men in her past and very likely the present, that might not have been a very important consideration. "Yes . . . it matters to me very much."

"You confuse me."

"I do? How?"

"I shouldn't feel this way, I—it's just bodies, after all."

"Not for me, it isn't."

"You're different?"

I thought of a loaded answer and dismissed it. "Yes."

Her arms reached tentatively forward, her hands brushing lightly down my bare chest. Standing so close and scented with roses, fear, and now desire, she was like a white candle and I was just beginning to feel its gentle heat. Her heartbeat drummed so loud in my brain I could hear nothing else. If she'd told me to leave then I doubt I'd have had the ability or understanding. Something primitive and as old as time overwhelmed all conscious thought and all caution, she was in my arms and nature was taking its course.

A hot minute later she pulled away. "Not here, not in his room—this way." We went to her room, and she locked the door and turned her back, lifting her hair out of the way. I undid a few strategic buttons and the white silk fell in a heap around her ankles. It was a happy surprise to learn that like Jean Harlow, she disdained the wearing of underclothes. In another second we fell into the bed.

My basic method of lovemaking was the same as when I'd been alive, and I'd never received any complaints, but knew this time from the signals my body was sending out that its ultimate expression had changed considerably. I was in the delightful situation of being able to lose my virginity twice in one lifetime. There had once been the incredible sensual joy of being on the receiving end of Maureen's special kisses. Now I understood why she'd been unable to describe what it had been like for her.

My lungs were pumping regularly, not to breathe, but to smell. The dark scent of red blood rushing swiftly beneath her skin was maddening. I was going too fast and had to pause, my lips were already seeking out her warm, taut throat. Shifting slightly, I took in the other pleasures her body offered, exploring her soft mouth and testing the firm muscle underlying her smooth skin. She was no stranger to the act and did all she could to please me, but as I learned long ago, my greatest satisfaction came from pleasuring my partner. I did my best, with the steady roar of her heartbeat stimulating rather than distracting me. She let me know she was ready, but I held off as long as I could, held off. . . .

The kiss was painless to her, but not without its own unique intensity, and her body shook from it for as long as I held her and drew into my own starved body the hot, salty essence of her life.

After many long, long moments I gradually pulled away. Her hands slid around my head to keep me in place, wanting me to continue, but I was afraid of going too far and taking too much. I was aware of my inexperience and didn't want her to suffer from it. She sighed acceptance finally and arched her back, pushing her head deep into the pillows. Through half-closed eyes she smiled, her lids drooped shut, and she dozed lightly, her heartbeat returning to normal. With an ear pressed against one soft breast I listened to the rhythm as declining waves of warmth surged and ebbed through me.

Earlier in the evening I'd ignored the first faint tickle of hunger, planning to visit the Yards later, but that would have been mere feeding. This taking of blood was lovemaking, and for a vampire, there was a chasm of difference between the two.

I eased my weight from her and lay on my side, stroking her hair with my free hand. It had been too long since I'd really touched anyone. So long that I'd almost forgotten how good it was to hold and be held. Distantly through the walls I heard the band playing something slow and sentimental, then the phone in her room began ringing.

"Damn," she said. "I have to answer that." I didn't ask why, but moved so she could get out. A minute later she returned and snuggled in again.

"That was the stage manager. I had a number to do and missed it."

"And you told him you were sick. Are you?"

"I think you know better. I never felt anything like that before that lasted so long."

"But you're not hurt or dizzy, are you?"

"I'm fine, I'm terrific."

I tilted her chin to one side with a finger, looking closely at her neck. The marks were surprisingly small and there was no apparent bruising. Her hand slid onto mine, which she drew up and kissed.

"I guess you are different. What did you do to me?"

"If it felt good, does it really matter?"

"I just don't want it to have been a fluke of my imagination."

"It was real. I take it you didn't mind that we didn't follow a more traditional method?"

"No, this was so much like it, but more . . ." She shrugged. "I can't describe it, I only know I want to feel it again."

"That might not be good for you now. I'll come tomorrow night."

Her face clouded. "What about Slick?"

"I can get rid of him."

"What do you mean? Kill him?"

"Why do you think that?"

"It's something you get to expect after a while. I have no illusions about what he is or what I am to him. We've used each other to get what we want. It's an old story."

"It sounds very empty."

She didn't want sympathy, and a hard edge crept into her voice. "I know it is."

"Do you have to use him? What is it you want?"

"I have it now. I'm the top singer in a top nightclub and I'm on a local radio broadcast once a week. Slick makes sure I meet the right people and I keep him happy. When he gets tired of me I'll use those contacts to move up in the business."

"But are you happy?"

"Yes, I think so."

"Is that why you were working that slot machine so grimly the other night?"

"That was just boredom. Even this place gets boring. I don't like all the people here and I get tired of being stared at, but Slick likes me to mingle. He likes to show me off."

"But he doesn't like you to get too friendly."

"At least with the wrong people. But sometimes it's good, it's really good, when I'm on stage and the spotlight hits me and the music comes up—that's what I really want. That makes me feel so alive and I don't care what I have to do as long as I can stay there and sing."

"He's in a dangerous business. What would you do if something did happen to Slick?"

"There are always others like him, and he's not so bad. My first boyfriend used to hit. Slick likes to roughhouse, but at least he doesn't hit me. Then there's the other owner of the club"—she went very still—"but I'd never go to him for anything."

"Who's he?"

"Slick didn't tell you? He's the fat poker player, Lucky Lebredo."

"Colorful."

"Just don't get in his way. Slick can be mean, but Lucky is worse, and he's a lot smarter. He's like some big spider, always watching things."

"He watches you?"

"What do you think? He hasn't laid a hand on me yet, and I don't plan on ever giving him the chance. I think he and Slick have some sort of understanding about me."

"Nice guys."

"You said it."

"Do they have an understanding about Gordy as well—about who he really works for?"

"Slick doesn't know about that and neither should I, but sometimes you overhear things."

"Like what?"

"I just caught the end of it, but Gordy and Lebredo were having an argument, or something pretty close to it. Lebredo asked him if he were planning to be awkward in the same way Mr. Huberman had been awkward, and then Gordy backed down, and I've never known him to do that with anyone before. Even Slick knows where to draw the line with Gordy."

I remembered the Huberman scandal; it had been the nine-day wonder tabloid editors dream about. Someone had thoughtfully provided them with some especially lurid evidence of Huberman's romance with a knockout of a blond who was not his wife. Tame enough stuff, it happened often enough, but not always to senior state senators. The real lid came off when the general public was made aware of the true sex of the blond. Huberman was found on the floor of his office with the muzzle of the gun still in his mouth and the back of his skull blown off.

"Does Gordy like girls?"

"Sure, he does. I see what you're getting at, but that's not it. Lebredo's got something else on him."

"Maybe it's time you left this place."

"Not now, but soon. I'll leave when I'm ready."

"But—"

Her eyes snapped. "Don't go all protective on me, I can take care of myself."

"Okay, I can see that." She was right, it was none of my business.

"Mrs. Smythe didn't raise no dummy."

"I'm not arguing."

She took me at my word and calmed down. "You going to tell me your life story now?"

"Not tonight."

Her hand went to her throat. "But I want to know about what you did. Is it because you're really different, or that you know something new that I never heard of till now?"

"Yes," I chuckled.

"To both? Don't be a kidder."

"I'm not."

"Then what's this about?"

"You ever hear the one about the one-legged jockey?"

"Yeah . . ."

"Well, I kinda have the same thing. It's a sort of condition—"

The sharp cough of the gun was the only warning we got.

Preoccupied with each other, we hadn't heard his approach in the other room or noticed the light under the door. Perhaps he'd come to check on Bobbi after she'd missed her cue, and then heard us talking. The second after the bullet blew off the lock, he kicked the door open and lurched into the room like a boulder coming down the hill, or maybe I should say mountain. It was Gordy, playing the watchdog for his boss.

He didn't know me in the dim light spilling from Morelli's room, but I was a man in a place where I shouldn't be and that was enough of an excuse for him to break things up. His gun was already up and aimed. I had barely gotten to my feet. I half expected the impact of a bullet, but he thankfully restrained himself and didn't fire again. Bobbi's breath caught in her throat, but she held back the scream. The room was dead quiet except for the squeaking hinges as the door swung a little in the aftershock of its sudden opening.

I raised my hands slowly, uncurling the fingers, tore my gaze from the silencer-encased gun barrel, and stared hard at his face. All his attention was on me. Good, I wanted him to ignore Bobbi altogether. A few seconds had passed, and I listened for the arrival of reinforcements, but none came. There was a chance for jumping him then. It was possible despite the distance between us, but there was also a big, bad chance of Bobbi picking up a stray bullet, so that was out.

He finally spoke. "Walk over here, pretty boy."

Better, he wanted me out of the room. I held his eyes with my own and moved slowly, hoping Bobbi would know enough to stay where she was. I didn't speak or look at her; the situation was tenuous enough, and I wanted Gordy to concentrate on me alone. For each step I took forward he backed up into the light of Morelli's bedroom. Bad. I wanted it dark. Pretending to squint, I kept my hands in front of my face. This made it harder to watch his movements, but by now I'd cleared the door and Bobbi was safely out of the line of fire.

He sensed I was planning something. The angle of the gun shifted downward. "Move and I'll blow your balls off."

Vampire or not, that kind of threat will stop any man in his tracks.

"Hands away from the face."

There wasn't any choice, I'd have to play it out and see what would happen. I straightened, lowered my hands, and looked him in the eye.

He still didn't know me right away, but then the last time he could consciously recall seeing me I'd been belly-up on a sidewalk, fully clothed and apparently dead. Now I was shirtless, disheveled, standing, and apparently alive. Small wonder the dawn came slowly.

The lids peeled back from his eyes. I kept very still, staring at him, hoping he was as unnerved as I had been. He took a backward step toward the door and kept on going until he was on the threshold.

"*Run,*" I whispered.

The idea must have already been in his mind. He flinched, turned, and retreated heavily down the hall.

Bobbi heard it; she was out of bed and peering past me, a few dozen questions on her face. I quickly grabbed up my discarded clothes.

"What did—"

"I can't explain now." I kissed her good-bye and darted out after Gordy. He was thumping down the backstairs. I pulled on the shirt without buttoning it and shrugged into the coat, not an easy thing to do while running, but I was able to keep up with him. He reached the bottom, looking indecisive, and turned for a backward glance. I ducked, dematerialized, and followed down after him.

Uncertain of his route, I hung close to his coattails and was able to stick right along with him. He went through a door into an assault of noise, and I guessed we were in the casino. Here he stopped and caught his breath. Maybe he only wanted people around him. At a more sedate pace he moved through the room and passed into a smaller and much quieter area, probably the cloak room.

"Hi, big boy, what's up?" a girl asked him.

He didn't answer, but pushed past her to an even smaller room where the coats were hung. I heard a click and sensed he was working at something with his hands. A little unsteadily, he began repeating a call sign. He was using some kind of short-wave radio and trying to contact the *Elvira*. I moved in close to hear both sides of the conversation. Unfortunately he began shivering, but it couldn't be helped.

They had a poor connection, and I hardly made out Morelli's voice.

"Yeah, Gordy, did you find out—"

"Boss, he was here, I saw him, I saw the kid."

"You *saw* him?"

"In your room—he was real, he was alive—"

"Shut up and get out here, I'll have the boat waiting."

"He's still up there with Bobbi—"

"*What?*"

"I caught them together, but I had to get out. Jesus, you shoulda seen his eyes."

"You left her?"

"I couldn't help it, I had to."

"Then get your ass back up there and get her out, you hear me? You get her out and bring her to me. . . ."

At this point I left, groping through the back door of the cloakroom and solidifying. The long, dim hall dividing the casino from the club stretched ahead. It gave backstage access to the bandstand and led to the farther of the stairwells. I raced to the far end and had to dissolve again because of two men sitting and smoking on the steps. I re-formed in the upstairs hall, hurtled into Morelli's room, and locked the door. Bobbi had just finished pulling on some clothes.

"Gordy just called Slick about us; he's supposed to take you to the yacht."

"So?"

"So I don't think he's going to throw you a party."

"Don't worry, I know how to handle it. I was more afraid that Gordy was going to shoot you just now."

"Never mind that, I've got to get you out of here."

"This place is packed with his boys. Tell me how you plan to get past them."

"I want you out of here."

"I know, but I'm staying put. I can handle Slick and I won't split on you."

"Bobbi—"

"If Gordy's coming up you have to leave. Slick won't hurt me, but he'll kill you for sure. I don't care what sort of deal you have going."

Before I could lose my patience, Gordy was banging on the door. He wasn't alone this time.

"Slick's closet—get inside!" She shoved me in the right direction, I felt like I'd wandered onto the stage of a French farce.

"Bobbi, I'm opening the door now," Gordy called.

"Keep your shirt on!" She opened it first.

For form's sake I got in the closet just long enough to vanish and was out again, keeping close to Gordy.

"Yeah? What is it now?" she demanded. She didn't sound at all like a woman who'd been caught doing something she shouldn't.

"Slick wants to see you. You're going for a boat ride."

She didn't ask why. While she threw on a light jacket, they searched the rooms, then hauled her downstairs to a waiting car. Invisibly, I went with them. She might have known how to handle Slick, but I didn't have her confidence in him. All too well I remembered the guy he'd beaten to a bloody pulp with his own gun.

When we got to the docks, I had a real check to face, the free-running water of the lake. Any and all instincts I had or had recently acquired were sending out emergency alarms, and it took a lot of effort to ignore them. I clung to Gordy like a lamprey as we got into the rowboat. I didn't care how cold it made him.

There were two men to handle the oars, but my presence aboard made it hard work for them, and they were panting from the effort by the time we drew alongside the *Elvira*. Bobbi was handed aboard, then Gordy followed struggling up the ladder as I hung on. I thought he was going to fall in, but he was very strong and someone lent him an obliging hand and pulled hard.

We both lurched onto the deck. The craft was big enough to give me some stability, but my back hairs—if I had any in this form—were still up. The whole yacht, big as it was, had given a shudder as I came aboard.

"Wind must be kicking up," someone remarked.

"I felt that, but there's no wind, that was current."

"Are they here yet?" I heard Morelli's irritated call from a short distance. Gordy moved toward the source, herding Bobbi ahead of him. We went below.

From the size of it, we were in the main cabin. I found an unoccupied corner and settled in to listen. Things were quiet at first, I could imagine Morelli giving Bobbi a good looking over trying to read her mind.

"Who was he?"

"You know already, Slick, so why play games?"

"You tell me his name."

"It was Fleming, the guy you sent me after the other night."

There was a long silence.

"Well, what's the matter? Didn't you want me to do it? He said you sent him."

"Shut up!" There was another long pause, his voice calmer and colder when he spoke again. "Did you screw him?"

"No." She sounded disappointed and disgusted. "Gordy interrupted things."

"Then get out of here. Go to my cabin." There was movement and the door opened and shut.

Morelli sounded tired. "Gordy, tell me what you saw."

Gordy was less excited than when he made his call. "She missed a show so I went to check on things. I heard them through the door and shot it open. He was in bed with her and got out fast. For what it's worth, his pants were still buttoned. I didn't know who he was at first, but then he came out and I saw it was the Fleming kid."

"Go on."

"I *know* he was dead on that sidewalk. You saw him. So how does he show up alive now? Is he twins or something?"

"Did you see how he got in?"

"No, and I don't know how he *could* have got in. Secret passages, maybe?"

Morelli's brief and obscene reply shut him up. He must have forgotten about looking for such passages only a little while ago himself. "He could have bribed someone, it happens. What did he look like? Was he normal? What was he wearing?"

"Pants and shoes, I didn't see no shirt or hat, but I wasn't there long."

"What was his face like?"

Gordy didn't understand what he was after. "It was a face, just like we left him, but God, his eyes—"

"What about them?"

"I swear, they were red . . . there was no white showing at all."

"Red? Solid red?"

"I saw him like I see you now. The light was good, better than this. I get the creeps thinking on the way he looked."

"Well, don't," he snapped. They were quiet, then Morelli started again. "Look, I know there's something weird about all this and Fleming, but there's no sense in going chicken about it. We'll stay on the boat for the night after we close the club, then tomorrow we'll really look into everything."

"Sure, boss."

"I'll be in my cabin."

I followed him out. The passage was short. He found another door and went through. I found another corner near to, but not quite touching, Bobbi, who was sitting on the bed.

"Well?" he said.

"Well what?"

"Gordy saw you two together."

"Being together doesn't mean we slept together."

"Maybe you didn't have time to sleep."

"What are you bellyaching about? It was your idea for the sleeping arrangements, not mine, and you've a dozen other girls up there since I moved in, and I've never said a word, not even when I was in the next room."

"You'd be in the same room if I wanted two at once. You like your job too much."

"Two at once, that's a laugh. You can hardly keep it up for five minutes."

"You were caught, you bitch, so start shedding and I'll show you what kind of damage I can do in five minutes."

"No."

"If you can put out for a dead man—"

"What do you mean, did you kill him?"

"Yeah, I killed him. He was shot dead in the street two days ago, or didn't he tell you that?"

"You're crazy."

"You can ask Gordy, he was there. You like to screw corpses?" There was a tearing of cloth and the struggling sounds of two bodies against each other. She slapped him and cursed, but he forced her back and down. His mistress or not, I felt compelled to interfere and closed around him like newspaper over a mackerel.

Seconds later he gave his first shiver. "What are you doing?" he asked. Vague as the question was, it was no surprise that she couldn't answer. He moved off her, falling back against a cabin wall his heart going fast. "You're here, aren't you? Why don't you come out? Come on, Fleming! I know you're here!"

Bobbi sat still, probably deducing she was locked in with a dangerous lunatic. I didn't want to push him too much, so I eased off to let him get over his chattering teeth. Neither of them moved; Morelli was listening and Bobbi was watching him.

"Are you all right?" she asked.

"He was here, I knew he was here. He didn't want me touching you."

"There's no one here, Slick. No one."

"Didn't you feel the cold? He was here, he's probably still here, watching."

"You're crazy. I'm going to my room."

"No! You'll stay here."

"What for, more roughhouse?"

"If I want it, yes."

"It's always what you want, isn't it?"

The argument started to build again and that's when I saw my mistake. All the guff between them had been some sort of ritual. They were quickly working up to another knock-down-drag-out. Bobbi had been with someone else and Morelli was reasserting his claim and using his body to do it. Bobbi had said she knew how to handle him, and as for Morelli, I suppose it was none of my business how he expressed his masculinity, as long as he wasn't really hurting her.

They were yelling now. She goaded him one step too far and then he was on her again and they got down to serious sex. I was not happy about the situation, but left them to it, exiting the cabin. No one had shown up to investigate the noise yet—apparently the crew were used to the histrionics.

Gordy was still in the main cabin, helping himself to the liquor cabinet before he dropped on a window seat to rest. He seemed to be facing out into the room, making an unobserved materialization difficult. I found my corner again, hoped it was out of his immediate line of sight, and tried to solidify.

I tried. It was like pushing a train uphill, caboose and all. I got scared, wondering if my remaining in a prolonged state of disembodiment had become a permanent thing. I tried again, harder. The train moved a little, but it was exhausting. The next time I really concentrated, visualizing each part of my body, willing it to come into being. There was weight. Arms felt like this, legs supported, eyes . . .

Like pouring cold molasses, I re-formed, the effort leaving me weak. Gordy spotted me right away, but he was surprised and it was little work to tell him to stay quiet and take a nap. He slumped over without a peep, leaving me to an undisturbed recovery.

Solid again, with my heightened senses running at full, I was immediately and urgently aware of the vast amount of water all around. Now that I had back hairs again, they were at attention from the lower spine to the top of my head. There was little I could do about the situation except to try and ignore it if possible.

The cabin was smaller than I thought, and I knew I'd been here before. My left hand, keeper of the memory, was twitching of its own accord. I tried to hold it still with the other. Outside I heard the occasional conversation of the crew, though I couldn't tell how many were aboard. Farther away were some distinct and unmistakable thrashing noises, and from the other sounds they made, they seemed to be enjoying themselves.

A glance around the cabin revealed the bar, table, and chairs and a safe squatting against one wall. Thinking it might have a similar alarm system, I checked the small desk next to it. Almost in the same spot was the on/off switch. It was off now and though there might not be anything valuable aboard, it was worth a try while I had the chance.

It was unlikely it had the same combination as the one at the club, but for the moment I could think of nothing better to do. The tumblers were clicking at the same spots, though, until I got to the last one and had to experiment. My mind wandered between the clicks. I was worried about the difficulty I'd had materializing. The fact that I was over open water was the obvious reason for the trouble, but some illogical twinge of guilt was nagging me about the fact I'd drunk human blood for the first time. Despite my extremely happy experience with Bobbi, I wondered if it made me some sort of monster, after all. As far as the books, the movies, and even the dictionaries were concerned, I was an altogether evil parasite. There was an extraordinary amount of bad press available on vampires and I was understandably worried. All I had to refute it was my own limited experience.

I didn't feel evil. True, I was a predator, but unlike other hunters, I left my prey alive and in one case, feeling pretty good afterward. I knew I felt better. Perhaps it was just the euphoria of lovemaking, but I did feel stronger. Maybe human blood was the perfect nourishment, it was hands down certainly more exciting and pleasurable to acquire.

The last tumbler clicked into place and the door swung open. Inside was a bundle of cash and unlabeled envelopes full of papers. This stuff looked more like Escott's specialty and there might not be a second opportunity at it, so I folded everything up and stuffed my pockets, leaving the cash. I was a crusading reporter, not a thief.

"Don't move," Gordy said behind me. My attention had wandered too far, and I'd forgotten to keep an eye on him. He told me to turn around.

For the second time that night his gun was on me. He was on the window seat, but far from relaxed if I could tell anything about his thudding heartbeat. Still, he was remarkably calm about facing the supernatural. I doubted I would have had anywhere near the same moxie. I thought about putting him to sleep again and turned it down. It was better to wait for Morelli to come; it was time to settle things up.

He called to someone topside and told them to get Morelli. From the straining noises coming from the cabin down the way, such an interruption would not be welcome. I suppose I could have delayed things for another crucial moment, but why should one of my murderers have any fun? I listened, trying to keep a straight face as the errand runner knocked on the door. Morelli breathlessly told him to go away. The runner delivered his brief message. Morelli told him to go to hell. The runner left, his job completed and the damage done. Morelli had to work hard to get worked up and now his concentration was thoroughly broken. After a short while, he gave up and things got quiet. In another minute he came charging in, loaded for bear.

"Goddammit, Gordy! What—"

Gordy just pointed at me with his free hand.

Morelli went all white in the face. I was getting used to seeing him in that color. He was looking rumpled already, with his hair messed up and wearing only a bathrobe. I hadn't improved things.

"Oh, God, it's him," he said out loud, but only to himself.

"He's the one I saw, Slick, except his eyes aren't red now."

No one moved. Perhaps Morelli was afraid I'd vanish again. It was tempting, but if I failed I didn't want to in front of them. The fewer weaknesses shown, the better.

"Look at his clothes, there's the holes and the blood's still there." Gordy stood to be in a more functional position to shoot.

Morelli was indeed looking at me. He noticed the clothes; I still hadn't buttoned my shirt and its tails hung sloppily out front. He also noticed that Escott's makeup job was gone.

"He looks real enough," he said, trying to generate some courage. His eyes dropped to my chest. "It can't be the kid, this guy's never been shot."

I beg to differ.

"Or there was a mistake on the street," said Gordy. "Joe never hit him, after all, the kid faked it."

"Then what about the other stuff?"

"Some kind of trick, like you said. He could have drugged the boys and robbed the safe. See, I got him red-handed just now."

Morelli looked past me. "Where are the papers?"

"In his pockets."

"Empty 'em," he told me. It was the first time I'd been addressed directly. I didn't move. If he wanted his papers he could damn well get them himself. He ordered me again, lost his patience, and came for them. As exasperated as he was, he approached me like a ticking bomb, giving Gordy plenty of target area in case I tried something. He threw all the stuff on the table and checked for other things. My wallet came out, my old one. I should have left it at home, but one can't think of everything. He looked at the papers inside.

The shock was almost physical. The wallet he held was supposed to be on a weighted body at the bottom of the lake, not in his own shaking hands. He dropped it and if possible, his eyes were bulging more than when he'd first walked in the room.

Gordy sensed the change. "What's the matter? Slick?"

Morelli's thoughts flashed over his face. He was trying to understand, trying to put reality right again and failing.

I smiled.

He broke. "Shoot him, Gordy! Shoot him now!"

The gun was already level with my chest. Instinct made me throw myself to one side. The bullet caused a brief bright flash as it crashed through my skull, leaving behind white-hot pain. The force of the shot and momentum of my dive carried me forward, out of control, and my head connected with a solid crack on the sharp corner of the wood table, with all my weight adding to the force. By comparison, the bullet had been a pinprick. I lay stunned and still by the sheer agony that enveloped me.

My body was turned over. My eyes stared at the light, unable to shut out the glare.

"Must have just glanced him," said Gordy. "There's a wound, but no hole. I coulda swore I hit him square."

"Is he dead?"

A heavy hand on my chest, then he shut my eyes. I couldn't have moved if I wanted to. "He's dead, see for yourself."

Before he could, there were quick steps and the door was thrown open. "Slick?" It was Bobbi's voice, frightened. "Oh, my God."

"Get the hell out of here! No, wait—look at him, is he the one? Is he?"

"Yes," Her throat was congested with tears. Grief for me or shock, I couldn't tell.

"Shut up and get out!"

Yes, Bobbi, get out so you don't have to see—

"I said get out!" The door slammed. She retreated down the passage, trying to stifle the sobs.

I'd been in such pain before and in this same cabin, lying helpless in the heat with voices and questions, the air thick with sweat and smoke, the stink of my own body burning my lungs.

I slipped into the nightmare, embracing the horror of memory like a lover.

Lover—Bobbi—

No, Maureen.

Maureen . . .

10

WE were laughing at some private joke. It was good to hear her laugh, she did it so seldom, but when I turned to look at her, she was gone and the smile within me died.

I woke from the cessation of motion as the train stopped. It was a familiar dream, I used to hate it, but not anymore because I needed the shadow memory of Maureen to know that I'd once loved her and felt alive.

She might have been saying good-bye this time, though. New York was behind me now, good memories and bad, and I wanted to start fresh again. That was what I told myself while threading through the crowded train station with my two bags. It wasn't much of a lie since I wasn't much of a liar, but the best for the moment, it would have to do.

Chicago was not windy today, it was late summer and the humidity was up to lethal levels. The walk from the station was unpleasant, the bags dragged hard on my arms, and the sidewalk threw the heat up in my face as though it were my fault. I was getting punch drunk from it until a hotel with the right price on the sign invited me into the shade. It was cheap, though not quite a fleabag. Later, if the money got too low, I'd end up in one of those, but not today.

Unescorted, I trudged upstairs to look for the door that fit my key. In these days of the Depression the hotel couldn't afford the luxury of a bellhop. The room was no worse than I expected, small and impersonal, with a sagging bed bolted to the floor, an ugly bureau and a chair to match, but it had a private bath and a phone and came with a fan, which I immediately turned on. I opened the window wide to let in the late-afternoon street exhaust and stripped out of my damp suit. I ran cold water in the tub and dropped in. Later on I'd hunt up a hamburger and read the papers to decide which one deserved to employ me.

The water was just rising past my chest when the phone rang.

I moaned and cursed, being one of those people who have to answer no matter what they're doing. It had to be a wrong number, the only person I knew in Chicago was the clerk downstairs. Lurching out and leaving a wet trail, I picked up the earpiece and said hello.

"Jack Fleming?" It wasn't a familiar voice.

"You got him, what is it?"

"Jack, this is Benny O'Hara from New York. You maybe remember at Rosie's bar about a year ago—"

Benny O'Hara, a little guy with big ears who gave me a tip on an arson story in exchange for five bucks and a drink. I'd let the cops in on it, they caught the guys, and I got an exclusive for the paper with a by-line.

"Yeah, Fourth of July, make it look like fireworks did it, collect the insurance. I remember."

"Listen, I saw you leave the train station and followed you. I thought you could help me—"

The same old story. He needed a soft touch, but I couldn't afford it this time. "I'm sorry, Benny, but I was just on my way out—"

"No, wait, please, this is important!" He sounded desperate, I hung on out of curiosity. "You gotta listen. I've got something big for you, a hell of a story, believe me."

"I'm listening."

"Can you come down and meet me in the street? I can't tell it all on the phone. Please, Jack?"

"What'll it cost me?"

"You mean what'll it give you? This one is red hot."

"Arson again?" I joked.

"Please, Jack!" He was in no mood for humor.

"All right, I'll be out in a minute."

"Just walk outside, turn right, and keep walking. I'll catch up with you."

It seemed overly dramatic, maybe he did have something important. If I came to an editor with a hotshot story ready to roll, so much the better my chances of getting a job, and with better pay. It was worth a try. I told Benny to hold tight and hung up, trying not to sound too eager.

Dried and dressed, I left the hotel, following his directions, scanning the faces around me for his. About a block later he appeared at my elbow.

"Don't look at me, for Chrissake!" he said in a low voice.

The glimpse I'd gotten was not reassuring. He always looked to be just this side of starvation, that was normal, but now he was haggard and twitching at the edges. I wondered when he'd last slept.

"Just keep walking and I'll tell you everything."

"For how much?"

"I'll tell you. When I'm finished you can take it or leave it."

Now, that was out of character. If I hadn't been on guard before, I was now. "Who's following you?"

"Nobody yet, I think, but we can't take chances. Just keep walking."

I kept walking.

"Ever hear of Lucky Lebredo?"

"No."

"He's a local gambler, owns part of the Nightcrawler."

"He owns a worm?" I said blankly.

"It's a nightclub," he said, pained. "Used to be a big speak, then it went in heavy on the gambling when he got part of it."

"Illegal, of course."

"Is LaGuardia Italian? Anyway, he's a name here to some people, but keeps a low profile and stays out of the way of the gangs, so not many people know him or his piece of the club."

"So what's this about, Benny?"

"Did Rosie tell you what I do for a living?"

"She said you were a locksmith," I replied with a straight face.

"Rosie's a swell gal."

"Benny—"

"Okay! I'm getting to it. I have to take advantage of an opportunity when it comes up 'cause there ain't that many of them these days for locksmiths. I gotta flop with this friend of mine, and every Wednesday he has room in his place for a big-time poker game. These guys use thousand-dollar bills like other people use matchsticks. Sometimes the game goes on for days. It's usually out-of-town guys lookin' for some fun, and there's different ones every week, but Lucky never misses a game. He's a real crazy when it comes to poker and he always wins."

"I've heard of people like that."

"You gotta see to believe this guy. I swear, one week he went home eighty thousand dollars ahead. You gotta figure he don't declare that on his income tax."

"How is it they let you in on this game?"

"I don't play. My friend tells 'em I'm a bodyguard. He lends me a gat for the duration and I hang around and look tough. Some of these rubes even believe it, they treat me like Capone himself, and they tip good to boot. Anyway, I keep my eyes open and one night I decide to follow Lucky home, just to protect him, you understand."

"I understand."

"Well, he goes on into this house, and for a guy with that much money it ain't much of a house, so I figure he must have piles of it lying around unspent and unprotected. Maybe he might like to hire someone to guard it for him when he's out."

"And you decided to apply for the job?"

"Naturally, but the next night when I went back he was gone, maybe off to the club, but I tried the door, anyway, and imagine my surprise when it just opened right up. I thought maybe something might be wrong inside, so I had a good look around to make sure there wasn't no burglars."

"Go on."

"Thank goodness there wasn't and a good thing, too, because—I swear this is the truth—he walked out the door and left the safe wide open. I mean, how careless can you get?"

"Tsk-tsk. Very careless."

"Now, I thought it would be a shame if all that cash were to disappear into the wrong hands, so maybe I should take care of it for him."

"Very thoughtful of you."

"I thought so, too. There were a lot of large bills there and I don't have nothing to carry them in, so I pull out this big envelope from the safe that looks empty. There's only two sheets of paper inside, they don't take up any room, so I start stuffin' money into it and the whole kit and kaboodle leaves with me. When I get back to my flop I count things out and that's when I get a good look at those sheets of paper."

"What was on them?"

"They look like some kid was playing with a typewriter. Both sheets are covered with a lot of punctuating junk and numbers top to bottom, both sides of the pages. I figure right away it's some kind of codes, and I like puzzles, so I try to solve it."

"And?"

"And it wasn't so easy, but I did it, and the stuff on those pages is enough to blow this state wide open."

"What is it, then?"

"A blackmail list. The names are big ones, ones you wouldn't expect to be there. It gives the names, where they live, the location of the stuff that's against them, everything. I checked."

"Oh come on, Benny."

"I swear! I got it with me and now I gotta get rid of it."

"Why? And why me?"

" 'Cause you're not on the list, 'cause you're new in town and none of these mugs know you."

"What mugs?"

"One of Lucky's boys and others. They're with the Paco gang, they've been after me for days, I can't get outta town. They've got the stations covered. I can't buy a car, boat, or bicycle without them finding out."

"And you want to foist this off on me? Turn it in to the cops."

"Don't you see anything? There's cops on the list—judges, lawyers, newspaper people—anybody with something to hide is on it. They'd bury it and me, too, if I went to them. I tried. But you're clean, you can do something with it, you can make a story out of it."

"What do you want from me?"

"Just some help getting out of the city. I can take care of myself from there."

I'd always been an idiot when it came to thinking out the long-term consequences of snap decisions. "What have you got planned?"

"You're a square guy, so I can trust you. I give you a couple of notes and you go buy a car for me, but in your name, then all we gotta do is drive outta town. You drop me in some burg in the next state, then I'm on my own and can lam it from there. For that, you keep the car and the list. Lucky and his boys don't know you from whosis, so you'll be safe, too."

"That sounds okay to me. When?"

"Right now. I gotta get out today before my nerves go. Take a turn into that alley ahead and wait for me. If things are clear, I'll be there in a minute."

I went into the alley, walking half its length before stopping and turning around. It was dim and quiet. I took off my hat and wiped at the sweatband with a handkerchief. My only company was a one-eared cat picking through the garbage. Down the middle of the alley ran a trickle of water, and overhead someone's laundry hung dejectedly in the still air. I hoped Benny would hurry.

Long before I thought of leaving, his scrawny figure appeared at the other entrance. His gait was a peculiar hopping walk, as though he were about to break into a run and always changed his mind at the last second. He hitched up close, puffing with his eyes darting all over in nervous jerks. He was looking down at the heels for all the dough he claimed to be holding and had the calm demeanor of a chain-smoker who'd just run out of cigs.

"Now we gotta be careful," he warned me, and gave me a thousand-dollar bill.

"Is this for real?" I'd never seen one before.

"Like Sally Rand's feathers. You might want to change it for smaller bills, but you can get a really good car with it. I can't cash 'em myself on account of I don't look that respectable enough, but for you it'd be easy."

Not that easy, but maybe if I changed into my better suit I could pass muster at any bank. "Okay, now where's the list?"

"Right here and welcome to it." He pulled out two sheets of paper folded double and gave them to me. I opened them up. As described, they were solid with typed symbols and numbers.

"How do I read this stuff?"

"It's easy, just substitution—"

Someone coughed off to the left. It was an oddly regular cough, coming three times very close together. Benny's small body jerked and three large red holes appeared in his head, chest, and stomach. He fell into the dirty little stream on his side and lay oblivious in the water, pop-eyed and forever surprised.

I won't defend my reaction, if it was cowardice or self-preservation, but I hurtled out of that alley and into the street as though my ass were on fire.

Terror is a great stimulant. Three long blocks later I was still pelting down the sidewalk at full steam, leaving a trail of disturbance and sometimes destruction as I negotiated obstacles in my path. I never looked back. The temptation was there, but it would have cost me speed and headway. I just couldn't take the risk. Heat and lack of endurance took their toll, though, and I was forced to slow down; my passage through the afternoon rush was too noticeable, anyway. I ducked into a big department store and tried to collect myself while still moving.

The list and the thousand-dollar bill were still in my hands. I tucked both away into my wallet and thought about calling for a cop. That might be a bad idea, though, since as a witness I was no good. I had, God help me, seen Benny die, but hadn't even glimpsed his killer. There could be more than one, from his talk. What story could I give, anyway? That I had accepted money from a thief to help him out? The truth wouldn't do at all, and from experience I knew I was a lousy liar. I kept moving, hoping to come up with some plan before somebody aced me.

I was just starting to feel safe and looked around. Even as a stranger to the city I had no trouble recognizing them. I'd seen the type in lineups in New York. They could look like anyone physically, but there was a hard-to-define attitude that set them apart from ordinary people. A predator's hardness, perhaps, but I had no time to analyze the quality because they were coming after me.

I located the back exits, tore through the stockrooms, upsetting employees, and burst outside onto a narrow street where freight trucks made their deliveries. The street ran into a larger one, with more people and hopefully safety. I heard feet pounding behind me and dived into the crowds.

We played this game for nearly an hour. There were five of them, three on foot and two in a dark green Ford that followed me after I jumped into a taxi. They were smart and certainly professionals. I was a stranger in their territory and really didn't stand much chance of getting away, but had to keep trying to avoid Benny's fate.

I thought of dropping the stuff in plain sight. Perhaps that was all they were after, and I was too unimportant to bother about. It seemed right, but there was absolutely no indication they would be so cooperative. I kept going.

I was getting very tired. The taxi dropped me on Michigan Avenue, though it had given me a small respite, I'd have to go to ground soon. I needed time to rest and think and a safe place to do it in. That's when I looked up and saw the massive limestone structure of the Chicago Public Library. Libraries had often been quiet sanctuaries for me, so I went in.

The first floor was useless, too open, full of newspapers and people reading them. I took to the stairs. The second floor was a haven for civil War relics, but not for me. I puffed up to the third landing and was greeted with the welcome sight of rows and rows of bookshelves. Like a fish returning to water, I slipped between their ranks and found a vantage point where I could watch the avenue and the stairs.

I owed the taxi driver a medal for losing the Ford long enough for me to get to cover. Far below, its green roof cruised up and down the avenue for half an hour before they gave up and moved on. No dangerous-looking types came inside and I relaxed and retreated deep into the shelves.

First I'd get rid of the list, then I'd get out of town until things cooled off; maybe even go home for a while and rest. I could write up a detailed account and send copies to the local D.A., the Feds, the papers, anybody I could think of who might be wondering who bumped off Benny O'Hara. It might not do any good, but it was as much as I was willing to risk at the moment. Seeing a man getting shot to pieces under your nose will take the starch out of anyone's backbone, and I never thought of myself as particularly brave. The last few hours had been so frightening I was ready to quit the papers altogether and go back to helping Dad at the store.

At the moment, though, I was getting hungry and felt that the promised hamburger was long overdue. The mind deals with the shocks, but the body goes on prosaically dealing with the basics of living.

Standing on my toes, I placed the two sheets of paper on the top of one of the shelves in the back. The aisle was clear, no one had seen me. I made a note of which section I was in, and left, knowing the goods were safe as they'd ever be.

I found a back stairway and used it to make my cautious way into the street again.

The coast looked clear, no green Fords, no hard men, but I kept pace with the thickest part of the crowds for many long blocks before relaxing enough to find a café. A small, busy place called the Blue Diamond smelled good so I went in and managed to get a table at the back. I ordered steak with everything instead of a burger, and while I ate I made notes on a napkin about what happened in my personal shorthand. I stalled over the meal, drinking coffee and having an extra dessert so as not to put off the waitress. When it was dark I left her a good tip and ventured into the streets.

Taxis cost, but walking back to the hotel was too much for my feet. Besides, I had no idea where it was, just the name of the street it was on. I gave it to the driver and hoped he'd take a straight route. It didn't take long, he knew his business and dropped me at the right corner as far as I could tell, although it seemed different in the dark. I was still nerved up and tired, bad combination.

I kept my eyes open, but wasn't too worried. The men who chased me couldn't know where I was staying since Benny had been so careful. Poor Benny.

And then it was poor me.

Two of them appeared out of nowhere. They must have been watching the whole street knowing I might come back. I was practically lifted from my feet and trotted forward. The green car came up, a door was pulled open, and I was hustled inside. The whole operation didn't take more than five or six seconds and I was being driven off to parts unknown.

The three of us staged an impromptu wrestling match in the backseat as I did my best to get out and they did their best to prevent it. Once I managed to get my hand on the door lever, but a fist hit the side of my head and another one gouged my kidneys.

"Hey, settle down back there!" the driver growled.

A few more hits and I was in no condition to continue the argument. They shoved me on the floor and kept me there facedown, their heavy feet resting with some force on my back and legs. I was dizzy from the punches and scared, and the swaying motion of the car in those claustrophobic conditions wasn't helping.

"I'm going to be sick," I said to the floor.

"What'd he say?"

A little louder, I repeated myself.

There was some laughter from the front seat, but the guys in back didn't think it was so funny. The one nearest my head took off my hat, turned it upside down, and shoved it under my nose.

"You get any puke on me and I'll pop your eyes out," he warned.

I gulped back my gorge and tried to get air in my lungs. It was a long, tough ride, but I managed to keep my dinner down. We pulled over once and the driver got out for a few minutes, leaving the engine running. The car rocked as he squeezed back behind the wheel.

"Frank says we bring him to the boat, then you guys take a hike until he wants you again. Georgie, you take the car back to the house for me."

"When do we get paid?"

"Tonight at the boat, as usual."

"Come on, Fred, we been after this guy all day."

"Then argue with Frank, I don't pay the bills."

Someone tied a rag over my eyes and I was hauled from the backseat with my arms fixed behind me. Two men had to hold me up since I couldn't balance. I smelled and heard the water lapping all around and had immediate visions of Lake Michigan and cement shoes. I tried tearing loose, collected a breath-stealing gut punch, and was dragged down some steps. The next few minutes were confusing as I was tripped into something that felt alive under my feet. I lost balance again and without my arms couldn't stop the fall. My left elbow hit something hard and so did my knees. I tried to twist to get upright, lost it all again, and my head snapped back and the hard thing caught me behind the ear. Despite the blindfold, lights flashed in my eyes before the dark closed everything down.

It felt like I'd been asleep for weeks and was only now coming out of it. Some men were talking and I was annoyed that they were holding their discussion in my private bedroom. I wanted to tell them to get the hell out, but my mouth wasn't cooperating yet.

"On ice and intact," a man said. I remembered his name was Fred.

"You call that intact?" was the ungrateful reply.

"He put up a fight, what can I say?"

"You boys been paid yet?"

"No, Mr. Paco."

"Okay, here, and keep your traps shut. Get lost and forget today ever happened. Fred, you stay with me. Georgie, take the car back home."

"Right."

Men shuffled away. It didn't sound like a very large room and I still had a slight feeling of movement all around, which I attributed to my half-conscious state. My head hurt and I was sick in the stomach, and the more awake I got, the more hurts made themselves known. I started remembering other things, none of them too pleasant.

"What did they do to him?" said Paco.

"He took a fall when we put him in the boat."

"Wake him up."

Some water was dribbled in my face. That was when I realized they'd been talking about me. I thrashed around and shot fully awake and painfully alert. I couldn't move much, being firmly tied to a chair, but the blindfold was off, not that what I saw was very reassuring.

The large lump holding the water glass was Fred. The shorter more bullish man behind him was Paco. Neither of them looked friendly.

The room was long with a low ceiling. The walls were oddly curved. I deduced we were on a boat and a big one. That explained the movement and my bad stomach; I was a poor sailor.

"He's awake," said Fred. He and Paco drew back from my field of vision. My chair was in the middle of the bare floor facing a table. Leaning on the table was another man, darker and thinner than his friends. He unhitched his hip from his perch and came over to me. I heard a click and a slender, long-bladed knife appeared in one hand. The edge was so sharp it hurt to look at. I stiffened as he bent down near me.

"Take it easy, buddy," he said, and cut the ropes. I could hardly move as they dropped away but tried flexing my limbs. Not a good idea, they went from numb to pins-and-needles pain as the blood started resuming its job.

"You want a drink?"

I managed a nod. He made a sign and Fred brought me a stiff double whiskey. I would have preferred water, but took what was offered. It was good stuff and made things comfortably warm inside. My benefactor smiled at me, I'd have smiled back if he'd put the knife away. Fred took my empty glass and returned it to the built-in bar. He was looking at Paco as though waiting for a signal. Paco was looking at the third man, whose attention was on me.

"I think you know why you're here," he said. He had thick long lashes on his eyes, a woman's eyes, and I didn't like that expression in them. "Stand up."

There was no reason not to, though I wobbled a bit and had to use the chair for support. Fred came over and pulled everything from my pockets and dumped it on the table. They went through it. I said good-bye to the thousand-dollar note. They looked at me and Fred was smirking.

"I knew the little shrimp passed him something."

"What else did you get off him?" asked Paco.

They found the napkin my notes were scribbled on, but it wasn't what they wanted.

"He's a reporter," said the third man. Fred laughed. They looked with interest at an old press pass he'd taken from my wallet and read my identification. "How long since you seen New York, Jack R. Fleming?"

"Look, I don't know what you want, I just got off the train today—"

"Did little Galligar call you in to help him?"

"Galligar?" Probably Benny's Chicago name. "I don't know what you're talking about. This little guy starts talking to me in the street. He's got some kind of crazy story right out of *Black Mask* that I don't believe and says he'll give me a thousand bucks if I can get him out of town. I figure maybe the bill is a fake and he's trying some kind of new con game, then somebody shoots him so I took off."

"Why don't you tell me the story?" he said, looking at my notes.

"He just said some guys were after him because he lifted some dough from the wrong people."

"Who's L. L.?"

"Louie Long or Lang, I think, I don't remember offhand." I sank back into the chair, tired. "The initials are only for my memory, I'll make up something later."

"What do you mean by that?"

"I'm a reporter, but I also write fiction. A real-life experience like that is too good to waste. I was thinking to do the whole thing up as a story and sell it to one of the detective magazines, maybe even make a book out of it. If I had to live on a reporter's pay I'd starve to death, so I write stories as well."

They stared at me. For a few seconds I thought they believed it, then Paco burst into laughter. The other two joined him and my hopes sank.

They next made me strip and I swayed for several minutes wearing nothing but gooseflesh while they went through my clothes. Piece by piece they tossed everything back, even my wallet and papers, except for the large bill, which remained on the table.

"I know he had it, Mr. Morelli," said Fred, using the man's name for the first time. He didn't seem annoyed at the slip, which disturbed me. I'd heard the name before and something of the man who owned it, but saw no advantage in letting them know that, figuring my best chance with them was to pretend ignorance. "The other boys with me will tell you that, too."

"Was he in your sight the whole time?"

"Well, no, but we were right with him and we got him—"

"Put a lid on it, Fred," said Paco. "You lost him long enough for him to stash it somewhere."

"Hide what?" I tried to sound frustrated and angry. It was easy.

"The list."

"What list?"

"The one Galligar slipped you."

"All he gave me was a cock-and-bull story and that money and then someone shoots him. I figure they'd shoot me, too, so I ran. Take the money, I don't want it, just let me go."

Morelli interrupted Paco's reply. "All right, Fleming, we will be happy to let you go and you can keep the money. I'll even give you another thousand for all the trouble we put you through. You tell us where you put the list and you can go."

"I don't have any list!"

"I believe you. Just tell us where it is."

"I don't know."

He sighed. "Then we may have a problem."

No problem for him, he just stepped back to give Fred enough room to swing. I tried to fight back and fight dirty, but he was too big, too experienced, and too fast. We broke some things up bashing around the cabin, but no one minded since I was the one falling over the stuff. I moved for the door, but he anticipated it, grabbed me from behind, whirled me around, and laid into my stomach. He stood back to catch his breath and I slid to the floor, unable to move. After a minute he hauled me up and dumped me into the chair.

Morelli bent down to my field of view. "You feel like talking yet?"

I couldn't answer right away, in fact there was only one thing I felt like doing at the moment. He saw it coming, said "Oh, shit!" and backed hastily out of the way. I had just enough strength to lean over the chair arm before giving up the steak dinner and the double whiskey onto his deck.

None of them thought it was particularly funny. I did, but wasn't laughing. I just hung over the chair arm and tried not to look at the stuff. The acid smell filled the room and drove out Morelli and Paco. They made Fred clean it up, having decided he was to blame. He wasn't a happy man and cursed the whole time, most of his more colorful abuse aimed at me.

When Fred finished he dragged me out on the deck. There were lights way in the distance, too far for me to swim in my condition, not that he gave me the chance to go overboard. He shoved me against a rail and bent me double so I was well over the water. With a heavy arm around my neck he pried open my mouth and stuck a finger inside and nearly down my throat. I bucked against this, choking until he pulled it out, and then I retched into the black water. He did this twice more until he was certain I was cleaned out, then let me drop on the deck.

Utterly exhausted and panting like a dog, I hated Fred more than I ever thought possible. If I had a weapon or the strength, I would have cheerfully killed him.

I never had the chance, he took me down below.

Morelli and Paco were there, Morelli with one hip resting on the table much as I'd first seen him. Paco was sipping a beer next to the bar. Fred practically carried me to the chair and dumped me in it. Except for a faint tang in the air, there was no sign of what had happened.

"You don't look so good, Fleming," said Morelli. He still had the knife out. He used it to slice the tip from a cigar and spent a minute lighting it properly. He blew the smoke in my direction. "Now, do you want to talk, or do you want to let Fred hit you some more?"

I didn't want either, so I kept quiet. Fred hit me some more. He stopped occasionally to catch his breath and Morelli would ask me his question, get no answer, and then Fred started all over again. I harbored some hope that he'd get tired and go away but when he did Paco took over—and he had brass knuckles.

They came as a bad surprise. Just when I thought it was impossible to hurt more he jabbed them hard into my ribs. The first time it happened I cried out and that encouraged him. He was still fresh, slightly boozed, and enjoying himself. I fell out of the chair and he kicked me until Fred put me back again. They were careful with me. They left my face alone, it'd be hard to talk through a swollen, battered mouth, and they wanted me to talk. I knew if I did and they got the list I'd die. It was a very simple conclusion, even in my present state I could grasp that. I kept quiet and let them hit me. I wanted to live that much. After a while I stopped reacting to the punches and Morelli told him to lay off. Good old Morelli, my friend, I thought before I stopped being awake.

They took a break, had a meal, and started again. The cabin got like an oven and the air was an unbreathable mixture of sweat, cigar smoke, and booze, though the windows were open. With surprise I saw clear blue sky and sunlight lancing through white clouds. It had to be an unreal vision. Men just didn't beat up other men on days like this; then I'd get a whiff of my own stink and know otherwise.

Morelli gave me some water at one point, my tongue felt like it was someone else's property. "You can save yourself a lot of grief, Fleming. Just tell me where you put it."

I must have been feverish. I heard someone laugh a little and say: "Where the sun don't shine."

He threw the rest of the water in my face. It felt good until I passed out again, which felt better.

I woke up. Something sharp in the air was burning my nostrils. I shook my head away but it followed. They'd turned up smelling salts from somewhere and were using them to keep me awake. It was necessary at this point, I kept conking out on them.

"Never mind that," Morelli said when my eyes finally opened. He had more water and gave it to me. It tasted odd, but I drank without thinking.

They left me alone and I started to drift away from the pain, never quite made it, whatever was in the water wouldn't let me. My heart started pounding hard and fresh sweat broke out all over, I felt breathless. The hurt numbed by a few hours' rest began anew. To my humiliation, tears began flooding down my face. Fred and Paco found it very funny. Morelli just sat and smoked another cigar, letting them do all the work.

By mid-afternoon they took a break.

"I don't think he knows," said Paco, drinking another beer.

"Don't be a sap. He knows, but he won't talk. If he didn't know he'd be making up another story about it or telling us he doesn't know. But this guy don't talk at all. He knows."

Fred yawned. "I gotta sleep," he said to no one in particular. He went out.

"Maybe we should go back and get Gordy," said Paco. "He's good at this stuff."

"Nah, Lucky's got him busy looking for Galligar."

Paco laughed. "He'll need a set of gills to do that. My boys took care of him good."

"They screwed up, you mean. If they thought to shoot both of them we wouldn't be stuck here now."

"I know, but we'll get him to talk. You wouldn't think he'd be this stubborn, would you? Stupid, but he's got some guts."

Their voices faded away. I dreamed about Benny, an uneasy Jewish-Catholic now buried forever without services from either faith, just another guy out of Hell's Kitchen scrambling for a buck.

I dreamed about escaping. If I could get overboard with a life preserver I might be able to make it to shore. Even the prospect of drowning looked preferable to another session with Fred and Paco. All I had to do was get up off the floor. Fat chance that, they'd done their work too well.

I dreamed about Maureen, dark hair and rare laughter, a nervous girl, looking over her shoulder, but needing love and giving fully in return. Was she safe yet?

I dreamed, but could not rest.

Hours later I opened my eyes. The lids seemed to be the only part of my body that could still move. I felt like a shattered piece of glass held together with weak glue. The wrong touch and everything would fall to pieces. It hurt to breathe and the air was hot in my lungs. The windows were still open, but there was no ventilation.

I wasn't thinking too straight, because even that hurt, but I wanted to get to one of the windows. Once there I'd think of what to do next.

It was only ten feet away. Three steps for a healthy upright man, a few miles for me. Under it was a padded, built-in window seat. If I could get to it I would . . . but I couldn't quite remember.

I squirmed forward six inches and rested. I'd have to go easy and keep the glue intact. Six more inches and rest. Repeat. My shoulders ached from the effort, but then so did everything else, tell them to shut up and cooperate so we can—what? Window seat. It was a little closer. Six inches and rest. Window seats have windows, windows have air, we need air. We need to rest. Oh, God it hurts. . . . Shut up. Six inches and rest. Tears again, waste of energy, but they wouldn't stop. Eyes blurring, from tears or pain? Where was the window? Rest. Don't move, just lay down and die, serve them right. Anger. How dare they reduce me to this? How dare they make me crawl? Twelve inches that time. Anger was good, stay mad and escape. Keep crawling and hate their guts for it. Crawl so you can come back and do this to them. Crawl . . .

But the glue came apart before I was halfway there and for a long time there was nothing.

"Jeeze, you wouldn't think he'd a made it that far." My admirer was Paco. I was looking at his shoes. I wished he'd give me a good solid kick in the head and end it all, but he was no pal to do me favors.

"Put him in the chair," said Morelli.

No, please don't bother.

They put me in the chair.

I fell out of it.

They tied me to the chair. Wrists and ankles. Rough hemp rope. I looked at it, not knowing what it was.

"Fleming."

Oh, go away.

"Fleming." He tilted my head back. I choked on some whiskey. Something had happened the last time I drank, but I couldn't remember.

"Wake up, Fleming."

I was awake, unfortunately.

"Look at me."

No, go jump in the lake. There was a lake all around us, which struck me as insanely funny. It hurt to laugh. Save it for later and laugh then, if there was a later. What was in the whiskey?

"Fleming, look at me or I'll cut your eyelids away."

That got my attention, but I didn't look at him, only the slender knife in Morelli's hand. Yes, it was possible they could hurt me more. The look in his eyes, his dark feminine eyes, promised that much. Lightly he drew the blade across the back of my hand, sure as a surgeon. Blood welled up from the cut. Yes, he could hurt me.

"Fleming, you've got to talk to us, you've got to tell us where it is. Believe me, we've been going easy on you. You've only got a bad bruising so far, nothing that won't heal. If you don't talk it will get worse and we'll start breaking things up inside you. You could bleed to death on the inside. Tell us where the list is and I swear on my mother's grave, I swear we will let you go."

I almost believed him. Talk and die or don't talk and die anyway. I'd be damned before I'd give them the time of day. They won't kill me, not unless I told them and I'd never give them the satisfaction. Stupid, Paco had said. Yes, and stubborn.

"Fleming, did you hear? Do you understand?"

I nodded or at least tried to. My head dropped so all I could see was my lap. He pushed and I was looking at the ceiling which kept moving around every time I blinked. Something went down my throat. I gagged and coughed.

In a little while my heart began to race. I was more alert. Fred put his hand in my field of view.

"You see these?" he asked.

Yeah. Brass knuckles. He gave me a good look at them.

"Mr. Morelli says I don't have to pull my punches anymore."

I caught a fresh whiff of stifling cigar smoke. "Talk, Fleming."

No, I'm too stubborn—

"Fleming . . ."

No.

"Fred."

Oh, *God*.

He hit me twice and we both felt the rib give way. I heard someone's sharp whimper and passed out.

*   *   *

It was daylight again when I woke. I was lying down, hot and shivering, with an ache all over as if my bones were too big for the skin and trying to bust out. Fred was looking at me. There was as much compassion in his face as a slab of concrete.

"What?" he asked, and leaned closer. I must have said something. I tried to remember.

"Leak."

"Tell me where the list is and I'll help you."

"I . . . can use the toilet or the floor . . . you want another mess to clean?"

He did not.

In the end he had to find a container to bring to me at the window seat. When he tried to stand me up it was too much to bear. I lay helpless and watched it dribble into a tin can. There wasn't much and it was dark with blood. I was sick again and thankful there was nothing in my stomach.

He went away and told them I was awake. Somehow they kept me that way, hours or days went by. I lost track of time when the fever set in. Morelli gave me some aspirin and had them lay off me awhile. My buddy.

The broken rib reminded me of its presence every time I breathed. Now and then I even thought of escape, but then we all dream when we're sick.

The day, from what little I saw of it, clouded over. There was some concerned talk about a storm, but no one made a move toward shore, except Fred, who, storm or no storm, wanted to go home. I heard something ominous about just one more try.

I was tied up in the chair again. The three of them were looking ragged, but still had the benefit of soap and water. I could only imagine what I was like with a thick growth of beard and no food for the past few days, not that I cared.

Morelli made his little speech, he had to repeat it several times before I understood. All I wanted was for him to douse that damned cigar so I could breathe.

Outside it began to rain. There was little wind with it, just the steady soaking kind of fall that farmers liked. Too bad it was all going to waste out here on the lake. It got dark. They turned on the cabin lights and added to the heat inside.

"Talk, Fleming. Where is the list?" He waved the lit cigar near my eyes. I thought I was past feeling more pain or even more fear until he twisted it down into the palm of my hand. My tongue bulged against my teeth, I tried to tear away, vision blurred.

"Where is it?" Again and again until my wrists were bloody and my hand red with burns. My throat was raw, I wondered if I'd been screaming.

"Talk, Fleming."

He stood back and let Fred have another try. Fred was out of patience and wanted to get to shore. He took it out on me and smashed in another rib. I felt things coming loose inside. He was finally going to finish the job, and I'd be out of my misery.

But I didn't want to die.

We were at the stern of the boat. They'd given up and were heading for shore. Morelli stood in the shelter of the hatch that led below, Paco was holding me up as Fred tied something to my ankles.

"Slick says we're not far from the house," Paco was telling Fred. "One of his boys will row you to the dock. You walk to the house and pick up the car and meet us at the pier by the club."

"Can't he call for his car at the club or get a cab?"

"He says that's out. Lucky's got his car to look for that damned list and we gotta get back before he wises up to what we're doing. Cab drivers, we don't want; they got eyes and ears."

"All this work and nothing to show for it."

"Yeah, well, you gotta know when you cut your losses." He lifted my face to his. "This is your last chance, Fleming. Where is it?"

Where was what? I couldn't remember.

"He's too far gone, Frank."

"Fleming? Ahh, the hell with him. Hold him up, there's one more thing I been wanting to do."

Fred help me up. Paco pulled out his gun, a big one and he aimed it at my heart. It finally dragged a response from me. My last scream drowned out its roar as he fired.

I felt nothing. A tug and a jerk of the body and then blessed release from the pain. My body was pushed backward, somersaulting into the dark water, and I sank quickly, leaving a stream of bubbles homing toward the surface. The weight of my ankles pulled me steadily down into cold, unbearable pressure. If I'd been breathing I'd have surely suffocated. The pressure grew and grew and I began to fight it. Something inside wanted out. I seized my inert form, encompassed it . . .

I floated, just another bubble compressed into a moving plastic sphere by the water. I was going to float to heaven.

I made it as far as the surface. The thing that saved me now drove me over the water. Some instinct rushed us straight to the nearest shore. My mind didn't question this, it was perfectly normal the way the most outlandish things are normal when you dream.

There was weight again. Solidity. Rain soaking my soaked clothes. Wind against my face, the same wind that drove away the clouds.

I looked up and winced at stars as bright as the sun.

11

THE silhouette of a head eclipsed the lights of the cabin. It looked familiar. I moved my hand in a feeble gesture to it, my fingers brushed against heavy satin. Not too far away I heard a woman draw a sharp breath, making a little surprised noise, the kind women make when they open a drawer and find a bug lurking in their frilly things. My fingers closed on the satin, but let go almost immediately because there was no strength in them. The angle of light changed on the silhouette and revealed some bony features.

"Take it easy, old man, there's no hurry."

Escott? What the hell was he doing here? I blinked and made an effort to get my eyes working again. He was a little green in the gills himself, and for some odd reason he was wearing that silly purple bathrobe of his. My hand had clutched at the heavy quilted lapels.

"Isn't that too warm for the weather?" I asked idiotically.

"There was no time to change."

"Why not?"

"My invitation here was rather abrupt."

I thought about that one and blinked fully awake. "What the hell are you talking about?"

"You're concussed. Just take it easy and you'll sort things out soon enough."

He made it sound as though everything were fine, but something was going on that was very wrong, and I couldn't take it easy until I found out what. I got my elbows on the floor and pushed. Escott helped and I was sitting up, resting my back against a table leg. Feeling for damage, I found a bloodied patch on my head. It was sticky and the hair was matted.

Escott moved and I could see the rest of the room. I was the center of attention of four pairs of eyes.

Bobbi caught my attention first. She'd been the one who gasped when I first moved; she couldn't be blamed for that since she thought I'd been killed. She was in a loose black garment, her version of a bathrobe. Her face was drained of color and pinched, her hazel eyes wide with whites showing. She sat rigidly on the window seat, her hands clutching the edge of the cushion with her shoulders up by her ears. I smiled at her and tried to make it reassuring with a slight wink, and she relaxed but only a little.

Next to her but not too close was Slick Morelli. His eyes were big, too, his whole body radiating tension. Of the two of them he was the most frightened. For him this was the third time I'd returned from the dead. God knows what was going on in his mind as he stared at me.

To the left, backed against the cabin door, was Gordy, his head crowding close to the low ceiling and his silenced .45 semiautomatic in his big hand. It wasn't aimed at me, but at Escott. Maybe he'd wised up somehow, I couldn't tell with him. He was looking more worried than scared and his eyes would twitch to one side, then back to me.

The fourth pair of eyes were sunk deep in gray hollows, studying me and missing nothing. They were eyes that should have belonged to a victim of starvation, but their owner was anything but underfed, chronically unsatisfied, perhaps, but not underfed. The brown bristle of the beard ringing his lower face camouflaged the spare chins and made his head look like it was growing straight from the shoulders without the convenience of a neck. The skin on his bald dome was dull, and I wondered if he was unhealthy or just shaved too much. He alone looked almost relaxed, but then he apparently knew exactly what he was dealing with, in his hands and cocked with the wood bolt aimed at my heart, was a crossbow.

Escott followed my gaze and looked apologetic. "Sorry, Jack. He turned that one up from my collection."

"How much does he know?"

"Rather a lot, I fear. Allow me to introduce you to Lucky Lebredo, the rightful owner of the list."

"I know he's the owner."

"Then you know I want it back," he said. He spoke as though the least amount of contact with me, even verbal, would somehow soil him.

"How did you find this out?" I gestured at his weapon.

His eyes flicked from me to Escott. "Tell him."

Escott sighed and settled himself against the other table leg. "I'm afraid it got started when you rescued me from Sanderson and Georgie. Mr. Lebredo, through channels he refuses to divulge, got my name from Georgie Reamer. Being interested in Paco's activities, he became curious as to why a relatively unimportant private agent as myself should be so permanently put out of the way, and how I managed to avoid such a fate. Georgie said I had help, and so Mr. Lebredo had a watch put on me and I was followed. He must have been a very good man, too. My trips to your hotel were noted and he became aware of our association, and had you followed as well."

"Even to—"

"Yes, even to there."

Lebredo had a look of supreme disgust on his face. It was fine with me; I didn't like him, either.

"He learned of our visit to Frank Paco and of the little incident in the alley behind the club which cost me a bloodletting. He learned that you had been killed, apparently at least, by Morelli's man during a clumsy attempt to obtain the list. The same day he visited your room to search for it and found you in your trunk and wondered how you got there from the street. The earth in your trunk struck him as being very odd. He is not an ignorant man, nor an especially superstitious one, but it did require some effort to piece his bits of information together to a logical, if unlikely conclusion. Your plaguing of Morelli confirmed his guess, and tonight he decided to make his move."

"So he kidnapped you to use as a lever?"

"Yes. As I said, I had little choice in the matter when three of his men came crashing through my door. I couldn't put up much of a fight with these stitches, either. I am most frightfully sorry about the crossbow."

I looked at Lebredo, he made me forget how much my head hurt. There wasn't much to read in his face except for disgust, and that got old pretty fast, so I looked at Bobbi instead to see how she was taking all this. She was holding up fairly well, considering she was learning some things about me the hard way, that is, if it was making any sense to her. Her mouth tightened. I think it was meant to be a smile, at least she wasn't afraid of me and that was something.

"I want the list," said Lebredo in a flat voice. "I want it tonight."

"It talks," I said.

The crossbow moved slightly, I was one finger twitch away from dying permanently. "Gordy," he said.

The .45 went off, the big silencer cutting the roar down to a manageable level. Escott jumped, jerking his hand. The bullet had gone between his spread fingers where they had rested on the floor. One of them had been nicked, he put it to his mouth. The guy had real guts, he wasn't even shaking. His eyes were on Lebredo, bright and cold. If their places had been suddenly reversed, Lebredo would have been dead and not easily.

The fat man ignored him and spoke to me. "I will give you that one warning. The next time Gordy will shoot off his arm."

Things were still, hearts and lungs were working hard. There were too many to tell one set from another, but I didn't need that kind of information to know he wasn't bluffing.

I drew in a short breath. "Okay. I'll get it for you."

"Jack—" said Escott.

"It's all right. I've remembered. Between Morelli and this boat, things jogged into place. I know where I left it." I looked at Morelli. "I also know what you and Paco and Sanderson did to me."

"But it wasn't—" protested Morelli.

"Be quiet, Slick," said Lebredo.

"But it couldn't—"

His voice raised slightly. "I won't tell you again."

Morelli shut up.

"That's better. Your skepticism is understandable, but your boundless stupidity is not. If you still need more proof, look at the girl's neck. The marks there are small, but not invisible."

Escott's eyebrows went up and his mouth popped open and shut before he blanked out his face, wisely deciding that my love life was my own business.

Morelli was not quite as liberal minded and he pulled at the neck of her wrap. Bobbi tried to shrug him off, but he forced her to hold still. When he saw them he let her go and crossed the room to get away from her. He even wiped his hands on his clothes. Bobbi glared at him—no woman likes that kind of rejection—then her eyes blazed at Lebredo.

"You fat, stinking bastard." She got up and went to the door, stopping inches away from Gordy. Gordy looked at Lebredo for cue, seemed relieved when he got one, and moved aside. She tore the door open and left. Morelli started to object, but Lebredo curtailed it.

"This is a boat, where can she go? Her faithlessness can be dealt with later, or need I remind you that you were the one to encourage it to start with? You have forgotten that women are very dangerous children and should not be trusted."

"Shut up!"

"For now, we'll consider how to deal with you. You and Paco betrayed me to get the list for yourselves—"

"And why'd you go to Paco for it, huh? You could have asked me."

"I'm not stupid enough to send an ape to look for a banana and expect to get it from him. I went to Paco because he obeyed orders as long as there was sufficient money, but he went to you, which was a very bad mistake. He found out exactly what he was looking for, then you both decided to keep it. I should have guessed at what was going on when you both disappeared for three days."

"We still didn't get it."

"That was very fortunate, or else I should have to take it back from you, perhaps even trying the same method you used with Fleming."

"Try it and see how long you live. New York wouldn't stand—"

"Your New York friends and I have an agreement. They understand how valuable I can be even if you do not. I made sure of that. They're running a business these days and have learned that hotheads like you are a liability. Don't rely on them to avenge your carcass, because your crude actions have put you in a very bad spot. Three times you had this man in your hands and you failed because you didn't take the trouble to look for his weak points and play on them."

Morelli shook his head and went over to the bar to pour out a stiff one. He drank it down straight and poured another, then lit one of his cigars.

"Put that damned thing out," I said.

He seemed surprised that I spoke to him but wasn't about to douse it on my order, so he kept puffing. I slowly got to my feet so as not to startle Lebredo. My head was still bad, but not unbearable. I went to Morelli, yanked the cigar from his mouth and crushed it.

"That is really a disgusting habit you got."

He hit me in the face with his fist, this time I didn't fake being hurt by the blow. It jarred my head a little, but for him it was like trying to punch out a tree. He yelped and clutched his hand. I grabbed the scruff of his neck and tossed him across the room. He smashed against the wall, sank to the floor, and didn't move. I went to the window seat and dropped onto it, tired. Lebredo and Gordy hadn't budged, which was fine with me.

"All right, let's go get your stinking list and clear this up."

"Where is it?" asked Lebredo.

"I hid it in the big library on Michigan Avenue, up on one of the shelves. I'd have to show you where."

Gordy shook his head. "He gave us that kind of story before."

"You weren't pointing a gun at my friend's head then."

"The library's closed now," said Lebredo.

"I have a way to get in. Let's go get it if it's still there."

"It had better be."

Morelli groaned and rolled over. That decided Lebredo, he didn't want to stick around for any debates. He took Gordy's gun in one hand, leaving Gordy free to find some rope. They had Escott stand and his hands were tied behind him and a gag was forced into his mouth.

"Gordy . . ." It was Morelli, looking groggy. "For Chrissake, kill Lebredo."

Gordy paused, not turning to look at him. "I can't, Slick, you know I can't."

Morelli got unsteadily to his feet, leaning on the table.

"I'm not going to forget you said that, Slick," Lebredo told him. "Gordy knows better than to cross me. He knows what defenses I have arranged if anything happens to me, and so do you."

"Damn you . . . Goddamn you—" There was a soft click and Morelli threw his knife. It was the last thing he said and did. Lebredo ducked and fired twice. Morelli twitched back from the impact and lay still. He stared at us and we stared at him. Lebredo gave the gun back to Gordy and we all filed out.

Lebredo either had control of Morelli's crew or replaced them with his own men; either way they got a rowboat ready for us without questions on the gunplay below. Gordy and Escott got in it first, along with a man to handle the oars. They reached the pier and their figures left the boat and slowly climbed the steps. They waited for us just outside the cone of light from the streetlamp. The boat returned and I got in, clutching the sides and trying not to think about the black water all around and the crossbow behind me. It took forever to row to the pier. My presence made the passage difficult for the oarsman. He was puffing and covered with sweat from the effort when we finally got there. I thankfully climbed up the steps. All I wanted was plenty of land between me and the water.

Morelli's big car was waiting for us on the road. Escott and Gordy got in the front seat, Lebredo in the back. They put me behind the wheel and the first thing I felt was the crossbow brushing my neck. I could have whipped around and grabbed it, but that would have left Escott with a stomach full of lead and a convenient lake to sink him in. Lebredo, poker player that he was, held all the cards. I started the car, worked the gears as smoothly as I could, and drove to the big library.

As directed, I parked on an empty side street in between the glow of the two streetlights. Lebredo told me to get out. I got out.

"No tricks, no funny stuff. You get in and come straight back here and I'll tell you where your trunkful of earth is."

"You took it?"

"Ask your friend."

Escott nodded in confirmation, his shoulders drooping. He was feeling responsible for the mess and could do nothing to make things right again.

Lebredo went on. "You wouldn't have had it if you didn't need it. I put it in a very safe place, just in case Escott wasn't enough of a lever."

A lot of things to call him came to mind as I glared at his impassive face. I might have been able to take him out, but was in a tactically poor position to take care of Gordy as well, and he was looking nervous.

I pushed away from the car and walked around to the front of the library. It was well after two, but there were still a few lonely cars cruising up and down the street on their own business. A block away a beat cop rattled doorknobs, but I couldn't ask him for help. Explanations would take too long and Gordy could cut him down easily enough if Lebredo told him to. The cop might even be one of his blackmailing victims, Benny O'Hara had made that much clear. For the moment I was stuck.

I went inside and re-formed, climbing the stairs quietly to the right floor and keeping a look out for a night watchman. I was still dressed in what was left of my haunting clothes, odds were the guy would either shoot or have a heart attack at the sight of me.

It was a big place; my steps echoed loud in my ears, the quality of sound giving me the creeps. I found the right section and went to the very back to the correct shelf. Raising a hand I felt along the top, but my fingers scrabbled over smooth bare surface. Nothing was there.

Partially dematerialized I let myself float up. The shelf was clean. Of all the lousy times to dust the joint . . .

I forgot to concentrate, went solid, and dropped to the floor with a jolt.

Lebredo would never buy it. Escott was a goner. I fumed and cursed and accomplished little in the way of coherent thought, wanting to tear the place apart, especially the jerk who had been cleaning. The papers could have gotten anywhere after all this time, most likely they were long lost to the garbage.

I sulked past the main desk. The wastebaskets were empty. Just for the hell of it, I rooted around. Some of the drawers were locked, but after seeing the handles were strong enough, I pulled them open anyway and discovered the lost-and-found box.

Envelopes, magazines, a purse, eyeglasses, and a sheaf of loose papers. The two sheets I wanted were mixed in with them. If I'd been breathing I'd have sighed with relief.

*   *   *

Lebredo's flat eyes took on a kind of gleam as he watched me return and get back in the car. Escott gave me a questioning look, I nodded, hoping Lebredo would keep his word and knowing that that was a long shot at best. Feeling naked, I turned my back on him and watched him in the mirror.

"Hand them over."

He took them and leaned back to examine them in the dim light. Escott's eyes were closed and the air hissed softly from his compressed nostrils. He wanted me to do something, but I was stuck until the situation changed. I was hoping Lebredo would not make his final move in the car.

"Very good," he said, folding the list into his pocket with one hand. "Now you will drive where I tell you."

This was it, the kind of one-way ride that Chicago had made famous, only I was the chauffeur.

"You got your stuff, let him go."

"No." A simple, unarguable refusal. "Start the car and drive. I can kill you both now or later, I think even you would prefer a little more time."

His undisguised disgust for me was reciprocated, but I did start the car. Teeth and gears grinding in frustration, I followed his directions. The route was familiar. Escott and I exchanged puzzled looks as I completed the last order and turned the car into the driveway that led to Frank Paco's big house.

I braked next to the front door. Gordy got out and pulled Escott with him. Lebredo heaved his way from the back and held the crossbow on me as I emerged. The place was dark and quiet except for the sound of crickets and our shoes crunching on the white gravel.

"Is my trunk here?"

"Open the door."

It was unlocked, the others followed me into a marble-lined entry hall. The air still had a sharp, smoky tang to it and the ceiling showed signs of discoloration from soot. The electricity had been fixed. Lebredo hit the lights. I blinked in the sudden brightness. He wasted no time, planting his broad feet carefully and taking aim.

I tried to buy more time. "Why here?"

"Why not? Paco's men found you here the night of the fire. They've been squealing that often enough to save their skins from the arson charge, so the police know it, too. You've been connected with Paco and Morelli, the police will jump to the easy and obvious conclusion that Paco's men killed you out of revenge."

"In an all-too-obvious location, don't you think?"

"A thin case for the district attorney's office, but a suggestion or two from me and the investigation will go no further."

"They're on your list, too?"

"A few key people."

"You don't ask them for money, do you? You don't really need it; it's being able to tell people what to do, to make them sweat."

"No doubt."

"But you don't have to do this. You must know I can be very useful to you."

"But the only way I have of controlling you is with Escott and possibly Miss Smythe, and such an arrangement would be complicated and clumsy. If I can't have complete control over someone, I don't bother; my present arrangement is satisfactory. It's much simpler to kill you, you're too much of a threat to me and everyone else."

"I can't see you doing this for the sake of saving humanity from my kind."

"That's right, I'm doing it for myself." He pulled the trigger.

I wasn't over running water this time, the second his finger tightened past the halfway point I vanished. The wooden bolt cut through the space where I'd been and imbedded in the wall beyond. At the same time a gun went off.

Escott.

I hurtled past Lebredo, materialized in front of Gordy, and grabbed the gun from him. He offered no resistance even when I shoved him hard into Lebredo. Both men staggered and Lebredo's hard-to-balance body went down.

I expected to see Escott dead or wounded because of my delay and Gordy's speed, but he was standing, white faced, looking out the open front door. Gordy did, too, then glanced down at the grunting man on the marble.

"Hey—somebody got Lucky."

I truly believe he never meant it as a joke, but outside someone laughed. Bobbi walked stiffly into the room, both her small hands held together clutching a gun. Her lips were knife thin, her face hard with hate. We all stepped away from her, except for Lebredo, who was gaping and glaring in sheer disbelief. He'd forgotten to take his own advice about women.

Gordy made a helpless gesture. "Bobbi, why'dya do that for? You know what'll happen to me?"

"I know how to take care of it," she finally said. She was having trouble talking. Her breath was uneven as she tried to hold back the tears.

Escott made an impatient noise. I pulled the gag out. It took a moment for him to work the saliva into his mouth to talk. I unknotted the ropes on his wrists. He thanked me and went to check Lebredo.

"*Keep away from him!*" Bobbi's voice went up to a near-shriek. Escott stepped hastily back and looked at me.

"Bobbi . . ." I said.

"I heard him in the car. I heard him telling Gordy what they were going to do with you and how they were going to get rid of Slick's body."

Lebredo twisted himself upright with some difficulty. "Gordy, take the gun from her. You know what will happen to you if I die."

"Oh, do be quiet," Escott said irritably. He had the right idea. The more Lebredo opened his mouth, the worse he made things for himself.

"Gordy—"

Bobby made a short, sharp noise, like she wanted to call him a name but couldn't think of one bad enough. Instead, she pulled the trigger. Lebredo yelled and grabbed his shoulder.

"For Godsake, Gordy!"

She fired again, clipping him in the side. Her eyes squinted slightly as some of the gun smoke drifted into her face.

Lebredo bared his short, blunt teeth. "You dirty little whore, I'll make sure you—"

She gave out a strangled half-scream of rage and fired again, hitting him square in the face. He flopped back spread-eagled, his big stomach jiggling a little, then going still.

No one moved for quite a while. Bobbi's face took on more normal lines. She seemed smaller in some way. Without looking at us, she carefully wiped the gun down with the hem of her black wrap, placed it on the floor, and walked outside.

Gordy chewed the inside of his lower lip and looked worried.

Escott heaved a sigh, then calmly picked up his crossbow and clucked over some scratches on the stock. He went through Lebredo's pockets, fastidiously avoiding the silent red explosions of the gunshot wounds, and pulled out the list, offering it to me.

I shook my head. "You keep it, I don't even want to see the damn thing." I gave him Gordy's gun and went outside.

Bobbi was leaning back against the car, her arms crossed with one heel resting on the running board. Her hair was a tangled, damp mess and her makeup had been smeared by a good cry. She was just beautiful.

I was hesitant to approach her, but she looked up and smiled wanly.

"I was afraid I'd be too late, I thought he'd gotten you."

"How did you get here?"

"The minute I was out of the cabin I rolled my shoes up in this robe and went overboard. It's not a long swim to the pier, and a person swims better naked." Feeling modest now, she pulled the wrapper more tightly around her shoulders. "I knew he'd use the car sometime, so I hid in the trunk."

"Are you all right?"

She nodded. "Now I am. I didn't think I could do anything . . . but when I heard him talking—it doesn't seem like I did it now, it's like it happened to someone else."

"He made it easy."

"I wanted to help you and to get back for Slick. He was a roughhouse, but sometimes he was good to me. I guess it's not just bodies after all."

"Where'd the gun come from?"

"It's Slick's. He always kept a spare in the glove compartment. The cops will think he did it." She looked at the open door of the house.

"He couldn't do it and be dead on the yacht."

"He can if we get Gordy to help."

"Gordy? But—"

"Lebredo's got some stuff on him, that's why Gordy had to play the stooge. I figure it's with his lawyer. You can imagine what kind of lawyer Lebredo had. We just offer him more money and buy it from him."

"And if he doesn't sell?"

"Then you can burgle the place. From what I heard you've got a real talent for it."

"You don't mind what I am?"

"I don't care about that. You are what you are. You don't judge me, I don't judge you. But could you tell me how you got this way?"

"Because of a woman."

She shook her head and laughed a little. "I guess we're starting even. I'm the way I am because of a man." She went tiptoe and kissed me. "Come on, let's get this mess out of the way. I'm tired."

With Bobbi's persuasion, we called a truce with Gordy. He drove us back to the yacht while she explained what she could do about Lebredo's lawyer. All Gordy had to do was transport Morelli's body to Paco's house so it'd look like they shot each other. I guess in a remote way they had.

"With any luck," she said, "no one's going to know they're dead for a couple of days at least, and by that time we'll have found your stuff."

Gordy nodded agreeably, he trusted her. He set the brakes and started out of the car, and I grabbed his shoulder.

"Where's my trunk?"

"Trunk?" He winced. I eased my grip.

"Lebredo took it," said Escott. "Where it is?"

"But he didn't, said it was too much trouble. He told me to go along with him on that. He just let it drop to keep you both in line."

I shook my head. "A bluff."

Gordy shrugged. "Poker was his game." We all got out and watched him walk down the pier to the rowboat. He started talking to the oarsman, telling him about the change of situation.

"I hope he remembers to leave his gun with Lebredo so the bullets match up," I said.

"He might also wish to clean the magazine and the unspent bullets left in it of any prints as well," Escott suggested.

"I'll make sure," said Bobbi. "We may need the car. Will you be able to get home all right?"

"Yeah, I'll call you tomorrow night. Promise."

She kissed me again and went to join Gordy.

"What a very remarkable girl," Escott commented as we walked slowly away, headed for my car that I'd parked near the club.

"I think so."

"You know this makes us all accessories after the fact?"

"Yeah, but do you think she should go to jail?"

"Not for a single hour." He looked like he wanted to say more, but he was tired and it was a long walk for him. He eased into the passenger seat with a grateful sigh, then pulled out the list and squinted at the figure-covered pages.

"Benny said something about substitution." I started the motor.

"Then it shouldn't be too difficult to solve." He nodded at the eastern sky. "You'll have to hurry, the dawn does not wait."

"*I* should be the one to say things like that."

"Yes, but you're not as melodramatic as I am."

"That's a shame. Considering what I've become, I really ought to go in for it."

His eyebrows twitched. "You're not seriously thinking of acquiring a black opera cape?"

I chuckled. "Don't be ridiculous. It's the wrong season and they cost too much anyway."

He looked relieved.

LIFEBLOOD

1

Chicago, September 1936

"BE a sport," I said to the bartender, not quite meeting his eye, "I'm nursin' a broken heart."

"Yeah, yeah," he replied, and continued polishing a glass with a gray rag.

"No foolin', I got the money." And I fumbled five singles from my shirt pocket and let them flutter onto the damp black wood of the bar. "Come on, that's worth a bottle, ain't it? I won't make no trouble."

"You can make book on it."

He had a right to be confident. We were nearly the same height, but I'm on the lean side and he was built like a steam shovel and just as solid. He thought he could take care of me.

He stopped polishing the glass and put it down next to the bills. I smiled and tried to look friendly, which was a hell of an act under the circumstances. This was one of those cheaper-than-two-bit dives where you take your life in your hands just by going to the men's room. From the smell of things, the facilities were located just outside the front door against the wall of the building, gentlemen on the left, ladies . . . I renewed my hopeful smile and rustled the bills temptingly.

He looked at them, then gave me a fishy eye, gauging my apparent drunkenness against the lure of the money. It was a slow night and the money won. His hand made a move for it, but mine was a little faster and covered three of Washington's portraits first.

"Wise guy," he said, and took a bottle of the cheap stuff down from the shelf behind him. Hell, it was all cheap, but that hardly mattered to me, I only wanted an excuse to hang around.

"I've had some, but not that much." I left two bucks on the bar, took the bottle, glass, and remaining money, and tottered to the second booth in line along the wall. With my back to the front door I settled in, using the careful movements of a drunk who wants to show people he isn't. I spent a lot of time counting my three dollars and putting them away before pouring a drink and pretending to imbibe. Ten cents for the whole bottle would have been an overcharge; the stuff smelled like some of the old poison left over from before repeal. I brought the glass to my lips, made a face, and coughed, spilling some of it down my well-stained shirtfront.

While I was busy dabbing at the mess with a dirty handkerchief, a big man in dark gray came in and went straight to the bar. He was in a suit, which was wrong for the neighborhood, and he was in a hurry, which was wrong for the hour. At one in the morning, nobody should be in a hurry. He ordered a whiskey with a beer chaser and took a look around. It didn't take long; except for me, seven booths, and the bartender, the place was empty.

He studied me like a bug. I pretended real hard that I was drunk and simple-minded and hoped he'd buy the act. It helped that I wore rough work clothes that stank of the river and past debauches with the bottle—just another country kid corrupted by the big bad city.

Apparently I was no threat. He knocked back the whiskey and took the beer to the last booth next to the back door and sat on the outside edge, where he could see people coming in from the street. I used the tilted mirror hanging over the bar to watch him. It was an old one with flecks of tarnish like freckles, but his reflection was clear enough. He hunched over the beer and drained it a sip at a time, with long pauses in between. His soft hat was pulled low, but now and then his eyes gleamed when he used the mirror himself. I kept still and enjoyed his slight puzzlement when he couldn't spot my image in the glass.

Another man walked in from the night and hesitantly approached the bar. He was also too well dressed, but was a bit more seedy and timid. He had a tall, thin body with a beaky nose that supported some black-rimmed pince-nez on a pastel blue velvet ribbon. He wore a cheap blue suit, the cuffs a little too short and the pants a little too tight. His ankles stuck out, revealing black silk socks peeking over the tops of black shoes with toes that had been chiseled to a lethal point. He affected a black cane with a silver handle, which would buy him eternity in this neighborhood if he waved it around too much.

He tried ordering a sherry and got a look of contemptuous disbelief instead. He had better luck asking for gin, then made a point of wiping the rim of the glass clean with his printed silk handkerchief before drinking. After taking a sip, he dabbed his lips and smoothed the pencil line under his nose that passed for a moustache.

He looked around, as nervous as a virgin in a frat house. He noted me and the man in the back booth, and when neither of us leaped out to cut his throat, he relaxed a little. He checked the clock behind the bar, comparing its time to a silver watch attached to his vest and frowned.

The bartender moved away, no doubt driven off by the scent of dying lilies that the newcomer had doused over himself. A cloud of it hit me in the face like exhaust from a truck, and I gave up breathing for a while.

He looked at the watch again and then at the door. No one came in. He removed his hat, placing it gently on the bar, as though it might offend someone. From a low widow's peak to the curl-clustered nape, his dark hair had been carefully dressed with a series of waves that were too regular to be natural. He removed his gloves, plucking delicately at the fingertips, then absently patted his hair down.

The bartender caught the eyes of the man in the booth and shrugged with raised brows and a superior smile as though to say he couldn't help who walked through the door as long as they paid. The man in the booth hunched closer to his beer and watched the mirror.

Two minutes later a lady walked in, probably the first one to ever cross the threshold. She was small, not much over five feet, wearing emerald green with a matching hat and a heavy dark veil that covered her face down to her hard, red lips. She carried a big green bag trimmed with beads that twinkled in the light. Her green heels made quite a noise as she crossed the wood floor to the tall man at the bar. He straightened a little, because polite men do things like that when a lady comes up to them, and he did look polite.

She glanced around warily, her gaze resting on me a moment. She must have been pretty enough to be noticed even by a drunk like me; at least she had a trim figure and good legs. I gave her an encouraging, if bleary leer and raised my glass hopefully. After that she ignored me and tilted her chin expectantly at the tall man.

He frowned, worried, but gathered up his hat, cane, gloves, and drink and followed her to the second-to-last booth at the end. She sat with her back to me and the man slid in opposite her with his back to the big man in gray, who was now pressed tight against the wall. She seemed not to have noticed him.

The gin placed his cane across the table, the curved handle hanging over the outside edge. His hat went next to it and the gloves were tucked into a pocket. I could tell he was nervous again from the way he fussed with things. He quietly asked the woman if she cared to have a drink. She shook her head. He repeated the gesture to the bartender, who then moved down to my end and picked up another glass to polish. He was watching me, but I was in a slack-jawed dream, staring into space, at least at the space occupied by the mirror behind him.

The man in gray leaned to the outside and craned his neck. He could see the bartender and was now worried that he couldn't see me as well, but it was too late to investigate the problem without calling attention to himself.

The woman stared at her companion, her breath gently ruffling the veil. Her voice was pitched low, but even at that distance I had no trouble hearing the conversation.

"Do you have it?"

The man cocked his head to one side, favoring her with the stronger lens of the pince-nez. "I might ask you the same question." His voice was flat and breathy, as though he were afraid the let the words out.

She didn't like him or his answer, but eventually lifted the purse from her lap to the table. With her left hand she pulled out a slim leather case and opened it for his inspection. It was no larger than a pack of cigarettes, and she held it ready to pull back if he grabbed it. He peered at the contents a moment, then drew a jeweler's loupe from his pocket.

"May I?" He extended a manicured hand. She hesitated. "I have to verify that it is genuine, Miss . . . er . . . Green. Mr. Swafford was very clear on that point."

She put the case on the table, her right hand lingering inside the big purse. "Just as long as you know that this is genuine," she told him, and turned the bag to let him see inside.

He stiffened, his eyes frozen on her hidden hand. He licked his lower lip. "V-very well." Slowly he picked up the leather case, removing the pince-nez and screwing the loupe into one eye. He examined what was in the case for ten seconds and reversed the motions, replacing it back onto the scarred tabletop.

"Well?" she said.

"It is genuine." He settled the pince-nez back on his nose.

"I knew that, let's get on with it."

"Y-yes, certainly." From his coat pocket he produced an envelope and gave it to her. She opened it and examined the contents in turn, pulling out one of the hundred-dollar bills from the center. A second later she looked up and grabbed the leather case.

"You can tell Swafford it's in the fire," she said in a voice like ground glass.

His eyes darted unhappily from the empty spot on the table to her veil. "But why?"

"These bills are marked. If there's cops outside you're a corpse."

"No, please, I didn't know about this, please wait!"

She didn't look like she was ready to move, but the man was unnerved. Behind him the big guy had shifted a hand to the inside of his coat, which explained why she hadn't noticed him; there'd been no need to notice her partner.

"I-I don't understand this. Mr. Swafford entrusted me to verify the stamp and to pay you—nothing more. I assure you that I had no idea—"

"I said it's in the fire."

"But wait, please, you have no idea how valuable it is—"

"Five grand. I only asked for half."

"I can help you. I know other collectors, ones who would ask no questions. They'd be glad to pay you its full worth. If I had the money, I'd buy it myself."

She took in his cheap clothes, her mouth becoming small and thin. "I'm sure you would." Her hand shot up and knocked the pince-nez from his nose, and his head snapped back a fraction too late to avoid it. They hung from the velvet ribbon, swinging free and hitting the table edge with a soft tick.

In turn his gray eyes hardened and his cowering posture altered and straightened. "We may still come to an equitable arrangement, Miss Green." His breathy manner of speech had been replaced by a precise English accent, and the prissy mannerisms dropped from him like sour milk.

"Like hell we will, Escott. Stand up and follow Sled out the back door."

Escott glanced up as the big shadow of the man in gray loomed over him. "I meant what I—"

"Shut up or you get it now."

He shot her a glum look and stood. He put on his hat and reached for the cane, but Sled grabbed it first, grinning at Escott's discomfiture. Sled opened the back door and started through a short, dark passage that served as storage space and led to the rear alley. The bartender watched me and pretended not to notice his other customers.

I gave up my drunk act and vanished into thin air. Maybe he could pretend not to notice that, either.

Escott moved slowly through the passage after Sled. The woman was behind him, presumably with her hand still on the gun in her purse. For the moment I was only aware of their bodies and general positions. The woman shivered as I passed her, the way they say you do when someone walks over your grave. Escott paused when I brushed past him and had to be urged on; it was his way of letting me know he was conscious of my presence.

Sled was out the back door now, waiting as Escott emerged with the woman. I didn't know if Sled had his gun ready yet, but hers was, so she'd have to be dealt with first.

I melted back into reality and solidified. From her point of view I just came out of nowhere, which was essentially correct. I slapped the gun from her grip, put a hand over her mouth, another around her waist, then half lifted her away into the dark. She made a nasal squeal of outrage, her heels flailing against my shins.

Sled's attention cut from Escott to her, and the gun jumped from the shoulder holster to his hand like magic. Escott grabbed it, forcing it down, and used his body to ram Sled against the brick wall of the dive. He was stronger than his thin frame promised, and the bricks did nothing for Sled's looks or disposition. He hit Escott with the cane, but it was at the wrong angle and he couldn't put his full strength in it. There was a meaty thump and gasp as Escott slammed the man's gun hand hard into the bricks. The gun dropped. The cane came down again. Escott took the blow against his side and at the same time led with a right that went halfway to Sled's backbone.

While they danced around, I tore the purse from the woman. Holding on to her was like trying to give a bath to an alley cat. I pushed her away from the melee, hoping she would have the sense to run. We wanted the stamp, not her. She was agile, though; one second she was getting her balance, the next she was making an unladylike tackle for Sled's gun.

She got it.

Her index finger slotted neatly over the trigger on the first try and she rolled and brought it up like an expert, firing point blank at me as I lunged. The yellow flash filled my whole world. I didn't hear the thing go off, maybe at that range it was too loud to hear. I felt the wrenching impact as the slug struck over my left eye and sent me on a slow, breathless tumble into white-hot agony.

Its duration was mercifully brief. I was writhing and solid one instant and weightless and floating the next. The shock and pain had knocked me incorporeal, temporarily releasing me from the burden of having a body full of outraged nerve endings. I wanted to stay in that non-place, but Escott's voice, distorted as though through layers of cotton, was dragging me back. He shouted my name once, and then the gun went off again.

I reappeared in time to see the smoke flaring away from its muzzle. Sled launched himself away from Escott, grabbed the protesting woman on the run, and dragged her off the battlefield.

Escott was leaning against the wall and had made no move to stop them. He was doubled over, struggling to breathe, with his arms curled tight around his stomach. His pale face stood out from the shadows like a funhouse ghost. Even as I found my feet he lost his and sank to the ground.

I was kneeling by him in a second, heart in my throat. "Charles?" My voice was all funny, as though it were borrowed from some stranger.

"Minute—" he gasped. He shut his eyes, let his mouth sag, and concentrated on drawing in air. I eased him more comfortably against the wall and tried to check his damage, but he shook his head.

"How bad?" I asked.

He showed a few teeth, but I couldn't tell if it was a grimace or a smile: with him it could go either way. His breathing evened a little and his eyes cracked open. "Where's the stamp?" he whispered.

Stamp? What the hell did that matter? "I'll get an ambulance."

"No need, I'm not hurt."

"You're doing a good imitation of it. Just hold on and—"

One of his hands came up. "Give me a minute and I'll be fine."

"Charles . . ."

The other hand came up. Clean. "I'm only winded."

"What the—"

"My bulletproof vest," he said with an air of stating the obvious.

I checked; under the rumpled clothes was a solid-feeling something encasing his torso.

"Unlike you," he continued, "I have no supernatural defense against flying bits of metal and must provide an artificial one."

I was stuck exactly at the halfway point between relief and rage. He wisely chose not to laugh at the expression I must have been wearing.

"I think I shall purchase a more effective vest for the future, though, this one seems a bit too thin for the job. Now, where is the stamp?"

Mutely, I handed over the beaded green bag. I didn't trust myself to say anything yet as it probably would have been too obscene. While he rummaged for the leather case I got up and checked the alley exit, putting some distance between us for a minute. On top of everything else, the son of a bitch didn't need a punch in the chops from a friend who was glad to see him alive.

Sled and the woman were long gone. It seemed like a good idea for us as well; their bartender friend might come out any minute, and we'd had enough excitement for one night.

Escott found and checked the case with its faded smudge of blue paper. "Philately is not a special interest of mine. I fear I am quite unimpressed, even if it is worth five thousand American dollars."

"Yeah, well, let's make tracks before that girl remembers and decides to come back."

He saw the sense of it. "Would you help me up? I fear the bullet caught me near that knife wound, and things are still rather tender there. What rotten bad luck."

"I'd say it was pretty good since it missed your head." I got him to his feet and retrieved his cane.

"Heavens, are *you* all right? I saw you—"

"She was using lead, not wood, so I'm just peachy."

He decided to ignore the sarcasm. I was justifiably annoyed with him and he knew the best thing was to let it run its course.

He leaned on my arm for support as we gingerly picked our way out of the alley. Though his was pretty fair, he didn't have my night vision and relied on me to keep him afoot. We found his big Nash a block away. He insisted he could drive, so I shoveled him behind the wheel and took my place on the passenger side with a sigh.

"What went wrong back there?" I asked.

"She recognized me, for one thing, but that's all right because I recognized her."

"Okay, I'm holding my breath."

He spared me a sideways look, started the car, and pulled into the street. "I can believe that. She still might have been willing to deal, but the whole business went wrong because of Swafford's marked money. I should have checked it earlier."

"You really think she would have chanced closing the deal after spotting you?"

"It was a possibility. Even knowing me, she might have taken the money and given you the chance to follow, but then the best-laid plans and all that. Swafford has his precious stamp and cash, but he's going to hear a few words from me about it." He suddenly swung the car in a wide turn. "I think we shall visit him now while I'm still angry."

He didn't look angry—a touch gleeful, but not angry.

"It's after one," I pointed out.

"Good, then it is unlikely we will be interrupting any of his other appointments."

He drove to a suburb that had the kind of big houses with hot and cold running servants, precision-cut lawns, and cars that always started in the dead of winter. He picked out a lumpy stone specimen, sailed through the decorative iron gates, parked, and motioned me to follow. Some lights were showing through the downstairs windows, but they were only to discourage burglars and to keep Jeeves from tripping over the Chippendale while answering the front bell in the very early morning.

The bathrobed butler opened the door, decided we were strictly servant's-entrance material, and was about to close it, but Escott got past him and requested to see Mr. Swafford.

"Mr. Swafford has gone to bed," he informed us in chilling tones.

"Then I suggest you roust him or I shall have the unpleasant task of doing it myself."

Both of them had English accents, but Escott's was genuine, and the butler knew when he was outclassed. He sniffed at us, a bad mistake, because Escott still smelled like a stuffy church on Easter Sunday, and retreated upstairs. After a brief wait, Swafford came down under escort and gaped at us.

"Who the hell—"

"You engaged my services to recover your stamp," Escott reminded him.

Swafford squinted, trying to peer through the disguise. "Escott?"

"And my assistant, Mr. Fleming."

"What is all this, Escott?" he demanded in a small, thin voice that didn't suit him.

"We merely came by to return your property and discuss some details on the case."

"Then you have it? Where is it?"

"I see you have a library. Perhaps we shall be more comfortable there." Escott led the way as if it were his own house. Swafford glared at his back and then at me, ineffectually. I just waited until he got tired of it, then followed him into the next room.

He was wide and stocky all the way down to his slippered feet, and even a fancy silk bathrobe had a difficult time making him look society smooth. My guess was he made his money the hard way and was using it now in an attempt to make people forget about the work. His library bore this out, and was done up like something out of a movie, with an eye to impress the audience. There was a Renoir over the fireplace, but its function was to hide the safe and not to express the owner's tastes.

"Where's my stamp?" Swafford asked, planting himself at one end of an acre of desk.

Escott was busy admiring the Renoir. "I rather like this one. What do you think of it, Jack?"

"Nice colors," I said noncommittally, keeping an eye on Swafford. He was awake enough now to know something was wrong and to try dealing with it.

Escott drew out the envelope full of hundreds and tossed it on the desk. Swafford grabbed it up and counted them. While he did this, Escott discovered a gold-plated candelabrum on an overvarnished table and lit all five of its candles. He carried it to the painting.

"Yes, either by diffuse daylight or by candlelight, that was how it was meant to be viewed." He placed the candelabrum on the desk. "I trust it is all there?"

"Yes, now where—"

"Then you may regard this case as closed."

Swafford looked up slowly and tried some hard thinking. "What happened to the stamp?"

"You signed a contract with me for my services, you should have read it. A good contract is designed to protect both parties should one attempt to defraud another. You defrauded me of your trust. Our association is ended."

"What are you talking about? Explain."

Escott gestured at the money. "That should be explanation enough. You had it marked and rather clumsily marked at that. The thief spotted it easily enough, realized I was not the philately expert, and gave me this." He exhibited the new ventilation on his coat and vest. "You should have trusted me; your money and the stamp would have been returned as promised. Now you have only the money. You've forfeited the stamp."

Swafford flushed a deep red that slowly faded to a muddy pink as he thought things over. "All right, what do you want?"

"A telephone call to have the charges against Ruthie Mason dropped."

"What else?"

"First the phone call."

"But it's—"

"I know. Wake up your lawyer, that's what you pay him for, have him set things in motion."

"If I do this, will the stamp be returned? Do you have it?"

Escott dropped the case on the desk. It thumped once against the thick blotter before Swafford grabbed and opened it.

"Empty!" He froze. Escott held up a slip of paper folded into quarters. He waved it dangerously close to one of the candles.

"For God's sake be careful. That's worth five thousand—"

"Get on with the call," Escott snapped.

Swafford got on with the call. Since he couldn't argue with Escott he took it out on the lawyer, and before five minutes were gone another Chicago citizen had had his night's sleep broken up. Knowing how fast some cops liked to work, it was a good bet that the lawyer would be tied up until well after breakfast. For that he would certainly gift Swafford with a whopping fee. Escott knew the art of a properly administered low blow. While Swafford was on the phone, Escott turned up some paper and a carbon from the desk and wrote out several lines.

Swafford hung up. "There, I've done it. Ruthie will be out in the morning."

"I doubt she'll wish to continue her employment here. Should that be the case, she will need references, and good ones."

"I'll have my wife do that—it's her job. The girl will have no trouble finding work."

"I also suggest a decent monetary gift to counterbalance her precipitant arrest."

"All right, you have my word . . . and there's your witness." He nodded confidently at me.

"Excellent. Now there is only the matter of my fee—"

"But you've been paid!"

"A retainer only. Under the terms of the contract I am within my rights to cover my expenses." His thumb emerged from the hole in the vest and wiggled. "Had I not taken precautions, you most certainly would have paid for my funeral, since your interference nearly caused it."

Swafford's face closed in on itself warily. "How much?"

He indicated the twenty-five hundred-dollar bills lying on the blotter. "I think that should cover it, but this time they're to be unmarked."

"But that's extortion," he grumbled.

"Earlier tonight you seemed eager enough to hand it over for the return of the stamp."

"At least then I might have gotten the stamp back."

"You may have that chance now; it depends upon how quickly you can open your safe. Our thief threatened to burn this when the marked bills were found; it occurs to me to be a very good idea. What a lot of fuss over a bit of blue paper the size of my thumbnail. Would the world stop spinning if I should commit it to the flames, I wonder?"

Before he could wave it near the candles again, Swafford had the Renoir swung to one side and was spinning the combination with nervous fingers. There was plenty more in the safe than twenty-five hundred, and he must have been worried we were after that as well. He gave me a wall-eyed look, and with good reason—I was still dressed like a hard-nosed punk, and the cheap booze stinking up my dirty shirt added to the image. I shifted my weight forward and tried to look tough. He quickly drew out a bundle of bills and hastily shut the safe.

Escott stood very close to the candles, their light and shadows making his minute smile look evil. "Would you mind counting it, Jack?"

I didn't. It made a tidy little pile: twenty hundreds and ten fifties: "It adds up right," I said, and pocketed it.

"Good. Now you will sign this, Mr. Swafford. It is nothing more than a receipt for my services, with a promise to pay that sum to Ruthie by to-morrow. I'm sure you'll find it as useful for your tax records as I do."

Swafford signed it and threw the pen down. Escott tucked away the original. He considered the folded paper between his two fingers, then suddenly put it into the candle flame. Swafford's eyes peeled wide and he choked, one hand raised as if he were taking an oath. The scrap burned down to nothing and Escott dropped the ashes onto the desk. He looked thoughtful.

"Odd, I had imagined five thousand dollars going up in smoke would look much more impressive."

His former client was beyond speech and looked ready to have a coronary.

"Well, no doubt your insurance can cover it—oh, dear, you mean it is *not* insured? How careless of you to have something so very valuable and portable lying around uninsured. On the other hand there are taxes to pay on these things. But surely as a good citizen you pay your taxes?"

"I'll sue you," he whispered. "I'll have your hide—"

"Next time, Mr. Swafford, I suggest you follow instructions to the letter when they are given to you. It is simply good business practice, especially when not doing so can cost you dearly. I hope this has been a lesson to you. Remember it."

Escott swiftly crossed the room and we let ourselves out into the hall, leaving Swafford frozen in place by the desk. The butler was waiting and locked the front door behind us. Escott paused, counted to five, and went back to use the bell.

The butler was too sleepy to be annoyed. Escott extended his hand and gave him a folded paper identical to the one that had been burned. "I forgot to give this to Mr. Swafford. Please present it to him with my compliments."

He took it without comment and locked the door with a solid and final click.

Escott was still chuckling as we drove away.

"One of these days it'll be one of your own clients bumping you off for that kind of showboating," I said. "That's no way to attract business, either."

He shrugged. "His sort of business I do not need. Swafford nearly got me killed tonight. I thought I'd give him something equally unpleasant in return. For his sort, being deprived of money by his own folly is the worst kind of torture imaginable."

"Okay, he goofed in a big way, but then I nearly got you killed when I got optimistic about her brains and let her go too soon."

"An accident, nothing more. In the dark she could have just as easily shot her partner."

"She also could have run, but didn't. The lady wanted blood, Charles. She tried to kill us both."

"Through no fault of your own," he insisted. "I'll admit to underestimating her professionalism, but I place no blame upon you or your actions tonight. Even if things had gone according to plan, I daresay she might have tried to kill me anyway. Had you not been along, I would certainly be lying in that alley this very minute."

I shook my head. "I'm too dangerous to have around; I'm only an amateur to this gumshoe business—"

" 'Gumshoe'? Really, Jack." He looked pained.

"All right, private agent, then. I'm supposed to be a journalist."

"I don't hold that against you."

I let that one pass.

He tilted the rearview mirror, stretched his upper lip, and peeled the tiny moustache off, rubbing the area with evident relief. "That's better, these things drive me mad. Would you mind opening your window? You may not breathe, but it's still a habit with me."

I cranked it down. "Between your cheap perfume and my cheap booze, it'll take a week to air this buggy out."

"Possibly. I hope it washes off." His nose twitched.

"The suit?"

"My skin. I'm considering the suit might be better off in the furnace."

"Isn't that a little extravagant?"

"You're right, I'll see if I can't have it fumigated and repaired, as this is an amusing persona; it's based on someone I saw once—the best disguises always are." With one eye on the road and the other on the mirror, he carefully removed his wig, lifting first from the base of his neck and bringing it forward.

"But she still saw through it."

"Not right away. She knew my name from Swafford's household, but had never seen me close up and had no reason to make the association. If he hadn't marked the bills . . ."

"So who was she? You got Swafford so upset he forgot to ask."

"Dear me, you're right. She was his wife's new personal maid, the one with the unimpeachable references."

I recalled a photo of the house servants he showed to me earlier tonight when he asked me to help him. The idea was to keep my eyes open should any of them walk into the bar where the exchange had been set up. "That little thing? She's hardly more than a kid."

"Yes, a mere child of twenty-seven, with a demure manner and a youthful complexion. The Swaffords were correct to suspect one of the servants, but I fear their accusations against Ruthie were purely racial in origin. The other girl worked and waited until someone new had been hired onto the staff; Ruthie came along, the stamp was stolen, and she got the blame. The thief's real name is Selma Jenks, and she's done this sort of thing before."

"You got a police blotter for a brain?"

"Just about. Anyway, Ruthie called Shoe Coldfield's sister for help and Shoe called me. Swafford may have hired me to recover the stamp, but I really consider Ruthie to be my true client."

"I wondered how you got the job. Swafford isn't your type."

"Too shady?"

"Too rich."

It was close to two when Escott turned the car into the alley behind his house and eased into the glorified shed that served as a garage. The interior was too narrow to open the car door very wide, and rather than struggle squeezing through, I disappeared and sieved out. I was sitting on the back bumper when Escott finally emerged.

He gave a start and caught himself with a sigh. "Damn, but that's—"

"I know—unnerving. Sorry."

"Quite all right. Let's go inside, I'm in need of something liquid and soothing."

"Like a bath?"

"Yes, that, too."

He cursed sedately as he struggled with the rusty lock on the back door. It finally gave way and we walked into his large high-ceilinged kitchen. His house was a big, roomy place; a three-storied pre-fire relic that in its better days (or worse) had been a bordello. As his time, money, and health allowed, he was gradually cleaning, painting, and restoring it into a livable home. But the kitchen was not high on his priority list and still retained an air of cobwebby disuse in the corners. Except for replacing the old icebox with a streamlined new refrigerator that crouched and hummed between sagging cabinets, he'd pretty much ignored the room.

In silent and common consent we peeled off our coats and dropped them on the battered oak table that had come with the house. An invisible cloud of booze and dead lilies filled the room and grabbed my throat.

Escott suppressed a cough. "Horrible stuff, that. Should I ever assume that persona again, I shall substitute something less lethal."

"Why use anything at all?"

"Attention to detail is the key to a good disguise."

"I think you poured on too much detail this time. You must have gotten perfume mixed up with cologne."

His brows went up. "There's a difference?"

"A lot, I think."

"What is it, then?"

Now I was stuck. "Uh . . . maybe you'd better ask Bobbi. She knows more about that kind of thing. All I know is there's a difference; one's stronger and you need less, or something like that."

"Hem," he said neutrally. "I know better than to offer you liquid refreshment. Do you mind if I indulge?"

"Go ahead. Just hold a glass under my shirt and I'll squeeze some out for you."

He declined with a polite but decisive head shake and smile, and went into the dining room. There was no dining table yet, just a stack of cardboard boxes that hadn't been unpacked and a large glass-fronted cabinet on one wall holding a modest collection of bottles.

"Think I'll go and change. It's getting late," I said.

"You're welcome to use the bathtub if you like. The water heater is almost reliable now."

"Thanks." I left him pouring out a gin and tonic and trotted upstairs. I'd scrub my face and hands off, but total immersion in a tub of possibly cold water was an experience I could do without.

My clothes were in a narrow bedroom next to the bath. The bed was long gone, leaving some holes in the floor where it had been bolted down and some rub marks from the headboard on the once florid wallpaper. There was no closet; my stuff was draped over a spindly wooden chair and more unpacked boxes.

Now that I was alone and changing back into familiar things, I felt a delayed reaction from the shooting tonight. I could avoid death in that manner, he couldn't. It didn't seem to disturb him, but I'd been thoroughly frightened, and I was far less vulnerable. If Escott hadn't been wearing that vest . . . Maybe he could treat the whole business casually, but not me. He hadn't seen the gun swinging up in his face and the muzzle flash searing his eyes. I touched the spot where the lead slug had passed through; all trace of pain was gone, the flesh and bone were smooth and unmarked.

My hand was trembling as it came away: half in wonder of what I'd survived and half in fear of what I'd become. A small mirror still clung to one wall, reflecting only the empty room, and nothing more. I shivered the length of my spine, turned away from it, and finished dressing.

Respectable again, I joined Escott in his downstairs parlor, where he'd stretched out on the sofa. He looked tired.

"This should cheer you up." I put the money on a low table next to his glass.

"What?" He turned his head just enough to see. "Oh, I'd forgotten."

I dropped into a leather armchair. "How can you forget twenty-five hundred bucks?"

"Twelve hundred fifty. Half of it's yours."

"Come on, Charles, I didn't do anything except get in the way."

A faint smile twitched in one corner of his mouth. "As you insist. But whatever tonight's outcome would or would not have been, you are still entitled to something for your services to the Escott Agency. I'd give you all of it, but thought you wouldn't accept it."

"Don't be so certain."

"I'll fill out some kind of receipt later."

"For tax purposes?"

"Of course. I have always been impressed by the manner in which the government finally managed to take care of Capone."

"What's that have to do with me?"

"With both of us, my dear fellow. Undeclared income and income without employment are things that are certain to be noticed sooner or later. A person with your particular condition should not call attention to himself."

"Okay, I see what you mean. What about that bundle we picked up from the Paco gang?"

"I said then we should consider it the spoils of war, but I plan to declare my half. I wonder if there is some sort of penalty in padding one's records in favor of the government?"

"In a bureaucracy do you think they'd notice? And it's gotten a lot bigger and more complicated since Roosevelt got in."

"I see, yes, what a ridiculous question. Still, I suppose the best thing is to store the lot in a mattress and declare it a little at a time over the years. Ah, well, here's to crime." He drained off his glass and grimaced.

"You all right?"

"Probably. I shall be stiff for a few days. Bad coincidence getting hit in the same spot."

"Let's have a look."

He'd already taken off his suit vest. Now he shucked the shirt and I helped him ease out of the bulletproof vest underneath. On his left side just below the line of his ribs was a thin red scar about four inches long where a thug's knife had cut him up not so long ago. He probed the area gently with his long fingers and winced a little.

"There, it caught me a bit lower than I thought. Nothing more than a bad bruise and some shock. Quite lucky, considering how close the gun was."

"Charles, about all you had going for you tonight was luck. If her aim had been a little better or worse she could have taken your head off."

"So you mentioned earlier."

"I'm gonna mention it again. You scared the shit out of me tonight."

"I truly appreciate your concern, but after all, nothing really happened, and I do intend to be more careful in the future."

"You mean that?"

"Certainly. This was an isolated incident. Before I met you the most violent encounter I'd ever experienced was a director with a vile temper who tried to kill me with his blocking of a stage fight."

I was verging on exasperation, but too curious to pass up the opening. He rarely spoke about his past. "What happened?"

"It was the difference between his opinion and my facts. The man had concocted some ridiculous fencing movement and I tried to point out something safer and more natural for the circumstance. Since I was only a very junior member of the company at the time, he got his way. On dress-rehearsal night I slipped in my felt costume shoes, fell into the orchestra pit, and broke the poor violinist's collarbone and nearly my own neck when I landed on him. I was never able to convince that director I hadn't done it on purpose just for spite."

I pulled my mouth shut to control the laugh. "Now you're changing the subject—"

"But I have not. My point was that tonight was an unfortunate set of circumstances, nothing more. In all fairness, how could the director or I have known that the stage floor had just been waxed? How could you have known the young lady was so murderously and athletically inclined? Believe me, if any future jobs like this should come my way, there is no one else I would rather have to back me up. I know you have doubts now, but you've a quick, observant eye and with a little training . . ."

I shot him a suspicious look. "What have you got planned? A little extra paint on the office door saying Escott and Fleming, Private Agents?"

"That would be interesting, but not possible. It takes several years of training to qualify for a license, and then you have to show up for the exam—in daylight. No, in practical terms that's quite out of the question for you."

"Then what is in the question?"

"I'm only proposing the odd job now and then, like tonight. I know you really consider this as just doing me a favor, but there's no reason why you can't make something for yourself out of it." He looked at the money and then at me.

"You trying to bribe me? Because it's working."

The faint smile appeared again in the same corner. "I had hoped you would consider it seriously. Of course one never knows what the future may bring; not all of my clients are as well off as Mr. Swafford, nor as easily bullied, but there should be enough coming in to keep gas in your car and so forth."

I put my half of the cash in my wallet. "This should buy a lot of so forth."

He smiled again at this obvious acceptance of his offer, briefly, this time in both corners.

2

It was nearly three when I left Escott's, but Bobbi would be awake. She may have left her job and her room at the Nightcrawler Club, but she still kept club hours. Her new home was a suite in a respectable hotel that provided maid service, meals, and a bribable house detective—everything a girl could want.

I crossed the marble-floored lobby, waving at the night clerk, who knew me by sight. The kid in the elevator was sound asleep on his stool, so I charitably took the stairs up to the fourth floor. Her rooms were to the left of the stairs, taking up a corner block of windows that fronted the building. Light was showing under her door. I knocked softly, heard her bare feet patter close, and a single hazel eye peered through the peephole. I winked back and the door opened.

"Hello, stranger, I was beginning to think you'd never show up." She pulled me inside and locked out the rest of the world.

"So you're taking me for granted, huh?"

"Uh-huh, just like the laundry."

"You dress up like that for the laundry?"

"This is dressing down; something informal, yet intimate." She was wearing some baby-blue satin lounging pajamas that made it difficult for me to think straight. When she walked, her legs made a pleasant susurrus sound. Slightly hypnotized by the rhythm, I followed her into the living room and we curled up on the sofa. At least she curled—I stretched my legs out and hooked an arm around her shoulder.

"What kept you so long?" she asked.

"Charles needed some help tonight."

"What did he do, drag you backward through a distillery?" She sniffed my hair critically.

"Just about. Thought I'd lost the atmosphere of the place when I'd changed."

"Into what?"

"What do you mean 'into what'?"

"A bat or a wolf—"

"What are you talking about?"

She pulled a thick book from under a pillow and tapped the lurid red letters of the title with one nail. "It says in here . . ."

Then I had to laugh and shake my head. "Bobbi, you nut, you can't be taking that seriously."

"Well, it's the only book I knew of about vampires."

"There are lots of others, but they're not necessarily right, either. Why are you looking at that stuff? You've already got the real article."

"I wanted to know more. According to this, you'll be turning me into one any time now." She said it like a joke, but I could see a real concern underneath. She waited for my reaction.

I took the book and flipped through until I found the right page. "There, read that part and try to ignore the scary language. Until we do this there is no chance of you ever turning into a vampire." I waited, listening to her soft breathing as she read, my arm close around her shoulders. She finally let the book droop.

"*That* scene wasn't in the movie."

"Too erotic."

"Erotic?" She sounded doubtful.

"Don't let the description put you off until you've tried it."

She looked speculative. "You want to do that?"

"Not unless you want to. It's your decision."

"What would happen?"

"One hell of a climax for both of us."

"And that's all? Not that there's anything wrong with a great climax," she quickly added.

"I'm glad you think so."

"Come on, Jack. What else is it?"

I rubbed absently at that spot over my eye. "Okay, it's got to do with reproduction . . ."

"You mean I could get pregnant?" That possibility alarmed her.

"No, I mean you could get like me. My taking from you is one thing, but if you should take any of my blood, there's a remote chance you could be like me after you died."

"Would it kill me?"

"No, of course not."

"How remote a chance?"

"I don't know. As I understand it, it almost never works because nearly everyone is immune. They'd have to be or there'd be more people like me around."

"Maybe there are and you just haven't noticed them. You don't exactly look like a vampire, you know."

"Not the Hollywood kind, anyway."

"I mean you don't stand out in a crowd."

"Oh, thank you very much."

She swatted my shoulder.

"Okay, okay, I know what you meant."

She settled in again. "This kind of reproduction . . . is that why we don't make love the usual way?"

"Yes," I said shortly.

"Hey, don't clam up on me, I was just asking."

"I know, honey."

I tried to relax and succeeded to some extent. She'd hit a sore spot, but it wasn't an unexpected blow. I wasn't—to put it delicately—fertile in the way that men are usually fertile with women. The pleasure centers and how they operated had drastically shifted. Oddly enough, I did not feel deprived, physically or mentally; I just felt that I *should* feel deprived, or that maybe Bobbi was losing out on things. There was no justification for it, so far our relationship was as mutually satisfying as anyone could wish for.

She snuggled closer under my arm. "If you want to know, I really prefer it your way."

"You mean that?"

She lifted my hand and pressed it against the soft, warm skin of her throat. "When you do it this way, it just goes on and on. . . ."

That was how it felt to me. As a breathing man, I'd had some great experiences, but they were hardly an adequate comparison to what I now enjoyed.

"Sometimes I think I'll go crazy from it," she murmured, kissing my hand.

My lips lightly brushed her temple, the small vein pulsed beneath them. Of their own will, my hands began to undo her buttons. "You sure you like it this way?"

"Yes, and for another good reason: I don't have to worry about getting pregnant."

"Hmmm."

She sat up straight, her top open almost to the waist and her perfect red lips curled into a sleepy, roguish smile. She nodded her head once toward the bedroom. "Come on, let's go get more comfortable."

Bobbi made a contented growl in the back of her throat, turned on her side, and burrowed close with her back to me, our bodies fitting together like two spoons. I draped an arm over her, and if my hand happened to end up cupping her left breast, nobody minded. We were in a lazy post-lovemaking afterglow and life was good.

"It's funny how you can get used to things," she said.

"I'm boring you?"

"I didn't mean it that way, and no, I'm anything but bored with you."

"Thanks for the reassurance. What is it you're used to?"

"I was remembering the time when I first noticed you didn't always breathe. It bothered me and now it doesn't. I just thought it was a funny thing to think of as normal."

"For me it is normal."

"Oh, I know that now."

"What else are you used to?"

"Umm . . . the no-heartbeat thing. But if you live on blood, how does it get through your body?"

"Beats me. Charles is speculating it's some kind of osmosis."

"What's that?"

I'd asked Escott the same question and tried to repeat his answer to her. It must have been garbled—laboratory biology and chemistry had never been my best studies—but she took in enough to understand.

"It sounds like the way a root draws water up into a plant," she suggested.

"Maybe so, just as long as it works."

"What about mirrors? Have you figured out why you don't show up?"

"Nope."

"Let me know when you do, 'cause I'm not used to that, yet."

"If it's any comfort, neither am I."

"You mean you can't even see yourself?"

"Nope."

"Do you know you need a haircut?"

"Hum a few bars."

She groaned. "That stunk."

"It's old enough. Anything else?"

"That's it for now."

"Until you can think of something else to analyze?"

"If you want deep intellect, go to bed with a philosopher."

"Thank you, no."

"I thought you'd say that." She was quiet for a while, resting her head comfortably on my extended arm. I nosed into the platinum silk she had for hair and began kissing the nape of her neck. She squirmed. "You want to go again?"

"It might not be good for you. Your body has to adjust gradually, even to a small blood loss. Too often . . ."

"But you don't take much."

"Neither did those doctors who killed a king from too much bloodletting."

"I heard of that, I think he was English. But this is different and I'm very healthy." She twisted up on one elbow to look at me. The satin sheet slipped down quite a bit.

"Yes . . . I can see that."

She made a face. "I'm serious. I've been eating liver like crazy, and I hate liver."

"I had no idea."

"So do you want to go again?"

"It's very tempting, but better for you if we wait."

She thought about it, decided not to push the issue, and wiggled back into my arms again. "Who taught you all this restraint?"

I pretended it was a rhetorical question and resumed nuzzling her hair. It smelled lightly of roses.

She went on. "I can't help but be curious about her. I won't ask anymore if you don't want me to."

"But you'll still wonder."

"Uh-huh."

"Her name was Maureen." The words dropped out like lead, as always when I talked of her in the past tense.

"I can tell you loved her a lot. It's the way you look when you think about her."

"It's that obvious?"

"Sometimes. You'll be looking at me and then I'm not there for you, and I know you're seeing her instead."

"Sorry."

"It's all right. Are we much alike?"

"Her hair was dark and she was shorter."

"I didn't mean like that."

"She needed love," I said lamely.

"Everyone does."

"She needed it like . . . I don't know. It was all that mattered to her."

"And you loved each other a lot."

"God, yes. But I didn't realize how much until—we were both happy, a long time ago."

"I'm glad you were, that you had something like that. I never did—until now." Her voice was soft, I thought she was drifting off to sleep.

I tried to remember Maureen's face, but it was like recalling a dream. The harder I tried, the farther it slipped away.

"I hope you believe me," she said.

"About what?"

"About liking your style better."

"Thanks. Are you sure you don't miss the old way, though?"

She shrugged. "Not much. It's apples and oranges; I like 'em both when it's done right."

My hands began wandering again. She rolled on her back and we did some serious kissing. Her breath came faster and her heart rate went up.

"I thought you weren't going to take any more from me tonight."

"I'm not, but maybe you'd like some oranges?"

"What?"

I kissed her again, one hand passing over her smooth flank, dipping at the waist and pausing briefly just below her navel.

"Oranges," she murmured. "Handpicked, of course."

Asleep, she looked younger than her twenty-four years. Sleep lent vulnerability and vulnerability brought youth. I watched her protectively, feeling a fierce, quiet joy at the sight of her relaxed features. A little makeup clung to the pale skin, a trace of powder high on one cheek and the faint line of drawn-on brows. Her own had been carefully plucked away to follow the current fashion. I had seen many pretty faces, but few classic beauties, and fewer still with brains and personality. She was beautiful, at least as I perceived it, with the kind of looks that artists sometimes capture, if they have the talent.

Her blond head turned on the pillow, the lips parting slightly then closing. They were light pink now; all the lip rouge had been kissed away quite awhile ago. From previous experience I could guess that if any were left it would be on me. I didn't mind a bit.

It was a hard chore to leave, but necessary—the sunrise was coming and with it my daytime oblivion. I eased out of bed, got dressed, and kissed her forehead in farewell.

Her eyes opened, but she was still nine-tenths asleep. "Are you a dream?"

"Yes."

"Thought so." There was a sigh and she slipped under again.

After being with Bobbi, it was always a rude jolt to come back to my own spartan hotel room. The essentials were there: a bed, rarely used, a chest of drawers, a chair, a bath, even a radio. For $6.50 a week it was luxurious, but not really a home.

Bobbi knew where I hung my hat, but had never been invited over. There was little reason for it since her own place was more comfortable and larger. For one thing, she did not have a three-by-five-foot steamer trunk taking up most of the floor space. More than once the bellhop had asked if I wanted to have it stored in the basement. I tipped well so he was always alert to do me a favor. A basement might be better to avoid sunlight, but was not as safe. During the day I needed a DO NOT DISTURB sign hanging from the doorknob and the door firmly locked against curious eyes. The trunk was locked as well, the key on a chain hanging from my neck. Once, after getting back too late, the sun had caught me out. I'd been unable to sieve inside as usual and suffered a painful and panicky search for the key, an incident I planned never to repeat.

I drew a hot bath, cleaned the remaining booze smell from my hair, and tried to get comfortable on the lumpy bed. The bellhop had left my regular pile of newspapers outside the door. I filled in the remaining time before dawn flipping through them. Nothing in the news held my attention, and that felt odd since it had once been my bread and butter. Times change, people change, and I had certainly changed more than most.

Automatically, my eyes scanned the personal columns, but as ever, there was nothing to see. Five years had gone by without a response.

The papers went into the wastebasket. I thought of Bobbi, and with a sharp twist of guilt, I thought of Maureen.

I remembered the touch of her body, smaller and stronger, with dark hair and light blue eyes. I remembered the long nights spent loving her and our hope that it would last forever. Together we decided to at least try to make it so. I had no guarantee that it would work for me, but the hope was there; it would have to be enough. After taking from me, she tilted her head back, drawing the skin taut, and used her fingernail in a deft movement over the vein in her throat. She pulled me close and I tasted the warmth of what had been my blood, filtered through her body and returned again. Its red heat hit me from the inside out like the rush of air from an open furnace. A shock of fire, a flash of inner light, and then the shimmer of her life filling me . . .

My hands clenched. There was no comfort in remembered passion, it was all gone. Maureen was gone.

But Bobbi was here, vital and loving. I wanted and needed her just as much. It was hardly fair to her to have my mind drifting back to Maureen at awkward moments, nor was it fair to myself.

I found paper and wrote out instructions. It took less than two minutes, and another three passed downstairs as I explained what I wanted to the night clerk. He promised to fix everything. A minute for each year of searching and waiting, and that was how long it took to break off my last hope of contacting her. I felt empty, but no worse than usual. With Bobbi to help I could put the memories away for good. It was time to let the past rest; let it rest or it would continue to tear me up inside.

Let it rest, because God knows I was tired.

"Mr. Fleming?" It was the bellhop's voice, sounding faintly worried. His knuckles rapped on the door. "Mr. Fleming?"

I had no twilight moment of grogginess; I was either awake or totally unconscious. I faded from the interior of the trunk, re-formed outside, and answered the door, pretending to look sleepy.

"Yeah, what is it, Todd?"

"Sorry to wake you, but you got this phone message and the guy said it was urgent. He's been calling all day. You never answered, so we figured you were out." He gave me a slip of paper.

I unfolded it and read Escott's name and the phone number of his small office a few blocks away. He wanted me to call or come over immediately.

"You say he's called earlier?"

"A couple of times since I came on at four. It sounded important and I've been trying—"

"Okay, thanks for bringing it up. Did Gus get around to that stuff like I asked?"

"Yessir, got 'em all, he said to tell you. You still want your usual delivery?"

"Yeah, go ahead with that," I said absently, rereading the brief note. Escott certainly knew better than to try contacting me during the day, so he must be in some kind of trouble. I dressed and shot down to wedge into the lobby phone booth.

He answered on the first ring, sounding perfectly normal.

"Hello, Jack, I've been trying to reach you."

"What's up?"

"Something extremely interesting. Another case, as a matter of fact. I'd like to talk it over with you right away."

"Sure, I'm on my way."

"Have you dined yet?"

"Well . . ."

"We could talk details over dinner—my treat."

I struggled to keep alarm from my tone. "Sounds great. Meet at your office?"

"Certainly."

My premature relief was blown to bits. His perfectly normal manner had not been for me but for the benefit of whoever was in the office and listening to the call. He knew I no longer required ordinary food and was unavailable before sunset, but the listener did not. It did indeed look like the start of an interesting case.

Dusk was taking its own sweet time; the sky was still harsh and bright to me when I started my Buick. I fumbled on my sunglasses to ease the light down to a comfortable level. It didn't take long to cover the distance to Escott's office and park around the corner from his door. I wanted to check things out first before barging in.

He had two modest rooms on the second floor, each with a window fronting the street. Both were wide open because of the warm weather, but the blinds were drawn. Slices of light showed through the right-hand room. The left, which served the back room, was still dark. Without hurry I walked until I was positioned directly under it, and since the street was momentarily clear, partially vanished.

By concentrating, I could control the degree of transparency. My body took on all the solidity of a double-exposed photo and about half the weight. My hand went out and I could see the bricks of the building through it. Like a helium balloon, but with gripping fingers, I went up to the second story. I did not look down. I hate heights.

I made it to the window and thankfully slipped inside, but retained my current state. This semi-solid form left me visible—if alarming to any witnesses—but did not deprive me of sight and speech and gave me agile and perfectly silent movement.

The connecting door between the rooms was wide open. A bright fan of light spilled in from the front, so I took care to avoid it and folded the sunglasses away for unrestricted vision.

Escott was seated behind his desk, his back to me and his head turned slightly to the right. A chair stood on that side, and from his posture alone I could guess it was occupied.

I vanished completely and got close enough to him to give him a chill. After a moment, he stifled a shiver and cleared his throat. I drew off to one side to see what he wanted of me.

He cleared his throat again. "May I go get some water?"

A woman answered him. "No."

"I thought perhaps you might want some as well."

There was no reply.

"You might not be able to get us both, you know. My associate is extremely fast when he wants to be."

"I remember how fast, but no one's this fast."

"Perhaps. The first shot will be the most important. After that . . . well, homemade silencers are notorious for problems."

"Not this one."

Escott was taking a hell of a risk apprising me of the situation in this manner. She could get the idea to shoot him first and then wait for me to come along later. If my scalp had been intact, the skin would be crawling.

Their conversation died, but had lasted long enough for me to get an idea of their relative positions. She was seated with her back to the wall next to the open window, about seven feet from Escott, close enough not to miss hitting him, but not so close that he could try taking the gun from her. There were also a few seconds of critical time in her favor, since he was seated so firmly behind the desk. As far as I could tell from a swirling sweep of the office, they were alone.

The problem wasn't too complicated. I could appear and grab the gun away before she knew what hit her. It was something I'd managed before, but a dark alley was a different situation from a well-lit office. She would wonder where I'd come from and how I'd gotten so close without being seen. If the cops got involved there might be more complications, and I could *not* risk coming to official attention.

"Where is he?" The ground-glass quality was back in her voice.

"Please be patient. It won't be long."

"It's been too goddamned long as it is. Call and see if he's left."

"As you wish."

I heard dialing sounds. Her attention would be fully focused on Escott. I got into place in front of the window. She was right-handed and that would be the one to grab. I readied my own hands—or what would become my hands—over hers.

Just as Escott said hello I reformed and twisted the gun from her grip. The hammer had been cocked back and the safety off. Hardly any pressure was needed to finger the trigger; my attempt to disarm her was more than enough. The thing suddenly jumped and coughed, and a neat hole appeared in the far wall. I yanked the smoking rod free and let it drop. It decided not to go off again.

She jumped up and both my hands were full, one cutting off her surprised and angry shriek and the other pinning her arms. Escott hung up the phone, came stiffly around the desk, dodged her kicks, and grabbed her ankles. We shoved her back down in the chair by weight alone, needing every pound because she squirmed and bucked like a hooked pike.

"I must confess that you are a most welcome sight," he told me, still struggling with her legs.

"Anytime. Now what do we do with her?"

"The police, I suppose. They still want her for that robbery."

"Can you leave me out of it? I'm in no shape for a court appearance."

"Yes, as you wish. But without you for a witness, this incident could end up as my word against hers, that is, if I press charges."

"With her record do you need to?"

"Let's put it this way: after what I've been through today, I would very much *like* to. Hang on a bit. I've some cuffs in the desk."

He released her ankles and dodged another kick as he picked up the dropped automatic. He took it off cock, removed the magazine, emptied the firing chamber of its bullets, and put it away in his desk. From the same drawer, he drew out and opened a set of cuffs.

I put pressure on her shoulders to keep her in place and nimbly kept my fingers away from her teeth. Escott clicked the cuffs over her wrists, then produced a washcloth and a long strip of bandage from the tiny bathroom in back. Between us we shoved the cloth in her mouth and tied it firmly in place so that her outraged screams wouldn't bring well-intentioned, but misinformed help. Some of the fight went out of her by then, but I wasn't going to relax my hold.

Escott was puffing. "This is certainly no way to treat a lady."

"I could debate that," I replied, sucking a finger. She'd managed to lock her teeth on it for a few seconds while we were gagging her.

Selma Jenks, alias Miss Green, glared hard and hatefully at each of us, and I hoped the daggers she was throwing remained wishful ones. Today she wore a now-rumpled blue dress; the remains of a matching hat were on the floor. The skirt part had hiked up in the struggle, revealing a nice stretch of leg and the gartered tops of her blue stockings. I made a move to pull the skirt down, but she threatened to start up again, so I left things alone.

Escott excused himself and went back to the bathroom for his belated glass of water and other things. He returned, his tie loosened a little, and painfully eased his cramped limbs. "She walked in at two o'clock and kept me sitting there all bloody afternoon. Five hours in one spot is certainly brutal on the lower spine."

"You sat there for five hours?"

He shrugged. "It was that or get shot. She was quite upset on how we'd crossed her last night and even more upset that we survived. She looked my name up in the phone directory and came a-hunting. It is my admittedly inexpert opinion that she is more than a little loony."

"Loony?"

"That's the word." He sighed deeply and drew a handkerchief over his face. "She kept me calling your hotel to get you over here, I did what I could to warn you."

"It worked."

"Thank heaven. Spending the day a bare two yards from a nerved-up woman holding a hair trigger is not my idea of entertainment."

"It isn't?"

He shot me a considering look and let it pass. "Well, I suppose it's time to call the police."

"What about her partner, Sled?"

"From the little she dropped in conversation, I got the impression he doesn't know about this, nor, I think, would he approve."

"That's something. So maybe he's not down the street waiting for her."

"Quite likely. He'd have been up here ages ago to find out what was taking so long."

"All the same, could you go out the back way and take a look around just to be sure? He might guess where she is, and if he's down there any cop car will spook him off. You could spot him better than I, you know the street."

"Well, just to be safe . . . I'll be back shortly." He went to the back and I heard the sounds of his exit. He'd equipped the bathroom with a hidden panel that opened onto the upstairs storeroom of a tobacco shop that faced the next street over. He used it now to make a discreet exit outside without exposing himself to anyone watching his regular doorway.

As soon as he was gone, Selma launched from her chair for the door, slipping from my grip like a greased eel. Catching her was no problem, but she was stubborn and full of fight, and in the end I had to lift her bodily and swing her down on the floor with a thud. She was small and that helped, but it was a hell of a lively wrestling match. I threw one leg over her knees, pinning them flat, used one hand to keep her nails out of my eyes, and the other clamped across her forehead. By a little twisting, we were intimately face-to-face. Her eyes were wild, the whites showing all around, but not from fear; her skin under the powder was flushed beet red from sheer fury.

She abruptly stopped fighting, her breath loud and labored through her nose, and stared at me with pure loathing, waiting for my next move. She knew nothing about me, Escott was gone, along with any protection his presence offered. I was someone unknown to her and taking advantage of the opportunity while it was available. No doubt from certain points of view I would be guilty of a kind of rape, but for me it would make things a lot easier.

My gaze on hers, I said her name.

Escott returned from a clear street in ten minutes and found us as before in the office. I still held her shoulders, but she had calmed down considerably.

"May as well call the cops," I said as soon as he came in. He dialed the number and asked for someone by name. He explained the situation and was told to expect a car to come right away.

"All the business at the station will take a bit," he said after hanging up. "I suppose a late supper will have to do for me."

I nodded in sympathy. "I'll wait till the cops are at the door and go out the back. You can handle this wildcat for that long."

"She's not so wild now," he observed.

"Probably tired herself out."

"Indeed. Thank you for coming. I hope it didn't disrupt your evening unduly."

Bobbi and I were going to the movies, we'd still be able to catch the second feature.

The cops showed up in due time. At the last second, Escott cut away her gag, tossed it to me, and I slipped into the back. I waited long enough to hear the opening questions, then went out the window the same way I entered. My car and I were long gone by the time they were ready to take Selma away.

Bobbi had wanted to see *Last of the Mohicans* because she liked Randolph Scott, but Escott's accent had given me a taste for Shakespeare, and I talked her into going to *Romeo and Juliet* instead. Much to her own surprise, she enjoyed it.

"You can understand what they're saying in this one," she commented during intermission. We'd arrived late and missed the newsreel and cartoon, but were in no particular hurry to leave. I bought her an extra soda and popcorn while we waited for the next cycle of features to start.

"Why not? The sound's good."

"Well, I saw this once as a stage play and it was awful. The actors were bellowing to reach the back row and talked so fast you couldn't understand a thing. This kind of stuff you gotta talk clearly so you know what's going on. I like it as a movie better than on the stage."

"I should get you and Charles together to discuss it."

"Oh, yeah, but he's a good egg, he'd let me win just to be polite."

"Don't be too sure, he's got some pretty firm ideas about the stage and Shakespeare in particular."

"Staging I don't know, but I could give him a tough time about Shakespeare."

"How do you mean?"

"Like this show, it was good, but the girl was a nitwit for not running away from home to start with. That's what I would have done. She was wearing enough jewels to live off of for years."

"It wouldn't have been a great tragedy, then."

"Romeo could have swiped her money, left her stranded—anything could have happened."

"That's kind of a negative view."

"It's more believable than gulping down drugs to fake your own death. I think it stinks that Shakespeare didn't let them get together in the end like they wanted, after all the trouble they went through. What made you want to see this instead of Randolph Scott?"

"He makes me jealous."

"No, really."

"They had the biggest ad in the paper and this is a fancier theater. I wanted to impress you."

She glanced at our opulent surroundings. "It worked. They could show a blank screen and people would still pay admission to sit here."

"They do."

"What?" She was half-wary for a joke.

"No kiddin', I knew this usher who swore to me that the ticket is for the chair you sit in, the movie itself is free."

"That's crazy."

"Nah, that's just the way it works out. This usher also told me that theaters make most of their money off popcorn sales."

"It must take a hell of a lot of five-cent bags to pay the rent on this joint."

"Eat up, then, I'll get you another. I like this place."

Another evening ended very pleasantly and as ever I was reluctant to leave. When I dragged my feet back to my hotel room in the small hours, though, I found Escott waiting for me. He was drowsing in my one chair, his feet propped up on the trunk.

I shook his shoulder. "Anything wrong?"

He blinked fully awake and alert. "I think not. Did you enjoy your movie?"

"How'd you know I went to a movie?"

He indicated the paper I'd left on the bed, opened to the entertainments section. "Or perhaps you went to a nightclub, but I recall hearing Miss Smythe state she was fed up with them for the time being."

"She is, but how'd—"

"Her rose scent is quite distinctive, and traces of it linger on your clothes. What film did you see?"

"*Romeo and Juliet.* It was pretty good."

"Yes, the principals were decent enough, if a little old for their parts, but the fellow playing Tybalt seemed to know what he was doing."

I had no illusions that he'd been waiting all night to deliver a review. "Charles . . ."

He straightened, putting his feet on the floor and fixing me in one spot with a look. "I came by to have you satisfy my curiosity."

"About what?" I tried to sound casual, but it wasn't working. He was far too sharp for me to lie to him, but I wasn't going to make it easy.

"About Selma Jenks . . . It was very odd, but when they began questioning her, she made a complete confession."

"She did?"

"In fact, she confessed to every robbery and extortion she and her partner committed since they teamed up. She then told the police where he could be found. They lost no time bringing him in, though he was not nearly so cooperative as Selma."

"Sounds like a good thing, though."

"Yes, an excellent bit of luck. But now I'm curious as to what you said to her after you got me out of the room."

"I want you to know that that was a legitimate request."

"I don't doubt it, but it was convenient for you. Did you hypnotize her?"

My tie suddenly felt too tight. I tore it loose and tossed it on the bed. He waited patiently, knowing there were some things about my nature I was reluctant to discuss.

"It seemed like the easiest thing to do. I didn't want her talking about me or giving you more trouble than you needed. I just calmed her down and gave her a few suggestions."

He was amused. I'd expected reproach. "Suggestions? Good Lord, you should be in the district attorney's office with that talent. You'd never lose a case. I doubt if a priest could have gotten so thorough a confession."

I shrugged. "But it showed. You knew."

"Only because I got so well acquainted with her that afternoon. Her behavior at the station was normal enough, but such a flood of information was hardly in keeping with her personality."

"You said she was a loony," I pointed out.

He got up, stretching his muscles with small, subtle movements. "Why were you so reluctant to tell me about this?"

I shook my head. "I don't know. I didn't want to tip her off to any funny business, I didn't want an audience, stuff like that. What I did, it's not something . . . well, it's . . ." I broke off with a tired and inadequate gesture for my feelings.

"Nothing you need be ashamed of," he quietly concluded. He let that sink in for a thick moment, then picked up his hat. "Well, this has been a long day—and night."

I grabbed at the change of subject. "You wait long?"

"No more than an hour."

"You could have called me at Bobbi's."

"It was hardly a pressing issue, I'd no wish to disturb you. Phone calls at late hours are bad for the heart."

"Thanks." I meant it for more than just his consideration.

He echoed my reply from earlier. "Anytime."

3

It was one in the morning and the same pair of headlights had been bumping around in my rearview mirror for most of the night. I noticed them first when I left Chicago, assumed they belonged to a fellow traveler on the same route, and forgot about them.

I stopped briefly at an all-night service station in Indianapolis, stretched my legs, and bought some gas. Owing to a wrong turn and getting lost in some downtown streets for a while, I didn't get back on the main road immediately. There wasn't much traffic at that hour, but my eyes were occupied with things in front of me, so the car hanging fifty yards off my rear bumper went unnoticed. Finally on the right road again and mentally congratulating myself for getting unlost, I settled in for the last part of my drive, starting with a routine check in the mirror.

Until the night I woke up dead, I'd never been very paranoid, no more than anyone else, so the familiar look of the car took awhile to penetrate my unsuspecting skull. It wasn't a conscious thought process; more like a gradual dawning. When the realization finally came it left me wondering how I could have been so slow.

My night vision allowed me to see past the glare of the headlights to the occupants of the car. There was little detail at this distance, I could only make out their figures: the slightly hunched posture of the driver, and next to him, a shorter man in a hat. They were in a black car, fairly new. I thought it was a Lincoln, but couldn't be sure from the foreshortened image in the mirror.

Not quite ready to believe that they might be following me, I decided a little testing might break up the monotony of the trip. Easing slowly off the gas, I dropped my speed to ten miles below the limit. Most drivers will keep coming right up your tail until they get impatient enough to pass. But this guy was on the ball and his speed dropped as well. When I came to a hill and crested, I hit the gas and let the momentum bring me up to the limit and over. I gained half a mile on him while he was on the other side, but when his turn came he easily caught up. There was a lot of power under his hood.

It could have been coincidence, but I was disturbed. If they really were following me, I wanted to know why.

About twenty minutes later I signaled a right turn and leisurely pulled off the road onto the shoulder. The black car—it was a new Lincoln—went past without the men inside turning to look. I saw only a dark, blurred profile that could have been anyone. They continued on until a long, wide curve took them from sight.

Just in case they'd stopped and were watching from a distance, I got out, stretched, and walked into some sparse trees that sheltered the side of the road. As I walked, I made fiddling movements with my belt and fly. I didn't have to go, but could pretend, and stood with my ears wide open. My hearing was extremely sensitive now, but the wind was blowing in the wrong direction for me to pick up any motor noises ahead. For the sake of my nerves, I dawdled another five minutes, leaning against the car and superficially puffing a cigarette for something to do.

Once back on the road, I eased up to speed with my eyes peeled, but there was no sign of them. I was still edgy. It had only been a couple of fast weeks since my life had been completely disrupted by some of the more violent members of Chicago's gangland. The thought that some grudge-bearing survivors of that fracas might be after me was not a comfortable one. They'd killed me once already, once was more than enough.

Briefly, I thought about turning back, then vetoed the thought. More than half the journey was behind me, and if it came to it, I could handle two jokers playing road games. I had an errand in my hometown that I wanted to get done. If I ran into a little trouble along the way, I could always rag Escott about it later. The trip was originally *his* idea.

The second night after our match with Selma Jenks, I woke up and again found him sitting in my old chair. I never minded his drop-in visits because he always had a good reason behind them.

"Good evening," he said. "At least I hope you will find it so. Things have cooled off a bit."

Fairly indifferent to temperature changes, I couldn't really tell, and found it hard to gauge the weather from the way he dressed. It was the middle of September, and though his suit was lightweight, every button on his vest was secure in its buttonhole. His neck was encased in a heavily starched detachable collar, which gave him a stiff and formal posture. He looked like a banker or a teacher of the old-fashioned sort. The intent was to boost the confidence of his clients.

"How's tricks with you?" I greeted in return, getting out of my trunk.

"I have no complaints, though I've been busy."

"New customers?"

"Old business. Since the influx of Mr. Swafford's cash is legally declarable, I've been able to afford a few modest home improvements and to clear some other details up."

"What details?"

"Your own case, for one. I've been tracking down the names on the infamous list you acquired—"

"I thought you were going to destroy it."

"I will, but not until I've provided a little peace of mind for some of my fellow pilgrims."

"Oh, yeah?" My tone asked him to enlarge on the subject while I brushed and gargled. My exclusive diet of whole blood sometimes made me subject to a slight breath problem. Thanks to modern hygienic products, I could still be socially acceptable, but had to be regular in habits.

The list had cost several lives, including my own. My breathing life and all the potentials that went with it were forever gone and I never wanted to see those scraps of disaster again. I should have been purposely disinterested in it, but a couple of weeks can be a long time. As Bobbi had observed, it was funny how you could get used to things.

Escott had long since broken the code it was typed in, revealing over two hundred names with skeletons in the closet. A smart blackmailer could make a fortune or wield considerable power, for without exception the names were those of important politicians, judges, lawyers, and cops, with a few big businessmen thrown in for good measure. Along with the names, the list provided the locations of the blackmail items, either incriminating documents or embarrassing pictures. Most of the stuff was stashed in a scattering of bus and train depot lockers throughout the area. He'd been collecting some of it today, and his briefcase bulged with enough scandals to keep the tabloids busy with hot headlines for months.

"I'm only halfway through it all; the hand delivery is what takes so long," he said. "It is sometimes very difficult to set up an appointment with these fellows."

"You've been giving it all back personally?"

"It's no great hardship. Posting it would be easier, but allows the chance that a letter or parcel might be innocently opened by a third party. The victim's life is either ruined by exposure, or they are still stuck with a blackmailing problem, but from a different quarter. It is not for me to judge the follies of my fellows, so I simply return the item, suggest they destroy it, and advise them to be more cautious in the future."

"But they might think you're the blackmailer, or in league with him if you run around doing that."

His eyes crinkled and he shook his head. "Hardly, because I don't look a bit like myself when I return the things."

"What do you look like?"

"Perhaps I shouldn't say, I might wish to try it on you sometime."

"Oh, thanks. What kind of stuff did you pick up today?"

"The usual run of evidence of extramarital affairs, illegal business dealings, and tax frauds . . . Nothing really outstanding, though the names involved are surprisingly interesting."

"Come on and drop one, I'm not a reporter anymore."

"Well, I could mention the name of Hoover, but I shan't tell which one or the nature of the blackmail article."

He looked smug and left me guessing which Hoover: Herbert, J. Edgar, or the vacuum cleaner. I finished dressing and someone knocked on the door. It was the bellhop with my regular pile of papers. I tipped him and shut the door.

"Good heavens, you read all of those?"

"I'm addicted, but trying to taper off." I opened the top paper to the personals page and checked the column of fine print. My notice was missing, but I was still hoping for a reply. I went through the rest of the stack in short order and dropped them to one side.

"What were you looking for?"

In answer, I fished an old paper from the trash, opened it to the right page, and pointed.

" 'Dearest Maureen, are you safe yet? Jack,' " he read. "I'd wondered if these were yours. This was the lady you knew in New York?"

I nodded. "That's from the other day. I've had the ad canceled."

He didn't ask why, not aloud anyway, but looked curious.

"If she were alive . . . she would have . . ." I wanted to pace, but the room was too small. Instead I took the paper from him and shoved it back in the trash. As an afterthought I threw the rest of them on top with it. "I *looked* for her. I'm no amateur, I know how to look for people, but this was like she dropped off the face of the earth."

"You still have doubts," he said kindly.

"I shouldn't after all this time. I've got Bobbi to think of now, I've got a different life ahead of me."

"And an unresolved question in your past. I would like to help, if you'll allow me."

"The trail's five years cold. I couldn't ask you to do it."

"I'm volunteering. I'm planning to go to New York, anyway. If nothing turns up you're no worse off than before, and if I do find anything, pleasant or not, it's better than not knowing at all."

"You know what it's like, don't you?"

His eyes flickered and settled. "I have an imagination." Whatever it was, he didn't want to talk about it, and changed the subject. "How is Miss Smythe doing these days?"

"Better since she quit the club. They put Gordy in charge of it."

"How fortunate for him."

"Anyway, she's been busy doing some local broadcast shows and stuff. Next week she's going to be on her first national broadcast. I'm going to drive her down to the studio."

"How delightful. I'm truly happy for her. She appears to have fully recovered from her . . . uh . . . adventure."

"I guess, she doesn't talk much about that night, and I don't bring it up if I can help it."

"For all concerned, it's probably for the best. Well, I did come by to ask a favor of you."

"What?"

"I shall be out of town for a few days next week—my business in New York, you know—and was wondering if you would mind staying over at my house while I'm gone. I'm expecting a shipment from overseas and would be glad to have someone there to receive it."

"They deliver after dark?"

"I could arrange that, yes."

"Sure, no problem."

"Thank you, I appreciate this. I'll have a duplicate key made up for you."

"Were you serious about looking for Maureen?"

"I can try, but I'll have to have her full name and description, where she lived at the time, and any other facts about her that could possibly be useful. Have you a photograph?"

"No."

"A pity, it might have helped." He shrugged his eyebrows philosophically and changed the subject again. "I've been reading Stoker's book—"

"You have my sympathy," I said dryly.

"Indeed, it does become turgid in spots, I had to completely skip over the correspondence between the two female characters—such a letdown after those terrifying scenes in the castle. But the idea of the multiple boxes of earth strikes me as very clever, and I came by to recommend it to you. You are quite vulnerable with just the one trunkful."

"It's not even that much, but I see your point. I've been thinking about that, but putting it off. After all, I'm hardly being chased by Van Helsing. Who believes in vampires in this day and age?"

"Myself, Miss Smythe, Gordy, and anyone else who might notice your lack of a reflection in a mirror or window and think it peculiar. Consider it a safety measure. Suppose there's a fire, or someone steals your trunk?"

"I'm sold, but where do I stash all this extra dirt?"

He had a ready answer. "I've plenty of room in my cellar until you can work out your own places. Are you planning to acquire a second trunk as well? The one you have is a bit large."

"You noticed. I'll look around for another tonight and see if I can locate something like a feed sack."

"What about some canvas bags?" He pulled one from an inside pocket and unfolded it. It was about eighteen inches long, with a rounded bottom six inches across. Around the opening were some things like belt loops. "They were originally made to hold sand, but should work just as well for your earth."

With that as a clue I realized it was the kind of bag that theaters used to counterweight curtains and stuff backstage. The loops were to be threaded with rope to attach it to lines.

"I have several dozen of these, you're welcome to them."

"It's perfect, but how did you happen to have so many?"

"I have a lot of odds and ends lying about that I'm trying to clear away. I found these while doing some unpacking today. Much of my kit is absolutely useless at the moment, but now and then it fills an unexpected need. It occurs often enough to justify the presence of so much rubbish."

So two nights later I was in my Buick with three dozen empty sandbags, a new shovel, some rope, and a new trunk. It was smaller than the one I'd initially bought to rest in for the day, which was currently in Escott's basement. The new trunk was easier to manhandle from the car, and though cramped, it was large enough to hold a body, namely my own. Inside, still in the original feedsacks, was my home earth, which for reasons I did not understand, I was compelled to lie in during the day. The stuff gave me rest and strength and was as necessary to my survival as blood; I could no more question its importance to me than anyone else could question the need for air and water.

I passed through a sleeping little town, one of the many on the road that rolled up the sidewalks at night. The reversed image of the welcome sign was receding in my mirror when the black Lincoln reappeared, this time with its headlights off. They were about a quarter mile back, and if they'd been after anyone but me they would have been invisible in the dark.

That clinched it, they were following me. The idea that they may have had their own brief rest stop and then forgot to switch on their lights was quickly discounted. On a night as black as this, human eyes needed all the help they could get.

Then I wondered if they were like me. That particularly uneasy idea held my attention for several miles before I filed it away for later consideration. It was not impossible, just unlikely.

My original thought that they were members of one of Chicago's mobs seemed the best explanation. But previous experience with them was in the nature of shooting first and never questioning later, so why just follow me? I'd have been easy enough to overtake on this lonely section of road. A few seconds of parallel driving would be long enough to deliver a .45-caliber greeting from a well-oiled Thompson, and they'd think themselves rid of me. They'd already had the chance to perform such an unsocial action outside Indianapolis. If their game was only to follow, it was becoming annoying, because I don't enjoy such games.

I kept my speed steady for many more miles, searching my memory for a clue as to who in the gangs would know me, and only came up blank. Perhaps it was some remnant of the Paco mob, or maybe something to do with Escott and that business with Swafford. I was getting more curious by the second.

Another hill loomed ahead and I hoped the far side would prove suitable. I stepped on the gas to gain a little more distance and time and topped the crest with the Lincoln half a mile behind. That would give me plenty of time, if my brakes were any good.

On the other side of the hill, I skidded to a stop and killed the lights, left the motor running, and got out. Standing in front of one taillight and holding my hat over the other to prevent reflections, I waited for them.

They came over the hill, their lights still off. My estimate of their common sense was less than flattering, but the lack of extra glare was fine with me; their faces were now visible.

The one on the left was a scrawny brown chicken of a man in his late fifties, wearing a hat with a brim too big for him. The driver seemed to be of average height, but looked larger compared to his companion. From the look of his pocked skin and wet eyes, he was hardly out of his teens.

Both men saw me at the same time, and both registered the same expression: wide-eyed terror. Had it not been so genuine I would have laughed; as it was I resisted the impulse to look behind me, instinctively knowing that I was the inspiration for their fear.

The kid had quick reactions, he hit the gas, and the Lincoln stormed past, gaining speed from the slant of the hill. I got back in my car and roared after them. Their headlights came on. The following game had been shot all to hell and the high speeds put an end to their stupidity. I left mine off—the starlit landscape was like day to me and I wanted to get close to them.

The older man was turned around in his seat, watching for my approach. I got a good look at his face, which seemed familiar, and then memorized their number plate. They were from New York. That opened up a whole new line of questions as I dropped my speed and settled in to follow them for a change.

The new speculations were as futile as the old—I could think of no one from New York who'd have a reason to be after me. Curiosity was giving way to frustration, with a dash of worry for taste. Their terrified reaction had not been lost on me. I'd seen it before in the faces of people who knew what I was, but that only took me back to Chicago again.

There was Escott, but I trusted him. Besides, these two bozos were too amateurish to be connected with him. The same thing applied to Bobbi. Selma Jenks and her large friend Sled came to mind, but first they'd have to break jail or send someone after me—nope, that was too screwy even for Miss Jenks. The only one left was a mob strong arm named Gordy, but it didn't fit with him, either. If he had a grudge on me, and he didn't, he'd handle it himself and much more efficiently.

The Lincoln's brake lights flickered, held, and then the big car came to a stop, bumping onto the shoulder of the road. I stopped as well and watched to see what they were doing. The kid backed the car off the road and it vanished behind a thick strand of trees and brush. It was just the sort of hideout that state cops liked to use to spring out on unwary speeders. My two friends were going to sit there and wait for me to pass.

I was pretty fed up by now and pulled off the road as well, shutting down the motor. The silence of the country jammed my ears. I got out, not quite closing the door—the slam might have carried to the Lincoln. Keeping low, I quit my car and tiptoed up to theirs.

Their motor was off and neither seemed inclined to any fact-revealing conversation between themselves. While they waited for the approach of my car, I crouched over their right rear wheel and performed a small operation. After unscrewing the cap in their tire, I located a pebble and jammed it inside at just the right depth and was quite satisfied with the faint hiss of escaping air.

Then I vanished.

It was a useful knack, and on occasions like this it was also fun. I materialized right by the open driver's window, clamped my hands on the kid's arms so he couldn't move to start the car, and asked a reasonable question.

"Who are you guys?"

Sometimes the element of surprise is not a good tactic. If your quarry is too surprised, the reaction you get is not necessarily the one you want.

Close up, the kid looked younger than I thought; his face still had the lingering softness of baby fat. There was a layer of smooth fat all over his body that didn't suit his years or his sex, and he'd have to lay off the sweets or the problem would get worse with time. Between that and a colorful display of pimples in various stages of development and decay, I didn't think he was much past eighteen. I'd seen younger thugs, but this guy didn't fit the mold.

His partner looked the age I guessed, past fifty or so. His hat was off now, revealing a thick growth of greasy hair that was too black to be true. His face had two deep scores on the cheeks, which were repeated countless times on the dry brown skin of his throat. He made me think of Boris Karloff in *The Mummy*, as though all the water had been squeezed out.

Both men confirmed that they knew what I was, and their reactions were again identical: utter terror.

The kid began yelling and fighting to get away. His legs had gone stiff and he was making a laudable effort at trying to levitate through the roof of the car. If Satan himself had appeared at his elbow in a cloud of sulfur, the reaction could not have been more violent.

His friend's mouth was wide open in shock. As a side issue I noted the yellow teeth and a number of black fillings. He was making incoherent, panicky sounds, and his hands were stabbing around the car interior, looking for something. He was searching for a weapon, as I found out when, in desperation, he tore off one shoe and began hammering at me with the heel. It was an ineffectual attack. Between the kid's struggles and my ducking, he kept missing. When he did connect, it was usually with the kid, and that set up a whole new series of howlings.

Loud noises at close quarters make me nervous, but I was game enough to try and last it out. I ended up joining the chorus, shouting at them to shut up. Nothing less than violence would bring that about, as I quickly deduced, and so suited action to thought. I freed one hand and punched out the old guy and his annoying shoe, and he slithered from sight somewhere under the dashboard. The kid freshened his own fight until I stuck a mild fist in his stomach and knocked the breath out of him. He doubled over, bumping his head on the steering wheel, and once again the country silence thankfully descended on us all.

While the kid worked to get air back in his lungs, I slipped the wallet from his coat and nosed through it. He was carrying thirty bucks and a New York driving license bearing the unlikely name of Matheus Webber. There was a small photo of two chubby people, who were probably his parents, a membership card to an athletic club, and a number of business cards from various New York bookstores. I shoved it all back in the leather folder and returned it to his pocket, then opened the door and dragged him out.

He was gasping for air and gray in the face, and I reasoned he must be a sporadic visitor to his club at best. Leaving him on the ground, I reached across the seat to the other guy and pulled him up. His wallet contained a hundred twenty bucks, and said he was James Braxton of New York and the owner of Braxton's Books in Manhattan. He still seemed familiar, though the name didn't jog anything in my memory.

Neither of them looked like gangsters.

Matheus was just getting his breath back and seemed likely to bolt, so I caught his collar and tie before he got his legs set and pulled him up against the Lincoln so that we were face-to-face. He stared, lips flapping, and nothing coming out.

"Okay, bub, why were you following me?"

He looked wall-eyed toward Braxton for some moral support but got none. His legs sagged and I had to straighten him up. I repeated my question until it finally penetrated, and then he only looked incredulous. He seemed to think I already knew why. This little act went on for several minutes; me asking variations of why and him blubbering and not giving out any answers. I probably wouldn't have liked them, anyway. He wasn't even attempting to lie, it might not have been in his nature. He must have been real cute when his mom caught him raiding the cookie jar.

As with Selma Jenks, I could force a way into his mind that would make him cooperative enough, but decided against it. There was no real harm done and I'd scared them far more than they had annoyed me. I'd try a more reasonable approach.

After saying the kid's name enough to get his attention, I eased my grip a little when I was sure he wouldn't try to run. He was as relaxed as he'd ever be with me, which wasn't much. I pulled out my cigarettes and offered him one.

He looked at it like it was a snake and barely shook his head. "I don't smoke."

I nodded agreeably. "It's a bad habit." He had some idea that I was an inhuman monster, so I lit a cigarette, because in my limited experience, inhuman monsters rarely smoke. I puffed and blew the smoke out downwind of his face, trying to look harmless. "I'm sorry I popped you and your friend, but things were getting out of hand, don't you think?"

He bobbed his head cautiously.

"Now, do you know me from somewhere? Do you know my name?"

Reluctantly, he nodded again.

"How do you know me?"

"Mr. Braxton told me."

"Fine, how does *he* know me?"

"I don't know."

"Why were you following me?"

"T-to see where you were going."

This was getting nowhere fast. "Could you be more specific?"

He had to think that one over, but I waited him out. "W-we were going to see where you went for the day."

"You mean where I was going to hole up?"

Another nod.

"Why?"

That one was too much for him and he tried to get away. I held him with one hand and advised him to calm down. After a minute he ran out of steam, his legs went like jelly again, and I let him sink down to the running board to rest.

I crouched to be at eye level with him. "You seem to know what I am. Do you?"

"Yes."

"Were you and your friend planning to make the world a little safer from vampires?" I should have been more diplomatic—his eyebrows were galloping into his hairline again.

"Please . . . don't . . . ." The kid was crying, actually crying, he was that scared. I felt sorry for him and a little embarrassed, and finally pulled out a handkerchief and gave it to him. He stared at it.

"Go on—it won't bite you."

He took it, suspicious of some kind of trick. When the trick failed to happen, he finally blew his nose.

I shook my head. "Van Helsing you're not."

He stiffened again. "You know about that?"

"What, *Dracula?* Yeah, reading it is one of the requirements for joining the union. Maybe you've heard of us, the International Brotherhood of Vampires. I'm with Chicago Local three eleven."

He stared. Well, *I* thought it was funny, but the kid was taking me seriously.

"Matheus—do they call you Matt?"

"No, they call me Matheus."

They would.

"All right, Matheus, I think you should listen to me very carefully so you can get this straight. You and your friend need to go back to New York and do business as usual. You're probably a very nice kid—you don't need to be chasing after vampires in the wilds of Indiana, you're not cut out for it. You got that?"

Now he was looking stubborn. Somewhere deep inside he had a backbone.

"Don't get me wrong, I think you've got a lot of guts to even be thinking of tracking me down. How did you latch on to me anyway?"

"The papers."

"What about them?"

"Your ad stopped."

This was a can of worms I hadn't expected. "Tell me about the ad."

"It stopped and we wanted to know why, so we called the papers and got your address."

"How did you know about it? What do you know about Maureen?"

"Nothing!"

"What does Braxton know?" But I was overanxious and the kid clammed up again. I counted ten and tried a calmer voice. "Did he know Maureen?"

"I think so, years ago."

"How long ago?"

"I don't know. Honest, I don't. But he knew you had been with her . . . that she had . . . had . . . that you might become . . . but we weren't sure."

My grip on him relaxed; the muscles felt like water. "Is Maureen alive?"

He shook his head. "No, she's like you."

"Is she alive?"

"I don't know!"

"Does Braxton know?"

"Uh-uh. He said he lost her trail, you were his only lead. When the ads stopped he thought you'd found her or that you'd died. . . ." The realization that he was talking to a dead man must have hit him all over again. He sat with his arms dangling, looking at me with helpless horror.

"How did you get on my trail?"

"Through the papers. We only got into town this afternoon, and spent the day looking for you. We got to your hotel, but they wouldn't help us, even when we described you, so we waited across the street for you to come out."

"So Braxton knew what I looked like?"

"Yes . . . but I thought you were a lot older."

The kid was right. I was thirty-six, but my condition and diet made me look about twenty-two.

"We saw you putting the trunk in the car and thought you were running away, but we weren't sure—not until you went to the Stockyards, then we knew that you were . . . you had . . ." He gulped the idea down. "We followed you, but when you got on the road you didn't act like you were running, so we just stayed back and followed."

"Biding your time until the dawn, huh? And then what? A stake in the heart and garnish with garlic?"

He squirmed, utterly miserable.

"Well, you ought to feel uncomfortable, that's just about the dirtiest trick I've heard of, and I've heard plenty. Have you actually *thought* about what you were planning?"

He had not.

"Come on, Matheus, I'm really a nice guy once you know me. I am not some kind of diabolical maniac; I even send money home to my mother. Think of it as a medical condition. You wouldn't try to kill me if I had polio, would you?"

Seeing things from my point of view was a whole new experience for him.

"Except for some physical and dietary restrictions, there's really nothing bad with being a vampire."

He acted like I'd said a dirty word.

"Would you be more comfortable if I said Undead or would you prefer something else? I know lots of substitutes, but they're harder to pronounce." I waited for an answer and tried again. "Come on, kid, if I could go back to being like you I would, but I can't, so I'm just trying to make the best of the situation. I'm not what you expected, am I?"

He shook his head grudgingly.

"Don't listen to him, Matheus!" It was the mummy, Braxton. He'd come awake and was struggling to pull himself together. He lurched from the car, looking ridiculous as he waved his shoe in one hand like a weapon. After a second he realized a shoe was hardly appropriate, so he dropped it and pulled a big silver cross from his pants pocket.

I stood up, uncertain how to react at this point. Crosses don't affect me unless they're large, wooden, and used as a club on my head. My theory on this is that I'm not an evil creature; the use of a cross against a vampire is primarily an invention of the stage and Hollywood. Having the vampire cowering away from one makes for a good dramatic scene, but in reality, things are far different. If these guys were ignorant enough to rely on one for protection, it might be in my best interest to play along. On the other hand, Braxton might just be trying to test me.

He pushed himself and his cross between me and Matheus. I moved back quickly because he practically shoved the thing up my nose.

"Back, you demon!" he said, and quite dramatically at that. Matheus was impressed. I refrained from laughing and gave them some room.

"And how do you do?" I inquired politely.

"Did he hurt you, Matheus?"

"Well, no—"

"But he *was* trying to hypnotize you."

"He was?"

"I was?" I echoed.

It looked as though Braxton was just the sort of dedicated crazy I was occasionally compelled to interview when I'd been a reporter. Even at this early stage in our acquaintance, his manner was easily recognizable. I tried to recall if I'd once talked to him while on an assignment.

"Leave us and trouble us no more," he intoned solemnly.

"Who wrote your dialogue? Hamilton Deane?" I countered.

Matheus looked at me doubtfully. He knew who'd written the play, *Dracula,* but he still didn't quite know how to take a vampire with a sense of humor. It went right over Braxton's head, for he was too caught up in his Van Helsing imitation to pay attention to what I said.

"Leave us," he commanded.

"Listen, buster, *you* were the ones following me. I was minding my own business. I'll be a sport this time and let you go, as long as you run straight back home and stay there."

"No, we will follow you as long as necessary."

That really wasn't the smartest thing for him to tell me. I sighed. "Matheus, maybe you can talk some sense into him. If I was half as nasty as you seem to think, I could just as well kill you both as stand around all night. I haven't got the time to waste trying to convince you of my good character, either. Just stay out of my way or I'll kick both of your asses all the way back to Manhattan." I turned and walked until I was lost to them in the dark, then vanished and floated back to listen in on what they had to say.

It took a few minutes for their nerves to settle and to convince each other that they were all right. Once the question of health was out of the way, Matheus gulped a few times and asked, "Was he really trying to hypnotize me?"

I could imagine Braxton nodding sagely.

"But it didn't seem like he was. He didn't say anything that sounded like it."

"You wouldn't remember it if he did. It's like falling asleep, you don't know you've been asleep until you wake up."

"Oh. What do we do now?"

"We wait him out. He has to come this way, and then we follow him."

"But how can we be sure he won't just double back?"

"He has become a vampire, he *must* seek out his home earth. I know he comes from Cincinnati—"

How did he know that? I wondered.

"—and this is the road that will take him there the fastest. He said he had little time. For us time is on our side."

He didn't know everything. He must have thought I'd changed only in the last day or so; he did not know I was merely augmenting my present supply of earth.

"Are you sure about this, Mr. Braxton? He could have killed us, like he said."

Braxton had a blanket answer. "Lies. He's only toying with us. They're very clever, these creatures, but you'll remember that he was the one to give ground before *us*."

I could almost see him waving his cross and puffing out his chest. Whether I was playing with them or not depended on how much they bothered me. Amateurish and ill informed as they were, they could still prove to be very dangerous. During my daytime oblivion I was completely vulnerable. My best chance of survival would be to lose them and hope they'd give up and go home. I had no desire to do them violence.

I left them and returned to my car, starting it up. They would hear the noise and be starting theirs as well. I drove slowly past, their white and defiant faces staring grimly back as I waved. Matheus was getting himself ready for the road race of his life.

It must have been a terrible letdown when their car swayed onto the road and with a lurch betrayed the presence of the flat tire.

I hit the gas and left them behind. It would take about ten minutes for Matheus to change the tire, probably a lot longer with Braxton helping him, and by that time I planned to have a healthy lead of fifteen miles or more.

4

LUCK was with me and I managed to avoid the notice of cops looking for speeders, arriving in Cincinnati with enough time to spare to find a place to stay. The best protection was with the herd, so I checked into one of the bigger and busier downtown hotels under a phony name. The Buick disappeared into a distant parking lot with a lot of other late-model cars.

A sleepy bellhop manhandled the trunk into a modest single with a bath. I dispatched him with a fair tip and hung out a sign to ward off the maid. My suit and body both felt rumpled from the long drive. I wanted a hot bath, a quick shave, and the inside of my trunk, and got them in short order.

Sunset seemed to come again a few seconds after I'd closed the lid.

While in my earth there was no sense of time passing, but the day had gone by as usual, since I felt rested and alert. I was in fresh clothes, checked out, and in my car in record time. My goal was to be back in Chicago that same night, so I hurried now.

What was left of my grandfather's farm wasn't too far from the city, but owing to the twists of the road, it was still fairly isolated. Once I turned off the farm-market road and onto the weedy ruts that led to the house, the trees closed in, and it was like going back in time. The Buick was a noisy intruder into a simpler and slower age, so I cut the motor and walked the rest of the way with Escott's sandbags in one hand and the new shovel and some rope in the other.

The place hadn't changed since my last visit in August. It still looked forlorn and overgrown, but not completely neglected. My father came out occasionally to check on things. He kept the grass trimmed in the little graveyard where we'd been burying our own for the last seventy-five years. The house was boarded up. It would have looked sinister except for the neat paint job. Even the three-seater outhouse in back had gotten a coat against the winter. It was as though it had only been temporarily closed for the season and the family would return in the spring.

I went to the cemetery. The earth near the big oak tree was vaguely scarred from my last expedition for soil, but not so much that the casual eye would notice. As before, I cleared another large area of fallen leaves and began scooping an inch of topsoil off and into the bags. I could have dug deeper, but that would leave definite signs, and I had no desire to accidentally include earthworms in my booty.

Whether dirt specifically from the family cemetery was necessary for me to survive had been a question in my mind for quite a while. My prior researches indicated that all vampires must be in their graves by dawn, and had I truly died, my body would certainly be resting here with the other Flemings. I suppose any of the earth in the immediate vicinity would have been suitable, but there was no time for experiments. I had a traditional turn of mind, anyway.

As I worked, my mind was already on the road, retracing the route back to Chicago and deciding which places to stop for gas. I vaguely wondered if I would again be plagued by Matheus Webber and James Braxton. They were worrying, but there wasn't much I could do about them until I could get their names to Escott. Hopefully he might be able to trace them down in New York while he was there, then I might remember where I'd met Braxton—

The work and thought were interrupted by several heavy objects slamming against my body like cannonballs and knocking me flat.

Two hard things caught me full in the chest, and a third had cracked against my head. In the very brief time between impact and hitting the ground I decided they were large rocks and that somebody really had it in for me.

The last rock must have been the size of a brick, but I hadn't been killed, or even concussed. There are undeniable advantages to being supernatural.

My body fell back and rolled. I glimpsed a whirl of leaves and branches that abruptly faded to gray and then to nothing. My body had taken things over again and I'd dematerialized from the shock of the sudden pain. No emergency called me back, so I remained disembodied and was glad of it. Floating upward until safely within the concealing branches of the oak, I slowly re-formed, arms and legs wrapped around one of the big limbs.

I was about thirty feet up, and once solid, had to endure a few bad moments of recovery. My head was the worst, I had to cling with my eyes squeezed tight until the dizziness passed. I *hate* heights.

While hiding in the tree and counting my blessings, developments were taking place below. Three foreshortened figures came into view and prowled uncertainly around my excavation. They were rough-looking men, each with a rock in one hand and a big stick in the other. Had I not vanished immediately they would have probably followed up with those clubs. The clubs were of wood and would have succeeded where rock had failed.

My headache rapidly subsided as I became interested in finding out who these guys were and why they'd attacked me out of the blue. Perhaps then I would work off the chagrin of being taken by surprise. They must have been hiding out the whole time I was digging, or else I'd have heard them sneaking up.

One of them cast around like a dog for a lost scent. "He musta rolled away fast after we hit 'em," he told the others. They agreed and made a swift search under the oak, then spread out among the grave markers.

"You sure we hit 'em?" asked another.

"Din' you keep your eyes open? We all hit 'em square. I know we did. Din' we, Bob?"

Bob grunted something affirmative and made a quick leap to look behind the big piece of carved granite over my grandfather's grave. It was the only possible hiding place, the rest of the stone markers being too small. They circled back to the sandbags and kicked at them curiously.

"What you suppose he was diggin' for, Rich?"

"How the hell should I know?" Rich was upset. He looked at the oak tree, his eyes traveling up the trunk toward me. I kept still, knowing he couldn't see me in the darkness among the leaves. "Go check his car," he told Bob. "Mebee he got some stuff we can use."

Fugitives from a local Hooverville or tramps off of any of the trains that passed through the city, they'd been looking for someone to rob, and I'd been handy.

Bob lumbered off to the car. The keys were still inside. I'd felt safe being back home, after all. Vanishing, I floated in Bob's direction, tracking the crunch his feet made on the gravel and old leaves. He was almost to the car when I re-formed in front of his startled face and gently knocked him out.

He was a gaunt, rawboned specimen and I'd have felt sorry for him had it not been for those well-aimed stones. Proving assault against them would be impossible, but I was, or at least I felt like, an outraged homeowner and they were trespassing.

I sandwiched Bob into one of the road ruts in front of the car, which gave me an idea: it was more of a childish impulse, but irresistible.

Rich and his pal separated, looking for my missing body and puzzling over the odd situation. It was easy to wait for a convenient moment and take the pal from behind. His unconscious body went next to Bob's in the adjoining rut. For an artistic effect, I folded their arms funeral style and decorated each with a large weed, as though it were a lily. When things were ready, I tooted the horn a couple times, turned on the headlights, then ducked into the cover of the trees.

Rich didn't delay investigating. He was complaining about the noise in a few short, coarse words, which trailed off when he saw his friends lying neatly in the ruts. He went on guard, held his stick at a threatening angle, and listened. It seemed a shame to disappoint him, so I threw a fist-sized stone at his legs. His yelp was more of surprise than pain, and he hopped to one side before twisting to face me.

I wasn't there anymore. By vanishing and shifting around I could move without being detected. In the darkness outside the glare of the headlights I was all but invisible by simply standing still. Re-forming a short toss behind him, I bounced another stone, this time off his butt. He had no appreciation for my marksmanship, though, and came charging at me with his stick. While he viciously assaulted the foliage, I moved back to the first hiding place and gave him another volley of rocks.

Not surprisingly, he got tired of this very quickly and bolted for the road, urged on by several parting shots. I couldn't let him leave without a personal good-bye and made a point to appear directly in his path. He had no time to stop and we connected solidly. He dropped, the breath knocked out of him, but he quickly recovered and took a swing at me with the stick. I went to a partially solid state and it passed right through, which was not what he expected. He stared at the stick, then at me, and tried again and failed. That was one too many and he ran away.

That didn't work, either.

I caught him at the front gate, swung him around, and pressed him face first against the bole of a tree, making sure he got well acquainted with the bark.

"Lemme go, I din' do nuthin'!" he squealed.

He struggled, but I had him firmly pinned and he eventually stopped. There had been a lot more fight in little Selma Jenks.

"Okay, I'll do what you want!" This was indistinct, as his mouth was mashed into the bark.

I whipped him around. He knew he was in trouble as his feet left the earth. I held him up by his stinking clothes, with his toes swinging free in the air.

"How long you creeps been here?"

"C-couple days."

"How'd you find this place?"

"Mailbox—sign on it says it's safe here."

"You're gonna change that, understand? It ain't safe anymore."

"Yeah—whatever you want."

My next action was pure show-off, but it also served to drive home the point that I was more than capable of handling him. I forced him over double and snaked an arm around his midsection. He was too dumbfounded to vocalize a protest as his feet left the ground again and he was carried like a sack of flour along the road to the mailbox. There, he eradicated a symbol scratched on the post and substituted another that meant "keep away" to any other bums that might happen by.

"That okay?"

He wasn't getting any pats on the head from me. We locked looks and I gave him a few choice words of advice, nothing as specific as those I shared with Selma, but along similar lines. I last saw him pelting for Cleveland at a dead run. If he kept up the pace he'd make it by morning.

His pals looked like they'd be out for some time, so I left them and had a good look around the house and barn. The barn was untouched, but the house had been broken into via a back window. Through it I could see signs of recent and very messy occupancy. This discovery inspired a lot of violent thoughts aimed at the two remaining bums. The only thing to do would be to give the cops an anonymous call and ask them to come out. They in turn would contact my father; by that time the bums would be gone, which was probably just as well. If Dad had come out for a visit alone, he might have been the one assaulted, not me. That idea had set my blood to boiling when I'd been talking to Rich, and now I stalked back to revive his two friends.

A little shaking did the trick, and I gave them no chance to run away. I had their full attention as I picked up the discarded clubs. They were heavy and hard, like baseball bats, but not so thick that I couldn't get my hands around them. I held them out front, making sure my guests had a good view.

"You boys get out and stay out, or I'll break your necks." At that I snapped the clubs in two with a sharp movement. The men were impressed, but didn't stay for an encore. If anything, they moved even faster than their leader as they ran for the road.

Satisfied, I threw the wood shards away and went back to my unfinished work.

Like a lot of chores, the digging took longer than anticipated and, coupled with the delay of dealing with the tramps, severely cut into my travel time. I could have probably made it all the way to Chicago the same night, but not without a lot of speeding. Allowing for state cops, unexpected flat tires, washed-out bridges, and other hazards, I could still easily make it to Indianapolis with a comfortable margin of time.

With the last dusty bag tied up and stowed in the trunk, I drove back to town in search of a phone, turning one up at a gas station. While a kid in greasy overalls fed the tank, I made a call to the Cincinnati police. After giving them the name of another farming family on the same road, I extracted a promise from them to investigate and, if necessary, roust the tramps from the Fleming place. They were given the impression the intruders were still there because it would do no harm for them to be cautious. I gave them my dad's name and number so they could inform the owner, and hung up.

Having the time and inclination, I decided to indulge in some nostalgia and drive through my old neighborhood. I needed some reassurance that the haunts of my youth were still there, still in use by another generation of kids.

I wasn't going to visit my parents, only look at the house and drive on. Visiting them would have been too complicated and painful. I'd be expected to stay the night and stuff myself with food and there was no way I could fob them off with some light excuse. I could also be honest and tell them the truth about myself and hope they'd understand and accept it, but that was something I absolutely was not ready to try yet.

Dad had moved off the farm years ago to be closer to the store he owned and to give Mom her long-coveted indoor plumbing. Their neighborhood looked smaller and dowdier to my eyes now, but still homey. There was ample evidence that the radio had not yet destroyed the quality of family life as had been predicted. There were plenty of people lounging on their front porches, seeking a cool breeze from the darkness. Windows were open and shades were up, their softly lit squares revealing a minute glimpse into other lives. I observed each with the detached interest of a gallery patron.

The detachment evaporated the second I saw the black Lincoln parked in front of my parents' house. Now I was really angry. They could follow and harass me, but not my family. I braked and was out of the car and halfway up the walk before common sense took over and counseled caution. My sudden appearance at the front door might send Braxton into a fit of cross-waving hysterics, which was the last thing my mother needed.

Crossing the yard, I stationed myself in the bushes just under the open parlor window. Like most families, our friends usually ended up in the kitchen for their visits; strangers were shown to the parlor. Mom was running to form, and through the gossamer curtains of the open window I could see them all, and my sensitive hearing picked up every word. Braxton and Webber had apparently only arrived and were just settling in for a talk. Braxton was doing most of it, the padded and polite kind of speech reserved for people that you want something from.

None of it impressed my father, for he dealt with salesmen every day.

"Mr. Braxton, you said you wanted to talk with us about Jack," he said, interrupting the flow of words.

"Indeed, yes, Mr. Fleming." Braxton's voice was smoother and more cultured than I'd thought possible, no longer strident with vanity or fear. It was that persuasive tone that kicked my memory into gear. "How long has it been since you last heard from him?"

"Why do you want to know?"

"At the moment that might be difficult to explain."

"He sent us a postcard just this week," said my mother.

"Did he mention anything unusual?"

"Like what?" asked Dad.

"An odd experience, perhaps?"

Mom was worried now. "Why do you ask? Has something happened to him? What is it?"

"Please, Mrs. Fleming, so far as we know he is all right and we are doing our best to see that he remains so."

Dad's temper was starting to flare. "Out with the story, Mr. Braxton."

"Of course, of course. Your son, unknown to himself, may have gotten into some trouble when he moved to Chicago."

"How so? What kind of trouble?"

"When he lived in New York he often wrote stories on the criminal element there for his paper. He had access to information sources that they would like to see eliminated, what we call informants and the like. Some of these criminals became very suspicious at his sudden departure and they are anxious to find out why he left. Matheus and I must talk with him about this and we must see him personally."

"His moving was hardly sudden," said Mom. "Besides, he moved nearly a month ago."

"Yes, unfortunately certain individuals from the underworld were arrested at the same time, and they are blaming him for their capture. Whether he was responsible or not makes little difference to them."

There was a pause as Mom and Dad exchanged worried looks.

"Then we have to warn him, send him a telegram or something," said Dad.

"No, you must *not* do that, such things can be intercepted. I know that from experience."

"What experience?"

"I work for the government; I must ask you to keep this meeting secret, of course."

"Government?" Mom echoed uncertainly.

"Here, my identification."

Dad looked at something Braxton passed to him. "You don't look like a G-man—neither of you," he added, to include Matheus, who was being very quiet about things.

Braxton chuckled easily. "None of us really do. For instance, young Webber here is one of our trainees. This is his first assignment, you know, so you see there is no real danger involved, but that does not lessen the importance of what we are doing. We must make contact with your son as soon as possible. We have to warn him about what is going on."

"We'll call him, then."

"I'm afraid he's no longer at the place he was living in. He moved out last night and we were only able to trace him part of the way here."

"He's coming home, then?" Dad was puzzled.

"Possibly, perhaps he learned of the trouble independently from us and he may try hiding out from them here."

"Or at the farm—no one would think to look for him there," Mom said helpfully. I groaned inside.

"Farm?"

Dad began explaining about the farm, with Braxton avidly listening, and I could see the next question coming a mile off. They didn't need to be nosing around my home earth and learning of my excavations. Before things could go further, I picked up one of the whitewashed stones that divided the lawn from the bushes and sent it crashing through the parlor window.

Mom screamed and I was sorry for that, but I wanted those bozos out of the house, where I could deal with them. Dad was roaring mad and the first one out the front door, with Braxton and Webber at his heels. But I wasn't hanging around, and bolted for the Lincoln. Opening the driver's door, I released the hand brake and pushed. It wasn't so dark that they couldn't see their car moving off by itself.

Matheus noticed, yelled, and gave chase. I had a good lead; he was out of shape and Braxton on the arthritic side. It was a good block's run before they caught up with the car. I ducked low, seeping into the backseat, and waited for them. They were both wheezing when they tore the doors open. There was no sign of Dad. They'd left him back in the yard looking in the bushes for the vandal.

"I'm sure I set the brake," Matheus insisted in reply to Braxton's irritated question.

"Well, start it up and let's get back there. I almost had him."

"But who broke the window?"

"I did," I said, leaning forward to clamp a hand over their mouths. For once the lack of an image in the rearview mirror had worked in my favor. They gave only a token struggle—I was strong and they were pretty winded after their dash to the car.

"I *told* you to go back to New York," I reminded them.

Braxton mumphed something loud and defiant. He squirmed and twisted, trying to get something from his pants pocket. I could guess he was after his cross again and shifted my hand until it was over his nose. He was already short of oxygen, in a few seconds he was weakly trying to tear free.

"You gonna behave?" I asked him.

He mewed desperately down in his throat and I eased off just enough so he could breathe.

I looked at Matheus, who was too scared to move. "Okay, kid, you drive to my directions, understand?"

He gurgled.

"You drive nice, or I'll break the geezer's neck."

Another gurgle. It sounded like an affirmative.

I let the kid go and he started the car without any argument. He seemed used to taking orders. Our drive was not a cordial one, and out of necessity I was forced to keep both hands tight on Braxton—one over his mouth and the other encircling his wrists. After several miles I was feeling very cramped.

We drove northeast until I judged that the distance was enough to keep them busy, then had the kid stop. He was visibly trembling and Braxton was sweating bullets. The area was well clear of the city, dark and deserted. They must have concluded that I was going to kill them and leave the bodies in a roadside ditch. It was tempting, but only as a joke. Instead I pushed them out of the car, got behind the wheel, and turned the big machine back toward the city. They gave an angry and halfhearted chase, but were easily left behind in the exhaust fumes.

If they got lucky they might turn up a ride in Montgomery, but in the meantime I planned to head for Indianapolis.

I left their car parked across the street from a fire station and had a brisk walk back to my own. By this time the neighborhood had settled down. The lights were still on in my parents' house, but the rest were dark, their occupants sensibly asleep. Dad had nailed a board over the broken window. I rolled quietly away to look for another telephone.

Dad answered on the first ring and I blandly said hello.

"Jack!" He sounded excited.

"Is something wrong?" I asked innocently.

"I'll say there is." He gave me a slightly garbled account of what had happened earlier and wanted to know if I knew there were some gangsters after me.

"Wait a minute." I tried to sound skeptical. It wasn't hard. "How do you know these guys were G-men?"

"He had an identification card, it said he was with the FBI."

"Those can be printed up by the hundreds in any joke shop. What did they look like? Was it a little guy and a chubby kid with bad skin?"

"That's them."

"Dad, I hate to say it, but you've been had."

"What d'ya mean?"

"I did a story on those fish last year. They're a couple of con men. Because of me, the cops went after them, a lot of their victims turned up in court, and these guys got sent up. Did they try talking you into buying anything?"

"No, they wanted to know where you were, and then someone broke the window—"

"That was the third man in their team. They'll be coming back and trying to sell you some kind of phony U.S. government insurance. . . ."

I gave Dad an imaginative account of their criminal career, stating that

Braxton was a dangerous crazy and that he and Webber indulged in some bizarre sexual practices. Then I held my breath to see if he believed it, because I'd always been a lousy liar.

Dad said a few well-chosen obscenities, but they were directed at his recent guests, not me.

"Watch out for them," I suggested enthusiastically. "The little one's a real weasel when he's cornered. If they bother you again, just call the cops. Don't let them back in the house."

"I won't, I just wish you'd called earlier. Why are you calling now?"

"I've been moving, I wanted to give you my new number."

"They said you'd moved. Where are you?"

"I found a nice boardinghouse. If there's an emergency they'll get a message to me." I gave him Escott's office phone number and told him to keep it to himself.

"What about the address?"

"I'll be getting a box at the post office, the landlord likes to steam things open."

"That's illegal."

"Yeah, but the rent's cheap and the food's good. How's Mom?"

He put her on the line and we exchanged reassurances and other bits of information. She thought I had a job at an ad agency and asked how it was going. I let her keep thinking it. Except for the Swafford case, my modest living expenses and the money I sent home to help them out had come from an inadvertent theft from a mobster and some engineered luck at a blackjack table. Neither of them would have won her approval.

I promised to call again in a day or two for further news and hung up, grinning ear to ear.

A few years ago I walked into a small bookstore in Manhattan. The window on the street was just large enough to display the painted legend: BRAXTON'S BOOKS, NEW & USED, and the inside sill held a few sun-faded samples of literature. In the last few weeks I'd seen a hundred hole-in-the-wall places like this; I liked them.

A bell over the door jingled as I entered. Dust motes hanging in the sunlight were stirred by the draft and I sneezed. By the time I straightened and wiped my nose he had appeared out of one of the alcoves formed by bookshelves.

"Good afternoon, sir, may I help you?"

He was shorter than me, with dark wrinkled skin like a dried apple. There was a suggestion of black shoe polish in his hair, but the world was full of people who didn't want to look their age.

"Got anything on folklore or the occult?"

"Yes, sir, in this first section." He indicated the area and watched with a pleasant smile as I went to look it over.

It was a fairly complete selection. There were copies of Summer's works on witchcraft and vampires, even Baring-Gould's book on werewolves, but nothing I hadn't already seen and read before. I checked the fiction section, drew a blank, and finished off with the occult shelves. They were also very complete, but only with the usual junk. I said thank you to the general air and started for the door.

"Perhaps," he said, stopping me, "if you're looking for something special I could be of help. I have other books in the back."

It was my day off, I was in no hurry. "Well, sure, if you don't mind."

"What are you looking for?"

Speaking the title always made me feel vaguely foolish. "A copy of *Varney, the Vampire* by Prest."

He knew what I was talking about, not surprising considering the contents of his well-stocked shelves. His brown eyes got brighter with interest. *"Or the Feast of Blood,"* he said, completing the title. "Yes, that is a rare one. I have a copy, but it's part of my own collection and not for sale."

"Oh," I said, for want of something better.

"May I ask why you are interested in it?"

The real reason I couldn't talk about, so I had a fake one practiced and ready. "I'm working on a book, a survey of folklore, fact and fiction."

"That is a very wide field."

"Not when you're tracking down certain books."

He looked sympathetic. "I'd like to help, but it could only be in a limited way."

Strings of some kind? He'd find out real soon I wasn't rich.

"You'd have to read it here in the shop, that is if you want to. I value it too much to loan it out."

"I can understand that," I said gratefully. "Are you sure it wouldn't be too much trouble?"

"Not at all, but it would have to be during working hours."

"That would be fine, thank you."

He offered his hand. "I'm James Braxton."

"Jack Fleming."

"Come in the back, I'll show you where you may read."

"You have it right here?"

"Oh, yes. Yes." He threaded past ceiling-high shelves, leading me deep into the narrow shop. He switched on the light over a desk and chair and swept some account books to one side. The light revealed shelves crammed with a faded patchwork of book spines of every shape and age. It looked like a duplicate of the folklore section out front, but more so. Some of the volumes were very old, with odd titles, others were recent and by skeptical writers. One shelf held only copies of *Occult Review*. He was more than casually interested in the subject himself, and I wondered if he sincerely believed in it. If so, I'd have to watch my lip.

He knew exactly where his copy was located and pulled it out, placing it on the desk. "I hope you enjoy it," he said.

"Thank you, you're very generous to do this."

"I'm just in favor of expanding knowledge in a neglected area," he smiled.

"You have quite a collection."

The bell on the door out front rang, interrupting his reply. He excused himself with a rueful smile, and for the next few hours was too busy to return.

I'd already read the first chapter in another book, so I skipped it and went through the second and third in short order. I was a fast reader, but did not plan to spend the rest of my life poring word by word through the book's more than two hundred chapters. In its original state, it had been published a chapter at a time for weekly consumption by the newly literate masses. A fast writer could keep himself employed for years with a popular series. In the previous century, the penny dreadfuls were just as popular as the current radio and movie serials were now.

I skimmed the pages, reading the brief descriptions given under the chapter titles, and touching on the dialogue whenever it popped up. The gist of it centered on the tribulations of the Bannerworth family as they nobly bore the attacks of Varney upon their daughter, Flora. A good family, but not too bright: if they'd simply moved away at the start they would have saved themselves a lot of trouble, but the plot dragged on regardless of such logic.

It was really better than I expected—at least at first, then the quality of the writing began to deteriorate along with the continuity. A cliff-hanger ending was never resolved and one of the Bannerworth brothers seemed to disappear completely from the story. When he did return, the author had forgotten his name. Whole sections written for no other purpose than to fill a word quota tried my patience and I skipped them altogether. I focused on the few scenes where the vampire appeared and had dialogue.

His blood requirements were only occasional, usually after he'd been killed and his body was carelessly left out in the moonlight, which revived him. The moonlight device had been lifted wholesale from Polidori's story and used shamelessly each time Varney was shot dead, or in one case, drowned. He had no trouble with running water, crosses, or garlic, not that anyone thought of using the latter two against him.

Eventually all the Bannerworths disappeared, to be replaced with a steady parade of beautiful young girls that he kept trying to marry, either in the hope their love would end his curse or because he was thirsty. Sometimes, the reason was a bit vague. He was usually kept from the nuptial feasts by an interfering old enemy, the man the bride truly loved, or the bride's suicide. He soon ran out of nubile prospects as well as European countries to ravage.

Tough, he was able to recover from mortal wounds with some lunar help, but he certainly lacked a talent for hypnotism. His victims always ended up screaming for help and interrupting his dinner. The one point I did find very interesting was that each time he was resurrected, he had to soon feed or die.

I shut the book with a slight headache and a sigh of relief just as Braxton was coming back.

"I was closing up for the day. . . . Surely you haven't finished it?"

"Not exactly." I explained my skimming method to him.

"Are you sure you got sufficient detail for your research? I thought you'd be here for several days, taking notes."

"I can hold it in my head long enough to jot the high points down later."

He registered mock disappointment. "And I'd been looking forward to some company. It is so rare for me to meet someone with a similar interest in the unusual."

"I couldn't help noticing your collection. . . ."

He was proud of it and this time able to talk. "Fortunately my business gives me an advantage over others. I often get advance notice of private collections going up for sale and can get first pick." He pulled out a volume, but didn't open it. "That's how I found this one. A friend of mine who arranges estate sales told me about it, and I made an early purchase ahead of the auction."

With a slight shock I deciphered the title; the script lettering was hard to read. "But I thought this was a fake, it has to be."

"As did I when I saw it, but here it is. It came from the library of a university professor. His relatives sealed up his house when he suddenly disappeared. The police thought he'd been kidnapped and perhaps murdered, but never found the body—the case is still open. His family waited seven years, had him declared dead, and settled his estate."

The story stunk like a barrel of very old fish. Braxton's friend must have taken him for plenty over that book. He had believed it, though, and expected me to as well. "What was his name?"

"I don't remember, this was years ago."

"Maybe he wrote it on the inside of the book."

"No, not *this* book."

"Mind if I flipped through it?"

He was uneasy. "I'd rather you didn't. The *Necronomicon* isn't just any book, you know. That does sound ridiculous in the broad light of day, I realize I must appear to be superstitious."

"Why did you buy it if it makes you uncomfortable?"

"I don't really know, perhaps it's the collector in me. I suppose I also wanted it kept somewhere safe, where it would not be used." He sucked in his lips and looked embarrassed.

He wanted to impress someone, anyone, and I was his latest effort. Projecting an air of mystery and implied danger concerning his possessions was his method, and it put my hackles up. I'd met people like him before; he was more subtle than most and probably had a small, handpicked circle of acolytes. I wondered where they held their weekly séance.

"Yes, I guess it could be misused," I commented neutrally.

He was relieved that I hadn't laughed, and replaced the book. "Some of these others might help you in your research. I wouldn't mind you looking them over."

"Thank you very much, but I'm afraid most of them are outside my immediate study range."

"Are you researching vampires exclusively?"

"For this book, yes. They're popular now."

"They always have been. Hardly a week goes by that I don't have a customer asking for a copy of *Dracula*. Business was especially good last month, when the movie began showing. It would seem to be the last word on the subject."

I knew better but said nothing. "Yes, I'm trying to locate Stoker's sources. I don't have the British Museum available so I've been hitting every bookstore and library in the city."

"Why are you interested in his sources?"

"To see if there were any true accounts of vampirism in them."

"Do you believe in vampires?"

I didn't like the way he focused on me. "In a way . . . I've read about people like Elizabeth Bathory and others. There's always going to be a few oddballs running loose, but as for the *Dracula* kind of vampire, no, I don't believe in them." And I said it with perfect sincerity, but his intense, inquiring look made me uncomfortable.

"You don't believe in supernatural vampires?" he pursued.

"No."

"But what if they exist despite your disbelief?"

"They don't."

He smiled tightly.

"You believe in them?" I asked.

"I'm not sure." He gestured at all the books. "I've read them, all of them, and there *is* a lot of evidence. Most of it is quite absurd, of course, but once sifted through, some of it refuses to be dismissed. I like to keep an open mind."

"To each his own," I said meaninglessly, trying to think of a polite way to end the conversation. Someday I might want to come back, though that possibility was not looking very attractive at the moment.

His expression was still disturbing. "But tell me, Mr. Fleming, and with all truth, what would it mean if there are such things? What would it mean to you?"

"I'd have to think that one over."

"I already have. I've thought a lot about it. We have this bright world of daylight, predictable and comfortable to us. Normal. But what do we do when something happens that simply does not fit into that world and makes us conscious of another world altogether, existing and blending closely with our own? A world we can but glimpse and then dismiss as a fantasy, a world we cannot sanely accept, for that would doom our complacent security. Its citizens are beautiful monsters, to be feared or laughed at as at a dream. But if their reality were to be proved to you, how would you react? You can deny it or accept the truth. One keeps your illusion of your world safe and the other . . . well, your hand might hesitate tonight before it turns out the light. How can you slumber in peace when you cannot see what the darkness conceals? Our eyes blink against it, our ears hear things that *might* be moving, our skin shivers and anticipates crawling things beneath the covers. Within that dark, which is as sunlight to them, they watch and bide their time until sleep takes you; they sense it as we sense the heat and cold. They approach, marking you, stealing your heart's essence to strengthen their own Undead bodies, and when the dawn comes they're gone . . . and one more part of your soul is gone with them."

It was past time to leave. The man knew too much and yet too little. He was perceptive enough to know there were other reasons besides a bogus book to inspire my research. Maybe he hoped I would confide in him, show him the marks on my throat and ask for help. That was out. I was not under any restraining hypnotic suggestion from Maureen, but I did have a share of common sense. Even if I told him the truth about vampires, it would do no good. He was the wrong sort to unlearn all the nonsense he had sitting on his shelves, such truth would endanger his illusions just as he said.

He read my face correctly and knew he'd gone too far too soon. Cultivating acolytes takes time. "I'm sorry, I do ramble on a bit."

"That's all right. It was very interesting, but I have to be going. Thank you very much for letting me read the book. I really appreciate it."

"Not at all," he replied, shaking hands. "I hope you'll come again?"

"Sure," I lied.

Social conventions sometimes come in handy. We smiled, said the usual things, performed the expected rituals, and pretended all was right in the world. It was for me as soon as I stepped out into the brisk March dusk to walk home. Braxton's outlook on reality was enough to throw anyone off center. If nothing else, he personified my own fears of vampirism and made me realize how groundless they were. Compared to Maureen, Braxton was far more frightening.

The relationship Maureen and I shared was hardly consistent with the popular image of vampire and victim. Our love-making was astonishingly joyous and normal, and if at its climax she drew a little blood from me what did it matter as long as we both enjoyed it? Maybe she wasn't a typical vampire, maybe there were others just as dangerous as Stoker's creation. I did not know.

I never mentioned Braxton to Maureen; I didn't want her to know about my fears, especially now that they'd been dispelled. She needed my love and support, not my insecurities. After a very short time, the incident faded from my memory.

AGAIN taking refuge in a large, anonymous hotel under a different name, I stopped for the day in Indianapolis. My car was left several blocks away in another hotel's garage. Not the best kind of subterfuge, but I was hoping Braxton was not that good a detective. My hopes panned out or I was lucky again; the next night I was back in the familiar and relative sanity of Chicago. My first stop was Bobbi's place.

I waved at the night clerk as usual, he nodded back, turned to a pillar near his desk, and resumed talking to it. This sort of behavior makes me curious, so I walked over to see what made the pillar such a fascinating conversationalist. Leaning against it, just out of my line of sight, was the house dick, Phil. He was a medium-sized, slightly tubby man in an old derby and a loose collar. He didn't look like much, but Bobbi said he could take care of himself and knew where to go for help if he needed it.

He saw me and nodded. "Morning, Fleming. You up early or out late?"

I shook his calluses. "I'm always out late. How's business?"

"Slow, but there's the weekend coming up."

That was when he made most of his tips. As long as the trysting couples were quiet about it, he was conveniently blind and deaf; disturb the other guests and the offenders were out on their ears.

"Good luck, then. Listen, could you do me a favor?"*

"Depends." His face was as carefully blank as the lobby's marble floor.

"There's been a couple of guys following me. . . ." I gave him an accurate description of Braxton and Webber and an inaccurate account of their activities. "They've already pestered my folks and I figure they might try bothering Miss Smythe next."

"They can try." The only thing Phil liked better than bribes was kicking pests around.

"I'd appreciate it if you kept your eyes open." I stuck my hand out in farewell and we shook again briefly. He pocketed the sawbuck I slipped him with the discreet manner that made him so popular with the other hotel patrons.

"I will do that," he promised. The only thing Phil liked better than bribes and kicking pests around was to be bribed to kick pests around. "Please tender my regards to Miss Smythe."

Phil and the clerk resumed their discussion, which had to do with the merits of various betting parlors in the city, and I completed my journey to the elevator. The operator put up a good imitation of being awake and he took me to Bobbi's floor.

"She's got guests tonight," he told me.

"Anyone I know?"

He shrugged and opened the doors. "They look the fancy type to me."

That could mean anything. I stepped out and immediately picked up the loud thrum of conversation down the hall. Bobbi had mentioned her plans for a little party a few days ago. Her idea of a little party meant inviting only half the city, not all of it.

The door swung open at my knock and a dangerous-looking female barred the way in. She sucked in a lungful of smoke from a skinny black cigar and let it blow out her nostrils to corrode the air. "Well, speak of the devil."

Not knowing how to respond to that one, I waited for her to stand aside, only she didn't, hanging on to the doorknob to look me over.

She had well-powdered white skin stretched over her bones, and dark eyes, which were made larger and darker by a liberal use of makeup. Her hair was jet black, shaped like a helmet with thick, severely cut bangs that just covered the eyebrows. The rest was leveled hard against her jawline. If any single hair dared to rebel, it had been rigorously dealt with by a dose of lacquer.

She wore something box shaped and bright purple, with green sequins edging a deep neckline that didn't suit her long face. The talons she affected were another bad choice, as they accentuated the developing witchiness of her fingers. They were painted the same color as her wide mouth: a deep maroon. I put her down as a case that was determined to look a young and sophisticated twenty no matter what her actual age. As far as I could tell under the war paint, she'd just edged her way over forty.

She'd finished assessing me as well, took a step backward, and swept her hand in a gesture to indicate I could pass. We locked stares for a second and she smiled. It was no more than a thinning of the lips, but it expressed her contempt as plainly as if she'd spit in my face.

Then Bobbi said my name, threw her body against mine, and I forgot about everything else for a few moments.

"You should have called." Her mouth was very close to my ear and I enjoyed the tickling of her breath. "I didn't know when you'd be back."

"I like surprising you."

"It *is* easier to catch them out that way," the woman said agreeably.

Bobbi pulled back a little, but kept her arms around me. "Jack, this is Marza Chevreaux. She's my accompanist."

I had wondered what she was. "How do you do?"

"Not as well as you, dear boy," she drawled sweetly, and held out her hand, forcing me to relinquish my hold on Bobbi in order to take it. It wasn't a fair exchange; her fingers lay briefly and limply in my palm and then recoiled to be better occupied at playing with the chain of her long necklace. She smiled again, took a step backward, pivoted on the same movement, and left us.

I hoped she was out of earshot and opened my mouth, but Bobbi beat me to it.

"You don't have to say it, I already know."

"I never saw her at the club."

"Slick didn't like her."

"Fancy that."

"She really is a good accompanist, once you get past all her dramatics. We're a good team and I got the station to agree to have her play when I sing."

"She said 'speak of the devil'; should my ears be burning?"

"A couple of the girls were wondering who I was dating, and I can't help but talk about you. Because of Slick, Marza doesn't think much of the men in my life, but she'll come around once she gets to know you."

"Do you have some less discriminating guests in the meantime?"

"Sure, come in and meet them."

"What's this about again?"

"Just a little pre-broadcast party, then afterward we'll have a post-broadcast party."

"I didn't know you were so social."

"Neither did I, but getting away from the club was like getting out of jail. I just want to celebrate." Then she kissed me again, linked an arm in mine, and pulled me into the living room with all the noise.

It wasn't as large a group as I thought, but they made up for it in volume. A half dozen were in the immediate vicinity, with several brands of cigarettes and perfumes, none of it too breathable, so I only indulged when it was necessary to talk.

Marza Chevreaux had taken up a station at the piano, but was clearly not about to play it. Her purpose must have been to prevent others from doing so. She clutched a drink and stared with glassy eyes at an intense-looking man crouched on the floor next to her. He wore thick glasses and had short skin-colored hair on the sides and long dark hair on top. It looked too much like a toupee to be one, so it had to be his own. He was making short, waving movements with his hands as he tried to prove a point of some kind to Marza.

"That's Madison Pruitt," Bobbi whispered. "Marza brought him along because he irritates everyone."

"He looks more than capable of it. Why is he so irritating?"

"Because if you give him half a chance he'll try to get you to join the Communist party. He's as bad as the Jehovah's Witnesses."

"You're kidding me, nobody could—" I hauled up short, staring at the mountainous back of a man on the sofa. "What's he doing here?"

"Are you angry?"

I thought it over. "Actually, no, just curious."

She was relieved. "He's my friend, Jack. I wanted him here. You don't have to talk to him, he'll understand."

"That wouldn't be polite. Besides, this place isn't that big and he's a hard man to duck."

"You going to be nice?" She was half-joking, half-serious. I felt like kissing her and saw no reason not to and followed through.

"I'll be nice," I promised, and walked over to the sofa.

He was taking up most of it, a big man with hard muscle under the tailored lines of his evening clothes. With short-cropped blond hair and a grim set to his lips, he wasn't the sort you invite to liven up a social occasion. His eyes were slightly sleepy from the drink in his hand until he looked up at me. They visibly sharpened, went on guard, then relaxed into a pseudo-dullness. I knew that to be one of his defenses, that dull look. People expected a big man like him to be stupid. He let them think what they liked and consequently learned more about them than they cared.

I put my hand out. "Hello, Gordy."

He registered a flicker of surprise, slowly stood, and shook hands. He was beyond trying to prove himself with a crushing grasp and gave me a firm, careful grip.

"Fleming," he returned. "Bobbi said you might turn up."

"Yeah."

"She says you're taking good care of her."

I wasn't sure how he meant that. Bobbi wasn't dependent on me financially, so he must have been referring to our emotional relationship. He was too polite where Bobbi was concerned to make cheap remarks on our sex life.

"She's a wonderful girl."

"Glad you know that."

"And if I didn't?"

"I'd sic Marza on you."

It was my turn for surprise. I hadn't expected him to make a joke. I glanced over to the piano and saw he was serious, after all. Marza was glaring at us, and from her expression, all she needed were some snakes for hair to turn us to stone.

"No, thanks." I hooked a chair so we could sit and be eye to eye. Standing with him was uncomfortable. I wasn't used to looking up at people, and Gordy was tall enough to give Paul Bunyan a stiff neck. "How are things at the club?"

He shrugged and settled into the sofa. "Had to put up with a raid last week."

"The casino?"

"It looks good for City Hall in the papers, but they should hold off until just before election, like they usually do. They grabbed all my slot machines and chopped up the tables. Take a few weeks to get new ones, but by that time the heat will be off. The club's still open, lot of the regulars still ask after Bobbi."

"You think she'll go back?"

"Not after all that mess with Slick. Can't blame her."

"Nope."

"You working?"

"Sort of."

"Need a job?"

"What kind?"

"What kind you need?"

I shook my head and smiled. "Thanks."

"About that mess with Slick—"

"No hard feelings, Gordy."

"Yeah?"

"Yeah."

"I mean, sorry if I hurt you. I was just doing a job."

"You didn't hurt me."

"I didn't? How come?"

"You already know that."

He took a long pull on his drink, studying me. " 'Sfunny, you don't look any different from a hundred other guys off the street."

"If I did, I wouldn't survive long. People notice when you're different."

"Hell, you don't have to tell me that."

"You always been big?"

"Ma said I weighed thirteen pounds when I was born. Damn near killed her. You wanna drink?"

"No, thanks."

Again the long study. "You eat anything?"

"Not eat."

"So that stuff's true, that you only drink—"

"Yeah, that part's true."

"What about Bobbi? Doesn't that hurt her?"

"If it did, I'd stop seeing her. Why not ask her yourself?"

"Nah, I couldn't do that."

"If you're worried, just look at her, she's healthy."

He looked. She was in a corner talking and laughing with a white-haired man with a beard. "She's not under some kind of spell or something?"

I made an effort to match his serious face. "None."

He digested this. "Okay. I just wanted to make sure about a few things."

"On the other hand, I could be lying."

His head went back and forth in a slight wobble, his version of laughter. "Hell, kid, you ain't no liar."

Bobbi introduced me to some names and faces, and a couple of the voices that went with them were familiar because I'd heard them on the radio. We made the rounds, and then it was my turn to do some steering.

"What gives?" she asked when I took a determined grip on her arm.

"You'll find out."

The only unoccupied place was the bathroom, not the most romantic setting, but it was private.

"Alone at last," I sighed.

"At least until the next customer comes—there's a lot of booze flowing out there."

"Too bad. I wanted to see you for a minute without an audience."

"Oh, so what do you think?" Hands on hips, she did a slow turn. She was in her best color, which was no color; something white and clinging, probably silk.

I shrugged. "It's all right, but the hem's too long."

She made a playful swat at my stomach. "Stinker, it's perfect and you know it."

"Only because you're in it." Then we took up where we left off when I first came in.

After a few minutes she came up for air. "Say, you *did* miss me."

"Very much," I muttered, nosing around in her hair. Her head tilted back and my lips brushed against the large vein of her throat. I ran my tongue over the two small wounds there, taking in the slight salt taste of her skin and feeling the strong pulse beneath.

Then the damn phone rang and made us both jump because it was so close.

"Hell, what's that doing in here?" I complained.

"Better in here than the bedroom. Hello?"

It was someone from the radio station working late. They hashed out a minor scheduling problem and hung up.

"Why the long face?" she asked.

I curled my upper lip back and made a mock growling sound.

"Oh," she said with vast understanding, and cuddled back into my arms.

"When can you get rid of your friends?" I lisped.

"As soon as the booze runs out, which shouldn't be too long with that crowd. Why wait? You can nibble on me in here."

"That's like going straight to the dessert and skipping the rest of the banquet. I want us to take some time and enjoy everything."

This disconcerted her a bit, and a blush fanned over her cheeks. "Dammit, sometimes I feel like a schoolgirl with you."

"Isn't it great?"

On this occasion, Bobbi proved to be a terrible hostess and ran out of drinkable alcohol before the guests had run out of party enthusiasm. But her guests were resourceful: one of the girls suggested removing to a nearby bar that she thought was still open and led an exodus for it. Bobbi and I promised to be along and somehow forgot about it the moment the last person was gone.

Her white dress was certainly beautiful, but since I'd arrived, the major thought on my mind had been how to get it off her. The fastenings were located on the left side instead of in the back, but she slipped away before my inquisitive fingers could accomplish anything.

"Help me search the place," she said from the kitchen.

"For what?"

"In case someone got left behind. That happened to me once, and it's damned embarrassing."

We searched the place and then later, much later, in a sleepy voice she said, "Welcome home."

"Thanks."

"I mean it. Move in with me."

"Move in?"

"I want you around all the time."

"What would the neighbors think?"

"Whatever they like, I don't care."

"Bobbi, I don't want to say no—"

"But that's your answer."

"It has to be."

"Why?"

"Because of what I am."

"Because you have to be up to your eyeballs in some cemetery by dawn, right?"

"Something like that. I'd be very dull company during the day. I just don't want you to see me like that. You don't let me see you in curlers."

"Listen, if I can get used to your not breathing—"

"This is different, it's different for me. What I've been through, what I've become—I'm still trying to get used to it. I don't know how else to explain why. This is nothing against you."

"I know. You've had a lot of things happen to you all at once."

"I need some time."

She sighed. "Then don't worry about it. If it's no, it's no."

"You can be pretty damn terrific."

"Yeah, and I just realized what sort of commotion would happen if someone like the maid happened to find you while she was dusting. Having a coffin lying around with a body in it might upset the hotel staff."

I laughed. "Good grief, I don't use a *coffin*."

"I thought all vampires did."

"Maybe they do, but not me—I have a more modern steamer trunk. It's smaller, just as light proof, and a lot less conspicuous."

"Very clever."

"I have to lay low for a while, anyway."

"What's wrong? Is it Gordy?"

"No, nothing like that."

We lay comfortably tangled together in the dark, and I told her about my trip and in particular about Braxton and Webber. "They can travel during the day, so they're probably in Chicago by now and looking around. I just want you to watch out for them, or for anyone asking after me."

"You're the one who needs to watch out if they're trying to kill you."

"They won't. I can lose myself in a city this big."

"Forever?"

"Until I can figure out what to do about them or until they run out of money."

"Look, I can call up Gordy. He and some of the boys can throw a scare into them—"

"Bobbi, my sweet, they are determined to track down a hideous, bloodthirsty vampire; a demonic creature of the night. Do you think they'll be intimidated by a couple of gangsters with guns and brass knuckles?"

"Who said anything about intimidation? Gordy can just have their legs broken."

"I can do that myself," I said dryly. "Just promise me you'll be careful. They may try to save you from my evil clutches."

"But I like being clutched by you."

"I doubt if they could understand that."

"Got any idea what to do about them?"

"I don't know, I'd like to talk it over with Charles first and see what he thinks."

"I'm glad you mentioned him. He called today, but I'd forgotten all about it because of the party. He wanted you to drop by when you got back, no matter how late."

"Even this late?"

"He said if the lights were on to come in."

"I hate to leave you. . . ."

"Oh, pooh, you'll have to go sooner or later, so come on. I'm hungry now, anyway." She rustled her way out from the sheets, and I obediently followed her to the kitchen.

What with our reluctant good-byes and some unexpected early traffic, it was close to six before I got to Escott's. My rearview mirror was clear all the way over, which was encouraging, and when I arrived, there were welcoming lights in the windows. He must have heard me pull up, for the door opened before I knocked and a cloud of stale pipe smoke and white dust billowed out along with his greeting.

"I finally got your message. Sorry I'm so late."

"Not at all. Do come in." He was dressed uncharacteristically in some ancient paint-spattered overalls and his hair was full of plaster dust. "Please excuse my appearance, I started the job today and it turned out to be more involved than I thought." He ushered me into the parlor.

"What are you doing?"

"At the moment, taking a well-deserved break. It seems the previous

owners subdivided all the bedrooms so they could accommodate more customers at one time. I've been upstairs knocking down a wall."

"You've been at it all night?"

"It's a very stubborn wall, if I may anthropomorphize it."

"When do you sleep?"

"Hardly ever," he said in an indifferent tone.

"What'd you want to see me for?"

"This. I'm not in a position to judge. It will be for you to decide what
to do." Before I could ask what he was talking about, he reached for a
folded newspaper and pointed to a circled item in the public notices. My fingers grew cold as I read it.

Jack, will you please call me. I want to talk to you about Maureen.

There was no name, only a phone and room number. I stared at the symbols
on the page as though they could tell me more.

"Sorry about the shock, old man," he was saying. "I knew you would
want to know about this as soon as possible, but I couldn't really give any
details to Miss Smythe."

I read the ad again, not believing it, but none of the wording had
changed. "How long has it been running?"

"It started the day after you left."

Then I stopped being stunned and things cleared up for me. "That old
bastard . . ."

"I beg your pardon?"

"Braxton must have planted it to try and trap me."

"Who is Braxton?"

"Someone else you can check up on when you go to New York. He
knew Maureen, or at least I think he did." I settled back and told him the
story of the last three nights of my life. "The kid said they began looking for
me when they noticed my ad was gone. This is probably just bait to flush
me out."

"I think not. I took the liberty of tracking down the number. It belongs
to a small but respectable hotel near the Loop. When I made inquiries, I was
told to go to room twenty-three, occupied by a Miss Gaylen Dumont. She
arrived two days ago from New York; a semi-invalid, she takes her meals in
her room and is regarded as a very quiet, trouble-free guest. The name sug-
gests that she is a relative of Maureen Dumont."

"Gaylen?" I repeated blankly. "I wouldn't know, Maureen never talked
about her family."

"People who don't generally have a good reason. In the simple cause of
common sense, I counsel you to be cautious about this."

"Hell, yes, I'll be cautious. Did you learn anything else?"

"She is in her seventies, listens to dance music on the radio, and doesn't
like fried foods."

"How did you—"

"It is amazing how much one can learn from a hotel's staff when the right questions are applied in the right manner. Have you any reason to think that Braxton might be connected with this woman?"

"If he knew Maureen, he might know this Gaylen. I just don't know."

"This could be bad timing or coincidence, but it will be safer if you assume it is not. You removed your ad and some people noticed."

"Yeah, but not the one that mattered." The paper twitched in my hands. "I'm checking on this first thing tomorrow night. Want to come along?"

"I was leaving for New York tomorrow, or rather today, but I can postpone the trip if you wish."

"No, I couldn't ask you to do that. I guess I can handle one old lady."

Escott looked out the front window. "Jack, it's getting lighter. If you've no other place to stay, perhaps we should move you in now."

"Jeez, I forgot."

My second trunk went into the basement next to the first, and between us we emptied the car of thirty-six bags of earth, piling them neatly in a corner. The faint gray of dawn was just beginning to hurt my eyes when we finished. Escott dusted his hands off.

"I'll bid you good morning now, I still have some cleaning up to do."

"It won't disturb me," I assured him.

"No, I daresay it would not. Pleasant dreams." He climbed the basement steps and shut the door.

As long as I had my soil around me I was past the point of being able to dream. All the speculations tumbling through my brain would have only given me nightmares, anyway. There were some compensations to my condition, I thought as I wearily lowered the lid of my trunk to hide for another day.

6

ABOUT thirteen hours later I emerged from the basement, drawn by the swish-and-crinkle sound of pages being turned. Escott was in the parlor, half-buried in a drift of newsprint.

"I thought you'd be on a train by now," I said, dropping into a leather chair next to his radio.

He gave out with a slight shrug. "I seem to be acquiring your habits. I was up late and overslept."

"The whole day?"

"Most of it. Knocking down walls is a very exhausting exercise. This afternoon was too late to make a good start, and by then my curiosity about Gaylen Dumont had grown considerably. If she has any useful information it could save me much trouble. I'd like to meet her, but if you would rather go alone, please don't hesitate to say so. I shall be more than happy to wait here for your return."

"Nothing doing, I could use the moral support."

He looked relieved, but covered it by picking up his cold pipe and fiddling with it. "I'll do my best."

The papers weren't thrown about haphazardly, but shuffled into stacks on the sofa and floor. A neat pile was on one end of the table, each refolded so that it was open to the personal column. I flipped through them, and each had the same ad he'd shown me the night before.

"They are all the papers that you had used," he pointed out. "Either she knew which ones or she is remarkably thorough."

"I'll find out."

His phone clung to a dingy wall in the kitchen, which he hadn't gotten around to repainting yet. With one of the papers in hand, I carefully dialed the number. A professional voice answered, identifying the West Star Hotel and asked if it could help me. I asked for room twenty-three and heard clicking sounds.

After five rings a woman said hello. Her voice jarred me to the core because it was Maureen's voice. I bit my tongue and counted to five until I could respond normally.

"I'm calling about the ad. I think I'm the Jack you want to talk to."

There was a pause at the other end and I heard a long, soft sigh being released. "Jack," she finally said. "Could you prove that somehow? I've had two crank calls already."

It wasn't Maureen. The voice and inflection were very similar, but this one had the reedy quality of age in it. "How can I do that?"

"If you could just tell me the color of Maureen's eyes—"

"Blue, sky blue, with dark hair."

This time there was an intake of breath. "I am so glad to hear from you at last, Jack. My name is Gaylen Dumont and I would like very much to meet you."

"Where is Maureen? Do you know?"

It was as though she hadn't heard me. "I am so very glad you called, but it's difficult for me to talk over the phone. Could you come over?"

There was no other answer but yes. I got her address and promised to be there within half an hour. She thanked me and hung up. I stared at the earpiece and wondered suspiciously what her game was.

"She wasn't too talkative," I told Escott.

"Some people don't like to use the phone."

I was more inclined to think some people don't like to deliver bad news on the phone. Maybe I could have stayed on longer and tried to get more information. I was vulnerable to making mistakes because of my emotional involvement and was very glad Escott was coming. He might help me to think straight. As we drove over, half-formed thoughts and questions and alternatives to what I should have said were running through my mind like insane mice.

The West Star Hotel was nothing to write home about; neither old or new, flashy or drab, there were hundreds like it all over. We parked, went in past the front desk and elevator, and walked straight up the stairs to the right room. I hesitated before knocking.

Escott noticed my nerves. "Steady on," he said under his breath.

I nodded once, shook my shoulders up, and tapped on the door. No immediate answer came from within. I knocked again and heard faint movements now: a shuffling, a muted thump, the knob turned, and the wood panel squeaked open.

The voice was softer and less reedy than it was on the phone. "Jack?"

I swallowed. "Yes, I'm Jack Fleming."

The small shadowy figure in the dark dress stepped away, turned slowly, and retreated into the room. Her heart and lungs were laboring. She was either very excited, very ill, or both. I stepped forward and Escott followed quietly, taking his hat off with a smooth and automatic movement and nudging me to do the same.

We took in her plain impersonal room with a quick glance. The window was open only a crack, and the air well tainted with the smell of soap and strong liniment. A radio on a table crackled out the news of the day. She hobbled to it, using a cane for balance, and turned it off, then sat down with obvious relief.

"I'm so glad you could come over to talk," she said. "I did so want to meet you, and it is difficult for me to get around."

A suitcase stood at the foot of the bed and beyond that a stiff and ugly-looking wheelchair. She noted where my eyes went.

"That's for my bad days. They come more and more often, especially when it's damp. I have arthritis in my legs and it gives me a lot of trouble."

"Miss Dumont, this is my friend, Charles Escott."

She extended a frail, yellow hand. "How do you do?"

Escott took it and said something polite, making a little bow that only the English can do without looking self-conscious.

She smiled, pleased at the gesture. "I'm glad to meet you, both of you, but you must call me Gaylen, everybody does. Pull those chairs a little closer to the light so we may have a good look at each other."

We did as she said and sat down. Maureen's eyes looked back at me, but the dark hair and brows had faded and gone white. The angle of her jaw was the same, and there were a hundred other similarities too subtle for immediate definition. Her face was scored with wrinkles, the skin puffy and gone shapeless with age—a face like and unlike Maureen's. It was an agony to look at it.

She was smiling. "I can hardly believe you're here. I hardly dared hope you would see my notice, especially after yours stopped. I was afraid you'd moved again."

I explained how Escott had pointed it out to me.

"How very fortunate. You see, it was only a few days ago that I saw it. I live in upstate New York, pretty much by myself, and don't read the papers often. My housekeeper had a stack of them for her chores, though, and I saw one opened to the right page, and Maureen's name caught my eye. I remembered she once knew someone named Jack years ago, and I had to find out. I called the paper and they said you'd moved to Chicago. By then I'd found some of her letters to me and I knew you were the right person, so I came out."

"Gaylen, do you know where she is?"

She bowed her head. "I'm sorry, I am so dreadfully sorry to disappoint you."

Everything inside me twisted sharply. "Is she dead?"

"I don't know," she whispered. "I haven't heard from her for nearly five years."

The twisting got tighter. "When did you last see her? What did she say?"

"I didn't see her, she called me. I don't know from where. She said she was going to be gone on a long trip and not to worry if she didn't write for a while."

I shut my eyes for a moment. When I opened them, I was able to speak quietly, lucidly. "Gaylen, tell me the whole story, tell me everything you know."

"I'm not sure that I know very much. I only wanted to see someone else who knew her, who could remember her with me. I'd hoped you may have seen her in the last five years."

I felt sorry for both of us. "You have the same name. How are you related to her?"

She seemed surprised. "I thought you knew. Surely she mentioned me?"

"She never talked about her past."

"How very unlike her. . . . Are you certain? Well, I am her sister—her *younger* sister, Jack."

"Younger," I echoed back softly.

"I'm seventy-two, Maureen seventy-six—did she tell you nothing?"

Her look made me acutely uncomfortable. "No, I'm afraid not."

She shook her head. "You poor young man, you must be starved for information. I'll try my best, but I hope you'll be as frank with me."

"How so?"

"When I told you her age, you were startled, but not incredulous. You are aware of her—her unusual state?" Her eyes went from me to Escott inquiringly.

Escott cleared his throat. "Please feel free to speak openly about your sister. Jack has made me acquainted with the facts. *All* the facts."

She regarded him soberly, pursing her lips. "Your accent, you're from England?"

He nodded once.

Gaylen's eyes were lighter in color than Maureen's. Now they faded to pale gray as she thought things over and made up her mind. "If it's all right with Jack . . . but some of my questions might be too personal."

"Questions?" I said. "No, Charles, stay, it's all right. What questions?"

She hesitated, struggling with something difficult within. She finally took a deep breath and said: "How close were you to Maureen?"

"We were in love."

"Then why did you separate?"

"It wasn't my choice, believe me. She left me a note . . . she said she had to leave because some people were after her. She would be back when it was safe."

"What people?"

"I don't know."

"And that was five years ago. Were you in school?"

"No, I was working for the—" I stopped and we looked at each other. Her expression was kindly and concerned, but I was in sudden doubt about how much I should confide in her.

She saw it and leaned forward. One of her small bony hands closed over mine, light and cool. "Jack, I'm old enough now to understand these things, and I hope wise enough to accept them. You can tell me, you loved each other. . . . Were you lovers?"

The words got stuck in my throat so I nodded.

She smiled. "Then I'm glad that she found some happiness. Could you tell me why you stopped the ad? Had you given up or was there another reason?"

"It's been so long," I said. "If there had been word, a single word from her, I'd have waited forever, but there was nothing. I had to get out of New York to try and start over, so I came here." I stopped, wanting to get up and pace. She patiently waited me out. "Well, I met new people and have new friends. I thought it was time to let the past go. If Maureen's alive, if she wants to find me, I left word at my old paper; they'd send her here."

"You don't think she's alive?"

"I don't know."

"Jack, I must ask you just one more question: you were lovers . . . did she *change* you?"

That was one I didn't want to answer, but my long silence was an answer regardless.

"If she did . . . well . . . it's all right. She was my *sister*. When it happened to her I still loved her; she was different, but not in any way that really mattered."

"Your older sister," I prompted, wanting to shift the subject around.

"Yes, it's hardly fair for me to ask all the questions. I should tell you some things as well. Go over to that table, bring me the picture on it."

I picked up an old-fashioned hinged frame for photos. It was ornate silver and just a little tarnished. I gave it to her and she opened it lovingly.

"You see?" She smiled and pointed at the soft, distant images on either side of the hinges. "I was just seventeen when we sat for these, and very nervous. I was afraid of shaking too much and ruining it, but it turned out very nice, after all. I'm on the left and this is Maureen on the right."

I knew her instantly. Her hair was different, piled high with a cluster of small curls over her forehead. She wore a high collar, and pinned to it was a gold-and-ivory cameo that I remembered her wearing. Her pose and expression were stiff, but it was Maureen, her face identical to the likeness in my memory. Escott leaned over for a look.

"Maureen was twenty-one. As you can see at the bottom, those were taken in the year 1881. Oh, but we were pretty girls back then, all the boys were after us."

"Did she marry?" Escott asked.

"No. Neither of us. We were destined to be spinsters. Sometimes it works out that way. You don't plan on it, it just happens. Our dear parents passed on and we were alone; we couldn't bear the idea of becoming separated by a marriage. Life just went on and we were busy with charity work and the church and the literary club and the sewing circle. There seemed so much for us to do back then and the years slipped by so fast, but then it all changed.

"She met him at one of the literary club meetings. They'd got to talking about some terribly popular book that had just come out, though I couldn't name it now if I tried. His name was Jonathan Barrett, and we had all teased him a little because of Elizabeth Barrett Browning, you know. He was very nice about it and so handsome and all the girls were silly about him, but it was Maureen that he talked to at each and every meeting. She was in her thirties then and he in his twenties, and I tried to tell her he was too young, but she didn't care. He was so charming and proper I couldn't dislike him or be jealous of her, and so he often stopped by our house in the evenings.

"You can probably see the rest, but at the time I did not. Our lives were changing and I didn't see it at all. Maureen was so happy then and I was glad for her and I suppose these days no one would be too terribly shocked at what happened.

"Now back then, ladies were properly courted. They had chaperons and other difficulties, it's a wonder anyone ever got married with all the manners, requirements, and formalities. Only 'fast' girls would think of meeting a man alone, and of course if you went beyond that you were no longer considered fit for decent society. But she was in love with him. I suppose I was, too, a bit . . . sometimes a look would flash from his eyes and that made me quake all over. If it had been me instead of Maureen I would have done the same thing as she, and we would have been lovers as they were."

I was not surprised at this news, but it was remarkably painful to hear.

"They saw each other for several years. He often had to be away on business—investments or something, he said—and in all that time he never mentioned marriage. Our friends speculated about it and I did, too—at least to Maureen—but she told me not to push her into things and forbade me to speak of it to Jonathan. Not to push her—this went on for eleven years, if you can believe it. Eleven years of courtship, or so I thought at the time.

"He only came at night. We'd visit, the three of us, then he would bid us good night and leave. Maureen and I would lock the doors, turn down the gas, and go up to our rooms. I suppose they waited until I was asleep, and then somehow he would come to her.

"I must have been completely blind at the time or it was my sheer innocence. Not once did I ever guess what went on, and it did go on for many years. It might still be going on."

"What do you mean?"

"If she were still alive . . . still breathing, that is. It was 1904—they say things were quieter back then, but it wasn't so, things were just as noisy in the streets as they are today. Wagons made such a rattle and rumble, especially on the paving bricks. People shouted, children played, perhaps if there had been a little less noise that day she would still be with me, who knows?

"We were just crossing the street, it was nearly Christmas, there were a lot of people around us, other shoppers. I remember a band playing on the corner to collect money for the poor. It was cold and we were wondering how the players could keep warm if they never marched around. We laughed and skipped along in step to the drum. What a sight we must have been; two spinsters in their forties acting so silly. We heard only the music, nothing else. Then Maureen turned her head to look up the street and suddenly pushed me. She pushed very hard, my shoes slipped on some dirty ice, and I was almost flying away from her. There was a rumble that drowned out the band and a bell was ringing and I was thrown up against a mass of people on the sidewalk. I was stunned and couldn't move; they said I struck my head when I fell. Some men carried me into a store; I fainted, and was then taken to a hospital.

"She saw it coming, but there wasn't enough time for her to do anything but push me out of the way. They said she couldn't have felt much, that it was very quick. I like to believe it did not hurt her. It was a firewagon and the horses were running at full speed.

"I woke up in the hospital ward. I thought I'd die when they told me she'd been killed. Jonathan came by that night and tried to comfort me, but I was so wrapped up in my own grief that I didn't notice his, or his lack of it. The funeral was held the day I left the hospital, but he didn't come, and I was very angry with him. He'd known her for eleven years and did not come to see her buried. I was alone, utterly shattered and alone.

"He came back again after a few days. It was a very difficult interview between us and he asked me some strange questions. He was talking about living after death, whether I would consider such a thing as a reality. He wanted to know if I wanted to see Maureen again. Then he looked at me— just looked—and it did not seem so absurd or horrible anymore. He told me I should be happy because Maureen was really all right. I was shaking my head and smiling; it was like dreaming, but he said he could prove it. He opened the door and Maureen walked in.

"She wore a new dress . . . it was blue, just like her eyes, and she was young, a girl again, and so pretty. . . ." Gaylen's head drooped, she looked very tired. She pulled a bit of lace and muslin from her sleeve and dabbed her eyes. "I'm sorry to get like this, it just all came back to me again."

"Can I get you anything? Some water?"

"No, I'm fine, I want to finish. They talked to me most of the night and I learned a great deal about things I'd thought impossible. But they were right there in front of me—Maureen had been changed by Jonathan and had returned from the grave because of it.

"They were going to go away; she said she could not be with me any- more, it was hardly something our friends could understand, and of course she didn't want any of them knowing about her. She had wanted to see me again, she couldn't bear the thought of me grieving for her. It was so hard, almost cruel to have her back and then lose her again. She wrote me often, from many places, and she mentioned meeting you and how happy she was. I thought perhaps you knew more than I did about where she went. I'd hoped so hard. . . ."

"I am sorry." The words were inadequate, but they were all I had to give her.

She took my hand again. "That's all right, there's nothing we can do about it. At least for her sake—if you don't mind—perhaps we may be friends."

"Of course."

"What happened to Barrett?" asked Escott.

She looked at him, her face blank for a moment. He'd been keeping very still throughout the whole story and she must have forgotten his presence. "He was with Maureen at first, and then I suppose they drifted apart. I asked—but she said she didn't want to talk about it—she acted unhappy and I didn't want to pry."

"So you did see her occasionally?"

"Yes, but not very often."

"I see," he said neutrally.

She turned back to me. "Jack, would you be able to confide in me?"

I started to act puzzled, but she waved me down with a gentle gesture.

"It's all right. I think you know I've already guessed. It was from the first . . . you have the same look about you as Jonathan; it's some quality that I've never been able to define."

"I do?"

"Perhaps you are yet unaware of it. How long have you—"

"Just after I moved here," I said quickly. It was damn hard for me to acknowledge the truth to myself, much less a near-stranger.

"You poor man, was it an accident?"

"No, I was—" But I couldn't tell her. It was an ugly story and I couldn't tell her the truth of how I'd died.

Escott broke in. "Jack doesn't like to speak about it, it was rather unpleasant at the time. The doctors diagnosed it as food poisoning. He remembers being ill, passing out, and then waking up in the hospital morgue. It was quite sudden."

I gave him a quick, grateful glance. He looked concerned, but with a touch of blandness. He was an excellent liar.

"It must have been horrible for you."

"Not really, just a surprise." It had indeed been a surprise, so I wasn't exactly lying. "Maureen told me pretty much what to expect and what to do if it happened."

"And your family?"

"They know nothing about this. They think I'm still alive—in the conventional sense."

"Yes, that's good. At least you're not completely cut off as Maureen was; you can still visit them. It may be hard for you in the future when they begin to notice you don't age."

"I'll let the future take care of itself."

She turned her eye on Escott. "And you, Charles, how did you come to know about Jack?"

"I happened to notice that he did not reflect in polished surfaces and became curious to make his acquaintance."

"But you don't care what he is?"

"Not really. I find the condition of vampirism to be a fascinating study, but not something to fear. Knowledge is an excellent cure for fear. On the other hand, Jack is the only vampire I know. If this genus of the human race is at all representative of the majority, then there might well be a few of whom we should be wary."

"You sound like a very exceptional individual."

He made a depreciative little shrug.

"Gaylen, I asked Charles along to meet you because he wants to help us find Maureen."

"After all this time?" She was very doubtful.

"I can make no promises, ma'am," he said. "But if you could provide me with enough solid facts about Maureen and perhaps the loan of this photograph—"

"But I don't understand. How can you?"

"I am a private agent, an investigator. I shall be leaving for New York tomorrow on business, and as long as I'm there I'm going to look into the matter of her disappearance."

"To New York? Tomorrow? You mean you're all prepared?"

"Yes, I've planned on this for some time. In fact, I was to leave today, but decided to stay to meet you. Your notice appearing when it did was very fortunate. Any information you give me about Maureen could be helpful."

"I don't see how. After all this time do you really think there's any hope?"

"We shan't know until I try."

"When do you plan to return?"

"In two or three days, sooner if I should be lucky."

"That seems a very short time."

"Not when one is digging through official records and documents."

"He knows his job," I added.

She took her eyes from Escott, visibly changing mental gears, "Of course I'll help in any way I can."

"For a start, what do you know about a man named Braxton?" he asked.

"Who?"

"James Braxton," he repeated. "He owns a bookstore in Manhattan."

"I've never heard of him."

A stray thought occurred to me. "You said you had some crank calls; could you tell us about them?"

"Why do you want to know?"

"Just tell us."

My insistence was not what she wanted to hear, and I felt frozen out for a moment. There was also a quality about her, a kind of authority that made me very much aware of our age difference. She swallowed it and decided to answer.

"The first call was a girl. She said she was Maureen and she didn't like people talking about her, then she giggled and hung up. The second was from some man who wanted to know more about the notice. He called yesterday with a lot of questions that were not his business, and I finally told him as much. He never said who he was and I didn't want someone like that bothering me."

"Maybe that was him," I said to Escott.

"It would seem likely," he agreed.

"Who? Are you talking about this Braxton?" she asked.

"Yes."

"Who is he?"

"A self-styled vampire hunter."

Her expression went from curiosity to complete horror and her heart rate shot up accordingly. *"What?"*

I smiled. "Please don't worry about it, he couldn't find his a—his head with both hands."

"But if he knows about you, if he's after you—"

I took her hand and made reassuring noises until she was calm enough to listen, then told her a little about Braxton and his acolyte, Webber. In the end, she was still upset, but mastering it.

"There's really nothing for you to worry about," I said. "They don't know where I'm living now, and in a city this big they never will, unless it's by accident."

"But he read my notice and connected it with you—he knows where I am and could be watching this hotel. He could already know you're here and be waiting outside."

"There's an idea," I admitted. "But I've been keeping my eyes open. If I spot them, I can lose them."

"But if they find you during the day . . ."

"They won't, I promise. I'm in a safe place, really. I am much more worried about them bothering you."

"But what will you do about them?"

I shrugged and shook my head. Since coming back I hadn't had much time to think about it, and there had been no real chance to talk strategy out with Escott.

"Can't you do something to make them go away?" she pleaded.

Her concern for my safety was touching and embarrassing in its strength. She'd just found someone she could link to a pleasant past and was in danger, at least in her mind, of losing him. She would worry, no matter how much I reassured her. I regretted letting her in on the story, but she was better off knowing about Braxton; at least now she would be on guard.

Escott pulled out a small notebook and pencil. "And now, Gaylen, if you can put up with a few questions about your sister . . ."

She blinked at him, distracted out of her worry. "Oh, yes, certainly."

It didn't take long. He gleaned a phone number and a couple of addresses from her memory, none of them familiar to me.

"I only wish I could be of more help," she said.

He gave her his best professional smile. "I'm sure this will be of great help, though I can make no optimistic promises."

"I understand."

"We have imposed upon you long enough, though, and must be going ourselves."

"Will you let me know if you find out anything?"

"Are you going to be in town when I return?"

"Yes, I shall be here awhile; it's a change for me. Jack, have you a number I can reach you at?"

"Um, yes, just a second." I scribbled down Bobbi's number. "You can leave a message for me at this one."

"And will you let me know what happens with this Braxton fellow?"

"As soon as I know myself."

Her eyes were shining. "Thank you. Both of you."

WE left her, neither of us saying much of anything. Escott must have been mulling things over in his head, and I was too drained and disappointed to want to talk right away, but not so tired that I didn't check the mirror now and then. There were plenty of headlights to fill it, but none of them belonged to a black Lincoln.

It was past Escott's suppertime, so I drove at his direction to a small German café a few blocks off the Loop. He gave his order in German, hardly glancing at the menu chalked on a blackboard above the cashier. We found a booth and settled in to wait for the arrival of his food.

"Thanks for the poisoning story. I was about to say it was a car wreck."

"Not at all," he said, absently aligning a saltshaker up with the checked pattern on the tablecloth. "An accident would have been acceptable, but she might decide to look up any records on it. There's the same problem with hospital records, but they can be more difficult to obtain."

"You don't think she'd check up on me, do you? She doesn't seem the type."

"Hardly, but if one must lie, it should be a simple one and difficult to disprove."

"What'd you think of her?"

"An interesting woman; she told a very pretty story. She seemed too good to be true."

"You didn't like her?"

"Emotions are the enemy of clear thought; my appraisals have nothing to do with personal affections."

"I'll put it this way, then: what bothered you about her?"

The pepper joined the salt on the checkered pattern. "She seemed terribly old."

"She *is* seventy-two."

"I speak of her state of mind. You can be seventy-two or ninety-two and still feel young inside."

"People are different."

"Mmm. Well, call it my natural caution at work. You were cautious as well. Why did you give her Miss Smythe's telephone number and not my own?"

I shrugged. "I didn't really think about it at the time. You're going to be gone for a while and I'm over at Bobbi's a lot."

"And perhaps you're worried that Braxton might trick or force my number from Gaylen and trace it down."

I frowned agreement. "There's that. I've got the house detective looking out for him, though, so Bobbi should be all right. The geezer's a little cracked, but I don't see him getting violent with an old lady."

"No doubt, but violence can emerge from the most unexpected sources. I can recall an exceptionally sordid case of two children knifing their grandmother to death to obtain her pet cat."

Escott's food arrived and delayed conversation for a while. Between the smell of the steaming dishes and his story, my stomach began to churn.

"I saw a drugstore on the corner and need to get some stuff," I said. "Be back in a few minutes."

He nodded, his attention focused on carving up his meal.

My shopping expedition left me with some mouth gargle, shoe polish, new handkerchiefs, and a handful of change for the phone. I folded into the booth and got the operator.

This time my mom answered, and for the next few minutes bent my ear as she reported the latest domestic crisis. Webber and Braxton had shown up at the house early the next morning, but unfortunately for them my brother Thom had dropped by for breakfast. The last three generations of Fleming males have been on the large side, and so he and Dad had no trouble throwing the troublemakers out. The yelling and language woke up any late-sleeping neighbors, but they were more than compensated by the show.

That same day the cops came, and at first Mom thought Braxton had called them, but they had different business altogether. Someone from the Grunner farm had reported vagrants on our old place, but the Grunners maintained total ignorance about the call. However, there had been a break-in as reported.

"Your father is fit to be tied over this, I can tell you," she concluded after giving me a full inventory of the damage.

"Is he fixing it, then?"

"Well, certainly, but it will take him awhile, and then there's no guarantee that the place will be left alone."

"Oh, yes, there is."

"What do you mean?"

"I mean, what would it cost Dad to install some real indoor plumbing?"

When we'd still been living there, Mom had known the figure down to the penny, but now she wasn't so sure. "What does it matter now, anyway?"

"Because if he puts some in he can rent the place out. That way it's occupied and you two have some extra income every month."

"You want a bunch of strangers running all over our old house?"

She'd never been so affectionate about the place when we'd been living there. "Better a bunch of strangers paying you rent than some tramps tearing it all up."

"Well . . ."

"Try to find out how much and I'll put up the money—"

"But you can't afford to—"

"I can now. I have a very understanding boss who pays bonuses for good work."

"In these hard times? He must be one of the Carnegies."

"Just about. Will you do it?"

She would, and when I hung up it was with a little more confidence in their future.

My personal future included immediate plans to visit Bobbi. I dialed her next and asked if she were receiving callers.

"That's a funny way of putting it," she said.

"I'm feeling old-fashioned tonight."

"Oh yeah? Well, come on over. I'm rehearsing, but I think we can squeeze you in."

I was disappointed, but kept it out of my voice. "You've got company?"

"Uh-huh."

"Marza?"

"Yes, that's it." Her phrasing indicated she was being overheard.

"Maybe I should stay away."

"No . . ."

"You mean if you can stand it so can I."

She laughed. "Sure, that sounds right."

"Okay, but if she threatens my life I reserve the right to withdraw to a safe distance."

She laughed again in agreement and we said good-bye.

When I returned, Escott was in deep conversation with a stout, bearded man wearing a white apron. They seemed to be talking about food from their gestures. They were using German and I only knew a couple of words. The man made some kind of point, Escott conceded, and the man looked pleased and left.

"What's all that about?"

"Against my better judgment, Herr Braungardt has tempted me into dessert, a torte of his own invention. This may take some time, I don't wish to tie you up."

"How long could it take to eat a dessert?"

"Long enough for him to try and persuade you to have a sample. I can find my own way home. Don't worry."

"If you need help, I'll be at Bobbi's." Grinning, I left him to his overstuffed fate.

I found a place that sold flowers and bought a handful of the least wilted-looking roses. They were cradled in my arm when I stepped off the elevator onto Bobbi's floor. The operator didn't have to tell me she had company this time, I could hear the piano and her voice clearly enough, despite the walls and solid door.

I thought to wait outside until the song was finished, but she cut off in mid-note. There was a murmured consultation, then the music began again.

Marza's voice was hardly recognizable, and when she spoke to Bobbi her tones were soft and affectionate and heavily sprinkled with endearments.

"You've got to hold the note just a bit longer, baby. Count one, two, three, then we both start the next phrase. . . ."

I knocked and a second later Bobbi answered.

She just looked at the flowers, and her face lit up in a smile that sent me to the moon and back. She accepted them gracefully, her hands lingering on mine. "Any special reason?" she asked.

"I felt sentimental."

"Do I do that to you?"

"Among a lot of other things."

She took my hand and led me inside. Marza was at the piano, just lighting a thin black cigar. Her posture was straight and stiff and she was wearing another V-necked disaster, this time in yellow. It was quite a contrast to the pink satin lounging pajamas that Bobbi had clinging to her rounded figure. Marza glanced once in my direction without making eye contact, then pretended to study the sheet music before her.

On the sofa sprawled her Communist friend, Madison Pruitt. He looked up doubtfully, having seen my face once, but unable to attach a name to it. He was holding a tabloid, apparently interested in a murder investigation that the police weren't conducting to the satisfaction of the paper's editor.

"Madison, you remember Jack Fleming from last night?" prompted Bobbi.

"Certainly," he replied, still uncertain. At the party he'd been too involved spouting politics to Marza to notice our introductions. I regretted that the present circumstances were not similar, and didn't relish the prospect of conversing with a zealot.

"I think we should take a break," said Marza, not looking up from her music. "My concentration's all broken. Some coffee, Bobbi?"

Bobbi took the broad hint and I offered to help, so we had some semi-privacy in the kitchen. It was cramped, but organized; she worked on the coffee, and I ended up scrounging for something to put the roses in. I found a container that looked like a vase and loaded it with water.

"Here," she said. "Put a little sugar in the bottom, they'll last longer. What's so funny?"

"Marza. I have to laugh at her or sock her one."

"I don't blame you, she can be a little trying at times."

"A little? That's like saying Lake Michigan's a little wet."

She stifled her own smile, and then we said hello to each other until the coffee was ready.

"Time to get the cups," she murmured.

"Couldn't we do this for a few more hours?"

"The coffee'll get cold."

"I don't want any."

"Yes, I suppose you want something else."

"Bobbi, you're psychic."

"Nope, I've got eyes. You're showing."

I snapped my mouth shut, trying the gauge the length of my canines with my tongue. Bobbi snickered and pulled out a tray, cups, and saucers. I carried it all in while she got the coffeepot.

Marza was next to Pruitt on the sofa and looked up. "What did you two do, go to Brazil for the beans?"

"No, just to Jamaica," Bobbi answered smoothly, filling the cups.

Marza approached her coffee delicately, tested one drop on her tongue, and decided to wait for it to cool. In contrast, Pruitt just grabbed his cup, leaving his saucer on the tray. I supposed he considered saucers to be an unnecessary bourgeois luxury.

"Your flowers, Bobbi, where are they?" Marza asked.

"Forgot 'em. I'll be right back." She slipped into the kitchen, but didn't come right back. Instead she was opening a cupboard, clattering a plate, and making other vague sounds.

"Flowers, such a thoughtful gift," Marza said sweetly. "You did know that Bobbi is allergic to some of them, or didn't you?"

"A lot of people are," I said evenly, and smiled with my mouth closed. I was speaking normally, but taking no chances on revealing the length of my teeth.

"Waste of money," said Pruitt, his nose still in the tabloid. "They die in a day or two and then you're left with rotting plants and no money. *People* are fighting and dying, you know."

"So you've told us, Madison," she said. "I don't notice you joining them, though."

"My fight is right here, trying to bring the truth to—"

"Cookies?" said Bobbi, just a shade too loud. She put the roses on the piano and offered the plate of cookies to Pruitt. It was a skilled move on her part—he had to choose between the plate, his coffee, or the paper. A hard decision for him, but the food won out and he dropped the paper. He was further distracted from his train of thought as he tried to figure out how to help himself to a cookie with both hands occupied holding the plate and his cup.

"You're not joining us?" Marza asked me as she wall-eyed Pruitt's juggling act. If he dropped anything it would be on her.

"No, thank you."

"Watching your weight, I suppose."

"No, I have allergies."

Pruitt finally gave the plate to Marza, then grabbed some cookies from it. They didn't last long and disappeared all at once into his wide mouth.

"You'll have to excuse Madison, he was raised in such a large family that he had to compete with his siblings for food, and learned to eat quickly in order to gain any nourishment."

"You know I'm an only child, Marza," he mumbled around the mass of crumbs in his mouth.

"Oh, I must have forgotten."

Pruitt nodded, content to correct her, having missed her point.

"What do you do for a living, Mr. Fleming?" she asked.

I couldn't say I was an unemployed reporter doing part-time jobs for a private investigator and opted for the next best thing. "I'm a writer."

"Oh? What do you write?"

"This and that."

"Fascinating."

"Need a writer," said Pruitt. He cleared his mouth with a gulp of coffee. "We need people good with words, articles for magazines, slogans—can you do that?"

"I'm sure anyone who knows even a little about the alphabet can help your cause, Madison," she said.

"Great. You think you could help out, Fleming?"

I could see how he was able to get along with Marza, since he was totally oblivious to her sarcasm. I was beginning to like him for it. " 'Fraid I don't have the time."

"For some things in life you have to take the time. People have to wake up from their easy living and realize they must join with their brothers to battle for the very future of man on earth."

"H. G. Wells."

"Huh?"

"That sounds like his *War of the Worlds*."

"Who's that again?" He pulled out a little book and scribbled it all down. "What else has he written?"

"Lots of things. They'll be in the library." I wondered how many English courses he'd skipped in school to go to political rallies.

"Madison can't go there," said Marza. "They won't let him in."

Pruitt got a look on his face that would have done justice to a New Testament martyr.

"Why not?"

"Because there is no true freedom of speech in this country," he said. "The people here think there is because their capitalistic lords say so, but that isn't really true."

"Why not?" I tried again, this time with Marza.

She shrugged. "The library didn't happen to have a copy of some book he wanted. There was no English translation available and they weren't planning to order one. Madison protested by setting fire to some newspapers in the reading room, and they had him arrested."

"I had to bring to their attention that censorship to one is censorship to all." He sniffed.

"His father paid the fine, but the library still won't let him back in again."

"Censorship." He shook his tabloid. "This story is a prime example. A man speaks his mind in a so-called public place, and then the police arrest him because his political views disagree with the established order."

"They arrested him because he shot at a heckler," I said.

"That's what the paper *wants* you to think. That 'heckler' was really an assassin for Roosevelt's Secret Service. He'd been sent to silence a voice of freedom for the masses and only got what he deserved."

My mouth sagged a little. Pruitt got the satisfied look of one who had scored a real point. A half dozen counterarguments popped into my head, but the best course was to say nothing. There was absolutely no point having a battle of wits with someone who was unarmed.

Bobbi put her cup down and suggested more rehearsal. It was gratefully accepted and the ladies returned to the piano. Madison stretched his legs out, crossed his arms, and yawned loud and long. The volume was sufficient for yodeling and the size of his mouth—a quantity of crumbs were still trapped in his molars—was an inspiration to well drillers everywhere. He wound up his musical solo and shut his eyes. From the not-so-subtle movements of his jaw, he seemed to be rooting out the last remnants of cookie with his tongue. I settled back in my chair to listen and wondered what the hell Marza saw in him, not that she was any social bargain herself.

Her true worth, as Bobbi had said, was as an accompanist. Her hands went solidly over the keyboard with expert ease, though she had to hold them at a low angle to keep her long nails from clicking against the ivory.

They did a warm-up on scales, and then Marza began one of the songs Bobbi would sing for the broadcast. It was a rich slow number and made a good showpiece for her voice, which was excellent. I sighed and let the sound wash over me, soothing and exciting at the same time. Perhaps later in the soft darkness of her room I would ask her to sing again.

They finished and held a consultation over it and I cast around for something to read, my eye catching on a fresh copy of *Live Alone and Like It* on the end table. I flipped through, noticing it was a gift to Bobbi from Marza. It would be. I was just starting to read a chapter with the unbelievable title: "The Pleasures of a Single Bed," when the room got unnaturally quiet.

Pruitt stared at some point behind me, mouth and eyes looking as if he'd borrowed them from a dead fish. Marza and Bobbi were also frozen and doing a reasonable imitation of gaffed sea life. My back was to the door, and with a sinking heart, I turned to see what inspired the tableau.

Advancing slowly from the wide-open door, with large silver crosses clutched in their hands were James Braxton and Matheus Webber. Both of them looked determined, but very nervous.

What made the bottom of my stomach drop out was the revolver Braxton held stiffly in his other clenched fist. His finger was right on the trigger, and I didn't know how much pressure it would take for the thing to go off. If the damned idiot forgot himself . . .

I stood up cautiously, my hands out and down and my eyes fixed on Braxton's. His were little pinpoints in a sea of white, gleaming with fearful triumph. Mine must have been just as wide, but without the triumph, only the fear. Unless that gun had wooden bullets, I had no concern for my own life, but anything else was another matter. If he shot at me, the bullet would pass right through, going on to Bobbi and Marza, who were right in the fool's line of fire.

From somewhere I heard myself speaking, pleading, "Please don't do anything, Braxton. These people are innocent, please don't shoot."

The seams on his brown face twitched a little, but I couldn't read him. I didn't dare try any kind of hypnotic suggestion—the least mistake on my part could kill Bobbi.

"I'll do what you want, just don't shoot," I told him. "These people . . . they're . . . they're not like me, I swear they're not. They know nothing about this."

"That remains to be seen, you leech," he said. He punctuated this by a wave of his cross and took a step forward. I flinched and fell back, but also stepped to one side. Bobbi and Marza were still out of sight behind me. Maybe they were marginally clear, but only if Braxton were a good shot.

Matheus was as keyed up as the rest of us, but he looked around and tapped Braxton's shoulder. "Mr. Braxton, look—they had coffee."

His eyes snapped to the tray and cups. "Is that true? Did you have coffee?"

Only Bobbi understood the significance of his question. "Yes, we did, and cookies, too. Didn't we Madison?"

Pruitt's head bobbed several times.

I heard Marza shift next to Bobbi. "That's right, we all had coffee and cookies." She spoke slowly, as though to an idiot child. In this case she wasn't too far off the mark.

Braxton shook his cross at me. "But not him."

I repeated my flinching act and moved another step to the side. "Braxton, they know nothing at all. You have no reason to involve them—"

"Shut up."

He had the gun and I still couldn't see Bobbi, so I shut up.

"You two—sit on the couch. Now!"

Bobbi and Marza made haste to join Pruitt. Good.

"What are you going to do?" Bobbi asked.

Braxton smiled at me. "I'm going to wait. We're all going to wait for morning."

"But why? What do you want?" demanded Marza.

He ignored her and stared at me grimly. Bobbi knew very well what such a wait meant, but hid it. The three of them fell silent, their stares divided between me, Braxton, and the gun.

"What kind of bullets, Braxton?" I asked.

"The best kind. They were expensive, but I judged them worth the cost."

"Silver?" I mouthed the word, not wanting the others to hear.

He smirked.

Bobbi moaned and her head swayed. "Oh, God, I'm going to be sick." Marza put a protective arm around her.

"What do we do, Mr. Braxton?" Matheus was bug eyed at Bobbi's white face.

"What?"

"I'm going to be sick." She gulped air and jerked to her feet.

"Follow her," he told the kid. "The rest of you stay where you are."

Bobbi ran to the bedroom with Matheus close behind, but she shut him out when she reached the bath and slammed the door in his face. He was still very much the kid and hardly had the gumption to go inside after her. Through the walls I heard her coughing, then the rush of water when she flushed the toilet. She took her time at it and Braxton started to fidget.

"Look," I tried again, "we don't need to be here."

"Quiet and keep your eyes down."

"What do you want?" asked Marza. A large chunk of her veneer had come off in the past few minutes. She looked much more real to me now.

Braxton pretended not to hear and called to Matheus. "If she's done, get her out."

The water was still running. Matheus knocked gingerly on the door. "Uh . . . miss . . . uh . . . you all right?"

Bobbi mumbled a no and turned on a sink faucet.

"You have to come out now." She didn't answer. He appeared at the bedroom door, shrugged helplessly at Braxton, and went back again.

"I'll go get her," said Marza.

"No." Braxton was not about to let the situation get any more out of hand.

"How did you find me?" I asked, distracting him.

"What? Oh, it was the old lady. I knew you would go see her eventually, so we waited at her hotel and followed you from there. This time we were more careful about it."

"Smart, real smart."

He made a little formal nod of acknowledgment like an actor in a play. He must have cast himself as Edward Van Sloan to my Lugosi. The only things missing were the accents and evening clothes.

"Miss? You've got to come out." Matheus sounded a little more impatient now, and that gave him confidence. "I mean it, come out of there."

The water cut off and the knob rattled. "Don't rush me, big shot," she growled. She pushed unsteadily past Matheus and stood in the doorway. The tableau hadn't changed. She took a step toward me.

I shook my head minutely. "You look done in, Miss Smythe, you'd better sit down."

She nodded, figuring out the reason behind my sudden formality. She had no wish to have Braxton breathing all over her neck looking for telltale holes. Things were safe for the moment; her lounging pajamas had a high Oriental collar. She glided back to the sofa, glaring at him.

"You mugs have no right barging into my home. My neighbors are bound to hear all this and call the cops."

He waved her down. "I have every good reason behind my actions, however strange they may appear to you. If you do not yet understand my mission, I promise you that you soon will, and when you do, you shall approve of what I am doing."

"It's the police state," said Pruitt, gaining a revelation from God knows where. "Who are you with, the Secret Service?"

"Secret Service?" said Matheus, looking blank. He was standing next to Braxton now, keeping me covered with his cross.

"Yes, the Secret Service, you fascist."

Marza spoke through her teeth, which were exactly on edge. "Madison, this is no time for politics, so shut up."

"I'm telling you—*ouch*!"

"I said shut up."

"Who's a fascist?"

"Matheus—"

"But he called me—"

"Everyone *quiet*!" Braxton must have felt the situation physically slipping out of control. He was already sweating from the strain and certainly not used to it. He'd never last until morning the way things were heading.

"Braxton, please listen," I said.

He liked the pleading tone in my voice and considered my request like a magnanimous ruler. "All right, what is it?"

"What Miss Smythe said was true, this is no place to settle things. There's a hotel detective downstairs—"

"*You* think there is leech."

So they had slipped by Phil somehow. It was time to change tack. "I can't help what I am, I've tried to tell you that."

He shook his head. "And I am sorry for you. I think I know what kind of hell you face each night. . . . I will end it for you."

Good God, he thinks he's doing me a favor. "No, not here, please, at least for the sake of the ladies."

"We will remain here. You seem to care for these people. I do not wish to use them as hostages for your behavior, but I see no other way."

He sounded very certain of his hold over me. He was either stupid or had an extra ace up his sleeve he hadn't yet shown. I was inclined to think he was stupid. He was badly underestimating my will to survive and believed crosses and silver to be a strong check. The only thing actually holding me back was trying to come up with a way of safely disarming him without revealing my true nature to Marza or Pruitt.

I glanced at Bobbi to see how she was doing. Perched stiffly on the edge of the sofa, her whole posture was tense, natural enough under the circumstances, but something in her manner struck me as odd. Her left arm lay across her knees, the right hand resting on the left. The long sleeves of the pajamas were pushed up to the elbows. Her gaze caught mine and her mouth twitched in an almost-smile and she winked, her eyes dropping to her hands. Her right index finger was tapping once a second against the crystal of her watch.

I got it, or thought I did.

"Matheus," I said, sounding reproachful. "I asked you to talk with him. I was pretty reasonable about it all. Remember, I could have hurt you then, but I didn't. Does that fit in with the things he's been saying about me?"

"It was a trick," he said. He spoke with the haughty conviction of a convert. "Besides, you left us stranded and stole the car."

"I left it at a fire station, for cryin' out loud. You two were bothering my family, I had to do something."

"We were trying to warn them about you."

"How would you feel if I did the same to your folks? Do they know what you're doing? What do they think of this quest you and Braxton are on? Do they approve?"

That one hit a sensitive spot and the kid went all red, right up to the ears. "They wouldn't understand."

"So you haven't told them. Maybe you should. Write a letter: 'Dear Mom, tonight Braxton and I held four people at gunpoint—' "

"Enough!" Braxton was actually stamping his feet. "Matheus, I warned you how he would twist things. He's one of the devil's own and will try and confuse you."

"Not me, Braxton, you've already done that. You don't want the kid to think for himself. You might lose your only hold on him."

"Shut up."

"I figure he's really smarter than you, but you don't want him to find that out."

"Shut up!"

I am not overly brave, and baiting a nutcase holding a gun is not something to do for fun, but it is a hell of an attention getter. Everyone was gaping at me, each with expressions varying from rage to puzzlement to worry, and one in particular of intense concentration. The last and most welcome face belonged to Phil, the hotel dick. He had just walked in the still-open door and was trying to sneak up on Braxton. In this hotel he never got much practice at being quiet, so it was costing him some effort. I opened my big mouth again to cover any creaking floorboards.

"Yeah, I guess the truth hurts. It must be nice to have someone around to agree with you all the time, or do you pay him money for it? There's not enough of that stuff in the world to make me want to put up with your kind of bull—"

Then Phil lunged, both hands grabbing Braxton's arm and dragging it down. Marza and Pruitt screamed as the gun went off and thunder and smoke filled the room. A furrow appeared in the floor near my left foot, and I foolishly jumped back from it.

There was a good fifty-pound difference between them, and Braxton's light frame didn't stand a chance. He went down like a tackling dummy, his knobby joints knocking hard against the floor. Phil was on top and his extra weight had pushed all the fight out of the little guy. A second later Phil was in possession of the gun and getting to his feet.

He dusted his knees absently, and glared all around. "Someone want to explain things to me, or do I really want to know?"

Matheus began to edge toward the door, but Bobbi spotted him. "Hold it right there, buster."

He held it right there and looked to Braxton for help, but his mentor was too busy getting his breath back and nursing his new bruises. Phil went to the door and checked the hall, keeping the gun out of sight.

"Nuthin' to worry about, folks, just a party trick. Sorry about the noise." He waved an apology at someone and shut the door.

"What *is* this all about?" demanded Marza, her voice shaking.

"They're just a couple of mugs from my shady past," I said. "The geezer here is a con man that I once did a story on. It blew his game to hell and he's looking to get back at me. The kid is just his latest trainee. The last I heard, it was an insurance scam. Looks like he's switched to religion. What are you doing these days, Braxton, swindling old ladies for church funds?"

Braxton flushed, jerkily stood up, and shoved his cross at me. I ducked back so it missed my nose. "Away, you demon." Somehow, he'd sounded a lot more convincing on that lonely road in the country.

"He's crazy," concluded Pruitt.

"For once, I'll agree with you," said Marza.

The cross jerked again and I stepped away from it.

"Braxton?" Phil made certain he could see the gun. "Sit down and shut up."

"But you don't know who or what this man is—"

"As long as he's not waving guns at the tenants, I don't give a damn, so clam up. What do you want I should do with 'em, Miss Smythe?"

Bobbi looked at me. I shrugged. "Call the cops?"

Pruitt suddenly found his feet. "I think I'll go home now, it's awfully late." He grabbed his hat and hurried out.

Marza stared after him. "Why, that no-good—how does he expect me to get home?"

"Oh, Marza," Bobbi groaned.

"What's with him?" asked Phil.

"He's crazy," said Matheus.

"So coming from you that means something?"

"He called me a fascist—"

"Shut up, kid," Bobbi told him. He looked hurt. "Jack, I don't think the cops could do much for us."

"They could take his gun away and lock him up if we pressed charges, but that'd mean court appearances, the paper—you don't need any bad publicity before your broadcast."

"Yeah. But what do *we* do with them? I could call Gordy."

"Don't tempt me. Phil, have you got some place you can stash these two?"

"Depends for how long."

"An hour?"

He nodded. "If you give me a hand."

"Sure."

We wrestled Braxton into the hall and took the service stairs down to the basement instead of using the elevator because the operator liked to talk. It was an interesting parade: I had Braxton's arms twisted behind his back and Phil was keeping the kid in line with the borrowed gun.

In the basement, Phil directed us to a broom closet that was made to order. Brooms must have been at a premium in the building, because the place was like a bank vault. Two of the walls were part of the cement foundation and the third was solid brick. It was about ten feet long and only four feet wide. We pushed them in with the mops and buckets and Phil locked it up.

"They gonna be able to breathe in there?" I asked.

Phil studied the blank face of the door for a while, then nudged it with one toe. "There's a pretty good gap at the bottom. If they get desperate, they can stick their noses down there."

We heard a thump and dull clang from within. Someone had tripped over a bucket. Matheus hit the door a few times and yelled to be let out.

We climbed upstairs. "Sure it won't be too noisy?"

"I'll make certain no one bothers them."

"Thanks. I'll go see if Bobbi's all right and work out what to do with them."

"I'll be in the lobby."

Four floors later I was back in Bobbi's apartment. She was just giving Marza a drink, then ran over to me, her arms open. We held on to each other, not speaking for a long while. Marza finished her glass, put it on a table, and stood.

"No more rehearsal tonight. I'm calling a cab."

Bobbi whispered, "She was really shook, can you take her home? Would you mind?"

When she looked at me like that I wouldn't mind walking over hot coals, or even taking Marza home. "If you'll be okay."

"I'll be fine. Marza . . ."

Marza got in my car and said nothing for the next ten minutes except to give directions. We stopped in front of her apartment building and I waited to see if she wanted me to walk her in or not.

"We're here," I said when she didn't move.

She stopped boring a hole in the windshield and tried it with me. I was getting another once-over, and the reappraisal was even more critical. "Why were they after you?"

"I told you."

"The truth this time."

I shook my head.

"Are you with the gangs?"

"No. This is some old business that followed me from New York. The guy is crazy, you saw that."

"Yes, I saw that. So what was it about? Why come after you with a couple of crosses? Why call you those names?"

"I said the guy's nuts. Can you account for all the stuff Pruitt lets out?"

"Madison's preoccupied with politics and being paranoid, so what is your friend preoccupied with?"

"With trying to blow my head off."

"And what happens to Bobbi when he comes back?"

"They're after me, not her."

"They were holding all of us. Do you think he won't try again?"

"He won't get the chance. I'm going to have a little talk with him tonight and straighten things out. Bobbi will be okay. I promise."

"I hope you mean that. I don't want her hurt. Not by them or you, you know what I mean? She's a beautiful girl and that's attracted the wrong kind of men to her in the past. Did she tell you what the last one was like and what happened to him?"

"I know all about it," I said truthfully.

"Good, because that's what I want to see her free from. You have no right to bring it all back."

Marza had some guts. If I'd really been like Slick Morelli, she was courting some broken teeth. "I don't plan to. I'm on your side."

She was anything but convinced, but there was no way I could prove my sincerity except to go back and deal with the problem. She gave me a "we'll see" shrug and got out. I waited until she was inside and drove a beeline back to Bobbi.

She unlocked the door after hearing my voice. "I thought you'd never get back."

"Same here."

"Thanks for taking her, Jack."

She was hugging me again. It was becoming a habit, a very nice one. Then it was time for my reaction and I couldn't stop it. My arms moved on their own, wrapping around her and lifting her from the floor. I held her hard, as much for warmth as for comfort. I was cold from the inside out and shaking all over.

"Jack? What is it? What's wrong?"

It was a long time before I had the strength of will to release her. I was damned near to crying. "That idiot . . . I was afraid he'd kill you."

Her light fingers stroked my brows and lids. "But he didn't. Everything's okay. He wasn't even aiming at me."

"He didn't have to, the bullets would have gone right through me. His silver is no more use against me than any other metal."

"You mean the bullets—"

"They're metal. The silver makes no difference. He's gotten vampires mixed up with other folklore."

"His cross held you back, though," she said in a small voice.

"That was acting." I looked around. She'd been cleaning up. The coffee service was gone and there was a throw rug covering the bullet furrow in the floor. On the table was Braxton's cross. He'd dropped it in the tussle with Phil. I carefully closed my hand over it and held it up for her to see. "There, nothing happens and it's made of silver."

"But why not?"

"I guess it's because God doesn't work the way Braxton thinks he should." I opened my hand and let her regard what lay in it. "I'm not evil, Bobbi. I have no fear of this, but I was afraid of losing you and can only thank God you're safe."

She came into my arms again and this time we did not let go.

I carried her to bed and tucked her in, which she thoroughly enjoyed. She was always a little sleepy afterward, regardless of how little I took from her. I sat next to her on top of the spread and kissed a few spots that had been missed earlier and made her giggle.

"Damn, you're good," she said.

"So are you."

"Do you have to go?"

"There's some unfinished business downstairs. Say, how did Phil know to come up here, anyway?"

"You forgot about that phone I keep in the bathroom."

"Then your getting sick—"

"Hey, you think you're the only one who can act if you have to?"

Her door was locked and I left it that way, slipping quietly through into the hall and taking the stairs to the lobby. Phil was behind his pillar, talking odds with the night clerk again. He saw me and nodded, then led the way down to the basement.

I planned to have him baby-sit Matheus while I had a private talk with Braxton. It wasn't something to look forward to, but I'd decided to try hypnosis on him. The man was stubborn and would be on guard, though. I was certain I could break through, but afraid of hurting him, of hurting his mind. The last man I'd done it to . . . well, the circumstances were different now, things were controlled, and I was emotionally calm. I had no wish to hurt Braxton, only to find out his connection with Maureen and then make him go home.

Plans are just fine when they work out, but this one would have to wait. The closet door was hanging open and the two hunters were gone. Phil stooped to examine the lock, holding a match to the inside of the door. He shook his head in mild exasperation.

"The old goat musta had skeleton keys. Who'da thought it?"

"I should have."

Braxton had underestimated me and I'd stupidly returned the favor. The man most certainly planned to kill me, and to do so he might have to break into almost any kind of building. He was sure to be outside to track me home when I left. The keys would jingle, the lock giving way to them, and then his shadow would fall across my trunk. . . .

"Can you keep an eye on four tonight—make sure Miss Smythe stays okay without disturbing her?"

"I can do that. What about you?"

"I'm going to get lost."

"Sounds like a good idea. I'll show you the back door."

8

HE let me out in a wide alley where delivery trucks trundled through during the day with their loads of food and linens. Things were comfortably deserted now, but I still felt like a shooting gallery target, and vanished as soon as Phil locked up.

I didn't know this area particularly well and being in a non-corporeal form only added to the disorientation. My sense of solid objects, even the push of the wind was heightened and extended, but since I couldn't see, it was hard to gauge distance. When moving, I had to rely on memory.

The alley entrance to the street was fifty feet to the left, with a row of garbage cans just before it, but the wind was throwing my direction off and to the right. Compensating, I drifted past the cans like smoke that wasn't there, then found the corner of the building. Left, right, or straight? Right. Move away from the hotel and car, float softly down the sidewalk, gain some space, and look around.

An alcove opened in my path, which meant a doorway. I entered the building and solidified in a closed pawnshop. The street looked clear; they might have returned to their own hotel for fresh strategy, but I couldn't count on that. They might also have my car staked out, so it would have to stay put. It was getting late for me and playing car chase with them might take too much time—was there anything in the car that would lead them to Escott's? The papers inside were in my name, with my old hotel as an address. No one there knew Escott except by sight. The car dealer could be traced, but that would lead them to the hotel again. I could relax. If they did break into it all they'd find was a dead end, along with some mouth gargle, shoe polish, and handkerchiefs.

All the same, having to leave my car behind was a disgusting situation. Braxton would have a lot to answer for the next time I saw him.

I took some bearings, disappeared again, and didn't reform until several city blocks were behind me. I checked the view, found it clear, and started walking.

Maybe I could have scoured the area until I found them, but there was no guarantee that Braxton didn't have a second gun on hand. If he used it the racket would bring all sorts of trouble. I shook the thought out of my head. One thing at a time, one day, or rather night, at a time. I was tired, the sunrise was coming, and I still had to make sure they weren't following me to Escott's.

I eventually seeped inside his back door and listened. The place had its own little creaks and pops, each loud in my straining ears. There were also small scratchings and a rhythmic gnawing sound; mice in the basement. Overall, it was a good normal silence, but it meant I was alone in the house. Where the hell was Escott?

My answer was propped against the saltshaker on the table.

JACK,

ALL THINGS CONSIDERED, I DECIDED TO TAKE A NIGHT TRAIN TO N.Y. AND CLEAR UP THIS BUSINESS. MY OVERSEAS SHIPMENT SHOULD ARRIVE TOMORROW AT 7:45 P.M. PLEASE CALL ME WHEN IT COMES. I'LL BE STAYING AT THE ST. GEORGE HOTEL.

ESCOTT

On my own again. Great.

There wasn't enough time to call a cab and find a hotel to hide in, I'd have to hope Braxton hadn't had Escott followed from the restaurant. And then there was Gaylen—had Braxton bothered her? I speculated briefly and irrationally if she had put him onto me, but shook that thought off as well. She'd been far too concerned for my welfare; no one was that good an actress. My troubles were my own; no one else could be blamed for them and no one else could clear them up. But that was tomorrow's problem.

Escott had given me the run of the house. I went up to the top floor, floating carefully over a patch of undisturbed plaster dust so as not to leave footprints. A small door at the end of the topmost hall led to yet another stairway, a short one that served the attic. There was dust everywhere and a number of interesting artifacts left by previous generations of owners. It looked suitable, but I still did not feel really safe.

I ghosted over to the one window at the far end. It faced another window in the next building just across the narrow alley. I gulped, tried not to think of the drop, and vanished, feeling a dull tug all over as I passed out of Escott's house to the one next door.

The attic was similar to the one I'd left: full of dust and domestic junk, but I felt much more secure. The place was occupied below, but I was more willing to chance spending the day here. It would be better to be found by Escott's neighbors than by Braxton, though from the condition of things they hadn't been up here in years and it was likely to remain so.

I went back to Escott's, retrieved a single bag of earth from the basement, and borrowed a blanket and pillow. The invisible nets that went out around me when I vanished, the ones that allowed me to retain my clothes and such, were sufficient to take in my light burdens. I floated directly up through the many floors to the attic again and moved next door, leaving no trace of my passage for inquisitive eyes.

Somewhere outside, the sun was creeping to the horizon, but the one window was deep in the shadow of the roof overhang and opaque with grime. The light would not be too bad. I had certain powers, but very strict limitations as well, and sunlight was one of them. It blinded the eyes and stiffened the limbs, and then the numbness beginning in my feet would travel slowly to the head until it mercifully brought unconsciousness. Being subjected to the unpleasant inertia of dying only happened if I fought to stay awake after dawn, or if I was without my earth. Since my change I'd tried staying up only once voluntarily as an experiment. It was not something I ever wanted to repeat.

Spreading the blanket, not for comfort, but to protect my clothes, I stretched out behind some old boxes, the pillow resting firmly over my face to block the light. The earth was in the crook of my arm and reminded me of the stuffed toy rabbit my oldest sister Liz had given me thirty years ago. They were her specialty. She'd made them for her own children and all the nieces and nephews of our big family. She was a sweet woman.

And then I surrendered all thought and became very still.

The pillow slid from my face as I sat up and listened. A car rumbled by down below, interrupting the neighborhood kids in their game of street tag. Another day had slipped past and they were playing all the harder at its end before their mothers called them in to supper, bath, and bed. The air was dry with the smell of dust and coming up from the kitchen was the odor of boiled cabbage and fried fish. I wondered if the kids would survive to adulthood on such a diet. I had, but maybe I'd been tougher.

My own diet was of concern for me tonight. The relationship Bobbi and I shared was not about keeping me fed. The small amount of blood she provided was for the purpose of lovemaking, and could not satisfy my nutritional needs. More blood than she could spare was required for that. Later on I'd have to visit the Stockyards, but my trips there were less frequent than they were before we met—only once every three or four nights, rather than once every other night.

Gathering up the bedding, I sieved across the alley to Escott's attic and sank down through the floors to the kitchen. It was a neat trick; if Escott ever went back to the stage we could make a fortune with a magic act. The only drawback was that I'd never be available for the matinees.

I worked the phone and Bobbi's welcome voice said hello and I said hello back and we each made sure the other was healthy.

"Phil told me you were going to lay low for a while," she said.

"Just until I can locate those bozos. I didn't have the time last night."

"You won't have to look far. Phil called and said they're parked down the street in a black Ford."

"Is he sure about that?"

"Fairly sure, and so am I. I took a gander out the window a minute ago and there's a heap there now that's new to the usual scenery. Phil thinks they're waiting for you to come back for your own car."

"Good conclusion. I'm just surprised that Braxton thinks I need it."

"What do you mean?"

"Considering his expertise, he's more likely to suspect me of traveling around as a bat or a wolf."

She giggled. "They might miss a bat, but a wolf's kinda noticeable out on the sidewalk."

"Maybe I should reeducate him. What do you think?"

"I think I'm going to take a cab to the studio."

"I'm sorry, I know I promised—"

"Oh, don't be a sap, this is an emergency. Oops, I just remembered, some woman named Gaylen called a minute ago. You running around on me?"

"Never. What'd she want?"

"For you to come by and see her tonight. Who is she?"

"It's something I'm working on with Charles. He's out of town, so I gave her your number for daytime calls."

"Wish you'd told me."

"We were kind of busy. . . . Did she say anything else?"

"Nope. You going to tune in and listen to me?"

"I'll be at the studio. I wouldn't miss it for the world."

"But what if Braxton follows me there?"

"Don't worry, I'll have taken care of him by then."

"But what if you miss him?"

"I said don't worry. You aren't going there alone, are you?"

"No, Marza's coming with me."

"Then God help Braxton if I do miss him."

"Oh, *Jack*." She was exasperated. "The man *is* trying to kill you."

"He won't. I'm only trying to keep him from hurting others."

"And I don't give a damn about others"—she cut off a moment and collected herself—"I'm worried about *you*."

"And about that broadcast, too. All this mess came at a bad time for you. Try to calm down and think about how great you'll be tonight. You don't have to worry about me, you know I'll be fine." I put a lot of confidence in my tone and it worked. We said a few things and she gave me directions to the studio twice and I told her to break a leg. It was a phrase picked up from Escott and apparently applied to all performers because she was glad to hear it.

I hung up and dialed Gaylen. She was upset because Braxton had been calling her, and now she wanted to see me. The little bastard was becoming a real nuisance.

"I'm pretty tied up tonight. . . ." I was also reluctant to face another emotion-laden talk with her.

"Not even for a little while? Please?"

A supernatural softy, that's me. Besides, she might have some useful news. "It may take me awhile to get there, and I can't stay long."

"I understand, I'd really appreciate it."

The schedule would be tight. Bobbi's broadcast was at ten and I was stuck in the house until quarter to eight, or at least until Escott's delivery came. In between I had to have a heart-to-heart with Braxton, and then go hold Gaylen's hand. If things went right I could go home with Bobbi, enjoy the party she was throwing, and still have time to visit the Stockyards.

It looked like a busy night ahead, and I wanted to get on with it; the waiting chafed at me like starched underwear. I filled in some of the time by cleaning up and changing clothes, but with that out of the way, the minutes dragged. At five to eight I was annoyed, and at a quarter after I was ready to strangle the driver.

Twenty after the hour a truck finally rolled into the street, stopped two doors down, and backed up. The guy inside squinted at house numbers. I went outside and he asked if I were Mr. Escott. To save him confusion I said yes, unintentionally puzzling any neighbors taking in air on their front steps. We gave them a good show and lugged several crates off the truck and into the narrow hall. He didn't say much, which suited me, and I signed Escott's name to the sheet on his clipboard. He gave me a receipt and drove off.

There was one last obligation and I was free. The operator put a call through to Escott's hotel, and then asked their operator to connect me to Escott.

"I'm sorry, sir, but Mr. Escott is not here."

"Then I'll leave a message for him."

"I'm sorry, but he has checked out."

"What?"

"Yes, sir, earlier today. He left Kingsburg as his forwarding address."

Now, why the hell was he running upstate to a little backwater town like Kingsburg? Gaylen hadn't mentioned the name. He was probably returning something to one of the many blackmail victims on that list. "Did he leave any messages for a Jack Fleming?"

"No, sir. No messages at all."

I hung up and pessimistically wondered what was wrong.

* * *

My visit with Gaylen was going to be brief, so I told the cabby to wait. He rolled an eye at the meter and agreeably turned me down, having been stiffed once too many in the past.

She was waiting at her door and I apologized for being so long.

"I'm just glad that you could come by." She eased painfully into her chair.

Nothing had significantly changed since yesterday, except for some watercolor paints scattered on a table with some brushes and a glass of gray water. A wrinkled sheet of paper taped to a board was drying next to it all. I expressed some interest, which warmed her.

"It's only a hobby, just to pass the time," she demurred, but held it up for inspection. The light gleamed off some damp patches. There was no model in the room of the pink, blue, and yellow flowers on the paper, so it had come out of her own head. As in most amateur efforts, it was noticeably flat, but the colors looked nice, so I complimented her and knew from her reaction that she would someday make a gift of it to me.

"Sorry I got held up, but I really don't have a lot of time," I explained.

She took the news without visible disappointment, because something else was on her mind. "That Braxton man tried to get in to talk with me. I had to have the manager throw him out."

"That's good. I'm very sorry you were bothered."

"Then he started calling. I kept hanging up until I finally decided to talk and tell him to go away."

"What'd he say?"

"All kinds of things. He was very excited and asked if you had hurt me, and practically begged for the chance to talk to me face-to-face. My legs were aching and made me a bit short with him. I said it was the phone or nothing. He asked if I knew what you were and what kind of danger I was in, and what did I know about Maureen, and if I would help, and a lot of other nonsense. I told him he was a very silly and stupid man and never to bother me again, or I'd get the police on him. After that he stopped calling."

"Good for you."

"But he still frightens me; not for myself, but for you."

"I'm safe enough. Anyway, the next time I see him, I'll talk him into going back to New York."

Her expression was sharp. "But how can you do that? What will you do?"

"Only talk to him, I won't hurt him. Please, Gaylen, don't worry about it."

Her gaze dropped and she looked away. "What will you do?"

Had I been breathing I would have sighed. "Remember telling me about Jonathan Barrett and how he talked to you just before Maureen came back? That's how I'll talk to Braxton."

"And you'll ask him about Maureen?"

"Yes."

She was quiet a moment, thinking.

"I'll let you know what he says. Charles says even negative information is better than none at all."

"What about him? Has he left yet?"

"He left sometime last night. I guess he was in a hurry to get on with things."

"But you haven't heard anything from him?"

"Not directly. I tried calling him, but he's gone to a little town called Kingsburg. . . . Does that ring any bells with you?"

She went still and thought, her heart racing. "I'm not sure. I think I once got a letter from Maureen from there, but memories fade—I don't know."

"It could be some other errand as well. He'll let us know."

"Yes, please, I want to know everything." But there was a hollow note to her voice, something else was bothering her.

"What is it?" I asked gently.

She made a brief gesture with her blue-veined hands. "This is hardly the time. . . . I wish . . ."

I stayed quiet. She would either talk or not, with or without my encouragement.

Her eyes had changed color. The blue had faded and now they were light gray. Maureen had been the same way when she was upset over something. "Oh, Jack, how can I put it in words? How can I ask you?"

"Ask what?"

"You can see how it is for me. I'm not well and it seems that with each passing day it grows worse; not just my legs, but other things. It's so awful to be like this, to feel so weak and helpless all the time."

I waited her out, for the moment unsure.

"And I haven't seen Maureen in so long. What if I never see her again? That *could* happen, I am so afraid it will."

What she wanted was right in front of me now, and I didn't want to look. She saw the answer in my face long before she could word the question.

"Oh, please, Jack, you can't deny me in this!"

I wanted to get up and put some space between us, but her eyes held me, eyes full of anguish and asking for something I could not be able to give her.

"I'm sorry."

"But why not?"

I had no answer. That was the really hard part. I had no answer, no real excuse—and she must have known it. "Because I can't. You don't know what you're asking."

"But I do. I'm asking for a chance to live. I'm asking for a body that doesn't hurt all the time. Is it so much to want to be young and healthy again?"

"I'm sorry." I had to turn away and pace or blow up. Her pleading gaze followed me up and down the small room until I stopped in front of the window to stare out at nothing. "You don't know what it's like. I'd give anything to go back, to walk in the sun again, to eat food, feel real heat and cold, to feel my heart beating. I have no stability. I can't go back to my family and will never have one of my own. Worst of all, Maureen's gone."

"And yet she changed you. If the life you have is so awful, why did she do that?"

"Because the kind of love we had would have made it all bearable. There was no guarantee that I even would change, but it was a hope we shared. At the very least we would have been together for as long as I was . . . alive. But something happened and she had to leave."

"And if she ever comes back, you'll still be here. I don't have that luxury. She *was* going to change me, she promised me that in our last talk. You are all of her left to me. All I ask is for you to fulfill a promise she could not keep."

"Why didn't she do it earlier?"

"I don't know." Her look held me steadily, still pleading, then dropped to her lap. "I don't know."

She knew and Maureen knew. I didn't and would have to go by my own instincts. A lot of emotions were getting in my way, and I wasn't sure if I was right to say no, or reading things into her manner that weren't there. I could do as she asked, the chances were very great it wouldn't work, but everything in me recoiled away from taking that step.

"I'm truly sorry, but it's impossible. I can't."

"No, please don't leave yet." She stopped my move for the door. "Please . . . will you at least just think about it?"

If I said yes, she would know it for a lie. I crossed the room, hat in hand, head down.

"Jack?"

I paused, my back to her. "I'm sorry. If there's anything else you need, you can call me. But not this." Then I walked out, my guts gone cold and twisting like snakes.

The cab dropped me within sight of a two-year-old Ford parked across the street from Bobbi's hotel. Gaylen's voice still lingered in my head. None of my reasons to refuse seemed very good now, but even after discarding them all, I was not going to do it. Something was bothering me; I wanted advice, or at least to have someone tell me I was right. Escott might be back in a day or two; I'd talk it over with him. Or maybe not.

Hands in pockets, I made myself small behind a telephone pole and tried to see the driver of the Ford. From this angle, he wasn't too visible. He was slouched down in the seat, it could have been either Braxton or Webber. They worked as a team; why was only one on watch? On the remote chance that there was a third member on their hunt, I copied the license-plate number in my notebook for Escott to check. The plates were local. They might have rented it, wanting something less conspicuous than the big Lincoln.

The Ford was parked in with a line of other cars. If Bobbi hadn't tipped me, I'd never have noticed it or the man inside. The rest of the street looked clean. No one was loitering in any doorways, it seemed safe enough to approach. I strolled along the sidewalk, breasted the open passenger window, leaned over, and said hello.

The man inside turned a slow, unfriendly eyeball on me. He wasn't Braxton or Webber and looked bored to death. I landed on my feet and asked if he had a light, hauling out my face-saving cigarettes.

He considered the request with indifference, then pawed around the car for some matches. It took some hunting before he found them; the seat was littered with sandwich wrappings, unidentifiable paperwork, crumpled cigarette packs, and smoked-out butts. I offered him one from my pack and he took it.

"Been here long?" I asked.

"What's it to you?" He lit his cigarette on the same match that fired mine, his long fingers shielding the flame from the faint night breeze. He was a good-looking specimen, with a straight nose, cleft chin, and curly blond hair. Up on a movie screen he might have stopped a few feminine hearts. I pegged him to be a college type, but he was too old and had seen enough to have a cynical cast to his expression.

"You're making the hotel dick nervous."

"I should if I'm doing his job for him. He send you or are you from Mrs. Blatski?"

"What's the difference?"

"He sent you then." He blew smoke lazily out the window.

"What if I am from Mrs. Blatski?"

"No skin off my nose. She has a right to hire someone as long as they leave me alone—or are you the guy she's sleeping with?" He eyed me with a shade more interest.

"You a dick?"

"Got it in one, bright eyes."

I pushed away from the Ford in disgust. Not Braxton or any connection to him, just a keyhole peeper trying to get the goods on his client's wife. Three steps later a crazy thought occurred and I was back at the window again.

"Charles, is that you?"

He gave me an odd look and I deserved it. A second and more detailed check on his face was enough confirmation that he wasn't Escott got up in disguise. The eyes were the wrong color, brown instead of gray, and his ears were the wrong shape, flat on top, not arched.

"What's your problem?" he asked, squinting.

"Thought you were someone else."

"Yeah? Who?"

"Eleanor Roosevelt. I was gonna ask for an autograph."

"Hey, wait up."

I waited up. He got out of the car slowly, stretching the kinks from his legs and back. He was average in height and build, but it wasn't padding that filled out the lines of his suit. He didn't look belligerent, so I wanted to see what he wanted. He came around to the front of the car without any wasted movement and rested his backside against the fender.

"Yeah?" I said.

"Nothing much, you just look familiar to me."

"I got a common face."

"Naw, really, you from around here?"

"Maybe. What's your game, anyway?"

"Minding other people's business."

"That can be dangerous."

"Nah. Like this job, nothing to it but following some old bitch around to see what kind of flies she attracts. She's filthy rich and all that dirt attracts plenty."

I nodded. "And you think I'm one of them?"

"It don't hurt to ask. Sometimes you can do a fella a good turn, keep him outta the courts, then maybe he feels like doing me a good turn."

A shakedown artist to boot. Well, it's a big nasty world and you can meet all kinds if you stand still long enough. "You got the wrong man this time, ace."

"Malcolm," he said, holding out a hand.

My manners weren't quite bad enough to refuse, so we shook briefly and unpleasantly. He had a business card palmed and passed it on to me.

"Just in case you need a troubleshooter." He smiled, tapped the brim of his hat, and went back around to the driver's side. "You never know." He slid behind the wheel, still smiling, his lips pressed together into a hard, dark line. He had dimples.

I barely smiled back in the same way, but without dimples, and took a walk. Creeps make me nervous and I felt sorry for Mrs. Blatski, whoever she was.

Oozing through the back door, I found my way to the lobby, kept out of view of the front windows, and got Phil's attention by waving at the night clerk. He crossed over casually.

"How'd you get in? The back's locked."

"Better check it, then. Any sign of Braxton?"

"He ain't in the car?"

"I had a look. It's some private dick on a divorce case."

"Then I ain't seen him."

"I guess that's all right, as long as they leave Miss Smythe alone."

"It doesn't mean they stopped lookin' for you, though."

"Yeah, but I'm being careful." We went to the back door, which I had unlocked once inside. Phil let me out and locked it again.

After five minutes of studying the street I tentatively decided that my Buick was unobserved. I was back to feeling paranoid again and went as far as checking it for trip wires and sticks of dynamite. Bombs were an unlikely tool for Braxton, but then why take chances?

The car was okay and even started up smoothly. There was little time left to get to the broadcast, but the god of traffic signals was with me and I breezed through the streets as quickly as the other cars would allow. Bobbi had left instructions with the staff about me, and as soon as I was identified, a brass-buttoned usher gave me an aisle seat with the rest of the studio audience.

The room was smaller than I'd expected, roughly divided between audience and performers, with only slightly more space given over to the latter. There was a glassed-in control booth to one side filled with too many people who didn't seem to be doing much of anything at the moment. Bobbi was on the stage, looking outwardly calm. She was seated with a half dozen other people on folding chairs, all of them dressed to the nines, which didn't make a whole lot of sense for a radio show. Across from them a small band was tuning up, and in between, seated at a baby grand, was Marza Chevreaux, flipping through some sheet music.

I caught Bobbi's eye and gave her a smile and a thumbs-up signal. She smiled back, her face breaking composure to light up with excitement. She was in her element and loving it.

A little guy with slicked-back hair and an oversized bow tie stepped up to a microphone the size of a pineapple. Someone in the booth gave him the go-ahead, he signed to the band, and they started up the fanfare of the show. For a minute I thought the little guy was Eddie Cantor, but his voice was different as was his style of cracking jokes. A studio worker in an open vest and rolled-up shirtsleeves held up big cards printed with instructions telling us when to clap or laugh. The audience liked the comedian, though, and hardly needed the prompting.

A deep-voiced announcer stepped in to warn us against the dangers of inferior tires, then the band came up again, and Bobbi was given a flowery introduction. She was standing and ready at the mike. Marza got her signal from a guy in the booth, and they swung into a fast-paced novelty number. It was one of those oddball songs that gets popular for a few weeks and then you never hear of it again, about a guy who was like a train and the singer was determined to catch him. Off to one side, a sound-effects man came in on cue with the appropriate whistles and bells. Before I knew it I was applauding with the rest of the audience and Bobbi was taking her bows. She'd gone over in a big way and they wanted more.

When the noise died down the comedian joined her, and they read from a script a few jokes about trains the song had missed. The tire man came on after them with his stern voice of doom, and that was when someone poked me in the ribs from behind.

Braxton had turned up another gun and was hunched over me with it concealed in a folded newspaper.

"Stand up and walk into the hall," he told me quietly.

He was damned right that I'd do what he wanted. We were in a vulnerable crowd, and all I wanted was to get him alone outside for just two seconds. Showing resignation, I got up slowly and preceded him. The usher opened the door, his attention on the stage. He must have really liked tire ads.

The hall was empty except for Matheus, who was clutching his cross and looking ready to spook off. Braxton had done quite a job on him.

"I give," I said. "How'd you find me this time?"

Braxton was smug. "We didn't have to. We've been waiting. Last night you said Miss Smythe was going to be in a broadcast. I merely called around to find out which station and when. There was a risk you wouldn't show, but it all worked out."

If he expected me to pat him on the back for smarts, he'd have a long wait. "Okay, now what? You gonna bump me off ten feet away from a hundred witnesses? The wall between isn't that soundproof."

He hadn't picked up on the fact that I wasn't as afraid of him and his silver bullets as I'd been last night. The gun moved a degree or two left. "In there, and slowly." He indicated a washroom across the hall.

"That'll be some headline," I grumbled, " 'Journalist Found Dead in Men's Room; Police Suspect Lone Ranger.' Matheus, you better stay out here, this could be messy."

"Shut up."

"Have some heart, Braxton, you don't want the kid to see this. Save him some nightmares."

The elevator opened at the far end of the hall and a man in a long overcoat got out. He noticed our group, looked at his watch, and walked away, turning a corner. He was just part of the background to me, but he made Braxton nervous. He was suddenly aware of the openness of the hall and didn't like it.

"Move," he hissed. *"Now."*

I looked past him to Matheus. Our eyes locked for an instant. It was long enough. "Stay out here, kid."

His expression did not change, nor did his posture, but I knew I'd reached him. He stood very still.

Braxton saw this exchange and his eyebrows went up, adding more lines to his dry, scored forehead. The gun wavered as he tried to decide whether to snap the kid out of my suggestion or shoot me outright. I saved him the trouble; when he came a half step closer and tried to urge me backward, I shifted my weight as though to comply and turned it into a lunge. It was faster, literally faster, than he could see and much faster than he could react.

The gun was now in my pocket, and he was staring at his empty hand as unhappy as any kid whose toy had been taken away. He looked up at me and thought he saw the grim reaper and made an abortive attempt to run, but I grabbed two fistfuls of his clothes and swung him around against the wall. His mouth opened and sound started to come out, but I smothered it with one hand.

Far down the hall I heard approaching footsteps. It was too public here, so I adopted his plan and dragged him to the men's room. The door swung shut and I rammed a foot against its lower edge to keep people out.

He was trying to struggle, his body bucking ineffectually against my hold. He was finally getting a clear idea of just how strong a vampire can be at night, with all his powers.

"Hold still or I'll break your neck," I said, and perhaps I meant it. He subsided, his eyes squeezed shut. From the pressure of his jaw, he was trying to hold his chin down. I was hungry, but not that hungry. It'd be a cold day in hell before I'd touch his blood.

His breath was labored, the moist air from his nose blowing out hard over my knuckles, and his heart raced fit to break. He needed to be calmer and so did I. Emotions, the kind of violent ones he stirred up in me, would only do him harm. I sucked in a deep lungful of air and let it out slowly, counting to ten. Outside someone walked past, the same steps that had chased us in here. They paused slightly, then went on, fading.

His eyes turned briefly on me, then squeezed shut again. He had an idea of what I was trying to do and was on guard. It might be too difficult to break through to him without doing permanent harm. I shifted my grip and his eyes instinctively opened.

"Braxton, I won't hurt you, just listen to me."

He made a protesting sound deep in his throat. My hand relaxed enough over his mouth so he could speak.

"Unclean leech—"

"Listen to me."

"Damned, you're—"

"Braxton."

"—damned to—"

"*Listen to me.*"

His muscles went slack, his lungs changing rhythm slightly. I'd gotten to him, but had to ease up.

"That's it, just calm down, I only want to talk."

He looked up in a kind of despair, like a drowning man whose strength has gone and knows you won't make it to him in time.

"Everything's all right. . . ."

I didn't understand how it worked any more than I understood the mechanics of vanishing at will, but I had the ability and now the need. My conscience was kicking up, but beyond moving to another state or killing him, there seemed no other practical way of getting rid of him.

"Everything's fine, we're just going to talk. . . ."

Without any more fuss, he slipped under my control. I relaxed and opened my cramped hands. His eyes were glassy rather than vacant.

"Braxton?"

"Yes?" It was the quiet voice this time, the reasonable one he'd used at my parents' house.

"Where is Maureen Dumont?"

"I don't know."

I was disappointed, but not surprised. "When did you meet her?"

"Years ago, long time."

"When? What year?"

"I was twenty-five or -six." He struggled to remember. "I opened the store in 1908, she would come and buy books and talk. She was so beautiful. . . ." His voice was softer with the memory. "She would talk with me. I dreamed about her. She was so beautiful."

What had he been like back then? The brittle body might have once been wiry, the seamed face once smooth. There had been a firm chin and dark eyes and skin; yes, to a woman he might have been handsome back then.

"Were you her lover?" I had to keep from touching him or he'd shake off the trance. Jealousy was foaming up inside; I couldn't lose emotional control of myself.

"I loved her. She was so—"

"Were you her lover?" *Stay steady.*

His eyes were wide, blind, searching inward for an answer. "I . . . don't know."

"What do you mean? How can you not know?"

"I was, in my dreams. I loved her at night in my dreams. She would kiss me." One of his hands stole up to his neck. "She would kiss me. God, oh my God . . ."

I turned away. I never meant to hear this. "Stop."

He became quiet, waiting and unaware while I mastered myself. There was no point in hating him, no point in condemning Maureen; not for something that had happened nearly thirty years ago. She'd loved Barrett and Braxton and then me. Were there others? Had she indeed loved me?

"Braxton . . . did you take . . . did you ever kiss her in the same way?"

"No."

It was something.

"She wouldn't let me."

Oh, Maureen. Yes, it was something. He hadn't been that important to her. She'd been lonely and needed someone to hold and touch, if only in his dreams. That was it and that was all.

"When did you last see her?"

"Which time?"

I made a guess. "The first?"

"A year after we met. She never said good-bye; the dreams just stopped, I forgot them. But she came back."

"When?"

"Twenty years later? Twenty-two? One night she walked into the shop. I knew her instantly and I remembered it all. She hadn't changed, not aged a single day, but I—she didn't know me, not until I said her name. I was frightened, I knew what she was, what she had done to me and what I would become unless—" He relived his fear quietly, the only outward sign of the inner turmoil was the sweat that broke out on his face. His heart was racing.

"Unless what?"

"I wouldn't be like her, feeding on the living, sucking men's souls from them. If I killed her first, then I would be free. I could die free of her curse. I began to hunt her."

"When? What year?"

"In 1931."

So this was the man. She'd run from him, leaving me standing in an empty room, a scribbled good-bye note in one hand and the life draining from my eyes. Five years of hurt, doubt, anger, and fear because this foolish man thought she wanted his soul instead of the warmth of his body when he was young.

"Did you find her?"

"No, but I found out about you. I knew what she'd done to you, but if I tried to help, you wouldn't have believed me. Your only hope was the same as mine—to kill her—but then you died first and now you're one of them. I'm sorry I couldn't have saved you."

It was pointless trying to explain it to him. Whether Maureen lived or died didn't matter; we'd exchanged blood, and hoped. She'd loved me, and had expressed it by giving me a chance for a life beyond life so we would always be together. But then something had gone wrong.

"Do you know what happened to her? Do you know where she is?"

"No."

"Are you the only one? Are there others hunting her?"

"Matheus, he believed me, he knows."

"Who else?"

"I don't . . . the old woman, she must know."

"Gaylen? The old woman here?"

"Yes. She knows something, she knew back then—"

"What do you mean?"

Something bumped against the door.

"I asked, but she wouldn't—"

Bump. "Hey, open up." A vaguely familiar voice, but not Matheus.

"—tell me. She wanted—"

"Come on out, Fleming."

"—life to live—"

"The kid says you're in there."

"Cheated. She was sick—"

"Who was? Of what?" The other voice was distracting, and I was losing the thread of Braxton's talk.

"—strong . . . frightening. I *told* her my story, but it was you she—"

"Fleming, it's now or I scrag the kid."

What the hell? I yanked the door. He was in a long coat, which changed him enough from the last time, so from a distance he was unrecognizable when he stepped off the elevator, looked at his watch, and walked away. A long coat, which was all wrong because it was only mid-September and still mild. But he wore it because that made it easy to walk into a building with a sawed-off shotgun concealed under it. He shouldn't have been here, he was supposed to be in a parked Ford waiting for Mrs. Blatski.

Malcolm grinned at my surprise, his dimples nice and deep, and without any more expression or warning he pulled first one trigger, then the other, emptying both barrels into the open doorway.

9

I was on the tile floor. It smelled of soap, cordite, burned fiber, and blood.

The impact of the blast had thrown me back against a washbasin, which altered the angle of fall and twisted me facedown. The agony of the shot passing through my body left me stunned as few things could. I fought to hold on to sanity and solidity. It was several long seconds before my shivering, jerking limbs recovered enough control to stand.

The door still hung open, and the air was thick with blue smoke. Ten seconds to find my feet, five more to stagger to the hall, but it was long enough. Malcolm was gone.

So was Braxton. He was on his back and not moving. The shot had all but cut his slight body in two. His blood flooded the black-and-white tiles. His face was calm and dreamy. Death had come so fast there'd been no time to react.

Matheus was on his side in the hall, one hand still clutching his cross. A smear of blood was over his right eye and a crimson thread flowed from it into his hair. Still alive.

The studio door opened. There was no time to explain, I vanished before anyone saw me, and sank down through the floors, hoping to reach the ground ahead of Malcolm. A few people were standing in the main lobby of the building. I took the risk of re-forming, but no one noticed; they were looking out the front doors. I pushed past and went outside. No Ford in sight, but there was a man running away, his long coat flapping. My legs gobbled up his fifty-yard lead and I hauled him up short and spun him around.

Watery eyes, a three-day beard, no chin, stinking of booze and sweat, he wore Malcolm's coat or one just like it.

"Easy, Captain!" he wheezed.

"Where is he? Where's the blond man?"

"Did what he said, was it good? I get another two bits if it's good. Was it good?"

"What'd he tell you to do?"

"Wait on the stairs 'n run, Captain. Lizzen fer the bang 'n run. Good joke, huh? Was it good?"

It was good, it bought Malcolm enough time to get out another way while I chased down the wino. I ran back to the lobby. The doorman was the first official-looking type, so I collared him, said there'd been an accident at the studio and to call an ambulance, then raced upstairs to look for Malcolm. It was a poor chance at best, he'd be gone by now.

The studio hall was in a mess. Men were peering into the washroom, and a small knot had formed around Matheus. Some woman was crying and another man was holding her. The stage was empty except for the chairs and piano. Crossing the divider between it and the audience, I was stopped by the man in shirtsleeves. He gaped at my shredded clothes.

"Sorry, you have to stay out."

"I'm with Bobbi Smythe, she was on tonight."

"She'll be backstage, but—"

The backstage door opened to a hall full of people all looking at me, questions on their troubled faces.

"Where's Bobbi Smythe?" I asked no one in particular.

"I think she left," a woman suggested.

"When?"

"She was here just a minute ago," someone else said.

There was another set of washrooms down the hall. I opened up the ladies' and called for Bobbi and Marza. No one answered.

"They must have taken the back elevator," the woman told me.

That was down the hall and around the corner, with more people in the way.

"What the hell happened?"

"I heard an explosion."

"Was it a bomb?"

"Nah, Big Al must be back an' havin' a party."

"Musta been a gun—Johnny said someone got shot."

"Goddamned drunks, screwing up the show."

I ignored their speculations and punched at the elevator button. This time I couldn't sink through the floors without getting unwanted attention, besides, the operator might have seen something.

He had, and told me about it on the way down.

"Yeah, the blond, a real bombshell—she stood out from that group like fireworks."

"What floor?"

"They got off on ground a few minutes ago."

"They?"

"She had some harpy with her. Seemed anxious to leave, and a couple of others, too. What's goin' on? What happened to you?"

We made the ground floor and I left him guessing. The back hall was empty, so I went around front. There was a cop in the lobby by now, asking questions. I waited until he was in the elevator then checked faces. No Bobbi, but the doorman was still there.

"Hey, did a blond in a red dress go out? She was with a black-haired woman in green."

"Haven't seen 'em."

"If you do, ask 'em to wait."

"Cops say everyone has to wait, nobody gets out now."

I went through the ground floor, again calling into washrooms, but with no luck. They should have left by way of the front; it was a busier street and more likely to have cabs, but then they shouldn't have gone at all. If she'd heard a man had been shot, Bobbi would have been on the scene to make sure it wasn't me. Marza must have dragged her out to protect her. Damn Marza, anyway.

The rear exit was ajar and unguarded—so much for the cops' instructions. It opened to another street busy with cars and nothing else. I called her name, but no one answered.

After wasting a lot of time, I finally wised up and drove back to Bobbi's hotel. It would be the place for them to go since it was closer than Marza's. Before I reached the elevator, Phil flagged me down.

"What happened to you?" he asked, staring at the hole in my clothes where the shell had gone through.

"Fight." I was in a hurry to get past him.

"Some kid brought this in a minute ago." He gave me a large envelope with my name printed on it.

"Has Miss Smythe come in?"

"Her friend did, she's—"

I broke away. The elevator crawled up to the fourth floor. Without knocking I went in. Marza was on the sofa and jerked to her feet. Her lacquered hair was messed up and her eyes were blazing fire.

"Who were they?" she demanded.

"Where's Bobbi?"

Her body was shaking inside the green frame of her dress. "*Who were they?*" If looks could kill, I'd be on a slab next to Braxton. She started for me, her hands reaching. One of her inch-long talons had broken, but there were still nine more left and aimed at my face. I dropped the envelope, caught her arms in time, and held her at a safe distance. She kicked and struggled until she ran out of breath, then her knees gave out and she sank to the floor, trying not to sob from frustration.

"What happened?" I asked. Somehow her raw display kept me cold and thinking.

"They *took* her," she spat. "Who were they?"

"When?"

"When we left the studio. He said to come here and wait for you."

Oh, God. "A blond man, long coat?"

"*Who was he?* He had a gun—"

"Anyone else? Was he alone?"

"The woman with the knife." She gulped air, still shaking and her head sagged. Near her was the dropped envelope and its meaning suddenly blossomed in my mind. I grabbed it up.

It was flat on the edges and slightly thicker in the middle and whatever was inside rustled against the paper. I tore one end off with stiff, clumsy fingers and the contents spilled out.

Marza went dead silent, not even breathing. Her hand shot out and caught a last tendril of the cascade of platinum silk before it sifted to the floor.

Neither of us could move, each staring with numb shock at the bright, soft nest between us. Marza swayed, her eyes flat from the faint coming on. I got her to the sofa, then went to the liquor cabinet and poured a straight triple from the first bottle I grabbed and made her drink it. She choked and pawed me away, but I made her drink it all.

"God, I *hate* that stuff." Her breath smelled of rum.

The dullness had left her eyes and she looked as though she might be useful again. I felt the shock hitting me now as I looked again at the pile of shining hair. A small piece of paper was lodged in the tangle. My guts were ice as I fished it out.

Sit tight or we'll give the whore more than just a haircut.

That was all. Marza whipped it from me and read. She was trembling, but trying to hold in the panic.

"Why? What do they *want?*"

There was nothing sane I could tell her. The fragments of Braxton's last words gave me an answer, but I was repelled by it.

Ring.

Marza flinched and stared at the phone as if it were a bomb.

I picked it up and waited.

"Jack? Marza?" It was *her* voice, breathless, strained.

"Bobbi!"

Marza stiffened and rushed in, trying to pull the phone from me.

"Oh, Jack, they're—"

And that was all, except for a muffled noise in the background and the final click of disconnection. Marza glared at me, for all the good it did her. I felt just as angry and helpless. We waited, but the thing didn't ring again.

"What do they want?" she repeated.

I shook my head and went to the bedroom to get away from her questions. Bobbi's rose scent hung lightly in the air. A couple of dresses tried on for the broadcast and then rejected were flung on the bed. The closet was open. I fumbled out of my tattered coat and shirt. Since I started coming over so often, she insisted I leave some spare clothes in with hers. I pulled on a fresh shirt, my fingers working mechanically, as I tried not to think.

Marza was where I left her on the sofa, head in hands. "Why won't you tell me anything?"

"You know as much as I do, even more. I've seen the man in the coat, his name is Malcolm, said he was a private eye. He shot and killed Braxton tonight."

She swallowed. "And the other? That woman?"

"What'd she look like?"

"I don't know."

"Yes, you do, you said she had a knife. What else?"

"About my age, bony all over, and hungry. Her eyes . . . she looked crazy. The man grabbed Bobbi and the woman put that knife to her throat, and they went out. He said to come here and wait for you."

"Was that all he said?"

She nodded.

Someone knocked at the door. Our heads swiveled and she went bolt upright. They knocked again. I signaled to her to stay put and looked out the peephole. It was Madison Pruitt. He saw my eye and waved and I opened the door a crack.

"Oh, Fleming, hello." He moved to come in, but I didn't stand aside. "Something wrong? Is the party still on? The broadcast stopped in the middle of—"

"Sorry, the party's off, Bobbi got sick at the last minute—"

Marza was at my shoulder. "No, let him in. Please."

I didn't exactly want to, but she looked like she needed him and pulled him inside. She wrapped her arms around him. He didn't understand what was going on, but instinctively offered what comfort he could.

"What's happened? Was there an accident?"

"Come on, I'll explain." I shut the door and made explanations. "There's going to be more people coming over soon, you'll have to get rid of them."

"But what can we do?" Marza asked.

"Just what I said. This guy's trying to make us nervous so we lose our heads. We do that and we lose Bobbi."

"And the police?"

"No. We don't dare."

The phone rang again. I picked it up before the bell had died.

"It's me, Jackie boy. Malcolm—you remember."

He got no answer.

"You gotta behave or I might get mad. Did you read my note?"

"Yes."

"And you heard her on the phone?"

"Yes."

"Good. Now you know we mean business. Your girlfriend got her ears lowered a little this time, but that's all—no real harm done. You do what we want and she gets to keep 'em."

"What do you want?"

"Nothing you can't handle, Jackie."

"What?"

"You gotta pencil?"

I wrote out the address he gave me.

"You come straight here and no cops. Just you or you'll never be able to find her again. Leave the other bitch where she is, out of trouble."

"I'll come."

"No smart ideas, either. We know all about you. That's why I aced the squirt, just to let you know. You see, I can't really hurt you, but the people around you is something else. No tricks. When you walk to the door you make noise and stay in sight, 'cause if you don't, your girl won't be using mirrors, either, but for a different reason. You got ten minutes to get here before she goes into surgery." He laughed, the line clicked, and my ear was pressed to dead air.

Marza's nails dug into my arm. "What do they mean? Where is she?"

"They want me, not her."

"But why?"

I memorized the address and tore the sheet from my notebook, folding it around Malcolm's business card. I scribbled Escott's name and the name of his hotel on the outside and gave it to her.

"This is a friend who can help us, but he's in New York. Call this hotel, they might be able to locate him. Say it's an emergency, life and death, but don't tell the truth to anyone but him. If he calls, give him the story, but no cops or Bobbi's dead. You got that?"

She nodded.

"He's got an English accent. In the meantime stay off the phone and keep the door shut."

"Yes, but—"

But I had bolted out the door, car key in hand and murder on my mind.

The address led to a warehouse that was a mountain of dingy red bricks and old wood held together by crumbling mortar and rusty nails. The street was deserted, the other nearby structures hollow and silent except for the rats. It was a good spot to kill someone. The river was only ten feet from the back entrance, and a body could easily be slipped unnoticed into the oily water on a black night.

The building was three stories tall, and a faint light shone in one of the top windows, outlining Malcolm's head and shoulders. He took his hat off and waved it. There was nothing else to do but go inside and see the setup. They knew what I was and what my capabilities were, but Malcolm was supremely confident, and that meant a bad situation for Bobbi. I glared at the grinning, waving figure, then tore open the warehouse door and left it on the walk.

The stink of wet rotted wood, oil, and exhaust filled the place. The exhaust was new and had come from Malcolm's Ford, the engine was still hot and ticking. Next to it was a paneled truck backed up against a loading bay, and beyond that, a freight elevator. Somewhere a motor whined into reluctant life, and the elevator descended from the top floor. It leveled and stopped. The doors opened horizontally like a set of teeth.

"Hey, it's the death of the party," said Malcolm, still grinning.

"Where is she?"

"I'll take you to her, Jackie boy." He gestured and I stepped onto the split, cracked boards, and he sent us grinding upward, to the top floor. He wrenched the doors open and motioned me to follow, feeling safe enough to turn his back on me as we crossed a hundred feet of empty storeroom. The dirty windows overlooking the street and river had been tilted open in an attempt to make a cross breeze, but the place was still stuffy. We approached a line of doors against the far wall; three on the right, four on the left, in the center an arched opening to a stairwell. Light seeped from under two closed doors in the line. He went to the one next to the outside wall and opened it.

A bare bulb hanging from a plain wire and socket disclosed a small bare room. Broken glass was all over the floor, and empty panes framed the sky and some buildings across the river. In years long past, someone had had a nice view. Malcolm followed me in to stand by the windows. He looked out and down, waved once, then turned to me.

"Where is she?"

"One thing at a time." He pointed at something on the floor. It was a flat parcel of folded brown paper. "You check that out first."

There was no reason to refuse; he had a purpose to his games and I had to play. I picked it up. It was very light and the paper came apart easily. Bobbi's red silk dress slithered into my hands.

I started for him and he took an involuntary step back, then recovered. "Don't do it, not 'til you see—"

My hands closed on his throat.

"See what, you shit?"

His eyes rolled toward the window and I followed their path.

The river was night black and smooth, stray lights caught in the surface barely moving. Below the window was a concrete loading pier with metal rings set in it. A length of rope was tied to one, and the other end went to an old flat-bottomed boat floating some thirty feet out. The woman Marza described crouched in the boat, leaning over its near side with her hand in the water. She was looking anxiously up at us.

"Let . . . go . . . now," he gasped out urgently, and his distorted tone suddenly convinced me. I released him and backed away so that we were clearly separated.

The woman in the boat took her hand out of the water and pulled on another piece of rope as though for an anchor, but instead a head broke the surface. It shook and shuddered, water streaming only from the nose, because the mouth was taped shut. Her eyes were bulging with utter terror.

Oh, my God.

Malcolm coughed, recovering. "And don't run down for her. She's tied like a mummy and weighted. The second you walk away from this window Norma lets the rope go, and down she sinks. You'd never get to her in time, not with your problem about crossing water."

I could cross water if I had to, but it was slow going. I'd never get to her in time. Never. I swung back on him, but he read my purpose and didn't look directly at me.

"No fish-eye, Jackie, I gotta stay in sight from now on. Norma has her orders, and if she thinks something's wrong with me, the girl is dead. You understand that? I gotta stay in her sight."

Numbly, I looked down, straight into Bobbi's eyes. They locked helplessly on mine, pleading. I called to her, not sure she could hear me. Her expression didn't change.

"Good," he murmured. "Real good." He took the dress from me, folding and rolling it into a ball. "I don't blame you. She's a classy twist. Nice, like I always wanted to get for myself. She needed a lot of help getting out of this. I had to hold her down while Norma did the honors. I like 'em to fight, y'know? That always gets me going. A body like that must feel good under you, huh?"

"Shut up!"

He abruptly stepped away from the window. Norma pushed Bobbi under. I grabbed for him, but he dodged.

"Say you're sorry."

"I'm sorry! Damn it, come back! *I'm sorry!*"

He eased back. Norma brought her up again. Bobbi's eyes flickered groggily, and her head lolled.

"Again, like you mean it."

"I'm sorry," I whispered sincerely, but it was to Bobbi.

"You promise to behave?"

I nodded. Tried to swallow. Couldn't.

His smile returned. "That's real good."

"What do you want?"

"Like I said, nothing you can't handle." In a louder voice aimed at the next room over he called, "It's all right, you can come now."

A door scraped open, a rubbing, grating sound crawled over the floor, and she rolled into sight. The harsh yellow light did funny things to colors and Gaylen's blue eyes had faded to a pale, cold gray. She was in her wheelchair with the rubber-tipped cane across her knees. She looked up, frowning. Malcolm turned to face the window, giving us a kind of privacy. Neither of us spoke, each holding still like actors at the end of a play before the lights go out and the curtain falls.

At last she drew in a breath and spoke. "I didn't want to do it this way. I really didn't, but you wouldn't understand, you—"

"You asked this of Maureen?"

Her answer was plain. There'd been fire in Marza's eyes, but Gaylen's held acid. Sometime long ago they had argued it all out, and Maureen had realized the truth and run. Her note said, *Some people are after me because of what I am. . . .* Turned another way, the meaning changed. It was not Braxton she had feared with his cross and silver bullets, it was her sister. Five years ago she'd left to protect me. Had she stayed it would have been me down there with Norma, and Maureen standing where I was now.

"I begged her. It was just one little thing, and I would have left her alone forever had she wished. I *asked* you, and is it so much? All you can tell me are the shortcomings. They're *nothing* to what I'm going through now. This body is old and crippled and I hate it! I want to live!"

"You have to die for that—if it works."

"What's death compared to the pain I feel whenever I move? And as for it working, it must! Maureen changed and I'm her sister, I *know* it would change me."

"What about Braxton?"

"I tried to explain to him and he was too pigheaded with his talk of contamination and souls to listen."

"He was never a danger to either of us."

"Never?"

"I was taking care of the problem when this . . . Braxton was a nuisance, but he didn't deserve to die."

"He did if I wanted to make you understand how serious I am. It could have been *anyone* else—someone walking next to you on the street, your detective friend—anyone. Time and circumstances made him a convenient target." She let that sink in.

My hands clenched and I longed for the luxury of closing them around her neck.

"But that's past and finished. I want you to think about the girl. You've seen her and you know there are no safe alternatives but one, and what I'm asking for is not so terrible."

I turned away as though thinking. I had no choice but to agree, but she expected reluctance and was getting it. "You don't know what you're asking."

But she'd heard that one before and had the same answer ready. "I *do* know, and I'm not asking now. Do what I want and the girl goes free. You already know what happens otherwise."

"You'd let them do that?"

"Yes."

My eyes were on Bobbi's face. "Will you free her unharmed?"

"Yes."

"All right."

She gave a sigh, very much like the one that came over the lines when I'd first called. "Good, then come here."

"Let her go first."

"No."

I glanced over my shoulder at Malcolm.

She shook her head. "No. He is to watch. If he thinks anything is wrong, he will take steps."

"Steps?"

"Whatever he thinks is necessary." She gave him her cane.

I looked at him. He was watching me, but not smiling as before, and I liked it a lot less.

"Come over here," she repeated. She extended her left arm, wrist up, blue veins bulging slightly beneath the thin crinkled skin. "Now. Do it now."

At least I'd be spared the intimate contact with her throat. To save Bobbi I would have done even that, but the thought of touching her in this way was sickening, and it showed on my face. She waited, though, until I moved a few reluctant steps closer. Her eyes took in every movement, as did Malcolm's. It was worse than being naked.

"Now, Jack," she whispered.

But my body was not cooperating. True, I had not yet fed; the hunger was there, but not the will. It would be many more days of fasting before I could overcome the physical revulsion with physical need.

My mouth came within an inch of the crepe-textured flesh, smelling faintly of some kind of soap and with a smear of paint on the upturned wrist. She painted pictures.

"Now."

Pictures of flowers. What had Pruitt said about flowers? Roses for Bobbi, fading now, and I had to do this or Bobbi—

"*Now.*"

Damn her. With cattle in the Stockyards it was simple feeding, a necessary chore. With Bobbi it was the means to express physical love. With Gaylen it was obscene and humiliating, and blinding white fury was the result. Most of my concentration was on holding in the rage or the old woman would find herself and her chair crashing through one of the walls.

She refused to meet my eyes, staring at her bared arm instead.

"Look at me," I said.

"*No.*"

"Look at me."

"Malcolm . . ."

His step behind me.

Bobbi. My eyes dropped.

"Wait, Malcolm."

He paused, then moved back.

Damn her. God *damn* her to hell.

Then anger tipped things and my canines emerged the necessary length and cut hard through her skin, tearing silently. It hurt and her arm jerked, but her free hand came down and she forced it to be still again. I swallowed her thin, bitter blood and tried not to choke. I thought of cattle and tried to pretend it was no more than a routine feeding, something my mind could handle to keep from retching, because if I stopped now I could not do this again and Bobbi . . .

The worst of it was that blood was blood, and my body began to accept it. Never mind the source, that didn't matter. This was food, all food and usable. Hot strength flowed down and through and I held on more firmly. She wanted me to take her blood, then so be it. Tonight I could and would take it all, and then I'd deal with Malcolm. I'd open his mind up like a tin can and not care what mess I made of it as long as he freed Bobbi.

"That's enough." Her teeth were set from the pain because I was not being careful with her.

No, now I make my own choice.

"Stop."

I'll drain you dry until there's not enough blood in you to keep your brain conscious and your head droops—

"I said enough."

—and your heart stops because there's nothing left to pump and everything winds down to a final stillness and all that's left is a hundred pounds of carcass and a bad memory—

"Malcolm . . ." Her voice was weaker, frightened.

—and I lift my head in time to see it coming as a blur, but he's already into the swing and it's too late to react. The thing hits me square and hard and sends my skull spinning into the light, and I fall—fall—and hit something hard—and lie still—

The yellow bulb burned my eyes; I was faceup on the boards, with the two of them staring down at me to see if I were alive. That's hard to do, since there's no pumping of lungs or beating heart.

Malcolm set aside the cane he used to crack my skull, waved out the window with his hat, and knelt closer.

"Jesus, look at his eyes."

"Yes, they get that color during feeding. It fades."

And when we make love, so Bobbi and I leave the lights out . . . Light—the damned thing was boring right through me.

"If he's dead—"

"He can't be. You said they were tough, that there's only one way for them." He passed a hand over my eyes. His pink fingertips brushed the lashes and I blinked. He looked relieved. "It's all right, he's just stunned. What went wrong?"

"Never mind. Are they coming?"

"Yeah, but I think Norma needs some help."

"She can handle it." She was wrapping a handkerchief around her arm to stop the flow. Her face was white and her hands shook. I'd been very close but could do nothing more. The room spun sickeningly with the light bulb in the center and I couldn't move. It was different from being hit with a stone, I wasn't vanishing to heal. Something about my nature and the nature of wood prevented it, but I knew I'd recover soon and the feeding would help. A few more minutes . . .

Malcolm grabbed my ankles and dragged me from the room. My arms fanned out uselessly over my head; I was unable to control them or anything else. He had struck with killing strength, leaving me helpless.

Grunting and straining, he got me through the door and around a corner into the stairwell. We were on the top floor, but there was still one last flight leading up to the roof. He struggled hard with my weight until the length of my body was stretched halfway up. My head hung off the angle of the step, turning the room upside down for me. My knuckles brushed the landing.

I tried to move and got only the smallest quivering along the muscles for all the effort. Not yet, perhaps in a few more minutes, but not yet.

"Hurry," she said. She had wheeled her chair into the landing, set the brake, and Malcolm helped her out. He was as solicitous as any boy scout helping an old lady across the street. She shuffled close to me and stiffly sat on one of the steps below my head. With icy misery, I realized what was coming.

Her breathing was hoarse and labored. I'd taken a lot of blood from her, after all. Now she was going to take it back. This was the exchange she had to have. It had been very necessary for Malcolm to hit me and keep me quiet or I would not have been able to stand it.

She hovered close with something in her hand, but kept it just out of view. She turned my head away and I was staring at Malcolm. His eyes were peeled wide with excited interest and he struggled to control his nervous laughter.

A tugging at my throat, a sharp sting, and then a strangled gag escaped me as she cut into the skin. I'd been placed head down so that gravity would speed the flow. Warm and wet, it trickled past my chin onto my face, filled a crevice in the corner of my mouth, overflowed, and skirted my eye and into my hair, tickling my ear and finally dripping onto the stairstep.

She drew a steadying breath and lowered her mouth to the open wound.

I didn't know how much it might take to secure the change she wanted, perhaps only a single mouthful was sufficient. She kept her lips hard on my neck, swallow after swallow, drinking quickly to keep up with the flow until it was too much for her and she had to stop. She was still alive and a living human unused to it cannot handle large quantities of blood, physically or mentally. She leaned back against the wall, eyes shut as she caught her breath.

Malcolm stepped forward and helped her back to her chair. "Can I—"

"No, later. I'll do for you later. I promise. Take me to the truck, I must rest."

"I thought—"

"Yes, you're right. Finish it."

The flow from my neck slowed and stopped. She must have used some wooden instrument to cut me—a sharp piece of ebony, perhaps. The pain in my head was subsiding, but not as fast as I wanted. Controlled movement was still a moment or two away. My arms were working a little, enough for the muscles to contract. It was a start. . . .

Malcolm's upside-down image was smiling at me; it grinned, it giggled. A long pole was in his hands, one chiseled end protected by a sharp metal tip to keep the point on the wood from splintering.

Panic roared up and took over. I tried to vanish and felt only a flicker of response brush over the nerves. The shock of the wooden cane had been too much. I needed more time and had none. My hands came up in a feeble effort to push away the tip of the pole. There was no strength in them. I was absolutely, utterly—oh, God . . . *no* . . .

With all his weight behind it, he rammed the thing into my chest and blood shot up and out. My body shook and bucked as if with seizure, hands clawed, legs kicked. A terrible suffocating weight settled on me, crushing and smothering out the life.

He pushed once more and the shattering, engulfing agony negated all thought and effort as a dying animal's shrieks filled the building; ugly, frightening screams that shook the walls and went on and on until there was no more air for the lungs to push out. The mouth hung uselessly open, and the last echoes hammered down the stairs and were finally lost in the darkness below.

10

FIRE.

Black fire.

Black fire you can't see or hear or smell, only feel, and by then it's too late. It's caught hold and is consuming everything.

Searing black fire that fills the chest from the inside out, until it should explode from the heat and end things forever, but doesn't. The silent body lies inert, enduring and somehow still conscious. Death is too far away for sanity to remain.

Gaylen's chair wheels grinding over the flooring, Malcolm's steps fading . . . crunch, bump, and they were in the elevator. The door was pulled shut and they began to descend. He would load her into the truck and they would go somewhere else. Somewhere . . . Bobbi . . . They'd pulled her out—their voices said as much in the distance. . . .

Move. Move *something*.

Bobbi had seen their faces, they couldn't afford to let her go. Gaylen would never take that chance.

But she had promised. She had—

Did a finger twitch? Or was that imagination?

My hands had only found movement at the end, when the wood stake plunged into me. The right one found direction, clawing to pull it out, and the left had convulsively torn through part of the steps. It was still there; damp river air curled around my fingers.

Doors slammed shut. The motors started, gears shifted, and they rumbled into the street.

Try to move.

Nothing. The body was still and dead, the brain was just taking a little longer. The cold was creeping slowly up my legs—cold and then numbness, something familiar and unpleasant. It was what had happened when I tried to stay awake past sunrise to see what it was like. I fought the numbness and clung to the pain. If I gave in and let the sleep take me now I would never wake up again.

Move.

Nothing.

Nothing at all for an infinity.

Alone in the dark with the pain and the cold and the fear for Bobbi. Would it be quick for her? Would they let her go?

Foolish thought.

Numbness from feet to knees. In a few hours it would reach my burst heart and smother the black fire raging there.

A soft crunch, conducted up through the stairs. It repeated and resolved; grit trapped between shoe soles and the flooring. Probably Malcolm returning at last to get rid of the body. I hadn't heard the truck coming back; must have blacked out for a while. I thought unhappily of the dirty river water closing over my head.

Scrape, scrunch. Pause. Not Malcolm, he wouldn't be so cautious. A tramp, then. He was in for a nasty surprise when he got to the top landing.

Numbness from knees to waist. Death was taking me an inch at a time and moving faster than I'd thought. Soon the ice and nothingness would flow over my brain. . . .

Move, damn it, *move*.

Someone breathing softly, listening at the foot of the landing below me, heart pounding, anticipating possible danger from above. Maybe he'd spotted my left hand poking through the underside of the steps and was having second thoughts about coming the rest of the way.

The first thin tendrils of cold streamed into my vitals like a dusting of snow off a glacier.

Heart thundering now, lungs taking short drafts of air, and then a long one as he came up the last flight and stopped because now he could see me. I heard in his voice some fraction of the agony that was holding me so helpless.

"Jack . . . Oh, my God . . . Oh, my dear God . . ."

I tried to speak, tried to move, but the slightest flicker of an eyelid was too much. The thing piercing my chest held me frozen. I could not tell him that some part of me was still alive.

Then Escott's hand closed around the stake.

God, yes, pull it out.

He pulled once, twice, then stopped because the gurgling sob that came out of me startled him. Coming back to life was almost as bad as dying. The third tug did the job, and it scraped between the ribs, shook the breastbone, and finally came free. Blood welled up coldly in the wound, quenching the fire there, and the body shuddered as the numbness retreated a little.

His hands went under my arms and he eased me from the stairs until my body was level, slowing the downward flow of blood I couldn't afford to lose. My eyes were open now.

He looked worse than I felt, with his paper white face and new lines formed by the horror of what had been done to me and what he had had to do. I'd read a lot of nonsense about vampires, but there was truth to the stories about those killed; when the end came, it came violently and loud, and mine had been no different. The walls of the stairwell were splashed with gore, and from the dampness soaking into my clothes, I knew I was lying in a pool that had formed on the floor below the steps.

The cold was coming back and I tried to tell him about it, but couldn't draw the breath to do so. Thanks for coming, Charles. It's too late, but thanks all the same. Maybe you can track them down before they kill Bobbi.

My eyes rolled up and the dark closed in.

"Jack!"

The lids twitched. They were so heavy. At least this time it wouldn't hurt.

He was doing something, making short, choppy movements above me. "Stay with me, Jack. Damn your eyes, *stay with me.*"

Fingers forced my lips back. He pulled my teeth apart and the first drops seeped into my mouth. I gagged, fighting him.

"Stay with me," he hissed.

It was hardly more than a taste, enough to seize my attention, but not nearly enough to do me any real good. I couldn't let him risk himself.

"Stay . . ."

I turned my head away or tried to, but his other hand grabbed my hair and held me in place.

"*Stay . . .*"

Then I accepted it. Fully.

My teeth abruptly pierced his skin, and the red warmth flowed more freely. He recoiled—perhaps from pain, perhaps from revulsion at what I was doing—then recovered, knowing that I couldn't help myself. I still desperately wanted to *live*. The instincts born from my changed nature had taken over and ignored the faint, dissonant warning that I could kill him if I went too far.

I ignored it—and I drank.

A heavy engine driving a heavier load. Men distantly shouting to each other. The lazy lap of wash as the barge passed along the river three stories below. The city was slowly waking, or maybe it had never really been asleep.

Some long time earlier I'd found the strength to push away Escott's lifeline, hopefully before it was too late.

My eyes were squeezed shut as much from the effort of recovery as to avoid looking at him. I wasn't quite able to do that just yet.

"Come on, Jack, no games. Are you still with us? Wake up."

His voice was thin, but conversationally normal. Some of the crushing weight on my soul melted away. I wanted to shout from the relief.

"That's it, open them so I know you're all right."

I did, but couldn't focus too well and didn't want to look at the stuff on the walls. The lids came down again like lead bricks. He, at least, was still alive. I was too shattered and sick to be very certain of my own chances.

He continued, trying to encourage me. "The bleeding in your chest stopped. It closed right up once I took that bloody great stick out."

He couldn't have meant it as a joke. My head wobbled from side to side as though to deny the thought. The cold and numbness were gone, but shock and weakness were left in their place. I could move again, barely.

"You'll be all right." He sounded very convincing, but I wasn't quite ready to believe him yet.

I drew an experimental breath to talk, and heard and felt a bubbling noise within. It developed into a spasm and I roiled on one side in a fit of coughing. One of my lungs had been pierced and was full of blood and fluid. This alarmed Escott, but I felt his steadying hand on my shoulder as I hacked some of it out. The business passed and I flopped back, exhausted.

I took another breath, shallow this time, to avoid coughing. It stayed inside without discomfort and wheezed out in what I hoped was a recognizable name.

He understood. "Your friends told me where you'd gone. They've heard nothing from the kidnappers yet."

I tried another breath, felt the cough beginning, and forced it to subside. "Gaylen did this—"

"You needn't explain, I found out a great deal about Miss Dumont in New York."

"Came back?"

"Yes, that's why I returned early. I thought things might be urgent, so I flew back. It only took five hours, but I'm sorry it couldn't have been faster."

He was sitting, his knees drawn up and his back to the wall about a yard away, a handkerchief tied around his left wrist. With a wry expression, he retrieved a folding knife from the floor.

"Hadn't time to sterilize it. If I get lockjaw, it will be your fault."

He tucked it away in a pocket and said nothing more of what else had happened.

"Did they give you any idea where they were going?" he asked.

I shook my head. "Took her away. Another woman with them. Malcolm—" I had to stop for the coughing.

"That's all right," he told me. "I'll see to it, I'll do my best."

"No cops?"

"No," he assured me. "Do you think you can move?"

"Can try." One thin, stained hand gripped the stair rail and pulled, the other pushed against the floor. He helped, but it was too much. The cough returned and the convulsions doubled me over.

"Have to wait." I whispered. "Weak."

He looked away, uneasy. "You can't wait long, the sun will be coming up shortly."

"When?" I had no sense of time passing. The whole night must have slipped by.

"About thirty minutes."

It was no good, I needed hours to recover—and my earth. "My trunk. Bring it here. I have to—"

"Certainly, if you'll be all right alone."

There wasn't much choice. He could probably carry me down to his car, but I was in no shape to move. The trip could kill me if I were exposed to the sun in this weakened state. I nodded yes, and hoped I was telling the truth.

It took him a little longer than thirty minutes. Though I was in a shadowed area, I was too feeble to fight the daylight blaring through the broken windows. I slipped into a half-aware trance, eyes partially open and unblinking.

He did finally return with the smaller of my two trunks, loaded down with two bags of earth. I must have looked really dead then, for he paused to check for a pulse and heartbeat before putting me into the trunk. There were none to be found, of course, but he was optimistic.

As soon as I was lowered onto the bags inside I went out completely.

The next night I surprised myself and woke up.

Escott was perched on a chair, peering at me. "How do you feel?"

A reasonably important question, I thought it over while checking things from the inside out. "Alive," was the conclusion. I didn't mention the ton of iron wrapped tightly around my chest or that my head felt like a balloon ready to pop. My nose and throat hurt as well, but they were much less noticeable.

"Bobbi?" I asked.

He shook his head. "I have been trying."

We were both silent. If Bobbi were not free by now there was little or no chance of her still being alive. After what Gaylen had done to Braxton and then me . . . The emptiness inside yawned deeper and blacker.

Escott saw and guessed what was going on. "Jack, I need you thinking, not feeling. There's still a chance for her."

"Yeah, just give me a minute." It took longer than a minute to shut it all down. I had to make myself believe she was alive. Anything else had to be kicked out or I'd be useless. Bobbi was alive and needed help, and that was that.

Escott got up while I was adjusting things. We were in his bare dining room, the only place on the ground floor with just one window. The panes of glass were now covered with sheets of cardboard to block out the day's sun. He pulled it all down, stacking the stuff neatly on a packing crate and twitching the curtains back together. Outside, a steady rain was streaming down the glass.

I was on a cot set up near one wall, on top of a bedsheet on top of a layer of my earth. It felt much more comfortable and civilized than lumpy bags inside a cramped trunk. My stained clothes had been stripped away and most of the blood on my skin cleaned off. Modesty had been preserved by a blanket tucked up to my chin.

He came back and sat down. Instead of the handkerchief, there was a neat padding of bandage circling his wrist. The skin on his face was tight, with dark smudges under his eyes from no sleep. Last night and the following day had been no picnic for him, either.

"I'm glad you're better. You looked quite ghastly earlier."

"How bad was it?"

"Bad enough. The blood loss was massive—it was as though your death a month ago had caught up with you." His eyes shifted uneasily away from the memory.

I dimly recalled my hand clutching the stair rail and noting its thinness. In retrospect, it was not so much thin as skeletal. I looked at my hands now. They were normal.

The movement caused a tugging at my cheek. "What's all this?" There was tape on my face and a rubber tube leading into my nose. The other end of it was connected to an upside-down glass bottle hanging from a metal stand. The bottle was half-full of some recognizable red liquid.

He stopped looking so grim. "It began as an experiment and proved successful. I borrowed the equipment from Dr. Clarson—remember the fellow who stitched me up—then made a visit to the Stockyards to obtain six quarts of animal blood. I daresay they thought I was more than a little mad, but they humored me and I returned here to set it up. You looked awful and I couldn't tell if you were alive or not, but thought it all worth a try. It did help you that time you were sun-blind. . . ."

I was astonished.

"You needed it. The first bottle was empty within a quarter hour and the others with decreasing slowness throughout the day, and each one filled you out a little more. With the lack of normal vital signs it was extremely encouraging. I originally considered trying a needle and tube in your arm, but decided against it. Your body, I suppose, has been adjusted to absorb and process blood through the stomach walls, and I was reluctant to tamper with the system by putting it directly into the veins. I'm still very much mystified by your condition. It really shouldn't work—not without a heart to pump and lungs to oxygenate, it really shouldn't."

He looked as though I should have an answer for him. I shrugged and shook my head, just as puzzled. "Beats me, but as long as it does work I'm not complaining. Where'd you learn to do all this?" I tugged at the tube, which itched where I couldn't scratch.

"Please, allow me." He began gently pulling the tube out; there seemed to be a lot of it. "I learned in a hospital when I was very young. I once thought I wanted to be a doctor, so one of my father's friends got me a job there, but it never worked out."

"Why not?"

He rolled up the tubing and unhooked the bottle. "Too squeamish," he said with a perfectly straight face, and carried the stuff off to the kitchen.

I sat up cautiously, my chest still aching. Some leftover fluid in my damaged lung shifted and burbled with the position change. When I didn't collapse into a coughing fit, I stood and followed him, but slowly, wrapped in the blanket like a refugee.

Near the sink were a number of similar glass containers, all empty.

"All that went into me?"

He turned on the tap, upended the bottle, and rinsed it out. The beef blood gurgled around the drain, and rushing water diluted it and carried it down. Involuntarily I thought of the walls in the stairwell and looked away.

"Nearly five out of six," he said. "There's one left in there if you need it." With his elbow he indicated the refrigerator. He'd been through a lot setting this up and then waiting to see if it worked. Faced with the same grim task and my inert and unpromising carcass, I might have given up before starting.

"Are you all right?" I asked him in turn.

He knew just what I meant. "A little light-headed when I move too fast, but otherwise there are no ill effects."

"Charles . . . I . . ."

He could see it coming and grimaced. "Please don't be an embarrassing ass about this. I only did what was necessary."

I nearly said something anyway, but held it back. He acted as though he'd done nothing more than loan me a book, and wanted to keep it that way. All right, my very good friend, if you insist. But thank you for my life, all the same.

The phone rang, and he answered.

"Escott."

The voice on the other end was familiar and not one I expected.

"Yes, he's up now. . . . He seems to be. What have you heard? Very well. We'll talk and I'll let you know." He put the earpiece back on the hook.

"Gordy?"

"You're surprised."

"The last time you saw him he was poking a gun at you."

"Forgive and forget. Besides, he never really wanted to kill me." Unconcerned, he crossed back with the bottles and busily loaded them into a cardboard box on the table. "From what you told me about him, I decided we needed his assistance. He has a large organization of eyes and ears and is more than willing to help us locate Miss Smythe. I called and told him everything that happened and he's been tearing this city apart since dawn. He just called now to inquire after your health, but unfortunately has no news for us."

Next to the box on the table were some of my things—watch, pencil, keys, wallet, and notebook. He'd made an attempt to clean it all but the notebook was a loss. The pages were rusty brown and stuck together. If he were so squeamish, how the hell had he been able to—

"Charles."

He paused, following my hand as I peeled a page open.

It was still legible. "There, I wrote it down and forgot it. Can you trace license plates this late? Can Gordy?"

"Is it Gaylen's?"

"No, her bullyboy. That blond crazy, Malcolm."

He remembered. "Yes, Gordy and I went to his office, but could trace him no farther. He was very careful about his personal papers; the place was cleaned out."

"This was to his Ford, the one he was in outside her hotel. Maybe there's an address other than his office."

"We can try." His voice was level, but charged with hope as he got back on the phone, relayed the numbers to Gordy, then quickly hung up. "Now we must wait. He'll call as soon as he has anything."

There was someone else waiting. "What about Marza?"

"She's still at Miss Smythe's hotel with Mr. Pruitt. She is upset, but in control, as when I talked with her last night. You'd left for the warehouse quite some time before I arrived, and I got only her version of things. I would be most interested if you could tell me what events led up to your being impaled in a stairwell in such a disreputable neighborhood."

It was the way he said it that made it seem funny. I started to laugh. It was probably just a normal release of pent-up emotion, but it turned into a coughing fit. I forced it all back, holding on to my aching chest.

"You should lie down, you're not nearly recovered yet."

"Nah, I'll be all right. Lemme get some clothes on and I'll tell you what happened."

I wandered up to the bathroom and tried not to think about Bobbi while I bathed, shaved, and hacked out the last of the junk in my lung. In less than thirty minutes I was dressed and in his parlor, finishing my story to him about last night's events. I stuck to the bare facts and left out the emotions. The earlier laughter was long gone by now, and my hands were trembling when I'd finished.

With a pipe clenched in his teeth, Escott listened, with closed eyes, stretched out on the sofa. The only sign he was awake was an occasional puff of smoke from his lips. It drifted up to get lost in the dusk of the ceiling. Only one lamp was on in the room, a boxy brass thing on a table by the window. The rain had slacked off a little, but in the distance, the sky rumbled with the promise of more.

"Your turn," I said. "Why did you leave for New York so suddenly, and what were you doing up in Kingsburg?"

He removed the pipe to talk. "It wasn't sudden to me. I was here digesting Herr Braungardt's excellent meal and thinking over our interview with Gaylen. The more I thought, the more my eye kept drifting to my packed bag. There was a night train leaving for New York and I simply saw no reason to delay."

"So you left."

"When I got to the city and began looking into things, it became obvious that Gaylen's information was useless. The addresses were nonexistent and the phone number a blind. The address you gave me was real enough, but by then I had reversed things and was intent on backtracking Gaylen rather than Maureen. It did not take long once I located the right papers and records, and then the reasons behind the falsehoods began to emerge. That led me to Kingsburg. Ten years ago Maureen had Gaylen confined to a private asylum located there."

"What? She put her own sister in a nuthouse?"

He opened one eye in my direction. "You know you have a bent toward colorful language that I find most entertaining."

"And you're funny, too. Go on."

He shut his eye and continued. "It was an expensive place, the sort that the wealthy patronize when they have inconvenient relatives. The patients, no matter how lively, are treated with velvet gloves, but kept under strict watch. The usual sort found there are alcoholics and drug addicts, but occasionally they take in someone like Gaylen. Her daughter, Maureen, had her declared mentally incompetent—"

"But they—"

"Yes, you and I know they were sisters, but I imagine it would have looked odd if Maureen gave that fact to the doctors."

"And if Gaylen insisted—"

"Which she did at first, according to the doctor I talked to, and that insistence only reinforced the reasons for her being there, at least for a while. It was there she became friends with another patient, Norma Gryder."

"The woman helping them. Why was she there?"

"Morphine addict. They escaped together in 1931 and vanished."

"Maureen found out and had to run to protect herself and me, to try and prevent what I walked right into."

"It seems likely. Perhaps all this time they were keeping an eye on you through your ad just as Braxton had been doing. She would also need more dependable help than Norma could provide and would be looking for someone like Malcolm. When your notice was canceled they had to find out why. I should never have brought it to your attention."

"You couldn't have known. They were worried, though. She was genuinely relieved when I showed up on the doorstep."

"And genuinely horrified about Braxton, and she lost no time in trying to persuade you to this blood exchange when she knew I'd be going to New York. My return or an untimely telegram would have ruined it all for her, but your own instincts made you turn down her request, causing her to make it a demand. Either way, you lose."

"Not me—Bobbi. Why didn't you send a telegram?"

"I did. One here and the other to Miss Smythe's hotel. Both must have been intercepted by Malcolm or Gryder. I received no replies and decided to take an aeroplane back. An interesting mode of transport, I quite enjoyed it, despite the noise.

"I checked with her hotel the moment I was back, and they told me she was out, then I went looking for you. This morning I called Gordy and he started his own investigation. We visited Gaylen's room, of course, but she was gone. She went to a great deal of trouble to set up the facade of a harmless and endearing soul, no doubt to arouse your sympathies before making her request."

"I suppose all that stuff about Maureen's death was a lie."

"I don't know. I had no time to trace down those records; perhaps on the next trip. At the moment we can do nothing. The management at her hotel hasn't seen Gaylen since she left yesterday evening. Her clothes are still there, but some few personal items, toiletries and such, are gone, and I doubt if she will return now. Gordy has men watching just in case, but if she's anywhere, it will be with Malcolm and Gryder."

"And Bobbi. It'd have to be isolated, maybe out of town."

His pipe had gone out. He sat up and fiddled with it. "Not necessarily.

You saw how isolated you were in the warehouse. I also checked on it. The owners are bankrupt and because of legal problems it's been unrented and empty for months."

"Then who paid the electric bill?"

"There's a generator in the basement. Gordy has two men waiting there as well, just in case Malcolm returns to dispose of your body."

"He didn't strike me as being that neat. What about the kid?"

"Kid . . . Oh, yes, the Braxton shooting was given an excess of coverage in the newspapers, but the police have little to go on. Young Webber received a concussion, but is recovering in hospital. He described Malcolm as his attacker, which is in your favor, as the police are looking for you."

"For me?"

"Several people could not help but notice your disheveled appearance as you tore around the building looking for Miss Smythe. The police want to talk to you and have inquired after Miss Smythe, but Marza told them she'd left town to be with a sick relative."

"She could have come up with something better than that."

"I believe it was Mr. Pruitt's suggestion."

"Bright guy. With him on their side, the Communists don't stand a chance."

"Hmmm."

"Has Matheus talked?"

"I wasn't able to see him, but did manage a brief chat with a hospital orderly who is fond of gossip. The boy is feeling better, but naturally upset at the inexplicable death of his friend. The police have been in to see him, but no one else except his parents has spoken to him."

"And everyone full of questions."

"True, but what can he say?"

"Yeah, if he tells the truth about hunting down a vampire, they'll think he's nuts."

"You had better hope they do," he said with meaning.

I took it. Either way somebody would be in trouble; me if they believed his story, and him if they didn't.

His pipe relit and drawing, he leaned back on the sofa. "How much time passed between Miss Smythe's call and Malcolm's?"

"Ten minutes, maybe less."

"There was no phone in the warehouse. I would guess they made the first call to prove they had her, secured her, and made the second call. Then they hurried to the warehouse to wait for you."

I lurched out of the chair, ready to put some holes in the walls, but hugged my chest instead. It still hurt. "Gaylen may have died by now. She wouldn't wait."

"Yes."

"She'll be like me, if it happens."

"Not like you."

"It won't be just her. From her talk she'll be trying to change Malcolm, too. If it works for him, they'll be the kind of monsters Braxton was after."

"You told me that acquiring this condition is difficult and there is no way to tell until after death."

"That's how I understood it. I'm thinking that it might work for Gaylen since it worked for Maureen. Malcolm I don't know about, but it's better if we include him as well, just to save us from any surprises."

"Unfortunately, yes."

There was one more thought left unspoken. If Bobbi were still alive, they would be keeping her as a food source. Oh, God.

The phone rang, I reached it first, but let Escott do the answering. Gordy was on the other end. Escott had once told me I had no real idea of the grip and influence the mobs had in Chicago. It must have been pretty strong—he had an address.

"I'm coming over," he said. "You got some iron?"

Escott said yes, but I shook my head and asked for the earpiece.

"Gordy, this is Jack. If what I think has happened has happened, guns ain't gonna work, at least not on one of them."

"So what can we do?"

"Can you get some shotguns?"

"No problem."

"And some extra shells?"

"No problem."

"And one more thing . . ." I told him what. Escott's brows went up in surprise and interest.

Gordy considered and again said: "No problem. I'm sending some boys over to watch the place 'til we get there. Sit tight 'til I come for you."

Almost as soon as we hung up it rang again.

"Hello? What? Oh, yes." He passed it to me.

I answered thinking it was Marza.

The masculine voice was a jarring shock. "Jack, I want to talk with you."

"Dad?" *Oh, hell.*

"What kind of trouble are you into?"

"Trouble? What's the matter?"

"That's something you can tell me. The cops were by here just now wanting to know where you are."

"Did you tell them?"

"Hell no. Not until I know what's going on. They wouldn't say and your mother's throwing a fit, so start talking, boy."

Hell and damnation. "Dad, this is just some kind of a mix-up to do with those two con men."

"I'm listening."

I suddenly felt six years old again with Dad towering over me, ready to get the razor strop. I had to consciously shake off the image and remember

I was thirty years older and a lot taller. "Okay, what happened is that the little guy Braxton got shot and killed, and the kid thinks I'm involved, so he sent the cops to look me up."

A long silence.

"That's the truth, Dad. The kid saw me in the same building. They were following me to make trouble, and then someone bumped off Braxton. The kid got knocked out. He saw the killer, but not the killing. He knew I was there so he gave my name to the cops, and yours, too."

The language that followed heated the lines up, and then he repeated the story to Mom, who began groaning in the background.

"Look, why don't you pick up one of the Chicago papers? They're full of the whole story—"

"I did. It's the 'Studio Slaying,' isn't it?"

"Yes, Dad."

"What were you doing there, anyway?"

"I went to see the show."

"Why couldn't you have seen the show on the radio?" he said illogically. "What are you going to do? Are you going to the cops?"

Double hell. "I don't know."

"What do you mean?"

"I mean this whole thing stinks."

"You're damn right it stinks," he agreed, his voice rising.

"I mean I need some time to get things straightened out."

"What things?"

"It'd take too long to explain. If my boss thought I was really involved with this I could lose my job, and I don't want to lose my job."

"And I don't want the cops coming around here again."

"I know. Look, could you just hold off giving them this number?"

"For how long?"

"I don't know."

"*Shit!*"

"Dad, I've got good reasons for staying out of this, but I can't go into them now."

He growled, hemmed and hawed, but in the end decided he could even if he didn't like it. Then we said good-bye.

I put the earpiece back. "This is ridiculous. The kid sicced the cops on my parents to try and find me."

"So I gathered."

"What a pain in the ass."

"Well, at least you have a father willing to help you."

"Yeah. I guess I'm going to have to talk with the kid and make him change his mind about me."

"Though it would seem the damage had been done. I do admire the way you did not quite tell all the truth and yet avoided a direct lie."

"Yeah, it must be all that journalistic training," I said, beating him to the punch line. "Except that bit about losing my job."

"I suppose if it came down to it, you could say that I am your 'boss.' Technically I am, at least on certain occasions, and you are correct; if an employee of mine turned up in this sort of mess, I would not understand."

"Tell me another one."

11

WE were ready when Gordy pulled up and touched the horn, but the weather wasn't the best for a long trip. Though I had a raincoat and Escott loaned me a hat, neither one was going to be much protection against a sky that had split open with a vengeance. I didn't like it and felt a sharp twist inside because it had been raining out on the lake like this the night I'd been killed. Such associations were hard to ignore.

Escott and I recognized the car; it was the same one that belonged to Slick Morelli, Gordy's deceased boss. It also stirred up bad memories, but it was just a car, so we got in. Escott sat in front with Gordy and I shared the back with some hard lumpy things. "Careful with that stuff," Gordy cautioned.

The stuff was covered with an old blanket. I pulled it back and Escott turned around to see. They were all from different makers but had the same basic look; sawed off, double-barreled, and at short range, appallingly deadly. Gordy handed me an oddly light cartridge box.

"Check this and see if it's what you want. They're loaded with 'em."

I opened the box, got a cartridge, and pried open the end with a thumbnail. The contents spilled into my palm. Less than a quarter inch in diameter and dull brown in color, there was just enough light to see the grain pattern in each one.

"They look like beads," I said, noticing the tiny holes drilled in them.

"That's 'cause they are beads. One of the girls at the club had this necklace. They gonna work?"

"If they're wood, they'll work, but only at short range."

"They're wood. We'll probably have to go for point blank, then."

Escott looked uncomfortable. Gordy noticed.

"You know how this could end up; stay in or get out," he said in an even tone.

Escott locked eyes with him a moment, then put his hand over the seat for one of the shotguns.

It was enough of an answer for Gordy. He gave me an up-and-down. "You look like hell, Fleming."

That was his way of saying hello, how are you. I shrugged. "Where are we going?"

He started the motor and shifted gears. "A house on the south side. Any of the guys down there catch my boys in their territory they might get annoyed, so keep your eyes open. What kind of iron you got?"

"This," said Escott, pulling out a huge, odd-looking revolver. It had a ring in the butt, which tagged it as an army gun to me. The cylinder had a kind of zigzag pattern to it and it looked like the top part slid back, as though for an automatic. It even had a safety. I'd never seen anything quite like it and neither had Gordy.

"What the hell is that?"

"A Webley-Fosbery 'automatic' revolver."

"Maybe someday you can explain what that means. How 'bout you, Fleming?"

"This shotgun's enough for me." I tried to sound confident, though I hadn't really held a gun since the armistice. "Did Charles tell you they've got a sawed-off, too?"

"Yeah, but the range on 'em's not so good."

"It's good enough to kill."

"So duck."

Pressing deep into the backseat, I inhaled a lot of air and slowly released it. My nerves were turning up with some sharp and useless edges, mostly because of last night. It'd been a long time since I last felt so physically weak, and it was unsettling.

We slipped through the nearly empty streets. Some stores and a few bars were open, their customers huddled inside near the comfort of the lights. Now and again a face could be glimpsed framed in a window, eyes raised to the sky. Rain crashed down against the roof and bounced from the hood.

"Lousy night," Gordy commented. It occurred to me he was showing some nerves as well in extraneous conversation.

"Quite," agreed Escott, making it unanimous.

It got worse. The wipers were doing their best in a bad situation, but there was just too much water coming down. Gordy slowed the car, muttering. A few blocks later we hit a clear patch and made up the time, then he took an abrupt turn, parking halfway down a long, empty block behind another car. He got out to talk to the men waiting in it and returned.

"That one," he said, his eyes pointing to a white house half-hidden in trees. All we could see was part of its wide front and a couple of brick pillars supporting the porch roof. There were no lights. "No one's been in or out. They think it's empty."

"We'll see," I said. "Stay in the car while I go look."

"But—"

"Let him," said Escott. "He's very good at it."

I got out, leaving the gun, and strolled casually on the sidewalk until I was even with the trees. The area was quiet, with only two other houses back at the corner where we had turned. No curious eyes were on us, the rain had sent everyone inside to listen to the weather reports on the radio. It was a good location: private, fairly isolated, and still close to the city. They would feel safe bringing Bobbi here. I wanted them to feel very safe.

The wind kicked up and tugged my coat. The storm cell we'd driven out from was catching up, and I felt wet enough already. I stepped under the dripping trees and melted in with the shadows. I kept enough solidity so the wind wouldn't blow me away, but was virtually invisible, at least to night-dulled human eyes.

The front windows were dark and the curtains drawn. It looked as deserted as Gordy's men had reported. Around the side, one of the bedroom windows was raised a few inches. I eased close and listened, but the rain interfered with any sounds within. There was screening to keep out the flies and curtains as well, but not the kind you could see through. I moved around to the back of the house.

We'd found the right place. I recognized the panel truck parked next to the open and empty garage. I sighted on it, vanished completely, and floated over, re-forming with it between me and the house. The motor was cold, the key gone. The front interior was clean but there was a box in the back; a box about five and a half feet long, a foot high, and two feet wide. I lifted the lid and was not surprised to find three or four inches of dirt lining the bottom. What was disturbing was the clear imprint of a body in the earth.

Gaylen had not waited a moment longer than necessary. I wondered if she had killed herself or given that task over to Malcolm.

Going back to the house, I went from window to window, shamelessly peering in, but with no results. They were all closed, except for that one, and the curtains were firmly drawn. I found one unobscured basement window, and it looked like a discreet place for us all to slip inside.

When I returned Escott and Gordy were anxious for even negative news. "Malcolm's car is gone, but the truck's out back. Her box of earth is in it—it's been used."

Gordy didn't like my tone. "Whaddaya mean 'used'?"

"He means that these guns and the shells in them are no longer a mere precaution, but a necessity," explained Escott.

"She's a vampire, then?"

"Yes, and every bit as potentially dangerous as our friend here."

Gordy looked at me, considering the possibilities. I didn't look particularly dangerous, but he knew from experience I at least had endurance.

"She will appear to be about Bobbi's age now," I said. "Maybe younger, and she could kill either of you without even trying. These guns give us a chance against her at night, but only a chance. If you get a clear shot, don't hesitate; I can promise she won't. If you miss and it looks bad, do whatever you can to get away, and let me handle her."

"Are they in the house?"

"I don't know. It looks deserted. If it weren't raining I'd be able to hear something inside."

"We shall have to break in, then," said Escott. "But quietly."

"I've got a window picked out, but I want someone to back me up while I'm checking the joint."

"Just lead the way."

Loading our pockets with shells, we took the guns, concealing them under our coats as Malcolm had done at the radio station. I cautiously led them around and pointed out the window. Gordy let out a startled "Jeeze" when I vanished and re-formed inside. The catch was a rusty mess and nearly broke off in my hand when I twisted it free and pulled. As it was, they had to push from the outside while I dug my nails deep under the painted-shut framing. There was a sharp crack and a creak and it opened. We all stopped moving and listened, but no one came down the stairs to investigate. When it was wide enough, Escott came through feetfirst, and as soon as they touched the floor he pivoted around to get his shotgun.

"Come on, Gordy."

His eyes went around the opening. With him next to it for comparison it looked a lot smaller. "Are you kiddin'? I'll watch things out here 'til you can get the back door open."

Escott nodded. "Very well, we do need a rear guard."

Rain spattered our faces, and above Gordy's huge frame the sky burned with lightning. The thunder that followed seconds later made me wince from the sheer sound, and even Escott paused and frowned.

"Lousy night," Gordy muttered, showing his nerves again.

I told Escott to stay in the basement while I looked upstairs, and left him in charge of the guns. He didn't argue.

The basement door was hanging wide open, which was a bad sign to me. Most people keep theirs shut because a large opening into a dark pit makes them uncomfortable, but only when they're home. The door led straight up to the kitchen.

No one was there, but they had been. The table, counters, and stove were all stacked with dishes, pans, and leftover food; a small garbage pail by the back door had passed the point of no return some time ago. I held still and listened, but the rain on the roof acted like so much radio static.

The back door was locked. I didn't want to chance any noise letting Gordy in, he'd have to wait awhile longer.

The kitchen opened onto a dark living room. No one was hiding in the corners. In the middle of the floor stood Gaylen's discarded wheelchair.

I went back, passing Escott, who waited quietly near the top of the steps with a shotgun ready in his hands, his brows raised in a question. I shook my head and pointed down the hall to the bedrooms and went there.

The first door on the right was the bath, the second a small empty bedroom. The bed was unmade and women's clothing decorated the floor and furniture. A crumpled mass of fabric on a chair looked like the flower-print dress Norma had worn last night. It was still damp and smelled of the river.

The door to the second bedroom was shut. I pressed my ear to it. Even with the rain, I was certain to hear anyone on the other side, but the wood was thick and the thunder made me jumpy. I vanished, slipped through the door, and clung close to it while trying to substitute extended touch for sight.

On the right was something large and square, perhaps a bureau; on the left, space for the door to swing and another square object. Ahead was empty space. I could hear, but only in a muffled sort of way, and by then I was imagining sounds. I had to see what I was into and tried for a partial materialization.

Standing out starkly on the walls and ceilings were red splashes—a lot of them. My eyes dropped to the body on the floor. She was on her back, half-covered with a bedspread, her legs tangled in its folds. The red dress still looked new, the bloodstains blending invisibly into the bright color.

Blood was everywhere.

Everywhere. There was no head.

I must have made a noise or been too long. I was dimly aware of Escott quitting the basement and approaching. I had no memory of leaving the room, but he found me on my knees in the hall next to the open door.

"Jack?"

I blinked. I was staring very hard at a corner where the wall met the floor. There was dust in the crevice. I had to look at that and concentrate on it or I would see her instead.

He stepped carefully past me and turned on the bedroom light.

"Don't." The word came out of nowhere. It was wrong to put light in that room; light would make what was there real.

He flinched, caught his breath, then looked back at me, but my mind and eyes were focused on a meaningless detail to keep the unacceptable at bay. The light went out and he remained still for a while, getting his breath back to normal. After a time he stepped away from the door.

"Come on, Jack. Come with me."

It was something simple to respond to, something undemanding. I got up and walked. In the kitchen he pulled a chair out for me. I sat.

He unlocked the door and went out. His voice and Gordy's drifted in. I could guess what was being said, but didn't want to distinguish the words because that would make it real as well. I stared at a bent spoon fallen from the counter. My arm brushed against a tray on the table and tipped over a coffee cup. I righted it again. There was lip rouge on the rim, I recognized the color.

The crash inside was louder than the storm and brought Escott and Gordy right away, but by then it was over. The table and all the junk on it were now in a shattered heap with the wheelchair in the living room. I pushed past them into the rain. Water streamed down my face. It was a good enough surrogate for tears that would not come.

Escott and Gordy trudged into sight, their figures distorted by the water on the windows. They got in, the car shaking a little from their combined weight and movements.

"Jack."

It was hard to raise my eyes, and when I did, Escott didn't like what he found there. He didn't ask me if I was all right; he could see for himself I wasn't.

"Jack."

I shook my head and looked out a window that faced away from the house, a window full of darkness and rain. I watched a drop slither down on the inside and disappear into the frame and waited to see if another would follow.

"I'd like to take him home."

Gordy looked at me uncomfortably. "Yeah, go ahead. I'm gonna stick around until she comes back for her box." He handed over the key and got out.

"Thank you."

He didn't quite shut the door. "He gonna be all right?"

Escott slid over to the driver's side and put the key in the ignition. "I'll park it behind my building, you can pick it up later."

The door slammed, he started the motor, and made a U-turn. I closed my eyes in time to avoid looking at the house.

The sky opened up in earnest as we crawled home. The streetlights did little more than mark where the sidewalks began, and lightning flashed overhead as though God were taking pictures of it all. Between the water hammering the roof and the thunder, conversation was impossible, but neither of us felt like talking. Escott refrained from the usual phrases of sympathy, his silence was infinitely more comforting. He would leave me alone or stick around, whatever was needed. He seemed to understand grief.

He pulled the car around the house, triple-parking behind the Nash and my Buick. He must have picked it up from the warehouse sometime during the day. He cut the motor and considered without enthusiasm the soaking dash to the door.

"I suppose we can't get any more wet," he said, but hesitated.

Maybe he was thinking about standing in the downpour and struggling with the stiff lock on the back door; it was that or the necessity of having to leave me alone for a few minutes. He opened his mouth again, but the sound died as his attention focused rigidly on something in the mirror. His head whipped around.

"Oh, good God," he whispered.

I stared out the back window. A pale shape lurched toward the car. Rain streamed past, blurring the view. The shape stumbled and fell against glass, and the face, anxious and white, looked inside. Our eyes locked with mutual incredulity.

Numbed only for a second, I tore out of the car, afraid she'd disappear, but she came into my arms, solid and real, moving, laughing, crying.

Alive.

Some joys are too much for the heart to hold and can even supersede grief for intensity. The tears that had not come before now burned my eyes and finally spilled out onto Bobbi's upturned face.

We clung to each other in the car while Escott watched with a mixture of happy indulgence and indecision. He looked ready to leave us alone, but Bobbi saw his intent, hooked an arm around his neck, and held him in place with a hug.

"Good heavens," he mumbled, embarrassed and pleased, and unsuccessfully tried to suppress his smile.

She finally released him and turned back to me. Her face was swollen and red from crying, and her chopped-off hair was limp and dripping, but honest to God, she was the most beautiful woman in the world. Escott offered her a handkerchief and she gratefully accepted and blew her nose.

"I thought they'd killed you," she told me with a hiccup.

"We had drawn the same conclusion about you," said Escott.

"What do you mean?"

"We traced down Malcolm's house. There's a woman's body there, wearing your red dress."

"Jesus, no wonder Jack looked so strange."

"Who was it? What happened?"

"That was Norma. We had a fight and she lost."

"Could you be a little less succinct?"

"Easy, Charles, she's all in," I said, annoyed.

"No," she gulped, "it's okay. The other two left, the man and old woman."

"She's still old?" I asked.

"I don't know, I only heard her voice. I'd heard what they wanted you for, what they wanted you to do. . . . Did you?"

"Yes."

She paused, her thoughts on her face.

"I had to, Bobbi."

Her fingers brushed my temple, and I caught her hand and kissed it.

"I heard you," she said. "I think it was you. It was after she pulled me from the water, that's when they said you were dead."

"They were wrong. Charles found me in time to save my ass. Just tell me what happened to you."

"It's hazy; I was drugged a lot of the time. They kept me tied up in that bedroom all day, and once in a while the man would come in and check on me. The woman, Norma, sometimes shoved some cotton wadding over my nose and I'd hold my breath."

"Chloroform?"

She nodded. "I didn't think it was perfume, so I faked sleeping, and they left me alone most of the day. I spent the time getting untied. When it got dark I heard them again, the other woman, Gaylen—"

"What was her voice like? Old or young?"

She thought a moment. "Young, I think. I was still pretty woozy, but it was strong, at least. She and the man left, and then it was just me and Norma. When she came in to check on me she had the shotgun, but I hardly saw it because she was prancing around in my new red silk. It was a stupid thing to get mad about after thinking you were dead, but it just set me off. I jumped her, the gun came up, I pushed it away, and it—just—"

I held her tight. "It's okay, we know."

"God, I was sick and I had to get out. I pulled on one of her dresses and started walking. I didn't know where I was and the rain—"

"How did you get here?" asked Escott.

"Some couple in a car saw me, stopped, and offered a lift." She began to laugh—with relief, not hysteria. "I told 'em I had to walk home from a bad date and they believed it. They took me here, because I had to see Charles about you."

"Do you know where Gaylen went?"

"No."

"Probably the Stockyards," said Escott.

I agreed with him and looked at Bobbi. "Come on, let's get you inside before you freeze."

"Could we go to my place?"

"Anywhere you want."

"And Marza, she looked so awful when they grabbed me. Could you call her? Please, I know she's worried sick."

Escott fingered his waistcoat pocket. "My key—"

"Won't need it." I grinned and left the car, dashed up the back steps, and sieved through, re-forming again inside the kitchen. I opened the door and waved at them through the screen, showing off. They couldn't see me very well, what with the darkness and rain—

"Hey . . . Escott." A man's voice. Behind me.

Again, no warning.

They must have been expecting him to come in the front way and been waiting there, then heard the back door open and quietly come up from behind. It might have been avoidable with no rain or with the lights on, but then the right man would have been killed. I might have even stepped out of it, but my thoughts were elsewhere, and all the emotional shocks had made me sluggish. There was no time to react before something like a sledgehammer slammed into my back at kidney level. The breath was pushed right out of me. I staggered sideways against a wall and slid down, my back on fire.

Legs gave out and crumbled with no strength, right arm hanging loose and useless, left one twitching—my nervous system was shot all to hell. What was it, what was wrong with my back? My hand flailed around the source of the pain and my fingers brushed against hard metal. It was sticking out of my back at a firm right angle and I didn't realize what it was at first. When I did, I moaned and felt a sudden sympathy with Escott's squeamishness.

Two other people were with me, but only one was breathing. I kept my head down and went very still.

"Is he dead?" She was across the kitchen. Any closer and she'd see who I was.

Malcolm's hand pressed my wrist. He was close enough, but it was dark and he didn't have her night eyes—not yet. "Yeah, let's go."

I had to wait. No matter how badly I wanted them dead, I had to let them get clear and hope Escott and Bobbi stayed out in the car. I might be able to protect them from Malcolm, but not from her.

The front door slammed shut behind them.

Get up, go after them. Push against the wall, get the legs under the body. Stand up, get control, *walk*.

It was more of a drunken reel. The table got in the way.

Rest a second. It's not that bad. Now *move*.

I shoved the table away and went to the front of the house, trying to ignore my back. I made it to the door and twisted the knob. They were down the steps and walking quickly to their car parked down the street. Her coat was too long, but her figure fit it; it might have been one of Norma's spares. Her hair was full and dark, her walk light and strong. I didn't have to see her face; it would look like the photo she'd given Escott. Her skin firm and smooth again, an image of a girl in her pretty youth.

Their heads were down because of the rain, so neither of them saw it coming.

A narrow alley ran between Escott's house and the next; kids were always charging through it in their games. Malcolm, no gentleman, was on the inside of the walk and closest to the opening when a noise like thunder, but much louder and briefer, happened there. Raindrops were caught and frozen for an instant in the flash before smoke and darkness obscured them.

It had been Escott. He'd seen something from the car and had gone around to ambush them. Unfortunately, Malcolm's body was in the way for the crucial second and took most of the blast.

He was thrown hard against Gaylen. She screamed from surprise or pain or both, and they went down together. She rolled clear, her coat full of small holes. He pitched onto his face, his head and part of one shoulder hanging over the curb in the runoff water.

Gaylen got to her feet, dazed and staring at Malcolm, then looked down the alley. She took a half-step toward it, but lights were coming on in the surrounding houses. Malcolm moved and moaned, pushing himself up and reaching for her. She hesitated; there was blood all over his left side, head to toe, but he was somehow still alive. He sobbed her name. She made her decision and got him standing and helped him unsteadily toward the car. They were too busy to notice as I followed in roughly the same condition. I glanced down the alley in passing, but Escott had sensibly left.

Gaylen started the car and began rolling away. It paused undecided at the end of the street, enabling me to catch up, but not long enough to get inside. I grabbed the spare-tire cover and got my feet up on the bumper's narrow edge, with most of my weight resting on the slick angle of the trunk. It was not the most comfortable or secure position I'd ever been in, much less in a rainstorm with a knife in my back.

The gears were grinding, I dug in with my hands and held on tight. The metal began to bend under the pressure. I tried to vanish and slip inside the car, but the knife was screwing that up somehow. I tried to find a way to hang on with one hand so that I could pull it out, but things were too precarious. Literally and figuratively, I was stuck with it.

Dirty water flew up in my eyes, blurring the spinning pavement. I squeezed them shut, not daring to spare a hand to wipe them. Headlights flashed briefly, then peeled away. A horn honked. The Ford sped up, skidded on a corner, and straightened with a jerk. My foot came loose from the fender. The damaged muscles in my back protested the sudden movement and again at the effort required to put the foot back again. Wind caught Escott's borrowed hat and sent it spinning. My hair got soaked and dribbled into my eyes. Bobbi had said I needed to cut it.

Bobbi—

Not now, I couldn't think of even her now. I had to hold—

A short skid, more headlights. A truck coming from the other direction; its spray blinding, its roar deafening.

A speed change. Brakes.

We slow and stop. Stoplight.

I stick a foot on the road for balance and reach around. Can't find it—there—close the fingers—*pull.*

The initial pain returns. I nearly fall, nearly scream. Bite my lip instead. There's no end to the damned blade.

Pull.

Fingers slipping, gripping, no time to baby it out.

Pull.

It's a goddamned sword. . . . There . . . the edge catches on something. . . .

There.

Gears. Car lurching forward. Grab at the wheel cover. Rest.

It didn't hurt so much now, but the nerves were suffering from the aftershock. I looked at the thing. It wasn't a sword, just eight inches of good-quality steel and heavy enough not to easily break. A solid chef's knife that was meant to be slipped between Escott's ribs so he couldn't tell anyone what he learned in Kingsburg. After the first hideous shock he wouldn't have felt much, maybe just a little surprise as the floor came up. Malcolm was an efficient killer, he liked to do it quick and then get away before the fuss started.

We made another turn, and the streets looked familiar. How'd that story go about the man walking backward so that he could see where he'd been? We were approaching the neighborhood where Malcolm's house was, where she had left her box of earth, where Gordy and his men were waiting.

12

THE car cruised past the correct turn and took the next one a quarter mile down the road. The shotgun blast had made Gaylen cautious. Someone knew about her and her changed nature and knew how to fight her. She was going to be careful not to approach her box openly. We rolled into an area thick with trees and darkness. Branches and leaves stirring constantly in the wind made it all seem alive and aware. We stopped cold in the middle of a deserted mud-washed road, the motor died, and their voices rose up in the relative quiet.

"Don't leave me here!"

"I'll be right back. I have to see that it's clear."

"God, I'm dying. You can't go now."

"You'll be all right." Her door opened.

"No! Do it now! You said you would—you promised! Gaylen!"

She got out. I was flat on the ground by the rear passenger tire pretending to be a rock. The door slammed shut on Malcolm's protests. From under the car I saw her feet slip on the mud, regain balance, and walk away. When I no longer heard her I stood up.

Malcolm was on his side across the length of the seat and hardly noticed when his door opened. He was still alive, and that was all that mattered to me.

His wounds were scattered and colorful and he was bleeding freely in several spots. The little skin showing through the blood was white and clammy with shock. He and Gaylen had been outside the lethal range of the wood pellets, though. His claims of dying were premature, at least for the moment.

"Gaylen, please—"

"She's gone, all you've got left is me." I wanted him to *know*, to see it coming.

He didn't know me at first, I was only an unexpected intrusion, then his eyes rolled fully open and he started to scream. My hand smothered his mouth and part of his nose.

"You said you wanted it. Does it matter where it comes from?"

He couldn't move. He was that scared and hardly flinched when my hand slid down his face to close around his neck.

"You want to be a dead man like me? I can do that for you, Malcolm." My fingers tightened.

He struggled for air, imagining my grip to be stronger than it was.

"I'm not as good at killing as you are, though. It won't be quick, and believe me—it's gonna hurt."

Simple words he could understand, and now simple actions. I brought the knife up so he could see. The blade was clean and shining now, the edge was so sharp that it hurt to look at it. He recognized the thing and realized the mistake he'd made in Escott's kitchen. I let it hover next to his face. He shrank back into the car seat, and when he could go no farther, the first pathetic mewlings of sound began deep in his throat.

"Where do you want it first? Your eyelids?" I pressed the flat of the blade against his temple, the razor edge brushing his eyebrow. "I could cut them away, top and bottom."

He jerked at the touch of the steel, causing a tiny nick in the skin. I drew back and let him recover. His breath was coming too fast, and I didn't want him passing out.

"That'd hurt, but there are better nerve centers to play with. I want you to know what I went through in that stairwell. I want you to know what you gave Braxton and Bobbi. You think you're hurting now—in a minute you're gonna wish it was this good."

I threw the knife in the backseat and used my bare hands and, God help me, I was laughing.

I crawled from the car like a drunk and leaned against it, still shaking a little from what I'd done. Maybe I should have been sickened by my actions, but nothing so normal as that touched me now.

The wind was damp and cool as it washed over my face.

I'd stopped in time. He was still alive. Somehow I just managed to shake free of the insanity that had taken me over. Malcolm hadn't been so lucky. I'd paid him back for all that he'd done and then some. I was free of the nightmare. He would always be its prisoner.

I sucked clean, moist air deep into my lungs and let it shudder out again, flushing away the last stink of his terror.

No regrets. None.

I pushed away from the car and went after Gaylen.

The rain had almost stopped, but the leaves above continued to drip, creating a false fall. I couldn't count on that to muffle any noise I made, and stepped carefully on soft grass whenever possible.

She'd heard his screams and was coming back to investigate. I saw her just in time, put a fat tree between us, and sprinted, closing the space. I got within ten yards and froze, peering out from a fork in the branches.

She stopped short of the car; one of her sharp new senses had tipped her off and her head snapped around, on guard for an unknown threat.

The old woman was gone. It was one thing to know that fact, quite another to see it. Her face was so very like Maureen's, especially now with her anxious expression. But she was someone else, not the gentle woman I had loved.

I stepped out from behind the tree and walked swiftly toward her.

The body and its inner functions may have changed, but her mind was still human-slow to react. I was absolutely the last thing she expected to see, and with good reason, since she'd watched me die. She was still rooted in place when I caught her arms. The touch confirmed my reality. There was some struggling, then she abruptly stopped and smiled, quite calm. That smile made me freeze in turn and I knew then why Maureen had confined her sister to an asylum.

"What are you going to do?" she asked. "Kill me?"

I held her fast. "I can try, and after what you did to Bobbi, I'll enjoy it. There's a lot of wood around here . . . haven't you noticed?"

She had. She was still smiling, though. Then her face rippled, faded, and became a shapeless *something*. The hair on my scalp went up. My hand no longer clutched arms, but closed through cold tendrils darker and thicker than any fog. Her body was gone and in its place was a floating blob of about the same size. She had vanished, even as I had done a hundred times before.

But I could *see* her. She might not know that. It was some kind of advantage to me if I could keep fooling her.

The gray thing hung in the air for a few seconds, then moved away like an amoeba swimming in fluid. It fell in on itself, shaping and growing solid again.

She was laughing. "You didn't expect that; I thought you would have. I can do everything you can. Did you think I'd just *let* you kill me?"

"Do you think I'll let you go? If I don't get you, Escott will. Malcolm missed, you know. Did you see him in the alley? His gun? You felt it. That wasn't rock salt in the cartridges."

"I'm not worried about him."

"Aren't you? You tried to have him killed tonight, but the next time you'll have to do the dirty work yourself. Malcolm's finished."

"I don't need him now."

She vanished again, or almost. The shape swung to one side and behind some trees, but didn't wander far. I kept staring at the spot she'd been in, even after she materialized, turning only when she made a sound. It was to test me. Apparently I'd passed. Pleased, she vanished again.

There were noises behind me, near Malcolm, but off to the left. I followed their direction, stopping, listening. A loud snap. A foot skidding over damp leaves. Silence.

A glimpse of movement against the wind.

The gray thing moved closer, coming across open ground to get close to me. It seemed larger.

I circled as though searching, but with my head turned enough to keep an eye on her. She would sense my presence and movement. I made it easier for her by stopping next to a tree and waiting.

She went solid and swung the broken branch at my head. I dropped a split second early, turned, and dived for her mid-section. Her club broke against the tree; she still clutched a two-foot length as we went down. I pulled it from her, raised, and struck.

The angle was bad; there was no force in the blow, nothing near what was needed. The raw edge caught her shoulder, not her head. She yelped and the splinters tore her dress and scraped her fresh skin, and then I was holding on to nothing again as she turned into living fog.

It slithered along the ground and rose into a rough human shape. I remembered to move around as though confused. A face began forming, and when there was enough for ordinary eyes to see I brought the branch down on its middle. That did no harm and she only retreated again.

Her direction was good, she was moving toward the house. She must have tired of teasing me and wanted to get on with her original business before she made a mistake. I let her get ahead and followed, keeping a prudent distance.

The backyard to Malcolm's house came into sight, its width sloping down at us, the trimmed grass giving away to weeds as the ground tilted sharply. The land did the same again from our side, forming a broad V shape. Down the middle, swollen and fast from the rain, was a brown stream. It wouldn't be very deep, two or three feet at the most, and in some spots no more than four feet wide. As far as she was concerned it could have been the Chicago River. Without help she'd find it nearly impossible to cross.

She stopped short at the very edge of the bank, the gray pseudopods probing and undecided. She was held back by the invisible barrier of free-flowing water. She went solid, with her back to the stream and her eyes on the woods to see my approach. I was hunched down behind a bush, keeping very still, and she missed me. Now she glanced side to side for a bridge of some sort, a fallen tree or stones sticking up, but nothing so convenient was at hand.

She turned again, checking for me and considering the car. She could go back for it and reach the house from the front, but would it be any easier? It was a long way back and I might be waiting near it. The truck with her box of earth was less than a hundred feet away, its nose pointing to the street, all ready to go.

Gaylen made up her mind and eased one foot tentatively in the water like a swimmer testing the temperature. She didn't like it, pulled out quickly, and again looked for an alternative. Nothing presented itself, so with a grimace she tried once more, right foot, left, the water churning up around her knees, then higher. For all her need of speed, she might have been wading through partially set cement.

When she was in far enough, I broke cover and closed on her with the club. She heard me and turned, or tried to; her feet couldn't keep up with the changing situation. The branch swung, she caught my arm, and no doubt at that moment tried to vanish. The confused surprise was plain on her face.

Had she been floating freely in the water, I'd have lost her, but her contact with the stream bed negated that option. The mud and earth beneath her feet held her solid.

I dragged free and struck again. She deflected it, but the force she needed threw her off balance, and she gave out a little scream and splashed full length on her side. The next scream was louder and filled with anguished pain. She fought to get up and out.

The branch caught her flailing hand, and she grabbed my arm successfully with the other and held fast, either to pull me in or make me pull her out. My own balance was tenuous on the loose, slippery bank. The fall was inevitable, but only my right arm and leg went in. They were more than enough.

I'd crossed free water before: above it dematerialized and rushing out of control to the nearest shore or clinging to the inside of a boat or sitting solid in a car to feel only its tug from one riverbank to another, but never by direct contact. It was a tremendous shock, like being dumped in the Arctic in winter. The actual temperature of the water had nothing to do with the freezing ice it felt like to me. I was different now and uniquely vulnerable to this element. I was instantly weakened. No wonder she'd screamed.

She clung to me, knowing I wouldn't go in any deeper if I could help it, and I inadvertently pulled her out a little as I tried to get free. My left hand closed on her wrist, squeezing and turning, trying to break it. Her grip on my shoulder loosened, then she took a chance, jerked free, and slammed her fist into my jaw. It was a solid hit and rattled my brain. I slipped deeper into the fiery cold on top of her.

It was utterly numbing. Our muscles were freezing up, our movements slowing to nothing. Neither of us could vanish and neither would let go. I pushed her under while trying to get back up on the bank. Breathing was no longer necessary to her survival, but such instincts are not easily overcome in a few hours. She pushed her body against the stream bed and her face came up, her hair matted and her teeth bared. With a free hand I hit her as hard as I could.

Her bones should have shattered under the blow. She felt it but ignored it. I hit her two more times before she knocked my hand away and stabbed my neck with stiffened fingers. She caught the Adam's apple, and I gagged a moment, then shoved her under again, hoping the cold would slow her down more than it was slowing me.

I used the leverage to free one leg from the water. The iciness abated a little, and I concentrated on holding her beneath the surface. She wouldn't drown, but a lengthy immersion might weaken her.

The branch was gone, lost in the swirling water, and there was nothing large or sturdy enough to take its place. Fingers closed on my ear and twisted hard. I hit at her face again and connected with a nose and eye ridge. It surprised her and broke her grip. My ear stayed attached and I seized her hand before it could do anything else. I had to look to see that I had it, for I was losing feeling fast.

Voices. Lights twitching above and to the right.

Gordy and one of his men had heard her scream and were investigating. They carried shotguns. It took them a full minute to find us; I was too busy holding her under to call out. My arms were nearly dead and I couldn't tell if my fingers were doing their job properly. At least her struggles had slowed.

Then my knees slipped in again and she exploded to the surface.

Her eyes were wide with flat, blank panic, and that gave her more strength than I was prepared or able to deal with. She wanted only to escape from the near-petrifying cold. Twisting and clawing halfway out of the water, her hands dug for purchase in the mud, tearing gouges in the bank. Wrapping arms around her middle, I kept her down, but she was kicking and I was already weak and battered.

Gordy was standing on the far bank, a flashlight disclosing the scene. His gun came up uncertainly.

"It's me!" I yelled, realizing he didn't know me for all the mud.

He knew my voice, crab-walked down the slope, and waded across, making it look easy. Gaylen's knee caught me under the rib cage, knocking my breath out. I couldn't warn him to stay back. One of her hands shot out and got his ankle. He yelped and fell, his body acting as an anchor as she began to pull free of the water.

I grabbed her a little higher, throwing my weight on top and smashing her face in the mud. We slid down the bank, our legs still in the stream. It was freezing agony, but safe. As long as she was held in it she couldn't vanish and escape.

Her face lifted, she spit mud and pleaded with Gordy. "Please help me, he—

I flipped her over, cutting off her helpless-damsel act. She was extremely strong, but when it came down to it, I was bigger and just able to hold her in the water. The man that had come with Gordy stared with openmouthed horror as I shoved her down again. Maybe Gordy had told him something, maybe not. He was unprepared for this kind of savagery and looked ready to run. Gordy stopped him.

"Hitch! Stay here and cover her." He got up, stepped back into the water, and kept his distance.

Gaylen fought her way up again, but this time she saw the gun. She remembered what I'd said earlier.

Gordy loomed over us, the muzzles centering on her chest. She tore and kicked against me.

"Fleming?" he asked.

Gaylen's eyes turned on me, frantic and helpless and with all the torment and wanting in the world in them.

I thought of Braxton staring sightlessly at his own blood on the tiles.

I thought of Bobbi being mercilessly shoved into the river water. The image was blinding.

"*Yes,*" I choked.

She was screaming, but without sound, even as I had screamed in the stairwell. Gordy put the barrels to her chest. There was no color in his face. The tendons in his hands were ridged to control the shaking. He was familiar with violence, but this was different.

The night roared once and went silent.

The rubber blade squeaked annoyingly as it dragged over the nearly dry windshield glass.

I was so goddamned tired. I was tired and sickened and cold enough to lie down and die, but he put his hand out and pulled me from the water, away from the red stains before they—

The window was a good thing to stare at; the movement of the wipers was soothing and hypnotic, even the noisy one. You could stare for hours at the fan shapes being renewed with each swinging stroke and not think of anything at all. You could forget the wetness and the clinging clothes and the earthy stink of mud.

"That shot'll bring the cops," Hitch had said uneasily, his eyes on me as I flopped bonelessly to the ground at his feet.

No time to rest. Things to do first.

Malcolm. I told them where to find what was left of him and what to do.

Back and forth. The squeak changed as some of the rubber loosened and trailed after the wiper like a piece of black string. First straight, then curled under on the return stroke. Back and forth.

"It's in the living room," Gordy told him. "Wipe it clean."

"Yeah, boss." He fled to the house, then stopped just short of it as a car pulled up and braked in the driveway. It was Gordy's, and Escott and Bobbi spilled out.

Gordy stared at her, his big face slack with stunned recognition. "Bobbi . . ."

Understanding his surprise, she paused long enough to give him a fierce hug, then knelt next to me, asking if I was all right. I couldn't answer and held on to her. Escott was explaining things to Gordy and was asking what had happened, until the sight of Gaylen's mangled body stopped the flow of words.

We all looked.

"Jesus," Gordy whispered, and stepped back from the bank.

The tangled hair was still dark, but the skin was changing. The smooth texture was sagging around the jaw, growing puffy under the eyes. Wrinkles formed as we watched.

It was as though your death . . . had caught up with you.

"She's dying," I said.

"She's not dead?"

"We take a lot of killing." I knew what she was going through and took no pleasure in the knowledge. "Charles, get Bobbi out of here."

He came and gently took her shoulders. She shrugged him off.

"I want to stay."

"Please, go with him," I said.

"But—"

"I know, but you can't. We have to leave, and fast. I'm all right, I promise, but I want you out of here."

She didn't like it but saw the sense. She kissed me hard. "I'll be waiting at my place."

"I'll come as soon as I can."

She smiled. It was a wan one, but still a smile, and she let Escott pull her away.

"What about her?" said Gordy, nodding at the stream when they were gone.

"We can't leave her for the cops. We can't chance an autopsy—not on her. And that truck with the box in it has to go."

"I'll get the boys to fix things."

Hitch came back then with another mug named Jinky and the shotgun used to kill Norma. Gordy sent them across the stream and into the trees.

"Put his mitts on it, and for Chrissake make sure he ain't got no spare shells," he ordered.

"Yeah, boss."

"And clean off that knife."

"Yeah, boss."

While they were gone we did what was necessary and did it fast.

The trail of rubber flapped and twisted, vibrating and adding its noise to the squeak. Hitch, who was driving, finally shut them off. We made a turn and the blanket-wrapped thing on the floor shifted with the direction change. I moved my feet so it wouldn't touch me.

Silly thing to do.

For the hundredth time Hitch checked the mirror. He was more worried about looking out for cops than not seeing my reflection. He made another turn and we swayed. His speed was cautious, but his driving technique clumsy. He didn't like what was in the back with me and Jinky.

Couldn't blame him.

Jinky was nervous as well and complaining. "This just ain't done, this cartin' around. Plug 'em and leave 'em, I sez."

"Shut up, Jinky," Hitch said wearily.

He shut up and kept looking sideways at me, uneasy from my silence. His hand never strayed far from the bulge under his armpit. Maybe he was picking up on my feelings of death. I looked at him once, he blanched, and the fear smell came off him, sharp and stinging.

Gordy was in the front passenger seat and turned his head, noticing something was wrong. I kept looking out the window.

"How's your mother, Jinky?" he asked out of the blue.

Jinky was gulping. "Wha . . . oh, she's okay."

"She's doin' okay. Still got that dog? What's its name?"

"Peanuts . . . yeah, she's still got 'im."

Gordy, not a great conversationalist, kept him talking until he calmed down. After five minutes, Jinky looked less likely to make a fatal exit out the door. I shut my eyes and pretended to nap, half expecting to fight off an army of ugly images from the recent past but finding sweet, warm darkness instead.

We drove north along the lake for a long time. I thought vaguely we were going to Wisconsin, but Hitch made a last turn onto a muddy, rutted road that curved into thick trees. The car bounced and slewed. The thing at my feet shifted again, but this time I didn't bother moving.

A little later, the four of us were slogging through more mud and wet leaves. While Gordy and Hitch carried the rope-tied bundle, Jinky and I used the flashlights. Jinky came along because he didn't want to be alone.

Twenty feet of dock and a boathouse waited for us at the shoreline. Gordy unlocked the boathouse. I couldn't easily go in since most of it was over the water, so I missed seeing them load the thing into the boat. Without any delay they rowed free of the house and out onto the lake.

I sat on the damp ground and watched them. They didn't start the motor until they were small specks in the distance. Human eyes could not see them in that dark, but Gordy was taking no chances.

Jinky alternately paced and squatted, wanting to stay near me for the company, but not wanting to get too close. He'd seen Malcolm, after all, and maybe Hitch had been talking to him.

Jinky was shivering; the wind off the restless lake was cool. He paced around, hands in pockets, jingling the change there. "We used to use this place a lot," he said out of nervousness. I let him talk; his voice took me out of myself. "We used to run some pretty good stuff through here from Canada. Mostly for the boss 'n his friends. Stuff that was too good for the speaks, they said."

The boat was at the edge of sight. The wind carried the thin buzz of the motor to us. The boat vanished.

He must have been wondering what I was staring at in the gloom. "Got hijacked once," he continued. "Early out. That was fun. Then we started packin' big rods and that hotted things up. We went to a lot of trouble over that fancy hooch and for what? You get drunk just as fast on the homemade stuff, faster even. Richer, too. Half those mugs never knew the difference."

The motor buzz was irregular now, the wind affecting it.

"There was this girl I had then, always after me for some of the fancy stuff. I took an empty bottle that still had the label on and put in some of the local make and some tea for color. She never knew the difference, but sure knew how to say thanks. Not too smart, but she was a lot of fun."

The buzz changed and grew. I blinked the flashlight a few times to give them a direction to aim for and kept it up until they were close. The motor cut and they rowed the rest of the way in. The bundle was gone and so was the boat anchor and its length of chain.

They got out and Gordy locked up. "Where to?" he asked me.

My throat was clogged; I had to clear it first. "Bobbi's."

He nodded.

The ride back seemed shorter.

BLOODCIRCLE

1

Chicago, September 1936

"... THEN the door opened and there was this crazy-looking blond guy with a shotgun just standing there, grinning at us. Before we could do anything he swung it up and fired right at Braxton."

"How close were you?"

"To . . . ?"

"To Braxton."

"Pretty close; arm's length, I guess. He knocked against me when he fell. There wasn't much room."

"And to the shotgun?"

"About the same."

"Go on."

"I fell back when he hit against me and cracked my head on a sink—sort of snapped it like this—and that's when things got fuzzy." I paused, expecting him to encourage me again in spite of my faulty memory, but nothing came out. Lieutenant Blair of Homicide, Chicago P.D., had the occupational necessity of a poker face, but I could tell he wasn't swallowing what I was dishing out. He waited and the uniformed cop hunched next to him at the foot of the desk stopped scribbling on his notepad.

I covered the awkward pause by rubbing my face. "Maybe I was dazed or something, but I ran after the blond guy, chased him downstairs and out the building. He was moving too fast and I was all shaky. I lost him. I went back and told the lobby doorman to call an ambulance. I returned to the studio, saw the crowd in the hall, and began looking for Bobbi—Miss Smythe. When I couldn't find her, I drove to her hotel, but she wasn't there, so I spent the rest of the night looking."

"You spoke to no one at the hotel?"

"Just Phil, their house detective. He had an envelope for me and I took it."

"What was it? Who sent it?"

"I don't know, I never bothered to open it I was so busy. I don't know where it is now."

The cop wrote it all down, trying to keep a straight face.

"I went up to Miss Smythe's rooms. Her friend Marza was there, Marza Chevreaux."

"Chevreaux," Blair repeated, and spelled it out for his man, referring from his own notes.

"She didn't know where Bobbi had gone, either," I continued. "At least that's what she told me."

"You think she was lying?"

I shrugged. "Bobbi and I had a fight earlier and Marza took her side. She doesn't like me much and wouldn't tell me anything. I got fed up with her and left."

"Where did you go after you left the hotel?"

I talked on, telling him of a lengthy search until I found Bobbi in a diner we'd once gone to and how we went out to my car and talked the rest of the night away. When Blair asked the name of the diner, I said I couldn't remember. The cop scribbled it all down until I ran out of things to say, but Blair hadn't run out of questions to ask. We were in his office, which was better than an interrogation room, but at the end of my story he looked ready to change my status from witness to suspect.

"When did you next see the blond man?"

"I didn't," I lied.

"Why did he shoot Braxton?"

"I don't know."

"Why was Braxton after you?"

"I don't know."

"You told the hotel detective, Phil Patterson, something else. You told him Braxton was a con man. Why?"

"Mostly so Phil would be sure to keep a watch out for him and keep him from bothering Miss Smythe. I thought that if Phil thought the guy was a troublemaker he'd be extra careful." At least that was the truth, and Blair seemed to know it. "Braxton was crazy, too. Who knows why he was after me? I never got the chance to find out."

He paused with his questions and I wondered if I'd tipped things too far. He looked at the cop and with a subtle head-and-eyebrow movement told him to leave, then settled in to stare at me. I stared back, attempting a poker face and failing. I'm a lousy liar.

Blair was a handsome man, a little past forty, with gray temples trimming his dark wavy hair, and full, dark brows setting off his olive skin. Too well dressed to be a cop, he was either on the take or had some income other than his salary. His upper lip tightened. He was smiling, but not quite ready to show his teeth yet.

"Okay," he said easily and with vast confidence. My back hairs went up. "This is off the record. You can talk, now."

I looked baffled, it wasn't hard.

"All I want is the truth," he said reasonably.

"I've been telling—"

"Bits and pieces of it, Mr. Fleming, but I want to hear it all. For instance, tell me why you waited so long to come in."

"I came when I saw the story in the papers."

"Where had Miss Smythe gone?"

"To some diner, I forget—"

"Why did she leave the studio?"

"She wanted to avoid trouble."

"What trouble?"

"*This* kind of trouble. She used to sing at the Nightcrawler Club, got a bellyful of the gang there, and quit to do radio work."

"Yes. She quit right after someone put a lead slug into her boss. It's interesting to me how death seems to follow that young woman around."

"You think she was involved with that mess?" It was meant to rattle me, but I was on to that one.

He just smiled.

"Then think something else," I said, leaning back in my chair. "Her boss gets scragged and she quits, there's no surprise to that. A couple of the other girls did the same thing. You can check."

"I have. She was Morelli's girl as well as his employee. . . . And now she's your girl."

It wasn't a question, so it didn't need an answer.

"Did you tell her to leave the studio?" Blair asked.

"No, I—"

"Why were you at the studio? You said you'd had a fight with her."

"It wasn't much of a fight. I went there to make up with her."

"And Braxton followed you . . ."

We walked through the whole thing again and I told the truth about what happened, but left out the motivations. Blair didn't like it, but he wasn't quite ready to get tough yet. He kept shifting around with his questions, trying to trip me somewhere.

"And then you went looking for her instead of—"

It was time to show a little anger. "Yeah, so I didn't stay put—I wasn't thinking straight. I see a man cut in two practically under my nose, maybe come that close to it myself, and I'm supposed to hang around to make a statement?"

"No, but you did go chasing after an armed man and disappeared for two days."

"Stop dancing and tell me what you're getting at."

He continued as though I hadn't spoken. "In the meantime, the man turns up in his car near his home, peppered with wooden pellets—"

"Huh?"

"—as though from a shotgun wound. Instead of rock salt or lead, someone loaded the cartridge with small wooden beads. Can you explain that?"

I shook my head.

"The man was half-dead from numerous other injuries and in a mental state one might charitably describe as shock. How did he get that way?"

"I don't know. Ask him, why don't you?" I was on firm ground here. That blond bastard would never put together two coherent words ever again. I'd made very sure of it.

Blair shifted the subject again. "Who was the woman in his house?"

"What woman?"

He pulled out a photo and tossed it to me. A sincere pang of nausea flashed through me as I looked at the starkly lit image on the paper. The harsh blacks and whites had their full-color match in my memory of the scene. I tossed it back onto the desk. "God, what happened to her?"

"Someone took her head off—with a shotgun; maybe the same weapon that killed Braxton."

"The blond guy must have done it."

Then who did it for the blond guy? Blair's expression seemed to ask me. "Why was this woman wearing Miss Smythe's red dress?" he asked aloud.

"What?"

"Miss Smythe wore a bright red dress to the broadcast; many people remember it. Somehow it ends up on this corpse. Why?"

"There must be a mix-up. Bobbi still had that dress when I found her. It must have come from the same store."

His eyes were ice cold, like chips of polished onyx. "Come along with me." He got to his feet and walked smoothly around the desk.

"Where?"

He didn't answer but opened the door and motioned for me to go out first. We walked down a green-painted hall and went into another, smaller room. It had a scarred table, three utilitarian chairs, and one bright overhead light, its bulb protected by a metal grille. On the table was a sawed-off shotgun, tagged and still bearing traces of fingerprint dust.

"Recognize it?"

"Looks like it could be the one the crazy used on Braxton, except when I saw it the barrels seemed about that big." I held my hands a foot apart to indicate the size.

"And what about this?" From the back of a chair he picked up a dark bundle that unrolled into the shape of a coat. The front lapels were ragged and an uneven hole the size of my fist decorated the middle of its back where the blast had exited. The edges were stiff with crusted blood.

"Looks like mine," I admitted, not liking this turn of evidence.

"We found it at Miss Smythe's hotel."

"I keep some clothes there so she can have them cleaned for me; she insists on it. I changed to another coat—I couldn't hunt for her looking like a scarecrow."

"Are you sure it's yours? Put it on."

I shot him a disgusted look, but decided to go through the farce.

"It fits you."

"All right, so it's mine."

He was busy examining the hole in the back. "Looks like the shot must have gone right through you."

"I had the coat draped over my arm at the time. Maybe it got between Braxton and the gun at just the right moment."

He shook his head. "The physical evidence we have doesn't support that, Fleming."

"What does it matter? You have the killer."

"Take that off and have a seat. We're going to discuss how it matters."

"You charging me with anything?"

"That depends on your willingness to cooperate. . . ."

He'd moved to one side so I could get to a chair, and stopped dead, his dark eyes flicking from something behind me to my face and back again, his jaw sagging. I could hear his heart thumping, though his breathing seemed to have stopped. Turning around I saw a mirror set in the wall behind me; a one-way job so someone next door could keep an eye on things. From Blair's new angle he could see the whole interrogation room reflected in it, and as far as the mirror was concerned, he was alone.

"Something wrong?" I asked, changing coats. I tossed the old one onto the table. As it left my hand its reflection appeared in the mirror, having jumped out of nowhere. That was interesting.

Blair had lost his voice as well as his calm confidence and hadn't moved a muscle except for his widening eyes. They kept twitching from me to the mirror. They settled on me one last time and he took a quick breath, reaching instinctively for the gun bolstered in the small of his back. A shoulder harness would have been faster, but it would have also ruined the lines of his suit.

I shook my head, maintaining a steady eye contact. "Don't do that."

His movement ceased. Completely.

I gulped. It wasn't easy because my mouth was bone dry. After a moment I was calm enough to work up enough spit to talk. "Let's go back to your office," I suggested. "You lead the way."

We went. I sat down; he remained standing until I told him to sit as well. He slipped automatically behind his desk, his face blank and waiting.

"About what happened in the other room . . . you hear me, Blair?"

"Yes." His voice was flat, distant.

"I identified the gun and coat to your satisfaction. You didn't notice any problem with the mirror, understand?"

"Yes."

"Then we came back here. My guess is the woman in the photo was murdered by the blond man. Her red dress probably came from the same shop as Miss Smythe's. That sounds right, doesn't it?"

"Yes."

"In fact, you think I've been very cooperative. You have got Braxton's killer, after all."

"Yes."

"That's good. You can relax now and do your business as usual—we're good friends." I had other people to protect than myself, so my conscience wasn't kicking too hard.

My hold on him melted away, but not my influence. He got on his phone and rattled off some instructions for someone to type up my statement and bring it in for signing. While he did this, I looked away and studied some framed items on the wall. A few were documents, the rest were pictures of Blair shaking hands with city-hall types. He liked to have his photo taken; he took a good one. On his desk was a studio portrait of a smiling and very pretty girl.

"You married?" I asked by way of conversation. I wanted to pass the intervening time on neutral subjects.

He looked where I gestured—normal again without my control—and literally brightened when he saw the girl's face. "Not yet."

"Soon, huh?"

"Not soon enough for me." His smile was sincere now, not the cold one calculated to put a suspect on edge. "Her name is Margaret."

"She's a real dish. You're a lucky guy."

We made small talk about his fiancée until the other cop returned with a typed version of my statement. I read it over and signed.

"Sorry it took so long," said Blair. The cop gave him an odd look.

"That's all right, I know how it is." I made to go, and Blair escorted me out of the building and even shook my hand. He liked me. Inside, I cringed a little at the power I had over the man and was glad to turn my back on him and walk away.

Parked down the road just under a streetlight was a gleaming black Nash. A man with a beaky nose and a lot of bone in his face emerged from it as I approached. He was tall and thin and almost as well dressed as Blair, but in a quieter style.

"How did it go?" asked Escott.

I sighed out my relief from habit rather than a need for air, but it felt good, so I took another lungful. "As Gordy would say, 'no problem.' "

"They believed you?"

"They didn't have much of a choice. I just sometimes wish I were a better liar."

"The way things are going, you're sure to have other opportunities to practice. Shall we go on to the hospital and see what else we can patch together?"

"Visiting hours will be over by now."

"We'll get in."

Escott was sure of himself because he seemed to know almost everyone in Chicago. I didn't question him. We entered the hospital without a hitch and even the most territorial and authoritative nurses gave way before him. He knew how to turn on the charm when he felt inclined, and we left the last of the guardians of good health giggling at her station.

"How did you do that?" I asked.

"I'm not sure, but if it works, I shan't try to analyze it. Perhaps it's to do with my accent."

"You mean if I learn to talk like Ronald Colman—"

"I do *not* speak like Ronald Colman."

"Sure you do, like just now with Tugboat Annie back there."

"Don't be absurd."

Escott's English accent was more clipped and precise and less leisurely than Colman's, but I argued that the effect was the same. Getting him to bristle was a novel experience for me. The debate kept us entertained until we turned the last corner and saw the cop in a chair next to a numbered door. He regarded us with interest and stood as we approached.

"I'm Dr. Lang," Escott told him. "Dr. Reade asked me to look in on the patient for him."

"Ain't it kinda late?"

"Yes, it is," he said wearily, "and this is hopefully my last call for the night."

"I'll have to see your pass."

"Show him my pass," he said to me.

I got the man's full attention and flipped out my old press card. "It's all in order, officer," I told him.

He didn't even blink. "Okay, you can go in."

"Thank you." Escott did so—all but grinning at the situation—with me right behind him.

It was a private room, furnished in cold steel and white enamel, with one small light glowing in a corner opposite the single high bed. The slumbering occupant was obscured by rumpled sheets and a mass of bandaging around the top of his head. His breathing was slow and deep, our entrance hadn't roused him.

Escott hung back by the door, ready to deal with the cop in case he walked in.

"I don't want to do this," I whispered.

He understood but shook his head, his humor gone. "But you have to do something. So far they're blaming the head wound for his story, but you can't let him continue to talk, especially if some of the more irresponsible papers get hold of it. You dare not take that chance."

"Yeah." Damn.

He was right. We'd been all over it before and couldn't think of any other alternatives. Indirectly, this would help protect Bobbi and Escott as well as myself, so that should have made it easier, but I'd still have to be very careful.

I cat-footed to the bedside and looked down at the sleeping boy. He was Matheus Webber, chubby young friend to the late James Braxton, and he'd come very close to death himself that night at the radio station. Both had been hunting for me with the mistaken idea that I was a menace to society. They'd assumed my normally friendly disposition to be false and had set out to kill me with the best of intentions and a lot of misplaced zeal. Their knowledge of my true nature and needs was limited, and they'd placed a superstitious reliance on crosses and silver bullets to control and destroy me. They'd been annoying, but nothing I couldn't handle until Braxton got in the way of another, much more effective killer.

Matheus was now telling the story of their hunt for the vampire to anyone who'd listen, but so far his parents, the medical staff, and the cops
thought he was crazy from the concussion he'd suffered. But if he kept talking, someone else just might begin to believe the story in the same way as
Blair. Once he'd seen a hint of the truth of things, it had all fallen into place
for him, necessitating my direct influence on his mind. There were too many
mirrors in the world for me to take any more risks.

I folded back the sheet and blanket to get a better look at the kid. What
I saw would have decided me if I hadn't already made up my mind. Escott
craned his neck for a look to see what made me stop and frown. He frowned
as well, but refrained from giving me an "I told you so" look. The patient
wore a big silver cross around his neck with a couple of bulbs of whole garlic threaded together on a string. He had at least gotten someone to humor
him. It was a step in the wrong direction as far as I was concerned.

The boy's eyes opened slightly. He didn't know me at first, mumbled a
sleepy question, and rolled onto his back. I put a hand on his shoulder and
said his name. He shot fully awake—but never got the chance to scream.

Escott was driving; his big Nash was one of the central pleasures of his life.
For the first time in several harrowing nights he seemed relaxed enough to
look content. His eyes were filmed over and far away, as though he were listening to music, but as always, his brain was clicking.

"You look like you've consumed a sour apple," he observed. "Was it
really so bad?"

"What solves a problem for me could make one for Matheus."

"In what way?"

"You know what I mean. I'm off the hook now, but what if he comes
out with psychological measles later because of my monkeying around?"

"You've read Freud, then?"

"Never had the time so I don't know about that. I do know I shouldn't
be doing what I'm doing. . . . It could be bad for the kid."

Just like Blair, Matheus's face had gone blank. It was easy, so damned
easy. I could put anything into his mind I wanted; twist it up like an old rag
for the garbage and leave it for other people to clean away. It happened before: by accident with my murderer and on purpose with Braxton's murderer. Both men were insane and not likely to recover. Matheus didn't
deserve that.

"I don't think you've done him harm," he continued. "You suppressed
no memories."

Which would have been too noticeable by everyone. If the kid woke up
with no recollection about his trip to Chicago with Braxton, someone might
get too curious. People tended to prefer the answers they already had to
dealing with new questions, so I played on that.

Instead, he'd wake up and realize that Braxton had been a crazy old
man using and misleading an impressionable kid. There'd be some un-

avoidable embarrassment for Matheus, but he was in the real world now, safe from the paranoid nightmares of a crackpot.

Go to sleep, kid. You'll feel a lot better about things in the morning.

"He'll soon put it all behind him once he's home," Escott added.

After all, there are no such things as vampires.

He hauled the wheel around and swung us close to the curb. "Our train leaves in two hours; I'd like to be there early to make sure your trunk is properly seen to."

"Hour and a half from now?"

He glanced at his watch to get the exact time. "I'll be back by then."

I almost asked him where he was going, but it was unnecessary. He was planning to simply drive. His eyes were already darting around the dark and nearly empty streets with anticipation.

"Please say hello to Miss Smythe for me."

"Sure."

The door shut, he shifted gears, and glided off. I crossed the walk to the hotel entrance and went in. Phil Patterson was at his usual spot, leaning against the pillar near the front desk. His crony, the night clerk, was making typewriter noises in the office and for the moment the lobby was dead. Phil nodded a neutral greeting in my direction.

" 'Lo, Fleming. Straighten things with the cops?"

"Yeah, we got everything all worked out."

"Blair tough on you?"

"Couldn't say, I don't know how tough he can get. We didn't have any problems."

He nodded, but there were a lot of thoughts and questions behind it. "Too bad about that little guy, Braxton. They ever figure why he got bumped off?"

"The killer's going to the nuthouse soon, maybe the head quacks can figure it out. Till then . . ." I shrugged.

"Guess we'll never know," he agreed, watching me hard.

"Yeah, too bad." My voice was a little tight and forced. He noticed, but let it pass. I owed him a favor, a big one for getting the muzzle of a gun pointed elsewhere besides my chest when it went off. I'd have survived the experience, but explaining why to a room full of people would not have been easy. Phil decided not to call in the favor just yet.

The kid in the elevator knew to take me to four without being told and hardly looked up from his magazine. He was deep into Walter's 110th Shadow novel, *Jibaro Death*. I'd have to remember to pick up a copy of my own to read on the train.

. . . the power to cloud men's minds . . .

I smiled and shook the thought out fast. That gimmick was strictly for the radio show and certain supernatural creatures of the night—not the book character. The main difference between me and the Lamont Cranston on the air was that he had fewer scruples about using his talent.

Bobbi's door was locked and no one answered my tap. The hall was clear so I vanished and slipped right through, which was a bad move. Marza Chevreaux stepped into sight from the kitchen just as I solidified. She was fiddling with the clasp of her necklace and walked like a movie holdup victim, elbows pointed up and head tilted down. She was a fraction too late to actually see my indiscretion, but nearly jumped out of her garters when she looked up and saw me standing in the entry way.

"Hello, Marza, I knocked—"

"I heard, but I was busy." She gave me a long, unpleasant stare, the kind usually reserved for roaches when they go spinning down the toilet. "That door was locked," she stated.

I glanced back and tried my best smile of baby innocence on her. "I had no trouble getting in."

She swiveled her head toward the closed door of Bobbi's bedroom and back to me again. "No, I suppose you didn't," she said in a nasty tone, and went to a table to dig through her handbag. She stuck a thin brown cigar in her mouth and fired a match.

For five seconds I thought unkind thoughts, but didn't voice them. That sort of indulgence is always wasted on people like Marza. "What put the bug up your butt tonight?"

Just like a dragon, she pushed blue smoke from her nose and snapped the match out as though it were a whip. "It's what you are."

"Which is . . . ?"

"A two-timing bastard who beds one girl while chasing after another," she said casually.

That was a relief. At least she wouldn't be coming after me with a hammer and stake. "You can hardly call it two-timing, since I haven't seen the other girl in five years."

"So you've told Bobbi."

"So I'm telling you. It's the truth."

"She believes you, I don't."

"Is that all that's bothering you?"

"You're leaving town to look for this other one. What happens to Bobbi when you find her?"

"That is none of your business."

"It is if Bobbi gets hurt."

"I don't plan to hurt her."

"Like you didn't plan for that goon to kidnap her?"

"Did Bobbi explain to you that Escott and I are doing this to make sure it doesn't happen again?"

"And do the cops know you're leaving town?" she asked sweetly.

"The less they know, the better it is for Bobbi."

"Don't worry, I'll keep my mouth shut for her sake—"

"That'll be nice."

"—but the best thing you can do for her is to go and stay gone. We don't know who you are. You hang around with Slick's old mob, you've got money but no job, the cops want you for murder—"

"I cleared that up tonight."

"You got Gordy to pay someone off, you mean."

"Lady, you're crazy. And I wouldn't be so hard on Gordy; if it weren't for him, we'd never have found the goon—"

She knew she was losing and grabbed up her bag, unlocked the door, and walked out, not bothering to slam it. I shut it, very carefully and very quietly. The woman was enough to make a preacher cuss, and at the moment I was feeling anything but Godly minded.

"Marza? Is that Jack?" Bobbi's voice floated out from her bedroom and had an instant brightening effect on me. I forgot all about Marza as Bobbi came out and rushed over to hug me.

"You doin' okay?" I asked the top of her head. Her silky platinum hair had been crudely chopped off by the goon, but she'd been to the beauty parlor for repairs and it looked fine now.

"God, I thought you'd never get here," she mumbled into my chest.

"We had a busy night."

"What kept you so long?" she demanded, pretending to sound nettled. "Was it the cops or that Webber kid?"

"Both, but neither should be any trouble now. How about telling me why Marza's in such a cheerful mood? She looked like a snake bit her, only the snake died."

"She's gone?"

"Once she saw me, she couldn't get out fast enough. Have I sprouted horns or something?"

"No, but it is because of you."

"So I figured. What's the problem?"

"She blames you for what happened to me."

"And not unreasonably. What'd you tell her?"

"Only what you said to say, that your old girlfriend's sister wanted something from you and had used me to get it."

"She want to know what it was?"

"Of course, but I said I didn't know and you weren't talking. It's hard on her, not getting the truth."

"I think it'd be a lot harder on us both if she did."

"Maybe she'd prefer knowing what you are to thinking you're in the mobs."

"Uh-uh. She's not as understanding as you. You sure that's all there is— she just thinks I'm in with Gordy's bunch?"

"No, I've talked with Madison, he said she was pretty upset that night. There was some kind of scene and you got her drunk."

"She was ready to take my face off so I made her drink something to calm down. It was purely in self-defense. I'm just glad Madison came in when he did, she needed a shoulder to cry on and mine wasn't available for various reasons."

"But you saw her like that, all vulnerable."

"Nothing wrong there."

"She thinks so. She's usually so in control of herself and now she's embarrassed because for once she wasn't."

"That's hardly a good reason to hate my guts."

"It is for her."

"Then she needs a doctor."

"It's just artistic temperament."

"I'd call it something else. What are we talking about her for, anyway? I came to see how you were doing."

"It takes my mind off things, Jack," she said, wilting a little against me. "I never said I didn't have nightmares."

"I wish I could help, baby."

"You do." She wrapped her arms more tightly around me. We ended up on the sofa, hanging on to each other as though it were the end of the world. Some of the feeling leaked out of her eyes, but she took my handkerchief and dabbed it away. "What'd you say?" she asked.

"I'm sorry."

"What?"

"I'm sorry that all this happened. Marza was right. If it hadn't been for me, you—"

"Jack." She pushed away to look me in the eye.

"Yeah?" I wasn't so sure I could look back.

"Shut the hell up and give me a kiss."

I double-checked. She'd meant it, so I stopped stammering and followed through. She let me know in no uncertain terms that everything was all right between us.

"Y'know," she said, coming up for air, "Marza thinks I should stop seeing you."

"What do you think?"

"I think she's an idiot butting in where she don't belong."

Then we picked up on things again, and the flat got very quiet except for Bobbi's breathing and the whisper of our hands.

"You staying the night?" she murmured.

"I want to, but I've got that train to catch. Charles is coming by later to pick me up."

"You sure he needs you along?"

"No, but he seems to think so. He says he wants my help, and it is my problem—what are you doing?"

"You're smart, you work it out." She pushed the lapels back until my coat was off, loosened my tie, and undid a few buttons at the neck.

"You sure you're up to this? I know you've been through the wringer."

"Let's find out."

She was wearing her favorite style of lounging pajamas, satin ones with a high Oriental collar. The top opened up with a minimum of fuss and, as usual, she'd neglected to put on underwear. She turned her back to me, slid free, and pulled my hands around to her breasts.

Her skin was all that a woman's skin should be, her strong body all any man could wish to know and possess. I knelt behind her, glad in a guilty way that her hair was short enough now for me to comfortably indulge in nibbling the nape of her neck. Even before my transformation made it a necessity, neck nibbling had been a favorite foreplay activity, among many others, which I now endeavored to put into pleasurable practice.

Quite some time later, she tilted her head back, drawing the white skin taut over the big pulsing vein. We both moaned as I softly cut into her.

2

THE hollow-eyed image in the dark glass of the train window was a sinister version of Escott's sharp face. I settled in opposite him. He glanced at me, then contemplated my apparently empty chair reflected between us. Beyond it the last lights of Chicago sped or dawdled past, depending on their distance from the train. We had the smoking car to ourselves and Escott puffed on a final pipe while the porter was busy elsewhere making up his compartment for the night.

"Something funny?" I asked when the corner of his mouth curled briefly. For him, it was the equivalent of a broad grin.

He gestured at the window with the pipe stem. "I was only recalling the night I first noticed this about you at the train station and what a shock it had been."

"Yeah, what were you doing there, anyway?"

"At the station? Using the train, of course. I had returned from the completion of some minor out-of-town case. It was quite a shock to look up and see something that wasn't there." His eyes traveled to the window again.

"Most people would have figured they were seeing things and shrugged it off."

"Most people see many things, but few ever draw sensible conclusions from them."

"And right away you concluded I was a vampire? Not too sensible."

"Hardly," he agreed. "I'll admit I did initially think your lack of a reflection was from some trick angle of the glass, but eliminated that option after a few moments of observation. The conclusion that you were a vampire was the result of an improbable line of reasoning. Improbable, but obviously not impossible. I've read my share of lurid literature."

I looked at the empty spot in the glass for a long time, cautiously touching the feeling of eeriness mirrors now inspired in me. After a month in my new life I was still not used to the way they ignored me. It was a constant and irritating reminder of my isolation from the rest of humanity. On those occasions when I was feeling particularly low, it was as if I no longer existed at all.

"And after all that reading you still wanted to risk meeting me?"

He rested his head on the back of his chair and closed his eyes. "There were many small indications that it was less of a risk than you would think. Trifles, really, but important trifles. A person's posture and movements reveal his soul far more clearly than his words, and once one has studied this alphabet of expression, the thoughts flashing through a man's mind are as easy to read as a child's primer."

"How'd you figure all this?"

"My theatrical background: in order to imitate life, one must first study it. When I first noticed you, your movements and expression suggested a deep preoccupation with some problem, but an energetic willingness to face it."

"Maybe I was worried about finding a victim to drain."

"Perhaps, but after witnessing your purposeful walk to the Stockyards, I concluded you had no need to subsist exclusively on human blood."

"Unless I was hunting up some handy worker there."

"Why go there when more convenient meals were strolling the crowded streets? If it were very difficult to isolate a pedestrian for some nefarious purpose, the crime rate for mugging would be strangely low."

"I hadn't thought of it that way."

"After you emerged from the yards, your posture had not changed. You still had a problem and it was not hunger. At that point I knew I wanted to arrange to meet you and to find out more, so I intruded myself—"

"I wouldn't call it an intrusion now. You just wanted to get my attention."

"You are most forgiving on that point."

"Why not? I got my earth back and you got your questions answered. Everything turned out all right."

"True." A lazy puff of blue smoke rolled slowly to the ceiling and his eyes opened a crack, studying me. After another puff, he said, "I was wondering if everything was all right now."

It was pretty vague and at the same time a pretty personal question, at least for him. "What d'ya mean?"

"I'm inquiring about your physical and mental state after that stairwell incident. Are you all right?"

A simple yes would have been the easy and obvious answer, but he wasn't one to ask casual questions, so I thought things over until I concluded I felt fine. It was crazy, too, considering I'd been staked in the heart and left to die by inches in my own blood.

Without passion I remembered the silent, paralyzing agony in the blackness, the near-insanity, and the final icy cold creeping up to claim me forever. Ultimately, in my mind, I saw my would-be killer as I'd left him: his face blank, his eyes staring pinpoints, and his mouth hanging slack. I'd left him as he had left me, except no one would come by to save him, now or ever. No one could.

It might be a popular conception in some circles that vampires are selfish creatures of pure appetite, that we can only take. In the brief time since my violent rebirth I'd learned that we are able to give of ourselves. I believe it's a way of venting off all the negative stuff that gets stored up in the memory, leaving only the memory, but not the destructive emotions. I'd freely given mine away to a man who deserved them. He was forever lost in my nightmare and would never wake from it again. I had no regrets.

"I'm fine," I said at last, and meant it. "Been reading my posture or something?"

"I did that on our way to the station."

"Yeah? So what trifles did you observe and what did you conclude from them?"

He kept his eyes on the darkened city slipping past our window. His tone was kindly and amused. "My dear fellow, there are certain things a gentleman just does not discuss and still expect to be considered a gentleman."

I went a little red in the face. "What about you? Are you okay?"

He dismissed his own feelings with a decisive wave of his pipe. It was what he didn't say that filled my head now. He'd read the papers and talked to the cops and doctors. By now he knew all about what I'd done to the man. Apparently he had no regrets, either.

We'd booked a double, but Escott had it all to himself. My place of rest was elsewhere on the train, and I remained in the smoking car long after he'd gone off to bed. It was lonely; no die-hard insomniacs were aboard, and the staff had better things to do than keep me company. I got busy reading a fresh copy of *Jibaro Death* that I'd bought at the station newsstand. It kept me busy over the next few hours, though it was poor occupation when compared to my recent time with Bobbi. Sometimes I'd drift out of the plot entirely and catch myself looking at nothing in particular, no doubt with a sappy smile on my face.

Toward dawn I moved on to the baggage car and slipped inside without getting caught. Buried deep among the tons of suitcases, crates, and other luggage was my own traveling bedroom—a lightproof and very sturdy trunk. It was large enough to hold some extra clothes, a sack filled with my home earth, and me, though it was less than comfortable to someone with my long bones. Standing vertically as it was now, I'd have to rest my rump on the sack with my knees crowding up by my ears. During the day the awkwardness of the position hardly mattered; as long as the earth was next to my body I slept the sleep of the dead.

No joke.

Outside the car I could sense the searing, blinding sun start to roll above the horizon line. I quickly folded away my magazine, sieved into the trunk, and let the rocking motion of the train ease me safely out of the world for another day.

I'd been alive once, in the normal sense of the word. In that time, I'd met a woman and fallen in love. All the clichés I'd ever read about the subject had turned out to be absolutely correct. Floating—not walking—around in a gauzy pink haze of giddy happiness, I could charitably understand how the power of love had changed the course of human history. I felt a kinship for other courting couples and pity for those who were still searching.

Maybe Maureen's nature set us apart and made us feel unique from all the others who'd ever been in love, but I didn't see it at the time and still don't. Love is love and I'd have felt the same about Maureen no matter what. You see, Maureen Dumont was a vampire.

Of course, she wasn't the kind of white-faced, blood-obsessed zombie found on the screen at the Bijou down the street; she wasn't the freckled girl next door, either. She was rare and special and so was our relationship, and we were smart enough to know it. We took steps then in the hope of making our love last beyond my own short life span. The one thing the books and movies do get right is our method of reproduction; it takes a vampire to make a vampire—only there's no guarantee it will work. You can get into bed, make love and exchange all the blood you want, but the change won't necessarily happen or there'd be a lot more of us around. Maybe it's like a rare disease and nearly everyone is immune to it.

In my case it was a success. One traumatic night I woke up dead—only Maureen wasn't there to see it happen. Five years ago she'd packed a few things together and vanished, leaving me a cryptic note with a promise to return when she felt safe again. She never returned.

I'd waited and then searched for her. Not knowing if she'd been caught by the people she'd feared or if she'd grown tired of me and wanted an easy way to say good-bye, the bewildering pain was still inside me, fresh and harsh after all the years in between.

I'd finally decided to try to leave it behind, desperate enough to quit my job with a New York paper in the middle of the Depression to attempt another start on life in Chicago. My efforts caught the attention of the people who had also been hunting her. One of them had been her younger sister Gaylen, who had been as murderous as Maureen had been gentle.

Escott and I had managed to survive that encounter, and now we were outward bound to pick up where he'd left off on his trail after Maureen. He was a professional, and damned smart, and I trusted him enough to take care of things on his own, but he insisted I come along this time. Between us was an informal agreement to work together, so I came, willing to render whatever help he thought I could offer, but doubting our chances of success.

We arrived in New York during the day, so I was completely out of things while Escott took care of the business of getting us routed to our hotel. His plan was to check in, then hop a train up to Kingsburg. Maureen had had Gaylen confined to an expensive asylum there, and Escott wanted to talk with her doctors again. He must have had a hectic time before he took off; when I came to at sunset my shoulders and spine were all twisted and aching. A sloppy wooziness sloshed between my ears and I felt oddly heavy all over.

Outside the trunk, a door opened slowly and closed abruptly and Escott muttered a pithy exclamation. My confined world lurched, tilted, and whumped solidly onto the floor. He clicked the key in the lock and pushed the lid up.

"Mm?" I said, still dizzy from being on my head.

"Terribly sorry, old man. I didn't have time to see you to your room. The train schedule was just too close. I distinctly told the fellow how I wanted your trunk placed and he deigned not to listen."

"Welcome to New York," I said philosophically and winced at the blinding dregs of a new dusk burning through the thin curtains. The sun was officially down, but more than enough light lingered in the sky to be painful. I fumbled for my dark glasses and found they'd slipped from their pocket and were burrowing into my ribs. One metal earpiece was bent, but they were still serviceable, and I slipped them on with a sigh of relief. Sometimes I really hate waking up.

"How are you?" he asked, walking to the open window and considerately pulling down the shade. A stale breeze made it flap a bit. It was the familiar used air of a big city, but some thirty degrees cooler than the stuff we'd left behind in Chicago.

I rubbed the sore place on my head and a few grains of dirt from my bag of soil trickled to the floor. "Gritty."

He liked puns, but only when he was making them. "Facilities are just over there if you wish to refresh yourself."

I did and got untangled from my mixed-up belongings and staggered into the bathroom to splash cold water on my face. "How was Kingsburg?"

He dropped into a fat chair, stretched his long legs out straight, and looked smug. "I have the address of Gaylen's next of kin—"

"*Next of kin?*"

"—to be notified in the event of an emergency."

"It's not Maureen, is it?" I'd read that from his attitude.

"No, it is not Maureen, but some other woman named Edith Sedlock."

I'd never heard of her and said as much. "Where is she? Have you checked on her?"

"She lives here in Manhattan, and I've not had time to look her up."

It flashed through my mind that Edith could be Maureen. "Let's get going, then."

He held up a cautionary hand. "You'd create a better impression if you had a quick wash and brush-up."

"Damn." But he was right; I looked rumpled and felt the same. Spending twelve hours packed in a trunk does that to a person.

He checked his watch. "There's a café off the lobby just left of the elevator. I'll wait for you there. Thirty minutes?"

"Fifteen."

He'd just finished his sandwich and I gave him no time to linger over the coffee. Playing native guide for a change, I led the way to the nearest subway station, taking the fastest route to the address we wanted.

"How did you manage to get it?" I spoke just loud enough for him to hear over the background noise of the train. "I thought doctors were first cousins to clams."

"By talking a great deal."

"The Ronald Colman bit, huh?"

"Hardly. I merely told them the truth . . . some of it, anyway."

"How much is some?"

"That I was hired by an interested third party to search for Gaylen's missing 'daughter,' Maureen. I had only to show them my credentials and a stunning letter of reference."

"Letter of—" Then the dawn came. "You mean you're still packing all that stuff from the blackmail list?"

"I haven't had time to return it yet and it seemed a waste not to use it in a good cause."

"But how could it be used?" I wasn't accusatory, just curious about his mechanics. As far as I knew, the stuff in his safekeeping consisted of nothing but embarrassing photos and indiscreet letters and documents.

"There *are* ways. I simply hinted around that my client was very prominent, but wished to remain anonymous. When pressed, I reluctantly revealed an important name on a miraculously appropriate letter, one of a most interesting series. It was child's play to keep my thumb over the name of the original addressee."

"Jeez, don't you take the cake. What did you learn from them about this Edith Sedlock?"

"They believe her to be Gaylen's other daughter."

"Other—Maureen's got another sister?"

"Possibly."

"She'd have to be a younger woman if the Kingsburg doctors thought her to be Gaylen's daughter. Then she could be—"

"Like you, yes, but I am not inclined to think so."

"Yeah? Why?"

"Because she was able to answer the phone during the day when they called to tell her of Gaylen's escape."

"Maybe she was rooming with a human friend."

"There's that," he conceded. "She instructed them to keep her informed on the situation, and that's all they were able to tell me about her."

"Would they phone her about you?"

"I'm sure they already have. Anyone else searching for Gaylen would certainly be of interest to the next of kin."

"Did Maureen leave any other address for them?"

"Her own—that is, the one you originally gave to me. All the bills for Gaylen's care were sent there and promptly paid via Western Union. Did Maureen always pay in cash?"

"As far as I know, when she did buy anything. We didn't exactly spend time shopping."

"Yes, and I know you hardly keep banker's hours. I did find out something quite interesting: the date of Gaylen's escape coincides exactly to the date you found Maureen's note."

That was no real surprise and made a lot of sense. "I wish she could have found some other way of handling things than by running."

"Perhaps she once tried."

"What d'ya mean?"

"In the same situation, what would you have done to neutralize Gaylen as a threat?"

"Same as I did to Matheus, I guess."

"But no matter what the provocation, she might have been most reluctant to do so with her own sister. You weren't happy with the idea yourself."

"Yeah . . ."

"Or perhaps Gaylen's will might have been strong enough for her to resist such an imposed influence. The woman was utterly obsessed with getting her own way and quite mentally unbalanced, considering the lengths she went to to finally achieve her goal."

"Tell me about it," I grumbled, and thought about Bobbi with a pang of guilt over what she'd been put through. "I hope to God we can clear this up now."

"As do I," he agreed, and left me alone with my thoughts until our stop came up.

We emerged in the east fifties and walked a couple of blocks south to Forty-eighth and a promising line of brownstones. It was a respectable working-class neighborhood with a few shops along the street, a drugstore on one corner, and a quiet little tavern at the other. We found the right number and went up.

Edith Sedlock lived in the back corner flat on the third floor, and her door remained firmly locked as she asked our business.

"My name is Jack Fleming," I called through the plain panel of wood. "I'm a friend of Maureen Dumont—"

"Maureen?"

"Yes, we've just come from Kingsburg—"

A key clicked and the door opened exactly four inches. Two dark brown eyes glared at us suspiciously. She had matching brown hair, bobbed short, and was nearer thirty than forty. Aside from the giveaway of her age, she had a strong and fast heartbeat. She was definitely not a vampire.

"What's this about?" she demanded.

"May we come in and tell you, Miss Sedlock?" Escott asked politely, his hat in hand. I took the hint and grabbed mine off.

Still doubtful, she stepped back, swinging the door wide and leaving it open after we walked in. She looked us over carefully, frowning, but apparently we weren't too threatening. She gestured us to a small lumpy sofa.

It was a simple one-room flat, and the place was littered with too much furniture, clothes, books, magazines, loose papers, and used dishes. A radio sang to itself on a table next to a tiny stove and sink. She turned it off and dragged a wicker chair from the table and sat facing us, her knees and ankles pinched tightly together and her hands yanking the hemline of her dark dress down as far as it could go.

"Our apologies for intruding on you, Miss Sedlock," Escott began.

She interrupted. "I've been expecting to hear from you. The sanatorium called me. They said you'd been asking after Gaylen Dumont. Are you Mr. Escott?"

"I am."

"May I see your identification?"

He solemnly opened his wallet, she peered at it, then at me. In turn, I peeled out my old press card for her inspection. She sniffed at both of them, vaguely dissatisfied. With her, it was probably a chronic condition.

"It's out of date," she said to me. She looked as if she wanted to find fault with Escott's but couldn't think of anything.

I put my card away.

"You're very observant," Escott commented neutrally.

"I have to be, I'm a teacher."

"No doubt you are quite good at your job." He was turning on the charm again, but keeping it to a low level so as not to scare her off. From the pallid pink spots that appeared and vanished from her cheeks it seemed to be working, too.

"How did the sanatorium come to give you my name?" she asked.

It was Escott's show, so I gave him the nod. He explained about our search for Maureen and that he had at least located her mother as having been a patient at Kingsburg. Since Gaylen Dumont was no longer in residence and since he had excellent references, the administrator there had every confidence in Escott's professional discretion. The doctor in charge had no qualms in giving out the name listed as Gaylen's next of kin.

"Yes, I'm sure *he's* got every confidence in you, Mr. Escott, but his lapse in releasing such information is nonetheless deplorable; hardly what I would have expected from a doctor."

"I agree, but the circumstances of this situation are most unusual. Believe me, we have no wish to impose upon you any longer than necessary." He was being utterly sincere. No doubt he found her just as grating as I did, but was better at hiding it.

Her frown softened a little, but not by much. "Well, at least they did call and tell me about your visit, though I think they should have first asked my permission before giving out my name to just anyone walking in."

"Quite so," he agreed, all sympathy.

She sighed, affecting a slightly world-weary exasperation at life in general and said, "All right, now that you're here, what do you want?"

"As I said, we are trying to trace Maureen Dumont. We thought—"

"First of all, I am *not* related to the Dumonts, and second, I have no idea where Maureen is. I haven't heard from her in years."

"How many years? And how did your name come to be—"

"July or August, 1931," she stated. "It was a little over five years ago. We were neighbors at the same apartment building back then and lived next door to each other. She asked if I'd mind taking deliveries and phone messages for her during the day if I happened to be at home. She worked at night, she said, and hated having her sleep disturbed. She said she had to follow a very strict schedule because of her health and get so many hours of sleep or become ill. She was quite serious about it, as I never saw her during the day, but her other hours were very irregular. She wasn't one of *those* women, at least, or I wouldn't have had anything to do with her. I don't know what she did, but she was a quiet neighbor, and that counts for a lot with me."

"What about the last time you heard from her?" I asked.

"I'm coming to that. When the crash came, it upset everything for me, and I had to move. I kept the same phone number, though, and so we kept the same message arrangement as before. I expect she got someone else to take her packages. As for the sanatorium, she'd asked if she could put my name down along with her own for next of kin. The idea was that if anything should happen to her mother and they called during the day, I could pass the call on to Maureen in the evening. It seemed a reasonable precaution, so I didn't mind. The only call for her was when her mother escaped. I immediately tried to call Maureen; it seemed enough of an emergency to justify waking her up, but I couldn't get hold of her till evening."

Escott nodded, soaking up every syllable. "Can you tell us her exact words?"

"No, not after all this time, but she was very upset. I thought she'd go right to pieces then and there. I asked if I could help in some way, but she said she had to think first and hung up. About three hours later, she called and left a number where she could be reached if they had any more news of her mother. She sounded a lot calmer by then, and made a point of saying I was not to give the number out to anyone. The old lady was quite dangerous and violent despite her years, and Maureen wanted to take no chances on being found by her. It's a terrible shame that she was so terrified of her own parent, but that being the situation, I promised."

"Would you object to giving the number to us?"

"What makes you think I still have it, Mr. Escott?" Her lips thinned a bit into a kind of smile.

"You have me there, Miss Sedlock," he admitted, responding with a warm one of his own.

She must have been trying to flirt with him. She liked his reaction. She went to a small phone table, picked up a flat address book, and brought it back to her chair. She flipped through the pages until she came to the Ds, and read off a number penciled in next to the neat ink lettering listing Maureen's name and former address. Escott carefully copied it down.

"That's a Long Island exchange," I said. "What was she doing out there? Did she say?"

"No, I don't think so, presumably she was getting help. It was a very short call, we didn't want to tie up my line in case the asylum had to get through to me."

"So she didn't give this number to the asylum?"

"Obviously not," she sniffed, "or she wouldn't have bothered giving it to me. Besides, Mr. Escott would have gotten it from them during his visit there."

Escott acknowledged her deduction and returned her out-of-practice smile with another of his own. She responded with a near-wiggle. "Did the asylum ever call you?"

"The next day, but nothing had changed."

"Did you try the Long Island number?"

"Of course I did. Some man answered, I asked for Maureen, but his manner was very off-putting, as though he were surprised. He asked how I'd gotten his number and I told him, then he wanted to know who I was, but I only gave him my first name and asked for Maureen again. He said she had left and wanted to know who *I* was, but I said Maureen would know and hung up."

"You have a very clear recollection of that conversation," said Escott.

"Yes, I do, don't I?" She considered it a moment. "I think it was because he was so insistent. It made me uneasy. I never called back."

"Uneasy?"

"Silly, isn't it? After all, he was only a voice on the phone; an ordinary voice, except for his accent."

"What kind of accent?"

"Almost like yours, but not quite."

"An English accent?"

"Not quite."

"Perhaps from another region there?"

"No . . . I think that it was more American than English, but I couldn't place it now. I just noticed at the time that it was unusual."

"And you heard nothing more from Miss Dumont?"

"No, and the asylum called only one more time. They'd notified the local police, of course, but they wanted to talk to Maureen, and by then I didn't know what had happened to her. I expect they were waiting for her to call them."

"Didn't you think it odd?"

"I most certainly did, but what could I do about it? I went by her apartment to see her, but she was gone. The landlord said he thought she'd moved out. She'd left behind most of her clothes and books and other things, so it seemed likely she might return. The landlord wasn't too concerned. She'd paid her rent, but he was planning to put her things into storage in the basement if she wasn't back by the end of the month."

"Did he have any theories?"

"No."

"And you didn't contact the police?"

"I thought about it, but didn't see how they could help. Besides, from what I heard, someone else was looking for her, and he'd have done all that. The landlord said that Maureen's boyfriend was always pestering him for news of her return."

I had trouble finding my voice, but just managed. "And you never thought to contact him?"

"Yes, I did, but for all I knew he might have been the unpleasant man on the phone." She sniffed again. "If she wanted to cut things off with him, that was her business, not mine."

I had a choice: I could walk out or strangle her.

I walked out.

Escott came down a few minutes later and found me hunched against a street lamp trying to light up a smoke. My hands were shaking so much I couldn't even fire the damned match. I finally threw it and the cigarette into the gutter.

"That stupid, idiotic bitch!"

Escott listened patiently while I raved along similar and much more obscene lines for some time until I wound down into coherency again. We walked for several blocks and the movement and damp night air helped to cool down my frustration.

"I am in total agreement with you," he said in a mild tone, when it was over. "She might have saved you a lot of anguish had she spoken to you then, but we've yet to see if her information is of any value."

"Then let's find out."

We went back to our hotel and Escott started out with a phone call. First he checked with the operator to make sure the number was still in service, and then he got an address and name to go with it.

"Emily Francher?" I said, echoing his inquiry. "No, I've never heard of her."

"You don't sound too certain."

"I'm not. I don't think I've met her personally, but maybe I saw her name in the paper or heard it on the radio. . . ."

"Perhaps it was an advertisement," he suggested, his gaze falling on the newspaper he'd bought in the lobby stand when we'd returned. He tilted his head, considering his own thought, and noisily attacked the paper, tearing open the pages in a sudden fit of energy. "There." His long finger stabbed at a name.

I stared at it awhile. "Naw, it couldn't be, not the shipping line Franchers, that's just too big. Maureen never mentioned she knew anyone like that."

"You've also stated she never talked about her past," he pointed out.

"Well, yeah . . ."

"It may only prove to be a coincidence of names, as it was rather easy to trace the number, but first thing tomorrow I shall check it out thoroughly."

"Tomorrow?"

"Indeed. The sources I intend to exploit are all closed by now—"

"But we could rent a car and drive out there."

"I plan to do just that, but only after I find out all I can about this Emily Francher first—and about the man who answered the phone."

"The one who made little Edith uneasy?"

"The same. Granted, the woman is certainly a touch paranoid as far as men are concerned—"

"You can say that again."

"—but for her, the form it takes is that of bossiness and a general hostility."

"I get you. Her normal reaction should have been to tell him off when he got nosy?"

"That or ignore him. But I'm getting ahead of my research. It is Miss Emily Francher I shall concentrate on in the morning."

I idly flipped the pages of the paper. "Then that's it for tonight as far as the investigation goes, huh?"

"Regrettably, it would appear so."

Disadvantages abound with my physical condition, and spending the day locked up in a lightproof trunk is the one that irks me the most. I miss out on a lot of life, and once awake and free, I try to make up for the lost time.

"The last thing I feel like doing now is to sit around in this fancy cage the rest of the evening," I told him. "What about you?"

"I hadn't really thought of it. I was going to unpack and perhaps listen to the *March of Time,* but if you feel restless—"

"Yeah, I'm restless, but it's no fun trying to cure it alone. I want to find some entertainment."

"It does sound somewhat more distracting." He glanced at his watch. "A pity, but it's past curtain time by now."

"A play?" I rustled the amusement page around, folding it to the outside. "This is New York, Charles, they've got more than plays going on. Here we go, *Swingtime* is playing at Radio City and a new place just opened called *The Paradise—*"

"Well . . ."

"Here, this is the one, *Folies d 'Amour,* three shows a night and dinner thrown in with the jokes and dancing girls."

He looked a bit shocked as he scanned the details of their ad. "Good heavens. Have you noticed the two-fifty cover charge?"

"You get what you pay for. Besides, this is my idea and my treat. You know as well as I do that I don't spend any money on food, so how 'bout it? I know I could do with some high kicking."

He chuckled suddenly. "It sounds most educational."

We took a cab and got there in time for the last half of the second show and stayed on for the third. Escott enjoyed his late supper and didn't seem too put out when he had to imbibe drinks enough for two in order to cover for me with the waiter. They had little visible effect on him other than a slight glazing of the eyes, but then he looked the same way when driving his Nash.

Outwardly he seemed more interested in the mechanics of the production than the show itself, and his conversation was limited to comments on the efficiency of the crew involved. It was hard to tell, but I eventually concluded that he was indeed enjoying himself. The glazing disappeared from his eyes at intervals, usually when the girls in their spangled costumes were strutting their stuff to the brassy music.

The wee hours were upon us when the place finally closed down. The air was a humid mixture of exhaust, oil, and hot tires . . . and something else, very faint and distant. In response, there was a familiar and insistent stirring in my belly and throat. I lifted my head to catch the scent again, but it was gone.

"Like the show?" I asked between my efforts to whistle up a cab.

Escott put a lot of thought to the question before coming up with an answer. "Very much. Next time it shall be my turn. I hope that you will then have no objections to seeing a play?"

"None at all. I wanted to see a show like this just to get the taste of Edith Sedlock out of my mind."

"It was an excellent idea," he said, enunciating carefully. "I must admit I do prefer a stage production of any kind to a film, though I've nothing against film as a medium for entertainment."

"Your acting background has nothing to do with it, huh?"

"It has everything to do with it, my dear fellow."

"Why'd you leave it for this business?"

"Why, indeed?" he asked the general air, looking just a shade sad.

"I mean it, Charles. From what I've seen, you're a born actor. Why'd you switch to being a private inves—private agent?"

"Because taking up acting as a profession is a good way to starve to death. The last company I was in folded for lack of funds—that is to say, the manager stranded us. I made it my business to find him. It was my first case."

"Did you find him?"

"Yes, after a time. I even recovered the money he'd stolen and divided it with the rest of the company. This, of course, after I'd indulged myself and thumped the miscreant a few times so he wouldn't object to things. It was interesting work, so I decided to go into it."

"Thumping managers?"

"Finding things; doing things for others." He waved his hand vaguely.

"Wouldn't acting be safer, though? I mean, since you took up with me, it's been—"

He laughed a little. "You've obviously never tried staging the battle of Bosworth Field in a barn full of drunken lumberjacks. When King Richard started calling for a horse, they were more than happy to oblige him with one. No, I much prefer to do what I'm doing now, there is a certain exhilaration to this kind of business that I never found on the stage." He took a deep breath, held it, and let it out slowly.

Perhaps he'd realized he was talking about himself and his attitudes rather than about things he'd done, which was his usual run of conversation. On certain levels, he was a very private man. I pretended not to notice and waved unsuccessfully at another occupied cab.

"I think it is long past my bedtime," he concluded after a long moment. "If I begin quoting Shakespeare to no good purpose, please bring it to my attention and I shall cease immediately."

A cab finally pulled up and I got the door for him and shut it. He gave me a questioning look through the window.

"I've still got a lot of night left to me. Thought I'd take a walk in the park."

He nodded, perhaps guessing the real purpose of my walk. "Right. Then I'll see you tomorrow evening."

The cab grumbled away into the night, its exhaust swirling around my ankles. When it had grown small and its lights had merged with dozens of others, I abruptly turned in the opposite direction. I walked quickly, my head raised to catch that tantalizing scent once more.

IT was nine long blocks along Seventh to Central Park. I covered it quickly, my mind focused upon what lay ahead. This sort of careless behavior can lead to a mugging or worse, but no one bothered me, not even to bum a cigarette.

There are stockyards of a kind in New York, but nothing that could be fairly compared to the huge landmark in Chicago. Cattle are shipped in by rail each day to be slaughtered, many of them to support the large Jewish population and their kosher requirements. Maureen had taken me there once, but I had no need to travel so far tonight in search of livestock; not as long as Central Park had pony rides and horse-drawn carriages.

I knew more or less where the animals were kept, and in due time my nose led me to some stables. It was the same smell that had caught my attention outside the club, carried to me by some freak of the faint wind. Maybe it was an unpleasant odor to some, to me it meant food. I slipped inside and quietly got acquainted with its half dozen four-legged tenants, picking out a healthy-looking gelding with a calm eye.

Having spent some formative years on a farm, I knew how to talk to horses; I almost didn't have to soothe him to quiescence. I did so anyway, just to be on the safe side. The animal stood placidly while I opened a vein in his leg and slowly drank my fill.

The hollow, near-cramp in my stomach vanished. The almost-ache in my throat eased to nothing. Most of the time, the symptoms of my hunger were negligible and could be ignored if I were busy, but I was careful never to let it go too far. It wasn't that I'd lose control and be tempted to drag someone into an alley to feed off them, I just disliked the physical discomfort that resulted from waiting too long.

It was my first taste of horse's blood and I liked it better than the stuff I'd taken from cattle. There *was* a difference to it; not so much in the subtleties of flavor and texture, but in the surroundings. This was a neat, straw-cushioned stable, not a soggy, stinking pen. The animal was clean and the hair on his hide short. When you have to get to your food by using your own teeth, that counts for a lot.

Afterward, he politely accepted being patted down in lieu of a more material show of thanks. Next time around I'd remember to bring an apple or some sugar cubes. It seemed only fair.

*   *   *

When I crawled out of my trunk the next evening I found Escott at his ease on his bed, showing no ill effects from his sedate debauch, and up to his neck in the papers.

"Good evening," he said cheerfully, hardly looking up.

"How'd it go today?" I asked, stretching,

"The *London Times* has finally dropped its pro-Hitler policy in favor of the Russians, who seem to be the lesser of two evils at the moment. It was that speech he made last Sunday at Nuremberg that did the trick."

"I *meant* with the—"

"Oh, yes, sorry." He folded the paper away. "Emily Francher, daughter to the late Roger and Violet Francher—"

"The shipping-line Franchers?" I interrupted.

"The same."

"I'll be damned."

He continued. "Emily was one of the better-dowered debutantes in 1913, and was sole heiress to the estate when her mother died in 1931."

The coincidence of the date wasn't lost on me. "When, in 1931?"

"I've a lot to tell you, but I'd rather tell it on the drive out."

"Out to—"

"Yes, the Francher house on Long Island. I've a map and hired some transportation, having assumed you would want to interview Miss Francher personally about that phone call. The sooner you are ready . . ."

"Okay, okay, I'm moving!"

I did all the usual stuff, and shaved with my eyes closed so I wouldn't have to look at the gaping emptiness in the mirror. It takes a little practice and a good memory so as not to miss any spots, but I was in a hurry and nicked myself this time. Vampires bleed red like anyone else, it just doesn't last as long from a metal cut.

"If they made safety razors out of wood, you'd need stitches," said Escott from the other room.

"How the hell did you know I'd cut myself?"

"By the timbre, volume, and quality of your language. Far be it from me to laugh at another's pain, but you are most entertaining when you choose to express yourself."

"Next time I'll charge admission," I grumbled.

Our rented Ford eventually got us free of the congestion of Manhattan and Queens, but it seemed to take forever. Escott had to concentrate on driving, while I kept us on course with the map, so we didn't talk much. Once past the worst of it and safely rolling on State 25A, I was ready to hear more about our destination.

"You said this Emily Francher was quite the dish in 1913?"

"I said she was well dowered. I don't know what she looks like. The money and her mother helped her to land a socially acceptable husband. In this case, he was an impoverished gentleman with a title from my own sceptered homeland."

"So maybe his was the nearly English accent Edith Sedlock heard on the phone."

"I think not. The marriage was at her mother's forceful instigation and short-lived. The blissful couple parted company a month after the ceremony, the bride taking up residence in London and the groom in the north to be near the races."

"Gambler?"

"Gentleman jockey. He broke his neck in a steeplechase later that same year and much to the disgust of his mother-in-law, the family title passed on to an obscure and fertile cousin with a surplus of sons. Daughter Emily was ordered back to New York and resumed the use of her maiden name."

"Where'd you dig all that up?"

"It was in the papers. The society gossips had a fine time then, but it was only a foretaste of what was to come. Roger Francher died in 1915 and wife Violet took over the shipping business and proved herself most capable. She also set about looking for a suitable replacement for her inconveniently deceased son-in-law. By this time, young Emily had suffered what we would now call a nervous breakdown and was sent off to 'rest' with relatives in Newport, who reported her every utterance to the mother. Efforts to locate another titled gentleman were thwarted by the war, but in 1920 the lady managed to befriend a French marquis and whisked him across the Atlantic to meet Emily."

"Did Emily have anything to say about this?"

"If she did, her mother was quite uninterested."

"And the Newport relatives?"

"Dependent upon Violet's generosity for their support. Another wedding date was set, but it all fell through when the groom was arrested. It seems he was not a marquis or even French, but an American with three other wives."

"Three?"

"And a number of children. They tried to suppress the scandal, but were unsuccessful with some of the less discriminating papers. Officially, the wedding was postponed for an indefinite period while he returned to France to 'settle his business interests.' In reality, I'd say he was lucky to only have to face the French courts and his several families and not Mrs. Francher. He might have gotten away with having a fourth wife had the lady been less publicity minded and not issued his picture to every society editor in the Western Hemisphere."

"*His* picture? What about Emily?"

He shrugged. "Perhaps her mother didn't think her an important enough participant in the proceedings. From what I could glean between the lines, the bride was once again less than enthusiastic over things."

"I guess it was just as well. What happened to her?"

"By then she had come into her own inheritance from her father's will and bought a house on Long Island. I think it was an attempt to make a life for herself away from her mother."

"Better late than never."

"Violet still tried to interest her in another titled marriage—she was a very single-minded woman—but was distracted from any serious efforts by her own involvement with the shipping line. When the crash came, she lost most of the business, and rather than doing her daughter a favor and leaping from her office window, she turned things over to the board of directors, officially retired, and moved in with Emily."

"Nice lady."

"Their past separation did seem to do the girl some good. Having her own money, she built a house for her mother on the same grounds as her own estate and invited her to take possession. The invitation was firmly declined, so Emily moved instead. It was just as well for her, because her former home burned to the ground in April of 1931 and Violet Francher along with it."

I thought awhile on that one. "You think Emily might have killed her mother?"

"That is always a possibility. The most vicious and unforgiving crimes often occur as a result of frustrations building up within families. Emily might certainly have had sufficient cause over the years to resent the woman enough to do murder. The investigation ruled it to be an accidental death."

"What do you think?"

"Not having had access to all the facts leading up to those results, I think nothing at all."

"Why was there an investigation, then?"

"It was the standard thing to do in such a case. A sum of insurance money was involved, though the amount was trifling compared to Emily's assets."

"Rich people can be greedy, that's how some of them get to be rich. How did Emily keep her assets through the crash?"

"She took to heart the maxim of Anita Loos's heroine that 'diamonds are a girl's best friend' and put her trust in safe-deposit boxes rather than her bank account."

"Smart girl."

"Since the fire, she's taken up the life of a virtual hermit, albeit a hermit in extremely comfortable circumstances. She still supports some of her poorer Newport relations, but never visits them."

"You learn anything about who answered the phone?"

He shook his head.

"What about that breakdown? Is she still loony?"

"I have no information on her current mental state. Her past experience might have been connected to the decease of her father. The story at the time consisted of a few bald statements about resting her nerves—"

"Which is the same as going nuts. I had an idea she might have been sent to Kingsburg instead of Newport for her rest cure. It'd give her a logical connection to Maureen."

"That's a good idea, but the dates involved are too disparate. There was also considerable documentation in the social columns pertaining to Emily's presence in Newport."

"Only if you believe everything you read."

"How much truth is there?"

It was a straight inquiry, not a rhetorical question. "In general, or—"

"In the papers. I should be interested in hearing from one who has been on the inside of things."

I didn't have to think long or hard on that one. "It depends on the reporter, his editor, and the kind of rag they work for. If you want to boost circulation—and who doesn't?—the truth can be victim of enough exaggeration to sell papers, but not so much that it courts a lawsuit. It also depends on the kind of information picked up. The best journalist in the world can make a goof if he's given false or incomplete information, or if he misunderstands what he gets. Unless editorializing is the main angle, we try to give people the truth. When you've got a deadline breathing down your neck every few hours you don't have time to make things up."

Since he'd exhausted his information about Emily Francher, the conversation shifted to journalism, with me doing most of the talking and Escott soaking it up as he drove. We were now passing through a different world from Manhattan; less than ten miles from the Queensborough Bridge were working farms and their villages. Minute museums housed in buildings dating from the American Revolution advertised displays of relics from that period.

Off to the left side of the road we got an occasional glimpse of Long Island Sound, smooth and sullen in the moonrise. I wore my dark glasses against the glare.

I checked the name of the last village against our map and a fast five minutes later I told him to hang a left. We began a tour through the exclusive country of the very rich. We were closer to the sound than ever, but couldn't see it for the trees that were packed so close to the road they formed a tunnel. Traffic was light, which meant nothing passed us coming or going unless you counted the rabbits.

"This is it," I said.

On the left was a fifty-yard stretch of brick wall, broken by a fancy gate with the name FRANCHER arching over it in white painted ironwork. Inside stood a very solid brick gatehouse, showing some muted lights. A white gravel drive twisted out of sight into the trees beyond. Escott tapped the brake, parked the nose of the Ford next to the gate, and hit the horn a few times.

A light came on outside the gatehouse and eventually a short man emerged and squinted at us. He wore an old hickory shirt, hastily buttoned, and gray work pants, stained at the knees. The lower half of his face was sunburned.

"What do you want to bet he's the gardener?" I asked, but Escott wasn't taking.

The man came within a few feet of the gate, trying to peer past our headlights.

"Who's there?" he called.

Escott introduced himself, said he was a private agent and that he needed to speak with Miss Francher about an investigation he was conducting.

"Huh?"

I gave him a sympathetic look. He cut the motor, got out, and went up to talk with the man. It took time and much waving of his Chicago credentials. The man dithered a lot and said "I don't know" a lot, and Escott got nowhere fast.

Another figure appeared from the house; a thin, sinewy woman with her graying hair braided for sleep. She wore the standard black of a maid's uniform, minus the white collar, cuffs and apron, and had shoved her bare feet into her thick-soled work shoes.

"What is this?" she demanded both of Escott and the man. By his behavior in her presence, it was likely he was her browbeaten husband.

Out of his depth, he made a partial start on an explanation, was shushed by the woman, then Escott had a turn. He repeated his introduction with his hat off and I noted he was emphasizing his English accent. This time it didn't wash and she suggested he come back tomorrow afternoon. Miss Francher was not in the habit of receiving uninvited callers after dark.

Escott wasn't put off. He mentioned again the vital importance of his case and asked that a message be relayed to Miss Francher. He would abide by her decision. He wrote something in his notebook and tore out the page. Frowning, the woman accepted it between thumb and forefinger as though it were especially dirty laundry. She snapped something at the man and stalked back to the gatehouse with him in tow.

Escott came over to my side of the car and leaned an arm on the roof and a foot on the running board.

"What'd you write?" I asked.

"A request to talk with her about Maureen Dumont. It tips our hand, but at this point it would seem to be unavoidable."

"What if Emily tells us to get lost?"

"Then we apparently drive away. You can quietly return later."

"And tiptoe up on her for a private interview?"

"You've acquired some experience at breaking and entering by now, and I know you have very little trouble persuading people to talk once you've gotten their attention."

"Yeah, but I'd rather go through regular channels, if you don't mind. I hate scaring people."

"With that attitude, you could give vampirism a bad name."

After a few minutes I caught the sound of a motor coming our way. The gardener was driving a rattle-trap old truck with shovels, rakes, and similar tools sticking out the back. They clattered and rolled around as the thing growled over the uneven gravel surface. He hopped out and opened the gate for us. The woman emerged from the house again to glare at Escott. She obviously wasn't happy, having been denied official sanction to tell us to go to Halifax.

She pointed at the gardener. "Follow him, he'll take you to the main house."

Escott wasted no time starting the Ford up again and driving us through the fancy iron bars. The woman closed and locked them, and we followed the little truck up the drive at a breath-stealing seven miles an hour.

The grounds were semi-wild; the grass was uncut, but the trees were trimmed and no fallen branches or brush cluttered the spaces between them. The drive curved, slanted slightly uphill, crested, and sloped down again to a large, unnaturally flat section of ground. An almost perfect square was outlined by scarred trees and stunted shrubs.

Escott nodded at it. "I can safely say that that must be where the burned house once stood."

Past the plateau marking the house, the land continued its long slope to the sound.

"Maybe Violet hadn't wanted to move because of the view," I said. "What caused the fire? Do you know?"

"They traced it to some worn-away insulation on a table lamp. It shorted out and set fire to a rug and then went on to the rest of the house. The mother was asleep upstairs and probably died of smoke inhalation without ever waking. The body was still in bed when they found it."

"Except for the plants, you wouldn't know anything had ever been there. That must have been some cleanup job."

"I expect the present mistress of the estate may have found the ruins somewhat depressing."

Another turn, more trees, and then a glimpse of buildings made of white stone with cream-colored trim. I made out a two-storied garage separated by the gravel drive from a much larger structure. The trees parted. Maybe it was modest when compared to some of the other houses in the neighborhood; it couldn't have had more than fifteen or twenty bedrooms at the most. Lights were showing on both floors and at the porte cochère-style front entrance. The truck stopped beneath it and so did we. The gardener escorted us to the open double doors, handing us over to a younger woman uniformed as a maid. She smiled a neutral welcome and gestured us inside.

The entry hall was only a little smaller than Grand Central and furnished with slick Italian marble and Impressionist paintings, which caught Escott's immediate attention. Beautifully framed, labeled and perfectly lit, I didn't have to ask if they were genuine; they wouldn't dare not be.

At the far end of the hall was a massive staircase, also of marble. The wall on the upper landing held a series of huge canvases that marched off out of sight on either side. They depicted fantasy scenes of people playing in gardens. I didn't know enough about art to put a date on them, but the white powdered wigs and wide skirts made me think of Versailles before someone invented the guillotine.

The maid had thoughtfully given us a moment to stare and get used to things, then led us to the right and to a smaller room. The marble floor was replaced by an intricate pattern of oak broken up by Oriental rugs. The fireplace was in use, and soft shadows from the antique furnishings danced in the far corners and were lost against the dark background of the paneled walls.

Under a single lit lamp by the fire, a woman on the young side of middle age sat in a massive red leather chair. She had shiny black hair, cut short and dressed in perfect waves along her skull. Her skin was sallow and just starting to bag along the jaw and stretch at the neck. She wore a long red velvet dress that clashed with the chair leather and enough diamonds to set the country's economy straight again. Hundreds of them hung from her neck and arms, catching the glow from the fire and throwing out glints and sparks like the Fourth of July. In full sunlight she'd have been blinding.

She watched our approach with a mixture of wariness and interest.

"Mr. Escott?" Her voice echoed her expression.

"Miss Francher?" Escott bowed very slightly and introduced me as his associate.

"Have you an affliction of the eyes, Mr. Fleming?"

"No, ma'am," I said apologetically, and folded away my dark glasses.

"That's better. You may sit down. Coffee or tea?" she asked without enthusiasm, and we declined the offer with thanks. Social necessity out of the way, she dismissed the maid and inquired about our business.

"As I mentioned in my note, I am working on a disappearance case," Escott began. "We're looking for a Miss Maureen Dumont, who vanished in the late summer of 1931. We know she made a telephone call to an acquaintance and gave your phone number to them—"

"You mean she called from this house?"

"We can assume she did. She said she could be reached at this number." Escott read it off from his notebook.

"That is my number, but I don't know anyone named Dumont," she stated flatly.

"She might have used a different name," I said. I described Maureen to her. She listened, but ultimately shook her head.

"I can't help you, I'm sorry. May I ask why you wish to find her?"

It was an effort to talk. "She was . . . she was special to me. Her disappearance was unexpected and unusual. I've been looking for her since then. This is the first solid clue I've had in five years . . . there must be something you can remember about that summer."

Emily Francher again shook her head, her expression clouding as she swallowed and looked away. "My mother died that year. Things were very difficult for me and I was on medication for much of the time. My memories of that period are most painful and I've done my best to try to forget them."

"I can understand that, but—"

She held up one hand. "I have led and continue to pursue a solitary life. I have very few visitors. I am certain that if this young woman had come to my house specifically to see me, I would have known about it."

"Even back then?"

"Most certainly back then. The only visitors I received were members of my family and my lawyer to settle up any legal matters. They were all people I knew—this Maureen Dumont was not with them. Now, either a mistake has been made on your part with the telephone number, or one of my staff is involved, in which case my secretary will help you. Jonathan?"

Two high-backed chairs were placed in the far corner of the room, turned away from the center of things. Until now, neither Escott nor I had known one of them was occupied. The man she'd called to stood easily and came forward to look us over.

He was too handsome to be real, that's how he struck me at first glance. His dark hair was perfectly combed, his features just uneven enough to be interesting and arresting. He didn't have to smile for me to know his teeth would match the rest of him for a correct turnout. He wore a sober, well-cut suit with a subtle stripe that picked up the color of his blue eyes. He was tall, with a good spread of shoulder and not much hip, just the type to have to beat women off with a club. Some twenty years younger than his employer, I could guess that he was secretary in name only. If rich men felt entitled to have mistresses, I supposed rich women could have their gigolos as well. It was no skin off my nose.

"Jonathan, this is Mr. Escott and Mr. Fleming. Would you please see to them?"

He nodded acknowledgment. "Certainly, Miss Francher. Please come this way, gentlemen."

Escott caught it at the same time and telegraphed it to me by a brief change in his eyes—an accent, almost English, but not quite. He swallowed back any objections to our summary dismissal by the lady of the house, bowed slightly again, and thanked her for her time. She waved a benevolent, if somewhat vague hand, and picked up a book from the table next to her chair.

Jonathan the secretary led us on a short hike to the second floor and ushered us into a cross between an office and a sitting room. It had more paintings on display, and Escott stopped and fairly gaped at a dim, heavily framed portrait of a man with a lumpy nose. Even my uneducated eye recognized it as a Rembrandt. It had to be genuine, nothing less would have been tolerated in such a house.

Opposite the door were some tall French windows softened by pale curtains. They opened onto a veranda that ran the length of the back of the house and overlooked a large, well-lit swimming pool. Though it was a cool night, someone was splashing around below. I wandered over to the rail for a better look and saw a slim blond girl cutting through the water like a seal, doing laps.

"That is Miss Francher's cousin, Laura," said the secretary, drawing my attention back into the room. "She's very fond of swimming," he added unnecessarily.

He politely settled us on a long couch and eased himself lazily into a padded banker's chair before a roll-top desk. The top was shut and a whisper of dust clouded its brass handles.

On closer look, and in better light, he was still a remarkably handsome man. His dark hair and expressive brows accentuated his pale complexion, and slender blue veins were visible under the fine-textured skin of his long hands. He suddenly seemed out of place in his fashionable suit and modern surroundings. He should have been on a movie screen swinging a sword around and romancing Merle Oberon or Greta Garbo.

"How long have you worked here?" I asked.

"Several years." He looked me over carefully in turn, holding on to a faint smile and not the least discouraged that it wasn't returned. "How came you gentlemen to this place?"

Escott may have picked up on my uneasiness and was cautious. "I believe you heard all that was said to Miss Francher."

"So I did," he admitted. "It was I who persuaded her to allow you in. She values her privacy very much and we are naturally worried about robbery, but I was curious as to how you know Maureen Dumont. She was a friend of mine."

He watched both our reactions, his eyes moving back and forth in a way that put prickles under my collar.

"Was?" I asked, trying to keep the thickness out of my voice.

"We were once very close."

"How close?"

"I've not seen or heard from her for some five years," he said, ignoring the question and watching me.

I started to say something, but Escott stepped in instead. "Would you relate to us the exact circumstances of your last contact with her?"

He dragged his gaze from me to Escott. "Possibly, but I would first like some information about the two of you." Now his full attention was focused on Escott. "Who are you? Why are you here?"

"My name is Charles W. Escott. I am a licensed private investigator from Chicago and this is my colleague, Jack Fleming. Mr. Fleming was a very close friend of Miss Dumont. In August of 1931, Miss Dumont disappeared. This took place within a few hours of her sister Gaylen's escape—"

"Charles," I warned.

He stopped abruptly and shook his head a little. I thought he was trying to put me off.

"Go on," said our host, leaning forward.

". . . escape from a private sanatorium in—"

I looked at Escott—really *looked* at him—and the skin on my scalp started crawling every which way.

"—Kingsburg. She—"

"*Charles.*" This time I grabbed one shoulder and turned him to face me. His gray eyes were empty. He was unaware of everything except the last question he'd heard and his absolute necessity to answer it.

"—telephoned her friend . . . telephoned . . ."

Hardly knowing what I was doing myself, I lunged at the secretary and hauled him from his chair and slammed him against the nearest wall. Escott's voice trailed off and stopped. An instant later the man's arm shot up and he caught me in the soft spot right under the rib cage. If I'd been breathing I'd have doubled over. As it was, the force of the blow surprised me and sent me staggering back into his chair.

I went right over in a crash and tangle, bruising my arm on an unpadded wooden edge. He started to come after me, but stopped short, as though undecided whether to help me up or belt me again.

"Easy now," he said, holding his hands with the palms out. I'd spoken the same way to that horse last night to keep it calm. We glared at each other for a few long seconds, and then I glanced at Escott. He was still on the couch and oblivious to what had just happened.

The man said nothing when I looked back at him. He was on guard, his white teeth showing in the kind of non-smile you see on a wolf. When I didn't leap up for another attack, he cautiously extended a hand down to me. I swatted it away before I could give in to the sudden urge to break the arm that went with it, and got to my feet without assistance.

"Easy now," he repeated. "There's no point to this, and you know it. The truth of things—that's all I wanted from him."

I knew what he was talking about, but wasn't ready to face it yet, not until Escott . . .

"Pull him out of it—and carefully, or I'll kick your ass into the sound."

"Very well," he told me. His voice was level, his rictus smile gone, but he wouldn't hurry to do anything until he felt sure of me.

After a moment I backed off. Slowly. I wasn't under his influence, but there was little else I could do.

When he was certain I'd stay put, he crossed to Escott, looked into his eyes, and said his name. Escott blinked, as though trying hard to remember something, and came quickly back to himself. He instantly noted the tension in the room and stood up.

"What's happened?" he asked.

"We hit pay dirt," I said. "He just pulled a Lamont Cranston on you."

"Then he's . . ." Escott didn't bother to finish as the realization hit.

The man's blue eyes flickered at me and held steady like the hot part of a candle flame. "How much does *he* know about things?"

"Enough," I snapped. "Charles, you get behind me, I don't trust this son of a bitch."

Without any questions, Escott did just that. Whether he was any safer with me in front was anyone's guess.

"Jonathan," he said, recalling the secretary's name. His head cocked thoughtfully and he regarded him with abrupt understanding. "You're Jonathan Barrett."

Maureen's lover, her ageless vampire lover of three decades past, nodded once as an affirmative.

"At your service, gentlemen," he said, and smiled mirthlessly.

4

BARRETT straightened a little and smoothed his clothes, not taking his gaze from either of us. "I apologize for the intrusion upon you, Mr. Escott." His tone was slightly hostile and devoid of any regret. "Perhaps you will both excuse my desire to protect myself."

I said nothing, it was up to Escott to pick up the ball.

"There was no real need to influence me into giving you information."

"Yes, but then I don't know you. The information could have been false or incomplete. It saves time and trouble when both sides know where they stand. For all I knew, you might have been friends of Gaylen, not Maureen."

"What do you know about Gaylen?" I asked.

"Enough," he replied, echoing me. "How is it that you know her?"

"She was looking for Maureen and found me instead."

"And what happened to her?"

"She's no longer a threat to Maureen."

"That hardly answers my question."

I ignored the sarcastic note. "Where's Maureen?"

He studied me carefully, probably gauging my past relationship with her, perhaps even trying to see me through her eyes. That was what I was doing to him. "I don't know." He could see I didn't believe him and said it again, spreading his hands for emphasis.

"When did you last see her, then?" asked Escott.

"On the night that Gaylen escaped from Kingsburg. Maureen stayed for the day, departed the following dusk, and I've not heard from her or of her since then—until you two turned up to trouble my innocent employer with questions."

"How so is she innocent?"

"Miss Francher and I have a complete understanding over certain matters: I maintain her privacy and she protects mine." He turned to me. "I know you can appreciate how important privacy and discretion are to those of our nature. You should be more mindful of those dark glasses. They are a dreadful giveaway."

"Tell us about Maureen," I said.

"That's a long story."

"I've got all night and so do you."

"Of course, but I must think on where to start."

"With yourself," suggested Escott.

Barrett frowned and shook his head. "*That* would take much too long and I am not inclined this night to confess my many sins to virtual strangers."

"The primary points should be sufficient. May we begin with your life and death?"

Something like amusement seemed to light Barrett's eyes from within. "So you do know that much about us. Are you Mr. Fleming's protector?"

Escott didn't reply.

Shrugging it off as unimportant, Barrett went to the French windows and shut them against the night. "Very well. Please be seated and make yourselves comfortable. May I offer you some refreshment, Mr. Escott?"

"No, thank you."

This time Escott picked a chair off to one side of the couch. I resumed my original seat, barely settling on the edge, ready to move again if necessary. I still didn't trust the man.

Barrett righted his banker's chair, checked it for damage, and rolled it back under the desk. Apparently feeling secure about us, he sank into the opposite end of the couch from me with a mock sigh of weariness, angling against the back and arm to be able to look at us both. His loose-boned, informal posture had its effect and I felt myself relaxing a little.

"Very well," he began, looking up once at the ceiling as though searching it for the right word. "I was a lawyer's son and destined to be a lawyer as well, though I had little taste for the work. I was sent to England to study. It was my first real experience of unsupervised freedom and I quickly grew to love it. There I learned to spend my allowance in ways my father would scarce have understood, much less approved.

"Those were wild, delightful days, and the nights were made even better when I became acquainted with a certain lady of astonishing charm who taught me some unique skills in the art of love. I was but a rough, untutored colonial then, for a time I believed that that was how all men and women enjoyed themselves—I grew wiser about such things later on.

"Then war came up and I was commanded home again, that or be left without funds. Being a dutiful son, I returned. I was so dutiful that it got me killed. My father was loyal to the Crown, y'see."

"What war are you referring to?"

"The one that sundered our respective countries, Mr. Escott. The American Revolution, as it is now called." He paused to let that sink in and enjoyed our reaction.

"How old were you then?"

His eyes drifted inward, briefly. "I was not old then, Mr. Escott. I was young; very, very, young." He shifted, crossing one leg over the other. "But I was talking about the rebellion. My dear father was a Loyalist and not a damned traitor to our God-appointed sovereign. Of course, his attitude may have been tempered by the fact that Long Island was then protected by British troops. We were safe and secure from the rebels, so they said, but they couldn't be everywhere at once. I was shot down in cold blood by a pimply-faced bumpkin cowering in some trees on my father's land. The cowardly, dishonorable, half-witted bastard thought I was General Howe."

After at least 160 years, his disgust was sincere and still fresh.

"I'll pass over the dramatic details of my death and return, and my first stumbling efforts at coping with the physical change within me. I was forever cut off from my family—if anything, I was too embarrassed to come forward and try to explain myself. By the time I'd decided to overcome it, the so-called colonial government had won their war and seized Father's property. He pulled a few pennies together and took the family back to England. I was tied to the land, though, and had to remain behind. I settled down, made a kind of life for myself, and even traveled a bit in later years when the chance presented itself."

"How did you support yourself?" asked Escott.

"That, sir," he smiled, "is none of your business. I did a lot of reading, trying to make up for my patchy and interrupted education. Decades later, my interest in reading eventually led me to meet the Dumont sisters at some literary club. I was immediately attracted to Maureen, her feelings were in happy correspondence to my own, and nature had its course with us for many contented years."

"What about Gaylen?" I asked.

He sighed and shook his head. "She knew something was going on, but never came out and asked anything. It worried Maureen, but there was little she could do about it. She chose to do nothing."

"What did you do?"

"Nothing. It was Maureen's concern and up to her on how to handle things. I merely followed her wishes. Gaylen was a strange woman. There were no doctors then who could be of any help to her. She was too clever to be obviously mad."

"What was she like?"

"Strange," he repeated unhelpfully. "Normal on the outside, but there was a soft and rotten core of sickness within that never showed itself until you really got to know her. She liked to use people, but only in petty ways, mind you. She'd never put on a manner to make you think she was imposing on your goodwill."

"What do you mean?"

"There are some people you like to do things for, simply because they're nice and know how to say thank you. On the surface, Gaylen seemed to be one of them. She was pleasant company, and careful never to go too far, but she was really using people in her own way. As an outsider to their family with some larger experience, I could see how she worked all things around her to her favor . . . oh, but she was ever so nice about it.

"Maureen did everything she could for her, but it was never enough. Gaylen enjoyed playing the sweet suffering martyr and craved the attention it got her. In later years, Gaylen practically clung to Maureen, 'as if increase of appetite had grown by what it fed on,' if I may borrow from the bard. When Maureen had her accident, it was too much for Gaylen; she completely fell apart."

"The accident that killed her?"

"Yes. She told you about the fire wagon? I'm surprised; she hated talking about it, even thinking about it made her feel sick."

Having suffered a violent death myself, I could understand.

"For me it was a miracle. I hadn't lost her to death. She'd come back to me, beautiful as ever, and young again. I helped her through her first nights, easing things when I could, but after a time she found she couldn't let go. She wanted to go back, to comfort Gaylen and to let her know she was really all right."

His expression had turned inward again; he was half-sad, half-angry. "It was a mistake and a very bad one, but she couldn't see it at first. She talked me into helping—pleaded, really—it was that important to her. So I helped. It was all right for a time, but when the happy shock of the reunion wore off and the implications sank in, Gaylen started to work on us both. She was slow and subtle about it, but she wanted to be like us. She said there was every chance of the change working in her since they were sisters."

"She couldn't talk either of you into it, though."

"It wasn't for want of trying, and finally she tried too hard. That was her mistake; that's when Maureen realized how sick her sister was in her mind. Things got very ugly, very fast after that scene, and she had to put Gaylen away in Kingsburg, which all but broke Maureen's heart. Gaylen was the cause of the rift between us; thereafter Maureen and I went on separate paths."

"But you kept in touch?"

"Out of mutual self-interest and because of what we'd become. Those of our kind are despairingly rare." His glance rested on me a moment and I couldn't read his expression.

"What self-interest?"

"Gaylen was full of mischief and I had little confidence in the security of that so-called asylum. Bedlam may have been noisy, brutal, and stunk to high heaven, but they knew how to keep a door locked. We each had to know where the other lived in case something happened—which it did when she escaped."

"Who paid for the asylum?"

"Maureen. She and Gaylen inherited enough from their parents to live in quiet comfort for the rest of their lives. When Maureen understood how things might be for her future with me, she made out a rather clever will that gave over her share of the estate to a nonexistent cousin. If the cousin did not appear within a year of her demise, then her share would go to Gaylen. It was easy enough to establish another identity in those days, and my background in law was proving to be quite handy for once. Maureen prepared for her change—if it happened, and so it did."

"It surprised you?"

"I was truthful with her. I told her there was no guarantee she would rise again; it was only a chance and we took it."

Escott stirred in his chair. "And the others?"

"What do you mean, sir?"

"Since your decease you must have been involved with women other than Maureen."

Barrett was amused. "Of course I was. I'd changed, but not into a damned monk."

"Did any of them return after they died?"

He didn't answer, but Escott continued to wait for one. "No, none of them," he said with a flare of anger. "Not one of them. D'ye want to know how many there were and all that we did together?"

Escott ignored the question. "What about the lady you knew in England? What was her story?"

"I was her lover, not her bloody biographer."

Escott was patient, which irritated Barrett.

"Her name was Nora Jones and she made her living by accepting such gifts as we lads could afford to give her, but mind you, she was no whore— don't ever think that. She was a lovely girl, truly lovely and lovable. Not all the students were poor, and I was doubly blessed with a bit of paternal lucre and good looks, both of which she took to like butter to warm bread."

"Did she not warn you of the possible consequences of her relationship with you?"

"No, she did not. It was her way; she liked 'em young and fairly innocent, and was pleased to keep 'em so. I've also come to think that she honestly did not know there would even be consequences."

"Your resurrection must have been quite traumatic for you."

His face grew hard at the memory. "It was, and I'd rather not speak of it."

"Then we shall return to the near-present: tell us about the night Maureen came here to you."

"There's little enough to tell. I'd obtained a position here some months earlier as Miss Francher's secretary. As you're already aware by now, she knows all about me, but however odd the hours might be, I am very good at my job."

"And it's safe here," I added.

He considered the remark. "Yes, as safe as one can be from life. We had our share of ill fortune that year. Miss Francher's mother died horribly in a fire that spring and I had my hands full for a time, helping her get through the worst of it and protecting her privacy. If not for young Laura it would have been impossible. She was only fourteen then, but a splendid child; the experience matured and strengthened her even as it seemed to drain her older cousin. Laura had been visiting us on her spring holiday that week and then stayed on. I arranged for a private tutor so she could finish out the year at home with us."

"What about Laura's family?"

"Her parents died ten years ago. Miss Francher's mother was her legal guardian. When she died, Miss Francher assumed the responsibility. It was easy enough, for Laura is a good girl. Things were just starting to settle down at the close of summer when Maureen showed up at the gate asking for me. She was in quite a state about Gaylen and hardly able to think straight. I'd said that things had gotten very ugly between them, she was afraid of what her sister might do to her. She wanted help and advice, and I offered what little I could."

"Which was?"

"I said she should set the police to watching her flat and to keep herself out of sight until they caught the old girl again. It seemed the most obvious thing to do, but she was that panicked."

"Did Miss Francher know of this?"

"I saw no need to trouble her with my personal problems. I told her Maureen was an old friend dropping by for a visit and she was content with that."

It sounded as though Emily Francher had been remarkably accommodating for one who demanded such privacy, and I speculated that he might have influenced her into her contentment. "How long did Maureen stay?"

"She didn't. I invited her to remain as long as she liked until they found Gaylen, and she accepted. With a place this big, there are any number of rooms she'd be safe and comfortable in, especially my own, which is well locked and fireproofed. The servants have standing orders never to go inside and they are paid enough not to be overly curious."

"Convenient." Again, I figured he'd have insured himself by slipping them some quiet suggestions on the side.

"Indeed. Maureen turned down the offer and picked another room. I saw that she was settled, did some work of my own, and stopped by to say good night and to see if she needed anything. She did not, so I went to bed."

"You saw her?"

"I called through the door and she answered."

That struck us both as odd and he knew it.

"She didn't really want to see me," he admitted.

"Why's that?" I asked.

"We had a disagreement, more of a quiet fight, really. She didn't approve of my job and I told her it was none of her business how I chose to live. Things rapidly deteriorated from there."

"And she still accepted your invitation to stay the day?"

"By then it was too late for her to go elsewhere; the time had gotten away from us. She stayed, but left right after sunset the next night. By the time I was up and about, she was gone."

"Without a good-bye?"

"Or even a thank-you. She must have been very angry with me, but then I was hardly feeling like a good Christian toward her myself."

"How did she leave?"

"Same as she came; by taxi,"

"Do you know where she went?"

"No."

"Anyone else see her leave?"

"Mayfair—that's the gardener—had to let them in and out. You may ask him if you like, though I warn you he's got a brain like a block of Swiss cheese."

"And you never tried to contact her?"

"I called her flat a few times, but she was never home. Later on when I called, someone else had rented the place. She never called or wrote, I expect she never wanted to see me again." He'd drifted away, as though he were talking to himself. I wasn't the only one Maureen had hurt.

"Did you ever think that Gaylen might have found her?"

"Not seriously, no. Once Maureen had a little time to get over her upset, I knew she'd be able to take care of herself."

"Was your disagreement serious enough for her to cut you off just like that?"

"I suppose it was, from her point of view. No woman likes to see herself supplanted by another in a man's heart, even a man she's long ago discarded."

"Are you referring to your employer?" asked Escott in that carefully neutral tone of his, which meant he thought his question was important.

Barrett fastened him with a cold eye. "As I told Maureen, *that* is none of your business."

Escott dropped the subject for another. "What about the phone call for Maureen you received the next night?"

"Call?"

"From her friend. Maureen gave her the number of this house as though she expected to be here for a time."

"Oh, that. I remember."

"You gave this person the impression Maureen was still here."

"I think I offered to take a message and I wanted to know who was calling. I was curious and I thought she might be involved with Gaylen in some way. Who was it?"

"She was not involved with Gaylen and she asked that we not mention her name."

He shrugged, uninterested.

"Are you not curious about Maureen and what happened to her?"

"Of course I am, why d'ye think I got the two of you in here to start with? A lot of good it's done me since you've no news of her—or have you?"

"Regrettably, we do not."

"That's no surprise." He turned his attention to me. "How well did you know her?"

"Very well."

"That's evident, laddie. You must have been something special to her altogether. So why hasn't she tried to contact you, eh? Had a fight with her, too?"

"She left to protect me from Gaylen, that's all I know."

"And you said you met Gaylen?"

"She met me."

"What about her? Did the asylum finally catch up with her? You said she was caught?"

I glanced at Escott. He left it up to me. "I said she was no longer a threat. She's dead."

He thought it over for a time, reading more off my face than I felt comfortable about. "How, then, did it happen? How did she come to find you?"

"It doesn't matter, she just did. She thought I might know where Maureen was, but I couldn't help her."

"Perhaps not to find Maureen, maybe she wanted your help in other ways—and don't look so dark, laddie, I knew her, too, and far better. I knew what she wanted and how badly she wanted it, and if you turned her down, I shan't think ill of you. I said she was sick. Sometimes death is the best cure for her kind of misery. You *did* turn her down? She really is dead?"

"She is," confirmed Escott. "Heart failure."

I felt my face twisting in reaction. Maybe not all of the nightmare had left; something perverse inside me wanted to laugh. I got up and walked to the French windows instead. The pool lights were out and the blond swimmer was long gone. The water was still and smooth.

"Death is the best cure sometimes," Barrett repeated. "It keeps her from passing her sickness on to others and making them miserable in turn. One can hope for as much at least."

Some distance beyond the pool was a bare, fenced yard with a few trees in it and the dark, rounded shapes of horses dozing on their feet. No doubt they were part of Barrett's food supply. It was very convenient and comfortable for him to have such an obliging patroness.

I could understand Maureen's reaction to it all. In her day she had been well off and certainly attractive. Then Barrett came into her life, offering her love and a possibility of eternal youth in exchange for her money and protection. It *could* have been that way, an old story with a new twist that Barrett apparently repeated if he had the same arrangement with Emily Francher. No wonder Maureen had been upset, but I didn't think she'd have simply gone off without a final word to him. She had manners as well, she would have surely left him some kind of a note.

I turned back into the room. They were both looking at me; Escott alert and Barrett . . . watchful. I focused my full attention on him, freezing hard onto his brilliant eyes, reaching into his mind.

"Where is Maureen? Tell me."

Escott held his breath. There was total silence except for his heart thudding a little faster than normal.

"You know how to find her," I said. "Where is she?"

Barrett looked slightly surprised, not blank, as I'd expected.

"Tell me."

His face darkened.

"Where is she?"

He stood up to face me square on: a tall man, well built, wearing modern, elegant clothes. Hard, primitive fury flooded and marred his features. I'd done exactly the wrong thing by trying to influence an answer from him.

His hands had worked into fists. He made an effort to keep his voice steady.

"I have already told you I do not know where she is." He was shaking from his anger, but holding himself carefully in check. "And remember this, Fleming, no one has ever called me a liar and lived. . . . Keep that in mind before you say aught else."

Something moved out in the hall, a light footstep as someone passed the door. Escott started breathing again, but his heart still thumped very fast. It was just distracting enough, so I did think twice about my next words and it was damned difficult to get them out.

"If . . . *if* you should ever see her again—" I paused, but Barrett held back, listening "—tell her Gaylen is dead. Tell her I only want to know that she's all right." My mouth was very dry. "If she doesn't want to see me again, I'll respect her decision."

Barrett was a perceptive man; he could see what it had cost me to say that. His expression softened and he gave a slight nod. "And you'll do the same for me?"

"Yes."

He nodded again. "If I should ever see her again, I will tell her that for you. *If* . . ."

And he left that last word hanging in the air between us with all its attendant uncertainty and doubt.

Our car rumbled slowly down the drive, gravel spreading and crunching under the tires as we followed the gardener's truck to the front gate.

"What do you think?" I asked Escott.

He replied with a shake of the head.

Fair enough, I felt about the same. "I can't believe the trail stops here."

We rounded the turn at the side of the non-ruins of the old house and rolled gently downhill at a slightly faster speed. The truck was now nearly up to ten miles an hour.

"Got any questions for Johnny Appleseed up ahead?"

"If you mean the gardener, yes, I have. As for Barrett, he said much that agreed with what we heard from Gaylen—the manner of Maureen's death, her separation from Barrett—on those points we can assume he was being truthful."

"And of Maureen coming here and leaving?"

"I don't know. Her abrupt departure is just odd enough as a story to be true. He could just as easily have told us something more plausible. Having never met her, I do not know if such behavior is something you'd expect from her. Is it?"

"She left me, didn't she?" Like a spectator standing apart, I noticed the bitter tone in my voice. Escott remained mercifully silent.

The gardener got out to open the front gate for us. Escott followed him and cornered the man. His wife appeared on the porch of the gatehouse and glared at them both, but Escott had anticipated her and carefully maneuvered the man so he was unaware of her presence.

Escott talked and got some mumbled replies along with head scratching, head shaking, and shrugs until the fellow caught sight of his better half and decided it was past time to go inside. Escott shook hands with him briefly. From the look that passed between them I knew he'd given him a private tip for his help, such as it was.

We drove out. Escott waved at him and got a guarded half wave in return.

"What'd he say?"

"A moment," he said, and a quarter-mile later pulled the car onto the road shoulder and cut the motor. "Lord, but that place was oppressive."

"And I thought it was just me."

My answer had to wait more than a moment as he got out his pipe, tobacco pouch, and matches. Soon he was successfully drawing smoke into his lungs and filling the car up with the aromatic exhaust. The excess floated out the windows into the cool night air of the woods around us.

He looked at the pale gray swirl without really seeing it. "Mr. Mayfair confirmed Barrett's story. It was a memorable spring because of the fire and death of Mrs. Francher, but things were more or less back to normal by summer. Unlike her mother, Miss Francher did not encourage visitors, and after her views were made quite clear to her various relatives, they ceased to call. Young Laura was the only one she'd have anything to do with. Again, he confirmed Barrett's statement that Emily took over the girl's guardianship."

"Did he remember Maureen?"

"Not by name, but he did recall admitting a young woman on Barrett's authority that summer. The circumstances were similar enough to our own arrival to bring the incident readily to mind. She arrived in a Green Light cab one night and departed the next, also by cab; a local called out from the nearest town."

"Green Light is based in Manhattan."

"Mr. Mayfair was aware of that at the time, which was another unusual detail for him to remember. He'd spent some thought on speculating how high the fare had been."

"Great. What else?"

"Nothing more to concern us, I'm afraid. Aside from the expected traffic of tradesmen, the only other visitors of note were the demolition men charged with the task of tearing down the burned shell of the old house."

"Can we try tracing the local cab?"

"I'll have a go at it first thing tomorrow," he promised. "Now about tonight . . ."

"What about it?"

"Our interview was fascinating, but I felt a bit shortchanged on actual facts about the household. I want to ask if you would mind returning to the house tonight."

"What? Pull a peeping-tom act?"

"Engage in further investigation," he corrected mildly. "I also cannot believe the trail stops here and would like to know more about the place and the people in it. I'm interested in the cars they possess and who actually owns them. How many servants do they employ? Do any of them actually live in the house? Barrett mentioned he had a secure resting place; where is it?"

"Oh, is that all?"

He chose to overlook the touch of sarcasm. "Any piece of information, no matter how trivial, may be of value."

"And if Barrett catches me?"

"See that he doesn't."

5

IT was easy for him to say, he didn't have to go over the brick wall up the road and bumble through the woods to reach the house—not that that was too much trouble. Most of the time I was incorporeal, and passed over the terrain the way Escott's pipe smoke drifted out the car window. In a bodiless state the wall was no problem, and my clothes were spared the rigors of a hike through the wilderness. I just didn't like my errand or anything to do with it; I was looking for things to complain about.

I had to pause and re-form often to get my bearings, but I made good speed, swiftly flowing between the solid bulk of the tree trunks until I was within spitting distance of the garage. After that I took my time. Barrett's night vision was equal to my own, and unlike normal humans he could spot me in my invisible state.

Creeping into the garage, I checked each of the cars: an early Ford on blocks, a Rolls, a Caddy, and a brand-new white Studebaker. I dutifully wrote their plate numbers in my notebook and looked over their paperwork. All of them were owned by Emily Francher.

The floor above the garage was occupied by two women, both comfortably asleep. They had separate rooms, but shared a bath and had black uniforms hanging in the closets that identified them as regular staff. I picked gingerly through their purses to get their names, and ghosted outside again without disturbing them. As a vampire hell-bent on finding slumbering maidens to drain into terminal anemia, I was a total washout.

The stables were next, and were just as quiet. The horses may have been used to late-night visits. Two stood in stalls and six more wandered loose in the adjoining corral. None of them did more than cock an interested ear in my direction.

Upstairs, a section had been converted to living quarters, and I found a young man happily snoring away in his bed. His place was cluttered with horsey-smelling clothes, riding boots in both English and Western styles, and other related junk. He had a modest collection of Zane Grey novels on a shelf and below them was a pile of magazines whose pictured contents were anything but modest. Again, I quietly raided a wallet for identification.

The easy stuff out of the way, I oozed through the back door of the main house and solidified in the kitchen. A small light over one of the electric stoves kept it from being totally dark. Various doors opened to a hall, the dining room, pantry, and the basement. I picked the basement, changed to a semi-transparent state for silence and speed, and sailed down the stairs.

The walls were very solid concrete and the massive house above was well supported by a forest of thick pillars. I went solid for a moment and listened, but caught only the irregular drip of water from the laundry room. A slightly musty smell hung in the still air, coming from some odd pieces of old furniture stacked against a brick wall opposite the stairs. It was only a basement and a waste of my time.

I was halfway back to the kitchen when it hit me: the place was much too small. I went down again and checked the brickwork. Not being an expert, I couldn't tell if it was part of the original building or not, but my curiosity was up. I disappeared and pushed forward through the bricks.

It was slow work, like walking through sticky oatmeal. I didn't like the feeling at all and the wall was nearly a foot thick. It seemed like forever before I tumbled into free and open space again, to re-form for a look around.

On this side the bricks were hidden by fine oak paneling, and the utilitarian presence of the support pillars had been softened by similar decoration. Some of them had been converted into four-sided bookshelves, each loaded with hundreds of titles. A thick rug covered most of the parquet flooring and several lamps held back the darkness. The chairs and sofas looked comfortable and the air was fresh.

Barrett had done very well for himself.

He'd said his room was fireproof and secure, qualities which struck me as wise precautions. It was no wonder vampires had a reputation for hanging around graveyards; few things are more fireproof or private than a stone mausoleum. But this basement location was a real luxury and far better than anything I might have planned for myself. I was frankly envious.

The entrance to his sanctum was a heavy industrial-type metal door covered in more wood paneling. It led to a carpeted hall and a flight of steps going up to a door with access to the ground floor. Both were locked, which was sensible. I went back down again and got nosy.

His quarters consisted of a large living area, bedroom, bath, and a good-sized closet. The bed was unusually large, with a fancy embroidered canopy. It was for use, not for show, since the nightstand held some personal clutter. His carpet slippers lay tumbled on the floor next to it.

I cautiously looked under the brocaded blue bedspread and plain white sheets and found a doubled thickness of oilcloth stretched over the mattress. It was sewn shut at the edges, but I could tell by the weight and feel that it contained his home earth. It was a very neat arrangement, one that I intended to adapt for myself, now that I had the idea.

Beyond the bedroom was a spotless white-tiled bath, supplied with the usual appointments, except that the cabinet over the sink lacked a mirror. It was an easily understandable omission.

His closet was stocked with a number of suits. He favored dark blues and grays for his business wear, had two tuxedos, and some riding gear. One long rack contained a rainbow of shirts, ties, and handkerchiefs. Almost everything was silk.

At the back of the closet was a big antique trunk. It was banged up, but in good, solid condition. It was also locked, but I could guess he had a spare supply of earth inside in case he felt a need to travel.

I heard a footfall just outside the room and damn near panicked.

Stupidly, I had an idea he'd use a key, but he no more needed a key than I did. He had slipped inside the same silent way. I froze absolutely still, afraid he'd hear my eyelids blinking. I could certainly hear his every movement. Two soft thumps indicated he'd removed his shoes and other, less distinct sounds I interpreted as him undressing. I had a wild hope he wouldn't bother with the closet and abruptly discarded it as he padded my way.

Abject fear can be inspiring; I made a fast and wild-eyed search for a hiding place and spotted a ventilation grate in the ceiling. In the time it took for him to grasp the knob of the closet door and swing it open, I'd vanished and swept up into the narrow shaft.

Even in a disembodied state it was uncomfortable, and I had some very unpleasant thoughts that it might lead to the furnace. I'm not usually claustrophobic, but a few minutes of such close confinement was more than enough for my rattled brain. I couldn't go back to the closet, but if I didn't get out soon, my attack of mental sweats would send me solid again. Since the shaft seemed to be only ten inches square, that was the last thing I wanted to happen.

I flowed along the metal tunnel, felt an upward turning, and took it, hoping for the best and trying not to think about furnaces. After that I got lost; in this non-physical state it's almost impossible to avoid. It's like turning somersaults underwater with your eyes shut. Before too long you lose all sense of direction and can surface for air only to bump against the bottom of the pond.

I streamed along, just barely maintaining control, and suddenly sieved into open space again, which was a great improvement. By extended touch I made out the shapes of large unyielding surfaces and guessed them to be furnishings. I slowly re-formed and found my guess to be correct. The room was unoccupied; I sank into a chair and spent awhile pulling my nerves together. The next time Escott wanted information he could damn well get it himself. Playing the rabbit in a tunnel was not my idea of fun.

After a few minutes of quiet, I was settled down enough to move on and find out where I'd ended up. A look out a window confirmed that I was on the second floor overlooking the front lawn, though I wasn't close to any inhabited areas. The rooms I checked were dark and very much underfurnished. It didn't seem to be from any lack of money, simply lack of interest. The house had been built for socializing and entertaining lots of guests, something Emily Francher actively avoided. I wondered why her mother had turned down such a gift.

Down one long hall I discovered Emily's suite of rooms, and like Barrett, she'd indulged in every comfort and convenience. More French windows opened onto the back veranda and were so heavily curtained as to be lightproof. If she stayed up to keep Barrett company at night, she was likely to be a very late sleeper, but just to be sure I checked under the bedclothes. No oilcloth flats of earth lurked beneath the sheets. Emily was quite human and during the day she slept alone.

Her favorite colors were red, gold, and white; the decor was expensive, of course, but not overpowering. I poked through drawers and found clothes and vanity items, but nothing useful like a soul-revealing diary. The bedside table contained a Bible, several used-up crossword-puzzle books, pencils, a copy of *Anthony Adverse*, and a big, nearly full bottle of sleeping pills.

Her walk-in closet was larger than Barrett's, held enough clothes to open a store, but even my uneducated male eye could tell many of them were years out of style. Two heavy-looking cases in one corner caught my attention. One was open and contained those few pieces of jewelry she hadn't worn tonight: a couple of gold bracelets, some rings, and a pearl necklace. The other case was locked and wouldn't budge. On closer look both proved to be made of thick metal covered with wood veneer and welded to a huge metal plate bolted to the floor. Emily was careless, but not stupid.

Leaving her room, I moved down the hall and invaded Barrett's private office. The roll top part of the desk was locked and I couldn't open it without making a lot of noise and leaving traces. The drawers were open, but only contained the usual supplies. If neatness counted for anything, Barrett earned his keep well enough.

I was starting down the central stairs to the front hall and nearly blundered into him again. A door below opened and shut, followed by swift, decisive footsteps. Backing up the stairs, I crouched behind the railings, keeping very still. He emerged into view, his boot heels making a clatter against the marble floor as he crossed the hall to the parlor. As for the rest of his clothes . . . I felt my jaw sag open.

The hall was too open and dangerous; I opted to slip outside again and moved around to the front to peer in through the parlor window. The curtains were thin enough; I very much wanted to get a second look at the man.

The lamp was off and the only light now came from the fireplace. Emily Francher had moved from her chair to a long settee, where she reclined, still clad in her diamonds and red velvet. For the first time I noticed the high waist on her garment, and it made me think of something from the Napoleonic era. The soft glow from the fire added to the illusion of the far past.

Barrett was leaning against the mantel. My initial glimpse hadn't been any hallucination; he'd changed his business suit for a costume from a long-lost century. He wore a flowing, open-necked white shirt with loose, full sleeves, some form-fitting riding pants, and a supple pair of boots. All he needed now was a fancy coat and sword, or maybe a brace of dueling pistols to complete the effect. With his thick hair now carelessly tumbling over his forehead, he looked like a friendlier version of Brontë's Heathcliff.

The intervening glass muffled things a little, but I had no trouble making out their voices.

"I don't think they'll be back," he was saying to her. "They just had a few questions about someone I once knew."

"What about her?" she asked. "That young man seemed very anxious to find her."

He shook his head. "I think they'll look elsewhere now."

"You're still troubled."

"Only because I don't want them to come back. I don't want them bothering you."

"My protector," she said, and broke into a sudden smile. It transformed her face and I could see strong evidence of the pretty young woman she had once been. He smiled as well and came to kneel on one knee next to her, taking one of her hands in both of his. Her eyes clouded with doubt. "Will it be different for us, do you think?"

He kissed her hand quickly, reassuringly. "I certainly hope so, dearest. I will do everything possible to make it so for you." He caressed her face tenderly and kissed her forehead. "I promise."

"Really?" The playfulness was back in her expression.

"I'll show you."

He undid her choker necklace and kissed her forehead again, then her eyes, then her mouth. His arms half lifted her from the settee, pulling her body close to his own. Her head tilted back and he moved lower, his lips closing possessively over the two faint marks on her throat that the choker had concealed.

Her own arms were wrapped tightly around him, one hand pressing on the back of his neck to help guide him to that special spot. His jaw worked and a tremor ran through her whole body in response. He stayed there, drinking from her, for what seemed a very long time.

My conscience was working a blue streak. How do you know where to draw the line between curiosity and voyeurism? I went transparent, pushed away into the darkness beyond the window, and floated around the corner of the house.

That they were lovers was no stunning surprise. Their style of going about it was much more sedate than some of the wild tumbles that Bobbi and I had shared, but to each his own. Despite their quiet method, the passion was there, and I could sympathize with it enough to get stirred up myself, but Bobbi was nearly eight hundred miles away. As for the horses in the backyard—they were for food, not sex. There is a very decided difference between the two, at least for me. I'd just have to hike around in the woods until the pleasant frustration wore off, and try to make up for it when I got back to Chicago. Bobbi wouldn't mind.

The other thing bothering me was Barrett's wish for us to stay away. Maybe he was afraid we'd be rocking the sweet little boat he'd gotten for himself as Emily Francher's secretary. On the other hand, he'd have to be a better actor than Escott if that love scene I'd just watched had been a fake. If he genuinely loved her, then he'd want to protect her from his past indiscretions and present troubles. Put in his place, I'd be doing the same.

Then there was Emily Francher wondering if things would be different for them. Was she talking about a better relationship than he'd had with Maureen or whether Barrett's attentions would bring her back when she died? I was inclined to think it was the latter, since she didn't seem to know all that much about Maureen.

Note that word—seem. Being lousy at lying myself often made me vulnerable to the lies of others. But right now I was too interested in finding Maureen to want to give anyone the benefit of a doubt.

The sound of radio music eventually tugged me out of my thoughts. It came from some open French windows on the second floor and reminded me that there was at least one other member of the household.

I drifted up and steadied myself with a ghostly hand on the veranda railing just outside the fan of light filtering through the lacy white curtains.

Laura Francher, the lithe blond I'd seen swimming in the pool below, was before a large mirror that nearly covered one wall of her bedroom. A balance bar ran in front of it at waist height, but she wasn't bothering with any ballet practice at the moment. Instead, she was swaying to the music of Rudy Vallee; her eyes shut as she danced with a pretend partner. Her feet were bare, but then so was the rest of her.

I hung back in the shadows and settled into solidity again. I only wanted to be able to hear the radio better. Honest.

I noted with quick interest that she was a natural blond. It was certainly fascinating, but I didn't think Escott would find that particular detail of much use in our investigation. My conscience was trying to kick up again, though at times I could be selectively deaf to it. What a pretty girl did to occupy herself alone in her room was her business—but the view was *very* absorbing. I reflected that this kind of detecting could easily become addictive. I'd give myself just one more minute and then move on.

When the minute ran out, Rudy was still singing and by then I was speculating what she'd look like performing a fast rumba when she abruptly stopped and scampered to a closet. She emerged a second later, hastily belting up a bright yellow bathrobe. Smoothing down her long hair, she opened the door.

It was Barrett and she let him in.

He was still in his poet's costume and looking less relaxed than he'd been with Emily. The whites of his eyes were solid red, still suffused with her blood. Their condition didn't seem to bother Laura, who shut the door behind him readily enough. The radio continued to blare, which was bad for me since I couldn't hear a word of their conversation. It was like watching a play through a telescope.

Barrett was obviously uncomfortable, but Laura appeared not to notice and settled in at her dressing table to brush out her thick, straight hair. Her loosely tied bathrobe was starting to come apart with the activity. She didn't bother to correct things. Barrett had called her a child, and so she must have been five years ago—not anymore. Her every movement indicated the confident maturity of a young woman who knows she is desirable.

He gently took the hairbrush from her hand, wanting her undivided attention. He'd finally worked himself up to say something, and it seemed pretty important. I ground my teeth, wishing I could read lips.

As he spoke, Laura's face grew cool and lost all expression. She studied her reflection in the mirror above the table. Barretts' own lack of reflection in it was nothing new to her, either. He ran out of words eventually and waited for some reaction. Rudy was replaced by Bing Crosby before the girl smiled and sighed out a reply.

Barretts' mouth opened; he was surprised and relieved at once. Their talk continued, apparently along the lines of questions and reassurances until both were smiling. He relaxed, lighter looking now that his errand was out of the way, and watched as she retrieved her brush and resumed work on her hair.

Her robe was still more than a little loose and her movements opened it wider. He spoke to her and she looked up and smiled at his concern. She had wonderfully large eyes, the kind that were made for men to get lost in. For all his age and experience, Barrett was no less vulnerable to them than anyone else, myself included. His hand went out and softly stroked the length of her shining hair.

She liked it but was content only to look at him and to wait for his next move. He obviously wanted her, his expression made that plain enough, but not just yet. He stood up, murmured something, and let himself out the door. She stared after him, then turned back to the mirror to smile patiently at herself. As far as she was concerned, his upcoming seduction was a foregone conclusion.

The car was at a slight tilt where it rested off the shoulder of the road. The night-shadowed landscape beyond the windshield looked askew from where I was sitting, which more or less suited my state of mind.

I talked and Escott smoked and listened, getting an earful. My description of the house and staff lacked for no detail, but when I got around to Barrett's relationship with Emily and Laura, I did some self-conscious editing. Escott noticed, but chose not to comment on what was left out, and kept puffing on his pipe. He continued to do so long after I'd wound down and stopped.

"Well?" I asked. The crickets out in the woods had held the floor long enough. "What do you think?"

His pipe had gone dead. Frowning absently, he tapped it empty and pocketed it for the time being. "I think this needs more study," he stated.

"More study?"

"But you've done some excellent groundwork." He paged through my scribbled notes, looking at each name. "I'll get busy with these tomorrow and try to follow up on the destination of Maureen's departing cab."

He saw my disappointment and added, "Our other alternative is to wait indefinitely on Barrett."

We'd given him the name of our Manhattan hotel and the mailing address in Chicago so he could send us word of Maureen. To me, it was nothing more than manners with no substance. We went through the motions, but I didn't believe anything would come of it.

"The hell with that," I growled.

Escott nodded agreement and started the car.

The next night I woke up in a strange room, which is very disorienting when you don't expect it, and I didn't.

My trunk was shoved against a wall too close for the lid to hinge back so I had to sieve my way out. I spent a few seconds gaping at the change of scene, then called to Escott to demand an explanation, except he wasn't there to provide one. He hadn't left a note, but since his suitcase was making creases in the homemade quilt on one of the tidy beds, it was reasonable to expect him back sometime soon. He knew my habits.

I was surrounded by dark, heavy furniture, old-fashioned wallpaper, framed scenes of us winning the American Revolution, and handmade rugs. Outside and one story down were huge trees, a gravel drive, cut lawn, fresh air, and a picturesque white picket fence. We were probably not in Manhattan.

The stationery on a tall bureau introduced me to the Glenbriar Inn of Glenbriar, Long Island, and a thin brochure pointed out sites of historical interest. It was so absorbing I dropped it flat the second Escott keyed the door and walked in.

"I was a bit delayed," he apologized. "I'd hoped to be back earlier in order to soften the shock."

"Too bad, I've used up all my double takes for the night. You missed a beaut when I came out and found this. What's with the move?"

"I thought it necessary and more convenient to the investigation if we could be closer to the Francher estate. This village happens to be where they do most of their local business."

"It must have been a million laughs getting me and the trunk upstairs."

"I had help, but I'd rather not go into details at the present." Slowly and painfully, he stretched out on the other, uncluttered bed, and I noticed that he was looking very green at the edges.

"You all right?"

"As well as can be expected after imbibing large amounts of coffee, tea, and beer, mixed with sweetbreads, biscuits, pretzels, and salted nuts."

I looked down with sympathetic horror. He managed not to groan or clutch his aching stomach, though he had every right to do so.

"Any reason why you put away all that stuff, or do you just go into a fit now and then?"

"The tearooms, inns, and pubs of this tour-minded place require plenty of custom if you expect to learn any of the local gossip. Did you know William Cullen Bryant used to live not far from here? They have a pair of his spectacles on display in a tearoom museum, which was urgently recommended to me as a pleasant diversion for the day."

"His spectacles?" I echoed, trying to sound impressed.

"Indeed."

"Well, well. Who'd have thought it?"

"Indeed."

"Charles . . ."

He raised one hand so I could bear with him one more time. "Tell me, *who* was William Cullen Bryant?"

"Editor of the *New York Evening Post* back in the last century."

"No relation to the orator of the Scopes trial?"

"That was William Jennings Bryan, not Bryant." I wondered just how much he'd had to drink.

He shut his eyes and gave in to a shudder. "Have you ever tried to turn a conversation around from spectacles to house fires?"

I admitted that I'd never had the opportunity.

"It does require some skill in order not to get caught at it. If people sense you are eager to learn something specific, you end up with too much information or none at all. Let them talk on their own and you learn everything you need."

"How can you have too much information?"

"Many feel the plain truth is too plain and requires embroidery."

"Does this mean you got more dope on the Franchers?"

"A good deal, mixed up with a half dozen other families, but the fire was an excellent point on which to focus their attention. It was quite the nine-day wonder, and once the subject had been introduced, one thing led to another."

"So tell me already."

Eyes shut and hands cradling his head, he began talking to the ceiling. "Violet Francher, the mother who died in the fire, was quite the proper and respectable dowager, but of the sort best admired from a distance. She had a sharp tongue, a temper bordering on the apoplectic, and I need hardly mention she had a difficult time keeping servants for very long.

"She was alone the night of the fire, as her housekeeper left her employ some three days earlier. Daughter Emily, ward Laura, and Mr. Barrett were all at their own house. Laura usually stayed with Violet during her spring holiday from school, but had moved in with Emily until a new housekeeper could be hired. The general consensus is the girl was very lucky, or she might have died along with her guardian."

"It took place at night?"

"I'm glad you noticed that. I found it of extreme interest in conjunction with some other facts."

"What are they?"

"I'm coming to them."

"Why wasn't the old lady at the daughter's house as well?"

"I'm coming to that, too. Sometime in January—this is in 1931—Emily hired Mr. Jonathan Barrett as her secretary. They met at a party given by Violet, who still attempted to maintain some touch with society. Barrett came as a guest of a guest, had no real references, but was obviously educated and cultured. Not long after his hiring, the rumors started that something was 'going on' between him and Emily. They circulated the servants' hall and into the town and eventually made their way back to Violet, who was all moral outrage.

"She immediately made her views known in considerable detail to her daughter, and the upshot was that Barrett had to go. Much to her shock and surprise, Emily flatly refused. For the next few months, neither woman spoke to the other, and when they did, they were usually trading salvos over Barrett."

"How did he handle all this?"

"He kept in the neutral background as much as possible. He turned down the most outrageous bribes, though the question was raised as to whether Violet actually had the money. He survived the investigations of a private detective hired to find something, anything from his past that might be used to influence Emily against him—"

"What about his influence on Emily?"

He got my double meaning. "Hypnosis is a possibility, but I put much stock in the fact that Emily was genuinely in love with him. Your report of last night's rendezvous makes that a virtual certainty."

"Unless they were both faking it."

"Granted, but to return—"

"Yeah, go ahead."

"All her efforts having failed to budge him, Violet assembled a trio of psychiatrists in need of funds for the purpose of having Emily declared mentally incompetent—"

"What?"

"A tactic that had every chance of working. After all, Emily did suffer one nervous breakdown years ago, why should she not suffer another?"

"Suffer is right, her mother must have been . . ." I was at a loss. Calling her crazy didn't seem strong enough.

"Right round the twist?" he queried. "Agreed. This was a woman who wanted and usually did exercise total control over those around her—particularly over her daughter."

"So what happened with the doctors?"

"It all fell through because of the fire and her death."

"Very convenient for Barrett."

"Yes, and something else struck me as convenient and suggestively odd: in the newspaper accounts of the fire not one of them mentions his name."

I chewed that one over. "He'd naturally want a low profile. . . ."

"Low to nonexistent. Also, there was no gossip connecting him to the tragedy. If anything, some people felt Violet had brought it upon herself—'God's judgment' for having such a foul temper and that sort of thing."

"But you think he did it?"

"I think," he said after a moment, "that if it was not an accident, then any of three people could have done it—or perhaps all three or any combination. Barrett is the most likely, more so than Emily or Laura."

"Laura was just a kid at the time."

"Remember that story I told you about the grandmother, her cat and the two homicidal grandchildren?"

I made an appropriate noise to indicate it was not something I was likely to forget. "What's her motive, though?"

"Violet Francher's overbearing personality? One cannot choose one's relatives."

"You could add a fourth, the housekeeper who quit."

"Ah, but she was very much elsewhere learning the duties of her job some ten miles away. On the other hand, that frayed wire could just as easily have been tampered with days earlier and left as a sort of waiting bomb, or the whole thing could have been an accident, after all."

"Look, is this anything we can really use?"

"It is knowledge, usable or not. Only time will reveal its value to us."

"So now what?"

Most of the green in his gills had faded and his eyes were sparking with new energy when he opened them. "We take a ride in a cab."

"We—you found the cab?"

"More important, I found the driver. His name is John Henry Banks and he is president, owner, and sole employee of Banks Cab Company. And"—he glanced at his watch—"he is due here in fifteen minutes."

"You talked with him?"

"I made an appointment by phone for him to pick us up."

"How in hell did you find him?"

"Sometimes in this type of work antic coincidence plays its part. One of the men I talked with today was part of the demolition and cleanup crew that worked on the burned Francher house. He mentioned that the day before they started the job, his cousin John Henry had been called out to the estate to pick up a fare. It should give you an idea of how exciting the pace of life is in Glenbriar that something so trivial is remembered."

"But it's a break for us."

"We shall see."

At seven-thirty a blue-and-yellow checkered cab pulled up outside the inn and a little brown man in gray work clothes and a peaked cap got out and stumped up to the front door.

"Call for Escott!" he bellowed, poking his head just inside.

I hoped Escott hadn't wanted a low profile for himself. If so, then John Henry Banks had just shot it all to hell. We'd already gotten a few curious looks from the desk clerk. Correction, I had gotten the looks. Escott had both our names on the register, but he'd been the only one they'd seen up till now. The clerk was giving me a fishy eye, trying to figure out where I'd come from.

We followed Banks out and Escott told him to drive to the edge of town. It took him all of one minute.

"Now where to?" he asked, looking at us from the rear-view mirror. I was squeezed flat against the door, but he got puzzled about the empty spot I should have been in and twisted around to make sure I was still aboard. Escott distracted him before things got out of hand.

"Mr. Banks, I have a question for you. . . ."

"Eh?"

"I need to know if you can recall a fare you picked up five years ago."

He gawked at us. He had a square face with a sharp nose and chin, thin brown hair, and large, innocent brown eyes. "You serious? Five years? I don't keep those kind of records, mister."

"Have you ever picked up a fare from the Francher estate?"

He started to roll his eyes and shake his head but stopped midway. "Here now, the Franchers'? The place where the old lady was burned up?"

"The same."

"I maybe could remember," he hazarded, his eyes flicking meaningfully to the running meter.

Escott smiled. "I'm sure you will, Mr. Banks, given the time. It's a fine cool night out and this country air is quite refreshing." He sat back in the seat as if it were part of a drawing room and he had all night to listen.

Banks responded with a grin. "Okay, as a matter of fact, I do remember that one."

"Please tell us about it."

"Why do you want to know?"

Escott now looked at the meter. "Then again, this air can be too much of a good thing. I shouldn't like to catch a chill, so perhaps we should return immediately to the inn. . . ."

Banks caught on fast. "Well, I was in my office—which is my house—and got his call. It's just me and the one car, you know, and business is pretty thin, so I'm open all the time. Anyway, this call comes telling me to come up to the Francher place, which I never been to before on account of the old lady and her daughter being rich with their own cars don't need any cabs. Course by then the old lady got burned up in the fire, my cousin Willie was gonna help tear down the old house—"

"The phone call, Mr. Banks?" Escott gently urged.

"Oh, yeah. I got out there, had to argue my way past Mayfair's wife—she's the housekeeper there, and what a temper she's got. You'd think she owned the place the way she throws her weight around. She went to call the house to see if anyone wanted a cab, and when she got back she looked like she'd just bit a bad lemon. Mayfair let me through and I drove up and saw the house—the burned one, and what a mess that was—"

Escott raised an eyebrow.

"Oh. Well. I got to the other house, the new place that the daughter had built, and there was this lady standing out front waiting—"

"What'd she look like?" I asked.

"I dunno. She was little, dark clothes, wore one of them hats so you couldn't see her face."

"With a veil?" Maureen often wore one to shade her eyes from the afterglow of sunset.

"Yeah. Looked like a widow at a funeral. She had a trunk, but I always keep some rope handy for stuff like that. It was some trouble I had trying to tie the thing in place—"

"Where did she want to go? What did she say to you?"

"She hardly said nothing, just told me to load the trunk on and to take her to Port Jefferson as quickly as I could."

"Where's that?"

"That's what threw me, too. I expected it to be at least to Queens, and this place is nearly sixty miles away in the opposite direction. It's along the north shore of the island. I asked if she was sure, and she nodded and got inside and told me to hurry it up."

"She was nervous?"

"I guess so. She seemed plenty interested in getting going."

"Was she afraid?"

"Dunno. Who could tell with that black stuff covering her face? All I can tell you for sure was that she was in a hurry."

"Did she say why she was going to Port Jefferson?"

"I asked—by way of conversation, just to be friendly—but she never answered, so I shut up. Some of these rich dames can be pretty snooty. She was quiet for the whole trip, and sixty miles is a long way to be quiet."

"Why did you think she was rich?" asked Escott.

"You think the Franchers would know anyone poor?" he reasoned logically.

"Where in Port Jefferson did you take her?"

"Now that's the funny part. She wanted to be dropped at the ferry."

"Ferry?"

"Port Jefferson has a ferry running across the sound to Bridgeport. It was full night by then and the ferry was closed down and I told her so. She just had me untie her trunk and leave it there with her on the side of the road. She paid the fare, gave me a five-dollar tip, and I drove off feeling pretty good."

"You seem to have a very clear memory of all this."

"I guess I do. I mean, besides this being the only person I ever picked up from the Francher place, she was the only person who ever gave me a tip that big. I ain't gonna forget something like that so soon."

Escott turned to me. "What would she want in Bridgeport?"

I shrugged. Why would she want to be crossing water by boat? It was difficult enough for me to bear going over on a bridge.

He went back to John Henry Banks. "You are absolutely certain of this sequence of events?"

"That's the truth, mister. Take it or leave it."

He took it, but neither of us liked it.

Banks drove us back to the inn. It was my turn, so I paid off the meter and gave him a tip equal to Maureen's, which put him into an excellent mood. He grinned and thanked us along with instructions to call him anytime if we ever needed another drive.

Escott strode purposefully up the stone-bordered walk. I caught up with him in the small lobby just as he was accepting a thin phone book from the desk clerk. I craned over his shoulder to see the pages.

He stopped at cab companies in the area—a very short listing—and Banks was at the top of the column, a fact Escott noted aloud to me.

"If she needed a taxi, she would consult a directory and the first listing might be her first choice, as it evidently turned out. How do you feel about a long drive tonight?"

"To Port Jefferson?"

"And possibly to Bridgeport."

On a boat. Across all that water. Damn.

"Or perhaps not," he added, noting my expression.

"I'm no Popeye the Sailor, but if Maureen could take it, so can I. I guess."

"Brave heart," he said, and signaled to the clerk to start checking us out.

While he was busy with that I went upstairs to bring down his bag and my trunk. I opened our door and stopped cold. Jonathan Barrett was standing by the window, hands clasped behind him and looking at me as though I, and not he, were the unwelcome intruder.

6

HE was back in twentieth-century clothing again, though a vestige of the past still clung to him with his ramrod posture and wind-combed hair. The five-second stare he gave me served as his only preamble. His eyes were cold, matching his tone of voice. "Last night I was made to understand that you were leaving for the city."

"We did." I quietly shut the door behind me. "And then we came back."

"Obviously. Why?"

"We had a little more checking to do."

"Yes, you've the dirty job of sifting through someone else's laundry. This is yet a dull village with gossip as the chief source of entertainment. It didn't take long for the story of your friend's pub crawling to filter back to our own servants' hall." He looked ready to belt me again and shoved down the impulse with a visible effort. "When *are* you planning to leave?"

"We're checking out now."

"For good?"

"Why are you so anxious about it?"

"I'm only protecting my—Miss Francher and her family. Having the two of you intruding into her private business is entirely abhorrent—"

"You mean about the fire?"

"Of course I do. What has it to do with your trying to find Maureen?"

"I thought maybe you could tell me."

"Tell you what? There's nothing to tell. The fire was over and done with long before Maureen ever came to see me."

"And you figure there's no connection?"

"How can there be?" He raised a hand. "No, don't bother answering that with another damned question. I can see you haven't the heart to care about the kind of damage you're doing."

"What damage?"

He started to shake his head in exasperation at my apparent stupidity, then caught on that I'd been trying to goad him.

"What damage, Barrett?" I pursued.

He said nothing and only glared.

"What are you afraid of?"

His face was hard now, nearly ugly from the emotions rumbling under the surface. He looked taller and I could almost feel the anger pulsing from him.

"If you were in my place, what would you be doing to find her?"

That one struck a chord. He paced the length of the small room once with slow steps, subsiding into himself. He stopped next to me, trying to bore a hole through my brain with his gaze. "You said you were checking out. Are you going for good?"

"I don't know."

"Why is that?"

"I can't really say."

"Because you lack knowledge or because you don't trust me?"

"You're sharp, Barrett."

"Yes, and I've had as much of you as I can stomach. Do what you must to find Maureen, but leave the Franchers out of it. Leave them alone and stay out of my way."

Or what? I asked him as much with my expression.

There was murder in his return look, and he took a step toward me to carry it out, or so I thought. The color abruptly faded from his dark clothes and his pale skin drained to the lifeless white of the truly dead. His outline wavered and swam in on itself, melting and merging into a shapeless, gray, man-sized *thing*.

Impossibly hanging in midair, it twisted like a slow cyclone and tore by me. The wake of its brushing passage pierced me to the bone with a rush of arctic cold. The gray mass slammed silently against the window panes, fell through them as though they weren't really there, and whirled away into the night wind. I rushed forward just in time to see it hurtle across the yard below to vanish into the cover of some intervening trees. A few moments later I heard the innocuous, ordinary roar of a car gunning to life. Its tires spun and screamed against the pavement, an audible expression of Barrett's anger.

Escott often complained that my disappearing act unnerved him. His limited human eyes missed most of the show, though. He didn't know about this, about what it looked like to me. I'd witnessed it once before myself, but not in the close, calm normality of a well-lighted room.

I was still shaking when he came upstairs to help with the luggage.

Sixty miles of bucolic country broken up by quaint towns and picturesque villages chock-full of historical significance can get to you after a while. An hour of it left me longing for the comfort of concrete, streetlights, and traffic signs. Barrett's visit had left a bad taste in my mind.

I'd told Escott all about it, of course. He listened but was inclined to shrug it off for the moment.

"The man has a point—" he started to say.

"But only if he's telling the truth about protecting the Franchers. It's more likely he's trying to protect himself. What I want to know is, what's he trying to hide?"

"Any number of things which we have discussed at length: his job, his regard for Miss Francher . . . and very possibly his condition."

"Condition? You mean—"

"Yes, the one you both share. That's a detail about yourself that you are wisely reluctant to reveal to people. I should imagine he feels the same way. An investigation such as ours could quickly place him in an untenable position. Would you not also be a bit nervous if someone started looking into your past and present?"

"Jeez, yes. But you said Violet Francher already tried to do that and it didn't faze him. So what's the difference now?"

"You, old man. You're the only one stopping him from fixing me with a basilisk gaze and instructing me to mind my own business. Perhaps he did do just that with Mrs. Francher's own agent. This time Barrett is denied the luxury and is no doubt suffering from the frustration of it all."

He was right, but I was still uneasy and promised myself to keep both eyes wide open if we went back to Glenbriar. I was safe enough, but if Barrett lost his temper, he could snap Escott like a twig—body or mind, take your pick.

Escott helped to make the rest of the trip bearable by reporting on his day and the other details he'd discovered about the Francher household.

"The maid, cook, housekeeper, and gardener are all employees of long standing with Miss Emily. When Barrett arrived, some horses were acquired, along with a groom to care for them. Barrett is the only employee to actually sleep in the house now. When the maid and cook were moved out to live over the garage, the natural conclusion was that they were not meant to see certain things, hence the gossip."

"Which has some truth behind it, from what I saw the other night," I put in.

He acknowledged with a nod. "Yes, though I may also add that there is a general sympathy for their employer because of the way her mother died. Few people seem ready to condemn the woman for keeping a handsome young man on the payroll."

"What do these people think of Barrett?"

"I can only report that hardly anyone outside the immediate household has ever seen him; which has also garnered the general approval of the locals. If there is something 'going on,' he has the good manners to confine himself to the Francher estate and is not attempting to spread his wicked ways among his neighbors."

"Does that include any society people?"

"Miss Francher has willfully cut herself off from her social and financial peers, so they are relieved of the unpleasant duty of making any public judgment of her private life. That Miss Francher is excluded from their tea parties and other events of import matters not one whit to the lady."

"And her family?"

"That is something I plan to check into—but discreetly," he added, catching my look. "I have no wish to call the wrath of Mr. Barrett down upon my head."

"Amen."

"As for the inhabitants of Glenbriar, Emily Francher may do whatever she pleases in private, as long as it stays that way. If she were anyone else, she'd find life a bit more hostile."

"The old Hester Prynne bit?"

Not having the benefit of an American education, he didn't understand the reference. I gave him a brief summary of Hawthorne's book until he did.

He agreed with the general idea, but added one of his own. "Perhaps it is closer to the point to say that her money makes the difference here. If a poor man does something out of the norm, he's condemned for a lunatic. When a rich man indulges in kind, he is affectionately tolerated as an eccentric. Thus we have it that no one thinks anything strange about the very late hours kept by the principals of the household."

"They're a pretty understanding bunch around here."

"The Francher bills are always paid on time. That counts for much in terms of tolerance and goodwill these days."

"These days more than most."

Conversation lagged for a quarter hour and I watched the woods on either side blur past.

"Sixty miles is a long way to be quiet," Escott quoted, breaking the silence by doing a perfect mimic of Banks. It jolted me, kicking a vagueness into a certainty.

"It's too much."

"What is?"

"The tip. Banks said he got a five-dollar tip from Maureen. It's too much."

"Perhaps she thought it to be a necessary compensation after such a long trip."

"No, think about her past, about the time she grew up in. In those days you tipped in pennies."

"Some women eschew the practice altogether."

"She wasn't one of them. I mean, she did all right for herself, but she was never one to throw her money around. In an extravagant mood she might have tipped him a buck, but never five, not unless she pulled the wrong bill out by mistake."

"That could well have been the case."

"Yeah." But I still had some doubt souring my mind and he knew it.

"What alternative do you suggest?" he asked.

"Like maybe five years ago Barrett called Banks out to the house and put it into his head he was taking Maureen to Port Jefferson. He gave him the fare and a five-dollar tip to help him remember it all the way he's supposed to."

"Complicated. Why should he do that?"

"So it looks on the level with Mayfair or anyone else who might have seen her arrive at the estate."

"Such as Emily Francher?"

"Well, figure it. Barrett's got a soft spot for himself with her, and then Maureen shows up. She doesn't like what he's doing and could queer it for him but good if she drops the wrong word in Emily's ear."

"Would she have done so?"

"That doesn't matter. What does is that Barrett thought she would."

"And you think Barrett—"

"Might have done something. Yeah."

"That he might have killed Maureen?"

After a long time I said, "Yeah," and I hated saying it.

Port Jefferson had a shipyard, some gravel pits, and the ferry, all dark now. Compared to Glenbriar it was a bustling metropolis, which wasn't saying much, but then some places aren't at their best at night. Escott and I split up. I took the hotels and he went to inflict more damage on his liver at the taverns. I advised him to find a diner first and line his stomach with the biggest, greasiest butter-fried hamburger he could handle. He didn't look thrilled at the prospect, but nodded agreement and walked off with a grim set to his jaw.

Maureen's stopover—if she had stopped—had taken place at the height of the tourist season. No one remembered a lone woman with a trunk arriving at night five years ago. I talked my way into examining hotel-registration books and learned a lot about kindness from various clerks and managers offering what help they could.

After running out of hotels, I checked out all the boardinghouses I could find, even knowing that Maureen would have avoided them as a matter of course. Like me, she would have preferred the relative privacy and anonymity of a hotel to spend her vulnerable daylight time. But I had to be certain. I covered everything.

Hours later, options exhausted, I climbed back into the car to wait for Escott. We had no set time to meet, though. When the first faint pangs of hunger started up I went in search of a meal.

No stockyards and no stables; it looked like the locals only ate fish, and duck—at least in the business district. I widened my hunting radius to less urbanized areas and soon caught the unmistakable scent of cow manure on a random puff of wind.

There were more stops than starts involved following it, but my nose eventually led me to an open field populated by several bovines clustered under a tree. I climbed through the fence, watched where my feet were going, and strolled up.

They seemed to know I wasn't there for an old-fashioned milking. As a cow, they all moved away. Picking one out, I optimistically followed. She proved to be quite agile for her size and energetic after spending the whole day eating her head off. Though country bred myself, I'd forgotten how fast cattle can move when they want to, and my dinner got away.

I picked out another, waited until it stopped, and calculated the distance. It bawled unhappily as though reading my mind. Disappearing, I rushed forward, felt its bulk loom close, and went solid with my arms reaching out to wrap around its neck.

The cow had other ideas and bawled again, tossing herself (and me) around like a rodeo trainee. She dragged me over half the field, deaf to my urgent pleas for quiet and oblivious to that special influence I usually have over animals. It only belatedly occurred to me that all the other animals had been in small pens with no place to run. I let go, managed to stay on my soggy feet, and old Bossy galloped off to be with the rest of the girls.

It was ridiculous. I had an easier job finding cooperative livestock in the heart of the city. After a few feet of weary trudging, I noticed the disgusting state of my shoes and opted to go transparent the rest of the way. The wind was in the right direction; I let it take me toward a group of buildings at the far end of the field.

By now I had trouble telling the difference between the yard manure and the supply I had with me. Each shed had to be examined by sight, not smell. Unfortunately, it is also almost impossible to take a casual walk through a working farm. You not only have to contend with uneven and odorous ground clutter and mud, but the local tenants as well. Never mind Farmer Jones and his shotgun, it's his animals that are dangerous.

Chickens are fairly brainless and confined to coops, but ducks are usually allowed to roam free to scavenge and play in their pond. It was just my bad luck that I blundered right into a flock and sent them on a panicky flight to safety. Mixed in with them were a few geese who made more commotion than all the rest together. In turn, they alerted a small pack of large dogs who charged in helter-skelter, baying in full voice. Their owner coming out of the house packing a gun with a double load of buckshot was a mere afterthought. I didn't stick around to see how the show came out, but vanished and shot up in the general direction of the main barn.

My amorphous form bounced unexpectedly against the vertical wall of wood, nearly sending me solid with the shock. I clung there against the wind and frantically felt around for an opening into the hayloft. It was just above me; I thankfully dribbled over the edge to re-form—and nearly rolled right off my perch. Instead of the loft, I'd shot too high and was hanging onto the roof, and oh, God, I hate heights.

Far, far below, Old MacDonald was circling the yard stirring up the geese and giving a lot of unexpected fun to his pack of semi-tame, lop-eared wolves. They were tearing all over the place, heads down and tails happily fanning, eager to show master how good they were at their job. So what if they never found a thing and only ended up anointing every likely projection turn in turn? It was a great break in the routine.

Shutting my eyes against the dizzy drop, I vanished again and seeped through the barn roof, inching down until I came in contact with a horizontal surface. A second later I ascertained that it was the straw-littered floor of the loft and fairly safe. I lay flat and rested body and mind until the circus outside finally died away.

The barn wasn't much different from the one I'd played in as a kid. I was aware of chickens and mice and another, much larger animal somewhere below. I could have used a ladder, but didn't want to risk making more noise and rousing the dogs again. Far better to disappear and float down to the safe, sane ground.

It was closed up against the night, but seeing in the dark was no problem for me. Over in one partitioned-off corner was a drab white draft horse only a little smaller than Escott's Nash. He was the four-legged answer to a hungry vampire's prayer, and I trotted toward him as though greeting a long-lost friend.

And stopped.

He moved restlessly, his head low and with his ears flat along the skull. His near-hind hoof was raised a little, all set to kick me into the next state as soon as I got in range. If his vocal cords had been designed for it, he'd have been growling.

It just wasn't my night.

Escott was in the car and taking a short snooze. He woke with a slight start when I crawled into the passenger side and flopped wearily back in the seat. My fatigue was mental, not physical.

"Good heavens, where have you been?" he asked, his long nose wrinkling.

"E-i-e-i-o," I muttered darkly, daring him to comment. He read the signs right and restrained himself.

It had been a struggle, but I finally persuaded Dobbin to part with some of what he obviously had too much of. He was a reluctant bastard and considered me to be no better than your average trespasser and thief. When finished, I made a fast and invisible exit from his stall, very mindful of his huge hooves. There was no point giving him a pat of thanks, he'd have only tried to take my arm off at the roots.

Escott had also been drinking, but was showing less wear and tear. As before, he had only a slight glaze to his eyes to indicate he was in no pain.

"You learn anything?" I asked.

He shook his head. "Did you?"

I shook my head.

"Care to go to Bridgeport?" he asked.

During his alcoholic rambles, Escott encountered a man with a boat who was ready to take us across the sound no matter what the hour. He'd had no similar requests five years ago from a lone lady and didn't know of anyone else who had. For a fee, the low, fast launch left over from his days as a rum runner was at our command.

I grimaced at the wide sweep of Long Island Sound. It was silver and calm under the steel-colored sky, a beautiful enough sight from the land. I hadn't always been afraid of water and could still slosh around in a bathtub with the best, but since my change, huge bodies of the open, free-flowing kind sent me into the sick miseries.

"I think I'd like to sit this one out," I finally answered.

"Really?" Escott asked, in a tone that wanted to know why.

Maybe it had to do with my basic need to be in contact with the earth, or maybe it's because I'd been murdered over water. I'd had some recent and very bad experiences occurring in or near water. Driving over it on a bridge was one thing, but crossing all of that bleak expanse in a tiny boat was quite another. I was hard put to suppress an involuntary shudder at the thought of only a thin shell of wood holding back such endless, smothering cold.

I tried to give him an explanation that made sense, but he waved me down after the first few stumbling words.

"That's all right," he said. "I understand."

"I'm not running out on you, am I?"

"No." He sounded fairly amused. "Of course you aren't. I know it's not easy for you at times—and I find that strangely reassuring."

I waved once at Escott from the shore as the launch started to cut its way across the sound. He was looking back, but didn't respond. Not having my night vision, he couldn't see me. With an inward smile, I got back in the car and drove off to one of the better hotels I'd found earlier that evening.

After some personal cleanup, I padded downstairs to find someone brave enough to scrape my shoes back to respectability again. The lobby was as deserted as a church on Saturday night. This was no city hotel with twenty-four-hour clerks to keep you company. The man who'd checked me in had worn his slippers, bathrobe, and a sleepy, resigned expression.

Not dressed for a walk, I was too restless to just sit in my room with the radio on. I was at a loss for activity until I spotted the pay phone. A whole pocketful of change was going to waste in my pants; I fished it all out and got an operator on the line.

Bobbi answered on the first ring and we exclaimed our hellos and "I miss yous" for a while, and she assured me she'd been awake, reminding me there was still a time difference between Chicago and New York.

"New York is old news," I told her. "We're on Long Island now."

"Why? You taking some kind of scenic route?"

"We're following up a lead."

"A good one?"

"Doesn't look it, but Charles wants to be thorough."

"What got you up there?"

"This and that. We . . . we turned up Maureen's old boyfriend."

There was a long pause on her end. "He's like you?"

"Yeah."

"How like you? I mean, what's he like?"

"Well, he's no Dracula, if that's what you're worried about."

"I was, a little."

"If anything, he's sort of a cross between a lounge lizard and Captain Blood."

"Captain *who*?"

Considering my dietary habits, it'd been an alarming reference to bring up. I quickly explained about Sabatini's pirate-hero.

"You don't like him much," she deduced, meaning Barrett and not Sabatini.

"It's mutual, believe me. He's all manners, but I'm watching my back."

"Then why would Maureen have gotten involved with him?"

That question had been eating at me as well. "He's just the type, I guess."

"What type is that?"

"The type who always has women stampeding to get to him. Right now it looks like he'll be stringing two of them along at once."

"Sleeping with both of them?" she asked, always one for clarity.

"It's heading that way—and try this on: they all live in the same house. One of them has money and the other's all ready to seduce him."

"Then he's some kind of a twenty-four-carat idiot," she sniffed. "The same house? That's just asking for trouble. Sooner or later his meal ticket'll figure things out. You can't keep news like that from a woman—we're naturally suspicious."

"You suspicious about me?"

"Of course not, I know you'll never meet anyone else who's better in bed with you than I am."

"You've got me spoiled rotten, sweetheart," I agreed.

And we steamed up the lines with similar talk until an operator broke in to say our time was up and did we want another three minutes? She must have been listening in; I could almost see the smirk on her face that her voice suggested. I dropped in more money and ignored her.

"Listen, Bobbi, I want to ask you something."

"You know the answer to that is yes."

"Thanks, but it'll have to wait until I'm back."

"Damn," she said cheerfully.

"I just wondered, would you ever tip a cab driver five bucks?"

She was shocked. "Five bucks? You think I'm one of the Carnegies or something?"

"Would you ever?"

"Only if I were delirious and lost on the South Side in a sleet storm on Christmas Eve."

"So what kind of woman tips a cabbie five bucks?"

"One that doesn't know what it's worth. You're talking about the idle rich, honey—someone who never had to work for it."

"That's what I thought."

"What's this got to do with things?"

"I'll find that out tomorrow night."

"So when are you coming back?"

"I don't know, baby. Expect me when you see me."

She made a rude noise to communicate her disappointment. "Then get yourself a raincoat. The papers say there's a hurricane moving up the coast and headed your way. I don't want you catching cold from all that wet."

I wasn't certain I could still catch a cold, but took the sentiment as it was given, promising to bundle up for her sake. We said good-bye until the operator cut in again, and then hung up.

The rest of the night went by like paint drying, though I spent some of it scribbling out a note to Escott about Bobbi's views on tipping. I didn't know how useful it would be, but thought it worth pointing out again. After his return I planned to make another visit to the Francher estate, with or without Barrett's permission.

I experienced déjà vu waking up in the Glenbriar Inn again. My trunk was in the same place as before, but pulled out far enough from the wall so I could lift the lid. Escott was there this time, stretched out on his bed, and contentedly up to his neck in newsprint, past and present.

"So what happened in Bridgeport?" I asked, when my few seconds of confusion passed.

"Nothing, as you may have gathered by our return here. I went to taxi companies and examined police, hospital, and as many hotel records as I could manage. I checked morgue records for Jane Does . . ."

He got a sharp look from me.

". . . as a matter of course. She might have thought to use an alias, so I searched for Barretts, Flemings, and Franchers as well as Does and Du-monts. There is no official indication she stopped at all in Bridgeport. She may have merely passed through it, but then one could say there is no real evidence she ever crossed the sound in the first place."

All that footwork and probably a hangover to boot, no wonder he looked stretched and discouraged. "What'd you think of my note?" I'd left it on top of my trunk in Port Jefferson for him to find.

Now he smiled thinly. "We have returned, have we not? I'm strongly inclined to agree with the insights the two of you have concerning that excessive tip. All our roads appear to lead back to the Franchers. A new beginning is in order and we need to start with them."

"That's what I wanted. I'm going out to the house again tonight to see if I can fix up a private little talk with Emily. You have to figure she must know something. Unless Barrett got one of the maids to impersonate Maureen, Emily's just right for the part."

"What about Laura?"

"Too tall. Maureen and Emily are about the same height and build."

"Excellent point."

"You get any more from the locals today?" I noticed that a general lassitude permeated his manner and movements and guessed that he'd been working his butt off in one of the taverns again.

"Most of the talk was about a hurricane that's been coming up the coast. The papers are forecasting massive death and destruction to arrive here soon, and people are busy tying things down in preparation. There's already been a little rain."

I groaned inside. Not so many nights ago, I'd had enough rain to last a few lifetimes; much more and I'd be tempted to move to Death Valley.

"Perhaps you should wait until it blows over," he suggested.

"Nah, I'm all ready to go do it now. I'll go crazy if I have to sit around a hotel room another night memorizing the wallpaper."

"I see your point."

"Look, Charles, this could take a lot of time. Did you really feel like coming along just to wait out in a damp car?"

"Put that way, it does sound most unappealing."

"Besides, you did all that work today; it's my turn now."

He surrendered without argument. "By all means go on without me. I could certainly use a quiet evening of rest."

Lightly put, but he was tired, and I felt better for having him safe at the Glenbriar—away from Barrett and any unforeseen problems.

I wore a dark shirt and black pants with my raincoat. The few tourists hanging around the lobby gaped at me as if I were an out-of-place mobster. They quickly huddled back into their mah-jongg game to resume discussion about how run down things were becoming with that Democrat in the White House.

The rented Ford was in a gravel lot behind the inn. I braved a stiff breeze and a few thick drops of rain and nosed it onto the road.

The possibility of Barrett discovering me going about my unlawful trespass of his employer's property kept my mind unpleasantly busy. Not that illegal entry was something to weigh on my conscience; I was simply shrinking from the embarrassment of getting caught. I planned to be very, very careful.

Preoccupied with the evening ahead, I took a wrong turn and found myself going in a miles-wide circle back to Glenbriar. The rain was coming down heavily and the wind gusted against the car, rocking it. I couldn't go back, the road was too narrow for a U-turn, and I didn't want to chance getting stuck in one of the steep ditches running along either side of the paving. I squinted ahead for a crossroad or driveway to use.

A mile later, the rain was pouring so hard that I was going less than half the posted speed limit. The wind drove the water straight at the front window, making the wipers useless. The headlights only bounced off a shimmering quicksilver wall, illuminating nothing. My night vision was no good for this kind of a mess. The speedometer pointer dropped down below ten miles an hour and I still felt I was going too fast.

Escott had had the right idea about a quiet evening resting up. It was past time to call it a night. At this point I wasn't all that sure of finding my way back to Glenbriar, much less getting to the Francher estate. Even if I did reach it, I was facing a long walk through the woods, and I could hardly conceal my presence while leaving a dripping trail throughout the house. Unless the hurricane blew it into the sound, the place would still be there tomorrow.

Its taillights were on—the only warning I had of its presence. I hit the brakes, skidded badly, but stopped just short of back-ending a car stopped in the road. I punched my horn once. They didn't move. Disgusted, I decided to pull around and hoped no one was coming up in the other lane to hit me.

A semi-clear patch opened in the shifting gray curtain of water. My headlights just caught the bright blue-and-yellow check design on the trunk of the car.

Glenbriar was only a small town and John Henry Banks was someone I'd be bound to run into again before our business was ended, but I suddenly got very cold inside. The uneasy feeling persisted the longer I sat and thought about it, getting worse instead of better as I tried to come up with a good reason for Banks to be out here tonight. Scowling at the rain, I swallowed back my fears and levered out of the car into the hurricane.

It was like standing under Niagara, except the water was horizontal instead of vertical because of the wind. I put my back to it, steadied myself with a hand on the car, and staggered over to the passenger door of the cab. It was on the lee side and offered some minuscule protection against the raw force trying to bowl me over.

I couldn't see inside the window for all of the water streaming down. I thumped on the door a few times on the off chance that I was interrupting a lovers' rendezvous and opened it.

As it turned out, I wasn't interrupting anything. It was all finished by now.

Banks was heeled over on his right side, one arm curled beneath him and the other trailing off under the dashboard. His eyes sagged open, looking at nothing. His pockets were turned out and a few stray coins littered the floor. Blood covered his head and face and flooded the seat where he lay. The red smell of it smothered my senses and jammed all thought.

Maybe I said something. I don't know. The shock had hit like a block of ice, leaving me stunned. As though someone else were doing it for me, my hand went out in a futile effort to find a pulse.

"Cha . . ."

I jumped like I'd touched a hot wire. Banks was alive.

". . . nged." Nonsense slurred from his slack mouth. His eyes were still open and fixed. He was unaware of me.

I leaned in close. "Banks, who did it?"

"Change," he said clearly.

Disturbed by me, a quarter dropped from the edge of the seat and hit the floor. The sound as it landed was lost, masked over by the storm.

"Who hit you, Banks? Who did it?"

"Not."

"Who was it? Did you know him?"

"Lie."

I didn't dare move him. I needed help, but didn't know where to go to find it. A house with a phone could be only yards away, but invisible in the rain. Maybe I could flag down another car if it passed by.

"Was it a man? A woman?"

"Tall."

"Who, Banks?"

"F-fine."

"Banks!"

His eyes were still open, but he'd slipped away. My hand was touching his neck and I felt it happen. The knowledge spread up from my fingers straight to the brain and coiled down my spine. One second he was a man with dreams and needs and desires like the rest of us, and the next he was an inert, empty carcass.

A slow and sticky kind of sickness started in my guts and began working its way up. I quickly backed out of the cab, holding on to the door for support, and sucked in drafts of cold air and rain. I did not vomit in the ditch running along the roadside, though it would have been a kind of release. My condition doesn't always allow me the luxury of a human weakness. The bile stayed in my throat, clinging to the back of my mouth, and wouldn't go away.

I checked Banks. He was dead, I'd not made a mistake. The side of his head was smashed in, hard. The killer had been very fast; so fast that Banks had had no time to blink. I reached in and closed his eyes with numb fingers.

The bile surged inside. Maybe I was going to be sick, after all. I backed out again, the rain whirling around me, and leaned on the cab for support.

I heard a close, sharp *thud*.

My feet slipped away from under me. I toppled forward against the cab, cracking my chin hard on the wet roof.

Thud.

I felt the second blow and sprawled flat on my face on the streaming road. Water bounced up from the paving, stinging and filling my eyes.

The third was much harder. My head was firmly braced against the un-yielding road surface. Whoever was doing it could bring a lot of momentum to bear with their downward swing.

The fourth.

I couldn't hear the rain hissing anymore. The world was reduced to cottony silence and the softly pulsing light beneath my eyelids.

The fifth.

The light was gone.

I don't remember the sixth or seventh.

Just as well.

7

RAIN pelting against my sodden coat.

Light.

A hand on my wrist.

Mitch, are they—

My God, Elma, get back in the car. Fear in his voice.

Footsteps. A door slams shut.

The man keeps saying *my God* over and over again before he finally backs away and leaves.

His voice raises in a shout, then a curse.

The wet rush and roar as a car drives quickly past.

Rain.

Wind.

Another car. The road under me announces its approach.

He shouts again. This time it stops. Light pierces my sightless eyes. Voices.

. . . get to a phone . . .

. . . Trent place, just up the road . . .

. . . police first, it's too late for . . .

More lights, more voices. Questions.

An eternity of rain and wind.

. . . thought something was wrong so we stopped . . .

. . . Johnnie Banks, don't know who the other fella . . .

Hands probe my pockets.

. . . out of town. Must be his car behind Johnnie's . . .

The light gets stronger. It beats on me like the rain. Hands turn my body. Rain strikes my face.

. . . cracked open like an egg . . .

Want to scream. Can't.

. . . multiple blows with a blunt instrument, both of 'em. That's as much as I can tell . . .

. . . musta been a robbery, but who . . .

Hands on my body, lifting me.

The rain stops. Full daylight. Blinding, burning, killing daylight.

Want to scream. Want to scream.

They drop a blanket on me. The rough fabric covers my face. Grunting and swaying, they carry my body out of the wind.

The blanket diffuses the light a little.

Can't move or talk.

A car rumbles under me.

Hands and movement. Hands tugging, pulling at me, at my clothes. No way to tell them to stop.

Searing white light cuts into my brain. Cold air on my bare skin. Icy water sluices over me. Nose and mouth clog with it. They turn my head. The water drains away.

Hands probe my broken skull.

Can't scream.

. . . we'd like to respect it, but in the case of a homicide, we have to have the doctor . . .

Arguments drift over me. One voice is vaguely familiar.

Someone closes my light-blind eyes. Red and black patches drift under the lids.

. . . notify his family . . .

. . . working for me, it's my job to . . .

The voices fade. They throw a heavy sheet on me. Out of sight. Out of mind.

The sun works free of the clouds. It beats silently against the covering.

Someone lifts the sheet. The sun flashes over me like a furnace. Something is shoved under me, firmly pushed under the small of my back.

It's the peace of the grave.

Out. Out. Out.

Sweet night.

A voice. A question.

And pain. Far too much pain.

". . . hear me? Jack?"

My head feels like a bomb crater. If I lie very, very still, it might not get worse.

The voice whispers anxiously.

I remember the rain and the road and yes, I can hear you, so shut up.

A hand touches my bare shoulder. He tries shaking me awake. It moves my head. I scream. It comes out as little more than a bubbling exhalation.

"Jack?"

Dear God, stop the pain.

"Can you hear me?"

More bubbles. The taste of mud.

"Jack?"

A series of small coughs. Someone whimpers.

The questions stop. He carefully turns my head to the left. It eases the pressure on the cracked and broken plates of bone. He's as gentle as possible.

It's too much.

Out.

A clock ticking. A heart beating. Both are nearby.

"Jack?"

The pain had subsided a fraction. This was heaven by comparison.

"Can you hear me?"

Leave me alone.

"Can you understand me?"

Yeah, now go away for a few weeks.

"Please answer me, Jack."

I inhaled to speak, but couldn't get the mouth to work.

"What's my name?"

If you don't know, you're in worse trouble than I am.

"Answer me."

Inhalation. "Charl . . ."

A long sigh of relief. Not from me. He'd been afraid. Of what?

"Do you know what happened to you?"

"Road . . . rain."

"Yes, you were driving."

And then I stopped. An accident?

"You found the taxi," he prompted.

John Henry Banks. Johnnie Banks. Slumped over, mumbling nonsense. His head smashed in . . . no more, I don't want to think.

"Do you know who did it?"

God, was that me asking Banks or Escott asking me? I really couldn't tell.

"Did you see them?"

"Hurt. I hurt."

"I know. Do you need blood?"

I needed something, like an aspirin the size of a boxcar. "Try."

He put a thin rubber tube to my lips like a straw. I drew the stuff in. It was no longer warm from being in the animal, but still wonderful. The blood spread through me with its promise of life and healing, and then I didn't think about anything until it was gone.

"Better?" he asked, his voice faint.

"A little."

He pulled the tube away and ran some water, cleaning up. He liked to have things clean and neat. The water stopped.

"Can you open your eyes?"

Why not? The darkness seeped away for an instant. Escott's worried face hovered close to my own and was gone.

"Did you see anything?" he asked.

"Yeah. Fine."

F-fine. The last thing Banks had said and then—

"Try it again."

I did. They stayed open a few seconds longer. "Okay?"

"Excellent. They're a nice healthy red."

The white-hot hammer and anvil on the side of my skull wasn't pounding quite so hard.

"Think you'll be able to travel soon?"

He had to be out of his mind. I didn't want to move for a month.

"I have to get you out of here before morning."

You'd better have a damn good reason. "No. Rest."

"Yes, at least for now. Do you know who did it?"

That question again. "Banks knew. They get me?"

"You were struck from behind. The doctor found wood splinters in your scalp."

Multiple blows from a blunt instrument. The phrase repeated through my brain like an echo from a dream. Wood. Deadly, deadly wood. No wonder I was so helpless. "How bad?"

"You've a hell of a fracture, they hit you several times. I was worried you might not be—did you see them at all?"

"No."

I noticed the general darkness, or rather the absence of artificial light for the first time. He was also keeping his voice low, almost to a whisper. Faint outside illumination came from a high, uncurtained window. The dimness turned his skin ghost white and simplified his features.

As I drew air to speak, the smell crashed in: formaldehyde mixed with the sweetness of old death. A chill shuddered all through me that had nothing to do with the cold air.

"Where?"

"I'm afraid we're at the local funeral parlor," he explained, as though embarrassed by the fact. "It doubles as the coroner's examination room in the case of questionable deaths or homicides."

"Deaths?"

"I'll go into details when you've rested. You're much better than you were, much better than I'd hoped. After that fresh blood has had a chance to work in you we'll see about getting you out."

"Out?"

"My position with the local authorities is anything but cordial, and I've no wish to be arrested for body snatching. It will be much easier for both of us if the body in question is able to move out under its own power."

The meaning and import began to sink in. Instead of a bed, I was on a high metal table wearing only an old sheet. "I'm dead—I mean, more so than usual?"

"As far as the law is concerned, yes."

I had a nightmare flash in my head of a sealed coffin with muddy earth being heaped on top.

"Not yet." He'd stopped me from moving. "We've time—almost the whole night, if you need it." He found a chair and sat down to wait.

Well, if he was in no hurry, neither was I. I rested and felt my battered head ache and listened to the clock tick. For something to do, I counted the ticks, getting up to thirty before losing track. This went on for as many times as I had fingers since I curled one up whenever I lost the count. When I'd twice made fists, I tried a little movement. My arms worked, the legs responded, but the head wasn't ready to coordinate anything more complicated than that.

The clock ticked and Escott breathed, and one by one, I curled my fingers. It was something I used to do to trick myself to sleep on bad nights. Sleep would have been a better way to pass the time, but I no longer really slept. I missed it.

After an hour, I managed to get my legs off the table and was trying to push myself upright. My head was impossibly heavy. Escott got up to help.

"Shoulders only," I told him.

"Right."

Supporting the base of my neck, he helped boost me to a sitting position. I wobbled dizzily like a baby, but didn't fall. The sheet slipped down a little and I wrinkled my nose in disgust.

"Christ, don't they ever wash this stuff?"

He took my complaining as a good sign. "I've some fresh clothes for you. The ones you were found in are a bit of a write-off."

"My wallet?"

"The police have your personal effects." He produced a sack, pulling out some pants, a clean shirt, and some slippers.

"My shoes?" I'd brought only one pair.

"They're locked in that room over there." He nodded at a closed door.

"How'd you get in?"

"Through a rear window with a glass cutter," he said casually.

The dizziness from sitting up gradually passed. I felt the back of my head with supreme care—even my hair hurt. It was still fiery and tender, but the hammer and anvil had finally stopped pounding.

"What'd they do to me here?" I was remembering the not-so-gentle probing hands on my scalp.

"You were given a preliminary exam on the scene and pronounced dead, then they brought you here for—" He stopped.

"Jesus, Charles, an autopsy?"

He could only nod, looking as queasy as I felt.

The doctor'd make a fast Y-incision and scatter pieces of me over the counters in jars full of preservative. Dear God. My arms wrapped tightly around my chest and stomach in reaction.

"What stopped them?"

"I did, I said I had to notify your family first, and then I told them you were a Christian Scientist."

My jaw dropped of its own accord, as it usually does when I don't understand something. "Huh?"

"I said they were like orthodox Jews in that their religion absolutely forbade autopsies."

"Does it?"

He suddenly smiled. "Actually, I haven't the least idea, but it worked for the time being, and that's all that matters."

"Why didn't you say I was an orthodox Jew?"

"I could not because you were out driving round after sunset on a Friday, the beginning of their Sabbath; something a practicing Jew would have avoided." He offered me the shirt.

I slowly dragged it on. It was clean and crisp with starch, but I still felt soiled. I wanted a scalding hot tub and a long vacation—in that order. He steadied me as I slid off the table to pull the pants up over my rump.

"We still staying at the inn?"

"Officially, *I* am. We'll just have to sneak you in somehow."

"They think—"

"You're dead. Yes, I've received much sympathy, at least in some quarters."

"What d'ya mean?"

"The police have told me not to leave town for the moment. They're probably strapped for suspects. It was fortunate for me that I was down in the lobby listening to the radio with some of the other guests during the critical time the crime took place or I would be in a very awkward position."

"Why should they suspect you?"

"Why not? Many people are murdered by their friends."

"And Banks?"

"I'm a stranger in town and Mr. Banks mentioned us to a few of his drinking cronies." His head went down and he leaned tiredly against a counter. "I should have been more careful. All my questions concerning the Franchers and that fire . . . I blundered badly and poor Banks paid for it."

"It might not even be connected to us."

"Can you believe that?"

I didn't answer that one. "You couldn't have known what would happen."

He shook his head, not really listening. "I am very much to blame for this, Jack. The police are not far off in their suspicions. The investigating officer is no fool, he knows I'm not telling him everything."

"And you can't, can you?"

"Not so that I would be believed and not without solid evidence. If Barrett is behind this, we need proof, and if we obtain proof, how may he be brought to justice?"

"If?"

"I am as yet uncertain of his guilt."

"After all this? Why?"

"I shall be glad to tell you, but elsewhere, if you please. Preferably at the inn so I can establish an alibi for part of this night. When they come in tomorrow and miss you, I shall certainly have to face some questioning. My strong objections to the autopsy will not have been forgotten in so short a time."

"What'll you do?"

"My best performance of moral outrage—after they inform me of the abduction of my poor friend's remains."

"Couldn't I just show up and say it was all a mistake and claim catalepsy or something?"

He shot me a look.

"No, I guess not."

"Do you feel ready to go?"

"After I get my shoes back."

"Perhaps you shouldn't. They're bound to notice."

"You think they'll worry about a pair of shoes when the whole body takes a walk?"

He couldn't argue with that one and nodded.

If I took things slowly, I could move. At the locked door, I leaned against it and seeped right through without even trying hard, which was a surprise. It took a lot more effort and concentration to solidify, though. Dematerialized, there was no discomfort, but I was reluctant to stay that way out of a sneaking fear of not being able to come back again. My head was tender inside and out and I wasn't planning to do anything fancy for a while.

The adjoining room was an office with wooden cabinets and functional furniture. My muddy, wrinkled clothes were scattered over a long table along with Banks's blood-spattered garments. Feeling sick and sad, I made myself look at them and remembered him.

I grabbed up my shoes, took off the evidence tag, and slipped them on. When I returned to the other room, Escott was just putting away a length of rubber tubing and a quart-size milk bottle.

"Is that what blood comes in these days?" I asked.

"It does when I collect it."

"How'd you get it this time?"

"I looked for and found a likely farm late this afternoon. If you were to recover—and I'm very glad you have—it seemed logical to provide for it. Blood appears to be the universal panacea for all your ills, and I wanted to be prepared."

"Thanks."

He shrugged it off, not one for gushing gratitude. It only embarrassed him.

"What'd you tell the farmer, that you were making blood sausage?"

"No, but that is a good suggestion. I said I was collecting blood samples from some of the area livestock."

"Didn't he think it kind of strange?"

"Yes, but fortunately the fellow was a Democrat, and that helped. I said I was a veterinarian working for the NRA and our branch of it was researching blood ailments in cattle. We needed samples for testing and offered monetary compensation for each pint collected."

"Sounds crazy to me."

"He must have thought so as well, but as they say, money talks. I got the samples."

"I'm glad."

"Well, you did buy me dinner the other night. . . ." He turned back to the table I'd spent the day on and swept up a small dark packet and shoved it into his bag.

"What's that?"

"A sample of your home soil. I managed to sneak it in under you when no one was looking."

"You think of everything."

"Not always," he muttered, and I knew he was mulling over Banks's death.

He climbed onto a counter next to the wall and pushed open the window above it. The way was clear and he wriggled through. I wasn't up to such exertions and did my usual vanishing act, reappearing at his side, but staggering a little. I'd had to fight to come back again, and it was draining. He caught my arm and led me away.

"It's a bit of a walk," he said. "They impounded the car as evidence."

"How far?"

"About a half mile. Can you make it?"

"I'll have to." I kept my groans to myself. I hurt, but was recovering incredibly fast. I'd been damned lucky.

We didn't talk and I concentrated on putting one foot in front of the other. The air was clean and cool, inviting me to indulge in a bout of breathing. It quickly flushed the taste of the mortuary from my lungs.

Escott followed a less direct route to the Glenbriar Inn, taking a back street running parallel to the main road. It was a longer, more discreet walk, but after five minutes, witnesses to his night raid were the least of our worries.

We were about to cross an intersection when I chanced to look up. I yanked Escott back, maybe a little too hard despite my current state. He nearly lost his feet as I dragged him into the thin cover of some trees. He choked off his protest and followed my example of crouching behind the thickest trunks.

"What is it?" he hissed.

I pointed. One block over, waiting for a stoplight to change, was Emily Francher's white Studebaker. Inside it was Jonathan Barrett, looking impatient. The signal turned green and he plowed ahead in the direction we'd just come from.

Escott had seen the car, but his eyes hadn't picked up on the occupant. I filled him in.

"He's headed for the funeral parlor," he said.

"Probably to finish off what he started last night."

"I think we're safe enough for the moment."

"Yeah, and I'm going to keep it that way. Let's go back to the inn and get your clothes and my trunk." I moved, trying to go faster than before.

He caught up easily. "Are you suggesting we do a skip?" The American slang jarred with his accent.

"Just for tonight. You can come back in the morning and square things up then."

"Would it not be better to simply square things up with Barrett tonight? We do need to talk with him."

"Like the *Titanic* talked with the iceberg? No, thanks, I'm not up to it."

He had more to say, but I didn't feel like an argument and urged him to hurry. We made the rest of the walk in ten minutes, but it nearly did me in. My headache was almost as bad as before, and I was so dizzy that Escott had to hold me up. It was in vain, though; the Studebaker had returned and growled to a stop on the street in front. Barrett got out and trotted up the steps of the inn. We watched and waited, but he never came out.

"He'll be up in the room," I said. "He'll be there the rest of the night."

"And you are in no condition to confront him. We can leave the luggage for the time being and shelter elsewhere. I've no objections to roughing it for one night."

"Roughing it?"

He took charge and helped me away to a small park close to the inn. We sank onto a stone bench in a dense group of trees and stared at nothing much for a time. It was too cool for crickets, but other night creatures moved around us; busy with hunting, feeding, and mating—busy with survival.

Escott was thoughtful. "If he asks for me at the front desk and they find I am not in my room . . ."

"You can fix it tomorrow."

"I wasn't thinking of the bill. When they open the parlor in the morning and find themselves one short, they'll come looking for me for an explanation. I was planning on having at least a partial alibi for my evening by spending it in the lobby again. Barrett has effectively prevented that."

"Then we get you another. Show me one of those watering holes you went to the other day."

"Are you really up to another walk?"

"It comes in cycles. Just keep it slow and stay out of sight of our window if you can."

He could. My head was not so dizzy now, but I'd soon want a place to stop and completely rest.

"Hand me that packet of earth," I said. He retrieved it from the bag and I shoved it inside my shirt and buttoned up again. It may have been a delusion, but I seemed to feel better having it next to my skin. "What's clinking in there?" I referred to the bag.

"Milk bottles, a large syringe, glass cutter, tubing, gloves—"

"Syringe?"

"For drawing blood. I found it at a local feed store. Some of the farmers do their own veterinary work."

"I thought you were squeamish."

"I am, very."

"So how'd you do that? Draw off the blood, I mean."

"My actor's training came in very handy. For an hour I pretended I was a vet and it worked. Be assured that I was quite ill after I'd finished and had the time to think about it."

Glenbriar was very close to the sound with a neat little bay and a sampling of bars and similar vice shops for weekend sailors. Escott picked a tavern called The Harpoon and led the way inside.

It was half for tourists, half for locals, with fake nets and stuffed fish on the walls, along with some other nautical junk. Escott bought a double something at the bar and carried it to the distant booth I'd picked out.

"Nothing for me?" I joked.

"This is as much as I wish to imbibe tonight," he stated. "There's little sense in both of us having a bad head." He sipped at the stuff—it was probably gin—and made a quick sweep of the other patrons. They looked like regulars, eyeing us once and returning to their own conversations. The bartender leaned on one elbow to listen to a man grouse about his wife.

"Real live joint."

"Better than the one you just left," he pointed out. "Would you care to tell me what occurred to you last night?"

I told him about the wrong road, the heavy rain, and how I found the cab. Shutting my eyes, I put myself there again and tried to repeat all of Banks's last words. "That's when I was hit. I must have gotten there right after it happened. Barrett saw my showing up as a piece of luck for him and he used it."

"Why are you so certain it was Barrett?"

"He knew to use wood, it had to be him. He also knew you were nosing around town and maybe found out that we'd questioned Banks. . . ." I read his face. "All right, why are you certain he's clear?"

"I'll grant that he is the likely suspect and he is tall—Banks would see him as tall at any rate—but the forensic evidence would indicate otherwise."

"Indicate what?"

"You and Banks had your skulls cracked by several heavy blows; I saw both of you today while the doctor was having his first close look. I don't believe Barrett did it because the blows were not heavy enough."

"They did the job."

"On Banks, yes, but not on you."

"I'm different from Banks."

"Exactly, and Barrett of all people is aware of that difference and would have allowed for it. Had he actually been wielding the murder weapon, he would have completely pulped your head to make absolutely certain you'd never get up again."

"I damn near didn't, anyway. If they'd done an autopsy . . . he might have been counting on them to finish the job." My shoulders bunched up and my stomach felt like caving in again. "Besides, he might have held himself back to keep it from looking too brutal."

"A single murder in this quiet pocket of the world is considered quite brutal enough, let alone a double one. In for a penny, in for a pound, you know."

"What's your point, Charles?"

"My point is that whoever tried to kill you was *unaware* of your special condition."

That hauled me up short. "Come again?"

He blinked. "I'd forgotten, you don't know the official theory on this."

"What's the official theory?"

"That Banks picked up a fare who made him stop, bashed in his head, then robbed him. You arrived on the scene while the killer was still there and were attacked in turn."

"A good Samaritan who got walloped himself?"

"Something like that. I believe the killer heard you speaking to Banks, or trying to, feared you'd get a clue to their identity, and decided to do for you as well."

"And they didn't know what I am?"

"Apparently."

"Which means it could have been a real robbery."

"I consider that to be a very small possibility, and so would the police if they had all the facts of our own investigation. We know Banks drove a woman from the Francher estate to Port Jefferson. Within twenty-four hours of giving us this information he is murdered. I believe the woman wanted him silenced, sought him out, and killed him."

I felt very tired. "Which means Emily Francher—"

"Or Laura."

"But Laura was only fourteen or fifteen back then."

"Yes, with some growing to do," he said meaningfully, only I wasn't up to catching on to it. "Banks said *change* and *tall*. If you speculate a bit on filling in the blanks, he might have been trying to say, 'She's changed, gotten or grown tall. She lied.' "

I shook my head, not the smartest thing to do. "What's her motive?"

"As far as Banks is concerned, she killed him to shut him up. She didn't want him to identify the person he took to Port Jefferson."

"Barrett could have hypnotized either woman into killing for him."

"That's a possibility. Our lack of data is most frustrating. If you've no wish to confront Barrett, then we must use this time to speak with the two women to find out what happened five years ago."

"I'll tell you what happened: Maureen got in that cab, went to Port Jefferson, and then to parts unknown. We show up way too late, ask some questions, and then some creep just happens to kill Banks and nearly gets me. We're trying to make this thing more complicated than it really is."

He drank his drink, listening until I'd run down and was out of nonsense. "Do you wish to drop this and go home?"

"I don't know . . . yes. I think so."

He pushed the glass aside, got out his pipe, and spent some time lighting it. He puffed and played with the match stubs with an absent finger. "I see."

But he didn't, and I started up another protest, which he cut off with a raised hand.

"I see that you're tired, upset, and frightened."

I glared at him.

"You've had too much coming at you in too short a time. Just because your physical nature has drastically altered is no reason to think your emotional nature shares the same advantages."

Advantages. Is that how he saw it? Confined to the night, avoiding mirrors, always having to plan out the next feeding, worrying that someone might get too curious about the big trunk in the corner . . . The whole business stunk and I was stuck with it, maybe forever.

"I'm just letting you know that I'm aware of how it must be for you right now. I'm also letting you know that if you do decide to go home, I won't be coming along just yet."

"And try to take on Barrett yourself? Maybe get killed? Is this some kind of blackmail to keep me here?"

"Not at all. What you decide for yourself is all right with me, and no hard feelings. My own decision is to stay. I can't leave anyway at this point. It might be open to misinterpretation by the police."

A smile tugged at my mouth. "Like charging you with body snatching?"

"I certainly hope not, but it is a possibility. They'll have no real evidence against me, of course, but I'll have to remain until they say otherwise. They could make a lot of trouble for me, and I've no desire to lose my license."

His investigator's license wasn't the only thing that kept him going, though. He had the same kind of curiosity that often got me into trouble. In the last week, a lot of it had been burned out of me and I was having trouble handling it in another person. Answering questions solved problems for him; for me it only seemed to make new ones. The emotional cost was distressingly high.

"You know if you stay you could get yourself killed. Barrett can do it without even trying."

He nodded a little, his gray eyes yellow in this light. Of all people, he knew exactly what he was up against, and it still didn't seem to bother him.

My breath exploded out in a sigh. "All right. I'll admit I'm scared. I don't like what we're doing and what might come out of it, but we both know that only a real bastard would run out now, and I'm no bastard."

He put down the pipe, maybe a little relieved after all.

"But," I added, "I've finally figured out that you are, when you want to be."

His eyes flicked up in surprise and went totally blank for a long second. I thought my joke had fallen flat until an abrupt bark of laughter burst from him. Heads turned our way from the bar and he stifled it quickly and returned to his pipe.

"So what's next?" I asked.

"Next I think you should—" He froze again, this time looking past me at the door.

I was careful not to turn around. "What is it?"

With a minimum of movement, he shoved the bag with the bottle, tubing, and other junk across the table into my hands. "They can't see you yet, so you can safely disappear for a bit. Nemesis is approaching and you might be recognized."

I managed to vanish a second before someone large stopped at our booth.

"Good evening, officer," said Escott in an even, untroubled tone.

"Would you come with us?" It wasn't a question.

"Why? Is there something wrong?"

"Just come along, sir."

"I would like to know why."

A silence. The rest of the bar, as far as I could tell from my muffled hearing, was quiet. "We got some questions to ask."

Escott made a knocking sound as he emptied his pipe. "Can you not ask them here? I don't understand."

A second man drifted up next to the first, both looming over Escott. They weren't taking any chances. "We'll fill you in at the station. Come on."

There was some movement and more puzzled protest from Escott. I hoped he wasn't overplaying his innocent-citizen act as they led him out.

I followed, clinging to one of the cops until we got into their car. He sat in the back with Escott. Eventually he shivered and complained about the cold, so I shifted over to the empty front passenger seat.

Escott made another attempt to get information from them and subsided with obvious disgust. The rest of our short trip was made in silence.

After stopping, I lingered in the car long enough to materialize for a quick look as they marched Escott inside. The station was tiny. The front windows disclosed a one-room office with a desk, phones, and files. Through a wide heavy door in the back wall were the cells. The ones I could see were empty.

We were in Glenbriar's municipal district. Conveniently across from the jail was the courthouse and next to that an ancient structure claiming to be the city hall. Down at the far end of the street, I abruptly recognized the Glenbriar Funeral Parlor.

All its lights were on, blazing away like New Year's.

Oops.

8

I quit the car, found a way around to the back of the jail, and slipped inside, too nerved up for the moment to worry about my sore head.

The place was all linoleum and painted metal; nothing to get excited about. The open door at the end of the cells led to the outer office, and I crept up to it with my ears flapping, only nobody was talking. I got in the angle created between the door and the wall and peered through the crack made by the hinges.

Within the narrow strip, Escott's profile and part of a uniformed deputy leaning his butt on a big desk were visible. The other man was out of view, but a squeaking chair placed him a few feet in front of Escott. They were all motionless except for breathing, and sometimes one of them turned that automatic body pattern into an expression of impatience by an occasional sigh. They made no offer to get coffee, which I interpreted as a sign of Escott's ambiguous status with them. A guest gets coffee and a prisoner you talk around like he's not there; Escott was neither and that put my nerves up even more. I couldn't tell what Escott was feeling.

A phone rang and the guy at the desk answered. He said, "Yeah," and hung up. Five long, silent minutes later a car rolled up and another man walked in. the deputies stood up and made room for him.

"Thanks for coming down, Escott," said the newcomer.

"I had little choice in the matter, Chief Curtis," was the dry reply. "What is this all about?"

"We want to know what you did with your friend."

"I don't understand."

And it went on like that until the cop got around to revealing the embarrassing fact that my body had taken a powder. Escott hadn't been kidding on his moral outrage. He was a real treat to watch, but Curtis expected an act and wasn't buying any of it.

"Put the lid on for a minute, Escott, and just tell us everything you've done today since four o'clock."

Escott choked a little. "You really think *I* did it?"

"You were the one so dead set against an autopsy."

One of the deputies snickered at the inadvertent joke.

"Yes, out of respect for his religious beliefs—"

"Which I think is a lot of crap. You know as well as I do we throw that out the window in a homicide case. Don't you want to find who killed your friend?"

"Of course I do—"

"Then tell us where you stashed the body."

"I didn't 'stash' it anywhere because I never took it. I've done nothing."

"Then tell us what you *have* done."

He gave out with a loose schedule of a walk around the town, dinner at the inn, and another walk ending with a drink at The Harpoon. As stories went it was pretty lousy.

"Anyone see you on these walks?"

"I suppose so. I wasn't paying much attention."

"Did you go past the funeral parlor?"

"I did. It's on the main street and I recall going down that way once."

"Did you go into the parlor, like maybe to pay your respects?"

"No."

"Did you want to?"

"Are you charging me with anything?"

Curtis ignored the question and hit him with a dozen more of his own, which Escott handled the same way; the truth, but not all of it. If I hadn't been the missing body all the fuss was about, I'd be starting to believe him.

I wanted a look at Curtis and chanced taking a peek around the other end of the door. It was safe enough, one man was watching Escott and the other was out of sight.

Curtis was smaller and slighter than his help, but with the kind of tough stringy body that reminded me of tree roots. He had short gray hair, a narrow face, and wore steel-rimmed glasses that caught the light and hid his eyes. He looked like the kind of person who could spot a lie and be ready to deal with it before it was out of your mouth. Escott was in for a hard time.

The deputy glanced up and I ducked back behind the door. Talk lagged while he came across the room for a look. I vanished, sensing his close presence for a moment as he checked the cells and turned away.

"What is it, Sam?" asked Curtis.

"Thought I saw something."

He'd left the door wide open so it was flat against the inside wall and I no longer had a place to hide and watch. I shifted to one of the cells and materialized on the lower bunk. Escott's bag was still with me and I took care not to let the stuff inside clink.

Talk in the next room resumed. Escott stuck to his bad story, Curtis let him know in very precise terms just how bad the story was, and neither side gave an inch. Having been in the same situation only a few days ago, I was all sympathy. Too bad Escott couldn't hypnotize his way out of this one. I seriously speculated on walking in the front door with a sad tale of concussion and a family history of catalepsy and amnesia. The consequences would have been amusing, but maybe not too productive to a low profile. I was distracted from further planning when the station door opened and another man entered.

"Well, Doc?" said Curtis expectantly.

"Brought 'em."

A chair squeaked and bodies moved.

"Out with your mitts," someone instructed, and there was a concentrated silence. I whisked from the cell and peered past the door with one eye, trying to be thin. Escott was standing at the desk having his fingerprints taken. He got a towel to wipe off the ink, but they ignored his request for soap and water. Curtis ordered him to be taken to the next room.

I jumped back into the cell, grabbed up the bag, and went away for the minute it took to lock him in.

"This is too bloody much!" he exploded as the key turned. "Am I under arrest? Answer me!"

I followed the deputy out as he shut the door, listening while they examined and compared. They were disappointed.

"Well, what did you think?" Curtis growled at them. "If he's smart enough to move a stiff and not be seen, he's smart enough to wear gloves. What about the others, Wally? Did McGuire take yours?"

"Yeah, and none of the prints match what we found on the table."

I grinned invisibly. Any prints on that metal table would be mine.

The doctor continued. "I'd just like to know why he did it, if he did do it."

"Who else? You said he threw a conniption when you started to cut."

"People are like that, they don't like to think about what we have to do. . . ."

"Like hell. This bird's no virgin, he's been in the business long enough. As for that religious scientist crap . . . he's hiding something."

"Then *you* try wearing him down. In the meantime I think you should see if there're any students spending the weekend in the area."

"Students?"

"As in medical. We got up to games in med school that would curl your hair."

"Students?" Curtis repeated unhappily. He had badly wanted to pin it on Escott and now had a new distraction to trouble him.

"Where do you want this stuff?" asked Wally.

"In the file over there."

Wally went over there and shuffled away the fingerprints.

"Now what?" asked the doctor.

"We let him wait and think. I'm going for my supper. I've been running my ass off since yesterday. Want to come?"

Curtis and the doctor left, and the two remaining men discussed their own dining plans. I drifted back to the cell, took the top bunk, and re-formed.

"You all right?" I whispered.

He was standing at the locked door, less than two feet away. He whirled, drawing a quick breath. "Not just then. You should knock or something, I nearly had a cardiac."

"Sorry."

"Have you been here long?"

"With you all the way."

"I thought as much when that deputy got cold and then started seeing things."

"I just came from the other room. They were trying to match your prints with some from a table. I think it's the one I'd been lying on at the parlor."

"With little success. I imagine the prints they found were your own."

"That's what I figure."

"I suppose I *could* suggest it to them. . . ."

"Don't be funny. The chief's gonna let you stew here for a while."

"I expected no less. They'll have to release me in twenty-four hours, though, or charge me."

"Only if they're nice about it. Some of these small-town cops can be regular dictators."

"One can hardly blame them in this case, as they are very much out of their depth—"

The outer door opened and I got scarce fast.

"Awright," said the deputy, "who you talkin' to?"

"My lawyer, if I'm allowed the chance. Where is Chief Curtis? He can't just shut me in here without . . ." He went on and on until the deputy left, slamming the door on his tirade.

"All clear," he whispered.

I reappeared on the floor, next to the lower bunk with my back against the wall. He was still at the cell door, his fingers threaded through the bars. They weren't the vertical type, but inch-wide iron strips in a latticework pattern that made the dark cell a claustrophobe's nightmare. The walls and ceiling were metal as well and covered with institutional green paint marred by graffiti. It was thickest along the bunk wall, with the usual initials, scratches to mark off passing days, and a crude figure of a woman to remind inmates of what they were missing.

"Not too terribly cheerful, is it?" he asked, reading my face.

"I'll get you out of here."

"A jailbreak?" He shook his head.

"No, I'll find Curtis and have a little talk with him."

"I'd rather hoped you might. Are you feeling better?"

"Yeah," I said, with some surprise. "It's funny, but I think my disappearing act seems to help—like taking an aspirin."

He was interested. "You do look improved."

"Will you be okay here?"

"Safe as houses." He removed his coat, folded it neatly, and stretched out on the lower bunk with a sigh.

"But aren't you worried?"

"Over what?"

"If Curtis checks your story at the inn, Barrett could hear about it. You're a sitting duck in this cell."

"I'm aware of that possibility, but pacing and tearing my hair will not help the situation."

"You still don't think Barrett is behind any of this?"

"Before forming an answer, I need more data."

I let it slide for the moment. "Speaking of which, you haven't filled me in on what happened today."

"What about Chief Curtis?"

"He's having supper with the doctor. I can't do anything until there's a chance of getting him alone. I can catch him when he comes back."

He nodded, approving. "That will be Dr. Evans, who is also the local coroner. He fancies himself to be a criminologist—"

"And nearly sliced me up for salami from what I've just heard."

"Erm, yes. Well . . . the less said on that the better."

"Sure, but thanks for heading him off. So, how did you spend your day?"

He squeezed his eyes shut. "I have the strangest feeling of déjà vu."

"Maybe you could tell me how I spent *my* day instead."

He jumped at the chance. "To summarize: you and Banks were discovered at about seven forty-five last night by a Mr. and Mrs. Malloy. Malloy was reluctant to leave the scene, tried to flag down a passing car for help, and succeeded on his second attempt. He sent the driver on to call the police. They arrived and the official investigation began.

"The two of you were pronounced dead at the scene and photos were taken. The hurricane delayed things and it was several hours before they could move the bodies. The worst of the storm hit around dawn. I was awake at the time along with a few other guests and beginning to wonder what happened to you. I thought you might have found it necessary to go to ground because of the weather, or that the car had broken down someplace. A deputy showing up to drive me to the funeral parlor to identify your body was the last thing I expected."

"Did you think I was dead?"

"Not after I saw you, but I knew you weren't at all well."

"How so?"

"That horrible shrinking and aging had not set in, so it seemed likely you would recover, given time and a little help. I was then invited to aid the police in their inquiries—"

"How did they know to find to you?"

"They traced the registration of the car to its hire firm, then to our Manhattan hotel, and ultimately to the Glenbriar Inn. They were less than satisfied with my story of a vacation, but had to settle for it, as it was all the information I was pleased to give them. They released me and I returned to the parlor in time to begin the first arguments against your autopsy. Dr. Evans was exceptionally busy because of the aftermath of the storm, and that helped. All he managed to get into the record was that you were probably dispatched by a blunt wood instrument of some sort, and the odd fact that after a period of more than eighteen hours, rigor mortis and livor mortis had not set in. He was mightily puzzled over that."

"We'll just make sure we keep him that way."

"I'm all in favor of—"

The door crashed open and the deputy bulled in. I barely squeaked out in time.

"Where is he?" he yelled.

"What are you talking about?" Escott's voice was mild.

"There's a guy in here, I heard you gabbing. Where is he?"

Escott didn't bother replying to that one and the man tore the place apart, which didn't take long, since it was pretty short of hiding places. In the end, he took Escott from his cell and locked him into another.

"Anything, Wally?" he called to his partner, who was outside beating the bushes by the jail windows. Wally came back distantly with a negative answer.

"What is the problem, Deputy?" Escott asked, with the polite blandness one reserves for idiots.

"You shut up," he ordered, and marched out, leaving the office door hanging wide open.

I resumed shape in the most sheltered corner of Escott's new cell. His face was grotesquely crisscrossed by the shadows cast from the bars, but he was silently and heartily laughing.

"Guess I forgot to whisper," I murmured.

He recovered enough to say, "We both did. I never thought jail could be so amusing."

"I'll get going before we drive them nuts."

"Good luck," he wished, and I winked out, taking the fast way through the front. Both men were very quiet and still, probably listening for more conversation from the cells. Unless Escott decided to treat them to a Shakespearean soliloquy, they were out of luck.

It wasn't late, but the streets were empty and had that post-midnight feel to them. Hard blue light from lamps around the station picked out broad puddles left by last night's storm, and a cool wind made the water shiver and stirred fallen branches. Not feeling it even in my thin shirt, I stood motionless under the shadow of a tree. I had nothing to do but wait and hurt and think and grieve. Down the block the windows were still lit at the funeral parlor where John Henry Banks waited to be buried.

A slow hour passed before the chief's car chugged up to its slot in front of the station. He was alone, which was exactly what I wanted. As he got out, I put myself on the sidewalk and called to him.

"Chief Curtis?" I used a light, friendly voice. I was someone with no real problems or gripes.

The car was between us. He shut the door and looked up. "Yes? Who's there?"

That reminded me about my superior night vision. He was squinting to see my face against the harsh, inadequate light of the street lamps.

"I need to talk with you, if you have a minute."

He didn't know my voice and was trying to place my body shape, comparing it with others in his memory to identify me. I was familiar, but he didn't know why.

"I got a minute, come into the station." He remained on his side of the car, unconsciously on guard. Some deep instinct within had raised the tiniest of alarms. I rounded the front of the car—a natural enough move—but it put the light squarely behind me and kept my face in shadow. His glasses picked up the brightness and threw it back.

"No need to go to any trouble, sir, I just had a question for you." I was almost close enough to start, but had to move to one side so he could see my face, half in light, half in shadow. He didn't know me, but I was now very different from the rain-sodden corpse on the roadside under the glare of his flashlight.

"What is it?" He was expectant. In another second he'd be impatient.

"I want you to listen to me," I said, focusing onto him.

Light flared over his glasses as I closed in.

The stone bench was cold and unforgivingly hard, but Escott cheerfully maintained its superiority over his padded bunk at the jail. His vest and coat were tightly buttoned and he was pretending not to feel the chill in the wind as we sat watching the Glenbriar Inn. The white Studebaker was still where Barrett had left it hours earlier.

My head had started its dizzy thumping again, adding to my worries. I hugged my precious packet of earth and longed for total rest deep in my quiet trunk. Chief Curtis had been less trouble than I'd anticipated, but it had been very draining.

A minute after I'd finished with him and faded into the night, he shook himself and completed the journey from his car to the station, unaware of its interruption. Escott was brought from the lockups and released, much to the puzzled annoyance of the deputies. Sometime tomorrow Escott would return to collect his car keys and my personal effects. I could have managed it all tonight, but didn't want to push things too far or too fast. There was always the chance that Curtis could be talked out of my influence by some familiar, sensible voice.

"I'm going inside," said Escott. His tone was relaxed and conversational, as though he'd only commented on the weather.

From this end of the place we could see the window of our room. If Barrett was up there instead of in the lobby, he hadn't bothered with the lights. I could easily imagine him sitting very quietly in the dark, facing the door and waiting for it to open. Escott had made his mind up and nothing short of my hypnosis could change it. I wasn't going to do that, but I couldn't let him go up there alone, either.

"All right." I stood up. Slowly. The nagging dizziness made the ground lurch. I'd used up a lot of precious energy dealing with Curtis.

"You don't have to, you know."

"I know. Let's get moving."

We left the park, going the long way around to avoid being in direct sight of our window. I kept my eyes wide open as we approached the back door to the inn, scouting likely corners and shadows for his presence. The memory of that amorphous gray blob so invisible to human eyes was still with me.

If Barrett was in the room, he would hear us come up the stairs. He could distinguish us from other guests by the sound of two pairs of shoes, but only one pair of working lungs. Our door opened suddenly and he stepped into the hall to look us over with his candle-flame eyes. He nodded and stood to one side, inviting us in.

Damn few things ever ruffled Escott; he murmured a polite good evening and did so, turning on a light. It took me a little longer to follow.

Our room was undisturbed. If for any reason Barrett bothered to search it, he'd been careful. Without thinking, I went straight to my trunk and sat on it; the soil within tugged at me like a rope. Escott sank onto one corner of the bed nearest the door and Barrett took a hardwood chair next to the window.

"I read the paper," he began. "I read all about the double murder and saw the name John R. Fleming, so I thought I should check it out and see if it was you. I'm glad you're all right."

My face must have been stone. "Are you?"

His lips thinned and his own expression hardened. "Yes, I see that you are. I'll go now."

"Wait." Escott arrested his move to leave. "Something else must have brought you here as well."

"It was the story in the paper," he stated, his voice even.

"Indeed."

Barrett didn't like his look and started to rise again, and again Escott stopped him.

"The other man who was killed, John Henry Banks—what do you know about him?"

"Only what they said in the paper. Why should I know anything about him?"

"He was the man who chauffeured Maureen away from the Francher estate five years ago."

The revelation did no more than raise one eyebrow. "He was?"

"We spoke to him at length. He remembered a small woman wearing a veiled hat who hardly spoke to him."

"What a remarkable memory he must have had."

"Only because of the unusual nature of his fare."

"How so unusual?"

"Because it had been a very long drive for them and she bestowed a rather large tip for his trouble."

Barrett shrugged. "It's a long road back to the city."

"But he did not take her to New York, he drove her to Port Jefferson."

"Port—"

"Why would anyone want to go to Port Jefferson?"

"To use the ferry to—" He broke off, his brows coming together.

"Would Maureen have had any reason to go to Bridgeport?" Escott asked, putting a very slight emphasis on her name.

"I don't know." He wasn't sure, though, and we both picked up on it.

"We saw you earlier tonight," I said. "You were going to the funeral parlor, weren't you?"

He all but grabbed at the change of subject. "Yes, when I read about your—your trouble. I thought you might need help."

"Did anyone spot you?"

He looked slightly embarrassed. "I'm afraid they did."

That explained why Escott had been picked up so fast.

"I got away and thought it best to come back here to wait for you."

"So you could be neat about things and take care of Escott, too?"

As a shock tactic it didn't work very well. He was surprised, but not in the way I'd expected. He gaped as though I was mentally deficient and looked to Escott for an answer.

"Jack believes you tried to kill him last night," he explained quietly.

Any breath in Barrett had seeped out and he struggled to replace it to speak, only he couldn't speak. His face was eloquent. Unless he was a better actor than Escott, he was an innocent man. Innocent of my attempted murder, at least.

"No," he finally whispered. "Why ever should I want to kill you?"

Escott didn't answer directly. "Banks was the intended victim, Jack only arrived at the wrong time and was attacked in order to shut him up. He might have seen or heard something that would have identified the killer."

"Why do you think it was me?" he asked, honestly puzzled. "Is it because of Maureen? Because we were once lovers?"

I hated him for being right. I hated the thought of Maureen in his arms, holding to him, responding to his touch—however long ago it had been. I hated that when she'd been in trouble she'd gone to him for help and not to me. I realized with shame that I could hate her for that as well.

Escott shifted uneasily and I looked away from them until the emotions cooled off. Given a chance, they lose their terrible intensity, but until then I'm not safe to be around.

"The paper said it was a robbery." Barrett was speaking to Escott. "You obviously don't think so. Why?"

"There's too much coincidence involved for my peace of mind. The day after we spoke with him, the man was murdered. I believe the killer found out about our investigation into Maureen's disappearance. That person did not want anyone looking too closely into things and cut off a source of information. This, of course, presupposes that Maureen is dead."

The only sound was Escott's heartbeat and the soft tick of his watch. Barrett was utterly still. Eventually he looked at me, hoping I'd deny Escott's words. I'd lived with the possibility for so long on the edge of thought that I felt nothing. Barrett had never once considered it and was having to deal with the idea as one solid blow.

He shook his head slightly, barely moving. "You think she's dead?"

I looked past him out the window, not wanting to see a mirror of my own old fears on his face.

"Why do you think that? Where's your proof?"

Escott stepped in and answered for me. "Jack has no other proof than his knowledge of Maureen and her feelings for him."

"But she was terrified of Gaylen, of facing her."

"If Maureen were still alive, she'd have returned to him despite Gaylen's possible interference." He switched back to me. "She loved you, Jack, she would have returned to you."

I nodded my thanks to him for that piece of comfort.

"Then who killed her?" asked Barrett. "If she has been killed."

"You could have."

Barrett wasn't threatened by the accusation. "Why should I?"

"To maintain your position in the Francher household?" he suggested. "Maureen could have upset that for you, especially if she ever suspected you of setting the fire that killed Violet Francher."

I felt the wave of pure shock roll from Barrett and flood the room.

"Easy, Charles . . ." I said.

Escott stared at the deceptively simple quilt pattern on the bed, using it as insulation between his mind and Barrett's feelings.

Barrett said clearly and slowly, "The fire was an accident."

"And a very convenient one for you, was it not?"

He was up and across the room faster than thought. All I could do was stand and take a step toward them, knowing that I'd be too late to prevent anything. At the most I might just be able to pry his fingers from Escott's broken neck, and I wasn't sure of doing even that much in my condition.

But Barrett stopped and did nothing more than stand over him. Unmoved, Escott continued to study the quilt, and Barrett's fists trembled for want of action.

"It probably was an accident," Escott continued, "and if not, then it was someone else who arranged it, not you. You have other means by which you may deal with such awkward problems. We know that. It would have been child's play for you to have influenced Violet Francher into accepting you. Why did you not do so?"

The answer was slow in coming, Barrett was still dealing with his emotions. "Emily asked me not to, and after my experience with Gaylen it seemed best to allow things to run their natural course."

"Did you know about the psychiatrists being brought in?"

"Yes, and if it came to it, I was more than ready to influence *them*. How did you come to know all of this?"

"Servants' hall gossip can be most enlightening."

Barrett snarled something obscene and returned to stand behind the chair, resting his hands on its tall back. I withdrew to the trunk. If he'd wanted to kill, he'd have done it by now.

"What was Emily's reaction to her mother's death?" asked Escott.

"What do you think?"

"I'm asking you."

"I don't know how to answer."

"Was it normal grief?"

"What's normal? I don't know."

"I think you do."

Barrett appealed to me. "How do you put up with him?"

"I usually tell him what he wants."

He shrugged. "For what it's worth, Emily took it very hard. She all but fell apart on us. Why do you ask?"

"Because *she* could have killed her mother," said Escott.

Barrett smiled, "No, that's impossible."

"You are very certain."

"I am absolutely certain, I was with her that whole night."

"But not during the day."

"No, but—"

"She could have rigged it all during the day, delaying things."

"No." He shook his head decisively. "No, she couldn't have done anything like that. You're completely wrong there. The fire started because of an old lamp wire shorting out."

Escott nodded, encouraging him to go on.

"Emily knows nothing about mechanical things. She's always had servants to do everything for her. She only has the vaguest idea of how to change a light bulb. Last year I tried to teach her how to drive and she was utterly hopeless at it. Besides, she's too gentle of heart. She could never kill anyone, nor even think of it."

Escott tilted his head to one side, looking directly at him. "Besides, it was an accident, as you said."

He scowled, knowing that Escott was patronizing him. "Why do you insist it wasn't?"

"Because it brings sense to what followed after: Maureen's disappearance and *why* she disappeared."

Things tumbled and lurched inside me that had nothing to do with my injured head. "Charles . . ."

He looked at me.

"No more," I said. "Leave it as is."

"You won't, by God," said Barrett. "You'll be telling me, and the sooner the better." His voice was low, but he meant every word and would tear it out of Escott if he thought it necessary.

Escott lifted a hand. "I can only tell you what I've been able to deduce from the inadequate data I have at present."

I waved him down. "No, Charles. What's the point? What's the good of it? Maureen's dead, this won't bring her back."

"I know." He was surprised, but not offended at my attitude. "Maureen, Banks, and nearly you—who's next? *That* is the good of it. That's the purpose and point, the one that I have to justify it all for myself—to stop her from killing again."

"Stop who?" Barrett demanded.

Escott started to speak, but his words could mean his own death, so I interrupted. "He's not talking about Emily, but Laura."

Her name echoed silently on his lips. The color had gone out of his already pale face, leaving him a cold, bloodless statue until he began to shake his head again. "No. You're both wrong again. You're too inept to find Maureen, so you invent nonsense to excuse your lack."

"Was Laura home last night?"

He stared me up and down, then sense and disbelief took over, and he smiled. "You're wrong, laddie. What you're thinking is impossible."

"It is not," said Escott. "Very sadly, it is not."

Barrett's finger found a seam in the wood of the chair back where two different grain patterns met. He ran the edge of one nail along the join, unaware of the nervous movement. "Right, I've nearly had my fill of this. Come and finish your terrible tale."

"It *is* terrible," Escott agreed. "And I am sorry to bring this upon you."

"Get on with it."

"I will speculate that in 1931 a fourteen-year-old girl returned to her adopted home for her school holiday and found herself in the middle of a very tense emotional situation between yourself, Emily, and Violet. Laura did meet you for the first time that spring, Mr. Barrett?"

He nodded.

"Did she like you?"

"Yes, but you know how schoolgirls are."

"Schoolgirls grow up to be women. A person's age does not invalidate the depth or sincerity of their feelings—you can certainly understand that from your own experience. You may not have been interested in her then, but she was interested in you. Is that correct?"

"She may have had an infatuation, puppy love—"

"And Violet was trying to send you away." Escott held up his hand to stem any comment. "We'll pass over the subject of the fire. Whether or not it was an accident, it happened and removed any threat to your remaining on the estate. From Laura's point of view, there was the secondary advantage that she no longer had to return to school. She was needed at home to help care for her grieving cousin.

"It was probably the best summer she'd ever known . . . and then one night another woman came into the house—a former lover, and a woman you were still very attached to in ways that Laura could only understand by instinct. You invited Maureen to stay as long as she liked."

"You're saying Laura was jealous of Maureen, but not of Emily? The girl wasn't deaf or blind, she knew we were sharing a bed."

"Emily was also much older looking than you. To Laura's young eyes she was no competition at all, but Maureen was young, beautiful and well acquainted with you. Laura must have eavesdropped on some of your conversations together, enough to see her as another threat."

"And for that you think she killed Maureen? Is that the whole miserable story?"

"The most important part, yes. Was Laura then aware of your nature?"

"She knew only that I was allergic to sunlight. Some people are so and are not vampires—"

"But what might she have heard if she'd been eavesdropping on you and Maureen?"

Barrett shut up. His face pinched in thought, he paced the room up and back, then sat in the chair. "Go on."

"She apparently learned enough from the two of you to figure things out easily enough. If there is anything like a decent library in that house she'd be able to pick up some basic data about your condition and your special weaknesses. She would know how to take advantage of them."

"But she was a child."

"And very intelligent? Precocious, perhaps?" Escott's voice dropped to a gentle, toneless murmur. "Sometime during the day she murdered Maureen."

"She did *not*! Maureen left the next night. Mayfair saw—"

"Mayfair and Banks only saw a woman wearing a hat and a veil; a hat to cover her blond hair and a veil to conceal her face. A woman was seen arriving on the estate and a woman must be seen to leave. There was no reason for Maureen to want to go to Bridgeport. Can you think of one for Laura?"

"Her boarding school was in Connecticut," he whispered.

"The route would then have been a familiar one to her and a logical one for her to choose because of its familiarity."

"How would she get back?" I asked him.

"She must have hired another cab in Port Jefferson. We only failed to find it."

"And what happened to her trunk?"

"I don't know. We shall have to ask her."

Barrett had been staring at the floor and looked up after he noticed the silence. "What?"

"I said we shall have to ask her."

It took a while to sink in and he was shaking his head slowly but decisively. "No. You're not going anywhere near her. You're both going to leave us all alone."

"And if we leave you alone, what will you do?"

But he wasn't ready to consider that. "No, you just get out of here and leave us."

"She's murdered two people, Barrett, possibly three."

"She has not. You've no proof for any of this. Only speculation, and what good is that?"

"Where was Laura last night?" I asked.

"At home in her room," he said too quickly, then realized it.

"What time? Was she in her room at seven-thirty or taking a swim? Was she out shopping or visiting a friend or just taking a drive in a hurricane? Or just maybe she was swinging a club at the back of Banks's head. There was a lot of blood . . . did she get it all off? Did the storm wash it away before she got home? Was her hair dry by the time you went up to her? Was she even in the mood for your company? Or maybe she was all excited and needed you to help work it off—"

The shock had come back to his face, then it swiftly evolved into white-hot fury. He was in front of me in one step, hauled me up, and knocked a fist square into my face before I could vanish. The room swung sharply to one side and a wall slammed me hard all over; or the floor, or both. I didn't care. Maureen was dead and I didn't care about anything at all.

9

"Fine," I snapped, and wondered what the question had been.

"Yes," said Escott. "Now hold still."

He was kneeling over me, undoing my collar button. Only an instant ago he'd been sitting across the room. Not even Barrett could move that fast.

The ceiling, which seemed very far away because I was flat out on the floor, twisted every time I blinked. I shut my eyes hard against the effect.

"This is getting to be a very bad habit with you," he chided. "Are you the sort who goes in for self-punishment, or are you just naturally stupid?"

There was no reason to answer that one. "Where's Barrett?"

"Halfway home by now. You provoked him into a fine temper by that last display." He punched at my tender forehead with a dripping washcloth.

"Ow!"

"Serves you right. I was going to talk with him and get him to see reason, but you've effectively canceled that gambit."

"So buy me a hair shirt."

He dropped the cloth smack onto my face and got up in disgust. I rolled to my left side, using my arm for a pillow. That damned hammer and anvil were at it again, and some thick, viscous liquid was sloshing messily around between my ears—probably what was left of my brain.

"What time is it?"

"After two."

Not late at all; five whole hours to sit around, stare at the walls, and wish I'd stayed in Chicago. Maybe I'd conk out regardless if I crawled into my trunk earlier than usual. Suppressing a moan, I eventually sat up, putting my back to the wall. It really wasn't as bad as my initial awakening in the morgue. I'd had worse hangovers when I'd been alive. Mentally I did want a drink, something 150 proof and painless till morning. I toyed with the idea of finding some animal, getting it stinking drunk, and then with all that booze in its bloodstream . . .

Someone rapped on our door.

Escott glanced at me. "Can you disappear for a moment?"

Why not? It was easy enough. No movement was required and therefore no real concentration; I was there one second and gone the next. The body with all its hurts was gone, gone, gone. Too bad I couldn't do the same for the mind and its memories. It was tempting to stay this way forever; floating, formless, and insulated from the countless ills caused by living, simple living.

The rap came again, and Escott answered. His visitor sounded diffident but official. ". . . heard a crash and asked us to check on things."

The neighbors had complained to the manager about the noise. At two in the morning, you could hardly blame them.

". . . frightfully sorry, my own clumsy fault. I tripped rather badly."

"You're not hurt?"

"It's really nothing, bang on the shin. More din than damage."

"We just wanted to be certain . . ." And the man apologized for the intrusion and expressed sympathy for my tragic death, and had the police found out anything?

"They said to expect some new developments anytime now."

Which was a diplomatic way of describing my body being absent from the funeral parlor. Tomorrow's paper would make interesting reading unless Chief Curtis decided to keep it all quiet out of sheer embarrassment.

"Can we expect you to be staying with us much longer?" He was not overly enthused, even less so at the affirmative answer. It's bad for business when guests get themselves murdered. Escott bade him good night and locked the door. Reluctantly, I faded back into reality. The aches returned, but they weren't as sharp as before.

Escott dropped onto his bed and pinched the bridge of his nose. For the first time I noticed the blue circles under his eyes and the general slow-down of his movements. He'd been up most of the night because of the storm, and then spent the day fending off the police and waiting for me to wake up, either as myself or as a brain-damaged responsibility he didn't need. The last twenty-four hours had sucked the energy from him.

"Sorry about all this," I said lamely.

He considered my own forlorn form, shrugged, and accepted the apology. "We're both tired. Tell me, was that show pure temper, or had you a purpose in alienating the man?"

"It was temper, but I had some idea it was the only way to reach him, to get him to see her through our eyes."

"There are subtler ways of doing it," he pointed out.

"I'm not so good at that."

"Evidently."

"What now?"

"Some rest. I want to give Barrett a chance to cool down."

"What's to keep him from skipping town between now and tomorrow?"

"That is not too likely, as it would be an admission of guilt and leave Emily and Laura undefended. I believe the man has a streak of honor in him."

"Or he could skip with both women and we never hear of them again."

He shook his head. "I don't read that off him at all."

"That streak of honor?"

"Exactly. I believe once he realizes the truth for himself, he will want to do the right thing. He only needs the time to think it all over."

"You figure he'll talk to Laura?"

He had a look in his eye that made me feel cold inside and out. "I am absolutely counting on it."

"I'll go out to the estate tomorrow and see what's happened."

"May I come along?"

"Yeah. I might need you to scrape me off the pavement again."

We'd planned to leave for the Franchers first thing at sunset, but he wasn't in the room when I woke up. It looked like the start of another disastrous evening.

I quickly dressed and stepped out to look for him, but being officially dead put a hell of a crimp into things. Walking up to the desk clerk to ask a simple question would only put the man into hysterics. While I dithered in the hall someone behind me said *psst*.

"This way," he whispered.

The top of Escott's head was just disappearing down the backstairs. He'd gotten the car back and had left it in the gravel lot with the motor running. We piled in and he ground the gears to get us moving again.

"Glove box," he said, before I could ask what was going on. His eyes were fever bright and there was a new tenseness to his body.

I opened the box and thankfully resumed ownership of my wallet, watch, and other junk. "This isn't the road to the Franchers'."

"I know, but something's happened." His lips had thinned to a single grim line and there was a brick wall behind his eyes.

"What?"

He tossed a folded paper in my lap. "The story's there. Emily Francher died today."

And he didn't say anything while I gaped first at him and then at the paper headline. The words swam. I couldn't make any sense of them. "What happened exactly?"

"I don't know, I've only just found out. There was some kind of an accident early this afternoon—a fall down some stairs."

"Shit. Where are we going?"

"The funeral parlor. For obvious reasons I daren't make myself too noticeable there, but you can get inside for a quick look."

"I'm not sure I want to. What am I looking for?"

"Any sign of Emily Francher's resuscitation or resurrection, or whatever you call it."

"Oh, Jesus."

"No need to be blasphemous, I only want your opinion on her condition."

Maybe he thought I was some kind of a vampire expert, which was true in a way, but I was not overconfident. "What if she has changed?"

"Then she might require assistance from someone who's been through it before. You said your own experience left you in quite a state of shock."

That was for damn sure. The night I had woken up dead, it took a hit-and-run murder attempt with a Ford to finally jolt my mind back into full working order. "What if Barrett shows up?"

"Tell him the truth of why you're there."

"And maybe ask if he's spoken to Laura yet?"

"I'll leave that to your discretion."

He dropped me in the street behind the parlor and promised to swing back again in fifteen minutes.

They'd replaced the window Escott had worked on with his glass cutter, but I had no trouble slithering through the cracks between the sash and the sill, emerging out of the air onto the sanitized floor of the morgue. I recognized the place with an uneasy twinge and was thankful it was empty. The adjoining office was also unoccupied, but not the whole building. Voices were coming from somewhere out front and I followed the sounds, tracing them through a bare linoleum hall.

Two wide doors opened onto a plusher room filled to the ceiling with the ultimate in vampiric clichés. They were stacked three high, and the ones on the bottom were tilted slightly with the lids up so that you could appreciate the linings. I counted nearly two dozen coffins, each with different styling, details, and prices.

I'd had no idea so much choice was available, from a simple native pine to a mirror-polished ebony with gold-plated handles. The one with scenes from the Sistine Chapel painted all over it with porcelain angels trimming the corners seemed overdone, but to each his own. I wanted none of it, preferring my cramped and homely trunk to such a constant and forceful reminder of death. The sight of a child-sized coffin and a tiny baby casket in a corner raised a sudden lump in my throat and I knew I had to get out of there.

The opposite set of doors led to a wide hall, this one with a white-and-gold carpet leading to the main chapel, or whatever it was. The walls were presently devoid of religious symbols, though I'd noticed a number of crosses, crucifixes, and even a Star of David leaning against a wall in the office. They were ready for all comers.

The voices originated from this room, where a man and woman were setting up folding chairs in neat rows. They were careful to stagger them so everyone would see the show up front. The line of chairs closest to the speaker's podium were fancier and non-folding. Painted white, with gold velvet upholstery, they were obviously reserved for the family. On a low, gold-draped platform left of the podium was a coffin.

The two people, apparently husband and wife and owners of the business, were busy discussing personal economics. I'd expected them to be quiet or reverent or something as they worked, but life goes on, even for funeral directors.

Clatter.

"I don't see how another dime will really hurt us," said the wife. "It's only one more dime a week."

Clack-clatter.

The man shook his head. "That makes for five-twenty a year on top of what she already charges. You've got to look at the whole picture."

"Four-eighty at the most, dear. There are no lessons on the holidays."

"It's still four-eighty."

"But think of the savings later, when she can play piano during the services. Then we won't have to hire Mrs. Johnson to do the music. This is actually a kind of investment. Besides, the extra business we've just gotten *more* than covers the expense for . . ."

Clatter-squeak.

The last chair finally went up and they left by a different door, still talking. I slipped across the room.

Escott had jumped the gun on things. The body in the casket wasn't
Emily Francher, but John Henry Banks.

Sometimes they look like they're asleep, but sleeping people usually
have some kind of an expression. Banks looked the way he was—dead.
They'd cleaned him up and there was no visible sign of injury, but he wasn't
going to smile or exclaim over a generous tip ever again. The responsibility
stabbed at me as it had at Escott, and I was torn between sorrow for Banks
and anger at the person who'd killed him.

I paid what poor respects I could and left before the man and woman
returned.

Escott rolled up and I got in. He found my report a disappointment, but
got us moving in the right direction, toward the Francher estate.

"I expect that she left very clear and specific instructions concerning the
disposal of her remains," he said.

"You can make book on it. I want to know exactly what happened and
to see how Barrett is taking all this."

"Yes, and Laura as well."

I had some very private plans for Laura and saw no reason to tell him
anything about them yet. "You don't figure Emily's death to be from natural causes?" He could tell that I didn't.

"I've no hard data yet to incline my opinion one way or another,
whether it was an accident, act of God, or murder. However, it does look
very odd, especially coming right after our interview with Barrett last
night."

The town faded behind us and the trees drew right up to the road and
closed overhead. Escott made the correct turning to take us to the Francher
house.

"He might have questioned Laura," I said.

"Which is something else I need to know about."

"He may try to protect her."

"Protect her?"

"Not everyone is as justice minded as you, Charles. Like it or not, those
two have become his family. A man will usually try to protect his family no
matter what they've done. I'm just saying this as a warning. Barrett's got a
hell of a temper and it could . . . could get away from him."

"As it has with you?"

I nodded, staring at the rush of gray shadows outside the window.

"Is that why you wanted to stop me last night?"

"Yeah, something like that. All I could see then was one big messy can
of worms being dumped out."

"And what do you see now?"

"John Henry Banks lying in a box forty years too soon."

Escott drove quickly and absently, with most of his concentration directed inward and not at the road. He almost passed the gate by except for my warning.

Mayfair was just inside sitting on a camp stool, ready to handle the incoming traffic. He had orders that only officials of the law and family were allowed in, but Escott's investigator's license placed him nominally in the former category. That and a generous tip persuaded the Cerberus in baggy pants to let us through, and he even parted with some minimal information.

"She died from a fall down the stair in the front hall," Escort repeated, slamming his door and shifting gears. "One of the maids found her and thought it was a faint until she saw the blood. Dr. Evans was called out and he brought in Chief Curtis."

"Why the cops?"

"Mayfair didn't know."

"So maybe it wasn't an accident. Are they still here?"

"Left hours ago, but the relatives from Newport have arrived in force."

"How much inheritance do you figure is involved?"

He gave out with a short, cheerless laugh. "You and I think along similar lines. I've no idea, but it is bound to be quite a lot. I'd give a lot for a look at her will and how she may have allowed for things in the event of her return."

Cars were parked haphazardly along the drive and on the grass, and the garage exit was choked. Almost every light in the house was on, and faces appeared at the windows to inspect the latest arrivals.

A different maid let us in. She'd left off the white starched collar and cuffs of her uniform and wore unrelieved black. Her round mouth was crushed and her eyes were red lined and puffy from her own grief. I recognized her as one of the two women who shared rooms over the garage. She didn't bother to get our names, taking it for granted that Mayfair had kept out the undesirables.

Emily had a lot of relatives. Some of them might have been there out of genuine concern, but none were readily apparent. A lot of booze was flowing, so it was starting to resemble an impromptu wake.

"You see Barrett?" I asked him.

"No. Do you see Laura?"

"Nope. Let's split up."

"Right."

Escort melted away into the crowd and I lost sight of even his tall, distinctive form in a few seconds. The big front hall didn't look so big anymore; it was literally a case of all the world and his wife showing up. I started to push my way through a sudden opening when a thin, hard-faced woman with gingery hair focused her sharp eyes on me and came over.

"Are you family?" she demanded sweetly.

"No. Friend."

"Then you shouldn't be here," she quickly said. "It's family only until the funeral."

"How are you related?"

"Poor Emily was my cousin."

"Second or third and only by marriage," an eavesdropper put in help-fully, and got a drawn-daggers look for his trouble.

"We were *very* close years ago," she defended smoothly to me. "And *that* makes up for a lot."

"But never as much as you hope," added the heckler.

She turned her back on him to face me. "Anyway, you'll *have* to go. It's family only, as I said. The maid will show you out." She waited expectantly with her hands neatly folded and her chin up and I struggled not to laugh in her face. Someone else did, loudly, and was immediately shushed. This made us the brief center of attention and my reluctant hostess went very pink, but held her ground.

Someone else latched on to my arm and I thought for a second that I really was about to be evicted.

"Why, Cousin Jules! I haven't seen you since the war, how you've grown!" A younger woman in dark blue tugged hard and led me from the scene.

"Yeah . . . it's been a while," I loudly agreed.

Once out of immediate earshot she said, "Don't mind her, Abigail is just your average inheritance vulture like the rest of us. Her trouble is that she pretends so hard she isn't."

"Thanks, Mrs., Miss . . ."

"Clarice Francher, Miss." We shook hands. "I'm a vulture as well, but then I'm more honest about it."

"How's that?"

"I admit that I never liked Cousin Violet and hardly knew Emily. I'm here for appearance' sake and so I can hear what people are saying about me behind my back."

She was a pretty woman in her middle twenties with intelligent eyes and a nicely rounded-out figure. She gave me a once-over as well and seemed to like what she saw.

"And who are you, Mr. . . . ."

"Jack F-flynn," I stumbled out, mindful that John R. Fleming was offi-cially dead and had to stay that way for the time being. She picked up on the hesitation, so I changed the subject. "Look, I only just heard about this, can you tell me exactly what happened to Emily?"

Her big eyes had narrowed. "Are you a reporter?"

"No, only a friend."

"Whose?" She was evidently aware of Emily's hermitlike life.

"Emily's secretary."

This got me a second and much harder look. "Really? So the mystery man has a friend?"

I glimpsed Abigail from the corner of one eye, straining to catch every word. "Acquaintance might be more accurate." Someone else caught Abigail's attention and she darted off to harp at them.

"Might it?"

"Yeah, we've got some business dealings in common. Now, about the accident—"

"Maybe you should talk to Mr. Barrett."

"I'd be glad to. Where is he?"

She shrugged. "Around, I suppose. I haven't seen him."

"I understand the police were called out here."

"Yes, they were, but it was just routine."

"Where did it happen?"

Clarice rolled her eyes, but with a hint of a smile. "You don't give up, do you?"

"It's what makes me so charming."

The smile became more pronounced. "All right. As I heard it, one of the maids found her at the foot of the stairs here in the entry hall. They called the doctor, but she was already dead—cracked her skull on all that marble. The doctor called in the police to look things over, but they didn't find anything funny. I think it was for show more than anything else. They probably wanted Laura to know they were on the job."

"Where is Laura? How is she?"

"Who knows? That tame dragon, Mrs. Mayfair, has been guarding her all day."

"When did it happen?"

"Sometime before two, because that's when the maid crossed the hall and found her. Good thing she did, or poor Emily might still be lying there."

"Where is she now?"

"They've put her in one of the side parlors." She nodded her head in the general direction.

"Would you mind taking me there, Miss Francher?"

"There're dozens of Miss Franchers here, you'd better call me Clarice." Somehow, despite her friendly smile, she made it sound like a threat. She linked her arm in mine again and we worked slowly through the hall. I got a look at the spot at the foot of the stairs and kept my eyes peeled for Barrett. The spot told me nothing, but the knot of people near it were entertaining and Clarice stopped to listen. Abigail was in the center of things, being her own sweet self.

"If you ask me, the little brat pushed her." She was obviously more candid and open with her opinions within the family.

"No one's asking you, Abby."

"Then you should. You don't know her, the stuck-up little bitch."

"Careful, Abby."

"What's the use? You know we're not getting anything from this because of her. If only cousin Violet were alive."

"We still wouldn't get anything, Emily's the one who got all of Cousin Roger's money."

"And she'll have left it to Laura or *that man*. He's nothing more than a gigolo, a fortune hunter."

"And what does that make you, dear Abigail?"

This brought about a furious response from Abigail. No one noticed as Clarice and I passed on to the parlor.

"They really shouldn't bait Abby so," she commented. "It's just too easy."

A corpse puts a damper on any party. As crowded as it was, no one was in the parlor when we entered. Clarice's fingers tightened very slightly on my arm as she reacted to the presence of death, and then let go.

Emily looked like Banks, dead. She wore some kind of white gown and held a white rose to her breast. They'd done a good job on her makeup; if she'd sustained any facial injuries or scrapes, they were well hidden. I looked long and hard, because her face did appear younger than I remembered, but she was lying down, and that would make a difference in the lay of the skin against the bones beneath.

The fine lines were still there under the powder, though. The mortician's artistry was simply undisturbed by movement or expression and gave only the illusion of youth. I touched her hand and said her name, but nothing happened.

She was cool, not cold; she'd been dead only a few hours. Her hand was still flexible. Rigor hadn't yet set in, but that wasn't unusual. It could occur anytime within ten hours of death starting in the jaw and neck, but I had absolutely no desire to test those areas.

"You liked her, didn't you?" asked Clarice.

I'd forgotten she'd been standing behind me and withdrew my hand from the casket. "I barely knew her, but I guess I did."

"A lot of us can say the same thing. Maybe if we hadn't been so blue nosed about that man she had . . ." She shrugged self-consciously.

"Yeah?"

"I don't know, maybe she wouldn't have been so alone in other ways."

"Did anyone in the family really dislike her?"

She was mildly surprised. "Not that I know of. There's jealousy, of course, but only because of the money. I think if she'd had a lot less of it, no one would have taken any notice of her at all."

"What about Laura?"

"What about her?"

"What's she like?"

She shook her head. "I saw her once as a kid at her parents' funeral. I really don't remember her. You sure you're not a reporter?"

Not anymore. "I'm sure. Thanks for taking me around."

"Leaving so soon?"

"I gotta look for a friend."

She smiled once more, her slight disbelief lending an interesting curl to the corner of her mouth. "Watch out for Abigail, cousin."

I craned a neck through the press outside for Escott or Barrett, and listened to bits of conversation as I made a way to the stairs again.

". . . call it a holiday? I tell you she had a complete breakdown and never got over it." ". . . wonder how much money she wasted on these trashy paintings?" ". . . the two of them carrying on with the girl right here in the same house." ". . . years younger than her, the poor thing, and it's not as though she didn't have a chance to find someone her own age." ". . . vicious old hag. Getting burned alive was only what she deserved. That's what they used to do with witches, you know."

A lowering of the general hubbub spread out from the center of the hall and heads swiveled toward a young woman descending the stairs. I didn't know her at first, but then the last time I'd seen her she'd been naked. Now she wore a severe black dress, and her lush blond hair was parted in the middle and drawn back into a demure bun at the base of her neck. She wore no makeup; her tanned face was drained and her eyes red.

"Laura, you poor dear!" exclaimed Abigail, and the thin woman rushed up to be the first to take her hand. Laura looked at her blankly, forcing her would-be and now-embarrassed comforter to introduce herself. "But of course you must be exhausted," she concluded, to excuse the lapse of memory.

Mrs. Mayfair appeared and without seeming to, managed to disengage Abigail, and led the girl down to the main hall. As soon as there was space, whether by accident or design, several people closed ranks behind her, cutting Abigail off from further contact.

Laura didn't notice and was busy collecting comforting hugs and murmurs of sympathy from her more recognizable relatives. Once the "hello dears" and "we're sorrys" were out of the way, one of them voiced it for all.

"What are you going to do now, Laura?"

Laura shook her head and shrugged. "I have a lot to think about, but Mr. Handley is taking care of all the legal matters for now."

"We hate to bring this up so soon, but one has to be practical about such things. What arrangements did Emily make?"

"I-I don't understand," the girl faltered, looking very young and vulnerable.

"Cousin Robert is talking about Emily's will, dear."

"Oh. I hadn't thought about it. Mr. Handley—"

"Is a stranger. We're your family. You need someone you can trust. . . ."

They weren't making it easy on her. Mrs. Mayfair stepped into the breach. "Miss Laura is still very much shocked by the accident. She really should be upstairs resting."

Laura drew herself straight, remembering why she'd come down. "I-I just wanted to thank you all for coming. It is a great comfort, but I don't feel well tonight. Mr. Handley is here and he will answer your questions on . . . on things."

It had the sound of a memorized speech and generated some muted tones of disgruntlement. The girl was no fool and did indeed know where to place her trust. At this official statement, Handley came downstairs; a stocky man in a vested suit with a stubborn mouth and Teutonic jaw. He had the fixed smile of a hard professional and slicked his pale blond hair back with Vaseline.

"*Lawyers*," hissed a woman, and made it sound like a curse.

"I know, darling," agreed another woman. "You can guess who's getting the lion's share out of this."

"Then there's no need for you to stay, is there?"

Handley said, "There are many arrangements to be made yet. Nothing can possibly be settled tonight, or at least until the poor lady has been laid to rest."

"He means we have to stick around till after the funeral to find out anything," a woman confided to her husband. She wrinkled her upper lip as though smelling a bad odor.

"When's that? Tonight?"

"*Shh*, Robert."

"This whole business is fishy—dead this afternoon and in her box by evening."

"Did you expect them to just leave her on the floor?"

"Miss Laura sincerely thanks all of you for coming and respectfully requests that you all return home until the funeral."

Objections rippled through the crowd. It was perfectly obvious to some that Laura's respectful request certainly did not apply to *them*. My sympathy went out to the hired help, who would have their hands full trying to evict them all.

Laura started upstairs for some peace, but Abigail had bided her time and darted in fast.

"My *dear* child, you really *shouldn't* be alone in this big house and you know that I—"

"Excuse me," I broke in, loud enough to distract even Abigail. "Miss Laura?"

"Yes?" Laura had a very kissable mouth and light blue eyes. Her pupils were dilated; Dr. Evans may have given her something to bolster her up for the mob.

"My name's Jack Flynn, I'm—"

"He's not family," Abigail put in suddenly. "He said so and he told Clarice he was a friend of that—of poor Emily's secretary."

The information woke Laura out of her daze, or seemed to. Much of it might have been assumed as a protection against the emotional clawing and tugging from all the people around her. She studied me with guarded interest and not the least sign of recognition, but then whoever had slugged me on the road had done it from behind. "You're a friend of Mr. Barrett's?"

"A business acquaintance," I clarified. "I came to offer my condolences and see him, if I may."

"What business?" Her tone was dull, but now I was certain it was faked because of her question. She was interested and not content to fob this off onto her lawyer.

"Nothing to bother you about, you're quite busy enough." I was acutely conscious of all the curious eyes and cocked ears around us. "Is he around?"

Her answer was slow, as if she interrupted her inner flow of thought to remember my question. "No. Actually, I haven't seen him all day. Sometimes his duties require him to leave on short notice."

The hackles went up on my neck at her easy tone. "When did he leave?"

"I really don't know."

"Does he even know about the accident?"

She blinked a few times, as though confused. "Why, of course he does."

"Has anyone tried to find him?"

Her blank, frozen look was back. "Mr. Handley has. Perhaps you should talk to him. Would you please excuse me?"

Mrs. Mayfair got between us and took the girl upstairs.

Handley came forward, his smile still fixed in place, but not at all neutral. "What business do you have with Mr. Barrett?" he asked.

Again I was conscious of the audience all around us. "It's personal. Any idea where he is?"

"None at all, I'm afraid. It's very inconvenient for him to go off like this just when he's needed the most."

"And even Laura has no idea where he's gone?"

"None. He left no message, but Miss Laura has told me that it's not unusual for him to do so."

"I need to find him. Would the servants know?"

"You may ask them. Excuse me."

A dozen steps up, I caught him again. We were still very much in full view, but no one was in immediate earshot. "Don't you think it's odd, him being away like this?"

"A little."

"A little? The woman's private secretary takes off the same day she makes a permanent dive down the stairs, I think it's pretty damned odd."

"Are you suggesting some sort of connection?"

"Possibly. Did you know that they were lovers?"

He was quite property shocked. "Mr. Flynn, I find your question to be extremely tasteless. To defame the character of my late client—"

"It can't be defamation if it's the truth. I want to talk to you about this."

His hard face got harder and the fixed smile twisted to express his distaste. "This way," he said in an acid tone, and continued up. I followed him to Barrett's office.

The rolltop desk was open now and littered with papers and ledger books. The French windows were also open to let in a faint breeze. Mindful of the veranda's connection to Laura's room farther down, I went out for a quick look. I was on edge not knowing where the hell Barrett had lost himself, and this was just routine paranoia—I really didn't expect to see the figure hiding in the deep shadows cast by the roof overhang.

10

HE was a perfect statue, standing exactly in line with a tall, potted plant. His subdued clothing blended with the darkness and made him as invisible to human eyes as anyone can get and still be solid.

The sight gave me a bad start and I had to choke back the surprise; then I wanted to belt him one for the scare. Escott read it all off my face easily enough and shrugged as though to say it wasn't *his* fault that I was so jumpy. He was there to hide from the lawyer, not to frighten poor nerved-up vampires.

"What is it?" demanded Handley, annoyed at the delay.

"Nothing, just checking the weather. We've been having an awful lot of it lately." I left the veranda to Escott and went inside to take a seat on the sofa. In order to face me, Handley had to turn his back on the open windows. He commandeered the banker's chair as I'd hoped he would.

"Now, what is this about?" From his attitude he must have thought I was warming up to try a little blackmail against the memory of his late client.

"Barrett and Emily Francher," I said.

"So I've assumed, since you suggested they had an intimate relationship."

"I stated they were lovers."

"Gossip is common, Mr. Flynn, very common."

"I know it for a fact."

"And have you evidence?"

"We're not in court, Mr. Handley, so just for laughs, let's pretend it's true. Can you think of any kind of errand that would keep Barrett away from here at this time?"

"He simply might not have heard the news yet."

"Laura just said that he had."

"Granted, but I can hardly supply you with the specific reason you seem to be looking for. Anything to do with the relationship of two people is bound to be complex, especially when such a disparate age difference is involved."

"More than you think," I muttered.

"What?"

"Nothing. Even with this talk of complexities, you think he'd run out at a time like this?"

"I really couldn't say."

"I'll put emotions aside, then. Let's say that his only attachment was to her money. There's a lot of it floating around here. I assume Miss Emily left a will?"

"You may assume correctly."

"Don't you think Barrett would want to stick around to hear it?"

"You presume that he is gone for good, young man. We don't know if he has. You also imply that Mr. Barrett is some type of fortune hunter, but I can tell you that Miss Emily was no fool in that regard."

"What do you mean?"

"Exactly what I said. Miss Emily was well aware of the kind of men who might prefer her money over herself, and allowed for it."

"I want to know what you mean."

"That is my business and none of yours, sir. Why are you so concerned?"

"Because I think it's damned funny that she should get herself killed at this time."

"What is so particularly special about this time?"

Watch it, I told myself.

"Are you suggesting there was something irregular about her death?"

"Convince me it wasn't. Convince me that someone didn't push her down the stairs."

He knew I was being utterly ridiculous. "Do you fully realize the serious nature of such a suggestion?"

"No one better. For instance, why did the doctor call in the police?"

"Miss Emily was a person of substantial standing in this community—"

"Bosh, she hardly left the house."

"She was certainly an important taxpayer, then. Dr. Evans called in Chief Curtis because he is a very careful, conscientious man. The nature of the accident was such that he wanted an informed professional to look at the scene in order to specifically allay the very rumors which you seem bound to spread."

"So he smelled something fishy, too?"

"That is not what I—"

"What'd the doctor have to say? And Chief Curtis?"

"You may ask them yourself, but I warn you now that if you are looking for some sort of cheap sensationalism in this tragic occurrence you are certain to be disappointed."

"Are you protecting Laura?"

"What do you mean by that?"

I was getting nowhere fast and lost my patience along with my scruples. "Handley, listen to me. Listen very carefully."

It was harder with some than others. He was on guard and didn't want to hear what I had to say, so I stepped up the pressure.

"This is very important. You must listen to everything I say. . . ."

He blinked once, twice.

"Listen to my voice. . . ."

His eyes softened, the stubborn expression gradually went slack, and his world closed and centered on my words and will. I told him to shut his eyes because I hate that dull look, like what the animals get when I'm feeding.

Escott was peering around the edge of one window. I motioned him in, cautioning him to silence. He nodded and came close enough to watch.

I kept my voice even and conversational. "Handley, do you know where Barrett is?"

"No."

"What did Emily leave him in her will?"

"Nothing."

That surprised us. Escott impatiently gestured for me to continue.

"Nothing at all?"

"No."

"What about for Laura?"

"Yes."

Playing twenty questions would take us all night at this rate. "Have you a copy of Emily's will with you?"

"Yes."

That was a relief. "Where is it?"

"My briefcase."

Escott spotted the black leather case and made short work of finding, drawing out, and unfolding the document in question. I left him to read it and kept Handley busy.

"What did the doctor say about Emily? How did she die?"

"She fractured her skull in a fall."

"Why'd he call the cops?"

"The man likes to dramatize, thinks he sees more than what's really there." Handley apparently didn't like Dr. Evans, either. I wondered if he liked anyone at all.

"Did they find anything odd or suspicious?"

"No."

"What time did it happen?"

"About two o'clock today."

"Where was Laura Francher at two o'clock?"

"Outside. Horseback riding."

"For how long?"

"I don't know."

"Anyone witness this?"

"Haskell, the groom."

"Where were the other servants?"

The maid and cook were in the kitchen, repairing linens and baking bread respectively. Mrs. Mayfair was there as well, working with the cook on the week's new menu. The gardener was on the other side of the estate picking up storm debris. At 2:10 the maid finished her sewing and left the kitchen to take the linens upstairs. Instead of using the servants' passage, she went through the front hall to see if Mayfair had restocked the wood for the parlor fireplace. She found Emily at the foot of the stairs and raised the alarm. At some point in the proceedings, Mrs. Mayfair sent someone after Barrett. His door was locked and no one could find the key. They assumed he was out.

"You get all that?" I whispered to Escott.

"The germane points. Did Miss Emily not have a key to Barrett's room?"

I asked, but Handley didn't know.

"Odd, that."

"Not if Barrett wants to keep his secret. He'd have allowed for an emergency like this."

"Hmm. No doubt we can ask him. I should like to arrange an interview with this Haskell for the exact time of Laura's ride and where she went."

"If we can interview Laura, we won't have to."

"True." He skimmed the closely typed pages of the will. "I believe I see Barrett's guiding hand in this."

"Yeah?"

"There are some personal bequests, a generous trust for Laura, pensions for retired servants, and one most unusual arrangement. There is a long statement here by Emily concerning a close friendship she formed with one of her British in-laws. She had a special place in her heart for a young cousin whose name was also Emily."

"You mean—"

He kept talking. "In the event of Emily Francher's death, her secretary has instructions to contact this person. If she appears within one year after the reading of the will, the rest of the estate goes to her. This person's fingerprints are on file with the Franchers' bank manager and with Handley so that she may be correctly identified."

"I can see the riot that's going to cause among her excluded relatives."

"Yes, this is hardly something they'd lightly accept."

"What happens if this other Emily doesn't show up?"

His eyes zipped back and forth. "Then the estate goes to Laura. In the event of Laura's death, and/or if the other Emily never appears, then it's to be sold off and the money distributed to a number of charities."

"You think Laura knows about this will? If she does, then she could have made an investment for her future."

"Unless Emily's death was an accident, after all."

"We'll find out."

He looked at Handley with some amusement. "I take it from your question to our silent friend here that you haven't found Barrett?"

"You take right. Nobody's found him. I'm thinking maybe he packed up last night and left."

"Why should he do that?"

"I dunno, maybe he talked with Laura, heard something he didn't like, and took off to think things over."

He folded the will and put it back in the briefcase. "Did you see Laura?"

"Yeah, I even had a fast word with her. She gave out with a song and dance that he was gone because of his duties, whatever the hell that means."

"She could be covering for him," he suggested.

"During the day, yes, but he'd be up by now. He might just be wanting to avoid the relatives, and I can't blame him for that, but it looks bad."

"True. I was considering that if Emily's fall were no accident, then Mr. Barrett is the only one in the house with no alibi."

"Except with us. *We* know he couldn't have done anything."

"Possibly. Can you guide us to his sanctum?"

"No sweat, but he won't want to see us."

We started for the door, but Escott abruptly stopped. I didn't understand why until he jerked a thumb over his shoulder at the lawyer, who was still on the far side of dreamland.

"Handley? You can go back to your work, now. Completely forget we had this little talk, okay?"

"Very well," he replied, sounding perfectly normal. He opened his eyes, swiveled his chair around to face the desk, and started shuffling papers. Escott and I slipped out and paced down the hall.

"What were you doing in there?" I asked.

"Virtually nothing, as I had no time to do it. I'd just gotten to Barrett's office and was about to search the briefcase when the two of you walked in. The rest of the time I was looking for Barrett. Were you able to get a look at Emily's body?"

"Yeah."

"And her condition?"

"She's really dead, as far as I can tell."

"Then God forgive me for not coming out here sooner."

"You think it was no accident, then?"

"To do so would be to make an assumption without the benefit of facts." he said stiffly.

Okay, he had to be logical about things, but at least one part of his mind had given in to conclusion jumping, and he didn't like that part one bit.

We went down by way of the main stairs. People still loitered in the big hall, catching up on family gossip and speculating on their financial future. I was tempted to tell them all to forget it and go home.

No one paid any attention to us, and after a little thought I found the right hall and the right door, the only one in the wing that was locked. I slipped through it, found the stairwell we wanted, and came back again.

"No key on that side," I said. "I'll just—"

"I think I can manage." He pulled out an impressive set of skeleton keys and picks from a worn leather case. Crouching in front of the lock, he began to experiment.

"Aren't you the regular Raffles," I commented.

"Ah, but I hardly ever steal anything."

"Look, I can just go down for a quick gander. If he's really gone you won't need to—"

"There!" He turned the knob and pushed open the door. "That was a bit of luck. Usually it takes much longer."

"Where'd you learn to do that?" I was impressed.

"You acquire all kinds of skills in the theater." He replaced his picks and shut the case. "We once had a leading lady prone to the sulks and locking herself in her dressing room. For the duration of her contract I was often required to get her door open so the stage manager could persuade her to go to work."

"Crazy world."

"Very."

"But where'd you get that?" I gestured at the case as we went down the carpeted stairs.

"Oh, they're sort of an inheritance," he dismissed. "Let's see about this one now."

I didn't bother trying to slip through again; I enjoy watching an artist at work. The wood-covered metal door at the bottom of the steps had a different lock than the one in the upper hall and took longer to break, but it was fascinating to see him do it. He had a definite air of satisfaction as it gave way to his efforts.

Barrett wasn't there to greet us.

"Bolts on the inside I see," he noted as he walked in. "I suppose if he were still here he'd have shot them and your special assistance would be necessary, after all. This looks most ominous."

A few bureau drawers sagged open, their contents gutted, and there were gaps in the closet.

My shoulders were tightening and I didn't think it had to do with Barrett skipping out. Something else had crept into the back of my mind and I couldn't identify it.

Escott went to the library/living area and returned. "He's quite the reader. These books are well used. He also did a bit of writing . . . I've found some sort of journal. It's odd that he left so personal an item behind, unless he's on a short trip. . . . Where are you?"

"Closet," I called. The something bothering me wasn't in here.

He looked in. "Good heavens, it's as big as my sitting room."

I pointed. "He left his trunk."

"Perhaps he has a lighter one ready for travel purposes, as you do. That thing doesn't look too portable."

"Yeah, maybe."

"But I concede that this is also odd. You said he has earth in his bed?"

"Sewn up tight in some oilcloth." A scent in the air—that was what was nagging me. Each time I breathed in to talk . . .

Escott went over to the bed and flipped up the linens. Everything was in place as I'd found it a few nights ago.

"As far as we know, this island *is* his home ground."

I breathed, trying to catch it again.

"He might yet retain title to some house or—"

Bloodsmell.

"—plot of land in the area and could have gone there."

I drifted over to the bath, opened the door, and looked in.

"But the journal in there bothers me. . . ."

It was wrong. The whole damned world was wrong.

"Why should he risk leaving such a revealing document behind?"

And I was just another poor bastard with the bad luck to keep bumping face-on into the wrongness of it all.

"Jack?"

"Poor bastard . . ."

"What is it?"

Then he was next to me, staring at the awful thing on the cold tile floor.

"Oh, my dear God . . ."

The color left Escott's face and he put out a hand to steady himself against the wall. A return wave of last night's dizziness hit me and I backed from the doorway, staggering to the bed. The alien soil was no comfort.

Escott kept staring at it and I didn't like the look in his eyes.

"I should have anticipated this." His voice was very soft, very weary. "I should have. I've blown this whole business."

"Charles—"

He shook his head, quickly, to cut me off. He drew a steadying breath and went into the bath. After a moment he called out, "Jack, I want your help."

Jesus, for what?

Barrett had been pulled in feet first so that his head was just inside the door. He wore plain blue pajamas, but the top had been partially unbuttoned. The expensive silk was soaked through with massive patches of blood, most of it concentrated on his chest. Some blood was drying on the floor, but wide smear marks and two or three wet towels wadded in the tub indicated a little preliminary cleaning had been done.

Escott knelt over the body, his long fingers delicately peeling back the stiffening shirt front. The skin around the inch-thick shaft of wood in Barrett's chest was parchment thin and just as dry. He was like that all over. His handsome features had shriveled up like an old monkey's; his teeth were locked into a false grin by the lips and gums shrinking back. I was very, very glad his eyes were clenched shut.

"What do you want?" I asked.

"To render first aid."

"Charles, he's dead. He's probably been dead all day."

He shot me a piercing look, as angry as I'd ever seen him. "Knowing what you know, how can you tell?"

That shut me up.

He gave me a second to think, then said, "I need to try, I have to. Will you please help me?"

I gulped back whatever I'd started to say. God knows I owed him plenty, and he never asked for anything in return. "All right, name it."

Some of the tension left him. "I daren't pull the stake out until we have some blood on hand. He's very fragile now; the extra shock could be too much. My kit with the things I used to help you is in the car, along with that livestock syringe. Fetch it out and go to the stables—"

"But I don't know how to use a—"

"It's only a syringe. All you have to do is find a vein and push the needle into it. Pull the plunger back slowly, though."

I nodded doubtfully.

"The stable lad might be there. Svengali him if you must to get his help, but hurry."

I shoved down the sick hopelessness inside and got moving.

The front door was more direct and faster, but I didn't want to be seen, stopped, or questioned, and opted to disappear. I tore through the big hall, weaving between knots of dawdlers until I hit against the entry door and slipped through. Our car was way off to the left and I maintained that general direction awhile before going solid. The cloudy darkness made the possibility remote, but I was wary of being spotted from the house.

The car was standing alone now on the grass. It looked like a long night ahead and I didn't want anyone noticing it.

Escott had given me the keys, so I started it up and scooted over the grounds until it was hidden from the casual eye by a break of trees.

Escott had stashed the bag in the back. It contained everything but the syringe, which I found in a metal box that had slid under the seats. The thing looked huge, but then large animals can require large amounts of medication. I dumped the case into the bag and ghosted up the road.

Rounding the bulk of the house, I went solid and saw lights on over the stables. Haskell, the groom, was in. I trotted up the stairs to his room and tapped on the door, calling his name.

He presented a startled face, all suntan and mussed hair and wore only his undershirt and workpants. "Yeah, who are you? What is it?"

"I'm a friend of Barrett's. Listen to me, it's very important that you do exactly what I tell you. . . ."

He might have cooperated without my influence, but I couldn't waste the time answering his inevitable questions. By now I was long past the point of worrying about the morals of using forced hypnosis; it was a tool and it worked. I gave him just enough time to pull on his boots and sent him down to the fenced yard to bring in the horses.

My hands shook as I pulled out the syringe. It was one thing to use my teeth, and I had enough trouble handling that idea at times, but it was quite another to use a needle to do the same job. Escott wasn't the only one who could get squeamish.

Haskell led in a big roan gelding and tied its halter rope to a ring on the wall. Its ears twitched, but I soothed it down with a little stroking and talking. Horses like to listen to nonsense, and this one was in the mood for it. When Haskell led in a second horse I stopped him and held up a milk bottle.

"Can you find me more like this? Clean ones?"

He stared hard at it.

"Any kind of bottles?"

He finally nodded and I sent him off.

I crouched next to the roan, picked out a vein, and decided on a firm fast jab over a slow punch and managed to get it settled somewhere in the middle. I was clumsy and the horse felt it, but kept still while I filled the barrel of the syringe.

It seemed to take hours, but there was no way to hurry things. When it was full I drew out the needle, shoved the point inside the milk bottle, and pressed the plunger. The process was far too slow with the blood coming out in such a tiny stream; it'd take all night to get six quarts. From the look of Barrett's dried-out and shrunken body, he'd need every ounce and fast.

At the base of the syringe, where the needle attached, was a gizmo that unscrewed it, probably for cleaning. Trust Escott to think about neatness. I opened it up and poured the rest into the milk bottle, filling it halfway.

Just as I finished, Haskell returned, carrying a case of amber beer bottles.

"Those clean?"

He nodded.

"You make your own?"

"Me 'n Mayfair, but don' tell his missus."

"My solemn promise. Bring in the other horse, will you?"

He did and I worked. I was getting better at putting the needle in right, but no one would give me points for neatness or speed. But at least the milk bottle was full, now. It would give Escott something to start with.

"Haskell."

He let go tying a rope.

"You see what I'm doing?"

"Yes."

"Think you can take over for me?"

"Yes."

"Great. Just fill it up and unscrew this part to empty it into one of your bottles. Okay?"

"Uh-huh."

"And wash the needle clean each time. I'll be back shortly for more."

He took the syringe and I grabbed up the milk bottle and Escott's bag.

The door to the kitchen was open and lights were still on everywhere. Not knowing how I could freely trot through the house with such a gory burden and unsure about finding the right hall again, I went down the cellar steps for a shortcut. With the bottle and gear hugged close to my body, I walked through the thick brick wall into Barrett's room.

Escott was at the writing desk flipping through a book whose pages were covered with fine, script-style writing. His back was to me and yet again I gave him a start.

"What are you doing?" I handed over the bag.

"Waiting for you and poking into things." He put away the book and returned to the bathroom.

Barrett looked worse than I remembered. "How are you going to do it?"

"Tube down his throat," he said tersely.

"Was I like this when you found me at the warehouse?"

"Not as bad. I'll hold him still, you pull out the stake. Keep it as straight as you can."

I pulled. The brittle body vibrated. The wood shaft sang against the ribs and came free. Unbelievably, there was more blood left in him to well up in the wound. We both looked to his mummified face for any sign of life. He never moved. Escott grimaced and placed the tube between Barrett's teeth and fed it down his throat.

"Isn't it supposed to go up his nose?"

"The tissues are too shriveled to attempt it. The problem we have here is that his glottis might be open and I could end up putting the blood into his lungs instead of his stomach."

"You can't tell?"

"Not unless he's breathing." He fitted the other end of the rubber tube into a stopper with a hole in the middle.

"How'd you get by for me, then?"

"I was lucky."

"You learn all this at that hospital?"

"I picked up some useful knowledge during my brief sojourn." He shoved the stopper firmly into the bottle and upended the thing, pinching the tube slightly to regulate the flow. "Can you get more?" he asked.

"Yeah, Haskell's working on it. I'll be right back."

Haskell had the first of the beer bottles full and was busy drawing off more from another horse.

"You're doing a good job," I said. "Ever have to before?"

"Yeah, I know a little about this stuff." His tone was different. He'd come out of the hypnosis sooner than I'd expected.

"Are you all right?" I asked.

"Yeah."

"Do you know why you're doing this?"

"No, but I figure you're trying to help Mr. Barrett."

"You know about him?"

He glanced up and I could see there was a brain working inside his head. "Maybe as much as you do?"

"What do you know?"

He drew out the needle, detached it from the syringe, and carefully poured the contents into a bottle. "I know I got a steady job here, the pay is good, and I have a lot of free time. How many people can say that these days?"

"Then you've seen Barrett—"

He nodded, tapping in a final drop. "Yeah, he's careful, but I seen him a couple times down in the yard."

"Doesn't it bother you?"

He shrugged. "It scared me at first, but not now. He don't hurt no one, he don't hurt the horses. This is a good place to work and he's a nice man, you know?"

"What about Miss Laura? What d'you think of her?"

Another shrug. "She's all right, maybe a little too full of herself."

"How do you mean?"

"She's just not the type to think about others, but I guess she's still young yet."

I took the bottles to Escott. "Any change?"

"Look at his teeth."

I did. Barrett's piercing canines had been even with his others, but now they were more prominent, as though ready to feed.

"Of course, it might only be a reflex of some kind," he cautioned. "I don't want to get too hopeful."

"What about his chest?"

Escott's own heart was beating very fast. "The hole has closed up."

I felt a grin start up on my face. "I'll go get another couple bottles."

When I came back, there was a definite change in Barrett's appearance. His face looked fractionally fuller and the skin was flexible to the touch. "It's working, Charles."

He nodded, but his own expression was still tight. "You were a long time."

"I was having a talk with Haskell."

"Yes?"

"He said he saddled a horse for Laura at one-thirty, and then she asked him to wash her car. He'd washed it earlier that morning, but she gave him some guff about dust and told him to wash it again anyway. It kept him busy on the opposite side of the house and he didn't see where she went."

"Interesting."

"Yeah, especially when you realize she'd have no problem getting back into the house from a patio door on the far side. I checked—"

Barrett's body spasmed and he suddenly gagged on the tube down his throat. Escott quickly pulled it out.

"Charles, you're a goddamned miracle worker!"

His face flushed. "Some days are better than others."

Barrett's lips moved, his teeth still prominent. Escott put the tube to them, but Barrett drew the blood out too fast and the tube collapsed from the suction. Escott detached it from the plug and put it straight into the bottle like a straw.

"We need more," he said.

"I'm moving."

In the end, Barrett drained away just over six quarts of the stuff, and I witnessed a faster version of the kind of recovery I'd gone through myself. The wrinkling smoothed, dry flesh-colored twigs turned into fingers, and stiff parchment filled out to became skin again.

He began coughing at one point, getting rid of the fluid that had built up in his pierced lung. It was a mess, but Escott grabbed a towel and I helped turn him on his side. The back of his pajama shirt was practically glued to the floor.

"How long do you think he's been here?" I asked.

"An expert could estimate from the condition of the blood, but I'm no expert. Perhaps it was concurrent with the incident on the stairs."

Barrett would be listening. Escott knew there was no need to hit him with the news of Emily's death just yet.

"Logically and practically, I would say it was done earlier, as this was a crime that was never meant to be discovered. Later than two o'clock and she would never have had the chance to be alone long enough to do it."

"And he's been here like this all day."

"He may not have been conscious."

He was only trying to ease my mind, but I knew better. Once his body had been dragged from the bed, Barrett's contact with his soil would be severed. He'd have been aware. Unable to act, but aware. For myself, there is no feeling worse than that kind of helplessness.

I stood and motioned Escott to come with me to the far end of the library, and kept my voice very low. "I need to go back upstairs again. Can you handle all this with him?"

"Yes, but—"

"I'm going to have a talk with Laura. It's way overdue."

"Agreed, but I'd like to be there myself."

"I know, but I need you to keep Barrett busy."

Whether he could read anything else into that, I wasn't ready to guess. The important thing was to say something that was halfway convincing so I could get out of there. He was distracted because Barrett was coughing and still needed help, otherwise I might have gotten more argument from him. Escott finally nodded, and if he knew what I had in mind, he chose not to comment.

"This might take awhile," I added, risking it anyway. A part of me hoped he would catch on and try talking me out of it.

He didn't, or wouldn't. "Very well. Take as long as you need."

I shut the metal fire door behind me and climbed the stairs up to the deserted wing. Inside me, equal portions of fire and ice went to war.

11

THE last of the relatives were gone and the staff had cleared away their debris and swept up. Except for the stale stink of cigarette smoke hanging in the air, no signs were left of the recent invasion. I made a careful and quiet sweep of the place to make sure Cousin Abigail hadn't lingered in some corner, but all was clear and silent. In a den off the main hall I found a third of a bottle of whiskey in a liquor cabinet and took it upstairs.

The door to Emily's room was locked, probably as a precaution against family souvenir hunters. The room was undisturbed and both jewel safes in her closet were firmly shut, but I wasn't interested in them. I pocketed what I needed and left.

I listened for a long time outside Laura's door to be certain that Mrs. Mayfair was gone and that the girl was alone. Water ran and splashed; she was having a long shower to steam away the day's troubles. The water sound cut off and softer, less distinct ones replaced it as she toweled down and padded barefoot around her room.

Her door abruptly opened in my face and her light blue eyes flashed on me in shock and fear. She nearly screamed, but didn't. The house was empty, no one would hear.

She was head to toe in black, her bright blond hair covered by a black scarf.

"Going to a funeral?" I asked.

Her heart jumped and she backed away, but I caught her wrist, swinging her around until she was pressed against the wall. Now she did try to scream, a normal reflex to the situation, but I stopped that with one hand and talked quickly, urgently, focusing in hard enough to crack through her terror. It eventually worked and she relaxed against the wall and I took my hand away from her mouth.

"Where were you going?" I asked.

"The basement."

"Why?"

"I have to get rid of him."

It was no galloping surprise. At this point I was just being thorough. "Did you try to—did you kill Barrett?"

"Yes."

"Why?"

"He knew—knew—" She was struggling against it and could shake it off if she fought hard enough.

"All right, calm down. Everything's okay."

Her breathing smoothed out.

"Go back into your room, lock the door, and sit down."

I followed her in. She chose to sit at her dressing table on a little satin stool much like one Bobbi had. I checked the place, keeping well clear of the veranda windows. The stables were at an oblique angle to them on this side, but there was a chance Haskell might look out and see my figure against Laura's curtains. It was very important that she appear to be alone now.

She was—at least in the mirrors.

It was a cheery place, with yellow flowers blooming in the wallpaper, and a thick rust-colored rug covered most of the floor. The bath was warm and damp from her shower, and that day's black dress was crumpled into a hamper. She'd rinsed her stockings herself and hung them over the shower rod to dry.

I found a chair and dragged it over to face her. In the mirror-covered wall it moved all by itself.

She was very still, waiting for me to speak. Her body rhythms were strong and even. After an active summer of swimming and riding, her skin was tanned and healthy. She was quite a beautiful girl and her youth attracted me even as it must have attracted Barrett.

"Laura, my name is Jack. You remember me from earlier tonight?"

She nodded.

"I'm going to ask you some questions and you will want to answer them. You can tell me the truth, to do so will make you feel very good."

She waited, disinterested and seeing nothing.

"Laura, did you kill Maureen Dumont?"

"Who?"

And that threw me until I realized she might never have heard the name. "Remember the summer of the fire?"

"Yes."

"Remember the dark-haired woman who came one night to see Barrett?"

"Yes."

"Did you kill that woman?"

She'd buried it deep and it didn't want to come out. Her breath got short, and for a second, real awareness came back to her eyes. I steadied her down and soothed her, keeping my voice low, but pitched so she had to listen. I told her it was all right to answer and repeated my question, and then she said yes.

I felt nothing looking into her blank eyes. Her face ceased to belong to a person and took on the smooth, bland beauty of a mannequin. The lost years and the emotional racking and the physical trauma had taken all feeling from me. The worry, fear, and doubt that had once driven me were gone, and I was empty. We mirrored each other now. All I had left were questions, and they weren't really mine, but Escott's.

"Laura, talk to me. Tell me about it. Why did you do it?"

She revealed no surprises. Escott had been right. She was in love with Barrett and had killed to keep him.

"Did you kill Violet that summer?"

"No, the fire did."

It was an odd answer and I picked a subtle change in her tone of voice, as though I were talking to a child. "Did you set the fire in the house?"

"No."

"How did it start?"

"The lamp cord."

"Did you do something to the lamp cord?"

"I fixed it."

"So that it would start the fire?"

"Yes."

"Then you did kill Violet."

"No, the *fire* killed her."

I could argue with her, but to no point. Her exacting logic was how she could live with herself, by shifting the blame. "Why did you kill her?"

For Barrett, all for Barrett. She'd wanted him that badly. She'd frayed the wires and fixed the rug so that air could feed in. All she had to do was turn on the lamp and wait. When the first flames sprang up she went out the door and snuck back to her room.

"How could you do that?"

She gave a little shrug. "It was easy."

Fire and ice inside me and now the same sickness I'd felt when Banks had died.

"How did you kill Maureen?" Someone else seemed to be talking to her but using my voice.

She'd read up about vampires that summer. She knew more about us than Barrett had ever suspected, and she knew what to do.

Being a strong girl, it had been nothing for her to lift Maureen's small body from her trunk to the bath in the bright light of morning. She'd filched a sharp stake of wood from Mayfair's work shed and she had a hammer. Frozen by daylight, Maureen had died without a sound. The only problem for Laura was the blood. Her clothes had been soaked with it and she was frightened she'd be found out. She'd spent hours cleaning it up.

In a cardboard box scavenged from the kitchen she hid Maureen's body. It was very light now, hardly more than a husk. She had no trouble getting it downstairs and out the side door, away from the servants' wing. Dragging it into some trees, Laura used their cover to take it to the ruins of the old house.

She'd been forbidden to play there, but such rules had never stopped her before. There was a broken spot in the floor above the deepest part of the cellar. It sagged under her weight, but she was careful to move slowly and test each step, pushing the box ahead of her. Grating against the soot and debris, it barely held together. She just managed to get it to the edge and pushed it in.

It had been a rainy summer, but the splash still startled her. She hadn't expected the cellar to be so full of water. A cautious look over the edge showed only a rippling reflection of the sky behind her head. There was no sign of the box or of Maureen's body. Laura was safe.

The parallels of what happened to Maureen and what nearly happened to me were all too clear in my mind. I knew *exactly* what she had gone through, and inside I was screaming for her. I stood and backed away from the girl. Not all feeling had died. The war was still going on between fiery rage and cold justice. Neither was canceling the other out, both seemed to be fusing together somehow.

"What about Maureen's things?" I asked, a calm stranger once more using my voice.

The only real problem was in getting rid of the woman's trunk. The earth she mixed in with the flower beds, the clothes Laura took to her room and hid under the bed. She spent the rest of the day reading and dancing by herself before the mirrors, as she usually did.

The household schedule was unorthodox, but regular. The staff did downstairs maintenance until midafternoon, when Emily woke up. After her breakfast, the maid was allowed to work upstairs. No one paid much attention to Laura or her activities. Showing up on time for meals was all that was expected of her.

She and Emily shared supper just before sunset, as usual, then Emily went downstairs to be with Barrett. Whenever Emily was with him, they almost always spent an hour or more together. Laura returned to her own room and changed into Maureen's clothes, called for a cab, and waited by the phone. Both Violet and Emily had been generous concerning her allowance. She had over two hundred dollars on hand. She took it all, not knowing how much it would cost to go to Port Jefferson.

The call came from the gatehouse. Laura answered on the first ring and gave Mayfair permission to let John Henry Banks through. The main danger now was that Barrett might break his pattern because of his guest and come up earlier than usual. He didn't, and she brought the empty trunk safely downstairs and out the front door.

Two minutes later she was on her way to Port Jefferson. Banks dropped her off near the ferry and drove back to Glenbriar to celebrate his five-dollar tip.

"What happened to the trunk?"

"I found stones to put in it and dropped it off the end of a dock."

"You take another cab home?"

"Yes."

She had the Port Jefferson driver drop her near the gate, snuck through, and walked back to the house without being caught. She listened to her radio and danced before her mirror, pretending that Barrett was her partner.

"What did you do with her clothes?"

"I pushed them into the house incinerator. Haskell burned them up the next day with the usual trash."

She watched the trucks and crews roll in and begin tearing down the ruins. The blackened shards of wood were torn away, and the broken glass was removed. What was left of the floor was pounded apart and allowed to cave in to the cellar, which gradually filled with the packed debris. A few days later more trucks came in with topsoil and covered it all like a grave.

All too fitting.

I found it difficult to look at her. "Then you just went on as before?"

"Yes."

"No questions, no guilt?"

She blinked.

"Didn't you feel bad about what you did?"

"Why should I?"

"You killed. You murdered an innocent woman you knew nothing about."

"Well, I *had* to."

No guilt, no regret. A job finished and a goal achieved. Barrett would be hers when the time came.

"What about Barrett? When did he start to notice you as a woman?"

She smiled at the memory. "He's always been looking at me. Always, always, always. I'm young and I'm beautiful and he wants me." The little-girl voice was back again.

"What about Emily?"

"He wants me, not her."

"But what about her?"

"She's dead."

"I know. Did you kill her?"

"I had to."

"Why?"

"She heard us talking."

"About what?"

Barrett had wasted no time last night. After punching me out he went straight home to Laura, finally hypnotizing her to get the truth.

She'd heard about the man asking questions about the fire from the house staff. The story of Banks and his memorable tip came up. Laura left to find him, to see for herself if he was a danger. She carried along a small suitcase. Inside it was a club.

Parking her car near a gas station with a phone, she called for Banks to come pick her up. They drove a little and she talked with him. Her questions about his Port Jefferson trip clicked things together in his memory, and he recognized her. He thought it to be an amazing coincidence.

She asked him to stop the car and he did so, still chattering about her and how she'd changed. She brought the club out of the suitcase and smashed it into the side of his head as hard as she could. She hit him several times to make sure, then took his money box to make it look like a robbery.

The storm was bad by now, but her car wasn't too far from where they'd stopped. She got out, but before she could get away, another car appeared and she saw the driver talking to Banks. She took care of him as well, then fought her way through the rain to her own vehicle.

Breathless, she tumbled into it and crept home again. She laughed to see a third car in line behind the others as she passed. The frantic man waving at her to stop looked so ridiculous.

Once home, she had the bad luck to be spotted by Barrett. He'd worried that she'd been caught out in the rain and they joked about her wet clothes. Things weren't so funny to him later.

The next night he pressed her for answers and Emily had heard them talking. She didn't know what was going on; she'd only heard the tone of Barrett's voice, and it frightened her.

"Silly old woman," said Laura. "She should have left me alone. It's all her fault."

"What's her fault?"

"She worried all night and then got up early to talk with me. Jonathan had told me to forget it, but then she started talking, so it's her fault."

"Why did he tell you to forget it?"

"I don't know."

"But you remembered when Emily asked you about it?"

"Yes."

Laura had only to lie again, to say that Barrett had been scolding her for driving out in the hurricane.

"Then what happened?"

"Then I had to do it again," she said wistfully.

Except for Barrett, Emily had the only other key to his rooms. Laura knew where it was kept and stole it and used it.

Her experience with Maureen left her better prepared to deal with Barrett. This time she stripped to the skin before using her stake and hammer. She cried while she cleaned up, because she did love him.

"I really did, but this was coming and I wish it hadn't happened so soon."

"You planned to kill him anyway?"

"I didn't want to, but he would have spoiled it all."

"Spoiled what?"

"It's Emily's fault, not mine. It's *her* fault he's dead and that I had to take care of her, too. She'd have found out, so I had to take care of her, and it's her fault, not mine, all her fault—"

"Laura, why were you going to kill him before?"

"*Because.*"

She was a complete child now, speaking with a child's voice and using a child's logic. Grown up in so many other ways, something within her was stunted or had never been a part of her at all.

"Laura, tell me why you were going to kill him."

"Because."

"Why?"

"He was going to marry her."

That rocked me back. Now I knew what Barrett had been telling Laura while I'd watched from the window and Bing Crosby sang from the radio. From that night, Barrett had been a doomed man.

"Were you jealous?"

"He was going to get what belonged to me. He was going to have me, but I wasn't enough and he'd get all of it when she died. He'd take it all away because she'd give it to him."

I'd been right; she'd made an investment for her future. She loved Barrett, maybe, but he was nothing compared to Emily's money.

"He should have said no, like all the other times—"

"You mean Emily proposed to him?"

"He should have said no, but this time he said yes and it's *her* fault, not *mine*—"

"Hush, now. It's all right, hush."

She trailed off, her face red with anger, the anger she'd hidden from him so well when he'd told her the news.

"Laura, how do you feel about murder?"

I had to repeat the question. She shook her head.

"Don't you feel anything at all about killing those people?"

Puzzlement. Another head shake.

"How do you think they felt?"

Her face was blank.

"Don't you think they had a right to live?"

She shrugged. It was like explaining light and color to the totally blind. She would never, ever be able to see.

"Are you thirsty, Laura?"

"A little."

"I'll get you a glass of water. Wait right here."

In her bathroom I mixed the stuff with the whiskey and stirred it around in a glass with my finger until it dissolved. I wiped everything clean and took the glass in wrapped in a washcloth. I told her it was cold water and that she was to drink it all.

"Will you write something for me, Laura?"

"Yes."

"Good."

She put down the empty glass and smeared dark pink lip color onto her dressing-table mirror, and I gave her the washcloth to wipe her finger on. The few words scribbled over the glass were for others to read and interpret. For her, they were utterly meaningless.

"You're tired, Laura. It's been a busy day. Go to bed now."

She stretched but didn't yawn, and immediately stripped off her clothes and tucked them neatly into the hamper. She'd dressed for darkness on her way to dispose of Barrett's body, but that task was forgotten as she got ready for a good night's sleep.

I looked under the bed and found the suitcase with his clothes. He was meant to disappear like Maureen. None of the Franchers would be sorry that the fortune hunter had left. No doubt his clothes would have gone into the incinerator for Haskell to burn. I put the case out in the hall and re-locked the door.

She brushed her hair, taking her time and staring at her body in the mirror. Her movements were growing slower and more unsteady as the minutes passed. She put on a nightgown but each action had to be thought out, and in between, she'd pause as though trying to recall what the next was to be.

She got into bed. The lights were on. I turned them off for her, using the cloth again as I had for the door. I left the bedside table lamp on.

Her gaze canted to the radio and her hand twitched. By now she'd lost muscle control. I turned it on for her, it warmed up, and we listened to soft dance music.

She was deeply asleep now. Her breathing was slow shallow even as her pulse speeded up. A thin sheen of sweat appeared on her serene face.

Instead of the sleeping mannequin on the bed, I saw Emily Francher.

I saw John Henry Banks.

I saw a last ghostly image of Maureen flash over my inner eye and spin away forever into memory.

I waited and watched and felt nothing.

Nothing until the time finally came and the room was silent but for the radio.

Nothing until I looked at the scrawl on the mirror and read the words I'd dictated: *I'm sorry. God forgive me.*

Then I bowed my head and asked the same for myself.

"How is he?" I asked.

Escott came in and sat across from me. I was in the red leather chair by the cold fireplace staring at the unswept ashes. The candles next to Emily's casket were out, but I'd put on a table lamp so she wouldn't be left in the darkness.

"He's better."

"That's good."

"He was cleaning up and getting dressed when I left him."

My voice sounded a little too normal. "Does he know about Emily?"

"He asked. I only told him she was dead. He did not seem too surprised. I expect he'll be up here before long."

"Did you talk about Laura?"

"Yes. He knew it had been her today."

"I thought he would. What'll he do?"

"I don't know."

We left it at that for a time and listened to the silence of the massive house around us. I'd long since shut off Laura's radio.

I got to my feet. "I'll go find out."

His face was very sad but he said nothing, and I was grateful for that.

I could have walked right through Barrett's door, but knocked and waited instead. After a long minute he said to come in and I did, leaving the suitcase with his clothes by the bed.

He was in his library seated on a long couch. He'd pulled on some pants and slippers, but his shirt was buttoned only halfway, as though he'd forgotten to finish the job. There was a new weariness in his expression, the kind that comes from a tired soul and not just a tired body. His arms hugged his chest, a gesture I could commiserate with; I'd felt the same when it had happened to me.

I stood in the doorway, hands jammed in my pockets. "Glad you're better."

He nodded. "Your friend didn't seem to want to hear it, so I'll say it to you: thank you for pulling me back."

I shrugged self-consciously, beginning to understand Escott's attitude. "He's the one who got me moving, Haskell helped a lot, too."

"Haskell? Did you influence him?"

"At first, but he woke out of it. He kept going, though. He knows about you."

"Well, well."

"Says he'd seen you with the horses."

"And he accepts me anyway. I'll be thanking him, too."

"Yeah."

He mused for a while and looked up, afraid to hope. "Is there any change in Emily?"

"Not the last I saw her. How long did it take for Maureen?"

" 'Twas on the same night she died."

"Same for me. For what it's worth, I'm sorry all this happened."

He accepted, numbly. "Thank you." He gestured, at chair. I declined and remained in the doorway.

"I need to talk to you about Laura."

He shook his head. "No, you don't, Mr. Fleming. Not one word. I've been a fool's fool over that girl and there's no excuse for me. You were both right. I wish to God I'd realized it earlier—"

"She . . . she pushed Emily."

He faltered.

"She remembered you questioning her; that's why she came here to kill you. Then she had to kill Emily to cover up your death."

The pain rolled off him like a tidal wave and I stayed there and let it hit me. I said nothing about the money or anything stupid like that because the man was falling apart in front of me, and I stared at the floor for the whole time and pretended not to see or hear him.

Later he mumbled something about talking to Laura.

"No, Barrett, stay here."

"I have to—"

"She's dead."

The man was in pieces already and it was my lot to smash them into smaller shards.

"I found her. She'd put some sleeping pills in a drink."

The truth, but not all of it. He didn't want to believe it and then he couldn't help but believe it. All he had to do was look up at my face and see it there. I stared at the damned floor and memorized the carpet pattern.

"I think maybe it was too much for her, and in the end she was sorry." The one thing I could give him was the cold comfort of a lie. He needed it badly.

Then it came pouring out of him, and I listened and let him talk because he had to get it all out. He repeated what I'd learned from Laura, everything about Violet and Maureen and Banks; the words tumbling swiftly until they ceased to be words and turned into an unintelligible drone.

"I wish I could have helped her," he said at the end.

"You could have," I said, adding one more lie to give substance to his illusion.

He accepted it.

Escott was cooling his heels in the main hall outside the parlor when I came up.

"Ready to go home?" I asked.

"What about Barrett?"

"We talked. He'll be all right."

"What will he do?"

"I don't know, but he'll be all right."

"Did you tell him about Laura?"

"He knows she's dead." Barrett didn't need or want the truth. Maybe he'd figure it out someday, but he didn't need it now.

Barrett walked up. His shoulders drooped, but he'd buttoned his shirt and tucked it in. It was a minor thing, but I took it as a good sign.

"I thought I'd ride with you as far as the gate," he said. "The Mayfairs will be long asleep by now and I'd rather not disturb them."

I started to say something, but forgot it—a small, soft sound distracted me. Barrett heard it, too, and automatically swiveled his head in the right direction. From where I stood I could see the parlor and noticed a white rose lying on the floor next to the casket. It was the rose Emily held to her breast. Somehow it had fallen out.

Barrett stared at us with sudden, agonized hope and dashed in to her.